A LATTICEWORK SHRINE

By
Parker J. Duncan

Cover art by Chris Panatier
www.panatier.com/home.html

ISBN 978-1-912964-83-3 (Paperback)

Published by Cranthorpe Millner Publishers (2021)

TABLE OF CONTENTS

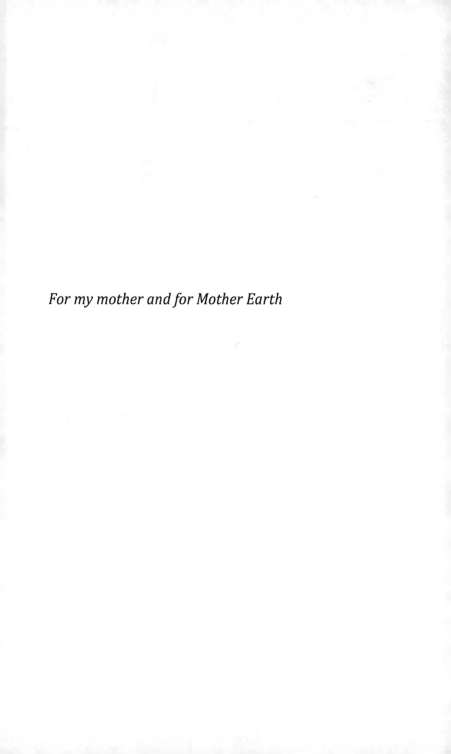

For my mother and for Mother Earth

June 11th, 2052 – Year of the Monkey

"I am the flail of God, had you not committed great sins, God would not have sent a punishment like me upon you."

–Genghis Khan

CHAPTER 15
GENERATION ZERO

In the dim light of early morning, a young man crouched low in a snowy wood. His breath shivered from his mouth like an icy ghost draping the grey forest floor. The full moon, yet to fall beneath the horizon, lay hidden behind the overcast skies that made the world a desolate realm of darkness and fear. The young man looked up as he held his left hand to his mouth. He breathed a quiet breath to warm it. His right hand held his bow, knocked with an arrow, ready to be drawn.

He crept on. The forest floor was a minefield of sound as he tip-toed over the mossy rocks. He attempted to avoid the crunching snow that covered dry leaves and sticks, but the dead Earth under him spoke like the crackling voice of an elder, as the bones of the old world decayed under sunless skies.

Five days the young man had hunted, competing with a small but ruthless wolf pack as they contended for dominance over the land. He had seldom seen them. A glimpse of a bushy tail flitting behind the thickets and folds of the mountains would pass without a sound. Then nothing again. He had become increasingly infuriated with the wolves, wishing they would attack him just so he could test his dagger against the starved beasts.

Under the faint glow permeating the clouds, he looked down at a deer track imprinted in the wind-blown snow. The track was fresh, and with dawn's subtle illumination, some depth could finally be perceived in the blackened wood. As he walked, a cold wind dove into the valley, scraping the treetops and throwing down broken sticks and needles. The deer had walked north toward the ever-dilating arctic circle. The young man sunk into his coat with a sigh and shiver, knowing back home a hot stew awaited him. Still, he followed the track. He could not remit his search for that rare and crucial ingredient, even if it meant scavenging among the crows for sinew.

Suddenly, he heard a branch break ahead of him. He stopped and held his breath, his heart beating loudly in his chest. Silence again. Nearing the edge of a frozen marsh, he stood for a moment, concealed in the shade of a patch of small black spruce trees as he watched the clearing with intelligent eyes. He could hear almost nothing but the hissing wind as the cattails broke in the sway. Dead branches moved stiffly against the wind, for the trees had been gutted and killed by swarms of pine beetles that had ravaged the continent before the great freeze. Some green grass grew at the center of the marsh, and it was there he focused his attention.

A shadow caught his eye. Off to the right of the clearing, a large dark figure was slowly making its way into the open. The young man's heart began to race. A moose; tall, dark, and beautiful. Its antlers stretched wide, and its face was rigid and long. The moose turned its head slightly toward the young man as it trudged into the clearing, revealing its pointy paddles and shavings of velvet still dangling from the tines like a bloody chandelier.

The rare creature made a few more steps as the young man drew his bow. He held it for a moment, breathing deeply, then set his arrow loose. Just as he released the string, he noticed there was a person sitting astride the animal. But it was too late. The arrow whistled through the air. To the young man's astonishment, the person atop the moose reached out and snatched the primitive missile with lightning-fast reflexes. The young man went to run, fearing a scout had found him, but made it only two steps before the rider's voice stopped him.

"Michael, you might want your arrow back." It was a woman's voice.

Michael turned around and pulled his dagger out slowly. He thought for a moment. "How do you know my name?"

The woman silently dismounted and stood serenely before him.

Michael held his dagger behind his back and yelled, "If you are here to implement a mandate from the Queen you must address your name and rank! You've crossed your bounds coming this far north!"

"You believe the Queen has bounds?" the woman asked. "Please, speak with me. I'm not here to hurt you." She spoke calmly, softly stroking the moose's neck.

Michael walked over to the woman and sheathed his blade, keeping his hand close to the hilt. As he drew closer, he viewed her in full and stopped. She was naked. He looked down.

"Oh...um. Do you need some clothes?" Michael stuttered, wondering what a naked woman was doing in the middle of the Yukon territories, and how she had survived this long in the freezing winds. He glanced at one of her hands. Nothing. Not even the slightest of shivers.

"Look into my eyes, Michael," she said in a rich, melodic voice.

Michael looked up and into the dark, cosmic eyes of the woman. She smiled wide as her long, messy,

4

black dread locks writhed around her head. Sticks and leaves poked up from the matte of hair and lichen grew on her forehead. Small mushrooms protruded from the largest dread lock that lay draped over her breast. Though unwashed and savage-like, she was lovely; her body appeared youthful, and her muscles were supple and strong. Slung over one of her shoulders was a leather satchel. She carried no weapon other than the whalebone spear-tip she had tied into her thick knot of hair. Her enchanting radiance was almost overwhelming to Michael, and he shifted his eyes to the moose standing beside her.

"Don't you see who I am?" she asked him.

Michael was speechless. Her nebulous eyes shimmered under her thrice woven neural-circuit lashes, caesious in their pulsing.

"I'm your mother," she said warmly.

Michael shook his head. "My mother died." His gaze flitted across the woman's body. He could not deny her beauty, despite her tundra-like flesh.

"Is that what Lily told you?" she asked.

"You know my grandmother?"

She approached him slowly and hugged him tenderly.

"Your father was Ezra James Beller and I was Ingrid McAdam Beller. When your father died, so did

Ingrid. Now I am Pavonis, a servant of salvation."

Michael stood wide eyed, staring at her in shock and confusion.

"I have looked far and wide for you, my son," she said, holding Michael close, "but I have been caught up in the complexities of worldly matters."

"Where have you been? I thought you died during the eruption?" He let go of her grasp slowly, unsure about the state of this woman's mind.

"It would be safe to assume so, but I did not," she said, walking over and petting the moose, who complacently nipped its large lips at the frosty marsh, uprooting mouthfuls of grass.

"What about Ezra, my father? What happened to him?" he asked.

She bowed her head sadly. "He fell. Just before the eruption. But he is with us in other ways," she said softly, looking up into the grey abyss, hoping for a glimmer of blue sky far beyond the toxic clouds.

Michael nodded shakily.

"I...I have so many questions," Michael said, still skeptical of the strange, moss covered woman. He knew not whether she spoke the truth.

"And I have so many answers, my handsome boy. But our time is limited," she said, coming back over to him. She looked deep into his eyes, bright green, like hers had been before her Sararan transformation. She cupped her hand under her son's chin. With the other, she touched his bow.

"Have you ever killed a man with this?"

"No," Michael replied warily.

"What about a woman?"

"Only if it were Queen Shakti herself."

"You're going to have to get over that," she said, caressing her fingers over the quartz arrowhead. "Don't think for a second that Shakti's lords won't castrate you and leave your severed sex for the wolves. If you're going to survive this war, you're going to have to kill women."

"What would she want with this empty land?" he asked.

"Once the Queen's foreign affairs are finished, she'll turn her focus back towards the hardened nomads of North America. I sense a surge from Caldera approaching, and she won't just be looking for males. She will be looking for you."

"This is all...too much to take in," Michael said, shaking his head. He began to believe that the woman before him truly was his mother. "Why have you not come sooner!?" he whimpered, feeling angry, hurt, relieved, and loved all at once.

"I'm sorry, Michael. I would have come a long time ago, but as you know, there has been a great war going on. You were too young for the worst of it. I have been fighting against the Queen's forces since the eruption. The last five years have been relatively quiet, and I fear her gaze is set to shift back to the Western world to rid these lands of its survivors." Pavonis spoke with strength; she had become a hardened war veteran, looking into the naïve young eyes of her son.

"You will come with me then, right? Back to grandmother's? Please, stay with us, I must know more!" Michael exclaimed.

She smiled at him calling Lily his 'grandmother', but she did not correct him.

"For as long as I am able to, without putting you and Lily in danger," she said. "Come, let us return to your home. I'll walk with you."

They set out towards Michael's home as the brisk winds raked the tarnished landscape of spruce trees. The grey sky illuminated their faces, and they studied one another, a dissociated mother and son reunited. The hungry moose followed closely at Pavonis' side.

"So, what has happened since the eruption?" Michael asked. "All I hear is rumors. Things people don't want to talk about."

"The world has been ruptured by an ancient cult.

The same cult that stole your father's blood to create the Aradians, the ultimate weapons against Earth's governments and resisters. The Aradians – those devilish twins – have been exterminating humans ever since. My role in this war has been in many forms. After helping your uncle, William, fight in the decade long Post-Eruption Wars immediately following the fall, we soon found that much more information and force was required for such an enemy. Most of the military surrendered, the government having been long since overtaken, and I hid away for some time. It wasn't until recently that I found a way to dismantle Shakti's reign. But I need your help, son."

"But I have to stay at the cabin and help Lily—"

"If you don't help us fight this war, Michael, there won't be a cabin to go home to, nor an opening in the abysmal cloud above us to view those wise constellations of light that have brought us here."

"What do you mean?" Michael asked. "What could I possibly do to help?"

"You must find your uncle. He is one of the commanders of the Rebel Marine Corps. He will teach you how to become a warrior. Meanwhile, you can protect those you love by staying far away from them. Now that you're of age, you are in danger, Michael. The faster you move, the better off you'll be."

"Of age? What are you talking about?"

Pavonis handed him a map.

"It's a long ways south, near the center of the Canadian Rockies. Obtain a good steed and you'll make the trip in a matter of weeks. I will meet you there in the coming months."

"What about taking a boat down the coastline first and then cutting straight east?" Michael asked.

"It's too risky, even with the detoxified seas. The Queen's navy patrols the coast. Alone, you will surely be found and captured if the sea itself does not devour you."

Suddenly, Pavonis looked up. The moose became skittish and looked at up as well. The wind came in gusts as the tips of the trees swayed northward.

"I may not make it for tea after all," she said, her face serious as she looked around. "For we are now prey."

After giving him the map, she reached into her satchel and handed him two grouse and a handful of rabbit carcasses.

"Put these in your bag and make haste. Do not stop for anything. You must ride home now and get your things and leave. I love you son. I know you'll make me proud!"

"Wait! I don't understand!" Michael said as Pavonis kissed his forehead and handed him the frail leather reigns attached to the neck of the moose. Michael put the dead fowl and rabbits in his knapsack and slung his bow over his back. He climbed atop the moose. With a small electric shock from the tip of Pavonis' finger, the beast lurched forward and began trotting away. Michael looked back at his mother, who smiled and waved goodbye before darting up into the trees, deft as the wind as she dissolved into the forest.

Michael felt jittery after his mother's abrupt departure, and a sinking feeling suddenly came over him, a feeling that he might never see her again. Or perhaps it was the storm building strength behind the mountain. As he crept through the wood he looked back once more to where she had just stood and wondered if what she had said was true. If the woman really was his mother, then he knew it would be worth venturing south to meet his uncle to learn more about his past. There he would learn more about his family, but he would also face the daunting notion of fighting against the Queen's army of merciless warriors. His one optimistic thought came as he rode home. 'If that crazy naked lady can fight the Queen's forces, anyone can.'

He smiled at the thought of his goddess-like

mother. Who was she? Why were her eyes as glorious as a clear night sky? Why was her skin so soft yet impenetrable, like the hide of a beast? Why was she covered in dirt and fungus, as if she were a forest sprite, born of the Earth's soil? He remembered the tales told by old men at the village tavern, tales of a new race of humans that became known only just before the eruption. To him, the stories had always seemed far-fetched and too thick with conspiracy to seem plausible, but they almost always mirrored what Lily left out of her stories of his own parents. Seeing his mother in real life made him wonder whether Sararans and Aradians maybe did exist in the world, and whether his mother was one of them. If that were the case, then it was the call he had been waiting for. Michael's one and only wish was to live in a world where the sun would rise every dawn, and at night, the clouds would part to show the stars and aurora he had only ever seen as a child, before the black clouds smothered the skies.

Michael tromped through the forest at a quickened pace. Something did not feel right. Far above, he heard what sounded like a jet engine, but planes hardly ever flew this far north. Michael slapped the reigns against the moose, whose long legs moved swiftly through the hauntingly colorless wood. He threw his hood up and nestled against the trotting beast so that his white skin could not be seen from above.

Back in Michael's village of White Horse, Lily awoke in her cabin with a short, fearful whimper. Heavy breaths ensued. She lay only for a few moments, then took a framed photo of Michael from beside her bed and kissed it.

"Come home today my sweet boy," she said in a weary voice.

She rose slowly, hunched, walking from her small bedroom into the octagonal shaped living room. At the far end of the room was a wood fired stove, and beside that, a simple kitchen, a couch, and a single chair. There were no power outlets or appliances. Almost everything was cast-iron, wood, or hemp twine material. The only functional relic they had kept from the twenties was a battery operated mp3 stereo they used sparingly during times of celebration. Seldom were days celebrated in their home lest the sun rose, an event that occurred rarely during the warm season. In the middle of the room hung a mobile of trinkets and relics, an archive of worldly treasures, that spun from the ceiling's center. Extinct bird skulls. Fossils. Dried flowers.

Gems. Antlers. Horns. Teeth. Ivory. Pinecones. Seashells. This was Lily's collection that she used to teach the children of the village about the natural world as they tried to understand what had existed on their planet before the great eruption. She was the only person in their village with a flower, for the community gardens yielded nothing but the occasional potato, carrot, or turnip, usually at odd times of the year.

Lily walked over to start a warming fire in the stove. She bent over to grab some wood and winced. She stopped for a moment, then knelt down slowly.

"These old bones will be the death of me," she said, lighting a piece of birch bark with a match and placing it under the kindling. She blew softly on the burning bark. The fire started crackling and popping into life. She put a few more logs in the stove and shut the hatch with a screech. After taking a few moments to catch her breath, Lily hobbled over to her kitchen drawer and took out a long pipe and her glasses before leaning on the couch and guiding her feet over to her rocking chair. She sat with a large sigh and slipped on her glasses, turning and snatching up a box of matches from the windowsill. The floor creaked with age. She lit the match and charged her pre-packed hashish pipe in the stale cabin air. The cherry burned bright in the low blue light.

A sound made her look up suddenly.

"Good morning." The sweet, soft voice came from the guest room entrance. It was Lily's young caretaker, Melody, who had clearly just risen, as she proceeded to sleepily stretch her arms upwards, greeting the day with a wide, dimpled smile.

"Good morning, Melody," Lily said, smiling back.

Melody was an eighteen-year-old Arabic girl with deep brown eyes and skin as soft as the shell of a glazed porcelain bowl. Her long hair was tied into a single braid that came over her shoulder, and she wore a green embroidered nightgown.

"Are you cold?" Melody asked, putting a blanket over Lily, and kissing her forehead.

Lily let out a large breath of smoke from her pipe and admitted, "No, just my hands."

Melody walked over to the stove and opened the door, letting the heat out for a few minutes to warm the room.

"Your back is hurting again, isn't it?" Melody enquired as Lily set down the pipe.

Lily nodded. "I'll be okay," she said. "Its Michael I'm worried about. He's not usually out hunting this long. Once, when he was twelve, before you arrived at our shores, he was gone more than a week. I was worried sick and asked a few men from town to find him. He was fine, of course. He'd killed a bull elk and was too small to pack out all the meat himself." Lily laughed.

Melody's face was serious.

"What troubles you dear?" Lily asked.

Melody's dark brown eyes locked onto the flickering flames. "I just hope that he's okay, that's all."

Lily smiled with squinting red eyes, studying the young girl's mind and heart.

"I know you are attracted to my grandson, Melody," she said.

Melody tried to hide her smile, but her dimples could not lie.

"No, no of course not...its just—"

"It's okay. I understand. He's becoming a man, and you're becoming a woman. He's handsome, loving, passionate, maybe a little arrogant, but that will get better in time."

"Yet I may choose any man I wish," Melody said nonchalantly with a tipped brow. "I'm one of the only women around here who is at the right age for courting."

"True, but is there a better man here for you?"

Melody smiled as she filled her teacup with the boiling water from the stove.

"You're not a princess anymore, you know?" Lily said, "Michael may be the closest to a prince you'll ever get."

"I know that," she said. "I just fear my past may catch up with me. I don't want him to get hurt."

"Did you ever consider that his past might catch up him as well?" Lily asked.

Melody was silent.

"The pain of love is taking those kinds of risks," Lily said, as she pointed the mouthpiece of the pipe at Melody. She took another puff of the hashish. The golden-brown substance bubbled and hissed.

"What were Michael's parents like? You are his father's mother, no?"

Lily blew out a thick cloud of smoke and coughed.

"Come sit my child, I have something to tell you." She set the pipe back down and looked deeply into the fire as Melody came and sat on the couch beside her." I am not Michael's grandmother. I was his parents' midwife. They abandoned Michael shortly after his birth, and I was left to take care of him."

"That's horrible! Who would do such a thing?"

"Well, it did seem a little insane at the time, but they were being hunted by assassins, you see. They wanted their son to be in safe hands. The reason I've not mentioned this before to either of you is because I'm not totally sure if they died after the eruption or not. I never saw them again. I fear broader repercussions if Michael's existence were found out. So, I tell everyone he's my grandson."

"You must tell Michael! What if his parents are still alive?"

"This is why I am telling *you*," Lily said cryptically. She slowly stood up and walked over to the stove, putting another log on the fire.

"Who were they?" Melody asked.

"Ezra was a good man. Though, he was not a man. He was the famous mercenary that saved Michael's mother during a mission in the Andes. For whatever reason, Ezra returned with a strange mutation, something to do with one of the jungles undocumented species. Ingrid was the only other survivor of their mission, and somewhere along the way, they fell in love with one another. Of course, the public knew little about the specifics of this mutation because the eruption took place less than a year after their return. I was part of both his and Ingrid's lives during their time in Montana, the summer before that fateful September day. I visited them often and took good care of Ingrid during the birthing process. It was a wonderful time in our community."

"So, the stories are true..." Melody gasped. "...about the hyper-evolved humans trying to take over just before the eruption."

"Yes, but there's far more to the story. Just after Ezra and Ingrid left for Neon City there were television broadcasts warning about 'Sararan' beings. There were two-million-dollar bounties on both their heads, and the FBI searched the Flathead Valley to find Michael and I. The eruption took place during their search. For a while, I was convinced that the eruption had something to do with Michael's parents, but I really don't think they could have caused it. Perhaps the truth behind their story is buried in the ashes of the great caldera. They were good people. You can see it in Michael. He has good roots. He holds his lineage true."

"Is Michael Sararan then?" Melody asked as she sipped her tea.

"He doesn't look it, but his father was mutated when he and Ingrid conceived him, so it is likely there is some Sararan genetics in him. I vaguely remember Ingrid mentioning that he may mutate when he gets older, at a 'peak age', but even she was uncertain."

"What did Ezra look like?"

"He had deep, reddish black eyes, like a shark;

strong, impenetrable skin, and crystalline fingernails. The easiest way to know a Sararan is by their radiant aura. You can feel their energy when they're near you. Its electrifying."

"Who else?" Melody asked, baffled.

"Who else what?" Lily asked.

"Who other than Ezra is Sararan?"

"The Queen is said to be," Lily said. "But, regardless of whether she is human or not, she is a malicious creature hiding in her stone palace where she conducts a vile sorcery."

Melody pondered for a moment with her brow furrowed. "If Michael were to turn Sararan, could he stop her?"

"I don't know. Maybe there are other Sararans out there, who knows?" Lily said, smiling optimistically.

BAM BAM BAM!

The loud knock on the cabin door startled the two women. Melody and Lily looked at each other fearfully.

"Is it the Queen's soldiers? What if they're looking for Michael!?" Melody whispered.

"It's probably just someone from town," Lily reassured her.

Lily stood up and grabbed the shotgun that

leaned next to the door, loading a shell into the chamber with arthritic hands, as Melody crawled under her bed frame. Lily breathed a deep breath, unlocked the door, and opened it.

Nobody was there. The dull morning light reflected off the snow and trees, but there was no one. She took a step out into the bitter cold.

WACK!

A silver arm swung from the side of the cabin and smashed Lily's face, knocking her back through the doorway and into the house. She hit the floor with a loud thud and shrieked. Wincing, she looked up with horror at the ruthless being who had assaulted her, the shotgun on the floor just out of reach.

A woman in full chrome plated armor stood over her, sensual yet menacing. A shimmering, red, rising sun inlay had been fitted into her titanium-plated forehead, glimmering in the faintest light of dawn. Over her slender contours, large, sea-blue lettering had been printed in an array of different languages. The words were written in a vertical column, starting at her collarbone, bulging over her right breast, and continuing past her hip, ending just above her knee. The first word was written in Japanese. The second read as 'TALA'. The rest of the words were versions of the same name. Aside from the markings, every other square inch of the woman's body was plated in titanium alloy armor. Even her face was masked, except her eyes, which shone with scenes of explosions and violence. The rest of her metal armor shone without blemish, save the arm she had painted crimson with Lily's blood.

"What do you want?!" Lily screamed. She looked up at the robot-like person, who shut the door behind her without further gesture. Melody whimpered with fear. Tala looked over at her. Melody screamed.

"Who...who are you and wha...what do you want!?" Lily stammered, tears of terror forming in her eyes.

The being looked back at Lily. She picked up a framed picture of Michael and dropped it on the floor. The glass from the picture shattered, spreading broken shards next to Lily's hand. She walked over and stepped on Lily's fingers, slicing her flesh and veins into the broken glass while crushing her old bones like twigs. Lily screamed whilst the being looked sideways at Melody. Melody sobbed and choked on her tears, trying desperately to wake up.

"It's just a nightmare...it's just a nightmare..." she muttered, climbing into hysteria and coughing on her collecting mucus.

The chrome woman crouched and picked up the photo of young Michael. She tapped Michael's face with her steel tipped finger.

"He went hunting!" Lily shrieked. "He won't be back for two days at least!"

The being rose and fanned her fingers impatiently, weaving her wrist's axis until her hand lay flat, as sheer as the rings of Saturn. She looked at the kettle boiling on the stovetop and knocked her open hand against the handle, causing the kettle to fall onto Lily's legs. The old woman shrieked as the boiling water burned her shaking legs.

"I promise." Lily had to reach for her words. She gasped. "I promise that he left here heading straight West. He was going to hunt his way to the ocean over the next few days, then try to trade with the merchants..."

Tala crouched down beside Lily's head and caressed her cheek with a delicate touch. Lily sobbed and continued to defend herself.

"I swear I'm not lying! He left a few days ago. Please spare us. We are simple people. We've done nothing to insult the Queen!"

Melody whimpered and looked down as the being stood and walked over to her, the orange firelight reflecting off every surface of the mysterious woman's curvaceous body. Just as she approached Melody, a blue light flickered on Tala's wrist. She stopped, backed away, and walked out of the cabin, slamming the door behind her.

Melody rolled out from under the bed and ran over to Lily.

"Dear God!" she sobbed while wrapping Lily's bleeding hand with a cloth.

"Melody, did...did you hear what I said this morning?" Lily said weakly, struggling to breathe.

"Shh, don't talk," Melody said, taking another towel and wrapping Lily's burnt legs carefully.

"I said...these old bones would...be the death of me. She...she broke my back when she...knocked me down," Lily wheezed.

"You're going to be okay, Lily! I'm going to get the doctor." Melody's voice was determined as she reached for her coat on the wall.

"No...it's...it's okay. I...I love you, Melody. Tell...tell Michael I love him too," she smiled, fading away.

Melody knelt in the shattered glass." Lily? Lily! No! Come back! Please! You're strong! Your heart is strong!"

Lily's eyes closed. Her blood stopped pumping. Her hand fell limp in Melody's.

"You are so strong...in your heart," Melody

whispered, feeling defeated.

She held Lily's hand in hers, sobbing. Each tear slowly washed the blood from their woven fingers, until Melody had no more tears to cry. In the silence that followed her distraught sobbing, she began to sing a soft lullaby to Lily, a song she had learned as a child. A somber melody, written solely to ease the pain of tragedy.

As noon approached, the fire turned to embers, then to a soft crackle of ash, and finally to cold, grey death. Melody knelt still, her knees digging into the shards on the floor. Unable to cry. Unable to sing. Unable to move.

Later that afternoon, Michael neared the outskirts of the village. He dismounted from the weary moose and whipped it with his bowstring, sending the towering animal trotting off as Michael watched it with tired eyes.

"You live to feed another day, forest king," he said.

He walked back to his cabin, his thoughts still racing, stopping suddenly as he caught sight of a mournful scene.

Melody stood in her nightgown and winter coat,

shoveling a deep hole in the ground, just a few yards away from the cabin wall. An old man knelt beside her, wrapping Lily's broken body in thin cloth wrap.

Michael ran towards them. "What happened?" he breathed, his heart beating frantically with anxiety.

Melody stopped shoveling and looked up. Her eyes were weary with despair and she stared as if she saw past him. The old man kept wrapping the body quietly.

After a moment of silence, Melody spoke. "Someone...or something...came to us this morning. They tortured Lily and then left. Lily didn't survive the blows."

Michael ran over to the body. The old man stood up and backed away as Michael clung to Lily's body and began to sob, a fury brewing inside him.

"What did they want?" he asked, his voice laced with menace.

"You," Melody replied, placing her hand on his shoulder.

Michael set down Lily's body and stood, taking a deep breath. He began to back away slowly, his whole body shaking with anger, until his rage crescendoed into a wordless scream of frustration, fury, and despair. He dropped to his knees, pummeling the snow with his fists as he sobbed a flood of tears.

"Shakti!" he screamed into the faceless woods. "Mark my words! I WILL find you, and when I do, I will tie your body to the ocean rocks and leave you for the tide you worthless monster! YOU'RE FUCKING DEAD!!" he shrieked. Snot and tears collected at the tip of his chin as his hysteria diminished, becoming heavy crying.

Melody cringed and stood silently, shivering in the cool air. The old man went back to wrapping the corpse, a murder of crows watching them all from their circle above.

As the afternoon waned to evening, the cold air brought a sullen mist over the village. Word of Lily's murder had spread through the town, and suspicion overtook the people as they locked their doors and prayed before their sun alters. Some left White Horse altogether for fear of invasion. Many stayed, for they were far more afraid of capture or ambush by pirates or the Queens probing militia. Then there were those who met at the tavern, as they would have done any other evening, their shotguns slung over their shoulders as they steeped themselves in pre-war plans and pungent spirits.

Michael and Melody sat inside their cabin, numb with shock and grief. Melody stoked the fire. Michael stared at the wall from Lily's chair, his face emotionless.

"What did it say?" Michael asked, after a long silence.

"*She* didn't say anything," Melody answered. "She simply tortured Lily and pointed at a picture of you. She wanted to know where you were."

Michael nodded.

"She was covered in shiny metal armor. She looked like a robot or something," Melody added.

"Probably one of the Queen's soldiers. My mother was right after all," Michael said. He suddenly stood up as if realizing something. He walked to his room. Melody followed.

"What are you doing?" she asked. "What do you mean your mother was right?"

"It all makes sense! This wild woman approached me in the forest this morning. She claimed to be my mother. She warned me, but I don't think the Queen expected her to beat them to me," he said as he started packing his satchel with supplies.

"Wait. Your mother is alive? Lily was telling me about your parents just today! No wonder the Queen sent her guards to get you! They know now that you are the heir to the original Sararans!"

"Lily told you my parents were Sararans?! That would explain my mother's cosmic eyes, and why she didn't need any clothing to protect herself from the cold! Of course! She really is the Goddess of life!"

"What are you going to do?" Melody asked, watching him pack his supplies.

"Avenge Lily's death and fight in the war against the Queen. My mother gave me a map to find my uncle. He commands the Rebel Marine Corps, deep in the Canadian Rockies. I will go there and train with him, until my mother meets us there."

Melody sighed.

"Yes...that would make sense...in case the dreaded creature returns."

"What's wrong Melody?" he asked, turning to face her. "Are you afraid they will return?"

"No! That's not it. I'm...I'm afraid they will find you," she said, hesitating a moment before embracing him tenderly.

Michael smiled and held her in return.

"Melody, before I go, I must tell you something," he said, as he sat down on the bed.

"What is it?" she asked, sitting close beside him.

"With this dreaded war going on, there's no

telling whether or not I will come back, and...well...I...I care for you, Melody. If you got hurt...I don't know what I would do. I guess what I'm saying is that if the Queen's army comes this far north, I want you to pledge your allegiance to her, so that your life may be spared. She accepts only women into her army, and based on your past—"

"Michael," she interrupted. "After what I saw today, I would rather die fighting them than bow down an inch."

Michael looked deep into her eyes and she met his gaze, her eyes bright with determination and desire. Without breaking their connection, Michael took her hand and leaned in to kiss her, but she grabbed his face and kissed him first.

"Why did you wait until now to express your love for me?"

"I could ask you the same question."

They each felt an invisible force surge through the marrow of their spirits, like a perfect knot unraveling between them, severing them from the cosmic twine that hung from the Immortals outstretched hands. What this love provided Michael and Melody was hope for the future; what it provided the planet was so much more, adding a whole new dimension to the complex struggle for survival faced by all life on Earth.

So began the new and unexpected resistance against Queen Shakti and her Aradians, with a single kiss between the son of the first Sararan and a middle eastern refugee, who through a cloak of ignorance hid a secret that would change everything.

CHAPTER 16
DARK SISTER TRINITY

Far across the Pacific, beyond the islands of trash where rib cages of whales pierced the plastic beaches like white tungsten; beyond the coast with its senticous barriers of shipwrecks rusting in the vicious tide, the self-proclaimed Queen Shakti was about to overthrow the last remaining powers of the world. She stood on a stage in the main hall of a plush government building in Tokyo, Japan, looking down at Mayari, who sat in the center of the hall, her titanium armor glistening in the artificial light.

The warrior looked straight up at the light above her, revealing a gold inlay of the Filipino star glistening on her forehead. Her eyes, like her sister's, were uniquely Aradian, though the two of them were opposites. Her sister's eyes were windows to her own violent past, displaying a sequence of images stored deep in the scars of her memory, but Mayari's eyes were mirrors to the world around her, reflecting everything like the suit that concealed her body. Besides the crest on her forehead, the rest of her armor had been scraped, dented, and caked with charred Earth from the brutal combat she had just experienced. Black lines and shrapnel riddled the suit, but the woman herself remained unbroken: an Aradian Goddess nearly impenetrable by modern weapon systems, with the ability to return a guided missile to its sender or scorch a sea into steam. She, like her sister, had become a being feared by all humans. Mayari was said to be even more powerful than Tala, and to some, she was considered the embodiment of God herself. The media powers of Japan idolized the Aradians in fashion, advertising, graphic novels, theatre, and film – layering truth with gimmick as the public's cultivated love for the Aradians grew. This growing popularity, however dubious, became increasingly helpful to Shakti, making it easier for her to recruit female officers from the Imperial City into her growing army.

Shakti, contrary to popular belief, was still very much human. Though powerful, present, and most foul, the Queen remained mysterious to the public and even her close followers. Who was this master of assassins unleashing the wrath of God, bleeding the Earth, and sparing few? What was her ancient belief system's final resolution? Her domination affected everyone, and those lucky enough to be alive kept these questions to themselves. Nineteen years after the eruption, the last of the world's humans had witnessed Shakti's genocide of billions and were certain Vishnu and his associates had influenced the disaster of 2033. It was no secret to anyone that the Zurvan Order was superior to every other nation. Even when nations had united under joint command, they had fallen to The Order. Shakti was feared, respected, and obeyed by nearly everyone. Those who refused to bow to the Zurvans were cut down. Nothing could stop Shakti, or so she had thought.

The Queen breathed deeply and walked up to Mayari. She wore a simple white Kimono, and her hair was tied back; she wanted to appear humbling in front of the Japanese officials coming to meet them. Golden embroidered cloth draped over the hall's long table, where dishes of the most delectable sushi had been set out. The Queen pulled a red silk cloth from her breast and began scrubbing the charcoal-stained metal from Mayari's battered suit.

"Tala found the boy's home, but he was out for a hunt. She has reason to believe Pavonis lives and is seeking her son."

"The forest deity was killed by Tala, master," Mayari said through her suit, her words bit-crushed and filtered to mask her true voice.

"In the Cascadian conflicts over twelve years ago, so I've been told. But she never gave me evidence, so I'm compelled to believe Pavonis remains alive, hiding somewhere beneath the tundra, somehow blocking her distinct Sararan aura and preventing you and your sister from sensing her presence."

Mayari kept still as her master stared at her with skeptical eyes.

The Queen continued. "The creature is probably so shell shocked she's completely given herself over to the land, nesting deep in the woods whilst her veins run with chlorophyll and her mind ferments like the fungus that grows from her scalp. She probably talks to the animals." Shakti laughed, continuing to clean Mayari's suit with the tenacity of a servant." I admit, her powers are strong for a Sararan, but she's alone in her fight. As long as she keeps replanting trees in the wake of our timber workers, she and I have a strange co-reliance in this fast-changing world, a symbiosis, really. If you find her, bring her to me unharmed. But it is the boy I want. To study a specimen born of Sararan genes intrigues me greatly, and my intuition tells me Michael poses more of a threat as a human than Pavonis does as a Sararan. Against someone like you, sister, neither are a worthy adversary. It is my wish to keep it that way."

Mayari nodded.

Shakti looked at her lovingly and smiled. "You, sister, are the fourteenth generation apprentice of Master Shaman Zou Cheng, who, as you know, lived to be over seven hundred years old. He taught the lesson of immortality to Vishnu, who in turn taught it to me, and I have now taught you and your twin sister. In your perfect cellular fortification of Aradian weaponry, you need not further education to pass the next threshold of your training, yet remember that these Taoist principles brought you here. Let this be known: your mutation is not an excuse to disregard the lessons you've been taught so painstakingly. And since you've no doubt surpassed my intellect, it is imperative that you gain full understanding of the importance of our cause."

Mayari sat quietly. She continued listening while Shakti buffed out the mud and charred black streaks in her armor.

"At the dawn of the thirteenth century, Zou Cheng was one of the shamans of the great Mongol conqueror, Genghis Khan. The Khan himself was said to be a shaman, but this rumor circulated only after Master Cheng's shamanistic powers were used to victorious effect on the road to war. On a cloudy summer day in 1204, a pivotal battle in Genghis Khan's life took place that would decide the outcome of his growing empire, and therefore the outcome of the modern world and its future unfolding. As the sun rose behind a black mass of clouds, a storm, said to have been conjured by the shaman himself, fell upon the enemy tribes of the Khan. Already in fear of the blood-thirsty Khan in his irrefutable rise to power, the enemies cowered as the sound of twenty thousand horse hooves thundered toward them. It was at that time the storm let loose like a ravaging beast. Heavy rains battered the enemy encampment. Lightning struck their lances. Strong winds pushed their shields back and carried Mongol arrows swiftly into their forces. The fighting tribesmen fell like pincushions onto the stained red Earth. After the battle, the Mongol people believed that God himself was on Genghis Khan's side. This rationalized the power of Zou Cheng, who grew much closer in diplomatic stature to the central Asian ruler. The Khan's relatives became distrustful of the shaman, and this caused much drama to unfold in the Khan's court. Zou escaped to Japan before an assassination could be executed, leaving behind his reputation as well as his promised sector of power and ties to the Khan's noble family.

Nearly eighty years later, Zou continued his practice as a Taoist monk in the mountains, when he heard news that the Mongol army, led by the grandson of Genghis Khan, was attempting to invade

Japan with a newly implemented naval force, ranging out of what is now Korea. It is not recorded whether any shamans were present during the first raids, as the brave but futile Samurai warriors fell to the Mongols and their advanced new cannons and explosive weapons systems. However, it is known that the Mongol invasion was halted due to a cataclysmic coastal storm, which resulted in the capsizing of hundreds of ships. Thousands of men died in turbulent seas, forcing the remaining armadas to return to the mainland, defeated. The mighty empire never claimed the island of Japan and thus the Mongol empire reached its full capacity on its eastern border.

I believe that Zou uprooted himself from the mountains to challenge the spirit of the Khan as a testament to his own powers against the heavenly. Had the Great Khan been at the mercy of God, Master Cheng would not have been able to manipulate the seas in the way he had, performing the same feat several years later as the Khan's navy failed once again on the violent seas. Zou's tactics were equally astounding. He combined geometry, scrying, and harmony to create a powerful spell previously unattainable by both Egyptian astronomers and Germanic sorcerers. Against the largest armies on Earth, led by the most powerful king, one man was able to stop their eastern conquest, and he did it all without pride or the desire for political advancement. Zou instead sought a student worthy of teaching the technique of immortality, a student whom he eventually found in the form of Vishnu, in the 1800s. Vishnu carried this knowledge well, and transferred it impeccably to me and thus to you.

If there were ever a being to reach the level of kung fu our master Zou Cheng had, it would surely be you, my apprentice of solar divinity. Do not let your sister's ineffable lunar powers allow you to feel lesser. Her stone is close to Earth, yes, but yours is a star. She envies you, Mayari. You have the power to manipulate every atom around you. You've become something more than even I could imagine. We will not only survive this great war but we will thrive in its wake. Our aim will be true, despite the betrayal I'm about to commit. It is a necessary betrayal, you understand?"

"Yes Master Shakti," Mayari said in her slightly raspy, auto-tuned voice.

"You are the true Queen of this world. You are the pure one. I am merely the face which every act of deceit may be known by. I am the betrayer of the betrayers."

Mayari nodded and stood up quickly, taking the position of a soldier ready for duty. A group of elaborately dressed military officers entered the hall.

"General Yoshida!" Shakti said, turning and bowing low. "Your punctuality is much appreciated."

Several soldiers followed the group of decorated men. The general bowed as he approached her.

"Please come and sit!" Shakti said, smiling, as she slowly raised herself from her bow, a Japanese formality hinting to her knowledge of the old way.

"Queen Shakti, your reputation precedes you," General Yoshida began. "Let me personally congratulate you on your seizure of all the American Embassies and U.S. government strongholds. You have done with a small group what no country has been able to do with alliances and millions of dedicated soldiers and civilians. To defeat The United States is the highest honor a Japanese national, such as yourself, has ever achieved."

"Thank you, General." She bowed again.

"The Emperor wanted me to invite you to accept permanent guardianship and an opportunity to command one of his naval fleets, should you desire the position. You are a hero in the land of the rising sun," he said, bowing once again. The men sat down quietly. Mayari stood like a statue, though seemed to glow with a golden radiance as her Aradian energy emanated from her third eye.

"Thank you, General. I humbly thank all of you for being present today and I am equally grateful for the Emperor's offering. However, I must reluctantly decline. I have managed to topple almost all the other major powers of Earth not with numbers, but with logistics, intelligence, and a very powerful weapon of my personal creation."

She walked over to Mayari.

"Modern genetic research has allowed me to harness the Sararan gene, augment its capabilities, and apply these super human abilities to my most gifted apprentice. I present to you the future of warfare, and ultimately, peace. The Aradian."

The men clapped. Shakti lifted her hand and opened it before Mayari, who suddenly levitated above the ground and spun steadily as if held in an invisible tractor beam. The men continued to clap and make quiet comments amongst themselves.

"Mayari is a combat engineer on a molecular level. She is able to manipulate the physical world in ways inconceivable to even the most advanced scientists of our time. This is Mayari, of course, and she is one of two models. Tala is currently deployed alongside West-Asian forces in Europe."

"And how is the campaign against the remaining Western powers going?" the General asked. "I hope that Japan's neutrality in the conflict does not insult the Zurvan Empire."

"I understand your nation's position, General. Your trade affiliations in Europe do not interfere with our operations. Your continued support, though quiet, is vastly appreciated. With an Aradian, however, you will never have to worry about security concerns again. Tala is gutting Europe from the inside out as we speak."

"Are there more of them?" the General asked.

"I have only two Aradians in my army because their cerebral activity must be implemented carefully. As you saw with the volcanic event in Wyoming, an Aradian is nearly five times more effective than a Sararan. Simply put, one can destroy the world, if one so chooses."

The men wrote down notes as she spoke.

The Queen went on. "I've loosely contracted, or herded rather, Daesh insurgents from Northern Iraq to help me with a short campaign in Turkey and Eastern Europe. I don't share the group's enthusiasm for fundamentalist Islamic doctrine, but their ability to do dirty work and execute aristocrats makes them a suitable regime for the Balkan front. Their forces are fairly robust, but I admit their methods are sloppy. I intend to personally see to it that their organization is eradicated by the end of the war."

"An interesting use of resources, Your

Highness," the General commented.

"I am very much an idealist, General. I opposed the use of nuclear weapons at the beginning of this war, and I will stand by my principles, even if that means hiring the devil to do God's work. My trusty Aradians will do ninety five percent of the fighting. They are undetectable by radar, faster than the speed of sound, and invincible against anti-aircraft artillery and most bombs, as they use their enemy's weapons against them via methods far beyond mortal understanding. No further resources are needed because an Aradian's energy is replenished by solar power."

"And how much are you asking for one of your genetic weapons, Queen Shakti?" The general inquired. Several other officers continued writing in their notebooks and making exciting revelations between themselves. Some guessed the price.

"That is where our deal may go cold, I'm afraid. I don't want currency, General, and I don't need the Emperor's good graces. I want your boys."

"Excuse me?" he asked, confused. The other officers looked up, puzzled.

"Vishnu wanted this world to go on without humans. But I don't think it is humans we must punish, but males exclusively. My goal is to live in a world without men, or at most, very few. The age of patriarchy ended the day Vishnu caused the eruption, and my Aradians will do everything in their power to ensure less than 2% of males survive this century. I have been collecting the most genetically supreme sperm in an underground vault, so I will not need them for anything, not even breeding. That is why your position as an ally to the Queendom of Caldera will be crucial when I attack mainland China tomorrow."

The men suddenly became nervous and whispered to themselves.

"With respect and honor, Queen Shakti, I understand your sympathy for the girls in China, and your resentment surrounding the cultural prejudice against them, but Japan will not trade its own citizens to satisfy our need for militaristic development, nor can it go to war with our allies in China."

"At least let me elaborate on the details of the offer, General. For half of your male population, I give you one Aradian. For complete viricide of your country, save the men in this room who will not live to see the end of the century anyway, I give you the twins; a fair trade for anyone seeking the throne of Emperor over the Earth. You would have as many mistresses as you wanted until the end of your days.

Just give me their names and addresses and I'll do the rest."

"I'm sorry, Your Graciousness, but as the Emperor's chief ambassador, I must decline your offer," the General said.

"Very well," Shakti said, pouring herself and her guests more warm sake. "Then I shall put down my arms when I finish my conquest to rid the world of Western evils. Let a new age of golden peace unfurl beneath our feet. Long live the Land of the Rising Sun!"

They all clinked glasses and drank as Shakti poured another for herself.

"One more thing, General," she said. She looked at Mayari, who had been waiting for her signal.

"Did you know your great grandfather was one of those who planned the massacre of Nanjing?"

The men looked up. Some squirmed uncomfortably in their seats.

"That was a travesty, Your Highness, a chapter in Japanese history of which I am deeply ashamed, never to be repeated. I'm sure you're mistaken however," the General quivered.

"I was visiting my uncle and aunt in China before the war. We watched the men come into the town on tanks and trucks. A Japanese soldier refused to argue with my mother over our papers, which he said looked forged. He instead killed my father, then raped my mother and choked her to death. I was five. They sold me into a slave trade, but I escaped, and eventually found refuge in the mountains of southern China. And here I am, looking at the great grandson of the man who sent those bastards to commit these unforgivable crimes. Forgive me for expending this long-awaited vengeance on you and your cabinet."

"No please!" the General screamed.

Suddenly, a sonic blast filled the room. The echo subsided after a few seconds, and Shakti rose from beneath the table she had ducked under seconds before. The decorated officers lay about, rendered unconscious by the immense explosion from Mayari's dangerous mind.

Queen Shakti bent down and took the General's sword and sheath, slipping them under her waistband and pulling out the katana with a loud metallic ring.

"Pack them onto the ship. When Japan's agents find them in a Chinese prison, they'll think we're siding with the Chinese. The Emperor will have no other option but to retaliate. We'll let the dogs of Japan bleed with the serpents of China. Then I shall ring the communist dragon's neck while stomping out North Korea and its puny leader."

"It will be done, master. And what of the new capitol? What Gem of the East shall remain unscathed?" Mayari asked.

"I don't think it's coincidence that Tala found the black spirit banner of Genghis Khan in a Siberian tomb only a few months ago, as we are about to shape the Eastern world yet again. I will take the spirit banner back to the Mongols, and let the Mongol Queens rule the world as they once did, in a world very much similar to the days of Genghis Khan's reign. The eternal blue sky shall once again be the people's cherished divinity, as the horsehairs from the banner's staff will be free to let the wind guide us to new battles. But no blood shall be spilled in the Mongol nation. For everyone else in the world, may God be merciful to the innocent, for I am not."

CHAPTER 17
GHOST FRONTIER

Michael awoke to the sunlight prying his eyelids open. He smiled and felt its warmth comb his face. The sun was a rare sight indeed. The brisk dawn gave way to the heat as the planet thawed slowly. A lark chirped from the nettle bush above him, and excitedly flew from branch to branch, for neither he nor the bird had seen such a day in months. It made perfect sense to Michael as to why.

"Good morning, Lily," he said.

Michael rose from the forest floor and packed up his sleeping bag, before tallying his pace counting beads and writing the value in a journal. Forty-five miles traveled. 1,342 to go. He would walk on foot until he found a horse, then start heading southeast. The way was daunting, or so he had been told. He did not know the kind of people that lived in those territories. With only a dagger, an axe, and his bow, he was ill-equipped against an enemy with superior weaponry. Secrecy and speed were his tactics to reach his uncle in good time. If he could make it by August, Michael would arrive at his destination before the acid rains performed their seasonal sweep.

Living in post eruption conditions was hard enough, let alone having to deal with July's extreme thunderstorms, when the sky lit up in a strobe of blue shockwaves, triggering episodes of epilepsy amongst the animals and killing off high mountain sentries who made the mistake of lifting their bayonets higher than their heads. The eruption of Yellowstone had brought Zeus to life, his anger sustained in a static bombardment that caused a buildup of nitric acid in the clouds, releasing heavily polluted downpours. If the conditions were not primed for rain that particular season, the dry, beetle-decimated trees would be engulfed by the sky licking flames of forest fires, ignited by the lightning. The burns would be inevitably put out by snow that held even more corrosive acids, starting around October. The smoke caused a vile reaction between the volcanic, sulfur dioxide snow and the nitric acids that pumped plumes of toxic air into the atmosphere – the helm of their wintry doom.

As Michael walked, the sun climbed over the eastern peaks and chunks of snow fell from tree branches. More animals came out of hiding, making small sounds and rejoicing at the return of their closest star. Were it not for those rare days of sunlight, all life in North America would be devastated. However, to his surprise, the further south he walked, the more living trees and foliage he found. There were berries for him to pick, roots to dig up, and game to hunt. He wondered why Lily had not chosen to live further south, where it was more sustainable and fertile. That afternoon, as he approached the edge of a large river, his question was answered.

As the early summer thaw melted the snowy mountains, a vicious torrent of rapids lay in his path. The river was wide and gnawing away at the bank with an erosive flood of muddy water. Large trees and branches tumbled swiftly downstream, breaking to pieces, and getting snagged on the banks for mere seconds before being ripped downstream again. Michael looked around for a way across. Swimming was not an option. He would surely drown. He figured he could make a raft, but that would take time, effort, and was not a much safer alternative. He wracked his brain for more ideas. None came. Having no other choice, he began gathering supplies for his craft.

He reached for his axe and then he saw it, a gigantic Douglas Fir tree, spinning in the turbulent water, with human body parts pinned to the trunk. Bloated and beaten, the bodies had been hung by nails and torn by the rivers rocky bottom, leaving the remaining flesh void of blood and shredded to pieces like wet, white cloth. A head missing most of its hair was partially intact, a railroad spike having been plunged through its mouth, its face unrecognizable as its toothless jaw hung by a hairline of pink fibrous muscle.

"Who could have done this?" Michael asked himself, fighting to hold down his breakfast as he watched the tree continue to roll downstream, carrying its clear and horrific message. He decided to heed the warning and turned back, using the sun to guide him another way through the vast wilderness. He left the shadows behind him, wondering if Melody would be in the path of the nameless decapitators up stream. Whatever evil plagued that land must have stemmed from Shakti, in one way or another. He began to realize that the further south he went, the more dangerous his journey would become.

Just when he thought he was far enough away from the stream, a loud sound boomed overhead. He looked up into the blue sky. Far above, an armada of bombers hummed like wheezing dragons, flying to the west. Their jet streams could be seen dissipating across the sky. Michael counted them.

"Thirty planes," he whispered, listening to the

engines growing louder. Suddenly, he heard far off popping sounds. They sounded to him like rifle fire, but louder. Brown smoke rose behind a ridge in the distance.

"What are they bombing?" Michael wondered aloud, looking around to see if there were any more of them. Hundreds of tons of explosives blasted the deep forest into a grey and brown haze.

The planes finished dropping their ordinance on the decimated ridge and turned back south. Their engines faded. A woodpecker was all that Michael could hear.

He referred to his map and compass to measure the distance. "Twenty miles away," he said, before continuing on.

Given that he was travelling through what he had come to realize was a warzone, it seemed rather ominous to Michael that he had not encountered anyone on his journey thus far, other than faceless bodies nailed to a tree and the Queen's pilots as they took advantage of clear skies. He was relieved when the bombers turned south, for even though Michael faced a gruesome quest, he was becoming far more concerned about Melody's safety than his own.

CHAPTER 18
DAUGHTERS OF THE GREAT KHAN

The noxious clouds over Beijing parted on a cool June day, and streetlights painted the air with reflective particles, as millions of masked humans raced to go about their morning motions. It was a city of consumption, and little else. Queen Shakti and her two Aradians emerged from the sea of suffocating citizens. The workers moved around the beings in a fluid motion, like a river against a prominent stone. But as the eyes of the civilians began to identify the deviants, suddenly the chaotic and steady motion of the mornings commute halted at the site of the awesome trio. Their screams carried a warning to the herd. As the women neared the center of the capital, crowds parted, the metal plated deities rising into the air like feathers caught by a gentle breeze. Cars stopped. People yelled to get away. Everyone suddenly knew what was coming. Panic spread, though a forty-foot radius of space circled the three deadly women.

Shakti wore a black hooded robe, with deer antlers wrapped in gold twine rising from her headpiece. Her Aradians shimmered in their chrome armor, reflecting the fearful faces all around them. Shakti walked with purpose, her legs moving swiftly, her posture authoritative, her body casting no shadow in the musty air.

The Queen's voice boomed out over the dispersing crowd. "Whoever hammers a lump of iron first decides what he is going to make of it; a scythe, a sword, or an axe. Even so, we ought to make up our minds what kind of virtue we want to forge… or we labor in vain."

A police officer ran up and attempted to shoot her, but Shakti unsheathed her katana and sliced his neck. She flicked her sword, sending a splat of blood onto a screaming woman's face.

"The Chinese used to be famous for their poetry, martial arts, and philosophy. But what have you now to prove your worth in the modern age? A metropolitan oven of smoke and disease to choke your children's lungs? A refinery built into the power grid as a systemic mechanical leech, sucking the life out of your once beautiful countryside?"

Tala stretched out her hand. A shockwave sent dozens of people into the air, and a crack of lighting emerged from Mayari's vulturous gaze, hitting the capital's steps. The sounds of screaming and return fire from the guards began as a barrage of ear shattering blasts rocked the area. Shakti slid unseen into a building as the advancing police brigades charged hopelessly towards the impenetrable Aradians.

Shakti ran down the hall and into one of the rooms. It was a classroom of first grade girls, no older than seven years old. They screamed and hid under their desks from the explosions outside. Shakti pushed the cowering teacher out of the room and shut the door. She looked around to make sure it was the right class.

"Good morning, cherry blossoms! I am your substitute teacher today, Mrs. Cheng. Today we are going on a field trip!"

Explosions erupted outside. Glass shattered nearby. The girls whimpered.

"Now don't worry lovelies, everything is going to be all right, at least for you. Based on your exquisite heritage, you've all been chosen to be Princesses of Asia!"

The young girls continued to cry and ask for their parents.

"I know, it's going to be a rough time, but you will thank me for this privilege when you're older," she said, as a large explosion hit the building next to them.

With the capital in flames, Shakti herded the ten girls onto the school's roof. Black smoke billowed from the streets below. The air filled with the cries of thousands of terrified citizens. Two helicopters awaited Shakti on the roof, pushing the smoke away as their engines roared and their propellers chopped the air. Shakti shuffled the girls onboard and then stepped in herself, patting the little ones on their heads as she passed. As the helicopters rose, the hovering Aradians flew beside them to guide them and cover their flanks. Everything had been timed perfectly, so that their attack on the capital would distract the Chinese authorities from the inevitable Japanese invasion.

Shakti looked above them. Through the whipping blades she could see tens of thousands of Japanese drones speeding toward the city from high above, blocking out the sun like an immense black specter. Their missiles dove in a hail of metal and fire, crushing the massive city to rubble as sirens blared in their wake. But Shakti was already gone. Bombshells cracked far behind them as they flew deeper inland and through a bamboo forest. The young girls were horrified but sat quietly, tears staining their cheeks. All ten children frowned as Shakti grinned, delighted with her crop of new apprentices.

In the basement of his castle, the leader of the Democratic People's Republic of Korea spun a silver coin on a table. His old hands shook as he ground his teeth slowly and stared at the blinking coin reflecting a single beam of light coming through the room's only window. A cigar sat burning by his side and the smoke rose into the stale air, drifting past the four soldiers who stood in the corners of the room. His sister sat in a wheelchair, looking into the pale light with opaque cataracts. She held a ballistic encased tablet that beeped excessively on her lap.

"They've hacked our system, your Majesty. All systems are shutting down," she said.

He sat, staring straight ahead, he eyes squinting in frustration and hatred. His sister looked at him once more before her head dropped to her chest, lifeless. The four guards followed suit, fainting into heaps of themselves as if poisoned. The door behind him opened.

"Keep your hands on the table," a voice said from the shadows.

"Tala, check him for cyanide capsules."

The Aradian walked up to his majesty and

sniffed his neck. He winced and clenched his teeth with fear.

Tala shook her head. Shakti walked in from the darkness and slowly rounded the table, looking into his eye's as she did. Mayari stayed near the door whilst Tala disappeared into the shadows.

The dictator looked up as Shakti sat down, her black silk robe shimmering like her penetrating pupils. She removed her headpiece and set it lightly on the table.

"So, the East finally falls to the all-powerful Shakti. You will not win, my people are loyal to me. I am their God," he said forcefully, mustering all the courage he had left.

Shakti smiled slightly. "Tell me, what is it like to be divine?" she asked, leaning into the light, her supple face illuminated, devoid of any blemishes save for a short scar that made a small slit through her left eyebrow.

"You mock me," he said, cracking a grin.

"No. I envy you. Though malnutrition, you've kept your population density low enough to maintain a level census. Fifty years in the making no doubt, all without an invasion or even so much as a serious investigation. Bravo."

"Know that the respect is mutual," he said, nodding slightly.

"You mock me," she teased.

"You conquered the United States. I am more than envious of that."

"How flattering!" she said, smiling widely.

They both laughed. Shakti's cackle filled the room. Suddenly, she lurched upwards and flung a small blade across the table. A five-inch spike buried itself into the dictator's forehead as he gasped in pain. Tala held him still as he squirmed in his seat. A red ribbon had been tied to the end of the blade with the leader's name written in black, using the charred bones of his people.

"Listen here, you fool! We are a triad of Goddesses! See us now, for it is our prophecy that will take root in the planet's tilled soils. Now, you will broadcast this message to your people, or this torture sustains itself for eternity!"

Shakti threw a small, circular, black microphone onto the table. Tala's magic fingers burned the words into the wood as the trembling leader screamed in pain. He fought to read the words as Tala grasped his head impatiently and pulled the spike deeper into his splitting skull.

"Good day children of North Korea! This is your Supreme Leader, making a final broadcast. I...I am no longer your leader, nor am I...God. I am a fat stubby man who craves childish, Western obsessions. I...am an embarrassment to world leaders and...am no use to the Zurvan Order, to whom I am relinquishing all my...territories and assets. Queen Shakti is now your Supreme Leader. If you are in good health and are...a woman...then you will be enlisted in Queen Shakti's...imperial army...to fight against impurity, as ordered by the Queen. If you bow low to your new Queen, and you show promise...as an advanced female specimen..." He flinched.

"Go on," Shakti said, her gaze pushing him onward.

"Then you will be sent to an isle in the Pacific Ocean to be used strictly as an artificially inseminated vessel...to birth only female babies. After your second child...you will be given a life of luxury. If you are a male and you surrender, Shakti will grant you a chance to be free under the new mandate. All uncooperative citizens...will be...exterminated. Report to your local market where food will be rationed in accordance with the Zurvan Empress's code of...communal wealth. Good day, and praise be unto the Earth, our true mother...and Goddess of all!"

Tala let him go and the dictator screamed as he ruthlessly pounded his head against the table to push the spike far enough into his brain to kill himself. His body flinched and his forehead oozed pink bubbles into the canals of the engravings left by Tala's smoking fingertips.

"I want that table as a keepsake," Shakti said, picking up the microphone.

"Don't clean it off though. It's not the words I need to remember."

Tala ripped off the top of the table, and the three of them left, leaving the dictator's corpse to rot in his grandfather's tomb.

CHAPTER 19
ESCAPE FROM WHITE HORSE

Only a week after Michael's departure, the young men of White Horse were already courting Melody. Word spread that Michael had left and would probably never return, but Melody felt otherwise. Nearly every time she went out, someone would be waiting to ask her for her hand in marriage. Every time she would say no. A man would promise her a new life near the coast, or boast his sizable potato yield, but nothing pleased her. She wanted a man she could love truly. She even considered following Michael south in silent tow. Eventually, her decision was made for her.

One morning in late June, Melody walked out to the well to fetch a bucket of water for cooking. A young, scrawny man in an oversized brown coat stood waiting.

"Good morning, Melody," he said, handing her a bouquet of half-dead dandelions. She took them reluctantly.

"Good morning, Allen," she replied, setting the flowers down and pulling water up from the well.

"May I help you with that?" he asked.

"I think I got it," she said, trying to ignore him.

"You know, a lot of the guys around here are wondering when you'll choose a husband. My father has a lot of land, and connections with merchants that travel all the way from the coast. We would live happily," he said.

"Allen, I think you're a nice guy. But I've already chosen. Michael is the one I love."

"He left you, Melody."

"He didn't leave me! He is on a journey to find his family. There is a difference."

Allen hung his head.

"Enjoy the flowers," he muttered, as he walked back down the hill towards the village, kicking the ground in disappointment.

Melody sighed and continued pulling the bucket up. Suddenly, she heard what sounded like planes far above. She looked up but could not see anything through the thick cloud cover. Then, she jumped. The first series of explosions came whistling down at the far end of town, not more than a mile from her. Dogs began barking and the church bell rang out in warning.

Melody's heart began racing as she took the bucket of water and ran back to the cabin. Once inside, she locked the door and looked out the window. A stream of smoke rose from the far side of the village. People were running and panicking, looking for their loved ones. The second series of bombs hit; this time at the towns center. The shockwave rattled the old windows in the cabin. Melody stepped back and quickly hid under the bed. A few moments of quiet passed, before the bombs came upon her in a thunderous cacophony. All the windows in the cabin exploded as Melody screamed. A fire started at the other end of the cabin where the log wall had been splintered to pieces. She ran outside, her hands and face slightly burned and her ears still ringing as the last of the bombs hit the other side of the hill. Houses and cabins lay in ruins, burning all around her, as the morning air filled with smoke. Hundreds of screams filled the air. A baby wailed and a legless child crawled up the hill, the school lying in a smoking pile behind her. Then, the shooting started. Machine guns fired into the city from what Melody could only assume was the Queen's army, making a northward push. Return fire commenced as the armed locals tried to protect their small village.

Melody turned from the village and ran into the

woods, stumbling over logs and stumps as the fear turned her legs into jelly. She kept running, looking back every few minutes to make sure no one pursued her. After a few miles, she was too winded to move forward anymore. She fell to the forest floor and listened, breathing fast, short breaths. The gunshots sounded distant, and smoke rose in a large column behind her. Melody's hands and legs trembled as she lay on a bed of dead leaves. A gentle wind pushed the clouds apart and Melody saw the sun for a moment, not for more than a few seconds, but long enough to give her fleeting glimmer of hope. She started sobbing silently as she lay there, not knowing where to go, or what to do. She curled up like a wounded animal shuddering in the wake of the massacre.

After almost an hour of being paralyzed with helplessness, Melody heard a sound nearby. She stood up and began to walk, trying to locate where the sound was coming from. Then she heard it again. It was a child weeping. Melody ran towards the source. A few hundred feet away, a small boy around the age of seven sat behind a fallen tree.

"Mama! My Mama! Mama!!" he cried. No one else was nearby.

"Oh God!" Melody gasped. She walked up to the boy and knelt beside him, hugging him close. "It's okay, you're okay, you're okay."

The boy continued to weep as he leaned into Melody's warmth, comforted by her presence. Melody looked around for his family, but he seemed to be the only survivor.

"I'm Melody. What's your name?" she asked gently.

The young boy reached down his shirt and took out a necklace.

"The Star of David," Melody whispered, identifying the small gold emblem hanging from his neck." Your name is David?"

The boy nodded, pouting and trembling with fear. Melody stood back up and looked around. Nothing but endless forest spread to the horizon. Neither an enemy nor a villager seemed to be close by. With a mission in mind, Melody took the boy's hand and began walking west. She thought that if she could get to the coast within a few days, there was a chance she might find the boy's parents still alive. 'But even if that were the case, what then?' she thought to herself. There was no home to go back to. Her lover was far away, already on his own journey. Odds favored that she would be either put into a refugee camp or sworn into the Queens army, in the same ranks as the soldiers who had just attacked and killed the people of her town. Melody wanted neither. As they walked on, she tried to think of a plan.

That evening, Melody and David stumbled upon an old hitch camper someone had abandoned. It was small, without a door, and was rat infested and falling apart, but it provided a better shelter than anything else around them in the dank, black-spruce thicket. Melody tucked David under the musty bed covers and lay beside him, wondering what to do. The day had beaten her spirit and forced her to see and experience things she would never forget. Though seemingly fragile, even to herself, Melody's heart was strong, and to give up would be the ultimate tragedy.

"Well slap my ass and call me Charlie, look what I found Burt!"

A gruff voice startled Melody and David awake the next morning. A bearded man with a shotgun slung over his shoulder looked at the two refugees with a creepy smile.

"Who are you?" Melody asked, her voice fearful but steady.

The man took off the withered baseball hat he

had been wearing and attempted to dust off the motor-oil stains.

"Howdy ma'am, the name's Lenny. What brings you ta this shit hole camper way out in the middl'a nowhere?"

Another man poked his head through the door.

"There's a woman?" he asked excitedly.

"Yes, Burt. A woman. A young, pretty woman who don't take kindly to the likes of scum brushers like you."

"Are you hurt?" Burt asked.

Melody sat up, her anxiety growing.

"We're fine...mostly. I burned my face and hands yesterday but I'll be okay. We escaped the bombings in White Horse."

"Ah hellfire! That town got bombed too? My brother's in White Horse!" Burt said smiling, showing off his rotten teeth and crooked eyes.

"Why are you smiling?" Melody asked, with a disturbed look on her face.

"Now I get the bastards assets! Wahoo, I'm gonna be rich!"

"No ya ain't ya dumb son-of-a-bitch. What the hell is a load of silver gonna do for ya other an weigh ya down? Ya can't grow food with it, so quit your talkin!" Lenny said, smacking Burt's thick skull with the bill of his hat.

"We got breakfast cookin bit of a ways downstream. You're welcome to some beans if it'd please ya," Lenny offered.

"Thanks," Melody said as she took David's hand and woke him, getting out of the bed and following the strange men downstream.

Lenny and Burt were middle aged, scarred and beaten by the constant harassment in their line of work. They were grossly unkempt, which was understandable given that a post-eruption merchant's life consisted of seasonal fishing in a nearly fish-less ocean and trapping and thieving in the short northern summer. Melody already knew this, but they talked of their ventures as they followed next to the stream.

"Yep, we had to head further inland this trip. Not enough trappers. Hell, not enough traders in general. We're one of the only businesses still regulated by the Queen. She taxes us so much that the only reason we keep working is the fact that she'll kill us if we don't produce. Well, how the hell are we s'pose to yield if there ain't nobody to trade with?!"

"Sounds like a pickle," Melody said, caring little for the merchant's pockets as she pictured her town being blasted in a whirlwind of death.

"Ha! She said pickle!" Burt said, laughing. His smile faded, "Oh man...I miss a good pickle," he said sadly, as a fond memory of the simple luxury of a cucumber soaked in vinegar entered his mind.

"Burt loved pickles," Lenny said.

"Pickled eggs too!" Burt said, "Mmm them things is delicious!"

They got to the camp where a pot of beans boiled over a small fire. A few other sleeping merchants were strewn about the camp.

"Don't mind these Sally's," Lenny said. "Just watch out for Chuck."

Melody looked over at the beast of a man who lay flat, holding an empty bottle of whisky to his chest as if protecting it. Breadcrumbs fluttered in his beard as his snoring battled a drunken slumber.

Lenny sat down and mixed the beans. Melody stared at the fire as he looked at her.

"So, they bombed your home. I'm sorry to hear that. That Shakti is one ruthless bitch I tell ya. Never gave a damn for another human heart as far as I can tell."

"Have you thought about rebelling?" Melody asked.

Lenny and Burt looked at each other and chuckled as Lenny poured some beans in a cup and handed it to David, who took it excitedly and slurped down the hot mush.

"The outcome of our efforts wouldn't be worth the cause. You think them bombers are bad? She's got these hench-women ya see. Fully plated in titanium armor n able to knock over a skyscraper or burn an entire forest to nothing. There's no stoppin them things."

"Titanium armor? I think one of them came to my house the other day," Melody said. "She tortured and killed the old woman living with us trying to get answers of his whereabouts."

Lenny looked at Melody in a skeptical daze.

"You sayin an Aradian came to your house? Lookin for who?"

"Michael Beller."

Lenny jumped to his feet, eyes wide. "You mean to tell me that you know a Beller? Listen here, young lady. I was a wild land fire fighter years and years ago. When Shakti and her cult started that fire in Yellowstone in '33 and killed those national guardsmen, I was there. I was there when Ezra Beller tried to stop her. Hell, we barely got out of there before the eruption...it was a horrible day for the world. If a Beller is alive, you wanna make sure you don't affiliate with them or else you'll be taken too! No wonder they bombed White Horse. They were trying to smoke him out!"

David leaned close to Melody and tugged on her sleeve.

"What is it little one?"

He pointed to the hill on their left above the stream, where a line of armed women in black armor stood pointing rifles at them. Melody gasped as the two men looked up with equal fear. Burt screamed like a small child. The rest of the sleeping men awoke, save the man still grasping the whisky bottle tightly and snoring away the morning.

"What a strange arrangement of humans," a woman's voice said, walking through her line of combatants and facing them. From behind the black metal mask, a crone with silvery blonde hair and cracked lips emerged. She wore a ram's skull headpiece, horns painted black as they curled around her rigid face. Her piercing blue eyes swept them like a Siberian wind. Printed in red on the collarbone of her black armor was her name, 'Sandraudiga'.

Lenny and Burt put their hands up.

"Lord Sandraudiga!" Lenny cried. "Please, if this is about the yield, we had to go a little further inland this time, don't be mad just cause—"

"This isn't about the yield, you miserable dicks,"

Sandraudiga scowled. "I have new orders from the Queen. Your services will not be needed anymore."

"I don't understand," Lenny said. "Have we not got ya what ya needed before?"

"Where are the rest of your men?" she asked angrily.

"We lost three in a fire fight with a troop of thieves. Seven more deserted us and four died at sea. This is all that's left."

"Very well," Sandraudiga said as she pulled out a pistol. She pointed it at Lenny and shot. Melody screamed. Lenny fell flat backward, his vest blooming red from the bullet that went through his chest. David began whimpering.

The men reached for their weapons, but it was too late. The line of women sprayed the encampment with bullets, sparing only Melody and David as the two stood in shock, unable to move.

"What is your name?" Sandraudiga asked Melody, smoke still rising from the barrel of her rifle. A soft rain began to fall, clinking on the various metal attachments of the assault weapons.

"Alisha," Melody lied, "And this is my little brother, Mark."

"Where do you come from?"

"White Horse. We escaped the bombings and

we're trying to get to the coast."

"Where do you come from originally, Alisha?"

"Umm, Nebraska."

"Nebraska? Really?"

"Yes ma'am."

"LORD."

"Yes, my Lord," Melody said, quickly correcting herself.

"Do you know who I am, Alisha?"

"Lord Sandraudiga?"

"Correct," she responded sharply. "So, it seems you've been acquainted with Michael Beller?"

Melody chose not to respond, shaking her head instead.

Sandraudiga turned and spoke to her second in command. "Take her to the camp and keep her for questioning. When I return from the coast, I'll deal with her myself. Kill the boy."

Sandraudiga turned and quickly left with her troop as the six remaining soldiers came down the hill towards Melody. One of them zip-tied Melody's wrists while the rest of the women kicked the bodies of the merchants and checked their pockets for valuables. One of them squatted down and ate some hot beans, for even the Queen's officers were malnourished.

"You're really going to kill a child?!" Melody asked the squad leader, her voice thick with anger and desperation.

"Men are a disease," the woman said as she combed her obsidian plated gloves through David's hair. The child wept but was so dehydrated that no tears could form.

One of the soldiers poked Chuck with the tip of her rifle and he opened his eyes widely. He quickly grabbed the rifle, pulled the soldier in close and stabbed her through the heart with his large bowie knife. In a quick motion he sat up and flipped the weapon around, firing off shots in all different directions at an incredible rate. Melody screamed but it was over as soon as it had started. All the women lay dead, including the squad leader who had two bullets through her neck.

After spitting out a large tobacco chew that had been under his lip all night, the large man slung the rifle over his shoulder and picked up David and Melody in his massive arms.

"We better get outta here quick," he muttered in a voice as crackly as the fire itself.

David and Melody looked at each other, half frightened and half relieved. Even though the man had a large belly and the body to support it, he carried David and Melody quickly, panting heavily and pushing himself onward like a titan pulling a mountain.

After a few miles of non-stop trudging through the thick tundra, Melody had to say something.

"You can stop and take a rest now. We have legs too, you know?"

"A children's foot prints are breadcrumbs for beasts in these lands," he said, barely able to pick up his feet as he jogged slowly down an old logging road. After a few more minutes, he gave in and stopped. David dismounted himself from the man's sweaty back. The man took a drink out of the canteen in his pocket before handing it to them and walking back.

"Wait! Where are you going?" Melody asked.

"Just wait a minute," he said.

He went back a few hundred yards and began erasing his tracks before making new ones in a different direction. He tied those tracks into a creek and walked up the stream before hopping on rocks back to Melody and David.

"In the Navy, I did some counter-tracking. Now they'll hopefully go the wrong way, and we can slow our pace for a short while."

"You were a sailor?" Melody asked.

"I was a Navy SEAL," he said. "Sea, air, and land special operations. We were some of the best in the world until the Queen created the Aradians. Every fighting force on the globe became obsolete after those things came about."

"Well, thank you for saving us. David is thankful too, he just doesn't talk much."

The man looked at them and gave a slight nod. He reached out his hand.

"Chuck Hartford," he said, introducing himself. "Call me Hartford."

"Good to meet you, Hartford. I'm Melody."

"Where does the little guy come from?" he asked.

"His name is David. I'm looking for his parents."

"Good luck. They're probably dead or they deserted him. Having a young boy around makes you a target. The younger they are, the more dangerous they are to be around."

"Is the Queen really going to try and kill every male on Earth?"

"Sounds like it. I have no doubts she'll succeed at this pace. But her forces aren't the only ones we gotta worry about out here."

"What do you mean?" she asked.

They walked on. After a while, Melody went to say something but he silenced her.

"Shh! Quiet!" he said in a loud whisper. Hartford looked around as if they were being watched. A long silence ensued. The only sound was a few dead leaves skidding across the ground, caught by a gentle breeze.

Just then, a shot rang out, and Hartford grasped his chest.

"Ah fuck, not again!" he yelled as blood dripped from his shoulder. He fell to the Earth a fallen giant. David dropped to the ground as Melody looked on in horror, before quickly dropping onto her stomach next to David. They looked up and saw their attackers.

A motley crew of a dozen or so young men and boys came out from behind the thin trees, as if they were born in the tamaracks' shadow. They were armed with mostly primitive weapons, along with a few carbines. They rested axes on their shoulders, and held machetes, still stained red with the blood of their victims. They were a group of orphans turned thieves of the new world. They wore human skulls around their waists, dried finger bones for necklaces, and all different kinds of clothing, ranging from the Queen's soldier's armor to high fashion trench coats, with wedding rings and women's jewelry stitched onto the breast pockets as mock medals for their transgressions steeped in sin.

"Do we have a treat for us today or what boys?" their leader said. He took off his sunglasses to show his beady eyes. He wore a tattered, grey wool coat, and a crown made of human jawbones entwined in his greasy, bloody hair. His stare would have forced a wolverine back underground. He walked down to the road and kicked Chuck's rifle away from him, then came right up to Melody. He stood her up and examined her. His breath was like the stale air released from a coffin.

"The Queen's soldiers are right behind us! You better leave now, or she'll kill us all," Melody warned.

They all laughed.

"We don't run from anyone, darlin'. People run from us," he said, smelling her hair. Melody shook with fear.

David got angry and stood up. He kicked the leader in the shin.

"Little fucking bastard!" the gang leader cried as he shoved the seven-year-old to the ground with his foot. David whimpered in pain and curled up on the ground as the thief ripped off Melody's coat. He licked her nipple as he caressed his dagger along her chest lightly. Melody froze.

"I don't think I've had a girl as pretty as you since I fucked that nigger in Anchorage," he said, licking his lips. His cohorts laughed and smiled as they watched.

"What do you think, Victor?" he yelled. "She cuter

than that nigger girl?"

"Oh yeah," one of the young men said behind her.

"Yeah? I think so too," he sneered.

"I...I...I have HIV!" Melody said desperately.

"No...you don't. But you're about to," he said as he slithered his tongue into her ear.

Melody screamed and the man pushed her to the ground, ripping at her pants with a forceful tear. "No!" she screamed.

The thief began to taste her body with his vile tongue, his foul saliva sticking to her skin.

Just then, a large arrow flew through the thief's neck, splattering Melody's face with blood as his jugular spewed. The man choked on his own gore and rolled over, dying next to Chuck, who still had a breath left in him. Melody covered her breasts and dragged herself away from the other men, who had turned their gaze from her, searching for the arrow's origin. They began to shoot their weapons into the woods, attempting to scare off the intruder. After a few seconds of random shots, they stopped and looked around. No one could be seen.

One of the thieves glanced upwards. "What the..."

Suddenly, a parliament of owls swooped on them without warning, like wide faced angels of death. The giant birds pierced the gang with their razor-sharp talons, pecking at them with their beaks. One managed to pluck a boy's eye from its socket while another knocked a boy to the ground and tore off his genitals.

Just then, a woman with a drawn bow jumped out of the woods and put an arrow through one of the boys' skulls. She fought as if she were dancing; her motion could never be predicted. She punched and kicked the men into submission while the owls continued their raid. She swung her foot around, cracking the chests of one of the men before sending a fatal punch into the throat of the last living thief. In less than a few seconds, it was over, and the woman stood in the center of the owls' feeding frenzy.

Melody looked up at her savior. There stood a tall, naked woman, with dark black dreadlocks and vines wrapping around her arms and legs. Her eyes were blue and green with white specks of light. Her aura pulsed with divine energy. Having eaten their fill, the owls silently retreated into the tree branches as they tended to the wounds under their ruffled feathers. One of them hobbled around with a broken wing.

"Ingrid?" Melody asked, gazing upon the sprite.

"Melody, I can only presume," Pavonis said with a smile as she helped Melody put her clothes back on.

"How do you know who I am?" Melody asked.

"Are you not the Princess of Qatar who famously escaped the Queen's takeover of the Arabic states?"

Melody did not answer.

"Your secret is safe with me, young Princess," Pavonis said, smiling.

"I've never told anyone that," Melody said. "And all the brave people who helped me were slain on the Alaskan coast..."

"I was there, Melody. I was the distraction that allowed you to run into the woods without being pursued."

"And now you have saved me yet again," she said somberly. "Thank you."

"Don't be disheartened. You are no warrior, Melody. At least, not yet."

Pavonis walked over to the thief, who was still gargling blood, and stomped his temple with her sharp heel, crushing his skull into a myriad of fractures. She stepped beside him.

"And who is this man who still holds onto the thread of life?" she asked, kneeling beside Hartford.

"This is Hartford. He saved us from the Queen's ruthlessness just earlier today. The pigs you just killed shot him. I don't think he's going to survive."

Hartford lay there with a sucking chest wound, his breaths separated by a faint tone.

Pavonis placed her hand on his naked chest, over the wound.

"What are you doing?" Melody asked.

"Preventing him from crossing over."

A strange sound and smell came from her palm as Hartford sat up, coughing. Pavonis pressed her lips against his and entered a large breath into his healing lungs. With a single breath she pushed life back into him with her efficacious Sararan qualities.

After a spate of coughing, Hartford looked at Pavonis.

"Who are you?" he asked Pavonis, who smiled back at him with his blood on her chin.

"I am the shepherd of this forest and all forests. You can call me Pavonis."

She stood and wiped the blood from her mouth. Chuck sat up and looked puzzlingly at Melody, who shrugged in return, equally astounded.

Pavonis walked to each of the thieves' bodies and assessed their weaponry. As she did, she spoke to Melody while Hartford regained his strength.

"Who is the boy?"

"This is David."

Pavonis came back with a few carbines and two daggers. She set the carbine by Hartford and gave a large dagger to Melody. The smaller knife she set by David. She knelt next to David so he could see her better, and she, him.

"You've had quite a time these last few days, haven't you?"

David nodded, crying to himself as the weight of the day fell on his already heavy heart.

"I'm sorry for not getting to you two sooner, but the forest is vast and saving humans is not my first priority."

"What should we do now?" asked Melody. "The Queen's troops are everywhere, not to mention these rapists and God knows what other evils."

"We will take a ship out to sea and follow the coast at a distance, southward. From there, we will go directly east, and meet with Michael and his uncle in the mountains. You would like that, wouldn't you?"

"How did you know that I knew your son?"

"Don't be so obtuse, Melody. I know more than you think."

"But what about the Queen? And the thieves?" Melody asked frantically.

"Shh. We don't have to worry about any of that now. I have fought worse adversaries than starving combatants and thickheaded thieves. It is the trek itself that will challenge you. Come now, we must move since all this commotion will bring in more attention than we need. Hoo! Hoo!"

As she spoke to the owls, the large birds rose from their perches and flew off in different directions.

"How did you get them to do that?" Hartford asked, looking Pavonis up and down in a curious way. He could not decide whether he was attracted to the tall naked woman, or scared of her, or both.

"They are my eyes and ears of the forest."

Pavonis picked up David as if he were her own child, kissing his forehead, and Melody helped Hartford to his feet, as the four of them walked on towards the sea. Melody wanted to believe that all the mayhem was behind her, but she would soon realize that being bombarded, ambushed by enemy soldiers, and nearly raped by Alaskan barbarians was only the beginning of her journey into the unknown. Luckily, she and David were being guided by one of the most powerful creatures to ever walk the Earth.

Pavonis, however, was not so complacent, given the ever-watchful gaze of the Aradians. Cautious measures had to be implemented at every turn; every creek crossing; every word spoken, and every breath taken. Pavonis knew all too well that, under just the right conditions, the range of an Aradian's sensory abilities could span a continent.

CHAPTER 20
NO SHADOWS

It was midnight in early July when Michael awoke to a strange rustling, only just audible over the chorus of cricket screeches. His fire smoldered as a string of smoke rose to the heavenly sky. With his awakening, his empty stomach lurched into motion, groaning, making it even harder to pinpoint the sound that had roused him. He heard more rustling in the bushes and picked up his axe and dagger. The beast sounded large, at least the size of a man. He assumed the worst. Maybe it was a bear or a bony mountain lion, eager for a fresh meal. Without waiting to find out, Michael aimed at the bush he suspected the sound originated from and threw his dagger.

"Ouch!" A yell came from the bush.

"Who goes there?" Michael yelled in response. "I'm armed!"

"And a terrible throw! Ya hit me with the butt of yer knife ya little asshole!"

Out of the bush stumbled a scraggly man with a rifle in his hand. His logger clothes were tattered, and Michael could smell the scotch on him.

"What do you want?" Michael asked as he stood up with his axe raised high.

"I saw smoke and thought I'd see who was trespassin on my property!"

"Your property?"

"Yeah, this is my piece of land. Been here for over thirty years! I should be the one throwin knives at you!"

The old man picked up the lantern he had dropped during Michael's attack, and kicked the handle of the dagger by Michael's feet. Once the man had set the lantern alight, Michael could see the man's scarred face. Michael put his axe down.

"May I stay with you in your home for one night?" Michael asked.

"Oh, now you ask!"

"Please sir, I'm starving and haven't eaten for three days! I will do any work that needs doing."

The man walked up and put the lantern close to Michael as he looked him over.

"The cabin does need a good clean," he said reluctantly. "You ever fix fence?"

"No, sir. I've never had to. I've never owned

livestock."

"It ain't hard to learn, it's just hard on this old body. Why don't ya come get some stew and we'll work somethin out. Gotta ice my shin now too ya god damned bush-wackin son of a bitch."

Back at the farm, Michael slurped down a serving of beef and vegetable stew, between sips of home brewed scotch ale. The steam from his bowl poured into the air.

"Slow down there, half-squat, you'll burn a hole in your gut! What the hell you doin way out 'ere anyways? Where'd you come from?"

Michael looked up at him and wiped his mouth, before taking another swig of delicious, frothy dark ale. He had not eaten a decent meal in weeks.

"I'm seeking my uncle, near some town called Barkerville."

"Barkerville?! That ghost town? How in the hell you gonna make it all that way before fall?"

"I need a horse," Michael said, tipping the bowl to his mouth and shoveling the rest of the potatoes and broth down his throat. He briefly choked on the bay leaf at the bottom of the bowl before spitting it out on the table. "Sorry," he mumbled, picking up the leaf and throwing it back into the bowl.

The old man shook his head. "You ain't never worked with livestock. How you gonna take care of a horse?"

"I'm a hunter and a fisherman, not a farmer. All a horse needs is food, water, and rest. It's not like I plan on beating it to hell or anything."

"Ha! You are if you're plannin on makin it to where you're goin before the acid rains! A horse needs a companion, someone to take care of it; someone to tend to its hooves when it throws a shoe, and give it the right medicine if it falls ill. If you don't know how to do these things, you better start knowin."

"Will you teach me?"

"I guess so." The old man shrugged, filling up Michael's beer mug from a small keg on the countertop and handing it to him. "What's your name, son?"

"Michael, what's yours?"

"Sean Cahill. I've lived here since the early '20s. My wife died in '24. Haven't seen too many people since the exodus. Just the few folks who come purchase cattle from me from time to time."

"I'm sorry to hear about your wife," Michael said,

wiping his mouth with his sleeve, satiated at last.

The man sat down and sipped his beer, looking over at an old photograph of his wife. His eyes were warm. "She was quite a woman. Liked rodeos and moonshine. Never gave a damn for the cyber age. We moved out here from Kentucky to escape all the bullshit happening. She started smokin cigarettes like a chimney after the miscarriage. Cancer got her quick...it was the hardest thing I've ever done, buryin her behind this cabin. I quit smokin after she died, but lately, with my health, I might be joinin her soon anyways. You smoke?"

"No, sir," Michael said.

The man sighed. "I haven't tasted tobacco for a decade. I guess it's for the better. I got a few packs stashed away in case there's some cause for celebration. Haven't had anythin to celebrate in a while I suppose. You get some rest for now. I'll be wakin you up before sunrise to start work."

"Will do, Sean. Thank you."

Sean stood up and set his mug down. Michael got up from the table and made his way toward the couch in the living room of the large cabin.

"Just work hard, get done what needs doin over the next few days, and we'll see about gettin you a horse for your travels."

"I'd appreciate that," Michael replied.

"See ya in the mornin," Sean mumbled, walking to his room with a slight limp.

The next day, the old man took Michael out to the stables. There were several horses, a few pigs, and a chicken coop. All the cows could be seen grazing in the distance, spread out across the hills. They walked down to where the horses were kept. There were two large mature horses, a frisky young stallion, and an old grey steed whose neck drooped with age. Sean walked up to the young horse. His hide was mostly a rich, red-brown russet, but his hind legs faded to startling white.

"This here is Apollo. He's a young Appaloosa. He's rare. Beautiful. He's got a lot of energy in him...and he's a pain in my ass. I'll make you a deal. You fix my fence and clean the cabin top to bottom, and you spend the rest of the time breakin him, he's yours. I've gotta use this time to get some vegetables growin while the suns out."

"I'll take that deal any day, Sean. And when I return, I'll bring you whatever treasures the south yields."

"The only treasure you'll find in those mountains is a tombstone with your name on it," Sean said, shaking his head. "You'd best head back north. Back home."

"The only family I have lives in those war-torn mountains. I'll stop at nothing to get there."

Sean nodded and said nothing.

"I promise to take good care of Apollo along the way, as best I can. Now, where's this fence at?"

Seven days later, Michael found himself shirtless and covered in mud, working on one of the longest, hottest days of the year. There seemed to be no end to the fence post pounding, beneath the sun he had once longed for; the sun he now wished the clouds would deny. Hauling hundreds of pounds of barbed wire across several miles and having to dig deep into the root-entangled earth slowed his progress. Insects by the swarm ravaged him as he labored. He would start before sunrise, end after sunset, and was fed by Sean only twice a day, having to forage his lunch as he worked. On the eighth day, just as the sun was setting over the rolling hills, Michael clipped the last coil of barbed wire and put his tools in his satchel, before making his way to the cabin.

Michael's sunburnt back faced dusk's waning glow, as his heavy tools clanked over his shoulder. After a four-mile hike he arrived back at the cabin, to find Sean sitting on the rocking chair on his porch, facing the sunset, a cigarette burnt all the way to the filter still held in his fingers. His frail, beaten body had finally had enough. He had spent his final moments taking one more puff of tobacco, before joining his lover in whatever afterlife he had been yearning.

That evening, Michael buried Sean's body next to the old man's wife, Mabel, laying a handful of budding lilac flowers on both their graves. As if it were plain sin to waste the home-brewed ale, Michael brought the keg out by the graves and drank it, the night's mournful quiet leaving him to ponder the infinitely beautiful thought of his friend being reunited with his lover in some higher plain of existence. Having drunk his fill, Michael went to the stables, setting all the animals free except for Apollo. The horse had mellowed over the past few weeks, becoming surprisingly gentle, and Michael soon fell asleep with his head resting on Apollo's soft belly, to the sound of a cricket's chirp and the distant howl of a lone wolf.

The next morning, Michael opened the stable doors, and Apollo presented the less amenable side of his personality. The young horse whipped his neck around as Michael struggled with the reins, kicking, bucking, and stepping about, always trying to free himself from Michael's pull. Just when he thought the horse would calm, as the cool morning breeze whisked gently over the terrified, sweating animal, Apollo would seize the reins and fight Michael for control.

"Come on, you menace!" Michael yelled, to no avail.

After many hours battling with the troublesome stallion, Michael finally figured out the problem. He pulled Apollo eastward, so the horse's face pointed towards the rising sun.

"Look, Apollo! There are no shadows!"

After a few seconds of calm, Michael cautiously approached the exhausted animal. He placed his hand gently on Apollo's neck and stroked him. Without being able to see his own shade, the horse breathed easily.

"We have no enemies in the face of the sun," Michael said calmly, letting his voice become recognizable to the frightened steed. "Our sun is a being that knows no equal. If there were ever a day to be guided by our friend in the sky, it would be this day. Set your heart to match its splendor, and our companionship will not be in vain."

Apollo dipped his head and nudged his nose into Michael's neck. From that point onwards, they never fought. The horse knew Michael as his master and friend, and through that fellowship, Michael would come to know Apollo as an equestrian God, who had concealed behind his braided mane a pair of eyes that raged with burning lust for war.

After two weeks of riding Apollo through the grey valleys of war-torn North America, Michael slowly crept his way deep into the wilderness, until at last he reached the eastern edge of the Canadian Rockies. The massive peaks rose behind a great wall of cast iron and ice: skeletons of destroyed airplanes, trucks, and electrical appliances lined the base of the great mountain range for five hundred miles in either direction, and the wind wailed through hollow car frames and razor wire, weeping with ice crystals. It was a clear warning to anyone who dared to venture into the heart of Sandraudiga's domain.

The snow fell lightly as Apollo pulled back, uncertain.

"Come on, boy. There's no turning back now."

Apollo whinnied nervously as he hopped from one to hoof to the other, but eventually allowed Michael to lead him into the mechanical graveyard.

As they journeyed, Michael spotted devices that he had only ever heard about from his elders. Computers. Televisions. Phones. Washing Machines. Chairs. Broken guns, of all sizes. Bullet shells. Helicopter parts. Roofing. Medical equipment. Everything was smashed and collecting rust, sinking further into the foot of the mountain with each passing year. Every so often, a bone would appear in their path, sometimes human, sometimes not, licked clean by rats and raiders.

An old highway lay in the middle of the barrier, the crude fencing at its edge having clearly been erected then torn down again many times over. Michael crossed the naked stretch quickly, mindful that the eyes of feral border raiders might notice him and decide to include both horse and man in their next meal. Having avoided imminent death, the two of them crossed the last walls of crumpled aluminum rubble, where an awning held wind chimes made from porcelain doll's heads, hung from the rusted links of a chainsaw chain. The ceramic heads clinked in the wind like a dismal lullaby as they passed.

They entered a steep, narrow canyon, and Apollo trotted anxiously through the passage between the peaks, before climbing upwards into a wood, where rotting trees leaned over them with cataclysmic patience. They crossed several creeks and rose into a high mountain valley, where a burn scar of a vast, charred forest lay before them. Thousands of blackened pine trees stood like splintered towers of darkness, and the landscape was coated in a thick layer of ash, muffling all sound save the occasional boom of a falling tower. Each time a tree fell, a vast plume of ash rose from the ground like lunar dust from a meteor impact. Michael walked Apollo through the empty waste, trying to keep a low profile as his boots turned white with ash. He felt a crunch and picked up his foot, to find the weakened bones of a child's skull shattered underfoot. More bones lay about him as he kicked his boot though the ash. All human; all gathered together in some mysterious mass grave. He knew not whether they had been killed by a bombing or the forest fire, or perhaps something worse altogether. He felt the reigns pull on him and he walked on, as Apollo urged him through the treacherous wilderness.

Once they had passed through the scarred pine

forest, Michael and Apollo began to spend their days resting, moving quickly and anxiously at night, with Michael following the constellations and his moonlit compass as best he could. They practiced this nocturnal behaviour for an entire week, until neither of them could sleep for fear of capture, both man and horse sharing a sense of urgency as they journeyed through that ominous and threatening land. From that point on they travelled constantly, moving swiftly through endless forests of solitude, where fresh violence churned on the horizon, and remnants of massacres and bomb craters could be found in every valley, the very air steaming with death's essence as if it were waiting for vulnerability, like a phantom drawn to innocence.

The weather itself had become a growing threat worth steering clear of. One day, Michael came upon the merging of two storm cells. Cold air blew against his back while warm air blew against his face, and the pine needles swirled in small cyclones around him. Somewhere in the distance, a mile wide forest fire pulsed relentlessly as it sucked one of the cells into its bulbous column. Sprinkles fell lightly as Apollo's tired steps brought them around a ridge onto an overgrown logging road. Michael thought it best to stay away from main roadways in the base of the valley, for he knew not how many enemies would be sitting in wait to ambush him on such open ground. Focusing his sense, he could just make out the faint trickling of a stream below the road.

Michael dismounted Apollo and they walked wearily down the slope, and under the canopy of the evergreens, they each took a rest, soothing their parched throats with a drink from the stream. The slight sting on his tongue told Michael that the water was more acidic than he was used to. He looked up as he heard the thunder coming closer to their highly elevated position.

"We might have to dive off this road soon, Apollo. Storm's coming in fast. I'll try to find a shelter while this weather passes."

Apollo stomped his foot and neighed in agreement. Michael looked around for a while and eventually discovered a large hole, boring straight into the mountain. He walked over to it slowly. The hole was taller than a person and had almost certainly been dug by one. It seemed abandoned, or at least vacant, for the time being. As he walked inside, Michael's face lit up with a relieved grin. A cache of ammo boxes, weapons, grenades, food, and other supplies littered the floor of the cave. Knowing the occupiers could be back at any time, Michael quickly grabbed some food, an AK-47 rifle, a few dozen magazines of ammo, a wide-brimmed hat, and a bandoleer of grenades, which he slung across his chest. He came out of the cave a twenty first century outlaw of no nation, with a Russian automatic rifle in one hand and a wad of beef jerky in the other.

Michael returned to the stream and led Apollo back up to the road, where he quickly mounted the horse. Sensing his master's urgency, Apollo set off down the road at a gallop. Though they had so far been lucky, it was still early. The rain fell heavier than before as the road gradually took them down to the bottom of the valley again. When they reached the valley floor, Michael directed Apollo to follow the river south. They clopped along a paved road, hoping to find an abandoned cabin where they might finally be able to settle for a night. Then Michael heard what sounded like the roar of a powerful engine and the clamor of a hammer on metal.

'What was that?' Michael thought to himself. He had never heard such a sound before. He knew it could not be a car, for a car's rubber tires did not make such a clatter on cracked asphalt. It was a vehicle of some kind, for sure. But what? Suddenly, it came to him. Tank tread.

Michael kicked the sides of his horse and Apollo began to gallop swiftly towards the river, his hooves splashing into the shallow water as he led them quickly away from their unknown assailants. Suddenly, Michael heard a woman's voice cry out to her soldiers. The tank stopped.

"Right flank! Stop him!"

The hissing of bullets flying past Michael's head followed an array of shots from far across the wide river. Apollo jumped up the bank and into the cover of forest, as the trees splintered around him from the distant machine gun fire. A loud shell pierced the air before exploding above them on the ridge. The tank had opened fire.

Michael's ears rang with the immense shock of the blast as Apollo ran faster and faster through the thick woods. Michael thought about returning fire, but it would be futile in the face of so many. His only option was to get up the mountain as fast as he could, to evade the hail of death.

Another shell exploded near them and loosened a tree's roots. The massive pine fell just a few feet in front of Apollo as the horse jumped over the heavily branched tree. They breached a plateau high up on the slope and Michael looked back to see a platoon of female soldiers crossing the river towards him. Apollo breathed rapidly and shifted in from hoof to hoof in fear.

"Shit! They're coming!" Michael cried. Just then, he looked above him to see a man in a camouflage suit and green faceprint lying beside a rock.

"Get behind me, lad," the man whispered.

Michael looked around to see an array of men, all camouflaged against the rocks and bushes around them. Two of them loaded a large, mounted machine gun, while several others pointed their rifles downhill. Michael found himself about to be caught in a battle between the unnamed forest warriors and the Queen's unsuspecting forces below. He dismounted and pulled Apollo behind a large boulder, resting his back against the rock while he loaded his own weapon.

"Open fire!" the man yelled to his men.

The mountain shook with a tremor of firepower as the fifty caliber machine gun rattled the rocks around them and pulverized the enemy forces below. Dozens of the men picked off the female soldiers attempting to cross the river, and a sniper rifle blew out the engine block in the small tank on the road. Michael turned from behind the rock, shooting blindly into the trees where he thought the soldiers would be coming from. He was far too afraid to stay out in the open for longer than a few seconds as return fire ricocheted off the rocks and whizzed past the camouflaged men. He took one of the grenades off his chest and pulled the pin, before lobbing it far into the woods below. He heard the explosion, followed by the scream of a woman's pain. Michael suddenly felt sick and hoped the woman had died quickly.

After fifteen minutes of exchanging fire, the remaining female combatants retreated across the river and snuck back into the woods towards their base. The group of men reloaded and stood up, walking over to where Michael lay shaking, his pants wet with his own urine.

"I'm sorry," Michael whimpered, fearing for his life.

"Sorry? You led them right into the open. It worked out perfectly," one of the gunners said as he locked in another massive ammo belt, his barrel steaming in the light rain.

"Who are you?" Michael asked, standing feebly before reloading his own weapon with trembling hands. Apollo stood silently, his head bowed in shock.

"The U.S. Marine Corps, 1st Division. What's left of it anyways," the man said.

"Thank the Sun I found you! Is there a William Beller in your ranks?"

A man at the other end of the formation stood up and walked over to Michael.

"Who's asking?" the large man said, behind a rugged, grey-tinged red beard. He wore green and black face paint and had intense eyes that held a furious fixation.

"My name is Michael Beller. I believe you're my uncle..." Michael said hesitantly.

"Michael...could it be?" one of the men gasped.

The bearded man scanned Michael from head to toe and back again, a look of deep concentration on his face.

"I swear I'm telling the truth. My mother told me—"

"Let's talk on the move," the bearded man said brusquely, turning towards his troops. "Bombers will be coming in any minute. Let's move men," he barked. He turned back to Michael. "Well? Are you coming or not?"

Michael quickly took Apollo's reins, following the bearded man and his band of rebels as they hurried deep into the mountain's innards.

CHAPTER 21
WAGING WICCA

About the same time Michael found his uncle, Melody and her strange troop found themselves sailing the Pacific on a stolen fishing vessel, having successfully escaped right under the watch of the imperial guard, by hiding in a fleet of other fishing boats. The vessel they had acquired was an old boat with a broken engine, but the sail worked well enough to propel them across the water. Out in the open ocean there was a lot of time for Melody to think about her future. Pavonis, however, was more interested in the young woman's past.

It was a calm day out at sea. Hartford managed the sail, while David swung on the rigging, his small giggles brightening their daunting journey, as the sunlight sparkled on the water, creating an undulating carpet of sapphires. Melody sat on the bow of the boat, looking far off into the distance, enjoying the rare sight of a whale coming up for air; watching as the immense creature breached the surface, then dove again, leaving cascades of toxic foam in its wake. She imagined the whale journeying leagues into the depths – through ragged trenches where strange creatures were said to thrive in boiling vents of pressurized darkness – further from that predator star and its ill propagations than any creature on Earth.

Melody closed her eyes for a moment. There was a whole world out there; numerous creatures existed on this planet...creatures that she knew nothing about. Her joy at seeing the whale quickly turned to fear as she hugged her knees, anxiety setting in with each rolling wave as the ocean triggered traumatic memories of her past.

Pavonis had at last clothed herself, with a dirty white gown she had found in the boat's closet. She came and sat beside Melody, her long sandy dreadlocks hitting the deck like chains.

"Good morning, dear," she said calmly.

"Morning, Pavonis. Why are you covered in kelp and barnacles?" she asked, looking at Pavonis' arms.

"I have to blend in with the common life forms of my environment. Otherwise, the Aradians will find me."

"I see." Melody nodded, looking back to the horizon.

"Does something trouble you?" Pavonis asked.

"I'm just worried about Michael. I hope he's still alive."

"I'm sure he is, Melody. He is strong, like his father."

"It's not just that. It's...Lily's death...why must those things be so cruel?"

"The Aradians are cruel because they have to be. They are stripped of emotion, operating on a level outside of human consciousness. It is for this reason that I believe they will ultimately disassociate themselves from Shakti's wave of destruction."

"One can only hope," Melody mumbled.

Pavonis looked over Melody with her starry eyes. "Tell me about your life before coming out West."

"I...I'm ashamed of my past. I'm ashamed of where I come from," Melody admitted, hesitantly.

"Speak, child. I won't judge you."

"Where to begin...my father...his name was Hasam Abu Bakr; he was a merchant, with strong ties to the local noblemen. Then, one day, he became one of them, a nobleman I mean. It cost him his morality; his will to be a good man. He became the economic advisor to the Emir of the United Arab Emirates. Then, after someone tried to assassinate him in Lebanon, he quickly fled. He made money by selling Israeli defense codes to the Iranians. He and my mother married just after the bombing of Israel. Father was later appointed Emir of Qatar, and he gained extreme wealth during the oil wars. I never really knew my parents; the Queen's agents captured and killed them when I was five years old. Luckily, I escaped with deserters of the local military, and we fled to India."

"How do you know all this?" Pavonis asked.

"My servants told me. Once in India, they were no longer obliged to follow strict Sunni doctrine, so they emancipated themselves, and chose to follow Sufism. Even at such a young age, I found God through knowing myself as a seeker, but I have also seen what religion has done to the world, so I hide my faith. To love Allah is...to live in the moment; to be free of all fears and full of love while at the mercy of the universe. This is what I desire for the world."

Pavonis placed her hand on Melody's shoulder and smiled. "So, are you a seeker?"

"Seeking Lily a safe passage in this life was all I sought. And being near her and Michael made me feel like I was home. But before that...all I knew was survival. When the war finally entered India, my servants attempted to save me by putting me on an oil ship and sending me West. I made it all the way to Alaska, but the Queen's forces were waiting for me.

It is there we were ambushed and almost everyone was killed, except for myself and a few others, thanks to the wild woman who I now know was you. I remember it like a dream. But after I saw you do what you did...I knew that Allah was only part of my journey. For this creature before me had to be a merciful Goddess, to whom I owe a great favor. Don't let me go on without returning it."

"It was a miracle of timing, Melody. I knew you had something special about you, though. Maybe not that you were a princess, but something. I'm sorry for not guiding you further inland to safety that day. I had to evade the area due to an imminent threat. I do what I can, when I can. I'm only allowed certain movements. Anything else is fatal."

"Lily found me not long after, lost in the forest, on a venture to the coast. She raised me as if I were her own daughter," Melody said, as she began to cry.

"Oh Melody, I miss her too. Lily was there when Michael was born. She took him under her wing and risked her life to ensure his safety. She was the mother I could never be."

Melody wiped her red eyes and looked at Pavonis. "What happened to this world? How did things become so terrible, in the years leading up to the eruption?"

"It all started long before this century. Long ago,

humans stopped caring about the Earth and began to desire more. More money. More land. More everything. More people meant higher demand. The rich enslaved foreign natives and ripped up the Earth's soil to use for agriculture, to feed their growing numbers. In the early part of this century, America was so close to embracing social justice and progressive responsibility as a nation, so close to what the United States was meant to be: a land of the free. But with politicians acting like children and false media triggering outrage, it was only a matter of time before the entire world felt its implosion.

There were still a few hunter-gatherers left, who lived in accordance with nature's balance, and had done so since the beginning. But even they were being phased out by industrialized nations and the principles of growth. It all led to an increasing amount of friction between those who wished to save their dying species and traditions, and those spearheading the new age by creating a reliance on a device-addicted population, latching itself to the cyber-grid that outlined and consumed civilization. The hearts of the hungry grew weary in the world's lethargic dismissal of them. The outbreak was just the beginning. Then it escalated to the oil wars. The media distracted everyone with stories that didn't matter, in order to cover up the issues that did, and things that should have never happened did happen. We all fell for it, and in turn, the United States fell for Vishnu's trap. There were over ten billion people in the world twenty years ago. Now, there are less than a few hundred million, and the number drops every hour."

"So many..." Melody gasped.

"The first billion went the fastest. They were killed off over a matter of months in some of the most gruesome fighting in history, and the rest have died from disease, starvation, murder, or poisoning, over the last seventeen years. It's hard to believe there were so many people living on Earth only two decades ago."

"So, Vishnu punished humans for what they had done...but why didn't anyone do anything about these issues? They sound complex, but history is riddled with impossibilities, made possible by those who seek an elixir," Melody said.

"Well, for a while, there were a few of us who tried. I was a biologist trying to save the oceans. Michael's father was a special forces operative, similar to Hartford."

"But they killed people. They were part of the problem."

"They were just players in the game of life, like you and I. Who lives and who dies by their hand is a malleable formula, subject to the individual and the agency they serve. For those who stay true to their cause, the ethos of men provides an unsaid pact once blood has been drawn. The warrior is therefore vindicated of murder so long as he is made vulnerable to the perils of war himself, and that higher calling which he worships forgives all desecration of principle, since no one can dispute him without entering that sphere of violence themselves."

"But that's just like saying might makes right!"

"Exactly. So, be mightier. Your conscience is the supreme law, Melody. I can see you are pure of heart, so do not fear the guilt of taking the life of someone who challenges you or your planet's safety. There were many who attempted to defend Mother Earth, and those who attempted to make change in their own ways, abstract or direct. I was a scientist trying to heal the planet of its toxins. Now I am of its essence and the healing never ends. This cycle is what allows for genetic superiority. Life prays on life, but apathy is infrequent in nature. You can exercise your mind and body until mastery, but without spiritual challenges, evolution remains on standby. The soul is hungry for a certain flavor of strife, and over time we lost this knowledge. What should have been easy was hard, and what should have been hard was easy. Everything became distorted by vanity and greed. There were no rites of passage, just candy-coated dreams created by marketing specialists."

"I'm not sure I understand."

"Did Lily teach you about The Holocaust?"

Melody nodded. "A little bit."

"Well, there was a day when the Jewish prisoners of Hitler's death camps put God on trial and sentenced God to death. I personally believe it was because they became Gods themselves, stripped of their humanity until only their souls remained. They understood that a merciful, omnipotent entity could not exist, and that heaven could only exist in their love for one another. The soul cannot be killed while on Earth, only displaced. But how does a soul find a vessel? It looks for hereditary traits and expounds on common grounds. What the human race lacked at the turn of this century was a sturdy bridge across the gap of human progression. Technology backfired. We traded God for the atomic bomb, and eighty years of peace ensued. But it was a dangerous peace, and while the wild lands took the brunt of this new flourishing, the disease of human conquest reached critical mass and was therefore beyond restraining. This sudden shift in the evolutionary path is the reason Vishnu took action against mankind."

"Why didn't people just change the way they lived?" Melody asked.

"Because it was never a choice. Their future was stolen from them. When the search for food ends at the grocery store; death can be defeated by advanced medical practices and comfortable living, and there is nothing but the slow sting of mortality gnawing at your withering bones to captivate your instincts, mental illness blooms, and solving those issues becomes a priority. Those fortunate enough to be raised in the more enlightened corners of the Earth – those who were educated and conscious of our hazardous trajectory – preached their ideals about sustainability and social progression. But greedy leaders, particularly those like your father, kept the ones actually trying to make a difference from doing so by inciting insidious social behavior and leading by intimidation."

"But why?"

"To turn a profit, of course. The torch of tyrants has been handed down from century to century, church to church, man to man. It was only when the Zurvans finally pulled the trigger, and decided to do something about the environmental crisis and over population, that actual change occured. They changed the world forever. Shakti's master, Vishnu, dove into a boiling pool in Yellowstone National Park and swam hundreds of meters under the surface. He emancipated himself from this life whilst causing the eruption to end *all* life. And while the U.S. began to fall from both the eruption and civil war's disputes, Shakti used Ezra's blood to create a hyper-Sararan gene called Aradia Complex B. She injected the gene into her two best apprentices and those creatures have been wreaking havoc on the world ever since. I suspect that, by now they've taken over ninety-five percent of the globe. It's just a matter of time now. Most of the destruction by the Aradians is from earthquakes, floods, tsunamis, and firestorms, so the Queen can make it look as though the extinction is occurring naturally. She'll curse the world with her false history. The Aradian Empire will surely be the first and last of its kind."

"What happened after the eruption?" Melody asked.

"While the caldera was polluting the region with toxic gases, Shakti engulfed the world in flame and smoke. She took down the Western powers in a matter of months, before creating an alliance with China and Japan, whom she basically held hostage. A few thousand U.S. Marines broke off from the main forces to fight the Zurvan advance. Together, they founded the Rebel Marine Corps: a few thousand men from the 1st Marine Division who traded their helicopters for horses and went headhunting through the cordillera with a bloodlust you couldn't imagine. I helped them fight in the Post-Eruption Wars, until their division was nearly wiped out and I was forced into hiding."

"Where are the Marines now?" Melody asked.

"They are somewhere in the Canadian Rockies, moving often and strategically picking their fights so their forces aren't completely destroyed by Shakti's massive army and high tech ordinance. The Marines had a sizable cache but now they're just scraping by. Within the next few months they'll be out of ammunition, which is why I have to take a break from healing the forest and help them finally make headway in this long war before they have to completely revert to a savage arsenal."

"What about the Queen's forces? Do they have ammunition to last them?"

"For now, but something tells me even she's running low. I haven't seen or heard nearly as many bomb runs since she directed her violence towards other lands. She's returning us to an earlier age each year, and soon all industry will collapse, even her own."

"Tell me what happened to you after the eruption."

Pavonis looked at Melody and breathed deeply, turning her face to look across the water. She could see the clouds in the distance so clearly and remembered how numb she felt on that eerie September day. "I couldn't see anything. I couldn't feel anything. I'd nearly forgotten about the weight of my brother on my back until he coughed awake somewhere near the Blackfoot Reservation line."

Nineteen years earlier, the plains of Northcentral Montana were a silent span of smokey blue fog. Ingrid looked back toward Yellowstone, her husband's grave, where with each passing minute, an ocean of toxic gases spewed into the stratosphere.

"We need to keep heading north," she said, her eyes sober.

"Wh...where are we?" Will choked, turning his half-burned head.

"Still too close. The deadliest of it will reach here by midnight."

"What time is it?"

"It's still morning."

"What are we gonna do?" Will asked, standing to his feet and revolving around his sister-in-law like a drunk interrogator, his brain still sloshing from the lightning strike that nearly killed him.

"Do you have any friends in the Marines still? Anyone in the military?"

Will looked at her, slack jawed.

"Friends? You mean, the ones that were killed by Vishnu's trap? Or my brother, who's also dead? Jesus Christ, Ingrid. We're wanted criminals!"

"What about Gadreel?"

"Oh yeah, great idea, a senior member in the Hood Battalion, which is owned by P.A.I.N., which is run by Cassandra Larson, the woman who had a fucking pistol to your head a few days ago," he yelled.

"We need to get in contact with him. He'll be loyal to us."

"Ingrid...what the fuck are you talking about? We need to find out where we are. We need a vehicle. We need to go to Michael. Face it, we lost. The Zurvan's pulled an end-all terror attack and there's nothing we can do now."

Ingrid watched the fog and said nothing. She breathed in through her nose and closed her eyes, picturing Ezra's face. She winced but held back her emotions. "We're going to enter Canada and get in touch with Gadreel or someone in the department of defense. We'll form a coalition with what forces we can conjure. Multiple armies from multiple nations. I need an air force. I need operators. And I need access to nuclear weapons."

"Oh, so, you're just gonna coordinate an international counterinsurgency on numerous fronts against an enemy that can make volcanoes explode? What makes you think you could do that even if you formed this coalition?!"

"Systems ecology."

"What?"

"I majored in systems ecology. The way species interact in an environment and how diversity shapes their behaviors. We have to erase the Immortals before they destroy everything."

"So, you have to die too then, right?"

"It will take one to kill one."

They marched north along an eroded precipice and up an old road, the smokey air cut with acidic rainfall. The drops stung Will's burnt, bald head and he held a piece of cloth to his mouth, eventually replacing it with a painting respirator he found in a pile of trash on the side of the road. Ingrid breathed easily with her filtering Sararan lungs and helped Will when she could, carrying him through the coulees like a feeble child when he became too dizzy to walk. He would repeatedly shake her off, stumbling about like a blind man falling, reaching for no object in that hopeless purgatory.

They approached a few old trailers where native families were planning their exodus. A limping dog greeted the travelers, looking at them with demon eyes, having already lived in a post-world realm for some time. The natives welcomed the Sararan and her brother, and it didn't take long for Ingrid to convince them that she could help them get into Canada. Will threatened to defect from the company, uneasy about Ingrid's promises, but she insisted he had to come, if only to salvage their virtuous creed.

They drove north to the Port of Sweet Grass and found a mass of vehicles and humans, all barred from entry. A blockade of tanks, ground support, relief units, and soldiers formed at the port, with helicopters circling above. Thousands of Americans teemed near the gate, as if it were some filter of noble right. Honking and screaming and the occasional gunshot could be heard through the mounting unease. Ingrid led the natives through the exodus and stood under the lights so the guards and militia could see her face clearly. A light rain fell, and the soldiers suddenly fixated their muzzles on the lone Immortal.

Ingrid spoke loud yet cautiously to them, volcanic rumbling growing behind her, intensifying the escalation. "If you don't let these people through, you'll have to live with the memory of being the reason they died untimely deaths."

A commander listened from behind a tank, knowing full well what Ingrid was capable of.

"I have a truce regarding the new Zurvan issue. Please trust me when I say that I am an ally to the U.S. and Canadian forces confronting this new threat."

A few soldiers slowly approached Ingrid and frisked her as she raised her arms. The gate opened and Americans rushed behind her but the guards pushed them away with their shields like a khaki-clad Roman legion.

"Hold up there!" a voice yelled.

A tall man, clad in an investigations uniform, confronted Ingrid from a distance. He smiled mildly, as if amused by the Immortal's stratagem.

"Mrs. Ingrid McAdam Beller. You've had quite a week. I'd like to know more about it."

They stared at each other for a moment. Ingrid's eyes swirled with nebulous catastrophe.

"Don't worry, we're not going to arrest you. Orders have changed. We need you. We need Ezra too. Do you know where he is?"

"My husband is dead."

"Is that so? So, Immortals can die?"

"Yes. Just as my husband and I can be killed, so can the Aradians. They are ammortal. Which is why you need me. I'm a Sararan, so I can help you to classify them, and if you understand their characteristics, from a biological perspective, you can eradicate them."

"What do you want in return for helping us go after the Zurvans?"

"I want to help unite a global coalition against these terrorists. I want to find my son. And I want you to let these people into Canada. If you don't, they will die. Every man, woman, and child. We don't have any time. Open the border."

"You're gonna walk away if we say no, aren't you?"

"Yes."

"I understand you've been wronged and don't know who to trust, but you killed a lot of good men yesterday."

"That's nothing compared to what you're about to do if you don't let these people through. Heading towards us is a volcanic wall of dust; inhaling the air will be like drowning on concrete. It's a slow and painful asphyxiation. These people...these families...will have to watch each other choke to death in a blizzard of ash. What are you defending here? Soon, these imaginary lines won't mean anything."

The man nodded and held up his radio. "You get all that?" he asked.

A voice emerged crackling as if it were transmitting from space. "Affirmative. Collect the asset and coordinate alternate routine."

The men stood down and transitioned their mission toward opening the border. The investigations man waved her forward warmly. Ingrid spat into her hand and held it out to him. The man reluctantly spit into his own hand and shook hers firmly. Ingrid had been pardoned, and the vetting of Americans into Alberta began. Those with a clean record were allowed into Canada, while those without were either destined to be buried in soot or smuggled across by other means. That night, Ingrid snuck back over the border and helped hundreds of native Americans who had been denied entry. Not everyone made it across before the storm of fine particulates and pyro-plastics swallowed them up like a great charcoal sea, and the natives prayed that the spirit of the Earth would treat their fallen brothers and sisters well and not allow the torment of their abysmal plight to besiege their departure to the afterlife.

The next morning, the five-mile-long military

convoy rode north to Calgary as the sky turned black behind them. When the sun finally burned away the fog, it became all the blacker. On the tarmac of Calgary International Airport, Ingrid met with the President of the United States and the Canadian Prime Minister to discuss hiring her as an asset, and all agreed that Ingrid would be best suited as a counter-intelligence officer when it came to dealing with the Aradians, since nearly all communications had been jammed and Ingrid could use her telepathic mind to warn allied forces about incoming threats. When she asked why they were not using satellites and radar, the President hinted that those were no longer reliable tools because of all the corruption that had occurred during the eruption. After a full security clearance, one of the Generals told Ingrid that Zurvan hackers planted inside U.S. agencies since 2012 had crashed their defense networks, using complex codes nearly impossible to untangle. He also told her that P.A.I.N. Security had fractured overnight, with those who had refused to stay loyal to Sandraudiga attempting to escape the unit before they could be executed. Those lucky enough to get out had rejoined the ranks of their former military branch. Gadreel had requested an immediate detail with special forces, but even they were dealing with cases of bad faith.

The government was in chaos. Planes were

grounded. Highways were clogged. The economy had shut down overnight. People were fleeing from fire and anarchy worldwide. Sky battles between modern warships and the dreadful Aradians were happening in strategic zones, but without any pattern. The only advantage the Allied Forces had was the knowledge that there were two of these Aradians; they could not be everywhere at once. But there were more enemies crawling to the surface than the twins. Shakti's hidden army was immense and willing to challenge the disorganised allied ground forces. Months before the eruption, Vishnu's cohorts smuggled weapons and Asiatic troops from across the Pacific. Tens of thousands in number. As the highly trained soldiers of the Zurvan Order marched from the coasts inward, they began wreaking havoc and confronting any police or military head-on, no matter the scope, picking apart an already conflicted society as communities struggled to attain stability. Children were shot in the streets. Entire cities were massacred. Any innocence left poured into the drainpipes of the city as the violence tore through soft civilization.

But the Allies did not deploy troops to those places. Instead, the armies of five allied nations convened at the tar sands a few hundred miles to the north of Calgary, to defend the petroleum reserves.

It was there that Ingrid would set her trap. At her request, Will was integrated back into the Marines and began piloting medical helicopters with only three weeks to prepare for what was to come. Ingrid took a crash course in special operations with a British Special Air Service team, passing every standard except the open water course, because the captain became furious when he found out she could breathe underwater. She then worked with communications experts to memorize the neural-DNA coding for each officer so she could transmit orders telepathically when communications went down. And although Ingrid's other requests had been met, not one of the men who went looking for Michael came back.

It was a dreary day on the tar sands when the fighting began. The thunderous percussion of hundreds of artillery cannons and rocket batteries sliced the air, bombarding enemy positions and shaking the Earth. Ingrid felt her body shudder at the drum roll effect of the vast guns, as soldiers raced through the sticky black mud from one end of the front to the other, passing messages. Their ears bled, but they did not seem to notice. Ingrid shifted between helping the forward combat controller in the field and aiding the wounded that had been moved behind the front, darting between healing and killing. She wore a black beret with an ambiguous lightning bolt insignia and a dark green uniform, a tight belt and pistol at her hip, resembling a guerrilla officer turned cold war proxy leader. The thick dark muck spread for miles over the flat waste, and Ingrid could see the blasts from the enemy trenches in the distance as the mud splashed from the heavy rain and zipping bullets. She sprinted out into No Man's Land and ducked into a fox hole where the battle's primary Joint Terminal Attack Controller was huddled up, monitoring the battle.

"I'm sensing at least five high-speed aircraft coming toward the southwestern zone of the front. No sign of the Aradians yet," Ingrid told the JTAC.

"Roger that. Wish I could tell someone about it," he said, knocking on his radio with his knuckles angrily.

"Right. I'll send a transmission to the general on my way to medical. There's a lot of wounded in there."

"No, you need to stay put. I'll need you if the Aradians show up."

Ingrid nodded and kept her head down, closing her eyes and feeling every painful soul crying out on that forsaken scrape of Earth. The shelling intensified and one of the enemy artillery shells landed near their position. A hail of blood and gore and mud smothered them. Ingrid wiped her face and shook her head in anger. A man screamed – his legs had been blown off – and Ingrid began to crawl to him, but the JTAC grabbed her arm.

"Let the other medics get him."

"I am *the* medic, sir."

"And I am *the* JTAC, ma'am. Chief medical officer is your secondary duty. Do you want to kill an Immortal today or not?"

Helicopters flew overhead and quickly touched down to pick up the wounded. Will had already conducted three rescues, each time taking heavy fire and collecting shrapnel and bullets in his ship. No Man's Land was a stretch of death, torture, and screaming, and even the medics were beginning to neglect their comrades cries for fear of being killed themselves.

At last, they came. A sonic boom quenched the chaotic air and anti-aircraft artillery traced the sky as the Aradians flew deft as sparrows into the clouds, bleeding a sharp hail of carbon crystals behind them. Through the redness, one of them came down and decimated a whole line of advancing troops, while the other flooded a trench with oil on the other end of the front, drowning hundreds in the cold black sludge.

The JTAC spoke quickly. "Okay, here we go. Pick your target and focus all your energy on a single Aradian. Don't take your eyes off them, even for second. I'm gonna take my targeting device and point it at your head, just like we practiced. Wherever your eyes go, that's where the missiles will go. Try not to move anything but your gaze."

Ingrid sat up and stared at the one they called Mayari. The silver-blue woman was taking a lot of fire and was gaining altitude to evade the bullets and artillery. The JTAC held the laser gun to Ingrid's temple as she fixated her eyes onto the Aradian. Another explosion struck near them but neither of them budged as more mud and gore poured over them. After a few seconds, three fighter jets rumbled overhead and began climbing behind the rapidly ascending Immortal. Two missiles fired from each of the jet's wings and the Aradian was now in a wild dogfight, flying away from six laser-guided smart bombs. She wove through the air and spiraled through the clouds before diving low and racing only a few feet above No Man's Land, causing each missile to bury itself into the ground as a line of explosions followed, creating a wall of dust and raining dirt separating the two sides. The deadly creature escaped and flew back up into the ether as the rumbling of the jets faded, the pilots having aborted their sortie. The JTAC pulled the targeting device away from Ingrid's head and sighed.

"Well, it almost worked."

They sat for a moment, listening to the clatter.

"We could try again, but I think we can expect similar results. We have implied clearance to initiate Plan B," the JTAC said.

"If all else fails, then we'll go that route. Until then, I have a better idea. Point your side arm at my head," Ingrid demanded.

He raised the targeting device again, but she pushed it away.

"No, your service weapon."

He hesitated but she stared him down. He pulled out his pistol and pointed it at Ingrid's head.

"Now rack the slide," she said. "Just do it!"

He racked a bullet into the chamber, sure to keep his finger outside the trigger guard.

"I was beginning to be able to read her thoughts. If I could just infiltrate her mind…"

Ingrid focused on being Mayari, not just seeing her, but knowing her, understanding her thoughts and emotions and learning her motives. She saw how powerful the twins' bond was and realized this bond was the source of their dominance; the Aradian gene only augmented this power.

"When I say now, pull the trigger!"

"I won't do that, Ingrid!" he yelled above the shelling, "Even if you kill her, there would still be another one. You are our only Immortal ally, and your blood would be on my hands!"

He pulled his pistol away and Ingrid snarled at him like a betrayed she-wolf.

"You coward!" she snapped.

"Think about it, Ingrid. I know you want to help, but perhaps preserving your life is the best thing we can do right now."

The fighting raged on, the Aradians causing widespread destruction among the ranks. Allied shelling was ramping up in preparation for Plan B. The sky cracked with gunfire and explosions and there were so many shell-shocked soldiers that the ships had to start transporting them back to medical as they were unfit for duty.

"Not that I have to ask for your authorisation, ma'am, but are you going to let me do my job now?" the JTAC asked.

Ingrid shook her head and wiped the mud from her mouth.

"Do what you have to do," she said in a defeated tone, her wet hair dripping from under her beret.

He pulled out a cell phone and texted a lengthy

code before pressing send to a private number. The man put away the phone and took out a fresh pack of cigarettes, lighting one, inhaling deeply, and laying back down as if finally free from something.

"Well...that was an expensive phone call," he joked madly.

"Aren't you coming back to the bunkers with us?" she asked him.

"Would you want to live after doing what I just did?"

Ingrid nodded and frowned.

"I will remember your sacrifice."

"I don't want to be remembered."

Ingrid touched his face with her hand and felt his cheek softly with her thumb as she looked into the mans pained eyes. He winked and smiled slightly as Ingrid crouched low and sprinted back to the front line. She entered the medical tent where she saw Will hauling in a wounded Canadian soldier.

"We need to get the wounded to the bunkers now. We're going with Plan B!"

"Did you tell the General?"

Ingrid stared at him.

"Ingrid, did you tell him that you confirmed the launch codes?"

Ingrid continued staring as if telling him not to spill her secret.

"Why wouldn't you tell him?"

She approached him and spoke into his ear.

"Because if all our forces retreat at once then the enemy will know something's amiss. We have to keep laying down fire so that the Engineers are caught in our trap. If we move only the medical personnel back, it won't look like anything unusual, and we can still save some of these men and women."

"That's not your decision to make!" he said as he started for the door. Ingrid stopped him.

"The man who just called in every nuclear weapon within two thousand miles did not make that choice lightly. This is the only way we're going to get them, and he knew it."

Will sighed and looked around. "Let's get the wounded onto the trucks then. How much time do we have?"

"Nineteen minutes."

They scrambled to gather everyone onto vehicles and helicopters, and although the word had gotten out that a thermo-nuclear air strike was inbound, the retreat was messy and slow. Will and Ingrid flew away from the base on a helicopter full of bloody bodies, the gunners firing away at enemy lines whilst nurses collected the bullet casings that bounced off the floor and the maimed bodies of the wounded, huddled up in piles.

When they landed, Will and Ingrid helped to carry the wounded down into the underground bunkers, until everyone was safely inside. Will went to shut the door and looked back at Ingrid, who was climbing into the helicopters pilot seat.

"Hey, what the fuck are you doing?"

"I'm going back for more."

"Not in that you're not!" he said as the helicopter's engine finally sputtered out. Black smoke rose from bullet holes in the aft compartment as it died. Will looked up and saw the bombers droning high above.

"You gonna wait around and get barbecued with the rest of them?"

"I have to try and lure both of the Aradians to me. It's the only way this plan will work!"

"You'll die in the process!"

"Two Immortals for the price of one! That's a good deal! Let's take it!" she said, as she ran down toward the retreating army.

"She's as mad as Ezra was. No fucking fear," Will said as he shut the door, continuing to curse up a storm as he walked down into the dungeon of screams and tragic pleas.

Ingrid sprinted to the top of a small knoll and slowed as she realized her efforts were ill fated.

Swarms of men and women ran past her, some in vehicles, some limping, all trying to get to the bunkers before the bombs dropped. Ingrid began backing up and quickly became afraid herself, running along with the mob and looking behind her every few seconds.

A flash of white light was followed by a catastrophic clap behind them. The boom resounded across the waste and a mushroom cloud rose and seemed to swallow the light from the sun in its atrocious ascension. Another one struck a mile to their left, and another to their right, until the warheads were detonating miles apart all around them, blinding and deafening the soldiers and driving them mad with fear. More warheads began hitting closer to Ingrid's position, until a massive wave of heat knocked Ingrid back, her strong but small body just a leaf in the wind, blown away with all the other leaves. The bombardment was like none the world had ever seen; somehow worse than the eruption. A man-made Godhead of destruction that heeded no equal.

Ingrid opened her eyes and screamed. She trembled violently as she looked down, lacerations decorating her torso, her whole body wet and sticky with blood. Her arm was broken. Her cracked skull throbbed. Blood poured down her face from her ears and her eyes were bulging and caked with ash.

Unable to stand, she looked up. All around her were thousands of dead bodies strewn across the ruptured earth and a few soldiers were still somehow living, standing before her like skeletons with their flesh hanging from their bones. A discordant ringing was all she could hear, the soldiers melted faces appearing mute in their sobbing. Ingrid screamed in agony, unable to hear even herself, and stared back at the ground, looking away from the zombies crawling along the fiery wasteland where boulders and rocks fell like fragments of a crumbling planet, spiting that battlefield of undead disfigurements. A sharp sting hit Ingrid's brain and a vision bloomed before her: it was Mayari speaking from beyond, that deadly Goddess who had somehow survived the blow of ten dozen nuclear bombs, now mocking Ingrid in her telepathic hijacking.

Ingrid stood up and stumbled back to the bunkers, across the expanse of fire and radiated soil. The atomic wind blew hard with a corrosive gale, and by the time she reached the door to the bunker, everything behind her was dead, and the tar sands were once again a steamrolled wasteland.

The first few weeks in the bunker went by quickly. There were fifteen men sharing the bunker with Ingrid; the dozens of other hideouts adjacent to them were unreachable, with over thirty feet of lead and dirt separating each bunker. Each had been packed with supplies, but the occupants knew they would only last for a limited time. Luckily for Will, and the fourteen other Marines, they had Ingrid with them. Once her body had healed her own wounds, Ingrid went to work aiding the others. She healed broken bones, hemorrhages, burns, and gunshot and shrapnel wounds, but some afflictions were simply too devastating to mend. They held ceremonies for each fallen Marine, burying them in the mud walls of the bunker.

In their extended privation, their camaraderie grew, and they helped each other through each day, none of them knowing how long they would be stuck there. They spent their eternal days telling stories of their past and reminding one another of the beauties of the world before the eruption. They often wondered how their wives and children were doing, but after some time they all agreed to never speak their names, in case the Aradians could hear them through the Earth's crust. Despite the deep friendships woven in those close quarters, Ingrid was not approached by any of the men. She was widowed and heartbroken, and beyond the desire for emotional distance that emanated from her, the men respected her superiority, recognizing her leadership capabilities and clear dominance as a Sararan amidst their mortal selves. But it was Ingrid who caught herself staring at the Marines, and they would stare uncontrollably back at her, her Sararan perfume-like pheromones impossible to ignore in the small space. Sometimes when Will slept, Ingrid would lay beside him and curl her body around his, imagining that he was Ezra. For a whole night she would dream she was with her husband again, until morning came, when she would retreat to her own corner of their doomsday cell. She would lay there and weep tears of blood onto the moss, praying to God that she would one day see the sun again. Will would wake up hours later, unaware of what had transpired.

Ingrid quickly realized they had more problems ahead of them yet, and that the men would not survive unless she fed and nourished them, so she went to work as a subterranean botanist, using the solar energy stored in her skin and the wet soil to pull the nutrients from the fallen Marines decaying bodies, growing medicinal plants and fungi to cure the surviving men's illnesses. She grew poppies and processed the saplings into opium to treat those with chronic pain, and at first, they would smoke the flowers' warm nectar purely for that reason. But as weeks turned into months, time slowed, and when the shellshock subsided, they began to rely on the chemicals for more than just pain.

Three hundred and thirty knife marks were scratched into the wooden support post of the bunker. They had almost made it a year, but sanity hung by a thread. Ingrid awoke at some odd hour and looked around. Her eyes were dulled to an opaque green wash from the lack of sun. She blinked, as if trying to change the exposure of the scene. Some men sat awake; others slept. Night and day were but obsolete. The constant green light was dim, but bright enough to nurture by, and nurture Ingrid had. She reached over and caressed her plants with an obsessive tenderness. Weed smoke filled the air, wafting over the masses of hallucinogenic fungi dripping from the ceiling. Ingrid and the Marines had turned into atomic shamans, sublimated by solitude, ingesting psychedelics and synthetic-opioid concoctions on a daily basis. Radiation absorbing fungi lined the muddy interior like fractal wallpaper, and the men who sat awake passed a pipe around, staring at the microcosm in wonder. The others stirred awake from the smell. Perhaps it was morning, but their timekeeper had gone mad and smashed all the watches. Will had found an archaic MP3 device in their supply cache and made speakers with the radios. They listened to 1960's rock and roll on repeat while blazed on a cocktail of mind melting substances.

Once all the men had risen from their restless slumber, they gathered around an oak bonsai tree Ingrid had placed in the middle of the room. After a long silence, she began a strange and dismal oration, explaining the need for new Gods in place of the old ones and how like a 'divine conductor' she alone could bring the world back to a state of pre-civilization. She surmised the fate of the Zurvans, and gave the Marines hope that by harnessing the powers of the sun and moon she could defeat her enemies and rule the planet. Her sermon continued like the ramblings of a Pagan cult lord, as she fed the men LSD from an aloe leaf and blessed each of them with a compassionate hand and prayer, proclaiming she was now Pavonis, reincarnation of Gaia, born from Chaos, threatening a maelstrom of biological warfare against the Zurvans like a prophet of some new and frightening revelation. She went on to claim that in her sun-fasting, she was able to see ghosts; spirits in limbo who had fallen on the battlefield and would visit her and beg for her to set their souls free.

That night, one of the men intentionally

overdosed on heroin. Will buried him in the wall and boiled the man's head, granting the man's final wish by carving his skull into a chalice. After a proper ceremony for their fallen brother, they asked Pavonis how long they could expect to be trapped, and whether the bunker was just a tomb. Pavonis did not have an answer, but simply reminded them that they were still alive. They were unafraid of death and yet unwilling to suck the dead air from the overworld.

For their remaining days they danced like a tribe of aliens in exile from reality, their imaginations augmented beyond their minds limits as they began crafting and cultivating their madness. They made instruments from bullet casings, bones, and sinew, strumming these pieces made from their fallen comrades and passing around pear wine in a skull cup, chanting loudly and giving each other tattoos with sharpened firing pins like an enclave of demented cavemen, hiding from the world until the darkness had passed, ready to rise again and become violent apostles for their new matriarch.

After over a year in hiding, Pavonis opened the bunker door and breathed the air. She could feel the sting of radiation in her nostrils and absorbed the violent neutrons by turning her skin grey with boron crystals. The other Marines climbed out one by one, skinny and malnourished, blinking around as if they had crash landed a spaceship on the wrong planet. It was unseasonably cold. Low stratus clouds cloaked the world in grey and they paced around as if not knowing where to go.

"May I?" Will asked, as he held up his phone.

Pavonis nodded as Will dialed a number.

"Hey, I have service!" he said excitedly.

"Because they control the towers. Make it quick," Pavonis said.

The phone rang and rang but no one answered. He tried again.

"Hello?" a deep, crackling voice said on the other end.

"Gadreel? It's William. Where are you?"

"William...my God. You're alive?"

"Barely. I'm with Pavonis."

"Who?"

"Ingrid, I mean, and a few men from the bunker. Where can we find you?"

"I'm with my team. We came out of the bunkers a month ago and set up camp in the mountains to the west. You should recruit everyone you can on your way. We need all the help we can get out here."

"Text me the coordinates and we'll be there as soon as we can."

"Okay. Be careful on your way here. The mountain front is constantly patrolled, and Shakti has given orders to kill every man in sight."

"How do we identify Shakti's units?"

"They're an all-female fighting force. Grey uniforms. No insignia. She confiscated the allied drones so either move on cloudy days or at night only."

"Any other resources she stole we should be aware of?"

"All of them. Tread lightly and I'll see you soon, brother."

"See you soon."

Will hung up, receiving a text of the coordinates immediately afterword.

"Lead the way, William," Pavonis said with a nod.

"I'm not the senior officer here."

"Who is?" she asked, looking around at the Marines.

They all smiled and looked at her as if she were joking.

William answered. "You are."

They moved at night and spent weeks navigating their way to Gadreel. When they found him and his small band of warriors they were dug in and engaged in daily fire fights with the enemy. All were Marines or mercenaries who had served in the Corps, so they had decided to name themselves the Rebel Marine Corps, mostly to piss off the Queen. Pavonis, Will, and the rest of the men they had been hidden with got stuck right back into the fighting, as if their year underground had been nothing but a strange fever-dream.

Eventually, their small numbers and limited resources forced the rebels to retreat north, and by the time they had established a base and began fighting again, they had to retreat even further north. This pattern persisted until the enemy forces bombed them into submission, and the Marines found themselves split all over the arctic in weakened divisions, trying to survive while fighting off animals poisoned by radiation and trying not to succumb to the enemy's psychological warfare strategy of starving them to death. Shakti's forces claimed a pre-mature victory over them and regrouped in Calgary, convinced the men and women of the Rebel Marine Corps would freeze or starve to death. Feeling defeated, Pavonis gave up her high status in the unit and snuck away through a blizzard one night, doubtful she would ever find her son and convinced that the Aradians would take over the world if she did not try and stop them.

Pavonis dipped her foot in the cool ocean water and looked at Melody. The young woman had listened silently to her story, a saddened expression on her face.

"For over a decade, I hid myself in the heart of a dead tree, my spirit broken from losing my true love, abandoning my son, and deserting the Marines on those isles of ice. All the while I hid, the Aradians scorched the forests, attempting to lure me out of hiding. But I endured their rain of fire." Pavonis smiled, her eyes fixed on the sun above the water. "Over time, the forest re-grew around me, and my DNA assimilated to a mass of infant organisms. I realized the Aradians could not detect me, because my energy matched the forest's. My Sararan genes disguised my identity, just as these barnacles do now."

Melody shook her head in shock and disbelief.

"When I finally came out into the open, I began to replenish the forest, nourishing the rivers with supplemental minerals and filling the soil with nutrients. I used my solar charged cells to invigorate the burnt crust of the land and sprout new plants and trees. I conjured winds to carry spores and seeds all over the continent. As the forest grew, the Queen sent timber workers into the old growth to harvest the larger trees that had survived the fires. I had to follow behind them and replenish what had been taken. I think she leaves me to my task to mock my existence, but she is unaware of my destructive capabilities."

"Can you do the same things the Aradians can?" Melody asked.

"I'm learning. During one of the Marine's retreats, I came upon a cottage in the wilderness. I inspected the abandoned home and realized the place had been built centuries ago. When I peeked between the floorboards, I found books buried in the dirt. I smashed the floor open and uncovered strange, fourteenth century scriptures: studies and spell books, on the subjects of witchcraft and popular folklore. I steeped myself in their knowledge for many months; I learned occult powers obtainable by those who wish to harness the energy of the universe. I practiced, again and again, until I knew I had found something remarkable: a feature of spiritual weaponry augmented by my Sararan qualities. A sorcery dangerous and powerful enough to overthrow the Queen and the Aradians, but only when the time is right."

"But...isn't magic just tricks and illusions?"

"No. What I found was real magick: Quantum-Divinatory Ionization. A great power kept in the shadows of time's deceitful pace. It can be met with some seeking, if one understands that its history is part fallacy. So often, in these late-Earth years, we consider our myths to be just that and nothing more, but in the correct hands, ancient practices can shift planets. Common-folk traditions were a lesser potent range of spells and potions, said to be widely useful for minor ailments or finding love. But there are women in history who have endured a great suffering and converged into covens to vacate from their patriarch, exploiting an identity all their own. Some took their craft to an unprecedented depth of enchantment."

"I thought practicing witchcraft implied that you worship Satan?"

"Melody, dear, that's religious propaganda. These practices are not necessarily conducted with negative or evil intentions. But know too that I will use whatever available energies within my grasp to accomplish my goal of slaying the Queen."

"So, what do you plan to do with these powers?"

"Firstly, I'm going to begin teaching them to you."

"I'm not sure if I'm comfortable with that. I'm a Sufi Muslim, not a Pagan sorcerer."

"You can be both. God was never meant to be cornered into the walls of a Mosque, Melody. Praise the almighty by healing the Earth in these starless times. Think of the prophets. Was Christ not a sorcerer? He who could turn water to wine and heal the diseased? Or Moses, who conjured locusts and plagues to cripple Pharaoh's power? These men may have known the rites which could transform the elements, yet they did not exploit their powers for personal gain. Compassion is the only way witchcraft can be justified. Used in any other way, and its immense multi-dimensional mechanics will ultimately consume its beholder through their own ruination or someone else's vengeance upon them. Why do you think I have waited so long to take on the Aradians? Eventually, they will have to turn, or face self-destruction."

With that, Pavonis stood up and walked to the edge of the boat, unclothed herself, and dove into the clear, salty water. Melody watched as her white skin disappeared under the deep blue cloak of the sea.

The Goddess resurfaced seconds later with two large fish in either hand.

"Lunch is ready!" Pavonis called as the princess in exile gazed back at her new master with a look of wonder and fear.

That evening, as the sun set low on the ocean's flat horizon, Pavonis stood at the back of the boat and watched a storm looming from the north. Melody and David were fast asleep inside the boat's cabin. Hartford sipped on some hot coffee and stepped outside to speak with the Sararan Goddess.

"Looks like a nasty storm headed this way," he said.

Pavonis watched the sky for some time before replying. "I might be able to shift its course," she said, holding her gaze still.

Hartford laughed. "You mean to stop a force of nature?"

"I stopped death from taking you," she said, turning towards him.

"I admit, that was some pretty biblical shit, but I don't know if that's the same thing as breaking up a storm cell. Thank you, by the way," he said, holding up his drink.

"You're welcome, Hartford."

The man peered longingly over the gentle waves as the sun's light cast a glimmering cadmium stream of foam across the water, like a vast tract arriving at some fierce portal, where the shadows of distant birds followed the course of Venus and were flogged from existence in that blinding, white evanescence.

"You fought for the Navy, as a SEAL?" Pavonis asked.

"Yes, ma'am. My last official deployment was in Oregon, right after the eruption, after everything went to shit."

"My husband was a special forces operative. I never understood his pain until the day Vishnu covered the Earth in ash. Then I fought in the war and I finally understood his suffering."

"You were in combat?" Hartford asked.

"I've been in a few skirmishes," she said modestly, crouching low and looking down at her feet, remembering how shell-shocked she had felt after the battle on the tar sands, and the years of resistance that followed in response to the Aradian carnage. She remembered the black clouds gathering around her as whole mountains were leveled by the Cold War-era ordinance of thermo-nuclear weaponry.

Hartford broke her silent reverie. "Word spread that Pavonis called in the airstrike meant to end the war..."

"It wasn't me. I tried to avoid the order...besides, the Aradians evaded the bombings like gnats in the wind and instead absorbed the radiation as if it were a delicacy. Only a direct hit would have proved fatal. Funny...it could be a .45 bullet or a nuke...if you could just put one in their spine..." Pavonis shuddered at the memory of how they had expended that energy, grinding her diamond teeth together before letting the thought go. "I fought for a few years with some very good men. But the twins are unstoppable. At least for now. Though the future seems bleak, I believe those who have been warmongering will ultimately have to face their end. Those who have been gaining power will become paralyzed. And I, the hermit shepherd lying in wait, will reign down a vengeance of a magnitude not seen since the nuclear strike." She looked up at him. "You will help us in our cause, won't you?"

"Of course I will. I owe you my life, remember?"

"You don't owe anybody anything, Hartford. Excessive deference to our league of resistance may just as well put us in the same predicament that brought us here. Earth is in command, no one else."

"Shouldn't there be...someone?" he asked.

Pavonis sighed. "If you fight for our cause, you don't fight for the freedom of a nation. This is a fight for all life on Earth. This is a different kind of war. That young boy," she said, looking into the cabin at David. "We must fight for him. He is one of the youngest males on the planet. We must fight for Melody, one of the last Muslims in the world not shackled by Shakti's oppressive regime. We must fight for these youth, who will someday lead the world back out of this darkness to form a free and unified Earth. The only way of doing that is without structure, without predetermination. Loyalty to one another and devotion to the cause will guide us and shape us. We must have faith in the principles of absolute anarchy."

Hartford looked at her skeptically. "What did them woods do to you?"

"Primal fears drive my dreams. The further the Queen moves forward, the farther we must reach back, until we once again believe lightning is the work of an angry God; fire is a healing process of rebirth, and water is a substance to praise above all other entities."

"I'm with you, Pavonis, don't think I'm not. But in all rationality, how will you defeat an army one hundred times the size of your forces? How will you fight against the Aradians, who could boil this very ocean or knock us off a mountainside with an earthquake? The Marines will be crushed without a well implemented plan. They can't hide forever."

"Though Shakti is undoubtedly intelligent, her craving for power has distracted her gaze. I have tricked her into thinking I am no threat to her."

"What strategy do you have to claim *victory*, Pavonis?" he asked impatiently.

Pavonis smiled then simply said, "Magick."

He looked at her with a puzzled stare and shook his head.

"More power to ya. I'm gonna go dig up some liquor."

"Will you wake up Melody and bring her out here? Tell her to bring a candle."

Hartford nodded, disappearing below deck.

Pavonis took a piece of charcoal and drew a circle on the boat's deck. She filled it with a large pentagram and drew old runic markings inside the center, symbolizing water and air.

"You called for me?" Melody yawned, as she brought out a candle.

Pavonis took the flame and set it at the center of her mandala.

"This shall be your first lesson in witchcraft. You see the storm approaching?"

"Yes."

"It's coming straight for us, but we're going to shift its passage to land. I will conduct the spell, while you sing the verse from this page. Once you start, please do not stop," Pavonis said as she handed Melody a folded piece of brown paper. The writing was in Latin.

"But there aren't any notes! And I don't even speak this language!"

"All that matters is that you sing the words with intent. Stay focused on your task and become a servant to the storm Goddess, then the melody will come to you."

Pavonis handed Melody a piece of hematite stone to hold while she sang.

"Go ahead," Pavonis said as she stepped aside, holding her hands up to the sky and closing her eyes.

Melody knelt down by the pentagram, holding the stone against her heart with one hand while she read the old scripture in the other. She sang the verse in a mournful tone. The dark black clouds pulsed with thunder in the distance.

Morriga, dea tempestatis, in omni forma auxilium peto.

Ut in lapide et in arbore exbibas atque ad aborem hanc procellam ex me procul expellas.

Averte rursus aequorem id.

Si autem dea mea consentit, tunc istud fac, mihi ostende.

Morrigan, goddess of the storm, I ask for help in every form.

Turn it back to the sea, absorb into the rock and to the tree.

Cast this storm far from me.

If my Goddess does agree, then manifest, make it be.

She finished and looked up at Pavonis, who motioned for her to stand. They watched in silence as the storm continued to roll their way, the sulking clouds in steady tow. The waves grew and slapped the boat as the winds gusted over the sea.

"How's that magic working out for ya?" Hartford asked as he emerged from below deck, taking a large swig from a half full bottle of rum. He smiled and leaned against the boat's cabin, shaking his head.

Melody looked to Pavonis, bracing herself for criticism. Perhaps she had sung the verses incorrectly? But the divine widow stood like a statue, her gaze fixed on the storm cell.

Nothing appeared to change, then quite suddenly, the winds calmed, the waves settled, and the cell swept east towards land. Pavonis and Melody watched for another hour to be sure it followed their desired path. Above them, the grey clouds dispersed and the dark blue sky opened to the stars' ancient light, the constellations casting their enchantment over them like a heavenly varnish, untainted by Earth's infirmity.

"See, Melody, witches can perform good spells too. And sometimes they work."

"I...I can't believe I just did that...that was me..." Melody stammered, looking down at the gem she still held to her chest.

"Superstition, nothing more," Hartford said, shaking his head as he finished off the bottle. Rum dripped from his beard as he went on. "These storms always head from northwest to southeast. I've spent years out here. It's not 'magick'."

"Not always. There have been many ships destroyed and crews killed out here," Pavonis reprimanded him.

"Sure, but there's nothin ya can do to stop it!"

Pavonis ignored him and turned to Melody.

"What did you feel?"

"I felt...slightly euphoric. But I'm not sure I read the Latin correctly."

"You did very well for your first spell, Melody.

You sing wonderfully. I can already tell you will be a strong witch. Focus more on preparation next time. Posture. Breathing. Line of sight. Also, certain spells require facing a cardinal direction, which I know is difficult on a moving craft, so just be mindful of the magnetic poles. We will delve more into the runic alphabet and other kinds of spells and potions later. This was a fairly easy one."

"Thank you, Pavonis," Melody said, bowing low.

Pavonis smiled softly. "Off to bed with you now, I've kept you late enough as it is." Her brilliant cosmic eyes were hypnotic, holding all of Laniakea's galaxies behind them.

Melody complied, heading down below deck again to find David.

"You want her to be the future of the human race and you're teaching her fake tricks?" Hartford slurred drunkenly, his left eyebrow pointing dramatically upwards.

Pavonis walked up to him and blew a handful of dust into his face. The large man fell into her arms as she laid him on the deck. He snored deeply in his wasted slumber.

"Passionflower and lavender; stored in the flakes of my skin and now running through your alcohol-infected veins. This universe was created through the marriage of magick and mathematics.

158

Your hangover will be proof of that."

She walked to the front of the boat and laid down to sleep. She had not dreamt for weeks. A night of rapid eye movement under the canopy of the stars was a way to reflect and be at one with the spirit of her lover, who she kept in a lotus flower, wilting in her perfect, cupped hands.

The next morning, Pavonis lurched as a splash of cold water hit her skin. A fresh gale pulled her gown against the contours of her body and massive waves pulled the boat this way and that as she tried to stand. She looked up. Dark clouds gathered overhead; a massive storm had approached them, seemingly from nowhere. She walked to the hull where Hartford was struggling to pull down the sail.

"This weather just moved in! We'll have to make our way to shore!" Hartford yelled.

Pavonis opened the door to the cabin and found Melody and David curled up in the blankets, frightened and shaking with cold.

"I thought you said the spell would drive the storm away!" Melody cried.

"When you send a storm to the east, it doesn't

mean another won't come from the west!"

"Can't we perform the ritual again?" Melody asked desperately.

"It's too late for that, we'll have to wait it out."

Pavonis walked back out onto the deck as the cool white water splashed over the railing. She looked up at the sail, which flailed helplessly in the wind. Hartford was nowhere to be found.

"Hartford! Hartford!!" she called desperately, looking all around. He had vanished. Clicking her tongue sharply, she used her echolocation to try and find him. After a few moments of nothingness, she sensed him splashing as he struggled to fight against the turbulent waters. She ran across to the starboard side of the boat and caught sight of Hartford hundreds of feet from the boat treading water between endless crashing waves.

Without wasting another moment, Pavonis jumped into the freezing water and glided towards Hartford, swift as a shark. The waves grew larger and wilder by the minute, pounding Hartford as he gasped for breath in-between the breaking white-water's wrath. By the time Pavonis reached him he was unconscious. She took him gently in her arms and kicked her feet like a propeller, jetting them both back to the boat. Pavonis jumped on board then hauled Hartford up and over the railing. She set him down on the deck and immediately began to press her hands down on his chest, trying to give life back into him. Melody came up onto the deck and watched with haunted eyes as Pavonis tried to bring the man who had saved her back from the dead.

"Come on you stubborn bastard! Come on!" Pavonis yelled.

Melody turned her face away, unable to watch. "Can't you do what you did last time?" she cried desperately, as sheets of rain and ocean water fell from the sky.

"He was still alive when I revived him last time," Pavonis said quietly, a whisper of resignation in her voice.

"There must be a spell to bring people back from the dead," Melody sobbed.

"There is. It's called resurrection, and it's not something I care to practice. He's not coming back, Melody. He's gone."

Just then, David walked out of the cabin door shivering, tears brimming in the corners of his eyes. He knelt beside Hartford's body and solemnly took off his star necklace, setting it on Hartford's ice-cold chest. Then the child wept for his fallen hero, his face crushed against Hartford's body, Melody crouched beside the boy, her eyes hollow, and gently placed a hand on David's head, stroking his hair soothingly as they mourned together.

When the storm finally passed, Pavonis cast their fallen friend into the ocean, wrapped in a torn American flag they had pulled from the ship's mast before setting their course for the shore, lest another storm drag them further from their intended path.

CHAPTER 22
THE REBEL MARINE CORPS

Will and his platoon led Michael deep into the wilderness, where neither roads nor houses had ever existed. Having been stricken with disease or immured by the conditions, animals were seldom seen, and a starved deer was considered enough to feed thirty Marines. Crows and other scavengers of the sky were the dominant fauna, feeding on the carcasses of the bombed. Bones of deer and elk scattered the land, their grey rib cages dripping with dew and sinew, unable to decay or bleach in the ridged wasteland. The hooves and severed legs of the newly dead were eagerly hung over the soldiers' backs, to be made into bone marrow soup when the team paused for the night.

One afternoon, as they journeyed across the bleak landscape, they discovered a slaughtered family, half eaten by the carrion that patrolled overhead. They left them to rot. The Marines believed the Aradians planted hexes in the corpses, and so dead humans were given a wide berth, treated as IED's that would cause madness if touched. Rumors of 'skin walkers' had spread. The Chippewa trackers claimed they had seen the dead resurrected before their eyes after a battle, led by the sorcery of the floating Aradian Goddesses. Their fear of the Aradian's was so great that they even feared Michael, turning their eyes from his gaze, his father's blood making him one of 'them'. Michael understood why his lineage might make him unwanted, but he was not sure why they feared him. He was only human.

At the end of the third day of hiking, their march ended in a low valley where numerous tents had been erected at the drainage edge, all decorated with branches and bushes to ensure they blended into the trees, making them indistinguishable from the rest of the forest if observed from above. Michael walked with Apollo as they passed a sign that read 'The Front', with arrows pointing in every direction. Another sign read 'Camp Draco'; another 'Days since eruption: 6,932 – Semper Fi'.

Will called over to Michael as they entered the encampment. "Michael, don't go wandering off. We've planted explosives in nearly every passage except for the east and west entrances to the camp."

"This isn't the same location that Pavonis' map

was leading me to," Michael said, confused.

"That's because if you had been captured, the Queen's officers would have found your map and gone looking in that location, which we left several months ago."

"But how would I have found you then?"

"Luckily you did," Will said gruffly. He pulled his beard lightly with his gloved hand and breathed with lungs like cracked lava, spitting a bloody drop of marrow from his upper lip before marching on. They entered the Marine base with heavy feet. Large wall tents, tarnished with ash and mold, had been raised in the small clearing between the strings of smoke from their deceitfully small fires. The other Marines had long unkempt beards and clothing made from animal skins and Michael noticed a set of freshly cut deer skins, stretched between the trees for tanning. One of the men wore metal chest armor layered with hawk feathers and blood dripped from his chin as he gnawed on raw squirrel meat. A few old Marines watched Michael walk into their camp guiding Apollo. They scoffed and made jokes to themselves, gazing at Apollo like he was a platter of steaks.

That evening, Michael strung his horse up by the edge of camp before heading towards his uncle's tent. As he approached, he noticed a tall black man with an eye patch standing nearby. The man's grey beard was dreaded with bones and teeth. He wore a long brown deel, and had a double barrel shotgun slung over his back. As Michael passed him, the man opened his one eye wide and reached out an arm, stopping Michael in his tracks.

"Are you Ezra's son?" he asked. "Come here, let me see your face."

Michael turned to face him, and the man examined him.

"Ah, you are much like him," the man said, smiling nostalgically. "I am Gadreel, an old friend of your father's. He was a great man, and perhaps something more. There were few as honorable and noble as he."

"Good to meet you, Gadreel. I hope that my presence is welcome here."

"Don't be too bothered by these old bastards. They haven't had a good meal or the warmth of a woman in a long time. Newcomers make them uneasy. We've had spies enter our camps before, often disguised as potential recruits or traders, or posing as whores. We always find them out, though."

"What do you do with them...when you find out who they really are?"

"Some of them are tortured for information first. All of them are killed. How long did it take you to get here?"

"Six weeks."

"You steal that horse?"

"No. A old man was kind enough to offer Apollo to me in return for some work. I wanted to make sure I found my uncle before the fall. I want to do everything I can for this unit, Gadreel. I want to be a warrior, like my father."

Gadreel nodded. "Just understand the sacrifice you are making by joining. I can promise you this: every man you see here will die in these mountains. But before we do, we will do everything we can to resist the tyranny wrought upon us."

"I am here to expend my vengeance upon my enemy. I've made it this far, and I will keep going as far as I need to."

"So it seems." Gadreel smiled sadly, as he examined the frail frame of yet another boy who was all too eager to become a man. "I'll be seeing you around, Beller. Take care."

"Thank you, sir."

Michael bid farewell to Gadreel and entered his uncle's domain. Potatoes boiled in an iron pot and the smell of whiskey and garlic filled the air. Candles and a small fire illuminated the officer's canvas tent, and a massive Kodiak bear rug lay sprawled out over the tundra. To Michael, Will seemed an odd mix of

Viking and Marine, survivalist and warrior, yet also a king to his small yet valiant band of brothers.

"So, Michael, it's been a long march. I know I haven't been too vocal during the last few days. It's just hard to see you and not think of my brother. I can tell you have the Beller blood in you." He handed Michael a cup of old scotch. "Please, sit," he said, pointing to a large log round that had been carved into a seat. "I'm glad to hear your mother finally found you," he continued, stirring the potatoes. "You know, she wanted to come and find you much earlier than this? But it was too dangerous. Shakti would have had you both killed. Your mother found the right moment, when she knew you would be able to make this long journey on your own."

Michael took a sip of the scotch and cringed as the fiery liquid sloshed into his empty stomach.

Will laughed. "You'll learn to love it," he said looking at his nephew with warm eyes.

"I'm eager to begin training, uncle. I want to become a Marine. I want to help defeat the Queen!"

"Defeat the Queen, you say? Michael, we can barely defend ourselves from her Northern Lords, let alone taking on Shakti herself!" Will came and sat beside his nephew, taking a healthy drink of the liquor before continuing. "But I like your enthusiasm.

The Marine Corps' current goal is to maintain a buffer zone between Lord Sandraudiga's troops and ourselves, until your mother comes back and implements a plan that will hopefully shift the tides of this drawn-out conflict."

"Who is Lord Sandraudiga?"

"She is the reason your parents abandoned you at birth. She sent assassins to their house the night your mother went into labor. After you were born, you were abandoned, because Ezra was being hunted. Ezra wanted to retaliate by killing Sandraudiga, but she tricked us with a decoy of herself. Your father killed the decoy, and from that point on, things went from bad to worse. Now, she lives to serve the Queen in all the territories north of Caldera. She isn't an Aradian, thank God—"

"My mother mentioned something about Aradians."

"A modified Sararan, basically," Will explained. "But even though she's still human, she's one cold hearted bitch. She orders her soldiers to nail the bodies of her victims to trees."

"I saw one of those trees floating down the river," Michael murmured.

"Where did you see it?"

"In the Cassiar Mountains, close to the Yukon

border."

"That far north? Damn," Will said as he took another drink of scotch. Michael took a long drink himself, his spirit illuminated with the throat warming liquid.

"Will...tell me about my father."

"Ezra was a great man, and he became an even greater man when he married your mother. Ezra was a fighter at heart. He was an excellent soldier, training and serving in all kinds of covert military operations. But your mother brought out the creator in him. He was a lover, and an estranged poet of sorts. It's rare to know a man with the qualities of both action and abstraction. I remember being so envious of him when I met your mother. I always wished to have a woman as amazing as she was. Here, look at this." Will opened up a duffle bag and pulled out some pictures of Michael's mother and father on their wedding day.

"That's dad? Wow," Michael said, his pained smile widening. "And my mother, she's so beautiful."

Will took out an old piece of paper and handed it to Michael. "This is your father's military file. It doesn't show everything, mostly because it's not a physical copy but one that was stripped from the government mainframe. But it gives you an idea of the kind of badass he was."

Michael read the file to himself, trying to decipher the acronyms and terms.

Will went on. "God knows we need men like Ezra now. We need more than a well-trained military to win this war. I just hope Pavonis can find a way to defeat or deter the Aradians. Those twins are the most dangerous weapons in Shakti's arsenal. They rarely attack us, but we have lost four fifths of our fighting force to them alone. The only reason they haven't wiped us out completely is because they're too busy taking over Europe, Asia, and the rest of the world. What you see out there in this camp is all that's left. Four thousand men willing to die for the cause."

"I'm willing as well, uncle. Train me to be one of them. Let me go through what every Marine must go through and I'll prove to you I can fight!" Michael said. The scotch spoke for him; he was empowered by the aged drink.

Will looked Michael over and smiled. He reached into his pocket and took out a knife. "This is your great-grandfathers knife, Eugene Ezra Beller. He carried it through Vietnam. Your grandfather carried it through the Gulf War. Ezra carried it across Africa and the Middle East during the global War on Terror. I've carried it through the carnage of the Canadian front, and when you're done with your training, you'll carry it into your own battles. May it serve you as it has served our forefathers."

Michael took the old knife and felt its deadly weight in his palm. He would never know the answers to the forsaken questions that swam like eels in his mind.

"Training will start soon for you, Michael. We have to get you ready for when your mother arrives."

"Yes, she mentioned she'd be helping you," Michael said.

"Helping? She's practically our commander in chief," Will said, chuckling.

Suddenly, a great fear washed over Michael, as he realized the horrors of war were just beginning, and that his fears were far from apex. He knocked back the rest of his drink and nodded in silent understanding, wondering how his mother had become so powerful and whether, through steady persistence, she could triumph against her enemy.

CHAPTER 23
PENDULUM SWING

Far to the east of Camp Draco, the ever-rising Pacific Ocean sloshed against the Cascadian coast, until its shoreline met the jutting mountains that halted the brooding tide. Under the cloak of night, Pavonis' fishing boat crept silently into a cove between the star-sinking peaks. She had used her talents in abiogenesis to erect a mast of conchs, mussels, and barnacles, supporting a thin but strong sail of spider web and mildew, which she had strung from her fingers like an arachnid maestro. The boat creaked as a soft wind pushed them through the corridor's retreat. Melody and David wrapped themselves in a blanket as Pavonis gripped tightly to her submachine gun. She kept her eyes peeled for any movement. As they entered the inlet, the lighthouse a few miles away flashed a rotating light, before the glimmer faded behind the trees. On the shore, an old Haida totem pole stood, half charred and tilted.

"We're going to dock here," Pavonis whispered. "I can sense patrols up ahead."

They quietly leapt into the water and walked ashore, weapons in hand. Even David held his dagger by his side. Not that he was expected to use it at his age. Pavonis had given it to him more as a metaphorical tool; if he was to survive in their harsh world, he would need to hurry up and learn how to protect himself.

The forest glowed eerily beneath a half moon as Pavonis led the trio inward, her eyes penetrating the dark woods. Once in a while, she motioned for them to lay flat on the forest floor, where they would stay for up to an hour at a time. Melody never heard anyone close by, but Pavonis could sense other beings for miles and took great caution in keeping them safe. This nerve-racking pattern of movement continued day and night for a week. Melody and David would only get a few hours of sleep during these times of silence before having to get up and keep moving. They grabbed berries and roots along the way for food, and occasionally Pavonis would kill a rabbit for them, which David and Melody reluctantly ate raw, unable to light a fire for fear of giving away their position. Whenever they came across an open area, Pavonis would pick up David and run with him, Melody following close behind, swiftly returning to the security of the forest to avoid being caught in the peripheral view of a sniper or signaled by a sentry.

When finally exited the coastal boundaries, they stopped near the edge of Nechako Reservoir, out of sight of the patrols. Pavonis led them into an empty drainage channel and built them a fire, cooking the two children fresh turkey and herb and onion soup. Having been finally fed a decent meal, David quickly fell fast asleep. But though she too was exhausted, Melody laid by the fire for a while watching Pavonis. The forest enchantress gazed through the flames and into the steaming coals, a glaze covering her spiraling eyes.

"Why don't you ever eat?" Melody asked.

"I don't need food," she replied, still staring intently into the fire's core. "My energy comes directly from the sun."

"What about when it's cloudy?"

"I still collect varying amounts of ultra violet rays. When I was hidden in that rotten tree, I felt like I was hibernating. I saved up years of stored energy."

"How do the Aradians get sunlight through their suits then?" Melody asked.

"I honestly don't know enough about their characteristics to rightfully say."

"Where did they come from?"

"They came from a poor village in Vietnam. They were torn from their burning straw huts when they were teenagers, before being kidnapped, raped, and starved. The two were then separated and sold as slaves on desolate isles in the South China sea. Shakti eventually saved them and taught them Vishnu's secrets. They learned immortality *before* the age of seventeen, and thus will resemble young girls forevermore, which can be quite deceiving on those rare occasions when they decide to dismantle their appliances. They harness a sacred Taoist wisdom which the Zurvan cult has survived by. *Winds of the immortals, bones of the Tao.* When their genetic transformation took place, they had already mentally and spiritually prepared themselves for their transfiguration. Now, they are able to manipulate the so-called 'laws' of physics in ways I cannot understand. They can fly at incredible speeds without thrust or wings."

"But how?"

"I don't know. They somehow repel atoms in the air around them, or harness a dimension I don't yet understand, which somehow gives them infinite aerodynamic conservancy. This is why they are the ultimate combat engineers. A single Aradian can construct, defend, divide enemies, multiply allies, and conquer whole nations. They can take the role of an assassin, a bomber, a hurricane, or an earthquake, all in a day. These are creatures that have been betrayed by mankind; they are more than just driven to punish us all. Who knows what one is truly capable of with that kind of ambition? They seem devoid of emotion, but I can see through their voided eyes. They must love something to achieve their impeccability...perhaps it is each other."

"Who else is in charge, besides the Queen and her Aradians? There must be more who have been delegated power."

"Well, you met Lord Sandraudiga in the northern lands, did you not?"

"The hag with the horned headpiece? She was going to have poor David shot!"

"That woman really is a cunt," Pavonis said bitterly. "Then there's Shakti's sister, Lakshmi, who is the Lord of Neon City."

"What's that?" Melody asked.

"Neon City is the metropolis surrounding what used to be St. Louis, Missouri. When the Queen destroyed all the major cities in the United States, she kept Neon City for some reason. I have yet to discern what that reason is. It's the only place some men are still allowed to occupy without segregation."

"How many people live there?"

"Well, seeing as it's the only populated city in North America, besides Caldera, I'd say probably around five million."

"Five million! That's so many…"

"There used to be hundreds of millions of people on this continent, Melody. Five million might sound like a lot, but when you factor in that Neon City is one of the only cities not totally destroyed by the Aradians, it is a tiny fraction of what the population should be. When you combine that with the fact that those people are nothing but substance abusing youths, apathetic to the apocalypse, completely numb to the world around them, the future looks very bleak indeed. Before the eruption, Neon City was a party city. Now it is a party city with an emphasis on 'spiritual cleansing'. City-wide speaker systems line the grid. Endless raves on rooftops are kept alive with rotating DJ sets."

"I have no idea what any of that is."

Pavonis continued. "They have an end of the world party every day, and Shakti uses the money she makes off of those drugged up kids to fund her army's hunger."

"That's so messed up."

"It's truly sad. Lakshmi has a police force that

runs a tight ship as far as most criminal activity goes. But when it comes to drugs, they all turn a blind eye. The police ship in both cocaine and heroin to begin the rotation."

"How is all this going on while people are being exterminated and towns like White Horse are being bombed?"

"We live in a terrible, cruel world, Melody. All I know is that there is a cause to fight for, and there is a new Earth waiting for David's generation."

"So, Lakshmi isn't Aradian?"

"Not that I know of. Based on her neutrality during the post-eruption wars, I'm convinced that she doesn't share Shakti's passion for world domination. I know she allows men in her city, so that's an obvious indicator of her more progressive policies. From what I know of her, I think she's just a woman who, like you, was plucked from a royal Middle Eastern family and given a wild destiny to fulfill."

"Hm. Maybe she'll join us," Melody said, hopeful as ever.

"I doubt it. She's smart enough to know not to go up against Shakti. But if just one of the Aradians took our side..." Pavonis sighed, not wanting to jinx her own hopes. She pulled out a small copper chain with an emerald stone at the end of it, holding the pendulum still for a moment. As she kept her hand clenched to the end of the chain, it suddenly began rotating in the air.

"What's that for?" Melody asked, her eyes squinting with exhaustion.

"Shh," Pavonis said, closing her eyes. She whispered something almost inaudible, then, after a few moments, she opened her eyes. The stone began rotating in the opposite direction. "This is a witches pendulum. It's a tool for divination. Through its movement, I can determine where the Marine base lies."

"And what does it say?"

"Almost straight east," she said, putting the pendant away. "We'll check it every day until we arrive. I'll let you try as well, and we'll compare results."

"Okay," Melody mumbled, drifting off to sleep.

Pavonis stood up and set her weapon down next to Melody, before walking quietly into the night to hunt for elk. Pavonis' nomadic lifestyle had become increasingly influenced by the primal instincts that had once led her ancestors through Europe. She tapped into that quantum memory and learned everything she needed to keep Melody and David alive and safe. She used the meat from the elk as rations to fuel the young ones' journey, and crafted proper clothing from the hide for both herself and the two children. She heated the hide with her radiant hands, tanning the inside as if she were the sun, then cut and sewed the pieces into a top and skirt. With the extra pieces she made pockets, in which to store her stones and other magick tools.

As she crafted, the runic alphabet played through her mind, and suddenly she saw through her third eye the faint outline of an ancestor, coaxing her into a cave. Pavonis walked between the mountains' fissures, unsure of what this being's intentions were. When she reached the cave, the specter dissolved, becoming one with the firelight that flickered across the walls of the chamber. Pavonis cocked her head, curious. How had a fire been created in the very center of this cavern without any trace of a man. She thought perhaps a lightning strike could have poured sparks into the underground , but she saw no strike tree at its entrance, and found no tracks leading in or out. This flame was not of mortal making. The fire burned bright blue as Pavonis let the ghost's hands guide her fingers like a savage scribe; they painted their conversation in rime stock with elk's blood upon the cave walls, united in that eddy of eternity as they moved to the low beat of the

Earth with somandric intimacy, utterly secluded from the stars.

Pavonis came back to the children's fire with her pelts, and saw Melody curled up next to David, fast asleep. She combed Melody's hair with her bloodstained fingers as she gazed upon them. Melody was her son's lover, but Pavonis often second-guessed herself as to why she had also taken David south with them. Perhaps the guilt of abandoning her own boy long ago had seized her heart, and helping the stranded child felt like doing for David what Lily had done for Michael. Perhaps this act of kindness would finally free her from regret. Then again, perhaps David too had a distinct purpose, and would end up playing a vital role in their world's climaxing theomachy.

CHAPTER 24
MOUNT LUCIFER

On the first day of August, Michael awoke before dawn to find the only clean-shaven man in the entire camp standing over him. The man was at least seven feet tall, freshly shaven, and bald, with skin like an albino serpent and a partially burn-scarred face. His bloodshot, heron eyes bulged as they dug into Michael's soul.

"Wake the fuck up, sunshine!"

Michael stood as fast as he could.

"Welcome to the Marine Corps, Beller! You are my one and only cadet, and because you are getting such a personalized version of United States Marine training, my eyes will be on YOU the entire time! My name is Master Drill Instructor Cassidy and from now on, I expect the only words coming out of your cock holster to be 'yes, sir' or 'no, sir', do you understand me?!" the muscular giant hollered.

"Yes, sir!" Michael yelled.

"Speak up and use your man voice for fucks

sake!"

"YES, SIR!" Michael screamed.

"Is that all you got? Sound off!"

"YES, SIR!" Michael screamed as loud as he could.

"Now hump up that mountain like she's a big bitch that needs ALL the love. Move motherfucker!"

Michael quickly dressed as the man continued.

"I'm going to be everything but joy to you. I am going to be the demon ringing your dirty little neck in the middle of the night! Do you understand me? I'm going to bury you and make you wish you'd buried yourself!" he yelled, pointing north.

"YES, SIR!"

Six miles later, Michael was panting hard as he ran up an old game trail. Cassidy ran next to him, a rifle slung over his shoulder. The run was closer to a walk for him because of his long legs and Michaels decreasing pace.

"You are one piss poor excuse for a human being. If I had the power to go back in time, I would fuck your mother so a real man could have grown in your place. If a diabetic walrus were racing you right now, you would have been lapped already! Can you go any faster?"

"Yes, sir!" he said, moving only slightly faster

than before.

"I don't hate you Beller, in fact, I'm half impressed you made it down here without becoming target practice. But I'm here to push you beyond your limits, which as of now are less than the operations of the Girl Scouts of America. Are you listening to me?"

"YES, SIR!"

"Turn around, we're going back down! Not that way shit stain, off trail!"

"YES, SIR!

Three miles later, Michael felt a sharp jab at his leg.

"TURN AROUND AGAIN, we're going back up the mountain!"

"YES, SIR!" Michael yelled, breathing heavily.

A few miles later, Michael glanced at the side of the trail as he stumbled up the mountain. He could still see his vomit from earlier. Cassidy yelled in his ear.

"Back down the mountain!"

"YES, SIR!" Michael screamed. He was so worn out he could hardly think. All he wanted was for the dreaded run to end. Back at the base, Michael jogged in with Cassidy leading him in. The other Marines watched and laughed as young Michael struggled to pick his feet off the ground.

"We're done with morning PT. Grab some chow and eat while I talk. Go!"

"Yes, sir!" Michael said, gasping for air.

Michael took some food from his satchel and stood while eating. His legs shook with fatigue, but he was too scared to sit down.

Cassidy paced along the grass in front of him as he spoke. The sun began to rise to the east behind him. "Just because the United States has been invaded by a foreign force does not mean the Marine Corps has forgotten its values. This is the strongest willed fighting force in the world. I don't care if those steel-titted chinks conquer every part of the world except this piece of land we stand on now. As long as the Marine Corps survives, they will not take the Earth from us entirely! We will fight until our last breath. We will fight even when there is no hope for victory. We will fight in the face of an enemy a thousand times our strength because that is what we do."

"Yes, sir!"

"The three values of the Marines are honor, courage, and commitment. You will honor those who have fallen before you in the name of freedom. You will honor the courageous men around you who still fight for the greater good of mankind. And you will honor the cause. We are up against a force that has infiltrated every part of this continent. The enemy you face is a fierce one. It will take immense courage to fight them, and to continue fighting them, in order to claim victory against the self-proclaimed Queen. You will commit yourself to becoming a Marine, because in the Marine Corps there is no tolerance for half-assing anything. You must operate on a fully committed level at all times, do you understand!"

"Yes, sir!"

"Get on your knees!"

Michael set his satchel down and dropped onto the cold wet grass as the officer grabbed his hair by his hand. Cassidy then took out a pair of medical scissors and began cutting Michael's hair.

"A Marine keeps himself in good condition. Only after you've finished training will I let you grow a beard, though I doubt your face will sprout more than a pussy hair. Do you know why these men are allowed to grow out their beards?"

"No, sir!"

"Because they are men, dammit! Are you a man?"

"I will be, sir!"

"Bullshit! Your entire training block is being condensed from three months to one. Do you feel lucky?"

"Yes, sir!"

"Well you shouldn't, because I'm going to make these next four weeks a living hell for you. I'm going to drown you in the river. I'm going to give Gadreel a bow staff and throw you in a pit with him and watch you try to defend yourself. I will harden you, Beller. I will make sure that you taste the bitter agony of all that is wrought with suffering in this world! How else are you going to learn to kill?"

"I don't know, sir!"

"How else are you going to destroy an enemy that beheads children without blinking?"

"There is no other way, sir!"

"DROP DOWN AND PUSH THE EARTH!"

Michael proceeded with the pushups, and when Cassidy gave him one hundred more after his first set, he puked up his breakfast.

"You disgust me!"

"I disgust myself, sir!"

"Good! You've learned that you are nothing! You are a squirming maggot. You are larvae more putrid than the ones that crawl beneath you. It is my intention that you grow beyond this phase, that you turn into a heightened version of yourself. Is that not the goal of all living things!"

"It is, sir!"

"Then I expect nothing less from you. Do you

188

want to be a Marine?"

"More than anything, sir!" Michael screamed in agony as he fought back tears.

"Are you down with the goat?"

"What, sir?" Michael looked up at him with a puzzled expression.

"ARE YOU DOWN WITH THE GOAT!? Lucifer is now your ally. Only once you have faced him and become that which you most fear can you rise to something greater than what you are now. But I have faith in you, Beller, because I have to. You may very well be the last Marine trained in the old way. You may be the one carrying the traditions of everything this fighting force has strived to achieve for two hundred and seventy-six years. The weight of this significance should scare you more than I ever could, that's why I'm training you this way. It will be grueling but rewarding. I will teach you how to be a brutal force, but also how to be surgical. I will teach you how to throw an axe, track an enemy, sew a wound, and survive in the wilderness, and to do all this swiftly and efficiently with only what you carry with you. The less I have to push you to meet the physical standards, the more we can focus on tactics and field work, because there isn't any more schooling after this. We're going to war. Meet me at the archery range at eleven hundred hours. Your combat training begins today. From now on, you eat, live, and breathe the Marine Corps. Do you understand?"

"Yes, sir!"

With that, Cassidy walked off towards the encampment. Across the field, Will and Gadreel stood outside Will's tent, talking and smoking tobacco pipes. Will nodded at Michael, who nodded back. Michael's face was wet with sweat and the steam off his back poured into the cool mountain air. He sat down for a moment, trying to catch his breath. For a split-second, he thought what nearly every Marine had probably thought on their first day. 'What the hell am I doing here?'. But then he thought about Melody, the war, and everything he held true, and he knew, deep down, that he would be fighting for a just cause. More than anything, he wished to be behind the tip of the lance, piercing Shakti's skull. But first, he would have to survive the next month.

Two weeks later, Michael found himself holding a boulder above his head as he forged his way into the river. His muscles were growing, and his body had hardened under Cassidy's ruthless training. He was constantly being tested.

Cassidy stood on the shore. "Is that pebble above your head causing you discomfort, Beller!?"

"No, sir!"

"Then drop it and grab a larger one!"

Michael went to walk towards the shore to pick up a larger stone.

"Did I say go the bank?! Reach under the fucking water and pick up a bigger rock, c'mon!"

Michael squatted in the chest high water, submerging himself in the current. He found a rock in the torrent and attempted to lift it, but it would not budge. He resurfaced.

"What's taking so long, sunshine?"

Michael went back under and flipped the rock over, so he had a better handle on it. The texture was slimy and hard to grasp. He lifted with all his might and pushed the rock above his head, splashing up out of the water with a furious yell. He slowly walked the next thirty feet to the shore, cutting his feet on the sharp rocks and fighting the slow but forceful current of the river. Upon reaching the other side, he turned and stood, the stone still raised over his head, staring at the drill instructor and awaiting orders. Cassidy just stood there and couldn't help but crack the faintest smile as Michael clenched his teeth and continued staring, his arms raised like cast iron.

On August the twenty-fourth, Michael's nineteenth birthday, Cassidy summoned him to his tent for his final training assignment to become a Marine. Michael entered the tent and saluted.

"Well, Beller, your archery scores are sufficient. Your swordplay has improved immensely. Your rifle scores are shit, but since our cache is nearly cleaned out and Shakti halted ammunition production, that doesn't matter as much to me at this point."

"Sir, those barrels have had far too many rounds though them to be accurate, I would like to try again—"

"Like I said, it won't matter soon anyway. We can work on that when the time comes. For now, I have one last assignment for you. Go to Mount Lucifer and live there for seven days without rations. All you get to take with you is your blade, your bow, and your canteen."

"Yes, sir!"

"Get going, and don't come back until the morning of the thirty-first."

"Thank you, sir!" Michael yelled. He walked back to his tent as a group of scouts nearby loaded their rifles with the cache's last bullets. Michael ate a quick meal, sharpened his arrow tips, then said goodbye to Apollo, before walking toward the massive peak to the south.

After hiking for a few hours, Michael reached the mountain. It loomed in front of him like a great white giant, defying the sky. The forest stopped at its base and gave way to rock and ice. This was to be his home for a week, a cradled valley beneath massive ridges that seldom allowed sunlight.

As he hiked along the western flank of the mountain, Michael suddenly heard a large crack above him. To his horror, a block of ice the size of a house tumbled and started an avalanche as it came charging like a cavalry of white horses towards him. Michael traversed as fast as he could to evade the crashing barrage. Just when he was about to escape the immense blow, a block of snow struck him in the leg, and he found himself washed away with the overwhelming tsunami of shattering ice.

Moments later, Michael peered up to see an ocean of bright blue sky above him. He had not been buried, but he felt a pain in his leg. He looked around as he scrambled out of the aftermath. He had lost his bow, arrows, and his canteen. Luckily, his long sword and sheath were still tightly buckled to his back. He lifted his clothing to view his pained leg. An icicle had stabbed into his calf and broke off. It was not a deep wound, but he decided to let the icicle melt rather than immediately pull it out. He wrapped his leg with his shirt and continued down the side of the slope, seeking out water. Turning around was not an option, because he knew he would be disbanded from training. Instead, he found a small mountain lake where he drank his fill of water, before making his way to a cave in the side of the mountain. There, he would be able to wait out his stay, and scavenge for roots and berries when he needed sustenance. He would look for his bow and his canteen when he felt nourished. There was nothing else but time against him. Avoiding infection was his number one concern, though he could hear the rumbling of more avalanches galloping down the other side of the valley.

His limbs throbbing with pain, Michael eventually reached the cave as the sun was setting. Under normal circumstances, it would not have taken him that long, but hobbling over jagged boulders and icy slopes with a wounded leg took time. The cavity was large and had multiple facets; Michael chose one and found some nearby sticks and pine needles to make a fire. It took him hours to make smoke with the bow drill he had fashioned from a nettle bush and an old pine branch, but his small fire grew as he fueled it with more sticks. Night had fallen, and the starry sky shone with millions of ancient suns; the Milky Way wrapping the mountains in a pinkish glow as the celeste moon rose from the east.

Michael began to drift off beside the warmth of the flames when he heard a strange sound, coming from deep within the cave. A shuffling of paws, then a low growl.

Suddenly, he noticed the deep black eyes of a creature moving toward him. The large, male brown bear lunged out of his den, roaring, his yellow teeth shining against the fire's glow.

Michael picked up his sword and yelled at the bear. "Stay back beast!" With a field of jagged rocks below him, Michael knew he could not escape the great bear's platform without injury. "Back I say," Michael yelled, picking up a large stick from the fire and swinging the torch in the bears face.

The bear growled and swatted at the stick, turning it into a snub of red embers with one swipe of his massive paw. As the large bear stood over Michael, the creature's razor sharp talons casting a terrifying shadow, Michael lifted his sword and swung, slashing the bear's leg as the weight of the bear came crashing down on him. The claws from the beast's other paw ripped Michael's chest and left arm, and both he cried out in pain. But just as the bear went to bite his face, Michael quickly slipped the sword into his right hand and stabbed the beast upwards, through the neck. The bear roared and tipped backwards, painting the granite walls of the cave with dark red splatters as its neck spewed blood. After a few more minutes, the bear collapsed and fell unconscious, never to wake again.

Michael panted and shook with adrenaline, and yet he was no longer afraid. The skin on his chest and arm had been torn, but it meant nothing to him. His stabbed leg was a forgotten scratch. He stood up and breathed rapidly as he took in his incredible moment of victory.

After heating his sword in the fire and cauterizing his wounds, Michael spent all night skinning the bear with his longsword. As the sun rose, he stacked armfuls of wood onto his dying fire and brought it back to life to cook the bear meat. As his breakfast of freshly cut loins sizzled and dripped with grease over the morning blaze, he processed the rest of the animal, pounding the muscle into tug and scraping marrow from the creature's splintered bones. He vowed to use his remaining time there to mend his wounds and meditate on the fact that he had been through some rite of passage, and at last began his quest as a warrior. No longer was he afraid of the Queen's army, her Aradians, or the wretch herself, who had betrayed his father and laid waste to all civilization. In the mountains bosom, Michael swore vengeance against the Queen, even if it cost him his own life. Even if it cost him his sanity. Even if it meant never seeing his beloved Melody or his mother ever again.

On the morning of the thirty-first, Will Beller was making coffee over a fire with Cassidy, Gadreel, and a few other Marine officers.

"What news of the northern scouts?" Will asked Cassidy.

"They haven't returned. I told them to stay until later this evening in case Sandraudiga wants a night fight."

"No bombers have been spotted for over a month," Will added. "Seems odd."

"Not that she's intending to level the playing field, but I think Shakti is running out of supplies too. Not just ammunition, but fuel, aircraft, parts, bombs...everything," Cassidy said, pouring the black coffee into his cup.

"You think she's cutting off manufacturing? Maybe something to do with the transition into the Zurvan prophecy?" Gadreel asked.

"That, and she is consolidating her forces. She doesn't need bombers or artillery or tanks anymore. She has her Engineers. We're one of her last resistances. She's gonna toy with us until the very end," Cassidy smirked.

"But why?" Will asked, shaking his head.

"Because she's fucked in the head, that's why. She wants to test us, and she probably wants to pick us apart to find your nephew," Cassidy said, sipping on his coffee as the warm steam from his cup rose into the humid mountain air.

"Do you think he's a liability?" Gadreel asked.

"Fuck no! Let him be the bait! We'll have Pavonis come up behind us and lay them all to waste!"

"How are the siege engines coming along?" Will said, looking back at the large catapult-like mechanisms. At the edge of the field, a crew of combat engineers were hard at work, getting the trebuchets ready for battle.

"We launched a boulder five hundred yards yesterday. They're tweaking the counterweight a bit to get one further, but seven hundred and fifty will likely be the max range," Gadreel said.

"Do you see any fucking castles around here? You aren't expecting us to haul that medieval cannon with us, are you?" Cassidy asked.

"I think it's more of a hobby if anything," Will said chuckling.

"Well if it isn't the archangel himself," Cassidy said, cracking a smile.

Will and Gadreel turned to match Cassidy's gaze. The whole camp did the same.

A man wearing a bear's hide and claw necklace walked into the camp. His stride had a dignified execution to it as he propelled himself forward, using his spear as a walking stick. His eyes were calm but hinted at a dangerous demeanor. His naked chest showed the blackened scars of singed and lacerated claw marks. The head of a bear was draped over his head, its long hide dragging over the wet grass behind him. The other Marines looked at Michael with approving grins. One of them shook his head in disbelief.

As he approached Cassidy, Michael stabbed his cave-made spear into the ground. He saluted Cassidy and Will and Gadreel, who stood up and saluted in return.

"Where is your bow, Cadet Beller?" Cassidy asked.

"It was taken from me by a snow demon. But I

have endured the mountain's rage. I have slain this beast I have awakened. And I have returned at the time you asked me to."

"Go back up and get your bow," Cassidy said, sitting down and drinking his coffee.

Michael was speechless. Hiding his fit of rage, he pulled the spear from the dirt, shrugged off the hide, and walked back towards the peak with a quick stride. After about fifty feet, Cassidy yelled to him.

"Hey, Beller."

The others chuckled.

"Yes, sir?" Michael yelled, turning about, still steaming with anger.

"Come back over here. I just wanted to see if you'd do it."

Michael walked back.

"But why?"

"Because you are stubborn. I like that .You just killed a bear and survived an avalanche and the first thing I do is send you back up to that forsaken mountain. Instead of crying about it, you were oriented to the mission. That's what being a Marine is all about: you meet inconceivable odds, go beyond your physical boundaries, stretch your mental capacity, then keep going."

Michael smiled.

"Gather up, Marines!" he yelled to the camp.

Four thousand Marines sat in the field as Will, Cassidy, Gadreel, and few other commanding officers stood before them in a straight line, their flat brimmed hats tipped forward, their stances serious.

Cassidy stepped forward and called out, "Will cadet Michael Beller step forward and face the Marine Corps!"

Michael marched up to Cassidy, saluted him, and turned towards the audience of hardened veterans.

"In recognition of completing his Marine Corps training and representing 3rd platoon, Fox Company, 1st Division of the Marine Corps, I hereby announce the latest graduating class of one man. A man that was not a man at the beginning of his training, but through arduous circumstance and a disciplined mindset, has become one. He has proved himself by demonstrating physical stamina, mental resilience, and constant dedication. What he lacks in team building experience, he will now be able to learn alongside his fellow Marines. We are the last of our kind, and to add another good man to carry on our tradition makes us that much stronger.

Congratulations, Marine," Cassidy said, handing Michael a set of aluminum dog tags made from a soup can.

"Thank you, sirs," Michael said, saluting his senior officers.

He shook their hands, excited and overwhelmed after experiencing the most intense four weeks of his life.

Will shook Michael's hand and handed him his great grandfather's knife. "Well done nephew. I'm proud of you."

That night, barrels of moonshine and other salacious liquors were rolled out, uncorked, and poured as the Marines welcomed their newest member. Michael told the story of the avalanche, the bear, and how he had eaten his way through the tough meat for six days. One of the Marines told him he would have to take his stories to Neon City someday and impress all the beautiful young women there. Michael almost told them about Melody but decided against it, and instead gave a toast to the Marines. Gadreel watched the ceremony with a satisfied look, as if he saw something in Michael no one else besides William could: the same ferocity as his father.

As the moonlight softly bathed the small encampment of bonfires and drunken celebration,

Michael rested against an empty stained oak barrel, his chest throbbing from his cauterized wounds, holding his father's knife to the flame light as if it were a wand, a treasure beyond all treasures. He smiled and watched the loud slobbering men sing old Irish drinking songs to a fiddle's warbling, and Michael knew at that moment he would forever belong in this company of lions.

CHAPTER 25
SYMBIOTIC THRUST

It was late August when Pavonis, Melody, and David finally reached the Canadian Rockies. They ascended the peaks until they reached dangerous altitudes, where spires sat mounted on razor ridges like pillars, and on either side of their path the cliffs dropped endlessly below. It was as if they walked the spine of a great serpent's tail. The clouds moved quickly through the thin air, yet the wind was light in that elevated realm of swirling cirrus mantle. Pavonis stepped above the inversion and saw the granite peaks poking above the clouds around them like islands in an albicant sea. An eerie feeling hung in the stripped atmosphere, and Pavonis could feel a certain electricity right down to her carbon woven bones. She continued to walk above the inversion, guiding Melody and David to her snowy perch.

The three of them all still wore their elk hide garments, appearing as a primitive tribe of nomadic time travelers, wandering the mountains with their daggers and rifles in hand. As they continued to round a thin spire, Melody spoke up about something she had been pondering.

"Pavonis, why are we taking this route high above the valley floor? It seems too treacherous."

"Sandraudiga's forces are scouring those valleys as we speak. As long as we stay up high, we can pass through the mountains undiscovered."

"I'm just a little scared of heights, that's all."

"David seems to be doing alright," Pavonis said as she watched David scamper about. He had picked up some glacier lilies from the rocks earlier, and handed one to Pavonis. She smiled.

"Thank you, David," she said, patting the little blonde boy on the head and slipping the flowers into her hair. The stems entwined with her dread locks and an entire line of the white flowers sprouted down her braid.

Melody gulped as they climbed through the rocks towards an eroded plateau between two valleys.

"The only real threat to us at this height is Shakti's drones, that and—" Pavonis stopped talking and stood unmoving. She held her fist inches from Melody's face. "Melody. David. Don't move a muscle."

Melody looked at her horrified face, then turned to see what she was staring at. An entity floated above one of the many spires that decorated the cloud dusted landscape. At last, an Aradian had found them. The woman's mirror-shine armor reflected the opaque world around them like a hovering doorway to some aneurysmal dimension. She did not move, but faced the trio directly, watching them with wind-bitten eyes.

"What do we do?" Melody whispered.

Pavonis answered quietly. "Run."

Pavonis took off in a full sprint as Melody picked up David and jumped down the rocks as fast as she could. Pavonis was already hundreds of yards in front of them, deserting the young ones without hesitation. She crossed the plateau and began traversing the side of a steep wall along the peak. She leapt down a ridge, jumping through the standing rock spires at rapid speed, her Sararan legs carrying her swiftly between the cliff's outcroppings and snowy ledges. Suddenly, the Aradian flew from behind the peak and struck her from the side like an eagle knocking a goat from its precipice. Time seemed to slow as Pavonis fell back-first along the mountain's fathoms. Her pollinated lashes opened and she saw a penetrating silver light beaming through those boiling clouds in requiem. Trails of blood crawled up her arms and broke forth from the surface tension of her fingertips, dripping upwards towards the diving fiend. She watched the deadly nepheliad fall at falcon speed towards her, the Aradian's shimmering fingers like surgical blades, slicing Pavonis down the center as an axe slices through old oak, dicing veins and vertebrae. At last, Pavonis knew her fate had found her as the ground loomed, the shadows of fir trees devouring her. She hit the forest floor with a thunderous clap as the Aradian's scraping metal hands pulled her spark from her soul. Her blood poured onto the forest floor and entwined with Mayari's mercury tears, collecting in a mirror pond at the center of that cage of thorns. As Pavonis lay dying, the Aradian whispered something in her ear.

In a flash of white light, Pavonis awoke to Melody standing over her, tapping on her arm.

"Pavonis, what happened? Are you okay?"

Pavonis looked around, realizing her experience was just an elaborate vision.

"You saw her, didn't you...the Aradian?" Pavonis murmured.

"Yes, of course I did. But she flew off and you collapsed. You were unconscious for about a minute."

Pavonis sat up and looked around. "She got into my head," Pavonis moaned. Her head pounded as a migraine emerged.

"The Aradian? What did she say?"

"It was Mayari. She simulated how she would have killed me. Then she spoke to me."

Melody fell silent as Pavonis relived the dreadful nightmare once again, telling Melody every gruesome detail of the fall.

"As I lay dying, the last thing she said was 'the world will be fertilized with your blood'."

They sat for a moment in the wet air in silence. David squatted down next to Pavonis and looked into her pulsing eyes.

"Fertilized with your blood? That's ominous," Melody admitted.

"I don't know if it's a provocation so much as a premonition. Her voice echoed a painful truth...of a life of trauma. So much pain. Whatever she's getting at, it doesn't hint towards what her intentions are. I think she wanted me to know that she could kill me if she wanted to. There was a message, surely, but I'm not sure what it is yet. The Aradians operate on a higher level, so it's hard to decipher their words and actions. We may never know her true motives."

"Which one was it?" Melody asked.

"The gold emblem on her forehead. The Filipino star. Yes...I'm fairly sure it was Mayari."

"So, what do we do?" Melody asked.

Pavonis looked long and hard into her apprentice's curious eyes. "We start using the energy around us in the ways that used to get women like us burned at the stake," she replied as she rose to her feet.

David stared blankly at Pavonis, for the words held no meaning to him. Melody, however, understood their Stygian origins. There was no doubt in Melody's mind that, through her occult practices, Pavonis was becoming something more than Sararan. She was becoming *Strega*: a high witch and student of dark magick.

CHAPTER 26
PRIMAL SAGE

On the nineteenth anniversary of the caldera's eruption, Shakti held a conference of esteemed women somewhere indiscriminate on the vast Mongolian steppe. Untainted by the twentieth and twenty-first century's quarrels and the fateful bombardment of the self-proclaimed Queen, the heavenly plains were an ideal place to hold that historic congregation. The sky was cloudless, more azure than a deep sea could ever be, more vulnerable than new love. The light of midday fell upon nine distinct matriarchs, who sat in a circle as Shakti stood at the center, wearing a red silk dress, her hair braided in Mongol fashion, her face painted white with a golden dot on her third eye as if the group were a colorful solar system and she were the ever-present sun. She dug her bare feet into the soil between the yellow and green grasses and rooted herself in the Earth, humbled by the feminine magi she had beckoned, transfixed by the sublime essence of the solennial day.

Having crippled China, Japan, Russia, and Europe into submission, she had at last conquered the world, faster and with fewer people than either Genghis Khan or the British Royal Family. There was not one continent her forces did not occupy. In Antarctica, she had hijacked Russian submarines and launched torpedoes into the ice, with some of the most important relics of human identity lodged into the projectiles' innards. The way she had fought the long war was explicit. Every mass-genocide wrought by the Aradians had been executed differently depending on the region. Cities crumbled easily to earthquakes: the first to be neutralized. Oceanic peoples were drowned by tsunamis. Desert folk, by drought and heat. Mountainous communities, by fire and ice. Inhabitants of the grasslands by tornadoes, locusts, and disease. The entire war since the Yellowstone eruption had been designed to look natural, so that Shakti could rewrite history from her chosen beginning. She deployed millions of women to burn, bury, and sink mankind's artwork, documents, and destructive devices, keeping only what had been made by women, or what she considered the greatest works, to be kept in her personal collection. Her combat troops were five hundred thousand strong; prior to the Post Eruption War they would have been the ninth largest fighting force in the world. But with her Aradians backing her, there was not a single threat left, other than Pavonis and the rebel Marines still plotting against her.

Shakti thought about the two decades of genocide, and she breathed deeply and forgave herself, before smiling and looking around at the women who had gathered. They were leaders of indigenous tribes: Amazonian; Apache; Hadza; Inuit; Kombai; Mongol; Samoan; Celtic, and Pashtun, representing all the bioregions of the world. All wore ceremonial garb that reflected the land they presided over.

"Above you is the eternal blue sky," Shakti began.

The women looked at her with placid stares.

"Our sky should look this beautiful forevermore, and so it shall be. Below you is the Earth, our mother. And in her fragile state, she has felt a terrible pain these last nineteen years. A pain my master Vishnu, and I myself, have bestowed upon her. But I ask that you see me now as a creator, and understand that I am not a tyrant, that I am not an instigator of evils for the sake of greed and power. My aim is sacrificial and sacred. Indeed, I resolve to delegate my power to the native peoples of Earth: the women, the plants, and animals. When my destructive work is done, you will be my successors."

A few of the women looked at her with unwavering stares. Some peered into the sky, as if searching for meaning in her words.

"And when you die, your heirs will be regional rulers, and the Mongol princesses shall be the ambassadors that communicate and negotiate between each other and their Queen."

Just then, a line of nine young Chinese girls walked over the hill and down to the circle, each holding a white rose. The tribeswomen looked on with curiosity as the girls walked around the circle and sat beside the women, before handing them the roses.

"These are your apprentices. Teach them your ways, your culture. Teach them to respect your domain, and to identify its natural balance. Treat them as daughters and their loyalty shall never be broken."

Another small girl, dressed in red silk, walked over the hill, her face painted white like Shakti's; her seven-year-old eyes falling upon the land that she would one day assume power of. She penetrated the circle and knelt graciously next to Shakti.

"This Korean princess is the most closely related human to the lineage of the Great Khan. Princess Parvati will be ruler of this world someday, but the way she rules depends on how you teach her to rule. So, I ask of you, will you train her to be a warrior, a healer, a diplomat, and a conservationist? These are the choices you will have to make as educators. I ask that you take these young girls and help them to build a new world beneath you, for when I am finished, almost no man shall remain alive; I shall only leave enough to maintain our species. Thus, I ask that, before you repopulate the world with the male creature, do not forget the strains masculinity has brought upon us: the war, rape, and patriarchal oppression we have endured for hundreds of years, for some of us, thousands. We must remain stronger than them. Now is time for the new age of matriarchy. Now is OUR time."

The city of Caldera breathed like a dying dragon, wisps of sulfurous clouds drifting upwards from the barren landscape. In the center of the valley, thousands of sheepskin tents circled Shakti's obsidian palace, which had been carved from a single bulbous mass of the terrible, glass-like, black rock. The mountains beyond glowed orange with volcanic vents that seeped toxic fumes into the air. No voices of the enslaved dared speak in the night hours, or wander too far into that circle of hell, the center of the Zurvan trinity's spectrum of power.

Inside the black walls of the palace, Queen Shakti sat upon a monolithic throne, cropped from the same stone as her castle, reveling in her glory after the long campaign in Asia. She tried to hold back her smile, but the seduction was too great. A warm glass of sake steamed next to her and she breathed calmly.

With a large whoosh, the Aradians entered Shakti's great hall and hovered for a moment, before planting their feet and bowing low. Shakti stood up and bowed in return.

"I have completed my reconnaissance assignment, master," Mayari said.

"So it is true? The woodland faery lives?" asked Shakti.

Mayari dropped her head in a singular nod of confirmation.

"And she seeks the brutes in the mountains. There is some interesting movement at play here!" Shakti laughed delightedly.

"We have reason to believe the devil dogs are harboring her son. What would you like done now, master?" Mayari asked.

Shakti stood for a moment, tapping on the tsuba of her katana and leaning on her arm rest, as if deciding whether to draw it or not...to attack or be patient when it came to the Marines. "Sandraudiga will be spending the next few months continuing the purification of the northern lands. The industrial sites west of Neon City have halted production, but this is exactly what was to be expected. Since our dream finally encompasses the entire world, machines and technology will be obsolete. The prophecy should remain our only fixation."

"Of course, master," Tala said, bowing.

"Sandraudiga arms her soldiers with swords and bows; she will plan a major offensive against the rebels over the next few months. But all of this must be timed correctly and dealt with delicately. If either Michael or Pavonis are killed, it may alter the events of the Zurvan prophecy. I want to study young Michael and test him. I need to know if he is truly human or not. He is of great importance to the scientific community. From now on, Tala will continue combat operations." She turned and looked at Mayari. "But I'm retiring you from active combat duty."

Mayari looked up as if insulted. Shakti turned to Tala.

"Tala, your assignment is to fetch Michael, since we have enough intelligence gathered to locate him. Mayari, you are now my lead counsel to the Mongolian princesses. Teach them the Zurvan way, and nothing else."

"Yes, master," Mayari said.

"Shal I bring Michael straight to you?" Tala asked.

"Take him to my sister, Lakshmi. I'll be going to Neon City in a week, and I want Michael rested and well-nourished before I bring him back here. A few days of pleasure will be a good mental shock for young Michael, or...how would the American's say it...a mind fuck."

Shakti dismissed her Aradians and called her white robed servants to bring her a fresh plate of delectable sushi and edamame. She ate the rolls and drank warm sake while shivering slaves huddled in nests of shredded blankets outside the walls of shocked lava.

CHAPTER 27
BLADES WILL SING

The morning after his graduation, Michael sobered up by taking Apollo for a brisk morning jaunt up the western trail. Dark clouds clapped with thunder in the distance, a sign of the oncoming autumn storms. There was an electric feel in the air as a lightning bolt struck within a few miles of them. Apollo growled at the sky and shook his head at the tremendous boom.

"It's alright, boy. We'll head back now. You better begin enjoying that sound though if you're going to be a war pony."

He pulled the reigns on Apollo and galloped away from the black cloud. Lightning struck behind them in ever closer increments. Scattered raindrops turned to sleet, and the storm cell swelled with darkness as they approached the camp.

When Michael arrived back at the Marine base, men were scrambling around for weapons and falling into their various platoons. There was much talk and commotion.

"What's going on?" Michael asked a fellow Marine as he dismounted his horse.

"Tie in with your senior officer. There's a patrol coming. We're gonna attack just to the north, in the basin."

Michael quickly ran over to Will, who was talking to some of the other officers.

"Beller, get your gear and check out a bow and quiver!" Cassidy yelled.

"Yes, sir," he said, running over to the cache.

Upon Michael's request, the man running the cache gave him a longbow and a quiver of arrows. The rest of the cache was empty besides a few long swords, some grenades, and broken arrows to be recycled for their tips. The man held up the last two magazines of ammo and shook his head.

"Today we step back into the iron-age." he sighed.

"Why can't the shells be reloaded?"

The man smiled. "You think we can spend time looking around for casings every time some hotheaded bitches wanna get in a fire fight?"

Michael shrugged. He looked behind him with a sense of urgency, but overhead was still discussing strategy. The Marine leaned in to tell him a story.

"Let me tell you something. It was years ago and, well...I wouldn't say we had it good exactly, but when we were low on bullets, your mother could turn charcoal and bat shit into gunpowder. She could make nitroglycerin from dead ferns and acid rain. I once watched that woman fill an entire mining flume with the stuff and into the shafts leading to the heart of a mountain. Nine hundred thousand gallons of it. All siphoned from the sky during a downpour. She split the mountain clear in half. To its roots. Cut off the enemy's supply chain by filling the valley with rubble while distracting the Aradians long enough for us to change our position. Whenever she leads us it seems like...like we have a chance. That's how it is now too. This war won't be won with rifles or bows."

"Can I have a grenade then?" Michael asked, looking at several boxes of the explosives behind him.

"That's the spirit," the man winked, handing four of them to Michael.

"Thank you, sir!"

Without skipping a step Michael filled his pockets with the grenades, checked his gear, and ran back to Will.

"Uncle, can I take Apollo with me?"

"You do realize he may run from the fight?"

"He's a good horse, I promise. I could send messages between platoons or transfer supplies quickly."

Will thought for a moment. "I suppose I'd rather him come with us in case we don't return to this camp. Use his speed. Lead your target when aiming. And remember that you'll be one yourself. Don't get caught out in the open."

"I understand, sir."

Michael mounted Apollo and walked behind his platoon as they marched north. They followed the bank of a small lake as the storm's sleet and hail pelted and splashed its surface. Once they had passed the lake, the other platoons veered off to cover more ground. They crouched as they entered the trees, slowing their pace as they became increasingly vigilant. Most held bows with arrows already knocked in their string. A few others towards the front had machine guns and rifles with only the bullets in their magazines to fight with, each precious casing ready to be stoked from the spent steel chambers. Michael's hands shook with fear as he held Apollo's reins. The harsh winds of the storm raked the tops of the trees and sent leaves idling to the forest floor. Waves of sleet fell and tinged lightly against their car-part armor. They were a hybrid force, equipped with both primitive and modern weapon systems, a hint at the transitioning age in which they lived and would continue to shape.

Suddenly, Will halted the platoon and motioned for everyone to get down. Michael jumped off Apollo and pulled on his stirrups to bring the steed low. Apollo knelt in the grass and dipped his head with the others. The sound of the wind whipping through the trees crescendoed as each of the Marines crouched in the bush. Michael's heart pulsed like a war drum between the swaying trees.

Will whispered to them. "The patrol is just up ahead. They're going to run straight into Gadreel's platoon, who will ambush them. Wait for Cassidy's men to engage, then we'll flank this side as Alpha hits them from the back. Watch your crossfire and yield for Alpha. Got it?"

The group nodded. Those with swords wrapped a piece of cloth around their wrists, tying themselves to their sword handles. One of the Marines stuffed a large cookie into his mouth, which he had found amongst a cache of packaged, freeze-dried meals. They waited patiently, listening for the muffled footsteps of the patrolling women.

Suddenly, gunshots could be heard to their left, followed by a scream.

"Attack! Get down!" one of the Queen's soldier's cried.

The fire fight exploded in the forest's gut. Will's men stayed crouched low and began shooting their arrows and bullets into the patrol's flank. Michael chucked a grenade high into the treetops, where it fell and exploded near a line of enemy soldiers. The return fire was mostly arrows, since they had attacked the middle of a patrol unit. While the other Marines were busy shooting at the main group, Michael saw a hooded woman running from his left side, trying to flank them. He quickly stood up and shot an arrow. The southern wind thrust his small missile through the air, and it sunk itself into the chest of the tall elite warrior. She instantly fell forward and disappeared into the foliage.

"Move in!" Will yelled.

The Marines stood up and unsheathed their swords. Like Germanic heathens, they ran screaming into the enemy, who were so confused at where each platoon was that their forces became both surrounded and divided. Michael mounted Apollo and charged into battle, his blood rushing with adrenaline as he ran past his troops.

"Michael, stay back!" Will yelled, but his voice was drowned in the immense calamity.

Michael unsheathed his medieval blade and steered Apollo toward a pre-occupied enemy soldier. When the woman turned toward him,

Michael swung the large steel sword and halved her head at its nucleus. Blood splattered his face and chest as other enemy soldiers around him shot arrows at his steed. The arrows whistled by his face and chest as he sped in a large circle around the panicking enemy. He raced toward a retreating soldier, trampling her into the forest floor as Apollo's heavy hooves crushed the soldiers's spine and head. Michael had killed the enemy commander as the Marines pulverized the confused squad in his wake. A myriad of arrows came from different directions and forced Michael to retreat back to his men. He raced over to where the platoon was still advancing and dismounted Apollo.

"Back to the base, Apollo. GO!" he slapped Apollo and the horse took off in the other direction. Will ran up to Michael as they hid under the brush.

"Nice work, Michael! But don't go out on your own again without my command. We operate as a unit. When you single yourself out, you become a liability. Now, listen up. Half of the platoon is going to split off to help out Cassidy's men who are pinned down. The other half will help out Alpha platoon. Go!"

They crouched low and made their way west towards the heart of the battle. As the Marines crested a small hill, Will had them hold up and take cover. From there, they could see Cassidy's men trapped behind a pile of rocks as enemy soldiers shot at them with an unrelenting hail of bullets and mortar rounds. The patrol unit had a large machine gun in their arsenal that chipped away at the rock pile with an air shattering clatter. The storm bent the trees and sent sticks and leaves flying down as the battle raged. It was as if the Earth herself had joined in the confrontation.

"Michael, let me see one of those grenades!" Will yelled.

Michael handed him the grenade and, to his surprise, Will took off running down the hill, hiding behind trees as bullets splintered the bark on the other side. He got within range and pulled the pin before lobbing the grenade at the machine gunner. In a massive explosion of metal and shrapnel, the gunner was obliterated, and the wind speckled blood and sleet upon the bodies like a bed of pink crystals.

"Charge!" Will cried, as Michael and the rest of the platoon descended on the enemy. The sword-wielding women soon ran out of ammunition and arrows, and the battle quickly became a blood bath of stone and blade. Michael watched as the Marines slashed, kicked, and clubbed their way through the enemy. To his horror, he saw a Marine's eye torn out of its socket by a woman with steel claws, and watched the man panic as he tried to push it back in. A tall enemy officer wielding a giant axe as her weapon cut the stomach of a fellow Marine, his intestines spilling out between the rocks and roots. As she approached Michael, he took two steps back and tripped over a dead body. But as the large woman raised her arms for the axe to fall, Michael felt a lurch on his body. In a matter of seconds, he found himself swept up and suddenly flying high above the trees. A metal arm wrapped itself around him as he ascended the hail filled skies. He looked up to see an Aradian holding him tight, flying quickly away from the battle and up into the turbulent storm cell.

Michael blinked wildly in the harsh wind as the being wove around the mountain peaks. He looked up at her face. The creature was completely concealed in armor yet looked back at him with naked eyes. In them were visions of cruelty, scenes that played out as the woman's memories were put on display. It was Tala, the eternally tortured knight, endangered and yet divine; she who was gifted with the opportunity to end mankind's aggression.

"Where are you taking me?" Michael yelled as they soared high above the rocky front.

"You will see in time," the woman said in her crackly robotic voice. "Now sleep."

The armor on the tips of her fingers slid back to expose her fingertips. She touched Michael on his forehead. His lashes closed as he fell asleep to the sight of the black storm swirling below him, a cyclical phantom swallowing the sky with each thunderous shriek.

Michael awoke and opened his eyes to a bright white luminescence burning against the shade of night. Towers of white, blue, and green neon lights reached high into the star filled sky. They had arrived at St. Louise, the last city still standing on the continent.

Tala held him tight as they flew below the clouds towards the light, like a moth beckoning its fate. Michael could hear the pounding of electronic music swelling from the city center, and the sounds of the cars that raced down the freeways and wound around suburban streets, as small aircraft zipped above them. The air held a series of levitating traffic lights, and small helicopters, drones, and single-seat hovercrafts lined the sky grid. Tala bolted past them, recklessly apathetic to the city's waking dream. As they flew into the city's depths, Michael looked about in awe. Windows with advanced screen technology covered the helix-shaped skyscrapers and lit the streets with mind-bending animations. Balconies wrapped around the abstract geometric architecture, squirming with hundreds of brightly clothed ravers, bouncing in unison to the heavy music blaring from seemingly everywhere, the synchronous speakers decorating the city in unison. The result was a chest-thumping beat that moved the society like a technological coral reef in an ocean of psychedelic spectacle.

The Aradian suddenly made a sharp upward thrust and flew to one of the highest floors of the city's tallest building. Hundreds of stories up, she touched down daintily on a balcony, where people of a higher class looked at the two of them with intrigued expressions and dilated pupils. An array of elegantly dressed women with fractal hair weavings and color changing contacts watched the chrome woman as though Tala were a welcome guest. The bar tender sported rolled up sleeves, showing off the nano-ink tattoo of an octopus on his forearm. The creature appeared to swim freely under his skin as the tentacles drifted over the contours of his knuckles.

Tala released Michael from her grasp. There was no escape. All he could do was whatever he was ordered to. After living all his life in the deep woods of the far north, hearing only far-fetched stories of the cyber age, Neon City was something of a culture shock.

"Welcome back, Tala," the hostess said warmly as she approached them, her rich brown eyes and subtle gold eyeliner perfectly complementing her honey skin. Her hair was braided in a complex pattern that made her seem tribal, yet sophisticated, and she wore a plush white dress with golden silk embroidery stitched into the sleeves.

"Michael, I presume?" she said, looking Michael up and down.

Michael was still in battle attire, his face and body decorated with blood, sweat, and dirt.

The hostess smirked at him. "You will behave, won't you?" She then looked to Tala, who said nothing, the images of burning grass huts and fleeing families in her eyes speaking for her.

"I suppose I have no choice," Michael said.

"Good. You had best come with me, we can't have you looking like that. And I'll bet you look gorgeous under all that filth. Come on, let's get you cleaned up for the evening. I'll take it from here, Tala." The hostess put her hand on Michael's shoulder and guided him inside as two security guards followed.

Tala walked behind them for a few minutes, but when Michael looked back, she had disappeared. The building's interior was a testament to the artistic endeavors of human design. Red walls with the texture of pure cashmere were hung some of the world's most famous paintings. Michelangelo's 'The Creation of Adam' covered the ceiling, and Michael wondered how they had managed to so carefully transfer it all the way from Italy. Ancient Etruscan sculptures of lions stood in the corners of the bar. The Rosetta Stone hung above the spirits, behind the bartender, who was in the process of cutting limes and herbs upon a slab from a six-thousand-year-old tree. Michael was speechless.

The hostess stopped beside an elevator and pulled out a hidden drawer from the wall, handing Michael a black silk robe from inside. "Here are some clothes. These guards will escort you to the spa. Wash up. Relax. Take your time there. Lakshmi has business to attend to so will not see you until later. Come back up here and get a good meal when you're ready. I've told the staff that you're an important guest here. If you need anything at all, call for Val. That's me."

"Thank you, Val," Michael said, confused as to why he was being treated so well. He suspected some kind of ruse, but there was nothing he could do about it. The massive submachine-gun-toting guards were not going to let him escape.

Michael entered the oscillating steel doors of the

elevator and down they went. When the doors opened, Michael was escorted down a hall of polished marble and exotic flowers. The walls were a limestone mosaic of fossilized insects and plants, and the atmosphere was instantly calming. The faint scent of burning yerba santa came from somewhere close by. At the end of the hall, a young red-haired woman sat playing a harp atop a small babbling fountain of gold painted rocks. To the right of her was a silver door; to the left, a bronze door. Michael watched, mesmerized, as the girl softly plucked at the harp's shimmering strings until he was shaken from his reverie by the stern voice of a guard.

"Go through the bronze door into the men's spa. There's no way out other than this corridor, so don't try escaping. We'll be waiting for you here when you're finished. No funny business."

Michael reluctantly turned away from the harp player as he walked through the door. Inside was a changing room with bamboo floors and rows of lockers. He changed into his robe and walked into the next room. The spa consisted of a large marble hot tub, surrounded by tropical plants. Twelve-foot-high windows gave him a clear view of the city's activities. Entering the steaming tub, Michael winced as the hot water splashed against his wounds, but after a few moments, the stinging subsided. He tried to relax as the warm water soothed his muscles, but he could not shake the tension he felt, his concern for his uncle and the Marines, his mother, Melody, and his own predicament, circling his mind in a whirlwind of anxiety.

A few buildings over, Michael noticed a rooftop rave, the flashing strobe lights cutting through the thick smoke that lay like a heavy blanket over the building. He wondered if they were using a smoke machine, or whether the smoke had simply accumulated from the vast quantity of weed being smoked. A hovering party bus floated by and someone hurled the contents of their stomach out of the window. Michael laughed and shook his head, imagining someone in the city below being rained on by puke.

"Sir?" A man's voice came from the corner of the room.

Michael stood up, alarmed.

"How are you, sir? Would you like a refreshment?"The servant continued, walking into the room with a small cart of clinking bottles.

"No, thank you," Michael said, slipping down into the water again.

The man poured him a glass of fine scotch and set it down. "Just in case you change your mind...are you sure you wouldn't like anything else, sir? Some cocaine, or a joint perhaps?" The man held out a mirror with three small lines of white powder running diagonally across it. "Here, sir," the servant said, handing him a straw made of polished hematite.

Michael waved him off.

"Are you sure, sir? It is pure Columbian product. Clean and uncut," the servant said, smiling. He took back the mirror and stood straight. "I'll be back shortly if you need anything." He turned the cart around and walked into the locker room.

Michael looked at the glass of scotch. He did not trust anyone or anything. He popped his neck and laid back into the warm water.

Just then, a thin man in his early thirties entered the spa and crawled into the water, seemingly exhausted. The servant came back out and offered him the same substances he had offered Michael. The man took everything: a shot, a joint, and a couple of lines to top it all off. The bitter drip ran slowly down the back of the man's throat s as he washed it down with some scotch. He looked at Michael.

"Quite the scars you got there, bruv," he said, in a raspy British accent.

"I was attacked by a brown bear."

The man nodded with curiosity in his eyes. He smiled slightly. "You tried the dope here, mate? It's dead good. Promise ya, will make you feel well decent," he said, taking a hit and handing the joint to Michael.

"No, thank you," Michael said, shaking his head.

"Hey, you look like one of those mountain men...you a Marine, mate? On some R and R or summat?"

"I wouldn't exactly call it R and R...but yeah, I'm a Marine. I don't trust these people. I'm not gonna drink anything they give me."

The man laughed. "Your loss, mate. They're just honey pottin ya, tryin a sweeten you up a bit."

Michael looked at him skeptically.

"Don't you get it? If they were gonna to trip ya gears, you'd been fucked up already. Take a hit, mate. Might as well lick the honey off the blade."

Michael reached out and took the joint, before inhaling hesitantly. He felt his lungs tingle and he coughed, handing the joint back to the man.

"Thas it, mate! Feel the weight lettin up off yur shoulders."

Michael sunk back into the water, the drug numbing his anxiety, combing his being with euphoric splendor. For a moment, he forgot all about the troubles in the north; the fact the world was in ruins, and that he was, unofficially, a prisoner of war.

After feasting on a dinner of worldly delicacies in the building's restaurant, Michael looked around for his security guards. They were nowhere to be seen. For an instant, he felt a glimmer of hope, adrenaline coursing through his veins. Until he saw the cameras. Of course. They were keeping track of his every move. Why had he even considered that they might give him a chance to escape.

He sighed, placing his napkin on the table, and waved down a waitress. "Ma'am!"

"It's Miss, sir. Ma'am is a term for an older woman," she said, smiling, her tone failing to hide her annoyance. She was young, blonde, and undeniably angelic, her mystifying aura drawing Michael in.

"I apologize. I come from a wild place. My manners elude me."

"It's fine. What can I help you with?"

"A whiskey, please."

"No problem. Would you like to close out now?"

"Val told me I was covered," Michael said.

"Wait...you're the VIP aren't you? Oh God! Please forgive me!" She bowed, trembling, and began to beg for mercy. "Please don't tell her that I corrected your language, or that I asked you for money! I didn't know! I'll be fired for sure, or worse—"

"Shh. It's okay," he said, looking at the young woman's terrified face.

The restaurant manager looked over at them with questionable eyes.

"It's alright, calm down. Are you allowed to take a break?"

"Yeah…" she said tearfully.

"Perfect. Come with me." Michael stood and gestured for the girl to follow.

Her manager watched them leave the restaurant and nodded. Employees were expected to be submissive to any and all of their special guest's desires.

Michael and the girl walked down the hall and through a door to a small balcony. Outside were two women, smoking cigarettes and looking out at the evening's delights. They looked over Michael with fluttering eyelashes and smiled at him, whispering conspiratorially to one another.

"Thank you for being so understanding, sir," the young waitress stammered, still nervous.

"It's fine, really," Michael said, lighting a joint that he had acquired from the spa earlier. He handed it to the girl, who took a puff and handed it back. Michael took a puff then handed it to one of the two gossiping women.

"Thank you," the woman said, eyeing him with a seductive smirk.

Michael blushed as she returned to joint to him, and turned back to the waitress.

"Oh fuck, I needed this," she said, lighting her own cigarette.

"Stressful night?" Michael asked.

"Always," the waitress answered. "Where are you from?"

"I was born in Montana, but I live in The Yukon," he said.

"Holy shit! Isn't it dangerous up there? What are you doing all the way down here?"

"I'm a prisoner of the Queen," he said with a slightly serious face.

The girl choked on some smoke and started laughing.

"It's okay, I don't expect you to believe me," Michael continued.

"I believe you... it's just...it doesn't matter."

"What?"

"I mean...do you feel like a prisoner right now?"

"No, I guess not."

"Exactly! We're only prisoners if we allow ourselves to feel that way. It's all a state of mind. It's like, I fall off this skyscraper tomorrow and die, this city won't change. Nothing will. Our existence is insignificant. The only thing that matters are the moments we share between one another."

Michael nodded and they finished their joints in silence. Stamping the ends of her cigarette into the ground, the girl pulled out a phone and began texting for long enough Michael began to lose interest and walk away.

The elevator doors opened with a loud 'ting' and Michael walked into the top floor bar where the two security guards and Val stood waiting.

"Perfect timing, Mr. Beller. I trust you are feeling refreshed?"

"Very much so," Michael said, his eyes glazed, and red as the cashmere walls.

"I'm glad to hear it. Follow me to Lord Lakshmi's suite."

They walked through the bar and down a long hallway. Maxfield Parrish paintings lined the walls, lit by softly glowing lamps, hanging from the ceiling.

Val opened the door at the end of the hall and gestured for Michael to enter.

The room was pyramid shaped, and at least fifty feet across. The angled walls climbed a hundred feet high, and at the top of the pyramid's apex were frameless, glass windows, showing the stars above. Below the windows, shards of ancient hieroglyphs covered the granite walls down to a floor of exotic animal rugs: tiger; lion; snow leopard; polar bear, and ibex. In the corners of the room stood eroded statues of Horus and Anubis, and between them, the cursed mask of King Tut hung above the hearth. In the center of the room was a large, circular, black couch with an octagonal malachite table at its nucleus. Staring straight at Michael was a gorgeous, dark-skinned Syrian woman, with emerald green eyes. She sat comfortably in a white and gold robe, her glyph inspired tattoos covering her arms and hands. She wore a golden diadem around her straightened, short, black hair. To Michael, she looked like a seraphic Queen: beautiful, powerful, and exulting. In front of her were two glasses, and a bottle of red wine.

"Welcome, Michael," she said soothingly. "Please, come sit."

"Is there anything else I can do for you, Lord Lakshmi?" Val asked.

"No, that will be all for now. Leave us, please," she said.

"But Lord Lakshmi, one of us should stay in case—"

"I said leave us."

The two bodyguards left the room with Val, closing the thick mahogany doors behind them.

Michael sat opposite Lakshmi while she poured him a glass of priceless 1988 vintage Bordeaux.

"What do you think of my city?" she asked, as she slid the glass toward him.

"I've never seen anything like it. The lights. The parties. The madness. I grew up in the countryside of the north, where we starve for half the year, so it's a bit unnerving to see people spending money on drugs while others die from hunger. We don't even have a use for money where I come from."

"I can sympathize with your anger, Michael. But this is a complex age. My sister has a strict plan, and the fact that she has allowed somewhere like this exist is beyond my understanding. She leaves the whole world to struggle through primal challenges while we mock the apocalypse with substance and spectacle. It is a society numbed by ignorance and therefore...bliss."

"Why are you helping her then?"

"I'm here because I was appointed to be here. Sandraudiga ranked up to become a General in Shakti's army. Shakti knows I am not the type to lead battalions into war. So, instead, she made me ruler of the last living city. The industries of the east coast spend their money here, where it circulates back into the economy."

"Why do you need money if the Aradians can just take what they want?"

"There is a level of honor behind every cruel act my sister and her engineers bestow. Europe, Africa, the Middle East, and Asia still have working citizens in functional industries, though they are almost all women who follow Shakti's guidelines. You would be surprised at how generous she can be, despite how barbaric her plan may seem. She's intelligent enough to know that the prophecy itself will take time to implement, and she's wise enough to understand some things will always be out of her control."

"So, what am I doing here? Am I a prisoner? Am I a guest? What are you going to do to me?" Michael asked, setting down the decadent wine.

"That all depends, Michael," she said, sensually licking the wine that had dripped onto her thumb.

"On what?"

"On whatever Shakti decides to do with you. But

Tala left you in my hands, and Shakti won't be here for a few days. For now, I control your fate. And what kind of host would I be to treat the son of Ezra as anything less than royalty?"

"Hence all the pleasures," Michael said, taking another sip of wine.

"What do you know about pleasure, Michael?" she said, standing before him and slowly unbuttoning her robe. It slipped off easily to reveal her naked body. Symbols of the chakra's lined her chest, all the way down to her pelvis.

Her womanly shape reminded Michael of a Goddess of Fertility; a sexual deity ready to quench all desire. He gulped nervously and his eyes widened as Lakshmi walked around the table and straddled him slowly.

"There aren't very many true men left in the world," she whispered. "Touch me with the hands of a real man."

She felt up his thigh, her breasts inches from his face, but Michael sat completely still. His blood ran hot and his skin reddened as Lakshmi began kissing his neck and face, massaging his crotch with gentle hands.

"Lord Lakshmi. Please stop this. You must," he said, hesitantly.

She leaned back, surprised at Michael's defiance.

Confused, Lakshmi walked back and quickly put on her robe.

"I'm sorry, but I am in love with another, and I must stay true."

"No man has ever been able to resist me. Who is this woman who is more beautiful than I?" she asked, downing her glass of wine, irritated yet impressed by his virility.

"You are beautiful, Lord Lakshmi. Goddess-like, even...but the one I love is someone who cares for me, someone who knows me. Yes, she is beautiful, but her inner beauty is what beckons me. When I think of her, I am like a ruby held up to the sunrise, not sure if I am still a stone or a world made of redness."

"I have heard this poetry before," Lakshmi said, her expression thoughtful.

"It is true. I speak the words of the great poet Rumi. But my heart does not lie."

"You really love her, don't you?" Lakshmi said, sitting and pouring herself more wine.

"Yes. Admittedly, I am a virgin. But I could only give myself to her. No one else."

Lakshmi smiled and nodded. She poured Michael another glass of wine and stared up at the windows in the ceiling's apex, her eyes sparking as she thought for a while to herself. "You have a pure heart, Michael. You are not a Sararan, and yet I can see why Shakti fears what you may become. You could change the course of this war."

"I doubt I can do much without the support of the Marines."

"You don't need them. What you have is a desire for truth, the greatest weapon of all. The truth is what my sister fears. She fears people knowing the truth. She fears *you* knowing the truth."

"What truth?" Michael asked.

Lakshmi's eyes then darted around the room as if looking for something. She searched in her mind for the right words. "You have something, Michael. I'm not sure what it is, but I know it has something to do with the prophecy. If I have one skill, it is that I know when to listen to my inner voice. It is telling me to let you free. But if I do this, you cannot go back to the mountains. Bad things are brewing in the northern lands. A terrible darkness awaits you there. You must travel west, into the desert."

"Why?"

"In the desert, you will find temporary salvation. I will give you a speed bike from my private garage. Head southwest as far and as fast as you can. Blend in with the locals; eventually, Tala *will* find you again.

Walk out of the door and go to the elevator. Go to the very bottom floor. I'll have Val meet you there."

"Why are you doing this for me? Won't you be killed?"

"I'll tell the Queen you escaped, then fire the guards. Now GO!"

Michael exited the room and quickly shuffled down the hallway, the security guards in rapid pursuit. One of them held his earpiece as he listened to Val's orders.

"Alright, Mr. Beller. Looks like you're getting let off the hook. Do you know how to ride a motorcycle?"

"I'm a fast learner," he said, his mind swirling from the wine and his decision to be abstinent in the face of what was surely every man's fantasy.

They entered the elevator and began dropping hundreds of floors down. Michael's heart raced as his inebriated mind tried to comprehend what was happening.

"I think I'm too drunk to drive, honestly," he said, looking helplessly at one of the security guards.

The gigantic guard reached into a pocket and pulled out a plastic bag filled with cocaine. He flicked it a few times. "This'll sharpen you up."

Michael sniffed the coke and choked as he felt the substance enter his lungs. The elevator door opened. Val stood there, stepping aside to unveil a large black speed bike. It was sleek and dangerous, a feat of modern technology and power.

"I hope your senses are keen, Mr. Beller. It's time to perform," Val said with a smirk.

Michael sped out of the garage, the bike whipping around the corner with ease, passing vehicles and threading through traffic like an aimless arrow. As he sped through the last green light of the city, the thumping music faded, and Michael pushed the bike to maximum as the empty freeway opened up before him. He shot into the void like a comet being swallowed by a black hole, into a place where time and the law held the same insignificance.

CHAPTER 28
GRACE

On a cool September morning, Will Beller stepped outside his tent, relieving himself as he watched the sun rise over the mountains.

"It's going to be a beautiful day," he said to himself, wincing as he felt the small piece of arrow lodged into his calf muscle, the broad head sunk into his bone. He resurrected his fire from the barren coals and boiled the branches of a youthful pine. After a short while, Cassidy came and sat beside him, pouring himself a cup of pine tea.

"How'd you sleep?" Will asked.

"Like shit," Cassidy said. "I bet the prisoner got more sleep than I did," he said, referring to the woman they had captured after the battle.

"Doubt it," Will sighed, shaking his head.

Cassidy looked up at him. "Don't worry about Mike. I'm sure he's alright. He's a tough kid."

"Yeah, it's just one of those things...the Aradian

could have wiped out the rest of us, right then and there. But she wanted my nephew instead. It's got to have something to do with Ezra, something to do with his heritage," Will said, gripping tightly to the knife he had given Michael. Michael had dropped it after being swept up by the metal witch.

"Well, on the bright side, we got to supplement the cache."

"I haven't seen the inventory since we set up camp yesterday. Any bullets?"

"Nah, they were using an old Russian 108mm. It was in pieces when we found it. I've got a few men collecting the powder. But the good news is..." Cassidy reached down behind him and picked up a sword he had brought to the fire. "Found a couple Samurai swords in the mix. Good quality too. Handmade. Tamahagane steel. Stone polished. You could put a face cut in a fifteen-inch grand fir with this man killer."

Cassidy handed the weapon to Will, who unsheathed the blade, listening to it warble with a slight metallic ring. He looked into the blade's mirror-like surface, his reflection distorted by the precision bo-hi cut in the sword's spine. He grazed the tip with his thumb. Though his touch was slight, he cut himself. It was as if the steel was hungry for his blood.

"Holy shit! You don't wanna be the person at the wrong end of this!"

"Have it. It's yours. I'm more of an axe guy myself," Cassidy said, sipping his tea.

"Who's watching the prisoner?" Will asked.

"Murphy," Cassidy answered.

"You don't think he'll try to fuck her, do you?"

"I put Murphy on watch because he's impotent," Cassidy chuckled.

"Was that to play a joke on Murphy or to protect the prisoner?"

Cassidy laughed and let his eyes wander into the abyss of forest around them.

"Do you think we've lost our humanity out here?" Will asked him.

"I don't wonder the discrepancies of another man's morality. What boundaries he sets for himself were created by him. A righteous man would never rape a woman, but the same man might use his righteousness to control people and steal the will of others without ever being tried for his exploits. No one dies innocent. Every creature on this planet is a survivalist at its core, and immortality is life's ultimate goal of sustainment. To be immortal is to write your own history, without relying on lineage. Time itself will foster this tragedy. See...we humans have the frame of a Sararan, just not the soul. Most people think it's the other way around. The human soul is what will destroy us. We're out here trying to kill Gods with spears. It's only a matter of time."

"Before what?" Will asked.

Cassidy breathed and sipped his tea, continuing after he had quenched his thirst. "When I was deployed in the Hindu Kush...must've been 2022...there was a terrorist faction we encountered that moved through the mountains like phantoms. They knew their territory well, and even with all our drones and recon planes and patrols there was no way to weed them out. It wasn't until we carpet-bombed the entire range that we finally killed them all. A few dozen civilians were found amongst the bodies. The blowback wasn't intended, but we'd resorted to a ruthless occupation. How else could we have won? Now, Shakti keeps us alive to mock us, to show us that we too can be the ones crawling through the mountains fighting a more powerful foreign occupation. Perhaps we are the demons with nothing left to lose, brought down to our lowest form. I have no doubt the Immortals will prevail. But just the attempt to kill them is worth even the most terrible death. If we are being punished for being men, then let us arrive at the gates of Hell."

Will nodded and drank his tea in silence.

Suddenly, a sentry ran up to the men.

"Sir! Two women and a young boy have been spotted just to the south, heading this way. They are armed."

Cassidy gave Will an inquisitive look.

"I'll go check it out," Will said, putting his new blade back in its sheath. "You and four others join me."

The sentry motioned for a few men outside a nearby tent to join the scouting party. The six of them descended from the camp in silence.

About a half mile down the mountain, the sentry stopped Will.

"They were back in those trees last time I saw them," he whispered.

They stayed put for several minutes, listening to the air and scanning their soundscape for anything: a rustling of leaves; a twig breaking, even a breath.

CLUNK!

A pinecone hit the top of Will's head.

"Damn trees!" he whispered.

CLUNK!

Another large pinecone hit him, and he looked up to see Pavonis, Melody, and David, all sitting high up on a large branch in the tree above him, their feet dangling carelessly.

"Hey, sis," Will said, a little embarrassed.

251

"Hello, William," she said in return, smiling.

"You brought...kids?"

"I brought hope," she answered.

The other Marines looked at each other and shrugged.

The group walked back to camp and Pavonis went straight to meet with the commanding officers. Gadreel walked up and kissed Pavonis on the cheek. She hugged him in return.

"Good to see you."

"Likewise, Pavonis."

Pavonis turned back to her troop.

"The young boy here is David. He's not much of talker, but he's got a lot of heart. The young woman is Melody. She is Michael's lover, and my apprentice."

"Pleased to meet you, sirs," Melody said, curtsying modestly.

"What's her deal?" Will asked, smirking.

"She's a princess," Pavonis shrugged.

"Where is Michael?" Melody asked anxiously.

Will looked at Pavonis, then at Melody.

"I'm sure you're all dying for some breakfast.

Come and get settled, you've had a long journey," he said.

Pavonis knew then that something was wrong, but she also knew that Michael was not dead. Melody did not share her patience.

"Well? Is he here or not?" Melody asked, in a more assertive tone.

Will faced her. "No. He is not. He was kidnapped." He turned and walked away.

Melody stopped in her tracks and stared at Will's back in shock, her expression pained.

"He's still alive, Melody." Pavonis said, feeling Melody's heartache, as David ran and grabbed Melody's arm. The little boy smiled and kissed Melody's hand, nodding encouragingly as he pulled her towards the center of the camp.

The waking Marines wiped their charcoal eyes and looked upon the strange group with astonishment. To those lonely men so displaced from the touch of a woman, Melody was a tantalizing feast for their eyes. Their stares made her uncomfortable, and she realized that some of these men had not seen a woman – at least, not one who was not trying to kill them – for over a decade. She drew closer to Pavonis.

"Officers, report to HQ!" Will yelled.

The Marine officers gathered in the center of the

encampment, forming a large, informal circle.

"We have some guests joining us for a while. I expect all of you, and your men, to treat them with the upmost respect. As most of you already know, Pavonis is back with us. Though she is not an officer, there will be times when I transfer command to her. She can see farther than you. She has more advanced hearing than you. She can tell if we are going to be shelled well before any enemy artillery is in place. Listen to her, heed her orders, and know that it is her goal to augment our capabilities. With her is Melody, and the boy's name is David. These guests will not be harassed or intimidated by your men in any way, shape, or form. Is that understood?"

"Yes, sir!" the Marines agreed.

"Get to your daily duties. Make sure inventory gets finished and I want a hunting party led by second platoon to leave at eleven hundred. Don't return until you have meat on your backs!"

"Yes, sir!" the men said, dispersing to their various posts.

The trio sat with Will around a small fire and Will handed the children a mug of steaming tea each. He told them how Michael had found the Marines; how he had undergone Marine training; how he had killed a bear and fought bravely in the battle north of Camp Draco. He told them about the Aradian scooping Michael up mid-battle, and that he had expected the other Aradian to show up and kill them all.

"So, the Queen has Michael?" Melody asked.

"It's safe to assume so, but we can't know for sure," Pavonis answered, as she thought deeply about her son's predicament.

"Around here, we don't call her 'Queen'," Will said to Melody. "She's no queen, she's a fucking tyrant."

"Language!" Melody said, pointing to David, who was picking grass and throwing it in the fire for entertainment. The boy smiled as he watched the green blades sizzle.

"He's surrounded by Marines. He's gonna have to deal with learning a few curse words while he's here. No way around it."

Pavonis directed the conversation back to the matter at hand. "Shakti will not kill Michael, for three reasons. One, she is playing mind games with me. Kidnapping my son is her way of trying to lure me out of hiding. An Aradian found us last week, but didn't engage us physically. Instead, she telepathically attacked me in a simulation of excruciating pain and violence. She gave me a strange message that I have yet to decipher. Shakti knows I'm on the move, and she wants me to unleash my powers. She doesn't see me as a threat, she sees me as a subject to research. She wants to see what a Sararan is capable of. Two, for all we know, this could be part of the Zurvan prophecy. I don't think even Shakti is fully aware of the details of this ten-thousand-year-old riddle. She knows it is a delicate plan, set in motion by ancient scripts and celestial movements. As long as she can line up the main players of the prophecy's forecast, her hopes are that the finer details will quantize and fall into place on their own. And three, Michael may not be human for much longer."

"Wait...you think Shakti will give him the Aradian gene and try to turn him against us or something?" Will asked.

"With some people, that might work, but not Michael." Melody said.

"Melody's right. His aim is set. Even if she did, that's not what I'm getting at. When I was studying Ezra, I made a hypothesis that Michael's transformation would happen later in life, when his body and mind matured, when he reached the pinnacle of his physique. Just as the Aradians stopped ageing when they learned the powers of immortality, Michael will turn Sararan at a crucial moment in his young adult life. I'm not sure what will engage it though. A celestial event perhaps, or some kind of triumph."

"Triumph? So, killing a bear with a sword isn't enough?" Melody asked, eyes wide.

"Perhaps not. But, like I said, it's just a hypothesis. Maybe Shakti has more confidence in the prospect of his transformation than I do. And Michael would be her own personal test subject, since I have no intention of going to Caldera until we defeat the armies of the north."

"What's your proposed timeline on the campaign?" Will asked.

"We should hit them hard sometime in the next six weeks, then lie low for a few months while the winter storms pass. The enemy will be inactive too, so we can regroup and stock up on ammunition and supplies. Then, mid-winter, we'll hit them when they least expect it, right in the heart of enemy territory. After Sandraudiga's forces fall, we mobilize to Caldera."

"And what about the Aradians?" Will asked.

"They won't interfere unless Shakti orders it. And since you should all be dead right now, it appears that will continue to be the case for the time being. Remember, there are only two of them, and there are other contested zones around the globe besides the Canadian Rockies."

"You were saying that sometime in February you want to attack Sandraudiga in her home territory?"

"Yes, but I'll need more intelligence."

"Well then, I have someone you need to meet."

They started walking away and Melody and David began to follow.

"This isn't appropriate for kids," Will said, stopping them.

Melody squinted defiantly at Will. "I'm not a damn kid."

Will stood firm. "Just stay with David, Melody. Trust me, you don't want to see this."

Pavonis and Will walked toward a tent at the edge of the camp. The grass bled dew as a hazy orange sun rose above the toxic horizon.

"Murphy," Will acknowledged the man guarding out front.

"Hello, sir."

"How is she?"

"She actually ate today."

Will looked at Pavonis. "We picked up a prisoner from the battle last week. She's a bit rattled, so prepare for that," he said.

Inside was an enemy soldier, tied to a pole. Her head dipped low as her greasy hair draped over her face like bog weed. Her black clothes were muddy and wet, and she was shivering in the cool morning air.

"Fetch a blanket, and hot water," Pavonis ordered.

Will turned to the guard at the entrance. "Murphy! Go get us a wool blanket and the pot off the fire!"

"Yes, sir!"

Pavonis placed her hand under the woman's chin and tilted the prisoner's head upwards.

The girl was no older than seventeen; it was likely she had been brainwashed, raised into the army at an early age. Her face drooped with exhaustion, but behind her cuts and bruises was an expression Pavonis recognised. Fierce and defiant, the young woman looked not unlike Pavonis herself, all those years ago.

"Hi," Pavonis said, smiling warmly. "What's your name?"

"Grace."

"Would you like some water, Grace? Maybe some tea?"

The girl nodded. Murphy returned with the

blanket and hot water. Pavonis put some herbs from her pouch into a cup and poured over the steaming liquid.

"Here you go," Pavonis said, gently dribbling the hot tea into the girl's mouth.

"It's hot," the young woman cried.

"Let's wait then," Pavonis said, setting the cup down on the ground. She knelt down to the girl's level. "Do you fight for your Queen with honor, Grace?"

"No."

"What will they do to you if you don't fight?"

"They'll kill me."

"So, not only are you getting tortured here, but if you go back after giving us information, you'll be tortured or killed. Correct?"

"Yes."

"And there's nowhere else for you to go, is there?"

"Lord Sandraudiga has patrols everywhere. They'd find me."

"They would find you, wouldn't they?" Pavonis said.

"Are you going to torture me?"

"No, Grace. I put a potion in your tea that will

force you to tell me the truth. It won't hurt you or have any other side effects. I need you to tell me where Sandraudiga is based, and how many soldiers she keeps there."

The girl started sobbing and swaying. "But if I tell you, they'll kill me!"

"Well, maybe you can stay with us for a while. Would that be alright, Will?"

"I'll have to clear it with the other officers, but I'm sure she can stay for a short while."

Pavonis continued to speak calmly. "So, Grace. If you stay here, you have to promise to be good. One wrong move and these men will cut your throat, or worse. Do you understand?"

Grace nodded.

Pavonis cooled the potion with an icy breath before letting the prisoner sip from the cup. Their eyes met and the girl saw the heavens in Pavonis' eyes.

"Good. Now tell me, where is Sandraudiga and what is the magnitude of her forces?"

"The fortress is in the valley of Banff. There are thirty thousand troops under the Lord's rule, but usually only ten thousand are based there at any given time."

"And where is the nearest post to where we are

now?" Will asked.

"At the base of Vega Peak. That's my duty station. There are three thousand soldiers there."

Will knelt down beside Pavonis. "That valley is narrow and has a great many weaknesses. Fire and gravity would be optimal offensive tactics."

Grace went on. "Exactly. If you showed up with everything you had, the commander would come out of that chalet she calls a base. She makes her soldiers put up tents like you do in the valley below. It's more of a communication's post if anything."

"Vega should be an easy victory. But Banff...it's the numbers we have to worry about," Pavonis said.

"Ten thousand is just a guess," Grace added. "It could be more, it could be less, just depending on the time of year and what the Queen has ordered."

"Is Sandraudiga supplying her soldiers with ammunition?"

"No, the Queen has ceased arms production. We are using the last of our cache, just as you are. They may have a few crates of ammunition left, but that's it. The rest of the army will have bows and spears, and shields made from the bones of the gilded age. Please don't make me return to them! Let me join your side! I hate the Queen! I hate her!"

"I want to believe you," Pavonis said gently.

"Please! I will help you! Don't make me go back there!"

Pavonis interrupted her hysterical plea. "Don't worry, we won't. Peace be upon you, Grace."

The tips of Pavonis' fingers turned purple as small barbules protruded from them, and she gripped the girl's throat. Grace squirmed in pain as white saliva began to bubble from her mouth.

"What the hell are you doing?!" Will yelled.

Pavonis pulled her hand away as the girl convulsed, shaking and kicking her feet haphazardly as she tried to escape from her bonds. Then, stillness. Grace's face turned white as slobber continued to drip from her motionless mouth.

"She's dead," Pavonis said, her voice devoid of emotion.

"Jesus fucking Christ," Will murmured, massaging his temples with his fingertips.

"Why do you care? She's your enemy. Did you really think she was going to stay here? We got what we needed from her. That's all that matters." Pavonis walked out of the tent, surprised at her ability to put on such an emotionless front.

Walking a short distance from camp, Pavonis knelt behind a log, where no one could see her, and let her blood-like tears stream down her face. She wept for Grace. She wept for Michael. She wept for herself, suddenly feeling the weight of her mission. How did she expect to defeat a superior enemy who only kept her alive to play games? She wept for the deceased and the living. But most of all, she wept for her lover, who she needed in that moment more than she had ever needed him before.

"Ezra!" she sobbed. "Come back to me. I need you!"

Her tears filled a small puddle in a dead leaf, and she gripped the ground, clenching her teeth, shaking with despair. She became more vocal with her weeping, moaning and choking between quick breaths. She lay back, her blood-stained face matching the yellow and red leaves of the autumn forest floor. Slowly, she calmed, watching a cloud drift over the sun. As the light disappeared, so did her sadness.

"Is darkness becoming my ally? Is light Shakti's crutch now?" she asked the sky. "Tell me, lover. Tell me what I must do. How did you hone your darkness?"

The sky turned grey, brooding with an oncoming storm cloud. Lying as still as the log that supported her shoulder, Pavonis felt the acid raindrops wash away her crimson splotches, resurrecting her heavy heart which beat to a new rhythm. She laid there in the rain for hours, watching a caterpillar slowly climb a tree, only to see it fall from a branch and start over.

It was high noon in the Palace of Caldera when Queen Shakti entered the Aradian's recharging chamber. Two tanks of illuminated orange ionized water stood in the center of a large hall. Bubbles from the bottom of one of the tanks spiraled around Tala's naked body floating in the tank's center, her head upturned toward the sun's rays, filtering in through a skylight at the top of the tank. Shakti walked past the pile of titanium armor next to the tank. She looked at the other tank. It was empty. She paced back and forth for a few minutes, looking around, her senses on high alert, seeking for any sense of betrayal. The black obsidian walls acted like a magnetic force, absorbing Shakti's frustration. After a while, Tala looked down at her master, her eyes flashing with the memory of when she and Mayari became separated. Shakti watched her eyes, already familiar with the Aradian's dark past.

"You and your sister have parted ways once again," Shakti said. She stood for a moment, looking into Tala's eyes, trying see beyond the Aradian's mind's projections. The anger in Shakti's eyes matched the suffering in Tala's. "Mayari hasn't reported for duty in almost two days. Tell me. Where is she?"

Tala kept floating, looking blankly at Shakti as though the Queen had not spoken.

"Lakshmi is a whore and liar, Michael has escaped, and Mayari is missing. Now tell me, WHERE IS SHE?!" Shakti screamed at the top of her lungs, her echo breaking the brittle rock walls into spiders-web cracks. The water in Tala's tank began to drain as Shakti breathed heavily. Her clenched teeth held still as her face shook with fury.

Tala exited the tank through the back latch. She sped the drying process by making her skin hydrophobic, and the water fell to the floor in seconds. She assembled her suit by pulling the pieces telekinetically against her body.

Shakti awaited an answer with vibrating, irate eyes.

"Mayari believes the prophecy has been compromised, master," Tala said.

"So, where is she?" Shakti asked intensely.

"Meditating at Burkhan Khaldun, your old training grounds in Mongolia. I regret to inform you that she has gone rogue, master. I have spoken with her and she has finalized her decision. Any moment now, she will attempt to fly into the sun and finish what Vishnu started. She plans to devastate the solar system."

"And you only decide to tell me this when I specifically request it? HAVE YOU NO DELIBERATION OF YOUR OWN!?" Shakti screamed. She glared at Tala, lowering her voice. "You will go after her," she said, turning away in an attempt to calm herself down, her eyes darting around the room for answers.

"And do what, master? What could possibly turn her?"

"Your words and empathy! Apparently, mine are not good enough! You are her twin sister. Remind her of her duty for the cause."

"She is immovable in her decision. The sun is her stone. She will use it as she wishes."

"You are the only one powerful enough to stop her," Shakti said.

"I would let the extinction of all mortal life unfold before hunting my own sister."

Shakti nodded, her decision made. "Come to my chamber."

They quickly walked to the Queen's throne room, where she sat gracefully, rolling up her left sleeve.

"The Prophecy calls for two beings of divine blood. I will make it so," she said, pulling out a dark red vial. "The Aradian gene will run through my veins, and I shall become the most powerful Immortal to ever have lived!"

Tala bowed down to Shakti as the Queen inserted a needle into the vial of unholy blood. She filled the needle's barrel and stabbed it into her vein, pushing the syringe's plunger down slowly.

She sank into her throne, her senses suddenly overloaded, overwhelmed by euphoria as the blood coursed through her, making tingling connections throughout her body and mind. She shivered for a few moments before placing her head between her legs. There she sat for several minutes.

Tala looked up from her bowing position.

"Master?"

Shakti laughed, a deep, rich, throaty laugh. She picked her head up slowly, her horrid laugh gaining volume, until the entire chamber shook with her mania. She turned her face to the ceiling, weeping bloody tears of joy from eyes as black as the obsidian walls surrounding her, a grayish haze at their center where the light was trapped inside them. Her evil chuckle eventually waned, her face assuming a purse-lipped expression.

"I should have done this a long time ago, Tala. A long, long time ago."

Tala stepped back and walked out of the chamber, dismissing herself quietly, as Shakti collapsed back into her chair, marveling at her stem-cell sorcery.

CHAPTER 29
MESCALINE SEDUCTION

Thin red rays of dawn illuminated the empty landscape as Michael continued his journey. He rode all the way into the heart of New Mexico, a land of lifelessness and ominous silence, where not even the rock clenching lichen had survived the decades of drought. To the north, the Rocky Mountains declined rapidly into the desert scape, bringing the southern horizon closer, warping Michael's perspective such that he felt he was traversing a small moon. The mesa's curved slopes cupped the morning star like a tomb mural of golden paint splattered across dried black blood. To the west, rounded hills shaped the countryside, emerging like swelling waves of rock, frozen in time just before breaking. Frail, remnants of juniper trees poked out from the chalky ground as tumbleweeds of rolled barbed wire caught on their stingy arms, blown across the waste by westward gusts.

Michael sped down the highway, followed by a

murder of starved ravens. He passed the bones of an ancient brick church that had been taken by time's whim. Through its doorless entry he could see yellow grass and the skeletons of cacti worshipping a wind that still whispered sermons of endless desperation. The bedrock of a canal revealed the mark of an old road, and a sharp wind lifted fiberglass and plastic sand through the sagebrush branches, filling in the shredded scars of asphalt with shards of modern man's misgivings.

Michael's bike sputtered as the engine choked on fumes. There were no gas stations in that corner of the Queens domain. He made it to the ruins of a small town before the vehicle finally died. He dropped his speed bike in the ditch and stood in the wind, whose howling pushed dust through the empty windows and doors of the old buildings. To his right, a range of mountains with snowcaps stood below a deathly grey sky. Though far away, snow meant water, which was what his body craved in his stark sobriety and panicked state of escape.

For hours he walked across that plate of shattered Earth. The mountains never seemed to get any closer after miles of what was becoming a funeral march. At times, he looked down to see slates of fossilized creatures, turned upright to the sky as reminders of an ancient epoch. He passed the bleached bones of an antelope lying on the banks of an empty riverbed. 'Will my life end similarly?' he wondered to himself.

The cold desert air scraped his lungs with each parched breath, and a light snowfall descended as the temperature dropped. With only a light jacket, he began to shiver in the cold. The mountains kept their distance and Michael's lip quivered for want of water. His eyes narrowed into a tunnel as a faint dizziness pulled him to the ground. He looked up into the sky. The clouds bubbled and morphed. He dropped to his knees and clenched the sand in his hands. Filled with anger and sadness, Michael shouted at the mountain.

"I will make diamonds from dust!" he rasped, trying to squeeze the grains into glass.

Exhausted and rapidly losing his grip on reality, Michael laid down beneath the grey sky, his black kimono flapping in the wind from under his jacket; his short hair collecting sand and snowflakes; his ears turning red in the frigid air.

"These stones will serve as my shallow grave," he whispered, as the thought of dying alone weighed down on him with the force of all gravity. He shivered as he retracted into fetal submission. The last water in his body collected in tears that fell upon the thirsty dirt. "Please, God...take care of my mother and Melody. Take care of the Marines. I wish I could have done more..." he whispered, before slowly drifting to sleep.

Michael awoke to fire light and a clear night sky. He was wrapped in a wool blanket. His eyes looked up into the galaxy's center before travelling down the stream of smoke which rose from a pile of crackling juniper sticks. Through the bending flames, he could see an old Navajo man watching him with a rigid stare. The man had a round head and deep brown eyes, and he wore a deerskin coat with turquoise beads sewn into the cuffs. Michael sat up and looked at the man, who pointed to a cup of water sitting next to him.

"Drink," the man said.

"Thank you," Michael wheezed.

Michael picked up the cup and drank the water with great thirst. The old man walked over and filled the cup back up with his thermos, then returned to his seat.

"It's tea," the man said.

"Thank you."

"What is your name?"

"Michael, and you?"

"I am Robert. I am a Navajo elder. What are you doing out here?" he asked.

"I'm lost."

"I can see that," Robert said, laughing. "You don't know what you're doing in this life, do you?"

Michael stared at his cup for a moment. "I have a destiny, but I'm not sure how to fulfill it. I want to save our species from extinction. I want to kill the Queen," he said.

The man chuckled. "Have you ever thought that perhaps killing the Queen won't save our species from extinction? What do you care about more, killing the Queen, or saving our species?"

Michael did not answer, sipping his tea in silence. It tasted odd, but he was parched, so he kept drinking.

"We Navajo live with freedom, more so even than when this land was ruled by the United States government. Shakti ended the reservations and made it so that all indigenous peoples can live as they please, so long as we follow the ancient ways. Even the boys are spared, so long as we abide by her rules."

"Then what is the right way? How can the killing and death end?"

"There will always be killing. There will always be death. Shakti is wiser than you think. Her tribe did something that had to be done. Humans would have destroyed the Earth within two hundred years had the Zurvans not committed the prophecy."

"But hasn't the score been settled? What more does she want?"

"The answer is in your cup, young man."

"I don't understand," Michael said.

"You will," Robert said, smiling.

Michael sat for a few minutes, sipping the awful concoction and gazing up into the night sky. Suddenly, his nerves started tingling, and the stars began swirling in circles. The smoke from the fire drifted into space and became nebulous, mixing with the blinking stars and purple hues of emptiness. The fire burped and consumed the screaming juniper branches in a swirl that took the shape of Melody's body.

"What's happening?" Michael asked, his pupils widening by the second.

"The sun god will accept you, but you must open your soul to the darkness first," the man said.

The old man suddenly morphed into a chuckling, horned toad as Michael's hallucinations increased, and without warning, Michael felt himself drifting through space itself, flying through clouds of colored gases and somersaulting over moons and stars. He tumbled through the ether as the chemicals wrapped his spinal column in a helix of euphoric embrace. As he settled into this new reality, he slowly dropped down from the sky and onto some strange planet below, where the gravity was lighter than Earth's. Michael touched down on a patch of pink grass. Purple plants sprouted around him as aspen trees swayed in a sweet-smelling wind. Across a small stream, white wolves chewed on and fought over a fawn's carcass. Michael stepped in slow motion across the grass. Each step was a tender kiss. With each breath he could taste heaven's air. The wolves gnawed at the dead animal without paying attention to Michael as he walked through the thick wood.

Eventually, he came to a clearing, where a throne made of stacked human skulls stood in the center. Naked women squirmed about the base of the black throne like an orgy of serpents, kissing and touching one another, and rubbing themselves with opium powder. In the throne's main seat sat Shakti. She was naked, save her large headpiece, and Michael stood before her in awe. The black-eyed Queen curled her finger toward him, licking her lips seductively. He walked over to her without hesitation. The crowd of women began touching him; tasting him; feeling every inch of his body with their faces and tongues. Michael crawled over the polished craniums into Shakti's open arms.

"I want you, Michael," she said, her eyes half closed as she touched herself.

He stood there for a moment, breathing heavily, his penis erect, and watched the Queen move like a lizard in heat. The red clouds above them cracked with green lightning.

"What's the matter, don't you want me?" she asked.

"I want you," Michael said, still in a state of ecstasy.

As Shakti closed her eyes and continued to finger herself, Michael slowly picked up a broken skull, its edges jagged down the suture.

"I want you dead!" he yelled, as he raised the piece high and struck Shakti in the chest. With a bellowing lurch, the wounded Aradian shrieked in agony. The sky turned from red to black as the women dispersed into the dark wood. Wolves by the hundreds ran into the clearing, howling in unison with Shakti's screams. Lightning struck the throne and Michael's vision dissolved.

Michael awoke with a scream. He looked around him. It was early morning. The Navajo man was feeding the fire with more sticks. He turned and looked at Michael.

"Did you get your answer?"

"Shakti...she's Aradian. I felt it."

"So?"

"So I must be mindful of how I conquer her. I need to understand what I'm up against."

The man nodded. "Come with me. You can stay with my tribe until you decide to continue your journey. Please, I insist."

He helped Michael to his feet, and they walked back to a small group of teepees in the base of the canyon. Although the man had secretly fed him peyote, Michael knew there was probably no safer place to be than with the tribe, since they had been pardoned by the Queen.

Though she knew not where Michael was hidden, Shakti saw him through her venomous gaze. She had entered Michael's mind, to test his manliness and mental malleability, through the shared dimension of their dreams. But the Queen's first test on Michael had only been a partial success. In order to execute her next test, she needed him in the flesh.

CHAPTER 30
SERRATED SKY

Weeks passed as the Marines prepared for a major assault on Sandraudiga's army, the first attack of such magnitude in almost a decade. After years of small skirmishes, Pavonis convinced Will the time for an aggressive push was coming. They began preparations by making thousands of arrows, and the blacksmiths took old car parts found on the river bottom in two-track ditches and pounded them into crude daggers and swords. A Marine martial arts expert began teaching the regiments how to fight with primitive weapons, and hand-to-hand combat drills were exercised daily. Even Melody began training, both with the Marines and with Pavonis, as her skills in magick steadily increased with each passing moon.

On a cool afternoon near the end of October, Melody followed Pavonis through the woods.

"We're here!" Pavonis said, her hands on her hips. She stopped by a large tree, with a massive bird's nest held high in its old branches.

"Where's here?"

"The spot I've chosen for your next lesson."

"What's the lesson?"

"You have a strong, beautiful voice, Melody, and you must learn to use it as your primary tool. You will sing a song to the raptor."

"What for?" Melody asked, looking up.

"The eagle will be our messenger. But first, we must convince it."

"So...you'd like me to sing it a song?"

"Not just any song, Melody. *This* song."

Pavonis handed Melody the lyrics, written on a withered piece of cloth.

"What is your intention with this?" Melody asked as she read the tune.

"I'm going to ask the raptor to recruit every willing animal within a thousand miles to join us in defeating Sandraudiga. Bears. Elk. Mountain lions. Eagles. Crows. Everything down to the last Badger. Hoof, talon, claw, and antler shall beat her army into the ground. With you, myself, the Marines, and the creatures of North America, we have a better chance of defeating the awful Lord."

Pavonis let out a loud, raspy screech. Melody jumped slightly as the ear-piercing sound caught her off guard. Two enormous black wings spread from the nest's center like a waking angel of darkness. The eagle lifted into the air, swooped around, and flew down into the clearing. Pavonis held out her arm as the eagle wrapped its flesh-ripping talons around it, yet she remained extended without flinching. She kissed the bird's beak and nestled her head into its neck. The bird responded warmly, as if greeting an old friend.

"Now, Melody, please kneel, then come and pet his back."

Melody timidly approached the raptor, knelt, and stuck her hand out hesitantly. The bird nipped her finger and Melody yelped.

"It's okay, Melody, he's an instinctual being. Go ahead, try again."

Melody slowly stuck out her shaking hand, this time gently caressing the bird's soft feathers. Slowly, the raptor warmed up to her touch, lowering its flared neck feathers.

"We have a request for you, oh father of the skies," Pavonis began. "Please, heed our words."

She nodded for Melody to begin. Hesitantly at first, then with more confidence, Melody began to sing the ancient words. As crisp as the wet air that clung to her lungs, the young witch unearthed the grace of the universe's vibrations and let loose the hymn into the canyon's descent. Her song echoed across the mountain walls, down into the valley, and further to the lowlands, where nothing more than a fragile whisper from the maidens divine request could be heard.

> *Behold all that is here,*
> *All that you know: between ice mirrors,*
> *Above clouds, below the lake,*
> *Find there these woeful creatures.*
> *The severed but standing, dead but awake;*
> *The furred, feathered, and fallen.*
> *Go long into tomorrow's glow,*
> *The lands of yesterday, and more so*
> *North into the aurora's veins.*
> *High as breath will take,*
> *Low as sand beneath the wake,*
> *Spread vast this old sermon.*
> *The red stag beckons war;*
> *She will bring back the forest floor.*
> *As one, we are Lord.*

Melody finished with a long, sustaining note that carried through the mountain hollow. The bird made a strange chirp and flew up into the grey sky, turning up sharply before diving down into the valley's forest, unseen.

"Did it work?" Melody asked.

Pavonis looked at Melody with a penetrating stare.

"What?" Melody looked at her mentor with a perplexed expression.

"I just had a revelation..." Pavonis smiled, then continued. "Yes, it worked. The bird knows the severity of our situation as its own. It will speak to the other animals and recruit them into our army. It will take several months for them to gather, but they will come."

"But how? Animals can't speak. How can they possibly understand what's at stake here? Why would they help us?"

"Oh, look who's suddenly the expert?"

"Well, no offense, Pavonis, but you've been teaching me a lot and I haven't seen any real evidence of how this 'magick' actually works. I have the right to be skeptical."

"You want proof? Here," Pavonis said, as she knelt down beside a patch of moss. She pressed her hand down and a myriad of flowers, fungi, and ferns began sprouting from its moist center. A vine wrapped around Melody's leg and she kicked it off.

"That's just your Sararan abilities growing plants! The storm manipulation; the speaking to animals. It's different. Its craziness!"

"Oh, is it? What about the Aradians then? They've mastered their bodies in ways that allow them to rearrange the physical universe. I'm merely taking my abilities and applying them in a different way. Just wait, my impatient apprentice. You'll see. You did very well today. Your message will be received, and when it is, you will begin to understand your capabilities."

Pavonis turned away and began walking down the mountain. Melody kicked a rock in annoyance and followed Pavonis back to camp.

Back at the camp, Gadreel and Cassidy were taking inventory of all their weapons and ammunition for the coming battle. A Marine close by was hunched over a bench beneath a deerskin awning, working tirelessly as he threw a freshly sanded stick into a mound of unfinished arrows.

"What's the count?" Pavonis asked as she walked into the camp.

"Forty thousand and counting," Gadreel said, nodding to the arrows.

"That's only ten arrows a man. We need to

double that in the next few days. Melody and I will help to gather more crystals and bones for arrowheads," she said.

"Good, because we will need them. Everything else is nearly completed, so we'll have everyone working on arrows exclusively in a few hours," Gadreel said, tallying up the swords.

Will approached them.

"Have you thought of potential strategies for the battle?" Pavonis asked.

Melody picked one of the finished arrows from the mound, examining the shaved stick.

Will pulled a map out of his pocket as the other three leaders watched Will's finger. "Well, at first I wanted to flank both the east and west, but that would involve splitting our forces at the initial mobilization, since we'd have to do that miles ahead of time to clear these mountains, making us subject to ambush from patrols."

Pavonis frowned. "I know it's a climb, but what about approaching from the hills to the north. We could use the terrain to our advantage instead of letting it get in our way. I say we post high up and use one hundred percent of our forces for archery and gravitational advantage."

"That's not a bad idea," Cassidy chimed in. "With a hillside that steep to work with, we can just start rolling boulders and sending every possible projectile downhill."

"So it's decided," Will said. "I almost pity our enemy. They have no chance of escape. We'll completely destroy them. We will mobilize in four days."

"Make it three, if possible. We should attack them on Halloween," Pavonis said.

"I like your style," Cassidy agreed, smirking with a foul grin, his sharp blue eyes eager for cataclysm. Gadreel smiled and shook his head. Will rolled up the map and patted David on the head, who walked up and wrapped his arms around Pavonis' leg.

"I missed you too, little one," Pavonis said, smiling.

David handed her a six-pointed star he had carved out of a piece of bark, then smiled, the pale light shining over his kind olive eyes.

Far to the south, smoke rose from the chimney of Camp Vega's command post. The up-valley winds beat at the canvas of a thousand tents, scraping the river bottom encampment with a dry scream. The gusts fled high up to the sickle peaks, then rolled back down with the warmth of the day. Samhain approached. As each hour passed, so did the thirst to harvest the souls of the damned. The Generals of Shakti's three army's congregated in the private loft above the main floor of the post, sitting at a long table made from a fir tree slab. General Sandraudiga sat next to General Fraus, a seasoned assassin and senior advisor to Shakti's personal guard. The two of them sat opposite the newly appointed and much younger General Lynx. Sandraudiga passed a letter from Shakti across the table to Lynx. Fraus poured each of them a glass of dark red wine, her silver rings clinking against the crystal. Lynx's eyes quivered as she read. She stood up and began to pace. Her cape billowed as she turned around in a whirl. She breathed hard with anger, her armor raising with her chest as she steamed.

"So, this is what it has come to? Ammunition manufacturing has officially ceased, and the Queen is grounding all air support? What the fuck is going on?"

"This was all part of the plan," Sandraudiga began. "I'm far more concerned about Mayari's sudden disappearance. If Tala follows her sister's exclusion, it won't matter how much artillery or close air support we have at our fingertips." She lifted her glass and drank.

Fraus walked over to the fire, tapping her crystal with her rings as her face glowed in the flames.

"But this is madness! How are my forces supposed to adapt so quickly?" Lynx continued. "We aren't ready for this! We've been trained with particular weapon systems and—"

"General, please. We're here to forge a strategy that provides leverage. If you need to consult your officers regarding supplies and training, do so ahead of time. There are three thousand women in this camp wanting to kill these men. We are here to adjoin our resources and come up with a plan. Leave the rest to your subordinates."

"As always, I'll do what's been asked of me, and more. But without a clear goal, the Marines will continue their advance, I'm sure of it. It's as if Shakti doesn't want us to win."

"Shakti wants what has been expressed in the prophecy."

"Which is WHAT?! Do either of you know? Have you seen with your own eyes the fragmented ribbons of this ancient prophecy? How do we know our Queen will not kill us all too when this is over?" Lynx darted her eyes between them, looking for an answer.

"It is a strange time of sudden movement and uncertainty. But be cautious of your frail loyalty,

General Lynx. Do not manifest the demise you fear. Not this late in the game. Not when you've come so far," Sandraudiga said, setting her glass down and standing.

"Admittedly, I feel betrayed. We've been given a short letter and then been left to fend for ourselves."

The fires crackling filled the room. Lynx sipped her wine and sat down again, resting her chainmail on her deer skin chair and tipping her head back to let her long blonde hair unravel as she sighed. Sandraudiga walked over and placed her hands on Lynx's ears gently and smiled. She bent slightly and kissed her forehead.

"What says the General of the Guard?" Sandraudiga asked, turning to Fraus.

General Fraus gazed into the flames. Her jaw line was as sharp as her stare, and she had tattoos in Russian on her neck and head, between scars where a knife had mutilated her ears. Her dark eyes sagged from sleepless nights, yet she gazed with lust into the yellow flame. She smiled and turned to them.

"General Lynx has hung some exquisite impressionist paintings on the walls. Berthe Morisot. Even some Bracquemond. These pieces of art suggest a feminine undertone that I find...charming. I wonder, however, if this is some defiant act against her masculine side, and she seeks impotence for the bull in her."

Sandraudiga tipped her brow as Lynx squinted her eyes in adversity.

"And why wouldn't she?" Fraus continued, slurping her wine like water. "We've been told for decades that men are the evil this world must rid itself of. And yet, in order to kill them off, we have had to become like them, perhaps worse; a ruthless tribe of blood thirsty monsters. What's more, we love it. The sensation of warfare is second to none. General Lynx, have you not felt a flux of testosterone in your system since the beginning of your campaign?"

Lynx sat silently and looked at Fraus with arid eyes.

"If this trend continues for the next few centuries, we'll have turned our warriors into the primary protectors of our people, biologically separating the Amazons from our nurturing mothers. In time, our fighters will become just as strong and courageous as the men who had shaped them. The honorable life of a warrior has always been the way of men, yet we have taken up that same dreadful mantle. Every woman in this army had the choice to become a breeder or a warrior, and in defiance of what has always been deemed a woman's 'nature', our warriors chose to kill rather than to give life. And why not? Why shouldn't they? A woman should have the freedom to decide her own fate, just as women should have the freedom to end the lives of their unborn children. We have the right to indulge in the pleasure of men's company without suffering any consequences. We are the masters of our bodies, and the masters of our futures."

Silence claimed the other two generals, and Fraus lifted her glass, expecting a dispute. None was forthcoming.

"Let me ask you this. When was the last time you had a good fuck, General Lynx?"

"It is not my wish to divulge such information...I mean...its surely treasonous to sleep with men—"

"We will succeed with our grand genocide, no doubt, and though we can store vast quantities of sperm for ages to come, don't you think that some men will be kept for pleasure? Some for slavery? And then what? Now that she herself has become an Aradian, Shakti is relieving us of our commitment to prudence. She has reduced us to our primal form. Who would have it any other way?"

Lynx shook her head and tried to stay on topic.

"I feel an attack is imminent, that is why I requested to speak with you both in person today. If you can give me at least one thousand more troops, I can do what you ask of me. I can defend this post,"

Lynx said.

"Fraus will be dissolving one of her regiments in a week's time. The two factions of her forces will be absorbed by our troops. For now, I suggest you fortify your defenses and put your supply order to use. You have archers and blacksmiths. Utilize them."

"Thank you, both of you," Lynx proclaimed as she lifted her glass to her superiors. "You will stay for the evening, won't you?"

"Unfortunately, we must get to the coast by tonight. I'm sure you understand the urgency."

Fraus and Sandraudiga finished their glasses of wine and walked to the stairwell.

"General Fraus, it was good to finally meet you. Thank you for your insight."

"You will heed my advice, won't you General?" Fraus enquired.

"About the Queen?"

"No, about men," Fraus said, looking back and smiling.

"Ah…yes…well, perhaps I'll indulge myself with a man if I ever find one worth hiding," Lynx jested.

"Be like a black widow spider," Fraus said as she turned to face her. "If I meet a man as deadly as I am, I fuck him. Then, I kill him."

Sandraudiga looked back and smiled and Lynx's shocked expression. Then, she and Fraus left, quietly, as if they had just stopped by to say hello, once again embarking upon their offensively ambitious undertaking.

The next day, General Lynx scrambled to get her camp up to speed. She called for one of her officers to transfer her orders down the chain of command. Someone knocked on the door of the loft.

"General Lynx? Major Alexandria, at your service."

"I ask for the Battalion Chief, and I get you," Lynx said, opening the door and looking the Major over.

"My apologies, ma'am."

"This is urgent, but also confidential. You will tell her what I tell you, and that is all."

"With honor and dignity, my word is sound ma'am." the Major assured her.

"From the south...the Queen has admitted that Mayari went rogue. In response, Shakti has turned herself Aradian. And the Marines are likely on the move again," the General said, leaning back in her seat. "Wine?"

"No, thank you, General. It sounds like a lot is going on."

"How many shields does your company have?"

"At least fifty."

"That leaves Venus and Saturn companies with only twenty-five each. We need more defensive armament. Is there anything salvageable close by?"

"We've salvaged all the airport ruins, and scavenged material from all the depots in the vicinity. Calgary and Banff have been totally stripped by Sandraudiga's army. There's not much left for us. The rest of it is scattered throughout the mountains. I don't see why the Queen won't outfit us with the necessary gear."

"Because we are on our own, Major."

"But, I don't understand—"

"She's playing games," Lynx explained, shaking her head before chugging half a bottle of wine. "We'll have to make do with crafting wooden shields for now. Where are the current patrols located?" Lynx set down the bottle with a hard thud and licked her lips, removing the remnants of the grapes blood.

"We have one squad that mobilized eastward an hour ago for Mount Hunter, and two that left yesterday for the northern valleys below Sunset Peak."

"Send out a scout to retrieve your east patrol. We are transferring to defensive maneuvers and we need everyone available."

"What of the northern patrols?"

"Send no one."

The General and the Major walked outside. It was Samhain, and the grey clouds hung like dark blue curtains of dread over their encampment. Thousands of tents sprawled across the valley floor. The soldiers stayed close to their own: eating roots, hemming ripped clothing, or sharpening their makeshift weapons. They were good soldiers and loyal; a sisterhood of modern warriors not unlike the wild women of ages past, who had run with wolves and made great sacrifices, despite the arduous epochs of revolving cruelty and oppression.

The Major watched as a group of the women formed a circle, holding tightly to each other's hands as they began to chant around the fire. They sang in unison, asking for guidance from the Earth. Lynx went over to them, sat down, and joined hands, to participate in their sacred song.

Far above Camp Vega, in the mountain's saddle,

Cassidy stood like a gargoyle on the cliffs edge, watching the enemy congregate. He had painted a large satanic cross in black paint on his face, and the mink fur collar of his coat wrapped him tightly, the fine hairs dancing in the icy winds that poured from the peak to the valley floor. He nodded at his archers, who drew their strings, each fitted with three arrows. Dozens of others wedged logs under boulders in preparation for felling the mountain and crushing the encampment. The wind hissed through the canyon as they awaited the final order.

General Lynx's hair stood on end and she parted from the singing circle, calling for the Major once again.

"Major, assemble the troops and brief them on the possibility of an attack. Outfit every soldier with some kind of shield. I don't care if it's a small hub cap or a piece of bark – they will need something."

"Copy that, General," the Major said, jogging over to talk with the other officers.

As the Major walked back to the outpost, she looked up towards the mountain, and saw something her eyes found impossible to piece together. A sky serrated by arrows was flying towards her, like a black cloud ripping through all other elements. They came without warning, the crystal and bone tipped missiles hurling down with the sound of five hundred short breaths of death. Screams erupted in the camp.

"Get down! Find cover!" someone yelled.

The General ran towards her outpost and held herself against the wooden wall. Looking out, she watched in horror as the arrows sliced through the tents and sent her troops into a chaotic swirl of panic. The hail of arrows seemed to come from straight above with ferocious velocity.

"Fetch me my blade!" the General yelled to her guard.

A woman crawled out from her tent, two large arrows lodged into her back.

"Medic!" she screamed "HELP MEEE!"

The very mountain shook with anger. Granite boulders between four and ten feet in diameter came tumbling down, crushing soldiers or tearing them in half as they rolled through the camp. Another wave of arrows fell upon them, and a full rockslide washed out part of the camp in a catastrophic massacre of rumbling stones. It was as if the Titans had been resurrected from their prison under the Earth's crust.

All around, the wounded shrieked and screamed in agony. Vega was no longer defendable. The wounded were doomed, and the living rapidly dispersed, retreating as the Marines charged down the mountain, their black and white face paint a fearful reminder of the legacy they carried.

Just as the guard handed General Lynx her blade, Pavonis herself dropped from the wall's totem, holding an oak scepter with a steel spike at its end. She sliced the guard across the face and pointed the scepter between Lynx's eyes.

"Who are you?" the General cried. "Please, whatever you want, I'll comply to your demands!"

"I am Pavonis, your true Lord! BOW DOWN TO THE QUEEN OF THE EARTH!"

"Yes, Lord Pavonis!" Lynx said, dropping to her knees.

Pavonis smiled as the woman bowed low, her forehead kissing the ground.

"Your fort is ours, and you will be the last to die."

"Please! Let me die with my soldiers!" Lynx begged.

"No afterlife awaits you," Pavonis said, as she held her scepter high and drove the steel spike through the woman's head. Brain and blood gushed from her split skull as the General's limp body fell to the side, twitching like a headless insect. Pavonis

298

could very well have touched her with the tip of her finger, poisoning her. She could have sedated the woman or left her to die in the wilderness. But the violence of war was brewing a deep hatred in Pavonis, an uncontrollable wrath and visceral lust swirled in her stomach.

From strategic development to tactical execution, Pavonis was getting excruciatingly good at warfare. But her freakish desire for blood on the battlefield led Will to believe she was becoming too warlike, as she fully indulged in the massacre, in her quest for vengeance against the Queen. During those years of hibernation, Pavonis had not just been accumulating genetic camouflage. She had been nurturing a deep resentment for the enemy. Will had known there was something more to her unique Sararan characteristics after he had watched her kill Grace. What he feared was that this was just the beginning of Pavonis' furious craving; that she would become something unstoppable; abominable. To what extent she commanded her vengeance was up to her, but her growing passion for witchcraft was shaping her personality in ways that scared everyone, from young David to the most battle-hardened Marine. Pavonis had called herself Lord to the General, to intimidate her enemy. But though she strived to be Pavonis, the constellation of salvation, it was clear that she was feeding off the Aradian's strategies. In truth, finding the balance between those extremes was her ultimate goal, but Pavonis had sensed that the only way to convince the Marines they had a chance of winning was to become what they feared the most; to become the as powerful as those they were trying to destroy.

On the southern slopes, the Marines lit fires at the grassy base of the foothills, which ran up the chimney canyons like dragon's breath, engulfing the retreating soldiers as they made their futile ascent into the alpine sanctuary. The sky turned orange and black, and smelled of burning flesh. Someone looted the outpost and torched it from the inside, leaving the paintings to melt in the swell. Will followed his invading Marines onto the field and looked over at his sister, who smiled and inhaled the smoke as she knelt down low, putting her fingers inside a soldier's skull, and tasted the blood of her enemy. With an urgent nod, Will coaxed his deviant sister back into the fray and they chased the retreating women one by one, sparing none as the swordsman and the Immortal cut them down like reeds, leaving none alive.

CHAPTER 31
CALDERA

The sands of New Mexico sizzled in the mid-afternoon heat. The temperature trends in the southwest swung like a naked planet in a forsaken solar system; negative temperatures rapidly increased, becoming unbearable Saharan heat by mid-day, then dropped again, the air becoming frigid by evening. Blinded by brightness, a lone vulture crouched on her telephone pole perch, where a calf's skeleton and thick tangled wiring served as infrastructure for her nest of cannibalistic chicks. The land was but an empty ocean floor, separated by islands of mesas, where behind gutted crevices, mysteries could be found in the form of petroglyphs and graffiti tags. One could find arrowheads or bullet shells, cast iron or car parts. To modern humans these were relics of distant past cultures without reference to a specific age, for the difference between a decade and a millennium gravitated the same intrigue in the eyes of a post-eruption child.

Strewn throughout the world were artifacts reachable by all man's means, left behind from a war that began too late and ended too soon and took too much. Without a museum or storyteller, the remnants of yesteryear were swallowed by rust, slowly erasing their solemn and crucial tale.

A round pond beneath the mesa sat mirror-like against the rocky cliff face, it's flat surface marred only by the movements of a horny toad, as the creature scuttled between a cactus and a dead juniper's shade trying to hide from the two beings walking towards it.

"Look, I found one!"

"That's not one," Michael said to his teenage companion. It had been a few weeks, and Michael's hair was no longer clean cut. He dressed like the Navajo and he had become accustomed to the tribe's lifestyle and practices, nearly suppressing all his fears and thoughts about his family.

"It is, I can tell by the numbers on the bottom," he tried to convince Michael.

The young Navajo held up a bullet shell to the sun as if it were a gem, gazing at its slender casing with a twinkle in his eye.

"Your eyesight is shit. Let me see that." Michael snatched the small brass casing and looked at the numbers rounding the primer. "This is a .300 caliber

302

shell. It's scratched though, see? Your dad reloads .308 shells."

"Damn. I thought we were close," the teenager said, tossing the casing to the ground as it clinked on the rocks.

"Keep looking," Michael said, sifting his hands across the ground, trying to feel for the super-heated brass baking in the afternoon sun. "Isn't this kind of breaking the rules the Queen gave your people?" Michael asked.

"Not as long as we scavenge for the casings ourselves and don't buy manufactured ones. It's still living off the land, just twenty-first century style."

"Where would you buy ammunition anyway?"

"Neon city cops. They'd sell them to us. But it's not worth getting caught. Shakti has eyes and ears everywhere. She would kill my whole tribe, even the young."

"I can believe it," Michael said, watching the horny toad crawl under a rock. "Well, shouldn't we start heading back soon, Derek? We don't want to get too far out at this time of day."

"I agree, let's boogie."

They hiked back to the village of teepees as the evening sun painted the sky pink and orange. The red rocks reflected the shifting color as the eastern horizon swelled with purple darkness that chased the receding light of day. Twenty teepees stood in a creek bottom where a small trickle of water ran between the sage and starving cacti. A woman was weaving a basket as they entered the camp. Small children played a game, rolling antelope bones on a satellite dish. The Chief sat complacently outside his teepee, smoking a tobacco pipe and gazing into his small fire.

"Derek. Michael. What did you find today?" he asked, his eyes and head still as a statue as he continued to gaze into the fire's center.

"I'm sorry, Chief. We looked hard all day but couldn't find any shells. We'll look again tomorrow."

"The creator will provide in time. Both of you, come sit," he said. He tapped the bottom of his pipe and emptied the tobacco into the orange blaze. "For too long our people have struggled against the white man's reign of cruelty. But now that this era is over, we face a new problem. It is an interesting problem. You see, there are too many women and not enough men," the Chief began.

"Derek. You have proved yourself a worthy hunter and skilled warrior. I want you to take my eldest daughter's hand in marriage."

Michael could not help but laugh into his sleeve on seeing Derek's terrified expression. They both knew the Chief's oldest daughter was the size of a prized sow, and twice as hideous.

"But I—", Derek began.

"No excuses. And what are you laughing at, white devil? I am arranging for you to take my youngest daughter's hand in marriage!"

Michael stopped laughing. "You mean Lydia?"

The Chief nodded.

"She's fourteen," Michael said, his eyebrow rising in surprise.

"And in a week, she'll be fifteen, the perfect age for marriage. We are planning a great celebration as you, Derek, and you, Michael, to take the future of this tribe to new frontiers!"

"I'm afraid I have to stop you right there, Chief," Michael began, clearing his throat. "I already have a lover, you see. I cannot marry another."

"And where is this lover of yours?" the Chief asked.

"Uh...back home, I hope? I'm not sure."

"If this woman is so important to you, you will go to her. If you stay, you must become a part of this tribe forever. If you leave, you must leave tomorrow morning and never return."

"I will leave in the morning, then," Michael said, standing.

"That's a bit harsh," Derek complained.

"Silence, boy! I understand he is your friend, but your bond must be broken if his path and yours are to continue. One day, you will be a great warrior, Michael," he said, turning to Michael. "But if you hold a significant adoration for another, your place is not here. Your destiny lies elsewhere. We love you, but you must go."

"Thank you, Chief. I will not forget what you have done for me." Michael hugged the Chief and walked off.

Derek followed, whispering to Michael as they passed the teepees. "I'm not marrying Mariposa: the queen of fry-bread!"

"And what do you want me to do about it, Derek?"

"Take me with you!"

"I don't think that's a great idea," Michael said. "If something happened to you, the Chief would scalp me!"

Just as they were about to enter Michael's teepee, a large girl with a single brow jumped in front of them.

"Hi Derek," she said in a squeaky voice.

"Hi Mariposa," Derek replied, forcing a smile.

"Did my father tell you the good news?"

Michael lowered his head in embarrassment, trying not to laugh.

"I don't mean to sound rude, but it's something I'm going to have to think about. You know, mull it over for a while," Derek said, in the sweetest way he could.

"Oh, I'll give you something to mull over," she said, giggling.

She walked off, and the petite young girl who followed behind her blew a kiss at Michael.

"Hi Michael," Lydia said, skipping away.

Once they were gone, Michael turned to Derek and whispered, "We gotta get the hell out of here!"

The glaze of morning ice thawed, wetted, and evaporated in seconds in the rising heat of dawn. Michael and Derek were still inebriated from the absinthe they had delved into the night before, which had prompted them to dance with the green faery and howl at the moon like wolves. Derek was the first to wake, slowly coming out of his daze. A red sun rose behind him like a demon army mounting in the east. Michael kicked the bottle of wormwood potion as he jolted awake from a strange dream.

"Derek?"

"Yeah."

"Did we finish the bottle last night?"

"By the sound of it clinking over the rocks, I'd say we got damn close," Derek said, rising from his mat slowly and spitting.

"Good God. Ever since I was taken from that battlefield I've been on a drug binge, trying to suppress everything."

"Is it working?" Derek asked.

"No. Not anymore."

"Then let's get the fuck outta here!"

As they rose, the hot desert sun tried to push them back down, but they resisted. Every time Michael blinked, he saw the green faery dance under his eyelids. It reminded him of his mother. He knew he needed to go back north to find her, and the Marines, even if that meant certain capture.

They walked for miles, seeking a longitudinal highway where some hermit might have a vehicle they could use to continue their journey north. Steep canyons stood around them and a kettle of vultures floated in the mesa's shadow, waiting patiently for one of the young men to drop in the scorching heat. They filled their canteens from an old well, sunken into a cavern of eroded shelves of dirt. The water was thick with minerals but passable. They walked on. Carcasses of cattle lay decimated, picked clean by scavengers. The empty canals of their skulls whistled in the dry wind.

By mid-afternoon, Michael had found an old license plate dusted in the red soil, an anachronistic breadcrumb in their search for a paved road.

"There!" Derek yelled.

In the distance, Michael could see a grayish black strip following the valley floor. Heat waves rose from its surface like a stove, creating a thick mirage that gave way to a false horizon.

"We should be careful. Between Shakti's patrols and the neighboring tribes, we're more likely to meet opposition than a tourist picking up hitch hikers."

"We'll be lucky to see *anyone* in these parts," Derek muttered.

Michael held the hilt of the dagger the chief had given him. He let go just as soon as he had touched it, for the bronze burnt his skin as the afternoon heat became unbearable. "We should find some shade before continuing to the road."

"I agree," Derek said, as sweat dripped from his face and evaporated as soon as it hit the red rocks at his feet.

They began walking to the shade of a large juniper when Michael noticed something in his peripheral vision. Far to the north across the great valley, he saw a glint of silver light. A few seconds passed and he saw it again as it flickered between the refraction of the mirage and the light reflecting from its body like liquid mercury. It was coming straight towards them at rapid speed. At first, Michael could see only its head, a helmet of pure chrome. Then the shoulders, its torso and legs hovering above the wavy surface like angel's wings. The menacing Immortal filled the canyons with a shrieking sonic boom in its wake.

"DEREK, RUN!"

"What?" the boy asked, puzzled.

"JUST FUCKING RUN! SAVE YOURSELF!" Michael screamed, pushing Derek.

"I'm not going anywhere!" Derek said defiantly, noticing the Aradian heading their way. He pulled out his dagger and gave a loud native war cry.

Michael froze, horrified, torn between the desire to run and the need to protect Derek.

The Aradian took only seconds to reach them, and as she rapidly decreased in speed, a gust of wind hit Michael and Derek with an incredible force, creating a small dust devil as the Aradian stopped only a few feet in front of them. A moment later, a sonic boom exploded through the canyon and nearly shattered their eardrums.

"Tala. We meet again," Michael said, bowing low. The Aradian stood directly in front of him.

Derek walked up to her bravely. "Go back to your Queen, bitch!" Derek yelled, spitting a large tobacco chew onto Tala's pristine suit.

Michael slowly looked at Derek, his eyes wide in disbelief. "Bow down, you fool!" he whispered.

Tala walked up to Derek until her face was only inches from his. Derek breathed heavily. He could see her eyes playing a slideshow of horrific events: a young girl getting her clothes ripped off as four men brutally raped her orifices in some abandoned motel room. Tala's metal mouthpiece slid aside, exposing the skin of her lips. She spit in Derek's face with the force of a shotgun blast. Derek dropped to the ground screaming, holding his hands to his burning face. The Aradian had turned her saliva into an acidic glue that had no end to its caustic bite. Thick niveous smoke rose from Derek's burning skin as he wailed. Michael could smell the potent chemicals searing his friend's flesh and he dropped his head to the ground, begging for mercy like an unworthy slave.

"Please, spare my friend!"

As Derek lay shrieking in agony, the rumble of helicopter rotors could be heard flying into the canyon.

"Rise, Michael," Tala said, her lips still exposed. Her unfiltered voice was soft and sweet, almost like a child's.

Michael stood as four massive Blackhawk helicopters hovered above them, aerial gunners pointing their machine guns from either side of the open bays like metal stingers. Red dust swirled in the wake of the rotor blades. As the ships touched down a hundred feet behind Tala, small rocks ricocheted off her armor with small pops and tings. The wind cooled Michael's body as the sweat dried on his skin.

"Where are you taking me?" Michael yelled, to be heard above the engines roar.

"We're going to Caldera," Tala said, picking up Derek by his long black braid as he screamed. She dragged him over to the helicopter and looked back.

"Don't make me herd you onto the ship Michael, unless you wish to be regarded as a sheep," she said, her metal lips covering her face once again. Michael dropped his dagger to the ground and followed reluctantly, his short hair catching grass particles and dust as he marched against the the rotor blades' turbulence. He shuddered as he stepped onto the blood-stained deck of the bay. Derek lay in the corner, holding his face as he moaned. They rose to the sky, Tala holding Michael's shoulder with a firm grip. Whether her intention was to prevent him from jumping to his own death, or to reaffirm her control over him, Michael did not know. All he knew was that he was going to the lair of his nemesis; into the terrible mouth of the sky shattering volcano from which Shakti had spread her conquest.

Michael looked at the gunners. The women wore full face masks and goggles to guard themselves from shrapnel and flack. They appeared as robots, save for the long black hair protruding from under their helmets. Michael looked back at Tala, who looked at him plainly. Her eyes showed a scene of her younger self, sitting alone in a room. But the room was a cage, a place where she was subjected to the horrors of slavery. Michael feared he too would undergo the same experience once inside Shakti's domain.

Michael stayed awake for the whole journey and Tala's hand never left his shoulder. He watched the landscapes of Utah and Wyoming pass below them, looking down at the small communities who appeared every so often, their teepees arranged in geometric patterns that told the Queen's air force who they were. Some orientated their canvases into large geometric patterns, others into the shapes of animals, depending on the size and type of tribe.

Derek had passed out from trauma and he lay in a small pool of his own bodily fluids, his face mutilated beyond recognition.

As they approached the rim of Caldera, Tala spoke to him in a sincere tone. "Welcome to Caldera, Michael, home to the last slaves on Earth."

The helicopters skimmed the crest of a hill, and Michael's heart began to beat faster, his fear rising as they passed over the cavity's edge and into the hellish valley. Slave quarters spread for miles in the form of sheepskin yurts and tents. Clothing hung from clothes lines, stained black, red, and yellow by the sulfuric ash and soot that still covered the crust of the land. Soldiers patrolled the streets, whipping the men who disobeyed the city's orders. Mounds of male bodies were being piled and burned in the ruins of a building. The helicopters flew through its black smoke. Michael had never experienced such a smell; the sulfuric hint of burning hair, the methane from the decayed guts, the iron from a fresh corpse. He knew he would never forget that scent.

In the distance, a great palace loomed in the center of the city. As they approached it, Michael could see the finer details. It was shaped like a gothic cathedral, carved from a single stone of volcanic obsidian. The awning support beams were shaped like bones; its entry doors were perforated with an intricate pattern inspired by classical Islamic architecture. The façade above the doors displayed a scene of detailed sculptures, with Shakti at its center and the Aradians standing like pillars to her right and left. Vishnu's statue stood above hers, twice as large and holding a large metallic crystal ball, made of perovskite; the mineral which makes up the mantle of the Earth. A large courtyard lay out in front of the façade, fenced in and gated with two machine gunners posted on either side the main doors of the palace.

Three of the helicopters flew to the air base, while Tala's landed outside the palace gates. As the rotor slowed, Tala gave Michael a slight push out of the bay. He looked back at Derek, who was being dragged by his shirt. The gunner holding Derek threw him onto the ground beside Michael.

"What will you do with him?" Michael asked Tala as the gated doors opened. Tala remained silent.

The courtyard gate opened, and Michael looked down a pristine marble path which lay between a set of pillars and an intermittent garden of dead roses. Wilted petals floated upwards as the winds of the helicopter's retreat lifted them high into the air. Beyond the dead rose garden, the mighty obsidian gates to the palace opened. From the shadows came forth two white robed guards and the Aradian Queen, dressed in an extravagant outfit of sheepskin and black lace, decorated with onyx stone buttons, which accentuated her slender body. Two thin braids rested over her shoulders, and the rest of her long hair was tied up in a rattlesnake's vertebrae, like some primeval czarina mocking Lady Liberty. She had eyes that could gouge, hands that could taste, and ears that could see.

"Michael. Welcome to the center of my kingdom," Shakti said, bowing graciously.

Michael glared at the Queen, refusing to bow.

"I'm so very pleased to gaze upon you," the Queen continued loudly, a few hundred feet from him still.

"I don't share the same admiration for a psychopath like you," Michael spat, scowling her.

An awkward silence filled the air.

Shakti nodded at Tala. Michael looked at her, then to Tala, as the Aradian picked up Derek by his braid.

"What are you doing? Leave him alone!" Michael yelled.

Tala reached out her free hand and motioned one of the gunners to hand over her weapon.

"No…please!" Michael begged.

Tala grasped the large pistol and stuck it to Derek's head. He knelt wearily, weeping from half empty sockets as salty tears stung the pink wounds on his lips and exposed cheekbones.

"Be strong, Michael. The Great Spirit is with you always," Derek slurred.

Tala stared at Michael as she pulled the trigger. The blast echoed through the courtyard as Derek's brains splattered the concrete. Michael screamed.

"You fucking bitch!" he yelled at Tala.

"Michael, make no mistake, that was my order," Shakti said, shaking her head.

Michael turned to her with his teeth clenched. He looked back at Derek's mutilated head, then turned to Shakti. "Fight me," he said.

"What was that? I couldn't hear you. Use your man voice!" Shakti yelled.

Michael faced her, his eyes aflame with anger. "You can do nothing to me, because I am nothing! Fight me, you miserable bitch!"

"That's more like it," Shakti grinned. "Gunners? Prepare to fire."

Michael walked towards Shakti as the gates closed behind him, his shoulders flexed like a beast. Black doves flew by his face, taking any peace with them. Watching Derek die was the last straw. He wanted nothing more than to strangle Shakti to death.

"This will be the first of many tests, young Michael," Shakti said.

"Do your worst."

Michael stopped. A calm wind blew through the garden. The sun poked through the black and red clouds, shining down on Michael and the Queen. The only sound to be heard was the falling of dead flower petals onto the stone courtyard.

Shakti raised her hand. "Fire."

Bullets pulverized the air. Michael ran towards the pillar on his left for cover. The bullets chipped away at the pillar's edges, deteriorating them with each burst. Michael was timid, for he knew from training that a bullet of that caliber only needed to be within twelve inches to sear flesh. He felt adrenaline pumping through his body, and when he blinked, he saw the green faery again. 'This is the grave of my father, but it won't be mine,' he thought, the absinthe still in his blood.

He heard one of the gunners stop shooting and reload. It would only be a matter of seconds until the other one had to reload as well. When the last bullet flew past him, Michael gave the silent air two seconds before running to the next pillar. He dashed across the path just as one of the gunners finished reloading. A blast followed his final steps as he sheltered in the safety of the pillar's shadow.

"Is that all you got?!" Michael yelled.

He ran diagonally to the next pillar, trying to gain ground even as the bullets flew through the air behind him. One of the bullets ripped a piece of his calf off. He screamed as he stumbled behind the middle pillar. He breathed heavily, the bullets scraping away at the edges of the stone monolith. As Michael sat there, his leg half blown off, he suddenly felt no pain at all. Michael's mind went blank. He did not feel the ground beneath him, nor did he hear the bullets screaming by his ears. He did not smell the sulfuric air. He could not see the opaque colors of the flowers in the garden. His senses went silent, and he went into a strange daze of spiritual purgatory. What was this state of unbecoming? Why now? Why here? These were questions he asked himself as he drifted, until he could not even think, and a singularity encompassed him. Love and gratitude suddenly grew from within his belly and stemmed outward in a leap of vital resistance. From his feet to his head he was revived, re-shaped, and reminded. Reminded of his love for Melody. Reminded of a power known seldom by the creatures of Earth.

Michael stood up. His leg stopped bleeding. His heart rate slowed. His eyes became alight like the forest fire that had killed his father on that very same ground. In a grand testimonial to his courageous spirit, Michael became what his mother had predicted. Through the power of the green faery, his overwhelming dedication to his virtues, and through a sequence of improbable events, Michael unleashed his dormant Sararan genes and felt the supremacy of being that rare and deadly species he was always destined to become.

As the gunners stopped to reload, Michael dipped out from the pillar's shade and ran like lightning towards the left gunner. He jumped high into the nest and kicked the woman in the neck, severing her spine with a deadly blow. The other gunner struggled to reload fast enough as Michael locked the belt of bullets in before she could manage. Michael aimed the large machine gun and opened fire, completely shredding the woman apart. The bullets shattered the other as well, destroying the post.

As Michael turned to Shakti, he noticed the gun had locked its rotation, preventing him from aiming at her. He jumped down and attempted to approach her, but Tala suddenly dropped from above and stood in front of him, blocking his path.

The Queen began clapping as Michael's fiery eyes gazed deep into Tala's pained visions.

"Bravo! You have passed the first test, and in doing so have become the first and only Sararan prince; a transcendence, born above his own father's tomb. It's exhilarating really," Shakti said with vigor.

"I am your foe, you unworthy shade! What do you have for me now? What could you possibly do, besides kill me, to keep me from doing good in this world?"

"I'm not going to keep you from doing good, Michael. I'm going to keep you from doing *anything.* You are my golden slave, and you've already omitted a detail of the prophecy by not succumbing to my sister; by staying so loyal to your young princess. You seem now impossible to break, which is of vast interest to me. My intention is to understand you. You are the most noble of all servants of science and divination, Michael, and if you think watching the brutal murder of your friend or challenging a simple soldier to a duel stirs you, wait until the real tests begin. I will mentally castrate you, but I promise it is for the sake of the future of life on earth. I'm going to introduce a unique dimension of captivity to you, and I will show you true suffering," Queen Shakti said, as she dipped back into the darkness of her black cathedral. Her ghost-like guards followed, holding antennae-like oak scepters, monitoring Shakti's hijacked air space.

Michael screamed in anger as Tala held him in place. His fiery eyes matched his Sararan identity, the image of flame locked into his memory: the same inferno reflected in the eyes of the great bear he had slaughtered; the fire he had gazed into before his peyote-inspired transfiguration; the fire that had killed Ezra, indistinguishable and forever consuming, before the beginning and after the end of all things. The fire that binds the universe concentrated itself within Michael, between the electrical pulses in his Sararan nerves and inside his blazing heart, pouring through the tetrahedron third eye opening in his mind's expanse. Michael closed his eyes and saw through that emerging organ his own father, obscure in the pale essence of the astral realm; he who had been defiled, his own powers used against him in the name of the Zurvan prophecy. Yet despite Ezra's ill fate, his mysterious DNA had indeed transferred to his son, who now not only carried the divine Sararan gene, but the virtues, strength, and vision necessary to quell the evil that provoked him.

Later that same evening, Tala walked pensively between the volcanic vents overlooking Caldera. The fissures spewed their toxic smoke as she gazed down upon the slave city, where thousands of wealthy white men had been stripped of their humanity and put to work until the air's cancerous compounds inevitably killed them. Though she did not outwardly display any compassion for the slaves, she did pity their plight, for she had been a slave herself and knew what foul orchestration it took to be an overseer. Her eyes showed a vision of her and her sister, reuniting after years of separation. The elation of that day was a significant memory, yet just a moment in her oceanic existence. She contemplated things that only a being of her divine nature could contemplate, and after some time gazing down at the black bulbous palace, Tala walked north, never to return to her master's decree. She was finally a sovereign being after one hundred years of struggle and fellowship. She was, and would be forevermore, her own master.

CHAPTER 32
PAVONIS RISING

The cold of the moon knelt upon the shoulders of a weary shade. She walked in silence across a burn scar of one hundred million charred trees. The black snags creaked in the soft breeze, telling the story of how they had once touched the sun. Now, the sky sat in a grey sea of nothingness. Slow clouds shifted for the dubious dawn as the horizon beckoned with an up-valley wind, fast shifting and sporadic, looking for leaves to be the instrument of its solemn song. Only skeletons of the strongest and oldest trees remained in that foggy valley of death. But where there is only death, life stands out. The shade, despite posing as one of the forests artefacts, was a diamond mist in that charcoal laden land.

The shade carried a great burden, an impossible task given to her by Queen Shakti. She was to seek the one who holds the powers of the river and the roots, and assassinate the deity. The shade had sought this mysterious being for five years, without intelligence from Shakti, comrades, or leads from locals. But if she could somehow outwit and kill Pavonis, she could become the Queen's apprentice and rise to the highest level of command. A feat it would truly be, to defeat the most famous Sararan, the most desirable of bounties.

Thousands of miles the shade had searched, and she would search thousands more if she had to. Her toes made subtle crunching sounds, aching from the stump holes and rocks that tore holes in her boots. Arrow knocked in bow, axe in hand, she wore her weapons well. She was seasoned and battle ready, anticipating becoming a spherical dimension of destruction at any moment; to shoot her arrow across the valley itself or swing her axe with a blow that painted the soil crimson.

Dawn showed no sign of lending its warmth, and the air turned a bitter cold as the wind whipped the assassin's face. Cinder cyclones swirled as the shrubs shook like trembling old hands reaching out of the ground. The wind faced her, the ash blasting her cheeks with carbon nettles. When she looked to the ground, she saw a few orange embers traveling on the winds schizophrenic current. Curious, she plucked the arrow from her bow and set it down. She looked ahead and slowly crept around a nearby snag, peering around the side. There was a stump ahead, but it was like no other around it. It was seven feet wide with embers still smoldering in its thick core as smoke billowed from its hollow center. The fire had died out weeks ago, or so the shade assumed. She could not see from the base of the mound what could be the reason for the phenomenon. The bark protruding from its white ashen halo had been slowly devoured by the fire and resembled a shrunken mountain ridge, meeting at hell's gate.

After scanning the area, the assassin carefully dropped an amethyst pendulum from a silver chain hidden underneath her robe's sleeve. It rotated in a perfect circle three times then stopped, perfectly still. She wrapped up the chain and held the stone in her palm for a moment, nestling it against her tattoo of a triangle with a short line through the top angle, symbolizing her devotion to Shakti. She silently dropped to the forest floor and pulled her scarf over her mouth to protect her lungs from the unsettled ash just centimeters from her lips, lest she cough and give away her position. Holding her axe tightly, she made her way to the mound like a slithering creature beneath the charcoal forest. The moon's crescent appeared as a cracked door emanating a purified light within. Storm clouds from the north soon engulfed the morning sky as they cast a shadow over the day, the moon's silver crescent shutting again like a boulder covering a cave entrance.

She began to scale the mound, using the compression of the fine ash to cloak her scent and the sound of her movement, in case the deity was lying quietly in the furnace of the old root's consumption, listening to the delicate omnipresence of the particle world. To ease her mind and her voluminous heart rate, she tried to focus on synching herself with the natural world around her; dwelling on the possibility that this could be a defining moment that would change the course of world events forever would almost certainly cause her to make a dire mistake. All that time spent searching, killing, and surviving would be for nothing. No man or woman could get close to Pavonis without her knowing, and even the Aradians, though more powerful, would have some difficulty outwitting the intuitive anti-hero.

The assassin crept on. The sun had risen behind the clouds to show a dim blue glow about the grey land. Smoke rose from insect borings and poured across the blackened bark, as if the stump were the mouth to the underworld. She crept slowly up the mound of ash, hesitating each movement until urgency forced motion into her feet. Once at the rim, she lifted her axe to ensure it could not be seen from behind the stump's shallow crest. But as she leapt up to fell the mirror steel blade, a hand reached up and grasped her wrist with a forceful lurch, corrupting her fatal inertia. Bats flew up from the stump in a helix formation and out of that sinful pit rose the beautiful and terrible Goddess, her skin blackened with carbon callous, her dreadlocks woven like a nest of spiteful snakes, her eyes nebulous and glistening blue, pulsing madly as if she had been stewing in a cave of mania for weeks. And she had been. She knocked the assassin to the ground with a sharp kick and held the primitive weapon behind her with her elbow cocked and wrist firm.

The woman lay on her back, coughing up blood that had exploded from inside her chest. Her shawl had unraveled, freeing her long hair which now spread over the ash. Pavonis walked down to her with authoritative footsteps, ready to annihilate her enemy mid-meditation. Inside her eyes, galaxies and star clusters spun, the reflection of everything that is within and around the universe of this and all other dimensions. Pavonis, however, was like so many creatures struggling for basic survival. She was alone, starving, and one of the last of her kind in that sick world. She stared at the assassin with emotionless eyes. The woman crawled to her knees and pulled out a cross linked to a silver necklace, hopelessly aiming for God's protection as the witch Goddess seethed in her woes, she who had been invigorating her Sararan cells in that cavity of embers like some yonic hell beast.

The assassin held up the cross, her hands clasped together in a silent plea for mercy. Her eyes were bulbous and her tears streamed and poured watercolor streaks down her ash-coated face. Pavonis lifted the axe and tilted it, swinging the hatchet as the woman let out half a scream. Ropes of gore followed the bloody crucifix as it flew through the air, the jangling chains muted by the thump of the assassin's head. Only the squirting of blood from the severed neck could be heard, as Pavonis dropped the axe and the headless corpse slowly fell to the ground. The body lay there, arms out and ankles crossed, as if Christ himself knew one day his significance would end without remission.

Pavonis stared into the blank eyes of the head on the ground and realized that it was now her time to lead. But she was no prophet, and she was no shepherd. She was a force of nature and her interjections now became as pure as the Aradians': without favor; without belief; without fraudulent holiness. She was on no one's side in that grand war, for she still praised the mother of all things, Nature herself, the archetype connecting all living things. Pavonis inhaled deeply, then sung a piercing note into the emptiness of the waste, kulning in short antediluvian echo's that carried through the valley, giving her a sonar perspective of the long mountain range. Towards her, through the mist, flew a golden eagle. It landed on the branch and nestled its beak against her cheek.

"The eastern passage is most promising?" Pavonis asked.

The bird screeched and pecked lightly at her arm.

"Thank you, darling. Please, eat," she said to the raptor.

The massive eagle swooped down and began shredding muscle and sinew from the dead woman's neck with its sharp beak. From the thick fog, a bear came hobbling into the clearing, thin and boney from hunger. It flared its nostrils, the smell of hot blood drawing it closer. From the west, a feral mountain lion came, and from the north, a pack of wolves, on and on until dozens of animals surrounded Pavonis, all eager to claim a limb or bone for themselves. The eagle plucked an eye from the assassin's head and chewed through the gooey texture as a light snowfall began to fall on the feast.

"This is just a taste, brothers and sisters," Pavonis said as two wolves growled at one another over a piece of the woman's calf. "There will be plenty to eat soon enough." She turned to the eagle as it swallowed one last piece of gristle. "Finish up and rally the troops, Hermes. I want this army in formation when I present it to my brother tomorrow."

She walked on as a rumbling symphony of hooves, paws, and wings stomped, galloped, and flapped behind her, erasing every memory of the assassin, save the crucifix and axe which Pavonis had left adjacent, so that any who wandered upon them would find those artifacts and guess as to the gesture of their staged orientation. Pavonis knew which symbol she worshipped. She knew its significance was closing in on her like winter barrage. The heave of unstable air walloping behind them would be Pavonis' primary weapon, and would at the very least lend her air force of diving falcons a decent tailwind.

CHAPTER 33
ALL BEINGS BOW LOW

Melody sat in a field on a warm summer's day. A soft breeze sent a waft of fragrant lilac flowers past her nose. It was June, and the flowers were blooming all over the field in mauve bouquets. There was a cabin a short distance away, and she felt an urge to go over to it, until she was suddenly gripped by a strange feeling. She watched the grass bend in the breeze, and the trees cast shadows over the edge of the timberline, turning the world into a theater of color and life beneath the perforated canopy.

"Melody..."

The whisper came from the woods, across the field. She looked behind her, towards the cabin. Michael was working away in the garden, picking radishes and carrots. He looked over at Melody and smiled. Melody smiled in return.

Then she heard the whisper again, coming from the trees. She looked away from Michael and began walking down to the forest's edge, where the wheat field met the ferns and forest, creating a natural boundary. The shadows behind the trees called out to her and she followed, as if entranced.

"I'm going to have the harvest ready soon Mel! Melody? Where are you going?" Michael called.

When Melody stepped into the shadows, she saw butterflies chasing one another and squirrels playing hide and seek. Nothing seemed out of the ordinary. Then, she heard the voice again, right beside her ear. Melody turned around to see Pavonis, lying in the grass, sick, disgusting, and pale. Melody screamed.

"You did this!" Pavonis said, her infected purple veins pulsing on her neck, her eyes like a dead snake's woeful lenses, cataract white with chasms of hatred sinking through their cold central slits.

"No!" Melody choked, stammering.

"Michael! She's poisoned me!" Pavonis yelled.

Melody shrieked and ran into the woods, but everything became blurry and faded as she ran. She suddenly did not know who she was or what she was doing.

"Melody, you did this?" a voice said as Melody

stirred awake.

"What!? No!" Melody gasped, sitting up and looking around. She was in a tent in the Marine camp. She looked at Will, who had come to wake her.

"This, whatever you call it," Will said, holding up a piece of paper covered with intricate writing. "You did this?"

The words from the dream echoed through Melody's mind.

"Yes, I did. It's Arabic calligraphy," Melody said, wiping her eyes and sighing.

He looked at her for a moment. Melody breathed and looked back at him, wondering what he was thinking.

"It's very beautiful. I appreciate your talents. I understand that Pavonis has been training you?"

"If you can even call it training. I'm not sure what she's teaching me sometimes. I understand the application but...why witchcraft? It seems like she's relying on elusive energies."

"You haven't seen half of what she's capable of, Melody."

"I know, but I just don't know if she's going about it the right way. Sometimes, she frightens me. She's spontaneous."

"Maybe you should take counsel with her then,"

Will said.

Just then, Pavonis walked into the tent in full battle dress. Her long dreadlocks were woven and wrapped in a crown of thorns and leaves.

"Pavonis! You're back!" Melody smiled, relived, and sat up straight, slightly on edge.

"Did you have doubt?" Pavonis asked, as David ran in and hugged her leg. "Hello button!" Pavonis cooed, looking lovingly down at David.

David smiled and blew a kiss to Melody. Melody waved good morning to the mute child.

"Will, would you take David, and prepare the other officers for briefing?" Pavonis asked.

"Yes, ma'am," Will replied, picking up David. They played airplane on the way out, and David laughed brightly as Will made engine sounds and swung the child through the air.

Pavonis closed the tent flap and sat down, across from Melody. She picked up an aluminum cup and filled it with water from a pitcher on the table.

"How are you?" Pavonis asked Melody.

"I'm good," Melody said.

"You're sick, Melody," Pavonis said, cracking a smile and tilting her brow.

"I'll be okay."

"Of course you will, dear. But we cannot afford

for any of the Marines to be taken ill before battle. You had a night terror as well, didn't you?"

"How did you know?"

Pavonis held the cup for a moment and heated it with her fingers. The water boiled slightly in her hand. She pulled out some herbs from her leather pouch on her hip and crushed them into a powder, before lightly dusting the water. She stirred in the herbs by tilting the cup slightly and rotating it.

"I was in the dream, Melody. That was a reality for both of us."

"But...how? Why?"

"We will both find out in due time, I suppose. All I can say is that I'm sorry, and I hope you can forgive me someday."

"I...already do?"

Pavonis laughed. "Not for that."

She took a small bottle from her pouch and poured its contents into the teacup, handing the cup to Melody.

"What's this?"

"Herbal tea and brandy. It's good for your lungs."

Melody took a sip and grimaced.

Pavonis laughed. "I didn't make it for the taste. You want to be healthy, don't you?"

"I think I'd rather croak!"

Pavonis rose and came to stand behind her. "Okay, head down," she said, as Melody bent over. Pavonis placed her hand on the back of Melody's neck for a few moments.

"Ouch!" Melody yelped, as Pavonis pulled her hand away. "Don't you have the power to make it not sting?"

"What do you mean, I didn't feel a thing!" Pavonis said, grinning.

"Thank you," Melody said, rubbing her neck where Pavonis had uprooted and expelled the virus, enslaving the sickness into her own cellular memory.

"Thank you, as well. That's a new organism to add to my collection."

"How many species have you copied into your DNA?"

"Over fifty thousand," Pavonis said, as she began to sew Melody's ripped clothing. "I've genetically archived everything, from mint leaf to Covid-19."

"What about animals?"

"That requires a host. I spread spores and seeds; creatures that can stand on their own do so without my intervention. I'm a fertilizer, not a filter. To me, directly modifying complex organisms is an immoral practice, which ironically is what I am."

"Then you and the Queen aren't so different,"

Melody said, half embarrassed that she had voiced the words aloud.

"You're partially right. The Queen is my opposite. Her obsession with the prophecy has turned the world into a churning swath of death, as she tries to strive towards what she perceives to be the answer to sustaining a utopian future for this planet."

"A process of elimination. She's finding the least common denominator," Melody said.

"Exactly. Which makes one wonder why we're alive and so is Sandraudiga. The Aradians have suffered beyond what I can imagine and have become masters of the atom itself. Because of my deep understanding of Earth's organisms, I am very close to understanding their abilities, and I believe after discovering this secret, I shall be far more powerful than any Aradian."

Melody shivered as Pavonis' voice turned cold.

"Where have you been, Pavonis?" she asked. "You've been gone weeks. We missed you."

"I've been recruiting, and charging my cells where I can find sunlight or moonlight. Both are rare this time of year."

"Then why are you planning this advancement? Are you prepared?"

"I spent the last few days charging my cells,

which is why it took me so long to return here, but everything will time perfectly. There is a storm from the north gathering. It's going to hit us tonight. But it's just a squall compared to the one behind it. A swell is coming in from the east: ocean wind currents mixed with a Siberian front from the north."

"You're going to try and harness it?"

"Yes. You, my dear, are going to lure it in and grant me its power so I can harness it."

"Wait...what? Why me?"

"Because you have the gift of song. You have a beautiful voice, you harmonize the pitches I give you, and you heed your astrological identity. You have been listening to my teachings and it shows. You have a talent for this. Did your calligraphy spell work?"

"Yeah, but Will asked me about it, which is weird," Melody said, itching her arm.

"It's only supposed to mildly allure. It could lure one who seeks friendship, or an even fainter form of relationship. Trust me, I wouldn't want one of these crusty bastards advancing on you in my absence."

"I really think Will wants to be in love with someone, though," Melody said.

"Everyone wants to be in love with someone, Melody. Those of us who are lucky enough to know what that feels like need to cherish that gift forever, even if it's just a memory."

Melody nodded, feeling a deep anxiety as she thought of Michael. "So, what's the next step in your plan?"

"This will be our last night in this camp. We're going to drink. We're going to sing songs. And we're going to give praise to this amazing life we have been given the chance to live. In the late morning, we will begin our journey south, hopefully arriving in Banff in two days' time. There, Sandraudiga will be awaiting our surprise attack."

"Then it's not really a surprise, is it?"

"The timing isn't the surprise."

After a small breakfast, Pavonis and Melody walked out of the tent. Pavonis' hilt clanged, the branched guard an amalgamation of charms, gold earrings, and military pendants, acquired from the Queen's high commanders and assassins that Pavonis had killed, welded with other silver relics. Her Persian style blade was the sharpest of all in their ranks, and contained gyroscopic mechanics built into a hollow mammoth bone handle, where two hematite spheres moved to the whim of Pavonis' iron blood. She had attached an amber pommel to instill fear in her combatants, for the fossilized resin was believed by many to contain the soul of a tiger.

Pavonis spoke loudly as her pace increased. "Are you comfortable around large animals, Melody?"

"I guess so. I like horses."

As they walked, Melody looked over to see a man straddling a buffalo. The beast snorted and groaned, steam puffing out of its nostrils like dragon's smoke. She stared for a moment before catching back up with Pavonis, who expounded on their new army.

"I have two squadrons of Kodiak bears and a half brigade of wolves. I have a regiment of bison ready to be utilized as cavalry, and I have a brigade of Big Horn sheep, mountain goats, and elk all getting their antlers and horns sharpened as we speak. You, Melody, will be assisting with air support, as the fleet of falcons and eagles will need their munitions re-supplied from a viewpoint above the battle. Someone will brief you and David on explosives this afternoon."

"Explosives!? But David is just a child!"

"Exactly. Those small hands. He's perfect for the job."

They walked by some mountain goats eating grass as they waited in a line patiently to have their horns filed by the blacksmith.

Pavonis went on. "I have Kamikaze hares, willing to do their duty for their Mother, field-engineer moles and mice, starling spies, and diseased coyotes."

"Why don't you heal the poor coyotes?"

"They'll be more affective as biological weapons."

Melody stared at Pavonis and shook her head fiercely in denial.

"Like it or not, Melody, I've found a way to turn nature's seemingly inferior creatures into an army of tactical beasts, each using their natural talents for the cause."

"But how? Did you give them the power of mutation?" Melody asked.

"No. I just listened. Everything was already understood in terms of current events. They're more in tune with the Earth than we are, Melody. It's been a combination of time and consistent loyalty that have made the animals of The Americas my formal allies. The last polar bear on Earth is here: a sow who lost her mate to humans not long after she lost her cubs to nature's whim. I have expressed my reluctance at her involvement, but she is well aware of her imminent extinction, and will fight with or without my consent. She will honor the legacy of her species by joining the others in battle."

They walked to the edge of the mountain's saddle and looked down into the valley below. Herds of bison, antlered elk, and deer grazed. Animals of all shapes, sizes, and colors gathered around the Marines, who were pouring hundreds of pounds of grain onto the field for the hungry animals. A few bears chewed on the remains of an elk calf who had not made the long journey. But the elk standing nearby did not seem too worried. No animal showed any animosity towards its companions in that odd camaraderie of fur and feathers. Even the Marines were beginning to feel at ease around Canada's remaining wildlife. A real union could be felt, as the men were each assigned to a bison.

After viewing the animal army, Melody and Pavonis sat down near a fire in the center of camp, away from the animals. They ate a second breakfast of pheasant eggs and raccoon meat, so as not to offend the various phylum, and Melody finished off some chokecherry jelly and a bread roll. They had managed to make the bread from stolen ingredients, acquired from enemy troops by a Marine scout patrol. It was the first time any of them had eaten bread in years, and the process of turning the flour into scrumptious rolls, and the grain into spruce tip flavored beer made with the high mountain creek water, had felt like a sacred act.

Just as Melody was finishing her meal, she looked up and saw a massive black bear lumbering towards her. She stood quickly and stared at the

343

creature. "Pavonis," she whispered, her eyes still fixed on the bear. "What do I do..."

Pavonis smiled. "You're fine, Melody. Just relax."

The bear was right in front of Melody now. Instinctively, she dropped the last of her bread and jelly into the great beast's mouth. The bear sat down on its rump and began licking the jelly off its lips. Pavonis chuckled, and Melody began to laugh too as the bear started licking her hand.

"I think you've found yourself a companion," Pavonis said.

"Or he found me!" Melody said, giggling as the bear scooted over and nudged her with his neck. "I'll name you Beau," she said, looking into the bear's curious eyes.

That night, a massive bonfire was built. The beetle-decimated trees lit up like dry tinder and flakes of birch and moss rose into the air, swirling around the stars like a mutiny in heaven. The Marines passed around the last few bottles of moonshine. Melody managed a swig but refrained from more; she held great disdain for the wicked drink, and one could understand why. The Marines cursed and yelled, beat each other, and chuckled loudly with beards full of grog. On the last round, they held a fiery swig in their mouths, trying to refrain from laughing as the liquid burned their tongues until the last man had taken his swig. Then they spat into the bonfire and yelled 'oorah' one last time as the pink alcoholic plume rose and forced back their long beards. The last of the food rations were presented and shared amongst man and animal alike. All cherished the experience, for they knew the march to Caldera would be the last engagement in the history of the Marines. They were tired of running and hiding; sick of fighting for scraps and digging themselves into the dirt under rainy fortresses; sick of burying their brothers in the tundra in the wake of their battles, knowing none of it would ever end. Pavonis knew the time had come. The Queen's inability to maintain control relied on the instability of her deteriorating cabinet. Wherever the Aradians were, they were surely preparing for their own version of the war's conclusion. Whether these conclusions intersected or aligned, only time would tell. The Queen relied on the prophecy. Pavonis relied on the Aradians. Everyone relied on the sun, and no matter the outcome, they all knew the first sunrise of spring would give enough power to someone to end the war once and for all.

Later, Melody sat by a smaller campfire, away from the crowd of drunken Marines. David and Beau slept by her feet, David's soft cheeks glowing in the dancing orange light as the large bear snuggled close, keeping him warm. Pavonis appeared suddenly from the shadows and knelt opposite Melody.

"Melody, have I ever told you about the left hand path?"

"No, I don't think so," Melody said, resting her hand on Beau's head.

"When one draws a bow, assuming one is right hand dominant, the left hand is the anchor and the guide. The right hand commits the act. One needs both for the bow to release the arrow. Without the sturdiness of the left hand, the right could not resist and pull itself into a draw. Without the deliberation of the right hand, the left would wander out of alignment, jilted with fatigue. They complement each other in an effective way, and yet require opposition. The left hand symbolizes the female power: balance, strength, and stability. A oneness with the Earth, and a root that grows deep. A nurturing power. The right hand symbolizes the masculine, the decisive and the timely essence of separation and delineation, of both fatal precision and the planting of seeds. We are women, Melody. We represent the garden of life. But that does not mean you have to be a mother. You can be the right hand and represent the change needed in this world."

"And what of the arrow? That which is the vessel for all change to occur?"

Pavonis smiled. "Perhaps your voice is just that, an arrow splitting and reuniting consciousness."

"If it were, I could only perform such accomplishments with guidance from you."

"It's already happening, my blossoming apprentice." Pavonis reached her hand over the fire, and Melody stood up,."I give you the power of the rain, the wind, and the Earth, and the strength to push fire into the heavens."

Melody touched Pavonis' hand and felt a small shock run through her body. "What was that?"

"I cast a spell that made you become a transceiver of atmospheric pressures. Together, we can break apart cyclones, combine them, or alter their path. It is a challenging skill to master, and it will take years before you can perform with accurate results."

"Won't the Aradians sense such a thing?"

"Rumors of our recent victories have surely reached both human and Aradian alike. I don't mean to frighten you, Melody, but one of them is watching us right now. They are like Gods to us, remember, so it doesn't help to worry over their actions. They are beyond us. And perhaps, if they are divine creatures, they know what is best for the planet after all. I just hope they believe in resurrecting the beauty still within this world, beyond our misfortunes."

Melody shook her head. "So, any one of those blue stars could be one of those death machines blinking at me? One of those monsters who killed Lily and billions of other innocent people? That is no just God!"

"Some of those are also satellites, the same machines that some governments used for warfare at the beginning of this century. This is a much more complicated affair than it seems on the surface, Melody. We lived in a world full of shifty technocrats. Now there are just two. And if you can believe it, Lily died so Michael could live. It was unknown to our enemies that you would follow him, and it is a wild and beautiful coincidence that I found you as well. You've become a key factor in the development of this so-called prophecy, Melody. Just know that I love you and will do everything I can to take care of you and David. Get some sleep and dream of my sweet prince. We are marching to Banff tomorrow."

A great brass gong echoed through the valley of Banff. Small snowflakes fell like rejected angels in patient descent to the sepia fauna below, covering the shattered pieces of what was once the Trans-Canadian Highway. The sky swirled in a sea of grey, severing the snowy alpine peaks with an unsettling mist, and called back to the mighty gong with an icy whisper. In the center of the valley lay a draw where the river had once run free, filled with rotting logs which had been coagulated in the last spring run, more than a decade ago. A grassy field spread in either direction, towards the looming tree line darkness separating the mountain's cloak from the rest of the landscape. There were no humans or animals to be seen. Yet, somewhere behind the forest's natural barriers, Sandraudiga's personal elite army of female Zurvan warriors were hidden, nestled beneath the tundra or tucked into granite crevices like thieves, their bone-weapons clenched in their teeth and their claws sharpened, ready for the frenzy.

Another splash from the gong reverberated through the windless canyon. There was no bird chatter; no rustling of animals in the undergrowth; no sound but the deep metallic toll. On the southern slope, where the trees met their end and gave way to the starved grass, a figure emerged. A cape rose lightly from the black-armored shade, whose rams-head helmet could be mistaken for no other. The lone woman looked into the valley clearing with piercing blue eyes. She spat onto the ground, the platinum chain connecting the tips of her ramshorn curls jangling in the still air. Tilting her neck slightly, she adjusted her headpiece. Then, with a small axe in each hand, tied tightly to her wrists with leather straps, she held up her arms and screamed.

"Show yourself, beast!!"

She stood impatiently, waiting for something to appear on the other side of the valley. Nothing. The snow began to fall harder. A sudden wind tugged at the tops of the trees and whipped the lone figure's cape into a spiral of fabric.

High above, on the other side of the canyon, Melody knelt on a large flat stone, watching Sandraudiga yell into the nothingness. Melody closed her eyes for a moment as another gong hit blared behind her. Will had struck the large plate one last time before crouching low to the snowy forest floor. He knelt in the accumulation and began wrapping the tsuka of his katana with a leather braid. He looked to Melody, neither smiling nor frowning, yet something in his eyes offered her some of his courage, for she too was now integrated into their militia and would soon be wrought in that plain of violence, and if not fragmented or flayed, she too would enter the sainthood in the halls of divine madness.

Melody's face was painted with red streaks, and she had braided her hair in rows, interwoven with bullet casings and bird bones. She wore the light leather armor Pavonis had sewn her, and her arms were dyed red up to her elbows. She reached out her hand and dropped an obsidian pendulum from within her palm, catching the length of the chain such that the pendulum was suspended in the air like a hanged man. It spun around the flickering candles protruding from the center of the fiery pentagram. Melody focused her energy southward. Crystals of various sizes and colors held down six tarot cards near the bottom of the last candle. The first card was the Queen of Wands, symbolizing loyalty, held down by an emerald stone. The second card was the King of Swords, symbolizing courage and resistance, held down by jasper. The third card was the Ace of Swords, symbolizing decision-making, held down by labradorite. The fourth card was the Nine of Swords, symbolizing pain and suffering, held down by a shard of iron pyrite. The fifth card was Death, symbolizing change and loss, held down by onyx. The sixth and final card was the Two of Chalices, symbolizing love and union, held down by the malachite, the stone of metaphysical transformation.

Pavonis remained behind her apprentice, dressed in white armor, sitting astride a strong necked caribou. The caribou's antlers had been sharpened and painted black; its face adorned with a steel mask, like some demonic Nordic stag. She nodded for Melody to begin.

Melody took one more deep breath and began her spell. Her voice echoed out with such sublime clarity that it pierced the static air and cut its way into Sandraudiga's ears and nerves.

> *White death from the North,*
> *Beyond the spine of this dying world*
> *Turning ever towards the Light,*
> *Heed our suffering and coldness.*
> *Fill your relentless winds in this void.*
> *Spare no beating heart,*
> *Grant this power to Pavonis.*
> *Unconcealed, she becomes a constellation of dread.*
> *Drown the wicked in snow.*

Pavonis tipped her head back and drank the snowflakes with unflinching eyes, as that prism of articulated ice crystals graced her view with meandering beams of light dripping from the heavens. She looked back down at the futile Lord and held her sword high.

"Creatures of Earth! We shall sew the seed of

tomorrow's forests with human blood today. Feast and kill. Show no mercy to this sage of wretchedness. Attack!"

Pavonis charged straight down the steep hillside, the eyes of her caribou steed burning with a passion for vengeance. Ravens' caws and wolves' howls joined the uproar as the bestial army made its way to the valley's center. Sandraudiga stood smirking, amused by the silhouettes of grey and brown fur darting between the distant trees shade. She held her axes up and called to her troops.

"Hold your positions and wait for my command!"

Just then, the General looked up and saw a line of falcons diving straight towards her from high altitude. The direction seemed affixed, yet their form dilated with each passing second.

"Shields up!" she yelled as she walked backwards slowly, hiding herself behind a tree's base. The falcons threw out their wings just before hitting the top of the evergreen canopy and dropped their arsenal in a grid like pattern: two grenades per bird, with fifty of them in a fleet, each fleet following in quick succession. A ripple of sound as explosions hit the mountainside followed the first wave. After the first fleet of falcons descended with their explosives, the larger eagle fleets came diving down behind them, carrying heavy napalm canisters. The entire mountain popped and burst; trees snapped, and chaos sparked in the Lord's ranks. Owls flew high above the other raptors, acting as tactical air control as they positioned themselves to indicate where enemy concentrations lay.

The bombing had a devastating effect on the enemy: the Zurvan soldiers screamed, releasing arrows into the air in a futile attempt to hit the birds; a fire started on a dry portion of the slope, and the assault caused Sandraudiga's troops to split ranks in the haze of wooden shrapnel and smoke.

Sandraudiga yelled above the myriad of explosions hitting all around her. "Charge! Now! CHARGE!!"

The army of grey-armored women poured onto the field, but Sandraudiga stayed hidden in the shadows, watching. Her troops sprinted towards the valley's center as Pavonis' army leapt onto the field from the other side. First came the Marines, riding atop the bison, stampeding behind their fearless leader; Pavonis rode her caribou without regard for the whistling arrows that flew past her cheeks and brow. The bears followed, hungry and enraged by food deprivation, caused by the Zurvan takeover. Then the lions, wolves, elk, and other animals marched out, ready to face the enemy with viciousness. Bombs planted by the moles the night before exploded, and the bodies of the Zurvan soldiers flew into the air. Some had yet to hit the ground before the bison made their first impact against the sword-swinging women.

The storm picked up the moment the two forces clashed. Bison hooves crushed the bones of the Zurvan women as the Calderan archers focused command fire on one human mounted beast at a time. As the horned beasts gored and crushed the enemy soldiers by the dozens, the wolves and cougars methodically chose their kills and gained strength with each bite of muscle they devoured. Gadreel swung his mace from atop his bison, crushing enemy troops with single blows and blocking arrows and poison darts with his large shield. Will held out his katana from his bison's perch, scalping women whose long hair flared like flowers of death before they were trampled into the field's soft soil. Will commanded his men to retreat then flanked the Zurvan's unsuspecting forces, luring more of the enemy out onto the battlefield so the raptors could identify their targets. The polar bear sow raged through the battle, a monstrosity of white death, her lips and face and paws stained red with blood as she smashed through the women's blockade and frayed their soft flesh with her claws.

Melody watched from above as the blizzard forced a fierce wind through the valley, making it difficult for the birds to maintain their course. She saw Pavonis spinning across the battlefield like a cyclone of death; a small tornado, casting ice crystals from her body, the entranced state given to her by Melody's spell making her one with the storm. Melody shuddered at the violence unfolding before her.

"Here comes the next fleet, David," she said with resignation, as David's head popped out of a thick coat. He ran over to the explosives box and carefully wheeled it over. The eagles and other raptors returned and perched on a branch for reloading. Melody and David quickly and carefully tied the napalm to the legs of the birds. When she arrived at one of the hawks, the bird's face was bloody, its beak was chipped, and its left eye had been blackened by fire. The bird's left wing had been torched as well, and its feathers ruffled and damaged.

"You poor thing. You're not going anywhere," Melody said soothingly, petting the large bird. It pecked at her and squawked defiantly. After Melody refused to tie the explosives to its leg, it leapt from its perch and flew high into the turbulent sky. Melody and David watched the hawk as it tucked its wings in tightly and fell, aiming its velocity at the battle below and using the strong winds to guide it. The hawk accelerated faster and faster until it hit its target, driving its beak and body into the skull of an enemy officer, killing itself and the human instantly. Melody shivered as she watched the eagles fly off for another bombing. Fewer and fewer birds were coming back. The battle was vast and brutal, but she and David felt safe at that distance, especially with Beau and two other Kodiak bears lying beside them for security.

Sandraudiga entered the fight, swinging her axes and killing two Marines who had their backs to her. She smiled and kept on. A wolf approached her, and she kicked it in the mouth, chopping it between the eyes. Two mountain lions latched onto her back and pulled her to the ground, but she cut them too, and rose with blood dripping from her trapezius muscles like a dishonored angel.

"Where is the demon bitch!?" Sandraudiga screamed. But Pavonis was on the other side of the battlefield. The Goddess had been fighting fiercely, but unbeknownst to Sandraudiga's army, she was only just getting started. Pavonis clenched the wind with a mere thought and spun around in a whirlwind of carnage, slicing her enemies with her sword as they were swept up inside her devastating cyclone of ice.

Closer to her was Cassidy, the tall, equally frightening, Nordic counterpart to herself. Cassidy's bison had been slain, and he stood in the middle of an enemy squad, splitting their bodies with an axe and growling with hateful vigor. Sandraudiga walked up quickly, and the Marine charged her.

"Let's go, hag!" he yelled.

She blocked his hit by crossing her axes and easily deflected him, pushing him off to the side. As Cassidy raised his weapon, an arrow suddenly plunged through his neck. He fell to his knees and choked for breath as his lungs filled with blood.

Sandraudiga came up behind him and whispered menacingly in his ear. "Look what is happening, you fool. You've lost the battle. Let this be the last thing you see: the end of your so-called 'proud' Marines!"

She pulled his head up so he could view the scene and Cassidy gasped, gargling blood as he took stock of the battle before him. One of the Marines was puking blood as four women stabbed him with broken arrows. The enemy combatants stomped on the injured animals, and he could see more of his men dead than alive. Just as Sandraudiga pulled the arrow from his throat, Cassidy reached over and cut her Achilles tendon with his knife. In those final moments of Bruce Alva Cassidy's life, he smiled and kissed the ground, listening to Sandraudiga's screams like a grave lullaby. Wounded badly, the furious Lord stepped around the polar bear sow, who lay lifeless on the pink ground, perforated with arrows, the creature's once white fur red and sticky with blood. Gadreel knelt with several arrows in his back, using every bit of strength left to erect his posture, unwilling to die before witnessing victory by his men. Sandraudiga lunged towards him and swung her axes, beheading him, before limping into the wall of snow and wind.

Melody tended to the raptors' wounds while they all waited for the winds to subside. Down below, a murmur of tortured, angry souls could be heard, their bodies hidden behind the veil of snowfall.

"Have I done something terrible?" Melody asked herself, her fingers tingling with a strange sensation. She was now convinced that practiced divination was not only real, but also dangerously accurate when executed correctly. The spell she had cast was the most powerful she had ever conjured, and though the energy had been bestowed to Pavonis, Melody could not help but harmonize with her master.

Pavonis stopped spinning, her tornado of death disappearing for a moment. A trail of severed limbs and halved torsos lay behind her. The air grew colder; the snowflakes thinner, becoming small missiles of ice that stung the battle torn faces of the soldiers. She saw bison lying dead, and wounded Marines attempting to regroup, having been outnumbered by Sandraudiga's reinforcements. Will tried to redirect his forces, but he was chased back into the trees by one of the women's contingents. Most of the animals had been slain, and a victory for the Lord was in sight. Pavonis growled, her face splattered with small crimson droplets; her eyes pulsing blue quasars. She saw the enemy Lord limping towards her, surrounded by several, tall, elite warriors. The wind whipped at Sandraudiga's cape, and she held her axes high.

"Gaze upon your Lord, beast!" she yelled at Pavonis.

As the first warrior lunged at her, Pavonis dropped to one knee and screamed against the ground, sending an ear-splitting cry into the warrior's ears, before jumping up with the speed and grace of a gazelle. She swung down and split one of the woman's heads, her sword dipping against her upward motion. In quick succession, she circled Sandraudiga and muted the lives of the elite fighters, beckoning the wind this way and that so that none could launch an arrow at her. After a few seconds of Pavonis' dizzying performance, Sandraudiga found herself staring down Pavonis' outstretched blade with a ring of dead bodies spread about her.

"Even if you kill me, you cannot kill the Queen. There is no elixir for what you seek!" Sandraudiga said, attempting to hide her fear. She dropped her axes in submission.

"*Your head* is the elixir," Pavonis stated as she kicked the woman onto her stomach. Sandraudiga cried out, her tears falling onto the blood-stained snow. In slow motion, Pavonis placed one foot on

Sandraudiga's shoulder blade and sunk her fingers into the woman's flesh, ripping out her spine like a stick being pulled from wet, woven grass. Blood and gristle dripped from the white bones as she held the piece like a rare trophy, the woman's face half shredded, still attached to the grim headpiece she had worn for so many years during her diabolical campaign. Pavonis held up the bloody head and screamed louder than she had ever propelled her voice, more so than on the day of her husband's death, when all the trees had bowed to their new leader. Her vocal cords vibrated to the point of breaking the sound barrier and suddenly the blizzard grew tenfold. It came as a falling planet, knocking down the remaining fighters and throwing man, woman, and beast against the trees. Icicles pelted the ground like bullets and Pavonis welcomed the pain of their cuts, her masochistic state of power and rage taking over her senses. She levitated in the frosty gale, unleashing the storm with a force that halved trees and buried the damned. The dead froze in the growing snowdrift. Pavonis stared into the screaming wind. She summoned it to be greater and greater, until even she could barely take its fusillade.

High on the mountain top, Beau and the other Kodiak bears surrounded the children. At first, Melody and David screamed with fright, but then they realized the bears were coming to warm them, forming a protective fort of thick fur around the children as they all waited for the storm to pass. Melody could see through a small hole above the leaning beasts, and eventually, the sky began to clear, the storm suddenly mellowing.

Pavonis felt the wind subside as the clouds parted, the dark blue masses of gas moving aside to reveal a stream of pure, white light surging through. Pavonis gasped as Tala appeared, bright and luminescent; holy as God herself; shining like the sun above that frozen scrape of Earth. The Aradian hovered for several seconds, the remaining snowflakes falling upward in an anti-gravitational manner. Tala stared down at Pavonis, and she stared back at the Aradian.

Suddenly, Pavonis heard Tala's voice in her mind. "You aren't as alone as you think you are. Trust your cause, Pavonis. Seek the treasure we all seek."

"But how?" Pavonis whispered.

"You already know. Heed my sister's word."

The brightness disappeared, and the storm returned, this time with hurricane force winds that Pavonis struggled to endure, the shreds of her white gown beneath her armor whipping like the blizzard itself. Her hair pulled at her scalp and the beads and bones in her dreadlocks snapped off into oblivion. The gale shrieked and pulverized the Earth, pulling trees from their roots and throwing them, stabbing or crushing the half-frozen survivors and those buried in the slanted, arsenic-white drifts that shifted like dunes. Soon, nothing was left alive. The storm seemed to have no end and no mercy. Melody and David fell fast asleep in their nest of resting bears, and when Pavonis finally dismounted herself from her invisible podium, all life lay frozen, dead in the drifts of snow. She walked back to the tree line as the storm wailed on. Somewhere, high on the cliffs, the owls had been buried too by the storm, their bones forever entombed there as jewels in the continent's crown.

The shrill sound of a grindstone against a dull blade awakened Melody the next morning. The resounding scraping ting made her wince with fright. Each burr on the blade had formed from severed bones and crushed skulls. Each burr meant a victory. Each burr meant a terrible sacrifice, yet Pavonis was as calm as the breath that escaped her heart shaped lips. The deadly goddess sat on a stump, still in full battle dress, sharpening her sword and humming a Celtic tune beside the warming fire she had made.

Melody walked towards the fire, wishing the day before had all been a nightmare. Tracks from the bears leading away from camp showed they had already left to rest in their dens for the remainder of winter.

A faint whisper of wind came from the north as she approached the soft morning flame. David ran almost gleefully from underneath Pavonis' cloak and over to Melody, while Pavonis continued to shed sparks onto the frozen ground.

"Thanks, David," Melody said, taking a seat by the fire as the young boy threw a blanket over her. David smiled and patted her on the head before plopping down into her lap.

"Why does David not suffer such trauma as I do?" Melody asked quietly.

"He is an interesting boy, isn't he? Amidst complete wreckage his spirits somehow stay high. He is, though, too young to understand what has happened, I suppose," Pavonis said. "I'll admit that even I was not prepared for yesterday's unravelling."

Melody's fists tightened as she stared into the fire.

"How could you take the lives of all those good men and poor animals just so that you could win the battle?"

Pavonis took a long breath, the steam from her nostrils forming white crystalline clouds of hexagonal prisms, which dissipated in the cold dry air.

"They were not completely wiped out. One remains. Will retreated near the end of the battle. He knew not to trust that I would ever put a cap on a spell like that. He was right to leave. When the Aradian came upon us, she amplified the spell to devastating levels. I'm convinced she's gone rogue, like her sister," she said, as she gripped the blade with her blood-stained hand. She passed Melody a cup of hot tea.

"What is this?" Melody asked.

"Pine tea," Pavonis said.

"Pine tea!" David shouted, dropping some blue spruce tips into his tea and stirring it with a bone he had plucked from the battlefield floor.

"D...David, don't use that, David!" Melody said, her shock at hearing the child's voice making her stutter.

"It's fine, Melody," Pavonis said. "He needs the marrow. And he knows it. He is a remarkable child."

David continued to stir his hot water with the shattered rib bone.

Pavonis set the blade and grindstone down, her shimmering sword as brilliant as a shard of platinum. She took a deep breath before speaking.

"The Marines would have followed me to Caldera and beyond. But their end was written in the stars, as are all things. Had I not done what I did, we would have lost the battle anyway, and the Grey Army would have been victorious."

"Do you believe you're evil too, for doing what you did?" Melody asked.

"Monsters are created to defeat monsters, that is Nature's way, and Homeland Security's come to think of it. All humans have good in them, but they also harbor something odious, and the good and the bad tend to overlap schizophrenically. Plants and animals were always easier to understand for me."

"Aren't humans animals?"

"They were. Ten thousand years ago, they turned their heads towards the sun-bathed fields and decided to farm that golden crop to its very end. They didn't realize there was no going back. Gradually, more fields meant more workers; more workers meant more food; more food meant larger

367

fields. Larger fields meant security. Which brought territorial challenges. War. Empires. And this defamation has come to back to haunt us. I want to believe there are people who are capable of understanding the concept of a balanced Earth, but also understanding doctrines that must be desecrated in order to move forward. Humans have forgotten the myths, the stories of who and what they are."

"And what are we, Pavonis?"

"Half beast, half God. Those who claim divinity go to war with the those who seek to destroy it. We currently stand at the pinnacle of this crusade."

"But we're barely standing," Melody said, shivering.

"Yet we are still standing. There will always be conflict, Melody. Even a self-critical thought is a simple but powerful force of opposing notions pulling at you. Don't be afraid to listen and make a sound judgment. The beast-thought may come adorned in gold lace, civilized, and masked. Be prepared to dismiss it, for in all likelihood it is not your true subconscious, but an animal instinct left over from your ape ancestors, telling you to survive."

"Then what is the God-thought telling me?"

"To die. Die and be reborn. As many times as it takes to ascend into your true self. Time itself, when given expanse, draws the fate of all things, man or God. When Ingrid died, Pavonis came to be. After Pavonis? None can say."

"Do you believe in a heaven?"

"I used to," Pavonis said, almost choking up for a moment. A single bloody tear fell down her cheek, her face half lit by the sun emerging from behind the thin clouds. Her tear absorbed back into her skin as she took another deep breath and turned to Melody.

David passed another cup of tea to Melody, who sipped it with great thirst, burning her tongue before spitting out the liquid in disgust. David laughed.

Pavonis continued as she stared at her apprentice. "True victory for the cause, Melody, comes from relentless dedication to our planet's balance amidst confusion, chaos, and impurity. Only through complete dedication can you defeat your foe, because human's reach their breaking point long before Sararans do."

"What about Aradians?" Melody asked.

"Their clairvoyance will be the death of them, at least in their current form. Anyone who can see the future but not control its outcome would surely go mad."

A long silence ensued. The sun poked out from the high cumulous over the eastern horizon and a fragmented black line appeared on its meridian, severing its waxing glow.

"What's that?" Melody asked.

"Birds. Thousands of them, ravens and crows mostly, drawn by the stench of the carcasses. They fly in a V to mimic geese. They'll be here in an hour or so." Pavonis continued in a soft, relaxed tone, unphased by the oncoming swarm of ravenous creatures. "Our sun gives us light and rakes our faces with warmth, and yet it is a constantly combusting ball of fire with radiation explosions ten thousand miles wide. Only through distance can you know that kind of love. Any closer and it would kill everything. Any farther and the cold you feel now would be every day of every year until all life went away. We haven't seen the sun in a while, have we, Melody? But the light will return. You feel pain, as do I, excruciatingly so. But the light will return to us, in time, reflecting the colors you've forgotten, the smells you could praise. For now, darkness has its own reflection. Inside of nothingness, you can learn to know yourself. There are symbiotic partnerships devoted to your existence, fungi, bacteria, and other lifeforms, working together on the complex biological interface that is your human body, dispersing only after your spirit has left its shell. Where your soul ultimately gravitates, no one can know for sure. But what remains are the stories you left behind. True immortality has nothing to do with keeping your cells and membranes bound together for eternity. It is won through legacy; through the memories of each generation, as they praise you for gifting the world with your explosive love. If the Aradians were in fact a product of Shakti's cheating science and created solely for violent intent, they would have killed me a long time ago. At the same time, I cannot predict their motions. Admittedly, they are far more powerful than I am. But it does not matter whether we are Sararan, Aradian, or human. Nothing lasts in this universe. For now, focus on the fact that you are what the cosmos has engineered, to rise above the natural cycle and complete it."

"But how do I do that?"

Pavonis pointed the blade over the fire at Melody's face and said, "Look at your hands."

Melody did so.

"Now take off your gloves."

She took them off.

"See them shiver? They are not so cold that they have gone faint. Can they operate?"

"Yes."

"Can they learn?"

"Yes."

"Can they do good?"

"Yes."

Pavonis flipped the sword around her wrist and

stabbed the blade into the ground. She walked around the fire slowly then knelt beside her apprentice. She held Melody's hands in hers and went on softly.

"Create, Melody. Build. Build life and burn. Feel the cycles of the seasons waft over your face a thousand times a minute. Feel the stars cast their ancient light. Pull in their warmth with the magnetism of a red giant. Feel the essence of Mother Nature pulse through your perfect veins."

Melody tried to smile as Pavonis stared at her with her intense celestial eyes, still possessed by the spell Melody had conjured the day before. She feared Pavonis would never return to her version of reality.

With her eyes still locked on Melody's, Pavonis walked back around the fire before continuing. "One night, you will see one of those diamonds in the sky disappear from that endless abyss. It will blink one last time then disappear forever. That light can never be replaced. But..."

Pavonis blew on the fire. David screamed and giggled with excitement as the fire fluttered its way towards him. Melody could not help but laugh a little.

"...it can be rekindled. See, we are like those stars. Sometimes, all you need is for a slight wind to direct a single lick of flame into your shivering hands, to make them shake no longer!"

They both smiled, and Melody felt oddly relieved.

Pavonis walked gracefully over to Melody and kissed her head before whispering, "The experience of being alive is what you seek, not the meaning of your life. The meaning comes from the experience. Revel in your existence. You can be the warmth and the light; the flower and the moon. You are Mother Earth's sweet Melody."

The love felt in that moment was enough to revitalize them for a short while, but the rising dawn forced them to begin their trek once more, at an ever-increasing pace. As Melody rode her caribou across the field, she dared not look down at the strewn bodies. She needed to maintain her resolve, for the way ahead was wrought with danger, the empirical territories looming before them in the form of a dark and damaged woodland.

Pavonis led them south, towards the sun's rising ecliptic alignment. Every few moments, the approaching fog hovering over the mountains would let the sun flicker over them, until the dense wet air shrouded them in darkness again. Suddenly, there was no sky, only a frosty forest canopy that muffled the roar of the mountains contour with snowy undertones. Melody looked behind them. She could hear the deathly screeches of the ravens in the distance as the corvine mass plummeted from the sky, scouring the battlefield and initiating their blood feast.

Pavonis rode alone alongside Melody and David's caribou, having passed the mantle of caring for the boy to her young apprentice. She had established that she could no longer be David's protector, as she had to be a lone unit, ready for attack in case of an ambush. She had already instructed Melody on how best to kill David and then herself, should they be over-run by the enemy. This was the world they lived in. But this violent way of life pushed them onwards, as did knowing Michael's tortures continued; knowing *the world's* tortures continued.

As the troop broke a path through the dead ferns, Melody noticed a flash of grey in the trees. She looked at Pavonis, who had seen another to her left. Many surrounded them, but none could be seen for longer than a second. Pavonis turned to Melody's worried face and shouted over the sound of the caribous' trotting on the snow and rocks.

"The timber wolves of Montana! They've come to escort us to Caldera. They refused to join the battle because they said it was a suicide mission."

"Then how did you summon them now?" Melody asked.

"I didn't! They came of their own accord!" Pavonis exclaimed vivaciously.

The pack stayed well hidden, dipping under rotten trees and racing over snowy quarries much too quickly for their eyes to follow. The black coat of the alpha male could not be seen in the shadows of the ancient forest. Only his bright yellow eyes give away his presence.

Melody held David tightly as they crept further towards the dead mountain mouth. A calm creek led the way upstream, and the valley's steep hillsides narrowed in on them. The box canyon eventually became a single file walk through a moss-covered rocky crevice, snow falling lightly through the deep cavern as the wolves led the way.

Somewhere along the way, the odd group gained an owl, who soared high above the cliffs, guiding them through. Pavonis smiled as she looked up, as did Melody.

"You no longer have to ask, do you? Nature is sending them a message herself."

"Precisely," said Pavonis. "This is a subtle indicator."

"Of what?" Melody asked.

"Divine intervention," Pavonis explained.

"I thought you didn't believe in heaven."

"Divinity doesn't come from the sky, Melody. No...this is a call from beneath us. She speaks through the mycelium in the soil, her sermon well defined. And we are her chosen disciples." Pavonis dug her heels into the caribou's side and quickened their pace down the snaking path, charging undaunted into the rugged sierra.

CHAPTER 34
MYRIAD CRUCIATUS

Michael sat in the far reaches of Shakti's dungeon, weary from its lightless exposure. He tossed a pinecone against the wall and pondered the fate of his loved ones. He had not eaten in months, but of course, he did not need to anymore. His veins craved sunlight and vengeance. The Queen had not spoken to him since his transformation, and he wondered what she planned to do with him. Hour after hour and day after day he waited. By pondering, he found nothing. From nothing, his Sararan blood whispered truths of underlying confidence, in between manic episodes of hope, desire, anger, and sadness.

Michael had found a window to the outside world, a small hole in the stone wall, showing him the rolling hills and dead trees covered in dirty snow and soot, his only taste of reality. The prolonged isolation gave him nightmares, and he gave up trying to sleep the days away. Waking life became a chore of managing his paranoid and helpless thoughts. All he could do was bathe in the memories of his beloved, and hope to be rescued by his mother and uncle before the Queen executed the next phase of the prophecy.

It was a late February day when Michael heard the clink of the lock on the iron door. It swung open with a metallic screech as he looked up with fiery eyes. The Queen walked into his cell, followed by her cloaked imperial guards.

"How are you feeling, Michael?"

Michael refused to look at her or acknowledge her presence. His bright orange eyes were buried in darkness, like a lion hidden in low grass, ready to pounce.

"I'm sorry if you feel neglected. I had some matters in Central Asia to attend to. Some raiders formed an alliance and attempted to kidnap the established nobles. It took longer than expected, due to the vast area across which these inferior tribes were scattered. Upon my return, it appears my messengers have received good news. Your mother has successfully defeated Sandraudiga in a great battle, destroying nearly every living thing within a two-mile radius in the process. Quite impressive, I must say. She has saved me a great deal of effort."

Michael looked up at her. "You're a fucking

monster," he said bitterly.

"We're all monsters, Michael. But it's not the ones with the sharpest teeth that will be remembered, it's the ones with the fiercest bite. And I want to feel your bite." She smiled a sensual and mischievous smile. "You know that your young princess is with your mother in the mountains, don't you?"

Michael said nothing, but looked at her with searching eyes.

"My guards here will help you clean up. Please don't harm them, or I'll make the next few days far more painful than they need to be. Join me for brunch once you're decent."

She walked back through the shadows of the dungeon. The guards walked in, and Michael noticed one of them scathing him with her liquid green eyes. The other's face was hidden by a curtain of fabric. Not even her eyes were visible.

"Don't you want to escape this place?" Michael asked the hidden figure.

She walked up to him. "This *is* the escape." She held up her hand and dropped her sleeve to reveal a stub of boney knuckles where her fingers had once been. "This is what happened to women in my country who showed their faces in public."

"So, if the Queen lets you represent yourself and practice whatever beliefs you choose, why wear the mask?"

She lifted the deceitful hood and showed Michael her mutilated face, burnt into a putrid, ghoulish complexion, her facial tissue melted and torn apart in some unknown disaster, leaving only a skeletal wiring breached by thin skin: eyeless, tearless, but alive.

"There's more to this war than meets the eye, Michael," she said, donning her hood and turning to guide him up the stairs. The guards stepped lightly, as if floating. Michael followed at a dissonant pace, feeling the weight of his imprisonment; drenched with doubt, like a cold-blooded mammal in an endless monsoon.

Michael walked into the Queen's dining hall dressed in a fine, blue silk robe. A quartet of sceptre-bearing women walked behind him, stopping at the doorway as he continued on. At the end of the long table, Shakti stood and bowed. Michael did not bow in return.

"Please, sit!" she said, sitting back down and

slurping some Miso soup.

Michael sat slowly.

"I'm aware neither of us are driven to consume such substances, but for me, it's ceremonial. You see, this is the beginning of the end, and I want to know that we both enjoyed a decent final meal before we reach the apex of all destinies."

"Do you plan to kill me?" Michael asked.

"I'm going to test you, and if you fail the test, you may die, or you will become far stronger than you have ever been before. If you complete these tasks as I have predicted, I shall consider you for my new apprentice."

"Just kill me," he said, staring at his food. His eyes flickered with orange flame and a hateful lust.

"Don't be bitter! This is a testament to your strength and fortitude as a Sararan. You're not some mutt I've bent over backwards for, just so I can modify them into another Aradian splice. Do you know what you are?" she asked, squinting. "You are the *only* naturally born Immortal. You didn't consume anything. You didn't plunge a needle into your veins and run the devil's dice, as my sisters and I did. You're the purest being in the universe, brought up by a lovely mid-wife who taught you values like perseverance and kindness—"

"Who you murdered!" Michael shouted across the table.

"I wouldn't take such actions personally, Michael. Tala had sensed a strong energy behind that door, and thought it was you. It turns out Lily was a venerable creature, an angel in God's eye. A mistake it was, yes, but then again, here you are. Tala never understood what was so important about you, Michael. But I understand. There are so many mysteries in your blood, and I intend to discover them."

"I'm not giving you what you want," Michael said, his eyes flaring.

"I'm not sure you are reciprocating the prestigious position this offering nominates you!"

"Well, both of your apprentices have left you, so what the fuck does that say about your leadership?" he asked.

The Queen closed her eyes and opened them. Her deep black pupils showed no emotion at all. They seemed to suck the very energy from Michael's body.

"Tala and Mayari have found strength in sovereignty, and I am honored to have been their master during the implementation of the prophecy."

Michael sat and drank some soup. He attempted

a new approach with Shakti. "When did it start, your prophecy?"

"Curious, suddenly, are you?" Shakti smirked as she drank a cup of sake.

"I want to know what my father died for."

Shakti smiled then began. "Firstly, it's not my prophecy, and it started ten thousand years ago, in story and spoken word. The exact origin is unknown, but an ancient Zoroastrian script, presumed to be a rendition of an even earlier version, resurfaced during the crusades of Latvia and Estonia. Vishnu's master, Zou Cheng, killed the Norseman who planned to burn it and instead offered the scriptures to the great Khan of the Mongol Nation. Though to some a vague concept, with the right eyes the prophecy is a guideline to achieve intonation between the Earth and its shepherd species. The idea is that the last ten thousand years were a massacre, so that the next ten thousand can be anything but. Just as the sun stays shallow in winter months then pulls flowers towards its warmth in the summer, the revelation of humanity required a grand elemental war to cleanse the Earth. Humans once knew this radical symmetry of the life-death-life cycle, far better than any modern man. At the start of this century, technological advances began reversing the evolution of the human race. This would have had dire consequences on the planet's climate, something far more dangerous to life on Earth than what the Zurvan Order has implemented in the last twenty years. It was Vishnu, praise be unto him, whose opportunistic spirit led him to ensure the prophecy was left in the right hands. He couldn't have done it without your father, Michael. In my eyes, you are royalty. You are the answer."

"Along with killing billions of people?"

"Ah, Michael...majority extermination was a byproduct of humankind's repeated mistakes and inevitable blowback. In my life, I fought in five major wars against the United States, not because I hated Americans, but because its government became an empirical state hell bent on digging its talons into foreign soils while destroying the planet's ecosystems. All of the major powers operated in this way. Therefore, they were eradicated."

"How do you know for sure that humans would have turned against the natural order of life? Aren't we all a part of that cycle, empathetic or not?"

"Of course we are. We are living it, are we not? When God sent the lamb, his powers of healing were later exploited and corrupted. The crucifixion of the Hebrew prophet backfired and brought another thousand years of war. The world needed a warrior king to bring back the divine essence that cusps humanity, and so it was that God gave the world the great Khan to connect the world under the eternal blue sky. But after he passed on, his greedy, self-entitled children who fought without heart reversed the global movement. And now, nearly one thousand years later, you and I sit at this table contemplating the fate of the world yet again. What you see as hypocrisy in my philosophy is in fact a carefully calculated course for the future of this planet and all the life forms it holds."

"So, you let your dogs of war loose on the world, your killing-machine twins who know more about death than life."

"You should respect those who are savvy in the arts divination, Michael. I have not hunted your mother since she became a protector of the North American forests and practitioner of the craft."

"How did she learn it?"

"By listening. There are ways to see glimpses of the future, places in time outside of time, where time does not exist." She gazed up for a moment, as if speaking to a specter at the table's center mount. "You see, while the citizens of the 'free world' lost sleep over what they had to lose, my people stayed awake long into the night, in poverty, with starved children, longing for a better life, studying the tools of our ancestors in order to fight the growing threats of both communism and capitalism alike. That is why my brothers and sisters were victorious. We Zurvans gave our enemies something to gnaw on and the wolves of war ground their teeth against their bloodied gums trying to kill us. I can give you specific instances. Lily taught you some history, didn't she?"

"She taught me enough to know that what you're doing is just like what Hitler and Pol Pot and Mao did; that you're just a new age dictator but without anyone left to control, so you toy with me instead. You're so pathetic that you've conquered to the point of loneliness. At this rate, you'll be the last one left alive on Earth. What then?"

Shakti sighed and shook her head. "You never witnessed the world in its late empirical days. It was beyond grotesque: hypnotic television screens; corrupt politicians, trading blood for oil; countless eradications of rare and irreplaceable species due to over consumption and mindless pollution. This infection of predatory industrialization sliced into the gut of the third world. There were child soldiers, manufactured diseases, drugs and ivory, slave trade syndicates, geo-engineered weather, and a mass media filter to slant it all and keep the wealthy living off the people's dependence on them. Humans were connected globally by commerce, while local cultures became less oriented to their artistic roots, either sucked dry of their resources or bastardized by the bright lights of entertainment and spectacle; the suburbs were replaced by slums, a violent mockery of the cities painted dream. Nothing people strived for contained a real version of what life is supposed to be; Neon city is proof of that. It's a living museum of what the whole world would be like if things had progressed as they were. I leave it, to mock humanity."

"It didn't seem so bad."

"And what did you learn from your experience there? Just how fake people can be when they're hypnotized by drug use? The treachery and lustful sins of my sister? The superficiality of humans who negate purpose for sensation? You see, Michael, the ones who taught me the important lessons about life were also the people trying to kill me. In turn, I will be teaching you about life."

Michael sipped his soup and stared at his bowl.

"Your passive aggressive defiance intrigues me. This passion within you, it comes from your father. He made incredible sacrifices to ensure you had a future. And I'm going to do the same to ensure you have an even better one than he could have imagined. I'm going to be famous for saving this world, Michael, and you will have the chance to be my successor. It may not sound attractive to you now, but I hope you will at least consider this proposal."

Michael took a drink of water and cleared his throat. "Whenever you're finished, I'm ready to start the first phase of your trial," he said, throwing his napkin on the table.

"Prepare yourself for a new kind of suffering, Michael Beller," Shakti said, rising like a tower in that Gigerian hall of black glass, her throne of shocked rock dazzling with a subtle rainbow sheen. She inspected him with her abysmal eyes, his reflection oscillated by their swirling fractal mechanics. "Come this way."

Michael stood at the gate of a large courtyard outside the palace walls. Winter's bleak light cast a pale hue across the land. The diluted sunbeams were enough to charge Michael's cells and prepare him for his occult tortures. A small mountain range rose in the distance, where vents still smoked and spewed pyroclastic flows in retarded continuation of the eruption decades ago. The smell of sulfur was prevalent in the cool air.

In front of Michael lay twelve granite stones,

388

positioned in a south-facing line, with zodiac signs engraved into them. At the end of the alignment, Shakti stood holding a black opal crystal ball in front of her chest with both hands. She breathed in through her nostrils like a hungry serpent.

"At any moment, I may choose to trigger an aneurysm in your brain. Your Sararan cells won't respond quickly enough, and you will perish. Do not exit the challenge prematurely or try anything unwise. Do you understand?"

Michael nodded.

"These stones represent the twelve signs of the zodiac, and each is tied to a different part of the body. You will experience pain in each area as lucidly as if you were wounded in battle, but I assure you, that pain will only be in your mind. If you can make it to the end, you will move on to the next trial. You cannot skip stones, touch the grass, or run across, so you had best learn to feed off your own suffering. Step onto the first stone, Michael."

Michael shook with fear. His quickly evolving cells would be of no use to him here. He often questioned his own faith in himself, but this was not the time, and he would not allow the thought to enter. There would be no way around this horrific illusion. All he could do was go *through*. He took his first step.

Michael's foot touched down on the rams' head engraving of Ares. Instantly, an ear splitting screech shattered his eardrums as the sensation of a dagger slowly entered between his skull's sutures. Deeper the blade sunk, and he could feel the blood trickling from his ears as he screamed like a wounded animal. He watched Shakti's body shift this way and that, as his eyes fought against his vertigo beneath the opaque silver sky of warbling planets. He conceived the horror of ten thousand deaths, his Sararan body attempting to fight the overpowering Aradian waves of mesmerizing inflictions swallowing him like a snake eating a mouse. He stepped to the next stone with urgency as the static throes became unbearable.

The dagger pulled away from Michael's brain with an icy lurch as he managed to step onto the bull-marked stone of Taurus. Suddenly, he found himself standing in a field of yellow flowers. The sun beat down on him with a warm embrace, and he could smell exquisite fragrances calling out in forgiveness. He reached down and picked up one of the small flowers. A hand reached around and slit his throat, the initial streak of pain followed by a warm gush of blood. Michael could not breathe. He choked and gagged as he attempted to step forward.

The Queen was laughing as Michael suddenly

saw himself back in Caldera, about to step onto the third stone.

"A hint: staying on one stone too long could get you into trouble, and stepping on two mixes the sensations. Find a balance that promotes ingenuity."

Michael's foot touched down onto the stone of Gemini, engraved with two people holding hands. He winced as his left arm became solid with frostbite, the creeping cold, black as plague, starting at his wrist and climbing up his shoulder. His right arm became scorched, his flesh popping, singed with burns so hot he felt his marrow boiling. His left arm nearly fell off from the cold as his right struggled to hold its remaining charred bones together. He could feel the rotting of his flesh pull at his shoulders. He stepped forward as tears of blood stained his face with each passing second.

His arms quickly went back to normal as invisible nails drove themselves through Michael's hands. He could feel the clenches of crab claws snap his fingers like twigs, the stone of Cancer holding him down. The forces were unseen; the pain only an illusion, yet the experience was as real to Michael as the cold air that wafted against his face. He shook off the invisible crustaceans and took his next step with an anticipatory gasp.

A misguided pulse stopped Michael's heart from

beating as he made contact with the lion's head on the stone of Leo, and he nearly tipped from his stone as he pounded his pained chest with his fist. In the corner of his eye, he saw Shakti raise her sword in warning. He began sweating, and could smell the grass as if his body was taking one last sensory photograph before death. He slowly slipped into unconsciousness as he stepped onto the next stone.

"What ills have I done to deserve such suffering!" Michael screamed, holding his stomach as if he were pulling his spilled guts back into his body.

Shakti stood without word or motion as Michael looked down at the stone of Virgo. He saw a woman, holding a plant. She reminded him of his mother. His insides burned in a cauldron of venom and he felt a hand on the back of his neck. He puked a vile concoction onto the ground, blood and bile mixing in a sticky black mass. Michael reached his foot towards the next stone, repulsed by the mystery of what lay ahead.

Michael's foot touched the stone of Libra, and to his surprise, he felt no pain. He waited for a moment, but nothing came.

"Your body consumed your own kidneys when it transformed into a Sararan. Lucky you. This is the center stone, Libra, the stone of balance and justice. I assume you're ready to go on now?" Shakti said impatiently.

"Do they get worse?" Michael asked, panting, tears of blood still dripping from his flaming eyes as he stood half naked in the cold, a ragged and tortured prisoner.

"That's up to your perception of pain, Michael. Now move!" she said, telekinetically pulling his foot forwards onto the stone of Scorpio.

Never had Michael experienced a worse pain, in his heart, body, or mind. The grisly act of castration cut his masculinity from him in one motion, shredding his ego and his manhood simultaneously. He clenched at the torn skin where his testicles and penis had once been, screaming in agony.

"Make it stop!" he shrieked, clinging to his groin as blood dripped between his fingers.

Shakti looked at him with a sadistic grin. "Yes! Cry out in your weakness! Overcome your pain through submission! Let go of your manly essence and accept what is!"

Michael continued to scream, choking and gagging on his own mucus. He forced his mouth shut, biting a hole through his lip as he hopped onto the next stone.

The dreaded centaur of Sagittarius roared into view as Michael stepped onto the stone. Both femurs cracked and Michael lost his balance. He wobbled about like a newborn calf, screaming in pain and desperation. His broken bones sliced through his skin and nerves as he tried to step forward, but his foot would not move. He grasped his thigh with both hands and picked up the dangling appendage, his head shaking as tears and snot collected on his quivering chin.

Just as the agony of the last stone was leaving him, Michael leaned onto the ram's headed sea serpent that decorated the stone of Capricorn and felt both his tibias break. The weight of his body was now held by two broken legs, as his fibulas pierced out of his shins and dripped blood on the beast's tail. Michael wailed in agony, unable to control his fear of the next stone, and unable to tell what was real and what was not. For a moment, he contemplated stepping off, and accepting death, until the image of Melody entered his mind and pulled him toward the next stone.

As Michael stepped onto the stone of Aquarius, both his Achilles tendons ripped in half, and his eyes exploded with yellow fire. His echoing cries could be heard by the slaves of the city, who began singing to drown him out, creating a mournful harmony in the distance.

The final stone was Pisces, hot as smoldering coals, and Michael's feet looked and felt like molten lava, oozing red and bubbling with heat.

Michael looked up at Shakti. "I have no fear of pain!" he yelled. "You have nothing left to scare me!"

Michael took another step and landed knees first on the ground. He dropped his head and body, crying like a small child on the bloodstained grass. All his body parts returned to their original sensations, but the shock had not yet left him.

Shakti nodded unenthusiastically. "A spectacular display of strength, not doubt, but it could have been worse. This test all depends on your perception. Mayari made it all the way to the end before realizing she was still standing on the first stone. But that was her perception, her choice. The mind is your most powerful ally, Michael, and it can betray you just the same as any other," she said, walking away as Michael continued to sob and pull at the dead grass with trembling hands.

That night, Michael finally slept. He dreamed deeply as his mind recovered from the harsh treatment he had endured. Even as a Sararan, such trauma required introspection and time for healing, especially since his life had taken so many rapid turns since his relatively simple days at Lily's cabin. He dreamed of some celestial yearning, as his body floated through pitch-black darkness, contrasted against the billions of stars gasping in the infinite beyond. The lights twinkled and warped as he felt the vastness and sorrow of ultimate seclusion. His fear was not death, but rather becoming the only Immortal left alive, forever trapped in an invincible shell of existence, until all his loved ones had passed, and extinction had taken his species; until all the energy in the cosmos had been exhausted, causing thermodynamic equilibrium in a universe of asteroids and gravestones colliding silently in the cold black.

Michael awoke in his cell to a visitor. General Fraus sat on the floor parallel to him on the other side of the bars, quietly watching him sleep. He stirred and reeled back into the darkness, his eyes ablaze, but she eased him.

"I'm not here to harm you, Michael. I came only to visit. Would you like some wine?"

He looked at her skeptically as she pulled out the bottle.

"Alcohol won't have any effect on me," he said.

"But it will have an effect on me, and I prefer not to drink alone."

She handed him a cup and they drank. Fraus studied him carefully, for she had been through the same training, the same tortures.

"What was your favorite part?" she asked.

"Favorite part? Are you mad?"

She drank her wine with a great thirst. "When I finished the trial, I wanted to walk the stones a second time. Only because the feeling after the last stone...it was incredible. It was the ultimate equilibrium of insanity and reality, of now and eternity. That feeling is Christ's submission and the Devil's resentment combined. It is God."

She drank again, as if in defiance of a sober thought, and Michael stepped into the light.

"May I ask why your ears are cut up like that?"

"Once, I was a bad listener, early on in my teachings. Only once. Now I hear everything Shakti says. And everything she thinks too."

"Then you should know her treachery."

"You have no idea how privileged you are, boy. The Zurvans will teach you lessons in accuracy most can only dream of. For a time, being caged isn't so bad. At least you don't have to share your quarters. Imprisonment teaches you things about yourself you never knew before. Trust me."

"You were imprisoned by the Zurvans?"

"That would have been pleasant, but no. I made the mistake of returning to Soviet Russia after betraying my comrades."

"Is that where you got your tattoos then? What was it called, the prison?"

She looked out the window, as if unable to answer; as if the light had stolen her spirit and she wouldn't get it back if she spoke its name.

"Why do you hate men?" Michael asked, taking another sip of wine.

"Masculinity is a dead ideology. You spend too much time thinking about who deserves what. Justice. Vengeance. Righteousness. None of these virtues will serve you in the post-world."

"What if cultivating these virtues among the hopeless is my true aim, my treasure and gift to the world?"

"And how's that currently working out for you?"

Michael drank, brooding silently.

"There is a deadly hemotoxin in your cup. And mine as well," she said. "We both should be dead having been given its course. And yet, here we sit. Alive. There is no sense to be made of this universe. Chaos creates form. Form matures and materializes, then disintegrates. And thus, more chaos is needed to create higher forms, be they planets, mountains, humans, or empires. Your toxic wine is like the injustices which exist in all partnerships and exchanges."

"My blood can tolerate poison. But if this is true, how would you still be alive?"

"Can you not taste the venom?" She smiled as she finished her cup. She made her way towards the doorway and turned back. "Don't go to sleep again. It shows the Queen your weakness."

Soon after the General's departure, Shakti's imperial guards came and escorted Michael through a long tunnel carved into the rock. Michael could feel the energy of the walls draining him. The sides of the brittle tunnel had been shaved into imperfect ripples that glistened a subtle rainbow of color through the opaque blackness. It was no wonder the guard's wielded spears tipped with the shattered gem; the edges were sharper than steel.

A small door at the end of the tunnel was opened by a guard, and the light from the outside world poured in. Michael walked out with the guards to find Shakti stand in front of them, dressed in a plain white kimono.

"Good morning, Michael. Since your trial yesterday, a thousand years have passed in my eyes. I have seen the destiny of this world, the problem, and the solution. You will suffer greatly by the end of it, but your suffering will be of your own doing. Therefore, you may go."

Michael looked at her inquisitively. She seemed genuine and gracious, but Michael knew some ruse awaited him. She began pacing slowly as the guards released their grip on Michael's arms.

"So, this is the next test..." Michael sighed. "What's the catch?"

"No catch. You're free to go. You can walk, or..."

Shakti whistled loudly, beckoning a steed from behind the northern pillar. The horse galloped gleefully as he ran towards Michael.

"Apollo?!" Michael cried as his horse ran up to him.

"You know this horse?" Shakti asked.

"Of course I know this horse! What did you do to him?"

"A retreating contingent saved him from the battlefield. Why did you abandon him?" Shakti scolded. "He's been well treated, fed regularly, and given proper medications. I think he is eager for a ride Michael. Go to Neon City where my sister can protect you. Go somewhere far away from this place. I want my apprentice to be safe—"

"Don't call me that," Michael said.

"Let me finish!" Shakti said, throwing a glance at Michael that sent him to his knees.

Michael screamed, his eyes engulfed in a supernova of pink flame as Shakti dosed him with a barbaric spell of skull rattling agony.

"I want to keep you safe because, when your mother arrives, I don't want you to have to witness her death."

Michael nodded weakly, the effect of Shakti's spell gradually wearing off. He climbed back to his feet with discomfort, and Apollo put his nose to Michael's chest.

"I missed you too, boy," Michael said, patting Apollo on the cheek before mounting him. Michael glared at Shakti.

"One day, you will be grateful for me. I see so much potential in you. Don't ever let anything hinder your soul's conquest, Michael."

"I'm grateful for your mercy, but with all my heart, I pray my mother is victorious," he said, as he tapped his heels against Apollo's side.

The horse began walking away in the other direction. As Michael kicked Apollo into a gallop, he dared not look at back. He knew Shakti was watching him, perhaps long after he had crested the hill that concealed his route north, towards his mother.

It was nightfall when Michael felt the wind strengthen on the foothills of the Rocky Mountains. Apollo drank water from a stream as Michael looked up at the treetops bending slightly in the gale. He chose not to light a fire. It was entirely possible the Queen's soldiers had yet to receive word of his pardoning, and besides, his thick skin defied the cold, holding in its own ignitions, storing them as though he were some kind of fire god. He breathed in the mountain air and felt the elements invigorate his Sararan body, which had not been adequately charged or given full conception within the bleak stone halls of the palace.

Michael noticed a bat flapping over his head. Then, several more came, until there were so many that one flew past him every few seconds. Michael stood and whistled to Apollo, who whipped his tail at the small, winged mammals that darted around like satanic doves.

"Come, Apollo!" Michael yelled. The bats seemed to be growing in number. Not knowing how long their colony had been without food, or how many of them there were, Michael quickly mounted Apollo and rode down to the prairie in search of cover. The bats followed him, their fast-flapping wings snapping next to his ears as they wailed their sonar chorus, seeking non-existent moths. Michael glanced behind as Apollo galloped faster. They were surrounded by thousands of furious mammalian bullets, purged from the mountain caves, swarming like black rivers eager to engulf the lone rider and suffocate him in their immense cloud.

Michael felt the pinch of small claws and teeth on his skin, and he quickly reached back and pulled them off. The screeching of their voices crescendoed, turning Apollo into a kicking bronco. The horse began to run awkwardly across the prairie as the bats gained momentum.

"To the left, Apollo!" Michael cried, pulling on his horse's mane as he noticed a rattlesnake coiled on top of a rock ahead of them. Michael held onto his saddle and reached down, snatching up the venomous serpent. He held it by the neck and let the snake bite his arm before throwing it back into the grass. Apollo ran with vigor; only his labored breathing gave away his exhaustion. The sea of bats swarmed over them and Michael lurched Apollo to a halt as they disappeared inside the mass of the vicious creatures. As the bats attacked their victims, Michael burst out of the swarm and waved his arms wildly, trying to touch every bat in the vicinity. His venomous hands slaughtered thousands of the creatures as he jumped through the waves of attacks, kicking, punching, grabbing, and throwing. He fought for several minutes, the piles of dead bats rising as the moon's light came into view and charged his cells amidst the screeching demons' silhouettes.

When it was all over, Michael looked around the open prairie, his heart beating fast but efficiently. There were so many dead bats that he had to pull Apollo from beneath a heap of the winged rodents.

"Apollo! No...shit, no!" he gasped, panicking.

The bats had bored a hole into Apollo's stomach with their savage little teeth. The horse looked up at

Michael with frightened eyes, nodding his head in pain as he kicked the sage grass and dirt with his hooves.

"Bastards!" Michael yelled, to the empty sky. He tried to think, to figure out how to save his horse, as Apollo slowly bled out onto the dry grass. Michael began to cry, holding his face in his hands. When he looked up, he saw the blood between the webbing of his fingers, and he wondered what would happen if he gave the horse his Sararan blood. Michael rested his hand on the hot wound in Apollo's side, focusing his energy on healing, as he let his blood mix with his horse's. In that quiet moment, Michael felt a deep connection with Apollo; he knew Apollo was no longer just some horse Michael had picked up from the old farmer. No. This horse was his comrade, for life. Apollo looked into Michael's eyes and stopped fidgeting, letting his head rest on the ground and allowing the reflection of the moon to guide his gaze upward. The horse's breathing eased and his body calmed as Michael took his hand away.

Michael watched Apollo as the horse rose to his feet and snorted through his bloody nose, splattering the lichen and rocks with crimson. Apollo whinnied, nudging his face into Michael's chest.

"Well I'm glad you're feeling better, pal," Michael said, smiling. He looked into the horse's eyes. They were aflame, like his own, but with a cardinal blaze at their centers, like seas of lava spewing molten rock and hardening into pinkish black crusts, before breaking apart again. "It seems as if we are destined to become closer yet," Michael said, looking at Apollo as the horse looked back with a faint telepathic notion of acknowledgment.

Michael jumped onto Apollo's back as he sped gallantly back towards the mountain front, jumping over large piles of poisoned bat bodies. Just before they reached the tree line, Michael looked up to see a star glinting at him. The star fell towards him, and he realized the growing bright light was Shakti, diving at him from some astronomical elevation, the friction of her descent burning the air around her like a downed satellite. She hit Michael like a meteor crashing into a planet, and Apollo sped off back towards the direction of the palace. He already knew what was to come. Michael crawled out of the smoking crater Shakti had made during her violent landing. He looked up at her with eyes ablaze, his ribs half crushed but already crackling back into place.

"Very resourceful, mimicking the rattlesnake's glands, Michael. But I can't have you riding north causing a ruckus and giving your priceless blood to horses. You're going back to your cell, where you could spend a very long time, if you don't start recognizing me for what I am."

"Which is what?"

"Your master," Shakti said, as she backhanded him, sending his face into the dust.

He breathed deeply and shook with anger. Then, fighting against his defiance, he loosened his muscles and rose slowly, his face half reddened from the blow.

"I'm sorry, master, I will not disobey you again."

Shakti smiled, and looked him over for a few seconds, to check his sincerity.

"You have almost everything you need to become a Zurvan apprentice. You're courageous, intelligent, passionate, and you possess a most valuable trait as a naturally born Sararan. All you lack is loyalty. I cannot sell it to you. You must desire it."

"I desire to follow in your great footsteps, master," Michael said, bowing his head. "I want to know the Zurvan's path."

"Very well, young Michael. We shall make our way back to Caldera. Your initiation will take place when we return."

CHAPTER 35
SICARIUS MAJOR

It was a typical winter night in Neon City. The fog rose from the low Missouri River, and the wind howled a hollow tone. The city was quiet. The raves had migrated below ground, taking place inside tunnels and aquarium plazas, built as many stories beneath the Earth as the skyscrapers had been built above. High in Lakshmi's tower, the glyph-shaped solar panels collected frost on their pyramid mounts. Between them, a window permitted the lone Lord a view of the misty city. She sat on the edge of her bed in a pontificating state. Not long after receiving news of Sandraudiga's loss, Lakshmi received a strange warning from a messenger. She drank a bottle of wine to herself and sat holding a golden rose. She wept at the sight of it.

"My Lord?" her guard stepped into the room hesitantly.

"Yes?" she said, her solemn stare unwavering from the shimmering rose petals, twinkling in her teary eyes.

"There has been a security breach. Were you notified?"

"Yes, I was, thank you."

"We are on high alert on all levels, my Lord. We're searching the building from the top down, with more law enforcement on their way."

"I trust you will find the trespasser," Lakshmi said lethargically.

The guard left the room and shut the door behind her.

Lakshmi looked up at the few stars uncovered by the drifting fog, the blue gaseous specks only visible on winter nights, freed from the steady beam of a million lights that usually obscured their glow. Just then, she felt the ice-cold bite of a blade caressing her neck.

"Don't scream," a voice whispered behind her.

Lakshmi dropped the rose. "Why don't you just do it?" she asked, calmly.

"Where is my nephew?" the voice asked.

There was a long pause.

"Michael is in Caldera, held captive by Shakti."

"And if I were to hold you hostage, would I be able trade you for him?"

"I don't think so. But there's still time to save

Michael," Lakshmi said softly.

The man orbited her, keeping Ezra's dagger held to her neck. William Beller had escaped the Battle of Banff and sped to Neon City, with the help of fast hooves and full fuel tanks, redemption in tow, racing on gristle and spoiled water like a Casanova wolf after surviving nearly two thousand miles of enemy movement and roadblocks. He had torn from himself the barbaric clothes he had been wearing and had donned instead a burgundy three-piece suit. His hair was combed back, and his beard trimmed; Ezra's sharpened dagger was his only device, and the light reflected from its perfect blade where the bloodstains of many complacent guards had been wiped from its surface. Will looked into Lakshmi's tired eyes with his own.

"What are you saying?" he asked at last.

"This long war can finally be over. It would be prudent of us to do the right thing before it's too late."

"Don't try and fool me. You helped your sister. You helped Shakti. You're part of her ridiculous prophecy."

"Am I though, William? Look at me. I'm a prisoner here, too. We all are. Neon city is Shakti's social experiment. The people are her lab rats. It didn't always feel like this...how she treated me.

Shakti rescued me when I was eleven years old. I was a Syrian refugee, fleeing the civil war in my home country. I was treated like trash in the streets of France, after the Paris terrorist attacks we were profiled everywhere. My mother and father had been arrested. I was alone. I was assaulted and beaten."

Will continued pointing the blade at her.

Lakshmi looked at him with sad eyes and continued. "But one day, a strange woman took my hand and led me into a close-bonded community. She gave me both discipline and education. I was never strong enough to become one of her apprentices. She was more like an older sister to me than a master. For a long time, I loved her as my sister, but so many of her choices have caused me dismay since the eruption. It has been mounting into a pain I cannot bear, and it's not worth living for. I do not wish to be nobility in her Queendom. I am ready to risk my life, in order to do what I know is right for the cause."

Will lowered the blade and looked at her for a moment. The silence was almost tangible. Then, quite suddenly, he dropped the dagger and lunged at Lakshmi, pinning her to the bed, his face inches from hers.

"You're lying!"

"No, I'm not. Shakti needs to die. Even she is

beginning to realize it," Lakshmi said, breathing hard.

"And what, *you're* going to kill her?"

"No. I have a better plan."

"Which is?"

"You and I go to Caldera disguised as imperial guards. Together, we free your nephew. Together, we can defeat her."

They looked at each other for a few seconds, their eyes darting around, suddenly aware of how close they were; of the undeniable pull drawing them even closer. Desire, true desire, was something neither of them had experienced in a very long time. Their pupils locked as Lakshmi grabbed Will's neck and pulled his face towards hers. She kissed him roughly, twirling her finger in his beard. Their bodies surged with sexual energy, new lovers caught in some impossible web of desire formed by anything but coincidence. Up above, the icy glass melted beneath the stars now shining undiminished. The extrasolar bodies reached down and pressed their frail blue light upon the lovers' naked skin, as Lakshmi shut off the lights with the snap of her fingers and embraced her former enemy.

CHAPTER 36
LUNAR MELODY

A splinter of fading sunlight threw orange rays into Melody's eyes, as she watched the dusk spread its embers over a cloudless sky. Some distance away, coyotes vocalized their raspy howls, hindered by soot and heavy breathing in the dry air. Pavonis played a wistful tune on her flute next to the fire, watching the changing colours of the rare purple stone she had set upon the paling coals as it reacted to the heat. She had not moved from her classical Roman pose in hours; her crown of laurel of leaves separated weave from braid, her knotted hair now a silken headdress of nerve endings, carefully aligned with the sutures of her modified skull. Next to her, David lay fast asleep, nestled in a bundle of blankets between the two caribou. Everyone was calm, but not content, for their warpath had conditioned them to a savage pace where rest came infrequently.

Pavonis remained hopeful of their conquest, but Melody's morale waned with each passing day.

Through the fragmented flames, she watched the moon rise slowly in the eastern sky. She looked up through sparks spiraling around the stars and saw her lover's face, as she wondered painfully about his fate.

Far to the south, Michael sat outside with his back against the palace wall. Around him lay a vast array of hills, mountains, and streams. He was allowed to wander the grounds, but not leave Caldera, having been warned that he would be forcefully returned. Still, the notion of freedom constantly taunted him. Michael gazed at the moon, longing for his beloved, as she longed for him. He wondered if her sweet touch was in fact tangible, and in that moment, attempted to broadcast some kind of telepathic message, telling Melody that he was alright; that his love for her was his sole inspiration, guiding him through those dark times.

Melody closed her eyes, then opened them. The moon seemed brighter than before. She could feel something, a strange sensation, like something was passing through her body.

"Pavonis, I think the moon is speaking to me."

"I feel it too," Pavonis said, laying down her flute. "But it's not the moon. It's Michael." Pavonis smiled. "Here. Hold my hand."

They held each other's hands and felt the warmth of Michael's love pour onto them.

"But, how?" Melody asked, smiling as the feeling enveloped her.

"He is no longer an adolescent human. He is a matured Sararan now, just as I predicted. Come, let us send him a return message."

Michael closed his eyes and saw his mother and Melody, sitting beside a fire. They held hands and smiled beneath the sky's ornaments. He watched Melody release a single tear onto her perfect cheek, and he wished he could reach out and wipe it away. He wished he could kiss them both and tell them everything was fine. But everything was not fine.

The Queen appeared beside Michael, like a phantom surfacing under the pale light of the moon.

"Having some pleasant thoughts, I see?"

"I'm broadcasting myself to Melody."

"Astral projection, a new skill you have achieved."

"Master, are you still able to love, as you once loved as a human?" Michael asked.

"Sometimes, I think I have lost the ability to love. Then I remember that, in the wake of the death I have brought to this planet, there will be a bountiful garden for all to enjoy. That warms my heart enough." She walked around him, wearing her tall black headdress of antlers and owl feathers. Her dress had been cleaned and her face painted with impeccable red lines and small black dots, a unique mix of runic symbols. "The time for revelation is nigh, Michael. Mayari has almost reached the sun's surface. Pavonis draws closer to Caldera every day. An unmistakable convergence of energies approaches. I must prepare you. Are you ready for your initiation?"

"I am, Master Shakti," he said, standing to his feet.

"Follow me," she said, smiling and squinting, her eyes like deep, dark crevices. She led him back into the palace, telekinetically closing the door behind them.

In the decades since the eruption, no ritual within the walls of the Calderan Palace had been as significant to the Zurvans as Michael's indoctrination into the order. At the height of their power, not even Shakti's transformation into an Aradian matched this new union, and the Queen had made sure her subordinates understood the gravity of this event.

In that grand hall at the center of all the World's power, two rows of imperial guards knelt low with their foreheads pressed against the hexagonal tiles that led up to Shakti's throne. Candles stood on the backs of the guards, burning purple in praise as the guards chanted a droning chorus which resonated through the chamber with its phrygian descent. General Fraus stood by the helm of her Queen, broadsword in hand, looking not unlike the Slavic barbarians she had descended from. Above her, upon her throne, sat Shakti, dressed in her silk ceremonial garb. She took off her headdress to reveal her hair, which had become one long braid, spiraling from the crown of her head into the shape of a helix, laying over her chest. She stroked the fine fibers subtly, watching the spectacle before her.

Michael entered as naked as the day his mother birthed him. A single path of black moss lay before him, and the smell of wet wood and sage smoke clung to the air. His eyes burned like the candles as he walked slowly over the moss, his stare affixed to Shakti's as she wove his soul through the cosmic quilt and into some forsaken dimension beyond the confinement of prima materia. He stopped and knelt at the steps of her throne, lowering his head in submission. He spoke with sincerity.

"Master Shakti, Queen of the Zurvan Empire and descendant of Grand Master, Zou Cheng. I, Michael Ian Beller, kneel before you. Henceforth, I shall refuse my identity, if you are willing to grant me acceptance into the Zurvan Order."

Shakti stood and reached her hand out to Fraus, who handed her the sword. The Queen walked down the steps and placed the sword on Michael's shoulder.

"I accept thee, Michael, King of Men, and Messenger of the Gods, for he is who is closest to God shall forever be so. His father betrayed him. His mother abandoned him. His master failed him. He is born anew. He is now the father, our protector, and our male ally in the war against inferior men. Rise now, Michael, and gaze upon me."

Shakti lifted the sword as Michael stood slowly.

He tilted his chin upward into the light. Crimson tears streamed down his face, the blood dripping onto the moss. He stood tall with honor and strength, despite his tears, as he held out his arm, wrist up.

"All rituals require blood. In most cases, this blade would be the tool of your letting," the Queen said as she reached out and lowered his arm. "But, as I look upon you now, I can see there is no pain greater than that which has brought thee to weep."

"No, master," he said, quivering.

"Let the blood of your passions be the vessel of your essence."

She handed her sword back to Fraus, took a step forward, and kissed Michael on his forehead.

"You are like a son to me," she said as she held him close, her white robes streaked with Michael's blood. The guards placed their candles around Michael and the Queen as their chanting faded and they made their way out of the hall, shutting the large doors with a boom. Fraus crept back into the shadows, leaving the Sararan and the Aradian alone in the darkness together.

The next morning, Pavonis and her troop walked through a vast, lifeless forest. Widow-maker

418

branches hung by mere twigs, clinging onto the charred trees. The ground on which they walked was devoid of color. Blades of grass were as rare as standing water on those massive slopes. The boney spine of glacial peaks before them stood like tombstones of shaved granite, climbing relentlessly into the grey sky. In the deep valley, so many trees had been bent or broken in a northward direction that the trio knew for certain they were drawing close to Caldera. The blast from the eruption had travelled hundreds of miles, turning the region to dust and leaving nothing but crumbled relics and ash-laden wasteland in its wake.

But, despite the decimation of the landscape, life found a way. A great helix of raptors and ravens flew over the valleys, hundreds of the scavenger's circling the sky in unison. The crows revolved around the base of the helix, smelling for rotten flesh; the eagles flew in the middle, scanning for victims with telescopic eyes, and a massive condor, one of the last, flew leisurely at the height of the helix like savage royalty, boasting its role as the superior species. All the birds' feathers were stained with charcoal from the eggs they had hatched from, tainted by volcanic toxins and nearly scorned by their starved mothers. They awaited the next tree of tortured bodies, which would eventually come rolling downstream, lodging itself into the beaver dam, inviting a frenzy of animals desperate for sustenance in the waste.

Pavonis stopped walking when she saw the slow tornado of scavengers.

"There is a clearing up ahead. Wait here," she whispered to Melody. She handed Melody her pendulum. The wolves and the owl were no longer behind them. They had abandoned the troop earlier that day, unwilling to enter the cursed lands.

Melody pulled the reigns on her caribou and patted David's hand, which was wrapped around her waist. David was looking around with wide eyes at the subtle death and chaos surrounding them. One tree leaned against another and creaked loudly in the smallest of morning breezes, its sword-shaped snags letting out a dragging, high-pitched moan. Nothing else made sound.

Pavonis walked up to the clearing. A highway of slaughtered trees ran from east to west, as the sun rose bleakly from its eastern stretch. They had reached the old border between the U.S. and Canada, and she immediately recognized some of the glacial peaks, though they held less snow now than she remembered. Pavonis whistled and Melody rode up to her. They walked down the tree-less path where the hills dropped down to the river's shallow banks. Pavonis hopped off her caribou timidly and calmly made her way up the bank, as Melody and David dismounted and followed.

"What is it, Pavonis?" Melody whispered, climbing to the top of the bank.

Pavonis stood before the foundations of five decimated cabins. Pots, pans, and parts of a stove were strewn across the ground. Although a forest fire had claimed the area before the eruption had, the remnants of the large boulders that had hurtled down from the distant volcano remained, lodged into the field and throughout the forest.

"Do you know this place?" Melody asked.

Pavonis walked up to a half-charred porch, where she had once spent the afternoons drinking lemonade and preparing for childbirth. The half-burnt boards still held some of the shelves, and she found the old plates and cups she had once laid out on the dinner table every evening. She picked up a teacup with the name Michael on it. Her hand flew to her mouth as a disturbed sadness washed over her, and she dropped the cup. The shatter made David and Melody jump, for the air was so vulnerable and serene that a single snowflake would have sounded like timpani to their eardrums.

"This was where I came to know Ezra. We married here." Pavonis looked across at the other ruins. "Here..." She paused, looking down river as if she could see something. "We were happy here;

everything was simple and beautiful. Before the horror of the prophecy swallowed our lives into Vishnu's masquerade of torture and war. I once knew this place for what it was: *home.* This is where Michael would have been raised."

"Pavonis, I...I'm so sorry," Melody said somberly.

They led the boney caribou down the shore a little way further. Where cattails had once grown, only dead grass remained. Where birds had once sung, only stiff branches held true, their stark movements a testament to the damage done after Vishnu's legendary act. Pavonis suddenly stopped.

"We must let Modi and Saya free. If they go any further, they'll starve to death."

"But we need them," Melody said. "Otherwise we'll never get there in time!"

Modi snorted.

"Sorry, girl. It's nothing personal."

"They have served their purpose. We're very close now."

"To Caldera?"

"No, we're still four hundred miles from Caldera. We're close to the Queen's range of view. She'll find us with or without her reconnaissance teams."

Pavonis stood there, looking into the decrepit wood, before walking up to where an old cedar tree had been decaying for decades. The large tree lay on its side, most of its bark having been eaten away by time and rot. Pavonis reached down and picked up a small piece of bark. She flipped it over. On the other side were her initials, and Ezra's, burnt into the grey bark. Within seconds, the wood was collecting droplets of blood in its etchings, as Pavonis broke down in tears. Melody came over to comfort her, with David close behind.

"I wuv you!" David said, hugging her leg.

Melody also reached her arms around Pavonis. "I love you too."

Pavonis was covered in bloody tears, shaking and sobbing, and as her legs gave way, she collapsed to the ground. In all her battles, and through all her losses, no moment in her life had ever been so dark and hopeless as that moment. She questioned everything, including how she could so deeply love someone who had chosen to abandon their child and leave her widowed, all to try and save an exposed and helpless world. Her soul spoke to her then, reminding her that, no matter his actions, Ezra's love for her and her love for him had been true. She knew what he would have wanted her to do.

"His death cannot be for nothing. It is our duty to stand for what he stood for," Pavonis murmured through her tears.

"I understand, Pavonis," Melody assured her.

Michael and Shakti walked down a long tunnel inside the Queen's black crystal palace.

"His death cannot be for nothing. It is our duty to stand for what he stood for, Michael," Shakti said.

"I understand, master," Michael said assuredly, as he followed behind her.

"Your father was the prophecy's long awaited catalyst. It isn't over yet. Did you know, a team of Japanese researchers went to the exact location where your father supposedly ingested the golden lichen, but found nothing of the sort? At first, I thought the story was a cover up; that Ezra was some government weapon. A super-being constructed in a lab; someone to fight for days on end without the need for food or rest. But my theory didn't add up. Our contact in the U.S. couldn't find anyone else in the super-soldier program with results as miraculous as Ezra's. His changes were too organic. They were too rich with ingenuity, a seamless design. Then, something struck me. In the mission report, your father documented that he and your mother spent most of their time in the rainforest hallucinating on potent psychedelics, not yet documented by science."

"You suspect my father tripped himself into believing that he could become an ever-evolving human?"

"With the amount of dimethyltryptamine they found in a single spore of the floating fungus, it is a valid possibility. Vishnu and I had achieved agelessness over decades of meditation, but what your father found was beyond our imaginations. Regardless of what the truth is, we must thank him for his sacrifice and his discoveries, as it has now opened up a universe of possibilities for the prophecy."

"I want to be a key player in the prophecy, like my father," Michael said.

"Maybe there's an important place for you in our plan after all. I must go and attend to some business matters. You may go to the dining hall. I suggest you use this time to open your heart and receive God's plan for you."

"Thank you, master," Michael said, bowing.

Shakti turned and bowed in return, winking at him before slipping through a secret door and leaving him to wander the quiet and ominous maze of gutted rock.

Later that night, the trio walked on through the wilderness. With her head bowed, Pavonis stared at the cold, dry ground, just about managing to drag her feet onto the warpath again. David tried to comfort her, clinging to her leg and laughing delightedly with every swing. But Pavonis kept on, without noticing the boy. Melody kept silent, following her disheveled master from a safe distance.

The mountains roared above them as they walked eastward. Pavonis hoped to reach the edge of the mountain front soon, for spring was fast approaching.

"Pavonis, shall we stop somewhere for the night?" asked Melody.

"We cannot stop now," Pavonis responded solemnly.

"But if we are too tired, we won't have the energy to keep going—"

"MELODY!" Pavonis exclaimed.

Melody and David looked up and David fled to Melody's arms in terror. Under the broken canopy of midnight's bloom shimmered a shining Goddess, radiating the crescent moon's aquamarine glow. She held in her hand a large moth, and a kaleidoscope of

Lepidoptera surrounded her celestial armor like enchanted faeries, drawn from the pores of the world.

The group stood in silence, unmoving. The Aradian looked at the winged insect in her hand and let it crawl over her thin fingers as she fanned them slowly; delicately, like an arachnid's legs just before the clutch of death.

"If butterflies are flowers personified, then what are moths?" Her voice was quiet, human, and astonishingly sweet. She sounded like a child. She stared at the creature in her palm for a few moments, before turning to the trio. "I did not block your telepathic senses to ambush you, Pavonis. On the contrary, I have come to give you a warning."

Pavonis looked at Tala without gesture or emotion.

"I would not try to betray everything you and I have fought to uphold," Tala reassured her.

"But you're not our ally either," Melody said, feeling instantly regretful and nervous about speaking in such a way to the Aradian.

Tala lifted her head and began walking towards them. Pavonis shook her head, disappointed in her apprentice's lack of respect, though no longer as frightened of the planet-pulverizing Goddess approaching them.

Tala stood in front of Melody and, in a very relaxed and steady motion, removed her chrome mask to let them see her petite, exquisite face. The lovely Aradian woman looked deep into Melody's eyes. In Tala's visionary globes, Melody could see her and her sister, meditating together in the Siberian wilderness.

"In Iran, I stacked so many human bodies that the sun set a half hour earlier, because the mountains of rotting flesh rose above the western horizon. I am no one's ally. I am bound to the process of fermentation itself."

"I'm sorry," Melody began.

"You have no reason to be sorry. But you need to know that if I *were* a true ally, it would not necessarily help the cause." She looked up to the heavens and smiled warmly before turning to Pavonis. "Several months ago, after weeks of deep meditation, my sister shed her sins on the cliffs of Mount Burkan Khaldun, in Mongolia. Using abilities I have yet to fully understand, she left Earth's atmosphere, in order to thrust herself into the sun. Though she deviated from Shakti's rule before I did, her upset was a cumulative one. Old emotions met with new horrors, and I can only guess that her aim is to destroy the entire solar system, while setting her soul at zero. That outcome would be the most just punishment and reward for this place, in her reality."

"Soul at zero?" Melody asked.

"At ten million degrees, the sun erases your spirit. The unfathomable heat and gravitational pull break up all cosmic identity, until the separated molecules of what you once were coalesce with new light photons in the super-heated energy of the sun's mantle, before redistributing pieces of your spirit throughout the universe. My twin sister will cease to be Mayari and every future incarnation. She has been traveling at a constant rate of about sixteen thousand miles per hour, and although she is mentally prepared enough for the task, I trust she will only make it within a few million miles before her body is incinerated by a solar flare. I trust the act will at last resolve her Icarus complex, though a part of me will surely die when she does."

"Are you sure she will not achieve this scheme of grand devastation?" Pavonis asked.

" She is an Aradian. Nothing is certain," Tala answered, sounding almost complacent. She looked no older than seventeen, yet she was over a century old. "I may not be the reincarnation of Zou Cheng, as my master had hoped, but the knowledge I carry contains an old wisdom, cultivated by centuries of concentric meditation," she said, tossing her mask onto the dry grass. "Just as I helped you in Banff, I am here to help you now."

Pavonis nodded. Melody kept listening. David sat with his little hands held under his chin, watching the glowing woman with fascination as his eyes darted between the fluttering moths. The winged creatures sparked the child's memory, reminding him of enchanting tales of forest nymphs, of which he knew more than the endangered creatures themselves.

"We Immortals were so focused on the size of the human population, and how to maintain it, we mistakenly overlooked the population problem that we present."

"But there are only—" Melody began.

"Four now. Michael, Pavonis, Shakti, and myself. Two Sararans and two Aradians are too many," Tala explained.

"So why don't you kill the Queen and leave," Pavonis said bluntly, still emotionally compromised from earlier, yet favoring logic.

"Not even that would be suffice, sadly. You see, there is too much energy conversion between Sararan and Aradian minds, especially complex beings such as yourself, Pavonis. With all the mental espionage and quantum engagement between us, there are instabilities that could influence the iron core of the Earth. The ramifications of this could be long term, and far from my premonitions. On a personal level, the phenomenon causes severe mental illness. You are sick, Pavonis, and you don't even know it. So is Michael, and so is Shakti. Even I myself am sick."

No one said anything for a moment.

"So, the solution to the overpopulation of our two, minutely limited species, is also the solution for solving the rest of Earth's creatures facing extinction?" Pavonis asked.

"Precisely. Lately, I have come to understand the true nature of Sararan DNA. I would tell you, but it cannot be said, for the inertia of your journey will find its way into this realization at the moment it is meant to. I have no place here. I will be at a distance, yet somewhere unmistakable. The rest of this prophecy is in the hands of you and Shakti, and hopefully not in my sister's." Tala smiled and began to walk away.

Pavonis looked helplessly at her retreating former foe.

"Goodbye, Pavonis, Princess Melody, and young David. Perhaps, one day, we will be able to see one another beyond our treachery," Tala said.

"What? You can't leave now! Tell us how to claim

victory! We must do this...for Nature! For the future of Earth and its people!" Melody yelled.

"Nature craves diversity, Melody. Follow that sacred rule, and hold true!" the Aradian cried, her voice becoming more distant.

"Tell us how to fix this, please!" Pavonis called out, her head aching, her eyes slanted in discomfort. She begged in desperation with her mind, but received nothing in return, for even Aradians preferred spoken conversation over telepathy. As the cosmic Goddess faded into the trees, she turned and spoke a few last words to them.

"There can only be two Immortals, and they must be lovers!"

With that, Pavonis' face widened, and she jumped with glee, hugging Melody tightly.

"I don't get it, what does that mean?" Melody asked, her face squashed by Pavonis' tight embrace.

"It finally makes sense! The evolution! The cycle of life! Soon the love of the entire universe will wrap itself around you, its light enveloping you, its tenderness melting you! We will see the world change before our eyes; plants sprouting by the millions; insects and amphibians pulled up from the fountains of spring; birds flying north again; herds of buffalo roaming, and sunsets and sunrises of all colors casting different harmonious, painting every night and every morning. People will grow alongside animals and become herders or tradesman in their local communities. All of the little things most poetic and obscure will return: the soft wood of a well pail, and the rough rope that pulls it; the maiden's sapphire eyes; her father's songs of the oppressed, now liberated through a fiddle's hollow lung, and teepees with fires lit like gems by the river's corridor to salvation. In the markets, children will run through serious conversations, to remind everyone of what joy we left behind! There is everything we could ever need or ask for under this soil, if people could just take care of it. There will be a new beginning, an age of peace and purity, as we reunite humankind with our Mother. Come now! Come my children!"

David joined them and they all hugged, feeling the warmth of whatever Pavonis knew. The enlightened faery looked east and saw there were still several hours until sunrise.

"We have time, but we must hurry. Put David on your back and I'll carry both of you. Let's go!"

David climbed onto Melody's back and Melody leapt onto Pavonis' strong rigid shoulders. The three of them seemed to fly through the mountains, Pavonis' confidence building with every step, her blood pressure dropping, her breath easing, and her lips muttering some haunting scripture in the low born forest's shadow.

Michael stood in the corner of the Queen's dining hall in painful anticipation. He paced for a while, then stood, staring at the door. He looked back behind him. On the dining table was a small, curious object, that had been placed on the edge closest to him. He walked over and looked at it. The ornament was made from carved bone and resembled a pregnant woman. Next to it, there was a note.

Michael,

This is the Venus of Hohle Fels, hewn from a Mastodon's tusk by Aurignacians over thirty thousand years ago. It is my gift to you, and proof of your acceptance into the Zurvan family. She is an icon of fertility and communal growth and will guide you to fruition.

With love and fortitude,
Shakti

Michael looked at the ornament again and

picked it up. There was a strange magnetism about it, an aura that warmed his hand. He placed it in his pocket just as the doors swung open. Two guards rushed towards him and he immediately put up his fists in defense, an eager flame burning in his eyes. As they approached him, they pulled off their white hoods and stopped.

"Will? Lakshmi? What's going on?" Michael exclaimed, hardly believing what he was seeing. Will ran up and hugged him. Lakshmi stood by and smiled as she caught her breath.

"Good to see you, nephew," Will said.

Lakshmi pulled out two pistols from her hidden hip holsters.

"Good to see you too! What the hell are you two doing here...together?" Michael asked.

Will stepped back and pulled off his robes. "We've come to get you the hell out of here. The Queen left the palace not long before we arrived. We have to pursue her! Her guards will be here soon. Where are the stables? You got horses here?"

"Near the gate by the north wall, follow me!" Michael said, hurrying towards the locked door, the taste of freedom tingling on his tongue.

Will handed his imperial staff to Michael and pulled a snub-nosed shotgun from underneath his robe, pumping a shell into the chamber then blasting the lock to pieces.

"Let's move!" Will said, kicking open the door.

The trio sprinted unhindered through the endless passages of the palace, until two guards suddenly appeared from a room, swords raised. Michael whipped around the white staff and knocked the swords from their hands, before knocking their heads against the wall. More guards appeared, but the three of them outwitted their adversaries with feline agility, racing swiftly though the maze of corridors like glorified runaways. Finally, they came to a cavity in the palace wall, bathed in golden light, and Michael found Apollo peacefully munching on some alfalfa under the awning of the stable. Apollo's fiery eyes matched Michaels as they shared a telepathic communication. A guard from the other end of the stable started running towards them but Will held up his shotgun.

"Don't you even fucking try it," he said.

The woman stopped, holding her hands above her head.

"Give me your bow!" Will yelled, not taking his eyes off the guard.

Slowly the woman slid her bow and quiver over to them.

Will handed them to Michael. "I trust you're quite the aim with this by now," Will said, winking, knowing that Michael's changes had yet to be acknowledged by a friend.

Lakshmi outfitted two white stallions as Michael rested his cheek against Apollo's neck.

"Are you ready to spin the world beneath your hooves?" he said softly, happy to see his horse; his blood brother.

Lakshmi and Will mounted saddles and Michael climbed onto Apollo, his connection with his horse such that a saddle would only hinder them. Michael realized he was still wearing the black kimono the Queen had given him and he pulled it off with a lurch, leaving him dressed in only his under garments.

"What's with your horse's eyes?" Lakshmi asked with an inquisitive look.

"My horse is half-Sararan, or whatever the next evolution of a horse is. I saved his life, and now he's one bad mother fucker," he grinned, as Apollo kicked the stall with a loud clank and strutted out.

"One more thing, Michael! You need to stop losing things," Will admonished him. "Like your horse...and your knife."

Will handed Michael his father's knife and Michael sighed.

"Thank you, uncle," Michael said, as he took the dagger and broke the tip off like a stick.

"Why'd you do that?" Will asked, shocked.

Michael took one of his arrows and replaced the obsidian tip with the shattered blade, wrapping the new arrowhead with twine and tucking the remaining knife handle into his loin wrap.

"If I only get one shot, it's going to be for my father."

"He would have been proud of you, kid. Have no fear. Momento Mori!"

Will nodded north but Michael already knew where to go. He kicked Apollo's sides and they sprang into a full gallop before even clearing the awning's shadow. Will and Lakshmi followed behind as they sped beyond the hills. When the Queen's guards realized what had happened, they ignored the orders of General Fraus, instead joining hands with the emaciated slaves and leaving the city and its stink behind. They were free at last; free from the atrocities of the past; united by common purpose; eager to begin a new life in a world that had been there all along, just beyond their reach.

CHAPTER 37
CREATION DAY

Early in the morning, on March the eleventh, 2053, Pavonis, Melody, and David emerged from the Rocky Mountains and walked out onto the vast expanse of the Great Plains, revealing themselves to Shakti's clairvoyant third eye. The sun's distant mercy cast a blue light over the sky as the mountains ceased their triumph with a halting decline. Rolling coulees stretched out before them, and the vast prairie of dull grass gently swayed in the thousand-year-old wind. The stars hung brightly, burning in ancient affliction behind cirrus clouds, scattering their cumulous in the wake of dawn's coming as the sun's light loomed like a forgone titan resurrecting ghost gods.

Pavonis stopped on a mount overlooking the great landscape and set her sword on the ground. She prepared for the ritual by falling into a sitting position, daintily as a feather, levitating inches above the ground and closing her eyes in deep meditation.

Melody followed suit, though she remained grounded. David sat with his legs outstretched, looking at the receding stars with wonder.

"Pretty sky," David said.

"This will be the brightest dawn this world has seen in a very long time. In this pure light we may sow the seeds of tomorrow's fortunes. When the Queen arrives, do not fear. She is swayed by the prophecy and its intricacies. When the moment is right, Melody, you must charge my blade with dawn's first glimpse and stab me through the heart. The spell is a difficult one, but powerful. It is all about focus and timing. The moment the light touches the blade you must thrust it into me. I will enter Shakti's body, she will enter mine, and she and I will die together on this hillside. A new world will be constructed from this day, a chance for humankind to be at one with all other life forms. And you will have become a true sorceress, sweet Melody. I cannot do this without you."

Melody sat, unmoving, her eyes still closed. A single tear fell from beneath her weary lashes.

"I am deeply grieved to request this of you, but I feel fortunate to have taught such a worthy apprentice, and to have been with you during these challenging times. I have confidence that you will succeed in casting this spell and reversing the damage Shakti has done to the Earth after I pass on."

"Stop talking like that! You'll live, you have to! You'll take over her body or something—"

"No, Melody. It doesn't work like that. This must end in sacrifice. My fate is tied to hers, just as Ezra's was tied to Vishnu's. I can't explain it. You'll understand one day."

"No, please!" Melody cried.

David came over to her and held her hand. "Don't be sad," David said.

Pavonis looked at Melody from her floating lotus pose. Her eyes were placid, with blue galaxies swirling inside them. "You know I love you don't you?"

"Yes," Melody said softly. "And I love you."

"If you love me, then you must do this. It is the only way to save the world."

Pavonis floated to the ground and embraced the children tenderly, the three of them clinging to one another in silence. Under the bright moonlight they took comfort in each other's presence, a nucleus of beings wrapped under Pavonis' tanned shawl, their hearts somehow still beating in that century's woeful antinode. The paths they had walked so desperately at first had led them to one another, two generations representing different stages of Zurvan oppression, each focused on resolve, however convoluted and daunting. Even behind Pavonis' cosmic eyes, Melody could find only a single glinting star of hope, defiantly announcing admonition, pulsing relentlessly like the heart of a dying animal.

An ill-favored wind turned Pavonis' eyes south, where a dark cloud followed a black figure, warping the sky behind it like a vacuum, devouring the world of ash and dust in its abrasive Earth scourging. The bubbling, catastrophic mass lacked all form beyond its fixation, as it crackled on the coat tails of a fearsome Gorgon.

Ninety-three million miles away, in the silence of deep space, a speck of light fell into the blinding luminescence of the sun's surface. During that long journey to the sun, Mayari had performed the greatest feat of any known being, with the intention of erasing that monumental act, and all other evidence of life on Earth forevermore. But just as her beautiful reflecting eyes became blinded by the coronal blaze, she did repent, and she refused to end all that the creatures of the blue planet had fought for in the epochs since the inception of the first single-celled organism. She thought of her sister, Tala, and what their duality meant to the world. She thought of her life as a prisoner, a refugee, an assassin, a weapon, and eventually a Goddess. She had no more resentment for man's wrongdoings, or for her own. At last, she understood a secret no human could ever know, thus succumbing to that enveloping shroud of heaven's ascent.

The titanium deity's armor melted and turned to steam. Her thick Aradian panels of skin disintegrated; her carbon bones shattered; her perfect organs and mind became nothing but puffs of ash in the face of that matured nuclear reactor of fusion and fire. Mayari became a soulless being, stripped of solar identity, her atoms pulled apart and consumed by the scorching surface. Her particles became wrapped in the guiding light of the sun, whose great flares threw pieces of her spirit back to Earth, just in time for someone to absorb those auxiliary rays and harness their charge.

Michael, Lakshmi, and Will had pushed their horses onward, with hardly any rest or water. Michael led the way, with his Sararan stallion charging ahead like a resurrected Bucephalus, his nostrils expelling atrous smoke and his hooves pummeling the ground with a thunderous gallop. The emerging light of dawn found its way to them as they raced along the northbound road.

"Slow down, Michael!" Will yelled. "We need to rest for a moment!"

Michael slowed. "Apollo's senses we are right on her tail! We are so close!"

"I understand, but these animals need water and food," Will said, dismounting. Will's horse laid down with a grunt and a sigh. Lakshmi's horse was just as exhausted.

Michael shook his head and looked around with his far zooming eyes. His breath caught in his throat. "There, on that mound at the base of the mountains! I see them! I see Melody and Pavonis, and a small child!"

Michael took off in an instant leaving Will to yell after him, "Wait! Michael! It could be a trap!"

Will and Lakshmi mounted their steeds and chased after him, their horses desperately trying to follow Apollo's seemingly winged hooves. Michael dove in and out of the coulees, pushing Apollo as fast as he could go, dawn's utterance fast approaching. Above him, a sonic clap sent his Sararan ears ringing as a black cape lashed at the clouds. It darted through the air like a crane of death, flapping toward the children and their protector.

The figure slowed as it approached the mound, and through its inertia one could see the face of Shakti. She landed lightly a few yards in front of the children and Pavonis.

"So, this is the ceremony to which I have been so carefully uninvited," Shakti said, her intentions unclear, her body clenching, her chin raised regally and her antlered headpiece directed toward the trio as if ready to charge.

"But you are invited, Shakti. You are an invaluable medium for this grand ritual," Pavonis said graciously.

Shakti stood still and stared at David, who held a small, frail lotus flower in his hands and smiled without judgment.

"This young boy...who is he?"

"He is one of the few that has survived your reign, Shakti. *He's one of the last.*"

"Then he is strong," she replied, almost sympathetically.

Pavonis knelt with her hands on her thighs. Melody stood behind her, the two of them facing the oncoming sunrise, the Queen's dark figure blocking out the horizon's coming light. Melody held the hilt of the sword high above her, so that Shakti's silhouette could not hinder its reflection, the tip pointed straight down at Pavonis' left shoulder. Melody's eyes poured tears of distress. David kept smiling at the Queen.

"I don't know if I can do this, Pavonis," Melody choked.

"You can. And you will. No one will attack you here. This is a place of divine transformation," she said calmly.

"It seems you have taught your apprentice well in the sciences of witchcraft."

"As you have taught yours," Pavonis said with respect.

In the corner of her eye, Melody saw the flash of a rider streaming across the plains, the dust behind him flaring orange in the coming light, like sparks from a furnace.

"Michael," Melody whispered, her heart fluttering.

"Focus Melody, the sun is almost risen. Watch the horizon! Watch for the first light!"

As the sun was about to rise, Michael came within shooting distance of Shakti. He knocked an arrow in his bow and drew the string back. Apollo bolted across the plain, falling into a trance of maddening velocity.

"Be kind to the world I have suffered to save, Melody," the Queen said calmly.

David slowly began walking towards Shakti. The tension in Melody's hands fought against her trembling. Pavonis took a deep breath. David reached out and Shakti grabbed the pink-petalled flower with reluctance, shedding a single, bloody, regretful tear as she touched David's hand softly.

Michael released his arrow with a furious scream, and it shot high into the air. Melody watched its flight as the light of the sun exploded over the horizon and bathed the scene in golden light. Melody thrust the blade downwards, slicing through Pavonis' thick skin and through her still pumping heart. Pavonis' face widened and her eyes became supernovas; shooting stars cast beyond the walls of her irises as the sun's pure essence wrapped her and consumed her. Pavonis smiled and mouthed the words 'I love' as the blade cut into her.

Just as the sword resurfaced below his mother's breast, Michael's fast flying arrow plunged itself through Shakti's back, and the once mighty Queen fell. Her blood splattered towards Pavonis and the bodies of the Goddesses hit the ground at once, their Sararan and Aradian fluids colliding in the air above that dry soil in a way that neither deity had suspected. As the drops touched the ground, plants and trees began sprouting, hundreds at a time, in a wave of growth that crawled over the hills and through the mountains, beyond the prairies and rivers, and far over the horizon. Grasses, ferns, pines, firs, aspens and larches sprouted from the Goddesses mixed genetic palates, unleashing a stream of organic consciousness, giving back to the fasted land what it had been craving since Vishnu's cleansing. Her master had changed the world through apocalyptic incineration; Shakti gave new life to the exhausted Earth as her cumulative symbiosis with Pavonis mounted and took shape, the judgment that had tortured Shakti all her life dripping away with the blood of her pierced Aradian heart.

The jungle of life bloomed past Will and Lakshmi as they rode in bewilderment. Pines erupted out of the ground like spears. Grasses and mosses drowned the rocks. Lichen and fungi swarmed over the previously dead land. Michael and Apollo bound through the lush landscape ahead of them to find a puzzling and disturbing scene. Amidst the dawn's light he saw the fallen Queen with his arrow in her back, David kneeling at her side. His gaze shifted a few feet away to his dying mother, held in Melody's arms, surrounded by the scent of pollen and petrichor.

"Mother!" Michael cried, as he approached them.

"It's over Michael. You did it! You and Melody...saved us," she said, blood dripping from her mouth as she gave in to her weakness.

"Michael, I'm so sorry! I didn't want to! Your mother, I...she told me...she said it was the only way!" Melody sobbed, tears streaming down her face.

"Shh, it's okay, it's okay. Come here..." Michael pulled Melody into his chest and embraced her, kissing her gently on the forehead. Then he walked over to his mother and held her head in his hands. "Mother look at me, mother, you're going to be okay! You're a Sararan, I know you'll be okay!"

Shakti looked up with a melancholy gaze as she drifted toward death, the arrow's white fletching rising from her back like a flag of surrender. David sat beside her, holding her hand tightly.

"Listen to me, Michael," Pavonis said, choking on her own blood. "My time is over...it's your time

449

now...you two...your time to rule...with the values you have been taught." She reached for the sword that had punctured her body, and cut her hand. She reached for Melody. "Come here, Melody," she said, struggling for breath. She took Melody's hand and sliced the young woman's palm.

Melody winced as Pavonis placed her hand to Melody's own and kissed it with bloody lips.

"You are now our planets protector and mother, Melody. Be better than I was but hold true the principles I have taught you. And you, my son," she said, smiling at Michael, the golden light reflected in her fading eyes. "My brave and handsome son."

"Mother..." Michael whispered, his own bloody tears streaming onto the foliage beneath them, each teardrop creating sprouts of bright red Indian paintbrush flowers.

"I love you, my son. I will always love you. Take care of your Sararan Empress," she said.

"I will, I love you. Please, stay with us a bit longer," Michael said, holding his mother's head in his shaking, cupped hands.

As the birds of the old forest began to sing and the wind once again found its song in the leaves and needles of the trees, the nebulous skies inside Pavonis' eyes were swallowed by black holes until they were no more. At the same moment, Shakti dropped the lotus, and each Goddess perished in equal resolve.

"No. NO!" Michael screamed as Melody held him to her, rubbing circles on his back and sobbing into his shoulder as she began to shake, the quickly assimilating Sararan cells inside her taking hold in a warm but overwhelming sensation.

Will and Lakshmi arrived soon after, and though they were saddened by the loss of their dear friend and sister, the wretched Queen had been defeated, and the war was finally over. They sat beside the young Sararans and grieved with them. Later, they determined the site to be a holy one, and left the bodies of the Goddesses as they were, so that their cells could continue to feed the forest in the way both of them would have wanted.

As the day passed and the group walked back into the mountains, they looked out upon the wake of seedlings that had spread and would continue to ripple across the world, into the oceans, over the continents, overlapping and recreating once again a semi-stable climate and wondrous paradise full of all the phyla that Pavonis had managed to archive in her blood before unleashing the sacred fluid onto the land. Just as Vishnu had scourged the world of its sins, Pavonis had replanted its soils through her virtuous undertaking, and just as she had hoped, all was becoming balanced in the world once more.

The few remaining humans put aside any religious scrutiny and past quarrels and joined hands as if the utopia was a gift from the sun itself. Perhaps much of it was. Perhaps each individual's offering provided the conditions ripe for a new world on that fateful spring day: Tala's reconciliation; Mayari's forgiveness; Pavonis' sacrifice; Shakti's atonement; Lakshmi's betrayal; William's perseverance; Melody's faithfulness; Michaels vengeance, and David's courage. Without any one of these being's virtues, the prophecy would have been compromised. With the death of the Goddesses, a new mythology began, as Shakti's submission at the sight of David's innocence once again proved that love and purity triumphs in the face of even the greatest Goliath of evils.

CHAPTER 38
A LATTICEWORK SHRINE

The world gasped in oxygenated awakening and exhaled its sour phlegm, each day spewing an inch of rain into the veins of the land. The high rivers swept waste out to sea, crumbling dams with their colliding tributaries of bitter water, pouring into catacombs of those hiding, bored of their burden. Around the world, news spread about the cause of the planet's sudden revival. Foreign peoples learned only the myth of the rejuvenation and did not see the changes until the sun pierced their cloaked atmosphere. Instead of thanking their Gods and prophets, new generations gave praise to the Sararans for defeating the Zurvan hierarchy. Pavonis was, to many, a bringer of light and hope; a true mother to all mothers.

The air once again became enriched with nutrients. Fungi and bacteria broke down the toxins built up in the soil, and the oceans teemed with life. People watched the biosphere pulse with change.

Vegetables and roots grew in such quantities no farmland needed tilling. Wild game could be harvested in smaller, less aggressive hunting parties. Fisherman came back daily with a sizable catch. People ate what made sense to their stomachs, as they performed great feasts, coming together for the benefit of one another as humans had done so during the birth of language. There was plenty of both song and spice to go around, thus through communion the world was made new, for words are easily swords and swords easily sheathed. History had shown its ugly face, and peoples very communication depended on the death of the damaging doctrines of the old world's lords. This included Shakti, whose army gave up their fight with only a few high-ranking Zurvans escaping into the mountains of Nepal to find refuge in Zou Cheng's hidden tomb.

Pavonis was the people's answer, their savior, and they gladly followed the two young people to whom she had bestowed her divinity. But despite Michael and Melody's new powers, it would take many decades to return the Earth to what it had once been before human dominance. The initial changes for the Americas were extreme. The fires of Yellowstone grew dormant, once again becoming geysers and mud pits, and the obsidian palace sunk into the earth, its great weight devoured by the thin soil. To the north, near Babb, Montana, a bloodstone jasper epitaph was constructed at the location of Pavonis and Shakti's resting place, its message of honor and sacrifice covered by vines within days of its placement.

For many weeks, Melody and Michael traveled the world to spread news of the great Pavonis. All agreed to have Michael and Melody become their benevolent rulers, their fear of a lapsing Aradian takeover driving them to side with the Sararan beings. In Africa, Melody visited the impoverished peoples of the savannah. She mesmerized the locals when she touched the baked soil and grew hectares of wheat and fruit. The tribes bowed to the young Goddess and praised her with thanks. All through the world, the couple continued this trend, winning allegiance from village to village and meeting at last with the eight-year-old Mongolian Queen Parvati on the steppe of Central Asia. They agreed upon a territorial dissection of land and sea, whereby the Sararans ruled Northern and Southern America, Africa and Western Europe, while Parvati reclaimed Eurasia as Mongolia, along with most of what had been within the Mongols contiguous empire at its height in the early fourteenth century. This split the world into two kingdoms, each equally in need of border deconstruction and enlightening policy changes. All rejoiced as beast and man came together, as humans integrated into the animal kingdom, rather than forcing themselves away by society's protrusion. That sacred bond still remained, thin and nearly broken by modern man, yet perhaps stronger since the post-eruption's decades of darkness. It would take many years for this bond of living things to solidify into a harmonized utopia beneath a sky still prone to interstellar dangers.

That May, Michael, Melody, David, Will, and Lakshmi resettled at the site of the old cabins on the North Fork river, where Michael's mother and father had once lived. Grasses and plants emerged with spring's fresh breath, and after the twenty-year winter, the river flowed clean again. From log debris, beavers and river otters made dams along its shores. Birds built nests in old trees, their numbers growing with each day. The sky was bright and blue and perfect. Wildflowers blossomed and bees returned, their honey tasted by children who had only read about the golden nectar, as they smelled flowers they had only heard of in song. Amphibians and reptiles once extinct came back to re-catalogue themselves into the planet's biodiversity. All life was multiplying and flourishing, with the exception of mosquitoes, for Pavonis had withheld the DNA of that insect of extermination, the only organism to cause more human deaths than all the Immortals combined.

Two cabins were built. Michael built one for Melody, and William built one for Lakshmi, as they gave praise to their female counterparts. The site once occupied by Ezra and Ingrid was to be the capital of North and South America, which they had proudly renamed Pavonia. Will had a hard time accepting the change to the free world, and he still kept a large American flag hung in his cabin, reminding him of his Marines and their sacrifices. Will and Lakshmi married in April, and the young Sararans were not far behind. It was late May when Michael and Melody tied the knot, and to call it the grandest wedding on the planet would be an understatement.

Orange and purple petals flared from the hands

of the child leaders of Eurasia, as they welcomed Melody down the aisle. They clapped their hands wildly and grinned, some with gap-toothed smiles. A crowd of people from the Pacific to the Atlantic watched on, hollering loudly for their heroes. Melody wore a pristine white dress and smiled softly as she walked, her dimples caving with joy. The wise old man who had married Ezra and Ingrid stood with Michael below a finely woven latticework shrine, welcoming Melody's gentle touch with his century old hands. Michael stood under the alter, wearing a green silk scarf over his black suit. He smiled at Melody, and she smiled back. The crowd quieted their clapping and the old man chuckled before beginning.

"A long time ago, I married a very beautiful couple in this very place. Now the son of that couple, and his soon-to-be-wife, have saved the world. I must recognize these young lovers as examples to all people; as prophets in this new age of peace. To see such wonderous beings fall in love with one other under the impossible circumstances that our time has allowed warms my heart beyond words. I believe this marks a new beginning for us all. David, the rings please," he said, smiling at the young child walking down the aisle.

A group of women almost spilled their

champagne as they cooed at the child's adorable face.

David walked up and handed Melody her ring. Michael took his and thanked David, who smiled and took off down the aisle, throwing the pillow into the air with excitement as he ran.

"You have both written your own vows, which you may now say to one another. First, Queen Melody," the old man said, stepping back.

"Michael, I knew you were a good person from the moment I met you. You are strong willed, determined, and you care about those around you to an extent I can only hope to achieve. My love for you is only limited by the lack of time I have been able to spend with you these last few months of war. But I believe our love will grow like the wave of life that escaped your mother's blood, and this age of peace will be guided by our ability to love one another and affect that kind of love. You were my inspiration through the toughest times, and even in complete turmoil, I found reasons to smile because of you. Will you be my husband for all of time?"

"I will," Michael said solemnly.

"King Michael, do you have something you wish to tell Melody?" the old man asked.

Half the crowd were in tears, even Will.

"Melody, you were born a princess, so it only

makes sense that you are now a Queen."

The crowd laughed.

"But you are so much more than that. You are a warrior in the truest sense. My mother taught you many things, and most importantly, she taught you how to make sacrifices and be the best person you could be. She knew it was no coincidence that she found you and helped you in your quest to find me. There is a want and a need that circulates through the universe. It is love. Love guides us and finds a way to defeat anything in our path. You are a strong, beautiful woman, who, like me, never had a true family besides the people we have met along the way, helping us through this strange life. I owe you my love, and I am forever yours, to have, to hold, to love, and to keep. Will you be my wife for all of time, Melody?"

"I will," she said, smiling at him and fighting back her tears as her eyes became outlined with scarlet dew.

"It seems to me you both love each other dearly, and through the passion that has molded you, you have connected on a deeper level than most people could ever know. You are the sun beings this planet has been waiting for, to bring back the cycles that bring joy to all. I announce you, Melody, and you, Michael, wife and husband. You may kiss one another!" he said loudly.

The married couple kissed deeply and the crowd of thousands erupted with applause as flowers were thrown and doves were let free from bamboo cages. A string quintet struck up a tune and the couple walked down the aisle in excitement. The cake was cut. Drinks were raised in toast after toast. Many cheers were given as people from all over the world of all different ages and colors and dialects danced in the warm evening air. Beyond the forest's shade the howling of many wolves matched the stroke of the fiddlers bow at the hearkening of dusk's cessation. The spirit of the wedding was a joyous one, vibrant and honey-dipped, and as much of a contrast to the cold world they had endured as one could imagine. The celebration was an achievement beyond a simple marriage, for the unification of the last two Sararans was the final act in reuniting Earth's humans and fellow life forms. Even the smallest of creatures depended on that beloved alliance.

Later that evening, Michael stood alone in the cabin loft, looking out at the full moon with wandering eyes. Down below, the guests had built a large bonfire, and the string players danced in time to their warbling as alcohol was poured from honey taps and weed smoke rose like slow angels with open wings for the clouds to envy.

Melody walked in quietly, and came to stand beside him. "Hello, King Michael Beller," she said, her eyes soft and glowing in the moon's caress.

"Hello, Queen Melody Bakr Beller," he said, smiling, gazing lovingly upon his dimple wearing bride, whose vine eyes could be drunk like the wine they cried, whose song had been sung with the tone of moonlight.

Melody's human body had been carefully replaced by that divine gene of ever replenishing fortitude, that compound of infinite focus and unrestrained emotion, always developing hence the make of its vessel, she who laid all demons to rest in the candling world.

"How did you know?" Melody asked curiously. "About me once being a princess?"

"Will told me bits of the story. I put some of it together in Shakti's prison after my own transformation. It seems our fathers designed our fate," he said.

"In a sense. Long ago, during the oil wars, Ezra attempted to assassinate my father, Hasam, but he missed his shot. Vishnu was there as your father's comrade. He took the miss as an omen, and purposely failed to destroy Hasam. He let Hasam live, a betrayer to the Zurvans, and yet a man who had a special lineage waiting to blossom. But was it my birth or Ezra's miss that gave Vishnu idle steps? One led into the other. Was it Vishnu or Ezra that unleashed the caldera's fury? Vishnu of course, but Ezra's involvement was crucial. Was it Mayari or Tala who was most dreadful? Which Goddess was most sparing? None will ever know. Was it Shakti or your mother, Pavonis, who gave the Earth back what humans had ravaged for so many centuries? They were codependent. Whatever the amount of luck, loss, or liturgy, Vishnu's plan was meant to save you and I. He saw the opportunity for balance in the world's youthful prodigies. He must have believed one of us could be the *reincarnation* of his master, and thus our place in the prophecy was vital."

Michael looked at the floor for a moment, processing the information as his orange eyes flickered with a calm blaze. "It's quite impressive, Vishnu's execution, so precise and well-drawn. Shakti nearly ruined it with her passions."

"Vishnu had a bit of luck in a lively and distracted world. Shakti endured the burden of all those deaths and the emptiness in her own soul until her only companion was you, the person aiming to end her reign. There might have been a way to paradise without Pavonis' death, but I have not been able to conceive one. I loved her like my own mother, Michael. I miss her deeply."

"Me too," he said sadly.

"I know you wish you had known your father. If I had the power to make it happen, both your parents would be here tonight. But it is because of what your mother and father did that we are able to be here now, in this wonderful moment."

"I know. I just wish I could have gotten to know my mother more, you know?"

Just then, Will appeared from behind the shadows. "I can tell you a lot about her, but if you share her love for all living things, you'll be with her in other ways." He walked in slowly, holding a glass of scotch, hardly aged but drinkable, for it was a spirit that reminded him of his brother. "Your mother was an amazing person. She knew the difference between a good apple and bad apple, just by looking. That's why it took so long for her to like your father," he said, chuckling.

They all laughed.

"Well, luckily I still get to see this side of him through his brother. Thanks again for everything you taught me, Uncle, and for being the person you are. I love you," Michael said.

Will hugged Michael warmly and Melody wrapped her arms around them both.

"You beauties gonna leave me out?" a voice said from behind.

They all turned to see Lakshmi walking gracefully into the room, and Melody opened her arms to welcome her into their embrace. Their love moved through one another in a circuit of warmth, passing between them with a steady resonance.

Will and Lakshmi backed away, holding hands.

"Once again, congratulations. We are old and it's past our bedtime, but you two have fun and behave yourselves. There's a few of Lakshmi's guests here from Neon City and they sure know how to party," Will said.

"Oh, I'm well aware of how they operate in Neon City!" Michael exclaimed.

"Goodnight you two," Will said, chuckling.

The couple walked off, hand in hand, into the darkness of the cabin's stairwell.

"So, what happens now?" Melody asked, her Sararan eyes glowing like an emerald centrifuge, much like Pavonis' pre-manifestation, matching the greenery around them.

"Well...besides Tala, who is probably meditating at the bottom of the ocean or something, we are the only Immortals on the planet. And, along with the

465

Princesses of Asia, who are still at the finger-painting stage in their development, we can make new laws and regulate goods for now. It's going to be a tough job, but I think we will be gracious and fair leaders."

"Laws and regulated goods? The world is full of tribes and communes, not cities. It will be simple and peaceful for a while. Can't we just enjoy it?"

"Yes, my love. Of course," Michael said, looking longingly into his beloved's eyes.

They gravitated towards one another under the full moon, Michael's fire eyes matching the passion in Melody's beautiful, floral gaze. She dipped her face into the mauve light, tightening her grip on her husband's hand. She wrapped her hand softly around his neck and from her finger a vine sprouted, weaving up and around their bodies before blooming into a lotus. The soft pink flower opened and settled under the blushing stars, framed in the windows oval arch above the young Sararan lovers, whose lips found fortune in a kiss as devoted as the sun itself. A kiss that seemed to last an eternity.

The party was dying down as the music softened and the guests in the teepee's dotting the field doused their fires. Sleep seemed to be the consensus at that late hour as Will walked about the grounds looking for Lakshmi. He found her by the river.

"I came back from the outhouse and you weren't in bed. Is everything okay?"

Lakshmi looked out across the water with a concerned expression on her face.

"Do you think they will be able to lead this world?"

"I'm sure they will do their best. Hey...what's wrong?"

"I'm just worried for them. I know Tala hung up her armor and Sandraudiga was killed in battle but..."

"But what?"

She went to speak, then paused. "What if...what if Shakti really did take over the world in order to save it?"

"What are you saying?"

"What if someone with that kind of power was totally blind to empathy. What if they were just using the life-long Zurvan training regimen to get closer to their own power and it had nothing to do with the prophecy at all."

"Who are you talking about, Lakshmi?"

Lakshmi watched the moon's reflection in the ripples. "Someone we shall not speak of anymore, for to say her name would direct her vision our way. No, we must make sure she has no allies and no recognition in this world. Forget I ever said anything."

With that they held one another tightly and watched the rivers flow, never again uttering the name of the jilted General, that shade who had chosen not to retreat with her clan to Nepal, nor to seek Queen Melody for pardoning, but instead chose to return to her origins in Chernobyl where she entered the abandoned building of Reactor Four, snuck down into the flooded basement, and slunk deep into that black pool of poison and broken down suns.

Along the Path

Along the Path

The Meditator's Companion to
Pilgrimage in the Buddha's India and Nepal

Kory Goldberg & Michelle Décary

Pariyatti Press

Kory Goldberg is a Humanities professor and Michelle Décary is a freelance writer, yoga teacher and organic gardener. They have been practising Vipassana meditation and travelling to the Buddha's Land since the late 1990s.

Pariyatti Press
an imprint of Pariyatti Publishing
867 Larmon Road
Onalaska, WA 98570 USA
Tel. [+1] 360-978-4998
www.pariyatti.org

First Edition 2009
Second Edition 2013

ISBN: 978-1-938754-58-6

Library of Congress Control Number: 2013912884

Updates and resources: www.pilgrimage.pariyatti.org

The authors wish to thank Aleksei Gomez for permission to use his illustration on the cover and title page of this book. Thanks also goes to the following artists for the images they so readily offered for use in this publication:

- Lluïsot Domènech: pages 20, 22, 50, 71, 73, 122, 156 and 313.
- Anita Ghanekar: pages 80 and 290.
- Aleksei Gomez: also pages 103, 114, 137, 164, 248, 301 and 315.
- Gary Gronokowski: page xxii.
- Nik 'the Bhik' Halay: pages 116, 144 and 282.
- Jenny Jeffs: pages 1, 88, 90, 93, 113, 143, 162, 212, 241, 278 and 366.
- Michael Pancoe: pages 42, 67, 124, and 367.
- Godelière Richard: pages 3, 77, 78, 170, 313, 347 and 348.
- Bjarni Wark: pages 61, 82, 135, 173 and 179.

Printed in the United States of America

Not all who wander are lost.

– J.R.R. Tolkien

Wherever you travel in this world,
Above, across, or below;
Carefully examine at all times
The arising and passing of all compounded things.

– Gotama the Buddha

Pariyatti Press

Enriching the world by:
- Disseminating the words of the Buddha
- Providing sustenance for the seeker's journey
- Illuminating the meditator's path

Contents

Preface to the 2nd Edition

During the winter of 2013 I received a wonderful opportunity to go on a three-week pilgrimage (while Michelle gallantly cared for our two young children) with twenty-nine experienced Vipassana meditators from twelve different countries. The aim of the tour, organized by generous and creative volunteers at Pariyatti, was to assist meditators deepen their awareness of the *Dhamma* in the places directly connected with the life and teachings of the Buddha and his Saṅgha. In the past I had always travelled to these places on my own, with Michelle, or at most, with a handful of friends, so I was initially reluctant when Pariyatti approached me to lead the group. Despite my reservations of travelling with such a large number of people, I accepted—apprehensively. Flying to Kolkata from Bangkok while my family was escaping the Canadian winter on a sunny and pristine Thai beach, I wondered what I was getting myself into. "Why travel with strangers during my sabbatical from teaching when I could be playing beach volleyball and swimming with my children?" However, as soon as I landed on Indian soil and saw one of my *khadi*-dressed Indo-Canadian travel companions smiling and waving at me through the security glass, I knew I had made the right decision.

Traveling and meditating with companions on the Path, especially in such a unique context as the *Majjhima Desa*, kindles life-long (and lives-long!) Dhamma friendships. The journey also enables meditators to cultivate and deepen their confidence in the Triple Gem. Walking in the Buddha's actual footsteps facilitates better comprehension of the background in which the Buddha lived, and doing so with a community of committed (and gentle, patient, humorous, and adventure-seeking) practitioners can be both humbling and uplifting. During this memorable *yatra*, our group formally meditated three times a day for one hour each time, although some days only two hours; many other days more—all depending on when and where we were. We always took turns reading a few select passages from *Along the Path* while at the sites—this helped us gain a deeper sense of the Buddha's teachings in the places they were actually given, and allowed us to better visualize what life may have been like 2600 years ago. At all times, we did our best to maintain silence and noble speech, thus increasing our ability to practice awareness and equanimity at these sacred sites.

During the *yatra* I kept a notebook to jot down my thoughts and observations of changes I noticed since my last sojourn to India five years earlier. Pages of my notebook began to fill up with gold nuggets that needed to be shared with future pilgrims. Not only did I come across recently discovered sites, but as for India itself, the country's infrastructure and services have developed, and continue to develop, at an unprecedented pace, making pilgrimage easier than ever before. Moreover, the standards, as well as the cost of travelling have increased, but anyone who pays attention to their budget and uses their hard-earned travel knowledge (coupled with pointers from this book) will still find India an affordable and gratifying experience.

Since 2009 when the first edition of Along the Path was published, meditators of all stripes imbued with a contagious love of Indian culture have written us. Their letters were replete with helpful criticisms, suggestions and praise, as well as personal anecdotes about meditation, travel, food and accommodation. Without their communication and support, I'm not sure we would have had the inspiration to keep the book alive, relevant and current. This second edition of *Along the Path* includes all of their feedback, and my own 2013 observations and conversations with local Indians and global travellers. It also features newly discovered pilgrimage sites to visit, as well as a few more stories from the Pāli canon. Many blessings and may this book serve you well along your path!

Kory Goldberg
Dunham, Québec
May, 2013

Prologue

The sites throughout the Indian subcontinent associated with the life and teachings of the Buddha mark the locations of some of the most important events in the development of human consciousness. Since the time of the Buddha, pilgrims from all over the world have been inspired to overcome all sorts of difficult obstacles in order to meditate, pray and pay homage in these places. The pilgrims of old had to endure many hardships in their travels, such as crossing hot deserts, traversing rugged snow-covered mountains, or sailing stormy pirate-controlled waters, often suffering intense exposure to harsh climates and life-threatening illnesses. Today's modern pilgrims, like all travellers, are likely to face some struggles during a journey to these lands. Getting there is made much more comfortable, however, by our easy access to air-travel and an extensive network of trains, mobile phones and high-speed internet, savvy travel agents and a wide range of guide books. Nevertheless, these 'luxuries' do not lessen the benefits of pilgrimage (*yatra*), nor do they necessarily diminish the evocative impressions many discover when visiting the sites and learning about what took place at each one. Experiencing these places firsthand, and feeling their continued spiritual vibrancy amidst the surrounding bustle of modern life, provides an entirely fresh dimension to any meditator's understanding of the Buddha, Dhamma and Saṅgha.

Visiting these places also enables us to appreciate the historical, social and artistic dimensions of the Buddha's life and teaching, which is difficult to comprehend while remaining at home. Witnessing the legacy of commemorative monuments, modern temples, monasteries and impressive artistic works—all bequeathed to the world by international adepts of the Dhamma—has the capacity to increase our awe of the Dhamma's magnitude, and to strengthen our own confidence in the practice of the Path.

The aim of this book is to assist the traveller, on different levels, along the pilgrim's route. In retelling the events of the Buddha's life, we have attempted to maintain the liveliness of the Pāli canon stories without compromising their meaning, theme and authenticity. We have revised the difficult and archaic language of direct translation, making the stories more readable for pilgrims, especially for those who are not native English speakers.

With regard to travelling we give pointers and tips to help meditators reach the sacred places with *fewer* hassles; however, nothing is guaranteed. Everything in life is uncertain, and even more so in topsy-turvy India, where things are always changing with great rapidity: names, numbers, addresses, bus/train schedules and all else in between. To prevent the book from being inaccurate or becoming too-quickly dated, we try to provide general, open-ended information in order to help free travellers from attachment to assurance in a land where nothing can be assured. This, in fact, is one of the benefits of pilgrimage in the Indian subcontinent.

We also want travellers to discover the Buddha's modern India for themselves, rather than follow a pre-scripted step-by-step tourists' track. Experience is obviously the best guide, and therefore the goal of this book is not to provide technical, archaeological, historical or economical details of these places (other books have already done a very good job of this), but to help enable the pilgrim to understand why these are important places to visit and in which to meditate. We hope that in this way, the mindful and receptive meditator can gain a deeper sense of the Buddha's teachings in the places where they were first given, and can reflectively visualize what life must have been like almost 2 600 years ago. These reflections, rooted in insight, can produce delightful and mature fruits of understanding. Rather than behaving like the average tourist *sight-seer*, who merely looks around and takes some snaps of India's historical skeleton—the ruins, the temples, the palaces, the Himālaya—we encourage the traveller to meditate in these places, becoming a *site-sitter* who *feels* the living energy of these tremendous sites for themselves.

The Buddha's teachings have only recently returned to India, and it is our belief that travellers who meditate are best equipped to contact the rich spiritual tradition of the Dhamma that lies at India's heart. Moreover, while travelling in these lands, meditators have the unique opportunity to not only grow in Dhamma themselves, but also to help the Dhamma flourish again in the land of its origin.

Wherever we are, whether in India or at home, we are encouraged by the Buddha's teachings to try and actualize, in our everyday lives, five requisites for practising the path of meditative awareness: proper devotion, good health, honesty, diligence and wisdom.

To begin with, we feel that it's important while on pilgrimage to consciously cultivate *devotion* towards the Triple Gem: Buddha, Dhamma and Saṅgha. Embracing these as centres of refuge means finding inspiration and protection in the quality and process of enlightenment. Without a sense of confidence and protection, one will find it difficult to plumb the depths of the mind. Taking refuge in the Buddha does not imply that the Buddha is a saviour or will extinguish one's suffering. The word 'Buddha' is a title that means 'awakened person,' or 'one who personifies being awake.' When we take refuge in the Buddha, we are taking refuge in the qualities of the Buddha, and not in the person himself. However, having respect for the person is also important, as the Buddha was the one who rediscovered and then compassionately shared this path of liberation with us. Taking refuge in, and having respect for the Buddha helps provide inspiration for developing the qualities of enlightenment in ourselves. It is said that all beings have the potential for enlightenment. This potential however, needs to be cultivated. By taking shelter in the enlightenment of the Buddha, we strengthen the process of developing our own enlightenment. When we explore the sacred sites with a mind committed to awareness and equanimity, every moment becomes an opportunity to achieve liberation.

Taking refuge in the Dhamma, the teachings of the Buddha, does not involve converting to a particular religion or following the ritual of any sect; rather, it is taking refuge in a universal teaching applicable to all. This teaching is divided into three interrelated parts: ethical integrity (*sīla*), concentration (*samādhi*) and wisdom (*paññā*). *Sīla* refers to a set of moral guidelines: abstaining from killing, theft, sexual misconduct, wrong speech and mind-altering intoxicants. When these pre-scriptions are properly followed, the mind is then able to become sufficiently calm, enabling the delicate task of self-observation. Without these precepts, a meditator will be pulled in two opposing directions: on the one hand, trying to concentrate

Pronunciation Guide

English, Pāli, Sanskrit, Hindi, and Urdu all belong to the Indo-European language group. While there are many similarities amongst all these languages, the Indian languages have particular sounds not found in English. The following list of Roman letters will help you learn the proper pronunciation.

Vowels

a	as in 'aware'
ā	as in 'calm'
i	as in 'sit'
ī	as in 'seat'
u	as in 'full'
ū	as in 'moon'
e	as in 'emanate'
ai	as in 'equanimity'
o	as in 'boat'
au	as in 'off'

Velar Consonants
(sound produced in the throat)

k	as in 'skin'
kh	as in 'kite'
g	as in 'give'
gh	as in 'dog-house'
ṅ	as in 'link'

Palatal Consonants
(sound produced at the palate)

c	as in 'chilly'
ch	as in 'switch-hitter'
j	as in 'jelly'
z	as in 'zipper'
jh	as in 'large-house'
ñ	as in 'nya'

Retroflex Consonants
(hard sound produced with the tongue curling back to touch the palate)

ṭ, ṭh, ḍ, ḍh, ṛ, ṛh, ṇ
(there are no English equivalents)

Dental Consonants
(soft sound produced with the tongue touching the upper front teeth)

t	as in 'tame'
th	as in 'Thailand'
d	as in 'determination'
dh	as in 'dead-head'
n	as in 'nice'

Labial Consonants
(sound produced from the lips)

p	as in 'pain'
ph	as in 'top-hat'
b	as in 'basket'
bh	as in 'club-house'
m	as in 'merit'

Semi-vowels

y	as in 'yes'
r	as in 'rope'
l	as in 'love'
v	as in 'very'

Sibilants

ś	as in 'shift'
s	as in 'save'
h	as in 'heavy'
ḷ	as in 'pearl'
ṃ	same as 'ṅ', but only found at the end of a word (i.e. *Buddhaṃ saraṇaṃ gacchāmī*)

and calm the mind down, and on the other, engaging in behaviours that agitate the equilibrium of the mind. *Samādhi* is accomplished by the practise of *ānāpāna-sati*, or 'awareness of the incoming-outgoing breath,' a universal object that is available to us at all times. *Paññā* leads to the total purification of the mind, which is accomplished when the meditator objectively observes mental and physical reality and comes to understand these truths: that everything is impermanent (*anicca*), unsatisfactory (*dukkha*) and substanceless (*anattā*). More on these teachings of the Buddha is included in 'The Middle Land' section of this book.

Saṅgha, the third refuge, translates as the community of noble people.[1] When we take refuge in this community, we are taking refuge in those who are walking or who have already walked on the path of purification, rather than in some particular sect. The Buddha taught that when our hearts are equipped with this type of devotion in the Triple Gem, visiting the sacred sites will be very beneficial to our spiritual growth.

Good health, the second requisite for a successful pilgrimage, is essential. If you become sick on your travels, stay where you are. There is no use continuing because it will only worsen your illness, and you won't be able to appreciate where you are and what you're doing. It's better to visit fewer places and maintain your physical and mental well-being than to visit a number of places and not truly be there. If you become sick, try not to worry too much, and maintain your awareness of *anicca*. It's during these times that our practice is most imperative. Illnesses common to travellers in India can be serious, so take care to be well-informed of possible problems before beginning your travels. Information about health is discussed in detail in the 'Travelling in India' section of this book.

Honesty is of utmost importance. You will likely encounter people along the way who will attempt to cheat and harass you, but try to leave their negativity with them rather than allow these disruptions to affect the balance of your mind. Try to develop love and compassion towards those irritating you and towards the terrible conditions that are responsible for their behaviour. It is important to maintain integrity. You will find that in most cases when you are honest with others, they will be honest with you in return. Be firm, and take strong action when necessary, but bear in mind that you are engaging with a culture different from your own, and make an effort to remove yourself from disruptive situations as quickly as possible. This is definitely not easy. India always has a way of pitching curve balls, and if we're expecting them we might instead get a fastball to *really* throw us off track. This is where *diligence* or effort, the fourth requisite, becomes so important. Continuous effort applies not only to our sitting practice, but also to the events that we constantly face everyday. The more we are able to increase our effort and maintain consistent awareness and equanimity, the greater our patience will be with all the challenges and obstacles with which we are presented.

The last requisite, *wisdom*, is the comprehension of *anicca*, *dukkha*, and *anattā* at all times. We should try to understand, in our own limited way, the clarity of the Buddha's teaching on the human psychological process. In this light, paying proper homage at the sacred sites means striving to understand the arising and passing of this mind-matter phenomenon of which we are composed. Obviously, only awakened beings are fully aware of impermanence at all times (*sampajañña*), but while meditating on the path, our fickle minds gradually settle into subtly, and we come ever closer to clarity and insight. For centuries, those seeking liberation along the path have found the pilgrimage places of the Indian subcontinent to be conducive to developing these qualities.

A fascinating paradox in this land of infinite contradictions is that while on *yatra*, practitioners often find it easy to effortlessly and peacefully meditate, while at the same time are also easily confounded by some of the most mundane situations, whether it be over a few rupees with a rickshaw driver or the noise and pollution of over-crowded cities. All these circumstances test our equanimity and are the real measure of our progress along the path of wisdom. By following the above requisites with a cheerful disregard for moments of both elation and depression, recognizing them to be equally impermanent, our time travelling in this incredible land will certainly be full of fruitful and memorable experiences. As home to about one-sixth of the world's population, India plays an increasingly large role in shaping world affairs, and travelling the subcontinent serves to enrich one's sense of this important, ancient and incredibly diverse culture. It has long been said that for true travellers, India is a rite of passage, and we know of perhaps no better place to put one's awareness and equanimity to the ultimate challenge of immediate experience...

It is our hope that this book will serve as a useful source of information and inspiration on this difficult road. May all the readers of this book gain inspiration and encouragement while travelling along the path! May we all come to fully understand the Buddha's ennobling message and awaken to ultimate reality! May all beings be happy, peaceful and liberated! May we be free!

A Note on Names, Language & References

In a train:

—Where going?
—Vārāṇasī.
—*Ah*! Kasi!
—No, Vārāṇasī.
—*Han*! Benares!
—No, no! Vā-rā-ṇa-sī!
—*Han-ji.*

Varanasi, is usually called 'Kasi' by locals, 'Benares' by out-of-staters, and is sometimes spelled 'Baranasi' or 'Banarsi.'

Those travelling in India cannot help but notice that any given place may be spelled in many different ways and may even be known by many different names. Many city names have been 'decolonialized,' including Bombay (to Mumbai), Calcutta (to Kolkata), and Madras (to Chennai).

Throughout the book we have tried to be both practical and traditional. We label each chapter by its modern name, and put the ancient Pāli name in brackets when the names differ. In the text, however, we often use both names, depending on the context. In presenting the stories surrounding the Buddha's life, we do not provide the literal translations from the Pāli canon, but attempt to retell them in a simpler narrative format without compromising their essence and authenticity. Nevertheless, we are deeply indebted to the translations of several great Pāli scholars: Nyānomoli Thera, Nyanaponika Thera, Narada Thera, Bhikkhu Bodhi, K.R. Norman, I.B. Horner, T.W. & C.A.F Rhys Davids, John Ireland, Maurice Walsh, and others. Without their invaluable contributions to the field of *pariyatti*, it would have been impossible for us to understand and narrate these inspiring stories the way we do.

At the end of each story from the Pāli canon, we provide abbreviated references for those who want to read the scholarly translations. The abbreviations are as follows:

A	Anguttara Nikāya	**S**	Samyutta Nikāya
D	Digha Nikāya	**Sn**	Sutta Nipāta
Dh	Dhammapada	**Thig**	Therīgāthā
DhA	Dhammapada Attagatha	**U**	Udana
I	Ittivuttaka	**VinMv**	Vinaya Mahavagga
M	Majjhima Nikāya	**VinCv**	Vinaya Culavagga

Acknowledgements

During the winter of 2003 at Dhamma Giri, we found ourselves relaxing under the shade of a large banyan tree, sitting between travel writer Carl Franz and Dhamma writer Paul Fleischman. Our post-course Dhamma discussions evolved into the usual travellers' talk, comparing nightmare travel tales with our ruminations of all the would-haves and should-haves. Then, rather suddenly, the idea came for this book. Carl was saying how he saw the need for a meditators' guidebook to India but didn't have the time to write one. Paul nodded towards us and said: "Why don't they write the book?" Thus our long journey began, weaving together inspiring stories from the Buddha's life with our travel reflections and lessons while walking along the path.

Along the Path has been six years in the making. Its momentum attracted friends from around the globe who have generously contributed, whether by sharing their stories, artwork, travel information and editor's eyes, or by simply supporting and encouraging us when the going got rough.

We would like to dedicate the merits accrued from this book to all those who helped out, directly or indirectly, with this project. While it's impossible to include the names of everyone, a few people deserve special mention. This project would have never been born if it were not for our Teacher, S.N. Goenka, who has been a constant source of inspiration to us, both on and off the cushion; Carl Franz for his introduction to travel writing; Austin Pick for his superb editing, restructuring and updating of the Beyond the Middle Land section, contributing his stories, and writing the section on Nepal; Amy Karafin for her razor sharp edits and comments on the travel section; Lisa Conway for her tireless and first-rate skills in text-editing, copy-editing and layout; Adam Shepard for his layout and marketing work; Ania and Irek Sroka for the cover design; Bill Hamilton, Gavin Turner, Nancy Rosen, Shauna Mahony, Jonathan Mirin, Jeremy Dunn, Kateri Snow, Jon Mirin and Alexandra Lapierre-Fortin for their enthusiasm and constructive feedback on the manuscript; Aleksei Gomez, Nik 'the Bhik' Halay, Lluïsot Domènech, Bjarni Wark, Godeliève Richard, Anita Ghanekar, Michael Pancoe and Gary Gronokowski for contributing their fabulous artwork; Jenny Jeffs for her magnificent map-making; Patrick Given-Wilson, Chris & Kerry Waters, Brett Morris, Jonathan Mirin, John Geraets & Karen Weston, Chantel Oosthuysen, Peter Buchanan, Sierra Laflamme, Leah Thompson, Elissa Crete, Kim Heacock and Eric Eichler for sharing their inspiring and touching stories; Jeff Glen for his patience and for helping us get through the publishing process; Brihas Sarathy for his time and technical genius; Dr. Panth for his wealth of knowledge; Pramod Bhave, Ity and the transient Dhamma Sikhara community for being there; the Dhamma Suttama community for being who they are; Catherine St-Germain for being a great companion along the pilgrimage route and for listening to us think out loud; Bhante Anand and Bodhgayā's Ladakhi Saṅgha for their shelter and great food; Jamna and Family in Sukeri for their sincerity; Ashwini and Family for their comfort and Bihari hospitality; Jamie & Nora Quinn at La Terre Bleue for their generosity; our cabins at Renouveau for their beauty and inspiration; François Thibeault for his pilgrimage conversations; Rick & Gair Crutcher, Tandon-ji, Rohi Shetty, Paul & Susan Fleischman, Bob & Jenny Jeffs, Laura & Parker Mills, Sally MacDonald, Jeff & Jill Glenn, Luke Matthews, Kedaar Ghanekar, Denis Ferman, Tutti Gould, Asawa-ji, Pushpa-ji & the Dhamma Bodhi staff, Vijay-bhai Shah, Manish Agarwala, and our parents for their general support, sharing information and believing in the project.

Kory Goldberg & Michelle Décary
Dunham, Québec
August 2009

Introduction

You don't need to go to India to look inside. But those who do inevitably come back transformed. Sometimes the changes are radical. Other times, their inner journey manifests itself in subtle details: a glint in their eyes, a silent presence, a fluidity in their stride, or a special glow (even if a few pounds lighter). They may be shaken by the poverty and suffering they have seen, and have vowed never to complain again about their petty problems. They may notice details that escaped them before, or see the magic in simple conveniences like a hot shower or tap water that can be drunk without worry.

Travel has a way of extracting us from our daily grind and making us look at our habits and ways of life. We re-evaluate everything that makes up our life back home—relationships, work, time—and decide we need to make some changes. Or, if we're lucky, the changes may just happen on their own.

Travel, however, can be especially moving when it is taken as a pilgrimage (*yatra*), not only through the outer world, but more so in discovering the inner world and the dark mazes of the mind. It seems to be in the nature of a pilgrimage to test our limits. But if we surrender to the journey, without looking for the final goal, we can find peace and joy in the present moment.

Using this Book

This book was created for people wanting to travel in India to meditate and volunteer at Dhamma centres, go on *yatra* to the sacred sites, visit old Buddhist caves and monasteries, and get in touch with the body by learning yoga, trekking in the Himālaya, or detoxing at a nature cure centre. In fact, when the Dhamma (the Buddha's teaching) becomes part of your trip, the entire journey becomes like an extended meditation retreat, with all the challenges and insights that come along with it.

We have included many illuminating Dhamma parables that may seem elementary to well-read meditators, but will, we hope, provide context for the novice. If you already know these stories, then either skip over them, or read them with a beginner's mind. Even if you hear the same teaching again and again, there is always something to catch in a new light. The same goes for the seasoned traveller: while you already know about train stations and *dhobi-wallahs*, the first-time visitor does not.

This book is not only a travel guide; it also traces the Buddha's life as it unfolded across these sacred sites. This is the land where the Buddha and original Saṅgha walked, meditated, taught, begged for alms, and lived, and those legends that can seem abstract in a book will come alive as you follow in their footsteps.

As well as the sacred sites, we discuss some of the Vipassana centres and interesting side trips in the area: the ancient Buddhist caves in Nasik near Dhamma Giri, the nature cure centre near Dhamma Sindhu, and the Triund plateau, good for hiking, near Dhamma Sikhara. There are so many Vipassana centres in India and Nepal, but we have included only the well-established ones here because the management is accustomed to foreigners. The workers at these centres usually know how to deal with foreign quirks and habits, and they usually have the discourses and instructions available in many languages.

The reader will notice our bias towards the Vipassana centres in the tradition of S.N. Goenka. This occurs for two reasons: first, it is the tradition with which we are familiar; and second, unlike the West and in South East Asia where differing insight meditation traditions abound, Vipassana in India is fairly limited to the method taught by Mr. Goenka. There are some transient Westerners offering Vipassana courses, but their courses are infrequent and irregular, thus difficult to include in this book. Nevertheless, we feel that meditators from all traditions will find *Along the Path* a useful tool to help navigate the pilgrimage terrain.

This book is meant to travel to India with you, to accompany you on bumpy bus rides and when you're waiting three hours for a delayed train. It's also meant to provide inspiration along the way, to support your meditation, and to be a reminder of why you came to India in the first place: to have equanimity with all obstacles India may throw at you. We hope it will be like having a veteran traveller along with you, sharing the information of the places s/he's been to, the stories s/he's heard, and the experiences s/he's had—the kind of friend we wish we would have had along on our journeys. Make notes in the book, tear out pages, or glue in maps. This will be useful when you exchange experiences with other meditators on the journey.

The best way to read this book is while you're on your way to your next destination. If you're heading to Rajgir, for example, use it to get acquainted with the important events that took place at Vulture's Peak and Bamboo Grove before you get there.

One thing we discovered while on pilgrimage is that the flow of pilgrims is what keeps these sites alive, both at the level of infrastructure—roads, transport, accommodation and food—as well as at the spiritual level. If no one walks on the path, it will be grown over again by moss, vines, and trees. As individuals, our role may be small and insignificant. As a community, however, there is nothing more important than taking that next step forward.

Part 1: Travelling in India

This first section contains useful information for the India pilgrim, including tips on planning your trip, visas and cheap flights, and practicalities about travel in India such as finding a room, riding a bus, buying a train ticket, ordering food, staying healthy and observing proper etiquette around monks and nuns.

Our aim in this section is not to replicate information already available in other guidebooks, but to add to your options. Many guidebooks warn you against salads and raw foods, prescribe scores of medicines and vaccinations, and tell you to drink only bottled water. We explain how to clean your vegetables, how to stay healthy naturally by focusing on prevention, and how to purify your own water. We want to provide alternatives to the information generally available.

Part II: The Middle Land

In the second section, devoted to pilgrimage in the *Middle Land* (Uttar Pradesh, Bihar, South Nepal), each sacred site has a chapter of its own which opens with important events that happened in that place and the teachings the Buddha gave there. We focus on stories that highlight the Dhamma, rather than archaeological or historical details of the particular sites. Sārnāth is important for meditators, not because there's a massive stupa of such-and-such a size or an elaborate temple built by such-and-such a patron using this-or-that stone, but because it was there that the Buddha set in motion the Wheel of Dhamma by revealing the Four Noble Truths. The stupas and temples are still important for the meditator, but they are only expressions of appreciation towards the Dhamma—not the Dhamma itself.

Part III: Beyond the Middle Land

The third section covers Dhamma sites outside the borders of the Middle Land. It includes ancient monastic complexes and modern meditation centres, as well as excursions and activities around these places.

Every chapter in the second and third section includes practical advice for pilgrims, under the headings **Site-Sitting**, **Sleeping & Eating**, **Coming & Going**, and **Excursions**. We've done our best to provide enough information to get you started, but circumstances are not permanent: hotels fold, monasteries burn down, programmes are cancelled, addresses and phone numbers change. If you find that something is not as we've said, please inform us for a future edition.

Site-Sitting recommends sites to meditate at and visit. The foot of the Bodhi Tree in Bodhgayā or Vulture's Peak in Rajgir are traditionally considered to be sacred meditation places conducive to mental purification, but the Delhi Museum may not be (although we have had a great sitting there next to the Buddha's relics). In any case, whether or not we're actually in the sitting posture, the heading "Site-Sitting" reminds us to be mindful at all times, even while moving from place to place.

One wise friend warned us before we went on pilgrimage: "Be careful; it's harder than a 45-day course!" Indeed, a *yatra* feels more like a Vipassana course than a vacation. But it's not exactly a retreat, either, since external challenges are added to the internal ones. This is why cultivating mindfulness and a conscious surrender are necessary at every step.

Coming & Going tells you how to travel to and from, either by bus, train, car, rickshaw, plane, or an exhausting combination of these. We give the names and numbers of relevant trains and stations, but no schedules, as these are always changing.

Sleeping & Eating provides a few names of hotels, guest houses, and monasteries, although our aim is not to be a directory. These are meant to assist pilgrims, especially those on a tighter schedule, to make best use of their time while travelling. It's far too easy to waste your time searching for a fairly-priced room. The recommendations are meant to be pointers to certain areas where you can find a room—we leave it to you to search and create your own experience. Besides, the best and most current information usually comes from other travellers.

We've grouped accommodation listings by price:

- Budget: Rs 350 and under
- Mid-range: Rs 350 to Rs 900
- Luxury: Rs 900 to Rs 2 500
- Top-dollar: Rs 2 500 and up

Excursions lists some interesting side trips. These are usually for meditators with time to spare and should not be taken as a checklist for the marathon *yatri*. If you're short on time, we recommend not trying to hit all of these: rushing about from one place to another can be very stressful and may lessen your connection to the site, thus making the place seem less a sacred site and more a pile of bricks.

Travelling in India

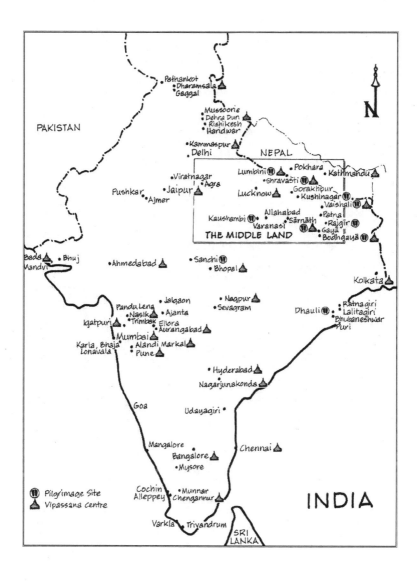

Planning Your Journey

Planning

> *I will visit a place entirely other than myself. Whether it is the future or the past need not be decided in advance.*
>
> – Susan Sontag

A friend of ours—a self described "travel-junky nut-case"—has an extensive collection of guidebooks in his house. He travels one or two months every winter, and the rest of the year is spent reading up on his next destination. Indeed, much of the fun of travel is in the planning and anticipation: on a dreary November day, the mind certainly enjoys fantasizing about palm groves and coconut water.

The danger of guidebooks, however, is that every single place mentioned seems so alluring that many people fall into the trap of wanting to 'see it all.' Although a vague plan is sometimes helpful, be prepared to chuck it if you find a place you like and want to stay longer. Travelling two days here, three days there can be done for short periods, but is exhausting in the end. Your memories of India will be of tiring overnight bus rides and dingy hotel rooms. If you visit fewer places but stay longer in each one, you will find that you start to befriend the *kelā wallah* (banana vendor) and the *chowkidar* (security guard), and life in India opens itself up to you. Or, you may meet a group of meditators who say, "Hey, why don't you come with us to Bodhgayā," while you were planning to visit Mysore. Be open—India is full of possibilities.

> *At no time are we ever in such complete possession of a journey, down to its last nook and cranny, as when we are busy with preparations for it. After that, there remains only the journey itself, which is nothing but the process through which we lose our ownership of it.*
>
> – Yukio Mishima, *Confessions of a Mask*

The more you move, the more it costs. Newcomers to India often cover about a dozen places in two months: from Igatpuri in the west, to Hyderabad in the south, to Bodhgayā in the east, and to Dharamsala in the north. Even though trains and buses are cheap in India, all that moving around still costs money.

Now, when we go to India, we almost don't feel like we're 'travelling.' We know the places we like and the friends we want to see, and we return to these for a stay of at least one month. Longer stays mean that you can bargain with the guest house for a reduced rate, or even rent a house and cook for yourself, which is much cheaper than eating out.

Choosing Your Dates

Most people go to India during the Indian winter months, when it is usually sunny but not too hot. Typically, visas are good for six months—the validity starts from the moment you get the visa, not from the date you land (so take this into consideration when planning your flights).

If you are interested in taking a long meditation course, check the long course schedule as early as possible and apply for admission. Once you are accepted, you can work your itinerary around that.

Seasons

Summer (*Grishma*): mid-May to early July.
An Indian saying from colonial times: "Only mad dogs and Englishmen go out under the midday sun." Summer is scorchingly hot, dry, and dusty. By early June, dust storms and electrical storms announce the coming monsoon.

Monsoon (*Varsha*): mid-June to mid-September.
Monsoon weather varies a great deal depending on where you are. In Bodhgayā, days are hot with regular short showers which cool down the temperature. In Dharamsala, it rains so much that you never see the mountains. Remember that travel in monsoon is uncertain, as torrential rains can flood the roads or railway tracks.

Post-Monsoon (*Sharada*): mid-September to mid-November.
Post-monsoon weather is warm and humid, with sporadic rain. It's a nice time to be in India, when it is not too hot, and everything is still lush from all the rain.

Winter (*Hemanta*): mid-November to early February.
Indian winters can get quite chilly in northern cities like Delhi and Jaipur. During the day you can wear long sleeves without sweating; at night, you will need a sweater, a shawl, or both. In the south, it is pleasantly warm, without being too hot.

Monsoon Mould

Dhamma Giri's constant downpour of heavy rain during monsoon creates a humidity of 85-90%, which is good for the skin, but also for mould: it attacks everything, from bedding to books and backpacks, and all leather items. A good trick if you're staying in Dhamma Giri over monsoon is to keep out only a couple of outfits (preferably made of synthetic fibres) and store the rest in large plastic bags with naphthalene (moth) balls until the end of the rains. Beware if you're bringing any electronic equipment—the humidity ruined the motherboard on our first laptop (*anicca!*).

Cool (*Shishira*): early February to mid-March.
The cool season is pleasantly mild—not too hot, not too cold. You start shedding the thicker layers, and before you know it, you're wearing a T-shirt.

Spring (*Vasanta*): mid-March to mid-May.
The spring doesn't seem to last very long in the plains before it starts sizzling again. High altitudes mean cooler temperatures. In the summer, the mountains are pleasant when the plains are sweltering hot. In the winter, the plains are temperate and the mountains can be terribly cold, especially at night.

Cheap Flights

Airlines usually have a few cheap seats on every flight, although you need to book well in advance because they sell out quickly. Fridays and Sundays are considered peak travel days, therefore are more expensive. Mention it to your travel agent, if you are flexible with dates.

It's a good idea to do a bit of internet research before seeing a travel agent; you may find better prices on certain flights yourself, or at least find a flight with only one layover instead of two or three. It's a good idea to buy directly from the airline's website, although there are some reputable *consolidators* that offer great deals. A consolidator is a company that buys tickets from the airlines in bulk or carries its own contract with airlines. Consolidators usually get very low fares and some of them sell these tickets directly to travellers. Finding the right ticket may require some virtual legwork—checking out different companies, different dates, different ports of entry—but you could end up saving a few hundred dollars. Be vigilant about the fine print when booking on-line, however: if the price starts to soar during the booking process, it's a sign to jump ship.

There are many advantages to E-tickets: they're easy to book, you can change your dates over the internet without having to pay a service charge, and you don't have to worry about losing that precious piece of paper. But if you have special needs or a complicated itinerary, a travel agent's personal touch could be worth the few extra bucks.

Flying Tips
- If you can, avoid checking baggage. You can usually get away with bringing a small backpack as carry-on. Remember that pen-knives, scissors, camping stoves and other 'dangerous' instruments can't be taken on the plane with you.
- Lock your bags. We have had things stolen from our luggage.
- If you have a preference for an aisle/window seat then it pays to contact the airline in advance or check-in early. For tall passengers on long haul flights, this is all the more important.
- Don't fly within twelve hours of dental work; the change in pressure can be very painful.
- Drink plenty of water on long flights. This helps prevent dehydration, which in turn helps recovery from jet lag.

- Stretching lightly during and after the flight, eating lightly at times that are normal for your new time zone, and getting fresh air and sunlight after the flight all help reduce the effects of jet lag.
- Melatonin and homeopathic remedies such as "No Jet Lag" help some people decrease the effects of jet lag.
- For ear-aches on the plane: chew gum during take-off and landing. If your ears don't pop, hold your nose, blow gently and swallow at the same time. One friend who suffers from ear-aches takes an antihistamine one hour before her flight whenever she has a cold or clogged sinuses.
- You may have to pay off a mysterious karmic debt by losing your luggage. Airlines usually compensate you for the inconvenience with a small financial reimbursement. When/If you retrieve your bags, go through them and make sure nothing is missing before you sign for them. If you find something missing, don't sign. Immediately call the airline to inform them.
- If you are expecting a long stopover waiting for a connecting flight, check out this website: www.worldairportsguide.com which can tell you what to visit and where to eat on a short excursion outside the airport.

Visas & Other Essential Documents

Well before leaving, ensure that your passport is valid for the duration of your stay; the application process for a new passport takes time.

Indian visas are usually issued for six months with multiple-entry. However, the exact details are different for every nationality and change from year to year. Americans and some Europeans can easily get one-year visas, and with a little paperwork, five- or ten-year visas. Contact your local embassy, or check on the internet, to find out the specifics. Always make photocopies of your passport and visa (and other important documents such as contact numbers, ticket numbers, prescriptions), and if you're travelling with a friend, exchange your copies, in case one of you loses your money-belt. E-mailing this info to yourself can also be a life-saver.

Is your six-month visa expiring soon and you want to stay in India longer? If it's only a question of a couple of weeks, it may be possible to get an extension on your visa. (Note that *possible* is not a guarantee.) Go to the Foreigners' Registration Office (FRO) at a local police station in any big city, but be warned that this can depend entirely on the whims of the officer-in-charge. Ask other travellers about their successes and failures. Some officers are infamous for refusing requests; others are more lenient and easily give extensions.

Hello, Photo?

It's good to travel with many passport-sized photos for visa applications, long course applications and other official purposes (like sticking one on the *Peace Planet* in Bodhgayā).

It's much cheaper to have passport-sized photos done in India, especially if you photocopy them. Or make many copies of the best snapshots taken from your own camera.

If you want to stay a few more months, you need to leave India and go to an Indian embassy or consulate in another country to apply for a new visa. By land you can go to Nepal, Pakistan or Bangladesh. Or you can fly to Sri Lanka, Thailand or Myanmar. The Indian embassy in Kathmandu has been flooded with hippies wanting new visas since the sixties, and it can be particularly difficult to obtain a new six-month visa—you may leave with only a 2–3 month extension.

If you will be studying in India, student visas are handy since they can be valid for up to five years. The disadvantage is that you need to register with the district police station. For example, in the case of Dhamma Giri's Pāli Programme, students need to register in Nasik. Once registered, you are not allowed to leave the district for more than 8 days without getting written permission from the man in charge of the FRO. Often, this procedure is much more challenging than it seems. When we were students at Dhamma Giri, the FRO was an hour away from our campus, the officer-in-charge at that time was rarely at his desk, and he generally refused to make appointments.

Packing

It's good to know if you plan on being in warm or cool climates; this will help you to pack more efficiently. It's no use lugging a -7°C sleeping bag if you plan to go south. If you think you'll go south but end up in the mountains, don't worry, you can always buy warm clothes, shawls and blankets on site.

What to bring?

Here are some of our travelling essentials:

- Sleeping bag
- Mosquito net and rope (you can find some in India, but the quality isn't the same)
- Meditation cushion (We like the Therm-a-rest™ cushion, and we have a tailor stitch a cover for it in India, very inexpensively.)
- Water treatment kit (drops and filter; e.g., SteriPEN™: a small, portable UV water purifier)
- Durable water bottle
- Shake flashlight/Flashlight with battery charger and rechargeable batteries (Indian battery chargers and rechargeable batteries seem to be reliable, unlike most Indian disposable batteries.)
- Pocket knife
- Travel alarm clock
- Small sewing kit
- Hair brush, elastics, barrettes
- Small first aid kit
- Good pens, notebook
- Combination padlock (Push buttons are useful when you don't have light, and are available at most lock shops.)
- Secure money belt

- A small photo album of our home and family, to show our new friends at the meditation centres or on the train
- We travel with three pairs of footwear:
  - Hiking shoes for travel and the mountains. (This is especially important if you have big feet because large sizes are very hard to come by.)
  - Good sandals for the towns.
  - Slip-on *chappals* (flip flops) for the meditation centres. Plastic *chappals* are also useful for bathrooms and showers.

What to buy in India?

- Heating coil to boil water in a metal cup
- Cup and spoon
- Clothes (travel/meditation)
- *Gomcha*: a multi-purpose cloth that can be used as a scarf, pillow cover, towel, meditation mat, light shawl, curtain, and table cloth
- *Lungi*: also a multi-purpose cloth that can be used as a sarong or skirt, bed sheet, and all the items listed for a *Gomcha*

Don't Leave Home Without It

After a Teacher's Self-Course in Dhamma Giri, we asked some seasoned traveller-meditators, "What is the one thing you would never leave home without?" The answers we got reflect a wide range of quirks and attachments, but by no means represent a checklist.

- Pumice stone (feet can get really dry)
- Peanut butter & herbal teas
- Natural mosquito repellent (essential oils like lemongrass, etc.)
- Ziploc® bags, all sizes
- Earplugs (for noisy buses/meditators)
- Tampons, sanitary napkins (you can now find these in big cities, or try the Keeper® or DivaCup™)
- Camera and extra memory card
- Art supplies
- Charcoal tablets
- Strong string to hang the mosquito net
- Toilet paper
- Melatonin (for jet lag)
- Wet towelettes
- Lip balm
- Scissors
- Men's shaving kit
- Therm-a-Rest® mattress
- Grapefruit Seed Extract, Acidophilus, Goldenseal
- Multivitamins
- Dental floss (difficult to find)
- Foot cream (again, cracking feet...)
- Bath plug (to plug the sink)
- Sunglasses, hat, sunblock
- Contact lens solution
- Cloth or paper face masks, for heavy traffic
- Duct tape
- Crazy glue (If you have a cut that needs stitches but are far away from any doctor, you can use it to close the wound!)
- MP3 Player with tiny portable speakers that don't require batteries

You're leaving home in two days, trying to pack your life into a 40-litre back-pack. Everything spread out on your bed is being sorted into three piles: can't-leave-without, would-like-to-bring, and only-if-I-have-room. The first pile keeps expanding:

— Should I bring my Discman for group sittings? Well, then I need speakers for when I have visitors...and an adapter. Hmm, maybe I should bring my collection of morning chantings...

Use strong determination to avoid these packing chain-reactions. Remember that you're leaving home to experience something *different*, and to fill up the jar of renunciation *pāramī*. India is India because it is not like home.

A Travel Routine

A travel routine is not necessarily a schedule; it is more about knowing your interests as well as your limitations. If you say, "I like to serve a course before I sit one," or "I like to visit old Buddhist caves," this is a travel routine. For example, we usually upgrade our standards for hotel rooms in big cities, knowing that we will probably spend much of our time in the room, and that it will provide refuge from the chaos outside.

The most important routine for a meditator is making sure to get in at least two daily sittings. When moving about, it is easy to come up with one pretext or another to avoid looking at the reality inside.

The Buddha mentioned six excuses that people often use to avoid meditating:

1. It's too cold.
2. It's too hot.
3. It's too late.
4. It's too early.
5. I'm too hungry.
6. I'm too full.

> *Most people never travel. They simply transport the mad loop of their brain's thoughts from place to place. To truly travel is to stand on the fields of yourself where you have never stood before.*
>
> – Speed Levitch

Try to see these excuses as dangerous enemies and make a strong determination not to be overcome by them. Even if you end up "sleep-sitting," the effort (*viriya*) and determination (*adhiṭṭhāna*) will be of benefit to you.

There are different kinds of travellers. Some people love to temple-hop and visit every single World Heritage Site in a 1 000-km radius, whereas others prefer to get to know the locals: how they live, how they eat, etc. Whatever your temperament, be warned that travel in India is slow, even when it is 'deluxe' or 'super-fast.'

Travelling with Friends

The Buddha said that creatures move and combine together according to a common elementary nature; people with high aspirations tend to gravitate towards each other. This is also true in nature: for example, you will never see a crow within a flock of parrots, or vice versa. In the same way, friends travelling together tend to share common goals and interests.

If you're planning a trip with friends, everyone should have a say in the preparations, so that nobody is held responsible when things don't work out precisely according to plan.

If you suddenly realize once you're on the road that the partnership is not exactly working out, then don't be shy to part ways.

Be sensitive to your travelling companion's budget. If you are travelling for a long stretch together, it's true that "Good accounts make good friends." But a "what-goes-around-comes-around" attitude is handy for short partnerships; you may treat someone to a 40-rupee rickshaw ride, and the next day, someone else may treat you to a meal.

Travelling Alone

As a deer in the wild, unfettered,
Forages wherever it wants;
The wise person, valuing freedom,
Walks alone, like a rhinoceros.

Without hostility from all four directions,
Content with whatever you get;
Overcome all dangers fearlessly,
Walk alone, like a rhinoceros.

If you can find trustworthy companions
Who are virtuous and dedicated;
Then walk with them content and mindful,
And overcome all dangerous obstacles.

It is better to walk alone
Then to be in the fellowship of fools.
Walk alone, harm no one, and avoid conflict;
At ease like a lone rhinoceros
in the woods.

M, 128; Dh, 328-30; Ud, 41

Don't be afraid to travel alone in India. Some people are natural loners, and others travel alone and find that they meet many more people. There are advantages and disadvantages to travelling solo. The single traveller is much freer to make decisions, cancel them at the last minute, or decide to join a group on a side-trip.

On the other hand, it's cheaper to travel with a buddy, sharing the costs of rickshaws and double rooms. It's also safer while in trains: for example, your friend can watch your bags when you suddenly have to visit the loo for the umpteenth time.

Women Travellers

India is a safe country for women, even when travelling alone. Of course, there will be times when you feel that your freedom is restricted compared to that of your male friends. Rather than take it personally and get upset about the injustices of sexism, it is better to shrug it off by reminding yourself that, "Well, this is just the way it is in India." Forcefully asserting your independence may be perceived as a lack of respect for local customs and could very well turn out to be counter-productive. This does not mean that you cannot have enlightening discussions with locals about gender equality.

Unfortunately, sensationalist media have created a narrow and somewhat distorted perception of Western women. Bearing this in mind, women should exercise common sense when dealing with men; who knows how an innocent conversation may be interpreted? Also, some men are eager to shake hands with foreign women; but in India a respectable *"Namaste"* with folded hands is more common and quite acceptable. Although it may seem rude not to acquiesce, remember that in India women rarely shake hands with, or have their photo taken by, unknown men, let alone have any informal conversations with them.

Although the normal precautions, such as avoiding walking alone at night, are advisable, being in India is generally not physically threatening. What can be draining, however, is male gawking. It's best to just ignore vulgar comments or provocative stares. If a man gropes you in a crowded train, however, then you might want to make a scene (with *mettā* and equanimity, of course) to embarrass the culprit and discourage him from doing it again. Those nearby will likely sympathize with you.

The way you dress will significantly affect the way locals—both men and women—perceive you, and consequently, the way they address you. Legs and shoulders are generally considered 'sexy' parts of a woman's body, thus, shorts, short skirts, sleeveless tops, or any tight and revealing clothes are inappropriate. In the meditation centres, women are asked to wear a bra (or tight-fitting undershirt) or shawl.

The *salwar kameez*, a long tunic over loose-fitting pants, is perfect for blending in and being comfortable. If you don't feel at ease in this traditional outfit, you can mix and match your own pants with some of the more modern tops and *dupattas*, the long scarves draped over the front. (The *dupatta* may seem like a mere accessory, but in the smaller towns, it is used to cover the chest or head.)

Indians love seeing a foreign woman in a *sari*, as long as it is worn properly. You may not see the difference in the pleats here and there, but they do. Ask an Indian woman to help you wrap it, and make sure that she gives you detailed instructions while doing so, so you can practise by yourself. The *sari*, although it looks cumbersome, is actually very comfortable (and it is still quite easy to go to the bathroom, just scoop everything up in the petticoat, and *voila!*).

Most Indian women swim fully clothed. It's best to do the same, unless you're at a popular 'foreigners' beach' where western swimwear is acceptable.

Travelling with a male friend changes your interactions considerably. You will find that some Indian men will address your travelling partner as if you didn't exist, "Hello, Sir. Rickshaw?" Instead of feeling offended, sit back and relax and let him do the exhausting work of haggling!

Travel
Sit with other women on buses and trains. If sitting next to a man, put a piece of luggage between you. Also, many trains have ladies' compartments. In train stations, there are usually counters for women; if not, it is socially acceptable for women to jump the queue.

Menstruation
Some women come prepared with duffle-bags full of tampons and sanitary napkins. Napkins and tampons are now available in most towns. If you use unbleached tampons, it's best to bring your own stock.

There are other options besides these throw-away bleached products. Re-usable methods, such as the DivaCup™ or cloth pads, are more eco-friendly, make you independent, and can save you a lot of money. For more information check this website: <u>www.divacup.com</u>

Still today, in some orthodox Hindu circles, there is a taboo surrounding menstruating women: they are not allowed into the kitchen, or the temple. In some villages they may even be confined to the porch or barn for three days.

Contact with Local Women

In the streets, trains, hotels, restaurants, markets—men are everywhere. But where are the women? You may find it difficult to make contact with the local women as they are a minority in the public sector. So how do you befriend the women? Working together, especially giving Dhamma Service (*sevā*) is the best way. The segregation of the sexes in meditation centres is a real blessing. While doing *sevā* with women—putting the cushions in the sun, preparing the Dhamma hall, eating lunch, or even just meditating with them—you are no longer merely a witness to their everyday routines but you actually become part of the team.

Travelling with Kids

While travelling with little ones, it is important to take into consideration the children's interests as well as the parents'. Kids will definitely be eager to go on a jungle safari or play at the beach. Unless your little ones have taken a children's anapana course or are really interested in visiting the sacred sites, a pilgrimage is not a good idea—bumpy bus- or car-rides and sitting motionless at a temple or pile of bricks is not a kid's idea of fun. Also avoid big cities for long stays. One thing you can count on is that all travel will be much, much slower than if you were alone.

You'll find that some aspects of travel become easier with kids. Without any inhibitions, they walk into someone's house, and then, when you go looking for them, you make friends with the local granny. People instantly trust you.

In Dhamma Giri there is a residential area where families can stay. Where, say, the mother can sit or serve while the father stays with the child and vice-versa. It is crucial that you make arrangements with the management before your arrival.

Precautions

A few precautions can go a long way in making your travels easier and smoother, beginning with the flight: take no chances. Choose a reliable airline and ask for a bulkhead seat (often called bassinette seat) if your child is under two and has no seat. This gives you extra leg space where your little one can sleep. If your child is sleeping at odd hours, no worries, it's a sign that they are already experiencing some fatigue and jet lag.

Once you reach India, the first thing to do is unpack and set up your mosquito net. Close it tightly. Indian mosquitoes are the least forgiving.

Food

Regarding food, go smoothly. Indulge slowly. It takes time to adapt to spicy Indian curries, but there are plenty of sweet or savoury options to start with: mangoes, papayas, guavas, *idli, dosa, puri,* and *upama.* If you prefer your kids to stay away from refined white sugar, you can treat them with jaggery-based sweets (but invariably, some kindly auntie will befriend your children by offering homemade, sugar-packed Indian sweets!)

If your kids are asking for soya milk, tofu, and brown rice, then you have to make some effort to shop. These are not available everywhere, only in select shops in big cities. Expect to pay 'western' prices, since these items will often be imported, although some restaurants in tourist spots make their own tofu and are willing to sell it at a good price.

Travelling by Train
Make sure to have reserved tickets, preferably in 2-tier AC or 3-tier AC for long journeys. Though AC class is more expensive, it is relatively clean and safe. The food on the train is okay, but it's a good idea to pack a lunch and many snacks instead. Don't worry if you run out of food though; you'll find fruit vendors at every station.

Accessories
Disposable diapers can be found in most of the pharmacies and big supermarkets, but they are smaller and less absorbent than the western ones, and toilet paper is expensive (one roll can go for as high as US$1), so be sure to bring a supply, or better yet, teach your child the diaper-free Indian way.

Travelling with Pets

When you see that cute six-week-old puppy playing in the sand, try to resist the temptation to adopt it. If you succumb, it will add many more logistical steps to your moving about. Expect to pay for an extra seat if you want to bring your pet on the bus or train.

Pets are not allowed in most meditation centres. And invariably, most guest houses will not appreciate your four-legged friend, even if you insist that it is toilet-trained and has finished teething. Moreover, we have seen Indian street dogs behaving quite nastily with domesticated dogs; ask yourself if you want to put your pet through this.

Travel Insurance

While travel insurance covering your ratty, old backpack may not be worth the money, a basic plan covering hospital treatment and a flight home is worth considering. If you live in a

> *If we do not find anything very pleasant, at least we shall find something new.*
>
> – Voltaire

country whose government provides a health plan, check what it covers while you are away. Canadian medicare, for example, will cover the costs of emergency treatments in other countries. If travelling in a country where health care costs are high—which is not the case for India—your regular medicare may not reimburse the full amount. Most credit card companies offer travel insurance. Check out http://www.worldnomads.com/ for inexpensive and flexible insurance plans.

A few simple precautionary steps will be helpful should you reap the bad karma of a severe accident or illness. Prepare a brief medical record including any allergies, medications you are currently using, your blood type, immunization history, etc. If you have health and/or travel insurance, include the company's name and your policy number. This info should fit on a small paper which can be kept with your passport.

Medications & Vaccinations

When you visit your local tropical disease clinic, the doctors there will usually recommend vaccinations for the following diseases: Polio, Diphtheria & Tetanus, Hepatitis A & B, Typhoid, Meningitis, Tuberculosis, Rabies, Japanese B Encephalitis and Yellow Fever.

This list is enough to alarm even the most laid-back traveller. Keep in mind, however, that it is the doctor's duty to anticipate every disease, even if it is only a remote possibility. Many seasoned travellers do not take any vaccinations at all, saying that they would rather run the risk of contracting a disease than dealing with the side-effects of the vaccinations. Ask your doctor's advice. For malaria and other illnesses, see the **Health** section.

You've landed...

India will bend your mind, assault your body, flood your senses, and shred your nerves, from the moment you step off the plane into its smoky unforgettable perfume of burning cow dung, diesel fumes, and a few thousand years of accumulated human sweat. And ultimately, if you're lucky, your old identity will break down like one of the decrepit, smog-belching auto-rickshaws that clog the Indian streets—and you'll have to walk on without it, through the twisting alleys of an unknown city, with cows eating empty juice cartons from street-side garbage dumps and ash-daubed mystics chanting mantras in the gutters. It's this breakdown and the attendant possibilities for transformation—more than a specific teacher or spiritual site—that's the real blessing India has to offer.

— Ann Cushman & Jerry Jones, *From Here to Nirvana*

Indeed, India has a way of always bringing you to your limits, like some "crazy wisdom teacher" asking you to stand over a precipice for a week without sleeping. Try to keep in mind that all the delays, wrong turns, and toilet runs are some of the most precious parts of your pilgrimage. Sometimes, we feel extremely grateful to the old man in the chai shop who gave us faulty directions. Then again, sometimes we do not. You just never know, and that's what this spiritual playground of saints, seers, and gods is all about.

The popular saying "In India, anything is possible," not only applies to the bank clerk hinting for a bribe, but to the daily miracles of bumping into a long-lost friend on a Himālayan mountain pass, or a car offering you a ride to exactly where you want to go after your rickshaw breaks down on a rural road in the dead of night. But the only way for these miracles to happen is with an unwavering trust that everything will be okay. The naïve traveller goes for the impossible by attempting to impose order on what is chaotic. The illusion of control, as you pack your bags, design a travel itinerary, buy your plane ticket and make reservations, is bound to be shattered within the first few days, as the simplest task becomes a day-long operation involving several bureaucratic layers. The following tips are meant to help the newcomer accomplish those missions efficiently and with the least stress possible.

Accommodations

Finding a room is often the first thing you do when you reach a place. There are many options: hotels, guest houses, family houses, and, in many of the sacred sites, monasteries. What is the difference between a hotel and a guest house? Hotels are bigger, and they are usually businesses run by employees; guest houses are smaller and usually family-run.

On the pilgrim circuit, many monasteries have a pilgrims' rest house on the campus. Staying in a monastery is our favourite option: it keeps you in the Dhamma atmosphere. Some of these may seem old, worn-out, and less opulent than the modern hotels and guest houses, but their warmth and hospitality make up for the material deficiencies. You may even become friendly with the local monks and nuns, who can show you places not found in any guidebook. (If you do, please send us this information for the next edition!) Guests are usually required to follow the basic precepts, and there may even be a shrine or meditation room for daily sittings. Plus, there's nothing like waking up to an early morning gong.

Some monasteries, however, are only open to citizens of their own countries, as is the case with many of the Thai monasteries.

Hotels & Guest Houses
You are exhausted from travelling, and all you want to do is bathe, eat and sleep. In this mental state, finding a room can often turn into an exasperating treasure hunt (which is why reserving a room in advance before you fly into Delhi, Mumbai, or Kolkata is not a bad idea). An operation such as this requires strategy: first, decide on your priorities.

- Price: What's your budget?
- Cleanliness: Can you live with cockroaches?
- Quiet: Do you mind roaring diesel engines or blaring music?
- Bathroom: Can you share a toilet with strangers?
- Hot water: Do you need hot water to bathe?
- Spaciousness: Do you need space for stretching?
- And any other unique quirks…

Sort these in order of importance to you. Inevitably, you will have a wonderful opportunity to develop renunciation here as that mythical 'perfect room' exists only in your mind. If you are really tired, you can take the first room you find and explore better options later when you are feeling fresh. A good way may be to ask a local shop owner, or someone who has no commercial interest in sending you to any particular place. Tell them that you're looking for a room: 'cheap and best.' If you ask for a 'hotel' in the street, you're likely to end up in a restaurant. It's better to ask for a 'guest house' or 'room.'

Tourist Information Offices often lead to crummy, over-priced, government-sponsored hotels.

When you find the room that looks within your budget and the desk clerk quotes you a price, it is sometimes open for negotiation, especially off-season. It goes something like this:

— Namaste, (Us, smiling.) Double room, how much? (Note the simplified language.)

— 300 rupees, Sir, hot and cold water, power 24 hours. (The clerk answers while straightening his moustache.)

— Three nights stay, you give good price?

— *Acchā*, three nights … (he stalls) Okay Sir … (tapping his pen on the desk) 275 only … (He adds this dramatically, as if this is a unique favour for us because we're somehow 'special.')
— Uh … can we look at room? (We have still not committed.)

Now, unless the room is worth more than this, we will continue to bargain, and probably end up paying 250 or 200 rupees.

Being indecisive can sometimes encourage the manager to drop the price, but if you overdo it, he will become frustrated and drop *you*. Ask to look at different kinds of rooms; for the same price you may get different features like a balcony or more windows. If the guest house is on a busy street, ask for a back room. *Always* look at the room before committing yourself to it. And don't forget the bathroom. Is it a 'bucket bath' or a stand-up shower? (And is the water pressure only a sorry excuse for a trickle?) Sometimes, sharing a damp, urine-smelling bathroom down the hall is a better option than having one attached to your sleeping quarters.

Check-out is usually at noon, but if you ask the manager in a friendly way, he may let you stay 'til one or two, if the place is not busy. Some guest houses are '24 hour check-out', or they may offer half-day rates, which are convenient if you're catching an evening train.

Keep in mind that the description of a guest house in a four-year-old Lonely Planet travel guide as having "clean rooms and friendly service" may not be accurate today. First, because of the free publicity, the staff and management may have become complacent and not made any necessary repairs. Second, because a five-year-old room that has never been scrubbed can be quite grimy. (At some hotels, their idea of cleaning is to dump a bucket of water on the bathroom floor.) Brand new guest houses are not necessarily more expensive, and are worth a look.

Unless you are staying with a family, you will be required to fill out the inevitable **C-Form**, with all your private information, including passport

> *Small hut, big heart.*
>
> – Ladakhi saying

and visa numbers. The guest house, or meditation centre, is legally obliged to bring it to the local police station within 24 hours of your arrival. Some Vipassana centres also ask to keep your passport while you participate in a meditation course. Don't be alarmed, this is only a formality. In case the police come to check on who is staying at the centre, the management does not have to disturb your meditation, but can simply show your passport.

The fancier hotels offer convenient services like money changers, travel agents, babysitters, couriers, doctors-on-call, laundry, room service, parking, internet and decent restaurants.

Renting a Place

It had been six months since we had left Nepal when we returned to Kathmandu for a third visa. It was December, and very cold. We had it all planned out: we would stay in Swayambhu, at the same Tibetan monastery for a month, where they had great veg-food, and hot showers to boot. This would provide us the seclusion and comfort needed to write. Although it was a little pricy, we figured that since it was low season, we could bargain down the price.

We got there however, and found out that an Italian monk and all his students were occupying the guest house. The only room left (at the regular price) had no hot water. We immediately renounced our plan and tried a new one, "We're here for a month, why don't we try renting an apartment?"

We set out for the hunt. Following an afternoon of visiting many great apartments with arched doorways and big windows that were already taken by other foreigners, we returned defeated and with our heads hung low. As a last resort, we decided to check out the place behind us, where we had enviously seen a foreign woman lounging on her terrace the previous summer. After enquiring around, we found the friendly Tibetan owners and asked them about the place. "Two German ladies are there now," he says, "but they're leaving tomorrow..." Anicca!

It was our refuge for a month. We rarely felt the need to go out, enjoying cooking for ourselves and waking up to the Tibetan horns and military trumpets. Our views of Everest on a clear afternoon never got tiring and even the company of sly monkeys who would steal our food didn't bother us.

KG & MD

You will find that when you stay in one place for a longer period you become somewhat part of the community, as opposed to being a mere tourist passing through. When you set up a daily routine, such as going to the vegetable market or cycling to a group sitting, this makes you familiar to the locals—they feel like investing the energy in getting to know you.

Ants in your bed?

Take some turmeric powder (*haldi*) and sprinkle it in a thick line around your bed: it has a strong smell that confuses the ants' scent trail. You will have to keep re-applying the powder, though, as they will eventually make a trail through it. If that doesn't work, put each foot of your bed in a small metal container (*katori*) and fill it with water. This solution isn't our first choice, as sometimes the ants drown in the water.

In most convenience shops, you can find Laxman Rekha, a stick of chalk-like substance with which you draw a line that repels the ants.

Finding a good place is often a combination of second-hand information, luck, and persistence. Ask around. Try to find some *videshīs* (foreigners) who are already living there; maybe one of their friends is moving on, or at least they can share the tale of how they found their place.

When you do find your ideal abode, and have settled on a price with your new landlord, don't forget to settle on who pays the utilities. If you're paying a month's rent in advance, ask for a dated receipt.

An added bonus when renting a place with a kitchen is that you can easily get into the routine of boiling your own drinking water.

Staying with Families

Some Indian families in or near tourist areas are quite open to having foreigners come and stay for a few nights, a few weeks, or a few months. Being in a home will give you the insider's perspective on what goes on behind closed doors. Life is very much communal, from eating to bathing and even relieving yourself (if there is no proper latrine), so much so, that you may find yourself craving solitude and some quiet time. The best way to find a balance is to communicate honestly (yet, sensitively) with your hosts.

You may stay and eat with families as a 'paying guest,' or simply as a friend: it should be clear to both you and your host from the outset. One friend was renting a room from a family, and the mother was constantly offering her food. As our friend was unclear about who was paying for the food, she offered to buy vegetables in the market. The mother brought her to a shop in which she purchased many household items such as incense and oil, ringing a bill of 1300 rupees, which she then presented to our friend.

When the arrangement is clear to both parties from the outset, such uncomfortable situations are less likely to occur.

Note that there is not much camping in India. Unless you're trekking in the Himālaya, a tent is just dead weight. (Although some resourceful meditators bring a tent for all-night sittings under the Bodhi tree—it keeps the mosquitoes away.)

Food

One of the best ways to get to know a country is through its culinary creativity and the rituals surrounding it: shopping in the market, ordering a meal in a road-side diner (*dhaba*), standing on a train station platform, mesmerized by the *puris* floating in oil, puffing up to the size of a football. As dutiful meditators, taste is the only sense that we have to indulge in; after all, only *arahants* can eat without craving and aversion, right?

India is a gastronomic paradise for vegetarians. Who knew that you could produce so much variety with grains and legumes? We suggest that even non-vegetarians stick to a veggie diet in India because bad meat is a prime cause of food poisoning: who knows what conditions the animal was brought up in, how the meat was stored, and how it was cooked? Even without meat, there is so much diversity from which to choose. To be safe, we try to go for 'Pure Veg' restaurants if we have the choice, which means that they don't use eggs or onions, and that the food has not come in contact with any meat.

Of course, the best way to sample Indian cuisine is by eating in family homes. When someone with whom you feel comfortable invites you for a meal, jump on the occasion; you cannot find these regional dishes in restaurants. The meditation centres also offer a variety of foods reflecting the local cultures.

I had the good fortune of being put in contact, by American meditator friends, with a meditator in Jaipur named Ravi. He was kind enough to pick me up at the bus station, give me a tasty lunch of vegetable curry, rice, lentils, and chapati at his home, and bring me to the meditation centre. After my retreat, I called him up and he invited me over for the following day, which happened to be the first and principal day of Diwali. I expected maybe another lunch, to meditate for an hour, visit a bit, then go back to my hotel. It turned out to be quite a bit more.

When I got there (having been picked up at my hotel by one of the workers from Ravi and his brother's workplace), Ravi's sister-in-law Manju was putting the finishing touches on lunch, which was rice pulau, spicy dhal, a cabbage dish, fresh chapatis, raita, and some really good Indian sweets. Indian sweets, by the way, are extremely sweet but have a subtle flavour from the careful use of spices. Afterwards, Ravi, Manju and I meditated together for an hour, then Ravi and I chatted for a while and looked at books. Not feeling well, Ravi went to lie down but urged me to make myself comfortable and stick around for the evening.

I did, and thus witnessed this Jain family's Diwali, including the preparation of their altar, under the charge of Ravi's dad Harsh. Harsh has sat one Vipassana course, but decided that he was happier with devotion to and worship of gods and saintly people than with this practice. Accordingly, he maintains an altar with various photos of saints like Sai Baba, statues of gods, sacred writings, etc. Diwali being a special occasion and a family occasion, the altar was set up with a thin mattress in front of it for the family to sit on during the pūjā (worship). Harsh carefully selected a postcard with images of Lakshmi, Durga, and Saraswati; a medallion with an image of Sai Baba; a statuette of Ganesha, the elephant god, and set up incense, dye/paint, and other necessities.

In due time, I sat down with the family, from the two apartments on this floor of the building, to start the pūjā. The women were all dolled-up in special saris and the older men were dressed in pure white traditional kurta pijama (that's the long roomy shirt with matching pants). Harsh officiated, chanting from sacred texts, while Ravi's brother Manoj and I took some photos. While it was a serious worship service, at the same time there was a light-hearted feeling, with all of us laughing and joking around, and people other than Harsh also taking turns doing some chanting or singing. Later, in the apartment next door where Ravi's sister and family live, we did the same thing, and the 16-year-old daughter brought out some Christian hymns in English from her Jesuit school to sing with me and friends who had stopped by.

All of this activity included much food, some of it in the form of prasad, or the blessed food (Indian sweets in this case) that had been offered to the gods and now was to be consumed by their devotees. Not realizing at first that food would be an insistent theme for the entire remainder of the evening, I filled up on the delicious sweets the first time around. Next door, more prasad was passed around; then there were snacks, a light meal of yogurt and a deep-fried-something plus poori (deep fried bread) and a bean/lentil dish, all pushed with relentless hospitality that I didn't want to refuse for fear of being impolite.

After playing with fireworks with the kids outside—some boys from the building had a box full of what seemed like quarter sticks of dynamite which they kept setting off about 50 feet away from us (there was no malice but even so, it was painful and I tried to plug my ears every time one was about to go off)—we all piled into two cars and headed off to another part of town to visit Ravi's uncle, an architect who had thoroughly redesigned the interior of his house after buying it. I was made to feel even more extravagantly welcome here, if that was possible, as though I were the guest of honour—photos were taken with me, and everyone followed me through the house when I asked for a tour, joking with me and listening to my comments with interest. Of course, I was practically forced to have more delicious snacks and tea. As Manoj was giving me a ride back to my hotel, I feared that I'd have to wretch out the window from overeating, but fortunately I was able to save self and hosts from such drastic embarrassment, leaving only pleasant memories.

– Peter Buchanan

Restaurants

The criteria for choosing a restaurant are the same all over the world:

- Choose a restaurant that is full—the continuous flow of hungry patrons means the food is always fresh.
- Ask locals where they eat—they know which kitchen is clean and which one serves two-day-old food.
- Trust your intuition.

Expensive Restaurants
You can recognize these by their table-cloths and multitude of personnel, all wearing neat uniforms and trying their best to look busy (and when you walk in, they're grateful to keep themselves busy with *you*, if only to stand next to your table, eyeing your every move...)

These restaurants vary widely in terms of décor and service, and the food is not necessarily better than what you could get at a cheaper restaurant. A credit card sign in the window usually means a larger bill.

Family Restaurants
These are good, clean restaurants that cater to families and business people. They may specialize in South Indian or North Indian food, which is served on a stainless steel plate called a *thāli* with little side-dishes called *katori*. A *thāli* is not complete without a representative of each of the six *rasas*: sweet, sour, salty, pungent, astringent and bitter. The prices may be a few rupees higher than the *dhabas* (see below), but the difference in quality is noticeable.

Tourist Restaurants
The tourist restaurants all over India have the same names—like Om Café or Welcome Restaurant—and more or less the same menu: a mix of Indian, Tibetan, Chinese and continental dishes. (Although just because you had a fabulous banana pancake in one restaurant doesn't mean that the next one will be as good.)

The quality of food in these restaurants is a gamble; the established places know foreigners' tastes and offer a cozy atmosphere, good food, and decent service, while other entrepreneurs just open up an eatery expecting to make a quick buck. Ask other travellers for recommendations.

Dhabas

The *dhaba* is the people's restaurant. Makeshift stalls of wooden planks, plastic sheeting, and aluminum siding decorated with wobbly benches and tables surrounded by posters of beautiful film stars and colourful Hindu deities, these eateries are set up wherever there is an opportunity to earn a few rupees off of a nearby trade. Dhabas usually offer *thālis* of ready-made food, which is displayed in huge aluminum pots at the entrance. These places are usually all-you-can-eat: the waiter comes around the tables with big pots and ladles, and scoops a generous portion of *dhal* (lentils), rice, and/or *sabji* (vegetables) onto your plate before you can protest. Dhabas sometimes also serve tasty snacks like *samosas* (fried pastry stuffed with spiced potatoes and onions) and *pakoras* (deep fried vegetables in batter).

Street Stalls

Many enterprising vendors won't wait for the customers to come to them; they go directly to the streets where they can tantalize the hungry masses with the smell of their fresh fare. You can find anything from snacks like tea, fresh juice, sweets and *samosas*, to a full meal of *puri baji* (fried bread and a vegetable dish) or even chow mein. It is normal in India to eat in public, but not while walking; just stand there and munch, or sit on the curb, have a picnic and enjoy your food.

Street food is very cheap: the vendor has no expenses like rent or staff—he *is* the cook, waiter and cashier. Street eating also cuts down on the formalities of restaurants like menus and ordering, and your imagination doesn't run wild about what's going on behind closed doors in the kitchen; you see your food being prepared right in front of you. (*Always* eat freshly cooked food or fruits that have not been pre-peeled—germ-carrying flies also like street snacks. Also, try to make sure that water does not come into contact with your food or drink.)

Ethnic Restaurants

You will only find specialty restaurants, like Chinese or Italian, in big cities or tourist towns, but don't expect them to be authentic unless they are run by Chinese or Italians who import their ingredients from home.

Ordering Your Meal

Between the menu and your hungry stomach lies the apparently-simple step of ordering. This is where being mindful could make the difference between a satisfying meal and a lingering disappointment. To help your waiter serve you better, be clear and patient.

- Decide what you want to eat before you order.
- Order what's on the menu.
- If all you want is a *thāli* and it's not on the menu, ask for one anyway; this could save you money *and* give you a variety of the cook's favourite dishes.
- Speak slowly, with as few words as possible.
- Don't ask too many questions, this will only confuse your waiter.
- Combine group orders, and if necessary, write them down.
- If you can't stand the heat, don't be afraid to insist that they don't put any pepper or chilli (*bina mirchi*).

Tipping
The Indian custom is to leave 5 or 10 rupees in the smaller restaurants, and 15% in the classier establishments (check if it has already been included in the bill).

Be Adventurous
Many travellers find one dish they like and end up ordering that item over and over. Unless you're feeling ill or homesick, try to conquer your fear of the unknown. Your bold trial of the hot *sambhar* may leave you beet-red with smoke coming out of your ears, but your courage will often be rewarded with a pleasant surprise. (We recommend sampling the mysterious confections in a sweet shop at least once—you'll then understand why there are so many advertisements for toothpaste!)

A friend was standing over the ice box trying to decide which ice cream he wanted. The vendor tried to guide him: "Best one," he says, holding up a frozen treat on a stick. "Most best one," he emphasizes, presenting another specimen in a cardboard cup. "This is pure best one," he says holding up a mango dolly, nodding his head with great authority.

A Nomadic Kitchen
There will be times when you're fed up of with eating out, and you think, "All I want is a fresh salad." With a few simple instruments, like a Swiss army knife and vegetable peeler, you can make easy dishes that will remind you of home: peel a few carrots into long strips, add some onion, cilantro and lemon, and *voilà*, a gourmet salad. (You can also sprout your own mung beans or lentils to add to it, see sidebox.) Use your imagination: add sesame oil, cucumbers, grated coconut, or tomatoes to create variety.

Sprouts

Sprouting is easy: the seeds and sun do the work; all you have to do is give water.

- Cut a plastic water bottle two thirds of the way up;
- Sift through the beans and remove any debris and stones;
- Soak the beans in purified water overnight;
- Place a cheese-cloth or screen over the bottle (secured with a rubber band) to drain the beans;
- If you don't have a screen, insert the top part of the bottle upside down.
- Keep rinsing your sprouts three times a day for a couple of days.

They're good to eat as soon as they're soft and a little tail comes out.

With immersion heating coils, you can boil water for herbal teas brought from home. Or, prepare a packet of instant *Maggie* noodles (easily found in most Indian general stores) mixed with some veggies.

For more elaborate chefs, remember that a camping stove is not exclusive to Himālayan hikers. Also, if you stay in one place, you can invest about Rs 500 for a propane stove and cooking utensils, which you can then sell or give away before you leave. In cases like these, it is good to bring dried herbs from home, such as basil, oregano, and thyme: they are lightweight and are a refreshing change from turmeric, cumin, mustard seeds, and chilli.

When you're on the go, fresh *chapattis* on the train platform make great bread for wrap-style sandwiches.

Purifying Veggies
An Israeli medical doctor once told us, "In India, you never know where the vegetables you buy in the market have grown; for all you know, they could have grown next to an open sewer!" This thought has helped us keep the discipline of purifying our veggies.

You can purify your fruits and vegetables with water purification drops of chlorine dioxide and phosphoric acid (like *Aqua Mira*® or *Pristine*, see purifying water in the **Health** section). Use 14 drops of each for one litre of water and soak your **uncut** fruits and vegetables for 30 minutes. This method is perfect for fruits that you can't really peel, such as grapes. You can prepare the mixture in a plastic bag and just soak them while you're on the train; you will then enjoy them without worry.

You can also purify veggies with iodine: soak them for 20-30 minutes, then let them air dry.

If you find yourself in a situation where someone offers you raw foods that have probably not been purified, and you don't want to offend the host, just muster up all your courage and *think* that they're pure; these mental *pūjās* haven't failed us yet.

Eating with Your Hands
Most Indians, from the poorest to the upper classes, eat with their hands. Although spoons are on the rise, most Indians will say that the tactile sensation adds to the experience of a meal. Just watch how Indians eat and try your best to imitate them. *Always* eat with your right hand (to know what to do with your left hand, see the toilet section…). Always wash your hands before a meal. For a second helping, never touch the ladle with your soiled hand; it is then proper to use your left.

What You'll Eat
An Indian friend living in Australia generously compiled this introduction to Indian food. Of course, the imagination of Indian cooks is unlimited, but these dishes are the most common.

SNACKS

Alu Wada	Boiled and mashed potatoes (*alu*) coated in chickpea batter and deep fried.
Bhajiya/ Pakora	Onions/spinach coated in chickpea batter and deep fried.
Sabudana Khichidi	Tiny white sago (tapioca-like) pearls mixed with peanuts and spices.
Samosa	A fried pastry stuffed with potato and peas coated in spices.
Timepass	Any snack eaten to pass the time.
Upama	Spicy or salty semolina porridge with vegetables.
Poha	Puffed rice flakes with turmeric and cilantro.

SNACKS (CONTINUED)

Vada Pao	Pao is a small bun. Vadas are mashed potatoes coated in chick-pea batter and deep fried.
Pao Bhaji	Pao is eaten with thoroughly cooked vegetables and HOT spices in butter.
Dahlia	Plain or sweet semolina porridge.
Dhokla	Spongy cubes made from lentil and rice flour, with coconut and cilantro, served with a tamarind sauce.
Idli	Fermented lentil and rice flour, steamed in circular shapes, served with a coconut chutney and *sambhar*, a lentil soup.
Masala Dosa	Fermented rice and lentil flour pancakes stuffed with dry potato curry served with different chutneys and *sambhar*.
Plain Dosa	Fermented rice and lentil flour pancakes served with chutney and sambhar.

MAIN COURSES

THĀLI	A platter including a combination of at least: 2 vegetables, 2 curries, 1 yogurt dish and 1 dessert, served with *roti* or *puri* and rice. Recommended as the best value for money.
Sabji/Bhaaji	Sabji just means dry vegetables cooked in spices. The most common vegetable is potato (*alu*), eaten by itself, or combined with any other vegetable.
Chillies	Known as *Mirchi*. Watch out for what looks like green beans, they may be fiery hot chillies.
Alu Jeera	Potato cooked with cumin seeds.
Alu Gobi	Potato and cauliflower.
Bhindi Masala	Okra (*bhindi*) cooked with spices.
Baigan Bharta	Roasted eggplant (*baigan*) mashed and cooked with spices.
Paneer	Indian cottage cheese similar in consistency to Feta cheese.
Navrattan Korma / Vegetable Jalfrezi / Kolhapuri Vegetables	Mixed vegetables.

CURRIES (EATEN WITH RICE OR BREAD)

Alu Matar	Pea and potato curry.
Matar paneer	Pea and Indian cottage cheese curry.
Palak paneer	Blended spinach in combination with Indian cottage cheese.
Kadhai paneer	Cottage cheese cooked in rich and creamy tomato sauce.
Chole	Chick pea curry. This curry is also known as *Pindi Channa*.

CURRIES (CONTINUED)

Rajma	Kidney bean curry.
Lobia	Black-eyed bean curry.
Dha Varan	Yellow lentil soup.
Tadka Dhal	Lentil stew garnished with onions and chillies in butter. Another popular combination is *Palak (spinach) Dhal.*
Malai Kofta	Cheese and potato dumplings in rich creamy sauce.

RICE DISHES

Biryani/ Pulao	Aromatic fried rice with vegetables, chicken, or meat, and sometimes nuts or dried fruit.
Chaawal/ Bhaath	Plain steamed rice, usually eaten with Dhal. (Dhal chawal/ Varan bhaat)
Tomato/Lemon Rice	Two popular alternatives to plain rice.

BREADS

Roti/Chapati	Wholemeal flat bread cooked on a griddle.
Puri	Deep-fried bread.
Paratha	Pan-fried bread, sometimes stuffed with potatoes or other vegetables.
Naan	White flour bread cooked in a tandoor oven.
Bhatura	Deep fried white flour bread.

ACCOMPANIMENTS

Yogurt	Also known as *dahi.* Dahi combined with anything is called *raita.* Common raita dishes are cucumber raita, onion and tomato raita, boondi raita (tiny balls of deep fried chick pea batter soaked in yogurt).
Pickles & Chutneys	*Achaar* and *chatni* are made of fruits and/or vegetables, range from sweet to extra-spicy, and accompany any meal.

DESSERTS (COMMON INDIAN SWEETS)

Halwa	Sweet flavoured semolina.
Khīr	Rice pudding with milk, dried fruits, nuts, cinnamon and cardamom (the black stones!).
Gulab Jamun	Brown deep fried dumplings soaked in sugar syrup.
Jalebi	Tiny whirlpools of batter deep fried & soaked in sugar syrup.
Rasgulla	White cheese dumplings soaked in syrup.
Laddoo	Round sweet balls in various flavours. They can be the size of a tennis ball.

DESSERTS (CONTINUED)

Barfi	Square milk cakes in various flavours.
Kulfi	Pistachio-flavoured Indian ice-cream.

DRINKS (TO BEAT THE HEAT)

Chai	Sweet, spiced black tea with or without milk
Lassi/ Chaas	Sweet/salty yogurt shake
Nimboo pani	lemonade
Sherbat	Flavoured cordial

TIBETAN (SAMPLE HEARTY TIBETAN COOKING WHEREVER YOU FIND TIBETANS)

Momos	Vegetable or meat dumplings either fried or steamed.
Thanthuk	Vegetable or meat soup, with square and flat homemade noodles.
Thukpa	Vegetable or meat soup, with long spaghetti noodles.

> *Wisely reflecting on this food,*
> *I eat not to distract my mind,*
> *Nor to indulge in my cravings,*
> *Nor to make my body beautiful,*
> *But simply for sustenance and nourishment,*
> *To help keep me going along the sacred path.*
>
> *Bearing this in mind,*
> *I dispel hunger without overeating;*
> *So that I may strive to live*
> *flawlessly and with simplicity.*
>
> A, 3:16

The feeling of being 'on vacation' and wanting to taste the local culture stimulates the appetite, yet tourists all over the world often complain of stomach problems. It is not uncommon to see travellers feasting on rich cashew stews, samosas with hot sauce, the sweetest sweets and ice-cream—and then complain about an upset stomach. Before accusing the restaurant and the country in general, try seeing if you are at least partly responsible for not listening to your body. This is particularly true after a retreat. When you have spent 10 days—or longer—purifying your mind and body, and then over-indulge, don't be surprised when your tummy rebels...

Before starting a meal, ask yourself, "Is this a special occasion or just another meal?" The Buddha said that *bhataṃ-attaññū*—knowing the proper amount of food one should take, neither too little nor too much—is one of the qualities of a good meditator.

Health

Before you read any further and become worried, let us assure you that it is not difficult to stay healthy in India. Most travellers will encounter the common cold or a mild case of diarrhoea, but with a little common sense, these will not be big obstacles.

Good health is one of the five requisites for walking on the path of Dhamma; therefore, it should be given proper attention.

Middle Path

The 'middle path' attitude is helpful in all decision-making. "I'm feeling tired, should I commit to an early day-trip tomorrow?" or "The centre needs servers for the next course, but I have a cold, should I go anyway?"

This does not mean that you should be a paranoid stick-in-the-mud. Just know your limits; listening to your body now will help prevent complications later.

Most importantly: be healthy before you leave!

Precautions

- **Sun**: Think ahead. Bring a hat with you. If necessary, use sun-block liberally, and always have a water bottle at your side. Protect yourself even on cloudy days. A friend travelled on the roof of a bus on a cloudy day for several hours and ended up with severe sunburn.

- **Footwear**: One traveller we know discovered tiny insects emerging from his thighs while he was bathing. When he went to a local Ayurvedic healer, the doctor said that he had not seen a case like this in 25 years. The doctor said our friend had caught these parasites from walking barefoot in the village. We should take S.N. Goenka's advice literally, "The path is full of pebbles and thorns. Protect yourself; wear shoes and walk over it!"

- **Carry your own cup** so you can enjoy the street chai, sugar cane juice and fruit juices without having those background thoughts of the *chai-wallah* washing the cups in dirty water.

- **Peel** or **purify** raw fruits and veggies, just to be safe (see the **food** section).

- Drink **purified** water (see below).

Purify your Water

You need to drink a lot of water in India. The problem is that if we don't like the taste of the water, we tend not to drink enough. Thus, finding a good way to purify it is essential. Boiling, iodine, filters, drops, or just plain faith, are some of the methods travellers use. The best and least intrusive way, of course, is to boil it for at least a minute, but this is not always possible. Iodine works well to purify water, but experts say that it should not be used for extended periods as it affects the thyroid gland. Filters on their own remove bacteria, but they don't remove viruses.

The winning method for us when we can't boil our water is to use the two-part drops—Part A is 2% stabilized chlorine dioxide, and Part B is 5% food-grade phosphoric acid—found in camping stores in the West, followed by a filter to remove the taste.

When parts A and B are mixed together, they create a solution of activated chlorine dioxide (ClO_2), which is used by many municipal water treatment plants as an alternative to chlorine. It purifies the water of any viruses, bacteria, giardia, and cryptosporidium. In only 20 minutes you have drinkable water. The tiny 30 ml bottles are quite affordable and can treat up to 120 litres. Although it is supposed to be tasteless, we find that the drops alone leave a pool-water tang, so we have started filtering it through a squeeze-bottle filter, which removes larger microorganisms, the chlorine taste and any sediments.

This solution can also be used to treat uncut fruits and vegetables, and sanitize your containers and dishes.

Camping stores in the West carry reliable drops, disposable filters, and filter bottles made by *Pristine®*, *Aqua Mira®*, and *Eddie Bauer®*. You can also order these on-line.

Does your water still taste bad?
- Squeeze a lemon into it, or
- Put a few cardamom seeds in your bottle, or
- Drink herbal teas. If it's too hot out, make ice tea.

Water in Meditation Centres
Most of the meditation centres use Aquaguard filter systems that blast tiny microbes with UV rays.

The Aquaguard system has three stages in the purification process:

1. The sediment filter strains out the dust, dirt and mud.
2. The activated carbon hinders bacterial growth, and reduces odours, colours, and free gases such as chlorine.
3. The Ultra-Violet (UV) chamber eliminates bacteria and viruses which cause water-born diseases, such as gastro-enteritis, dysentery, typhoid, and Hepatitis A.

When properly maintained, this filtering system is very safe. The advantage of Aquaguard over boiling is that it retains the natural salts, calcium, and magnesium.

The problem is that most Indians don't understand the dangers of water on foreign bellies, so the filters are not changed as often as they should be. If you are not the volunteer who is taking care of the water filters, it might be worth it to continue treating your water in meditation centres, if only to put your mind at ease.

Under the Weather?
Before dashing off to the nearest 'chemist' and committing yourself to a series of medications, decide whether all you need is a few days of rest. Relax, read a book, fast for the day, *meditate*. A wise Vipassana teacher in Nepal once told us, "Equanimity is the best medicine."

Having said this, the 'just observe' approach should not be taken to extremes either. There are times when the body can use a little help and you need to see a specialist. But who to see?

Allopathic, Ayurvedic, Tibetan, Naturopathic, or Homeopathic? In principle, we start with natural medicines and use chemical pills only as a last resort. In India, antibiotics are used much too liberally. For small ailments, the local 'chemist shop' should be able to recommend something herbal. For serious illnesses, it is better to consult a doctor. To find one, just ask around. Some big hotels have doctors on call, or at least can recommend reliable practitioners. Government hospitals are quite a lot cheaper than private clinics, although you may spend an entire day in a gloomy waiting room. Private hospitals and clinics are more efficient, quicker, and expensive.

If you don't have any first-hand references, visit Delhi's US Embassy website—http://newdelhi.usembassy.gov/medical_information2.html—which lists all the hospitals and physicians in India with which embassy staff have been satisfied. It is an excellent site to have on hand in case of major *dukkha*.

> ### Medicinal Plants
>
> When the physician Jīvaka was studying herbal medicine in Taxilā, his teacher decided that his student's period of study was coming close to an end and that it was time for his final examination. He said to Jīvaka: "My pupil, walk for one *yojana* [about 7 miles] in the eastern direction and bring me back a plant with no medicinal properties."
>
> After some time, Jīvaka came back and said: "Respected teacher, having walked for one yojana, I have not found any plant that has no medicinal properties."
>
> The teacher told him to go to the west, then to the south, and then to the north. Every time, Jīvaka came back empty-handed. After the fourth time, the teacher proudly announced that his pupil had finished his medical training, as he could now identify the medicinal properties of every plant.

Whichever method you choose, have faith in your doctor. Bear in mind that medicines like Ayurveda, Naturopathy, and Tibetan aim to restore the body's balance and harmony as opposed to merely dealing with symptoms, therefore, these treatments are often longer and slower. Once you have chosen a particular treatment, stick to it and give it a chance to work for you—even if it means chewing bitter herbs for a month. Even when you begin to feel better, don't stop your treatment (unless you have a serious reaction to it).

Allopathy
Allopathy means conventional, 'western' medicine: the remedies usually relieve symptoms quickly.

Ayurveda
Ayurveda is the ancient medical science of India. It focuses on prevention according to individual body types, and treats the cause of illnesses with herbs, diet, exercise, yoga and massage. To learn more about Ayurveda, read Dr. Robert Svoboda's *Prakriti: Your Ayurvedic Constitution*.

Tibetan Medicine
Tibetan medicine stems from both Ayurveda and Chinese medicine. It sees disease as an imbalance in different bodily humours, and focuses on healing the physical as well as the psychological. Afflictive emotions such as desire or hatred are seen

as the causes of many diseases, so developing positive mental attitudes are part of the pathway to health. Diagnosis is done by checking the tongue, eyes, pulse, and colour and smell of morning urine. It is a slow acting treatment, which uses mostly herbs and minerals (though sometimes non-vegetarian ingredients) that come in the form of small, bitter tasting balls produced through an intricate process of alchemy. Acupuncture, massage, and prayer are also used. To understand more about Tibetan medicine, read Dr. Yeshe Dendon's *Health through Balance.*

Naturopathy

It is difficult to define naturopathy, as it means different things to different people. In general, practitioners aim to cure illness through natural processes like fasting, enemas, steam baths, saunas, herbs, diet, mud packs, massage, and so on.

Homeopathy

Homeopathy was developed in Germany in the 19th century but has gained widespread popularity in India. The idea is that "like cures like"—which means that a substance that can cause certain symptoms in a healthy person can cure similar symptoms in an unhealthy person. Although most homeopathic remedies are made from herbs, roots, and minerals, a few are made with animal products. A great reference guide for pilgrims is *The World Traveller's Manual of Homeopathy* by Dr. Colin B. Lessell.

Your First Aid Kit

You can find a wide range of pills, syrups, and powders for every conceivable complaint; if (when) you get sick, you will almost always find a remedy on the spot (as well as non-stop advice about what you should take and what you should stay away from, such as "Papaya is good for diarrhoea," from one local friend, and "Avoid papaya at all costs," from another). So, since you can find remedies for almost any problem, you don't need to bring your entire bathroom cabinet to feel secure. However, you should bring your preferred medicine if you have a particular recurring weakness. Also be aware that brand names for certain medicines may be different in India: if you are not bringing your own medications with you, be sure to note the key ingredients so that you are able to request them in India.

If you're the type who likes to take multivitamins or health tonics, we recommend these traditional Indian tonics: **Chyawanprash** in the winter and **Sheetalprash** in the summer. The recipes for these tonics are over 2000 years old. They are made mostly of *amla* paste (Indian gooseberry)—which is very high in vitamin C and a great antioxidant—as well as different herbs and spices.

Altitude Sickness

Altitude sickness is caused by the lack of oxygen in thin mountain air. It can affect everyone, regardless of age or physical condition. Symptoms are flu-like: headache, nausea, vomiting, dizziness, breathlessness, physical weakness, mental confusion and general fatigue. The symptoms may not be immediately noticed—they may even appear a couple of days after the body has started to suffer. Altitude sickness usually last about three days.

We know people who have flown from Delhi to Leh (3 500 m high) and spent a week in the hospital with altitude sickness. Ladakhi friends of ours say, "When we fly home, we spend the day in bed, even if we don't feel sick." Those who land and think they feel fine and spend the day on the go, end up regretting it later.

Most people who suffer from altitude sickness will only need rest. If you have severe symptoms, you should see a doctor, but generally speaking, these tips help:

* Avoid alcohol, sleeping pills, and narcotics.

* Drink plenty of clear fluids as dehydration at altitude is very common and increases the likelihood and severity of altitude sickness. (Do not drink diuretics like coffee as that will make you lose more fluids.)

* Eat high-carbohydrate foods (rice, pasta, cereal) and avoid fatty foods.

* If nothing else works, you can return to lower altitude—even descending 500 m can make a difference.

A note for trekkers: A quick ascent to elevations above 2 500 m can cause pulmonary and cerebral oedema. These patients need to see a physician for oxygen therapy and descend to lower altitude. To avoid this, the general guideline is to not ascend more than a final total of 500 m per day: it is the overnight rest that helps your body acclimatize.

Bites and Stings

Most insect bites are just a test of equanimity rather than a real danger. Everyone will give you different advice on how to soothe the pain: half an onion, lemon juice, coconut oil, eucalyptus oil…but equanimity is the best anti-inflammatory.

To soothe itchy bites and stings:

* Wash the bite or sting with soap and water.

* An ice pack will help stop the swelling.

* Make a paste of water and salt, baking soda, activated charcoal or even just plain clay, and apply it to the bite.

* If a bee has stung you, scrape the stinger out with your nail.

Scorpion Stings

Scorpion stings can be very painful, but are rarely fatal. If you are stung, relax; panicking will only make it worse. Clean the area with soap and water or crushed garlic and lemon juice. If you can find ice, apply it to the sting. Lift the limb to heart-level. Take a lot of Vitamin C. People used to scorpion stings treat them like wasp stings; painful but not life-threatening. If you have trouble breathing, you can take an antihistamine. If you don't feel well, consider fasting for a day.

Scorpions like damp and dark corners, so be careful when walking in the brush or around rock piles. They are nocturnal hunters, so check your bedding before hopping in, inspect your clothing in the morning, and shake out your shoes before slipping them on.

Protection of the Aggregates
(Khandha Parittaṃ)

On one occasion the Blessed One was dwelling near Sāvatthī at Jetavana monastery in Anathapiṇḍika's park. At that time in Sāvatthī, a certain monk died from a snake bite. Then, an assembly of monks approached the Buddha. Having paid their respects, they sat beside him. So seated, those monks spoke thus to the Blessed One: "Here, Bhante, in Sāvatthī, a certain monk has died from a snake bite." The Buddha replied,

Indeed, monks, that monk did not permeate the four royal snake clans with thoughts of loving-kindness (mettā). Had he done so, that monk would not have died of a snake bite. What are the four royal snake clans? They are called Virūpakkha, Erāpatha, Chabyāputta and Kaṇhāgotamaka. Indeed, monks, that monk did not permeate these four royal clans of snakes with thoughts of loving-kindness. Had he done so, he would not have been bitten by a snake and died. Monks, I enjoin you to permeate these four royal clans of snakes with thoughts of loving-kindness, for your safety, for your preservation, and for your protection.

My mettā is with the Virūpakkha,
And with the Erāpatha too;
My mettā is with the Chabyāputta,
And also with the Kaṇhāgotamaka.

May my mettā be with all footless beings
And with all bipeds too,
May my mettā be with all quadrupeds
And also with all many-footed creatures.

Let not the footless do me harm
Nor those that have two feet;
Let no quadruped harm me,
Nor those creatures with many feet.

All beings, all living creatures,
And all those who merely exist,
May they experience good fortune,
May no harm whatsoever come to them.

Limitless is the Buddha, limitless is the Dhamma, limitless is the Saṅgha. Limited are creeping creatures—snakes, scorpions, centipedes, spiders, lizards and rats. I have guarded myself, I have made my protection. Move away from me, you beings. I pay respects to the Blessed One and to the seven Sammāsambuddhas.

The tiny black scorpions that you find in some parts of the Himālaya, such as Dharamsala, have a very benign sting—you may get a bit swollen, maybe slightly dizzy, but that's about it. Homeopathic remedies work wonders for these, when taken immediately.

Snake Bites

The most dangerous snakes in India are the Russel's Viper and the Indian Cobra. Even though snake bites kill around 20 000 people every year in India, travellers have little chance of even seeing a snake, let alone being bitten by one. Some Indians consider seeing a *nāga* as a sign of good luck, as the wriggling creatures are considered semi-deities. The snake is usually much more afraid of you than you are of it, and prefers escape over attack.

If you are bitten:

- Stay calm and lie down to retard the spread of venom (if there is any).
- Allow the bite to bleed freely for 30 seconds.
- Wrap a bandage (not too tight) above and below the bite.
- Remove any jewellery and tight clothing.
- Immobilize or splint the bitten limb and keep it at heart-level if possible.
- Put a cold pack on the bite; it will reduce the swelling and slow the spread of venom. Don't leave it too long or it will damage the tissues.
- Do not take alcohol, medicine or food.
- Get to a hospital.

Bleeding
Apply pressure and elevate the wounded area higher than the heart. Clean the wound with antiseptic such as povidine-iodine (not Dettol™ as that is too harsh); if it is shallow and stops bleeding, allow it to air dry. Otherwise, bandage it with gauze and medical tape, apply pressure, and seek help if the bleeding doesn't diminish.

Burns/Sunburns
Flush with cold water for 15 to 30 minutes to stop the burning, but don't use ice or ice-water—they can make the burn worse.

Gently wrap the burn in thick gauze and then leave it alone for 24 hours. After a day, gently wash it with soap and water once daily, then keep it covered, dry and clean. Aloe vera is a natural anti-inflammatory, anti-septic and analgesic: good for minor burns and sunburns. Don't pop your blisters—the fluid inside protects the burn.

You should see a doctor if the skin is charred or a creamy colour—this indicates a third degree burn. These are usually not painful, because the nerve endings have been destroyed. See a doctor if there is any sign of it becoming infected.

Cholera
Although cholera is endemic in India, the overall risk for travellers is very low— basic food and water hygiene should ensure that you won't contract the disease. Cholera is most commonly transmitted through contaminated water. A huge dose is required to cause illness in a healthy person. Only those travellers drinking the local water or living in unsanitary conditions are at risk.

Symptoms include profuse, watery diarrhoea, nausea, vomiting, and sometimes fever. If left untreated, it can cause serious dehydration. Take oral rehydration salts as soon as possible to replace lost fluids and electrolytes. Serious cases will require intravenous fluid replacement and antibiotics. Prompt treatment ensures rapid recovery.

Common Cold
There is a saying that goes: "A treated cold last seven days and an untreated cold lasts a week."

If you treat it as soon as the first signs show themselves, however, you have a better chance of defeating it: take plenty of *Amlaki* (a great source of vitamin C), and *Tulsi* (Holy Basil, an expectorant), which can be found in any chemist shop. Rest. Drink 6 to 8 glasses of water, juice, or tea (without milk) per day. Garlic has an antibiotic effect: you can eat it raw, or take 2-3 capsules three times a day.

For a sore throat, gargle with warm salt water 3-4 times daily.

Constipation
While many travellers get the runs, some also get constipated (especially during meditation retreats). A popular Indian remedy is *Isabgol* (Psillium husks) taken in a glass of warm water after meals. Psillium is a concentrated form or fibre, and, unlike chemical laxatives, is non-addictive. When Isabgol is taken with yogurt or cold water, it blocks you up.

Some herbal ayurvedic remedies, such as Herbalax and Triphala, are very effective.

Make sure you drink enough liquids: warm water helps to lubricate the digestive tract. Take a walk—it will move food towards the bowels faster. You can try doing forward bends, and the "boat pose": balancing on your sit bones, with your legs extended and your feet half a metre from the ground. This contracts your abdominal muscles, working as a massage for your intestines.

Cough
Persistent coughs often crop up after a change in climate, such as after monsoon, or because of pollution or dust (in which case it's a good idea to wear a face mask while in traffic). There are a variety of Ayurvedic lozenges like Kadiradi Goli, Koflet® or even Vicks®.

Cuts & Scrapes
Wash well with soap and warm water. Apply antiseptic if necessary. Aloe vera is a good natural antiseptic that is widely available.

Diarrhoea
If you experience intestinal turmoil, don't jump on 'gut paralysers' such as Immodium®—your body is trying to eliminate something toxic, and you are preventing it from doing so. Let it come out. It is actually a purging process. Fasting for a day or so is a good idea (you probably won't feel like eating anyways). Rest and recover for a few days.

When you actually feel like eating again, start slow. Avoid dairy products (except yogurt), as well as oily, spicy and raw foods (bananas are an exception). See *Kanji* and *Kicheri* recipes below.

The most important factor is to prevent dehydration (the yellower your urine, the more dehydrated you are—it should be light yellow) by drinking plenty of electrolytes. You can find these oral rehydration salts in the chemist shops (Elektral®, lemon flavour) or you can make your own with two tablespoons of sugar, half a teaspoon of salt and some lemon juice in a litre of purified water. Keep sipping your re-hydration solution throughout the day.

Another option is the two-in-one anti-diarrhoea cocktail: add half a teaspoon of honey (or sugar) and a pinch of salt to a glass of fruit juice. In another glass, add one quarter teaspoon of baking soda to a glass of water. Keep sipping alternating from one glass to the other.

If the diarrhoea persists, or you find mucus and/or blood in your stools, or if the stools are white or black, see a doctor and get a stool test at a hospital or lab.

Traveller's diarrhoea, popularly known as *turista*, is recognized as a natural reaction to change in environment. One meditator, who is also a medical doctor, said that he takes inactivated cholera to prevent "Delhi-belly" two weeks before he comes to India. It sets up antibodies without any side-effects. "It's called Dukoral™. Just remember 'oral dukkha'. You put it in water and drink!" he says, laughing. See www.dukoral.com

Kanji: The Ultimate Stomach Soother

Kanji is soupy rice. Take it during the initial recovery stages: it rehydrates and is easily digested. Even the kitchen novice will find it easy to cook: one part rice, six parts water, two teaspoons of salt, and cook for about an hour until the rice has completely broken apart.

Kicheri: Yogi Food

When friends of ours were experiencing a mild case of traveller's diarrhoea, they didn't believe us that *kicheri* would probably be better than medicine. After some persistent nagging and cajoling, they tried it and were convinced. They wanted nothing else after that, only *kicheri, kicheri, kicheri!*

Kicheri is a good transition to 'real' food because it is so easily digestible, and the mung beans also provide protein. (Avoid all other legumes when you are having problems; they irritate the stomach.)

Soak some mung beans for a few hours (be sure to clean out the insects, debris and tiny stones!), add an equal amount of rice, with a couple of teaspoons of salt and turmeric. You can also add ginger and cumin if you like. Cook until it has become one big mush. It may not look that appetizing, but your stomach will love it.

Kicheri is good whenever you are experiencing digestive storms. If it's not on the menu, just ask, the cooks may be happy to make it for you.

Curd (plain yogurt—*dahi*) is also good because it reintroduces good bacteria to your digestive tract (Indians like to mix in a couple of teaspoonfuls of Isabgol – psillium husks). But don't mix Isabgol with anything hot, because then it acts as a laxative. The upset tummy also likes bananas.

After a year in India, we had a mild attack of homesickness. The cure turned out to be staying away from guest houses and restaurants, finding a simple apartment with a kitchen, and eating healthy food of our own creation.

Feeling weak, we made it our goal to get back into tip-top health, studying yoga nearby for 3 to 4 hours a day. After another fit of diarrhoea, we sought the advice of an Ayurvedic doctor, who made it his personal mission to send us away "with rosy cheeks" in three weeks. After examining us he proclaimed, "You two are a perfect match—you both have the same low blood pressure!"

He put us on a strict diet of rice, mung bean soup, banana and yogurt for three weeks (and no mangos, even though we were in the middle of juicy mango season). He gave us various herbal remedies that he mixed himself, and a bonus of crushed Iranian pearls, that soothed our stomachs, cooled our heads, and gave our faces a shiny glow!

– MD & KG

Fever
Rising its temperature is one of the body's defence mechanisms against infection. The best thing to do is to let the body do its job. If the fever lasts too long, however, you may want to take some paracetamol to break it.

Wet compresses to the forehead, wrists and calves help the body to dissipate heat—change them as they reach body temperature. You can also try sponging these areas with water (not alcohol), as the evaporation has a cooling effect.

Food Poisoning
The symptoms of food poisoning are: cramps, nausea, vomiting, diarrhoea and dizziness (see the diarrhoea section). The symptoms should disappear in a day or two. If symptoms persist, see a health care professional.

Gas and Indigestion
You're sitting in the meditation hall with 100 other students, and suddenly your stomach starts its symphony and you have an extreme urge to pass gas. But do you hold it in? As one lovable granny used to tell us, "Better to fart and bear the shame, than not to fart and bear the pain."

Even if you bear with it, however, there are Ayurvedic herbal remedies that, at the very least, will make the gas smell fresh and minty. **Pudina Hara** is a combination of spearmint and peppermint oils that enhance digestion and prevent bloating. **Amritdhara** is made of ajowan, mint, camphor, and eucalyptus oil and relieves flatulence, abdominal bloating, and stomach pain. It also reduces stomach acidity.

Heat Exhaustion
Heat exhaustion happens when the body can't dissipate heat properly, often because of dehydration. If left untreated, it progresses to heatstroke, which should be treated by a doctor.

The symptoms of heat exhaustion are: intense thirst, headache, fatigue, nausea and vomiting, muscle cramps and irritability.

If you feel you've had too much sun, you probably have. Find a shady spot and start sipping water and oral rehydration salts continuously—not in big gulps. Eat fruits: they have a high water content.

Infection

Avoid infections in the first place. Wash all cuts and scrapes well with soap and warm water. Keep them dry; antiseptic creams are less effective in the tropics.

Urinary Tract Infection (UTI)

You feel you have to go, but when you try, nothing happens, or when it does, it burns.

Minor UTIs can be flushed out by drinking lots of water and coconut water. You can try soaking in a hot bath (time to splurge on that luxury room!). Take lots of vitamin C, and if necessary, a dose of anti-inflammatory. You can try the Ayurvedic medicine Chandrapabha Bati or the Allopathic medicine URAL. If it doesn't go away, have a lab test your urine and then bring the results to a doctor.

Yeast Infection

The little yeast fungus lives naturally in our gut and in women's vaginas, in harmony with the local bacteria. The problems arise when there is an imbalance in this micro-ecology: antibiotics, for example, kill the bacteria and leave room for the yeast to take over. Here are a few tricks to avoid this:

• Wear cotton panties
• Bathe regularly
• Wear loose, breathable clothing
• Eat unsweetened yogurt

Douching is not really used anymore to treat yeast infections, but if you do, do not douche during menstruation when your cervix is open—it could push the infection into your uterus. An alternative to douching is the sitz bath. Put half a cup of salt in a shallow warm bath, and sit in it, knees apart, until it gets cool. If you have a chronic problem with yeast or thrush, it should be treated at home before you leave.

Lice

The best way to avoid lice is by not sharing combs, brushes, linen, towels and hats. If other travellers around you are infected with lice, wash your hair regularly and rinse it with apple cider vinegar and water (2 tablespoons vinegar to 2 cups warm water). Adding 5 drops of rosemary, lavender, or tea tree essential oils into your shampoo bottle is a good idea.

If, after all your precautions, you still get lice, try taking the homeopathic remedy: 2-3 ledum (30c potency) pellets, 3 times a day for a week. Five drops of a goldenseal and echinacea tincture in a glass of juice or water, twice a day for a week also works, but don't do it if you are already taking ledum. If the above remedies aren't available, take garlic, which has anti-parasitic properties that will help fight a lice infestation. Consume a raw clove 3 times a day for 5 days.

You can also try applying a mixture of olive oil (4 oz) and rosemary, lavender and tea tree essential oils (1 tsp each) to your scalp. If you can't find these essential oils, try vinegar or kerosene. Then cover your head with a shower cap or plastic bag for at least 12 hours (24 hours is better). Then use a nit comb (available at any pharmacy) and comb through the hair. Wash out the oils with tea tree oil or special lice shampoo and rinse with rosemary tea (don't rinse the tea out). Comb hair again with a nit comb. Repeat each night for 1 week and once a week after that for 3 weeks.

Rubbing 2-3 drops of the essential oils into your hairbrush also helps deter lice, as does blow-drying your hair for 5-10 minutes a day for 10 days.

Malaria

The states of Madhya Pradesh, Maharashtra, Orissa, Gujarat, Bihar, Rajasthan, and Karnataka report the most malaria cases. Symptoms include delirious fever, headache, chills, muscle aches and vomiting. Get tested immediately if you think that you've contracted malaria. Serious illness or death can be prevented if the disease is diagnosed and treated early. Malaria is more prevalent during and after monsoon—mosquitoes need water to breed. Your best protection is to prevent mosquito bites: sleep with a mosquito net, and wear pants, long sleeves and socks, especially at dusk and dawn when the mosquitoes are most ferocious. You can try catching them with a cup and paper, or, as one meditator does, with a butterfly net. If you didn't bring citronella from home, it may be necessary to use chemical repellents with DEET—a popular cream called Odomos™ is widely available.

The high altitude states of Himāchal Pradesh, Sikkim, and Jammu and Kashmir are free from malaria since transmission is minimal above 2 000 metres.

Acquaint yourself with the possible side-effects of Mefloquine/Larium, Malarone, and Doxycycline, which may include nausea, vomiting, dizziness, headaches, insomnia and nightmares. For some people, Larium causes depression, anxiety, psychosis, hallucinations and seizures. These symptoms may persist even after you have stopped taking the drug. Below is a list of alternatives, but we recommend that you consult with a tropical disease specialist 4-8 weeks before travelling for the latest conventional and natural prophylaxes.

• *Malaria officinalis 30c* (3 pellets in the morning and 3 pellets in the evening, once a week) and *Cinchona officinalis/China 8x, 6c, or 30c* (3 pellets each morning and 3 pellets each evening, taken the other 6 days of the week) are homeopathic medicines that work in a similar way to a vaccine: they initiate a specific immune system response causing the antibodies to attack malaria parasites, as opposed to conventional malaria drugs which attempt to kill the parasite directly by acting as a controlled poison. These are used both as a preventative that helps the user develop a resistance to malaria, and as a treatment for malaria attacks. They have no side-effects and can be used by children and pregnant women. These treatments begin 2 weeks before travelling and continue for 6 weeks after returning home. It's best to consult a homeopathic practitioner before starting the treatment.

- An ancient Chinese herb known as Qing Hao, sweet wormwood, or *artemisia annua L.* is being grown in China to help fight malaria. The remedy is known as **Artemisinin**. The fern-like plant has been recognized by the World Health Organization as an effective alternative to quinine-based drugs (to which the malaria parasite is now becoming resistant).
- Eating lots of garlic may help ward off mosquitoes.
- To prevent bites, use citronella, lemongrass or DEET sprays.
- Malaria mosquitoes only bite at night—so make sure to use a mosquito net.

Motion Sickness

If you are prone to motion sickness, the best thing is to eat something that will sit well in the stomach before taking to those winding mountain roads or hopping on that bobbing ferry.

Fatigue increases the effects of motion sickness, so make sure you get a good night's sleep before travelling. If you feel sick in a car, move to the front seat and focus on the road ahead or the horizon. Breathe in fresh air. You can try sucking on lemons or cloves, or chewing ginger or betel-nut.

If you frequently suffer from motion sickness, you have less chance of getting sick if you travel at night.

Oral Ulcer

Dissolve several teaspoons of salt in a glass of warm water and rinse out your mouth several times a day.

Feeling Overpowered?

The Buddha said that there are eight things of nature which we should not let overpower our minds:

1. Intense cold
2. Intense heat
3. Intense hunger
4. Intense thirst
5. Intense wind
6. Intense sunshine
7. Mosquitoes and flies
8. Wriggling creatures

Try to keep this in mind when you are sitting under the tree in Bodhgayā, sweating profusely, feeling hungry, and being bitten all over.

I, 31

Strains & Sprains

A strain is an overstretched muscle, a sprain is a stretched ligament; both involve swelling and tenderness, and are treated in the same way. Always remember the RICE treatment:

- **R**est
- **I**ce the area for 20 minutes to reduce swelling. Repeat on and off.
- **C**ompression. Immobilize the injury by placing a firm bandage—moving the damaged tissue aggravates the injury.
- **E**levate the injured limb to heart level.

Dentists

Indian dentists are qualified, hygienic, and cheap (and we're not talking about the local toothpuller). Their reputation is growing as an increasing number of foreigners are adding a visit to an Indian dentist to their itinerary. As a general rule, dental treatment is about one third of the price the same treatment would cost back home. One friend had three crowns done for US$800, instead of US$2500. She said, "What I saved on my dental work paid for my plane ticket!"

For a simple cleaning and x-ray, most places will be satisfactory. Some popular treatments among foreigners are crown replacements, root canals, and corrective surgeries. For these serious operations, it's probably best to have a reliable reference.

Optometrists

In India, glasses and contact lenses usually come out to about a third of the price they would be in western countries. One meditator who suffers from nearsightedness brought her fashionable frames from the West and had her prescription filled in India. Although she went to a specialist because her case is unusual, most optometrists will do regular pairs of specs. One tip: have your glasses made upon arrival, it leaves you enough time to try them on, and, if needed, to have them adjusted.

Barbers & Hairdressers

Maybe it's the way they hold the razor with such confidence, or the way they flick the cover sheet with a grand flourish, or the way they give a professional head and face massage after the job. In any case, a man can feel safe in the hands of an Indian barber. Indeed, they know a handful of haircuts and have developed that art to a tee. Foreigners will walk out of the barber stall looking like all the other Indian men, down to the razor-straight neckline. If you don't like your do, you can't complain when a shave goes for around Rs 10 and a haircut about Rs 20.

Good haircuts for women are not so easy to come by, since most Indian women wear their hair in a long braid. Big cities have some decent beauty parlours, but make sure the hairstylist has experience working with foreigner's hair, as it is usually finer than the beautifully thick dark Indian manes. A haircut can go for anything from Rs 150 to Rs 1 500. Sometimes you can find foreign hairdressers in tourist areas.

Travel: Trains, Buses, Rickshaws, etc.

Travel in India is relatively easy and cheap. You can always find a way to get to where you want to go, even if it's in the back of a dusty truck or ox-cart. If you keep an open mind, you will find that half of the thrill of visiting a remote site is in the journey getting there. Travel is also the best way to get into close contact with locals. Without a doubt, your toughest travels will make your best stories when you're sitting around a table sharing a *chai* with fellow worn-out travellers.

Trains

We always travel by train when we have the choice; it is far safer and more comfortable than buses. The train is more scenic, the passengers more relaxed; watching the constant stream of food vendors—each promoting his goods over and over like a mantra—is better than a book; if your legs get numb you can walk up and down; it's less noisy than the incessant honking on the roads, and the toilets are there if you need them.

India's railway system is actually one of the best in the world. You can almost always find a direct train from one place to another. And they're usually on time too, except in monsoon or foggy winters. Basically, there are three types of trains: Express, Mail, and Passenger. Unless you have a particular interest in rural train stations, avoid the passenger trains as they stop at each and every small town, thus turning a 2-hour journey into an 8-hour one.

Indian Railways offers many different classes, depending on the type of train and the length of the journey. Let's say you want to travel from Delhi to Mumbai. You looked on the internet (or in your trusty *Trains at a Glance* train schedule), and you settled on the *Golden Temple Mail (2904)*, because it is a daily train that leaves from—and arrives at—a major station, and the times are convenient for you, leaving Delhi at 7:15 a.m. and arriving at Mumbai Central at 6:05 the next morning. Now, this train offers many classes, the same ones you will most likely come across for long journeys:

- **2-tier AC.** This means that each compartment accommodates four passengers, two on each side, one on top of the other like bunk beds. Each compartment has a curtain to close it off from the aisle (where there are two more bunks). AC means heat in the winter and cool air in the summer. These cars have plastic double-pane windows which make them very quiet and dust-free, but also cut you off from the scenery unfolding before you. In this class, you receive two sheets, a pillow, blanket and hand towel. You can also tell the attendant where you're getting off and he'll inform you (or even gently wake you up) before your station. On this particular journey, the fare for 2AC is Rs 1 775. Aisle seats are not really worth it here as they are the same as in 3-tier AC. The ticket will indicate SB (side berth) rather than UB, MB, or LB (upper, middle, lower).
- **3-tier AC**: This class is basically the same as 2-tier, except that each compartment has six passengers, and there is no curtain separating these from the two in the aisle. For the *Golden Temple Mail*, the fare for 3AC is Rs 1 140.
- **2nd class sleeper**: In this class, you have a reserved seat during the day, and bunk at night. There is no AC, but a barred window, which can be both good and bad, depending on the season and time of day. Each compartment officially seats six passengers plus two in the aisle, although in the daytime you may find that people on a 1- to 3-hour journey will edge themselves into a seat in your compartment; and you are expected to be gracious about it. (You shouldn't be too attached to your seat, who knows, you may have to rely on someone else's mercy one day. But be firm if someone tries to share your

bunk at night.) Second Sleeper is about 2½ times cheaper than 3-tier AC. On the *Golden Temple* journey, this berth will cost you Rs 425.

• **General**: There are no reserved seats in general. And no maximum number of passengers, either. There are people everywhere, sleeping in the aisles, blocking the doors, or monopolizing the bathrooms. At times, the fight for a seat can get a little vicious. People crowd around the door and squeeze and elbow themselves to the front. When the doors are locked before departure, many enterprising passengers will throw a hanky or newspaper through a window onto a seat and later claim it as their own. For shorter journeys general may be tolerable, although for a few rupees more, it's better to have a reserved seat in 2nd class, unless you're looking for a story to impress folks back home...

Note that some daily short-distanced trains (Mumbai–Pune or New Delhi–Dehra Dun) usually have three options for seats: AC Chair, 2nd Class Reserved Chair, and General. The AC tickets are more comfortable, quieter, better food is offered, and are about three to five times the price of 2nd Class Reserved Chair, which is about double the price of General. The main advantage of 2nd over AC is that you can store your luggage under your seat instead of over your head, which is a consideration if your bags are really heavy.

It is before the Teacher's Self-Course at Dhamma Giri. It is also Diwali, India's biggest holiday, when entire families will embark on a cross-country journey to spend a few days with their relatives. It is impossible to get a reserved ticket on the next train from Mumbai to Igatpuri. The train pulls into the platform; all the doors are jammed shut from the overload of bodies inside. The whistles blows and we scamper on with our backpacks, desperate to find some opening. Finally, we plunge into the pantry car; the waft of fried oil envelops us like thick fog.

After a few minutes, we think that there must be a better place to sit than this masala sweat lodge. We edge our way to the intersection of the next car where the toilets are, but this is as far as we can go; beyond is just too crammed. "Hmm, the toilets are reasonably clean, no usual stale urine stench," says one. "And the air is much fresher and cooler than the pantry car...," adds another. Four of us stand in the lavatory, with our packs, for three hours, sharing a few good riddles, word games, and Dhamma stories to occupy the time. Before we know it, the Igatpuri station rolls up and we're back at Dhamma Giri.

- MD & KG

Reservations

You can buy train tickets at the railway reservation office at the station, or in computerized reservation offices in some tourist towns, or you can do it through a travel agent for a nominal fee. It's best to book train tickets in advance, especially during holiday seasons. The earliest you can reserve is two months before the departure date, the latest for a reserved ticket is 4 hours before departure at any reservation office, and one hour at the reservation counter of the station from which the train departs. You can get a general ticket up until the train leaves, or if you're late, just hop on and pay the ticket collector on the train as well as a small fine. Major stations have special counters or offices for foreigners and 'Tourist Quota' tickets, meaning they reserve seats for tourists. To get this sort of ticket, you need the passports of all the people whose names will appear on the ticket, as well as an encashment certificate or ATM slip if you want to pay in rupees.

To make a reservation, you must fill out the form with your name, gender and age, as well as the train's name and number, the departure date, and which class you prefer (you can find train information in the handy timetable *Trains at a Glance*, found in most guest houses). You could always look on the old decaying boards for the train name and numbers, but these are often written only in the local script.

A Riddle to Contemplate

What is:

* Higher than God, but lower than the Devil
* The poor have it, but the rich need it
* If you eat it, you die …

For the answer,

e-mail pilgrimage@pariyatti.org

You can also specify if you have berth preferences. We prefer the upper berths as they allow for more privacy; you can always sneak up and read a book if the compartment gets a little too crowded below. It's also a vantage point for discretely observing the spectacle below without being the main attraction yourself.

If the train is full, you might get a waiting-list number. These are dangerous unless the number is low. Or, you might get a Reservation-Against-Cancellation (RAC) ticket, which means that you initially have a guaranteed seat for the journey and only get a berth if there is a last minute cancellation. To check the status of your ticket, look on the Indian Railways website (www.indianrail.gov.in). You'll need to enter your PNR number found on the top left-hand corner of the ticket.

Sometimes you can get a general ticket and upgrade it through the Train Ticket Examiner who has a chart of all the cancellations and will assign you a seat number. (The TTE—or one of his subordinates, the TT—are the men wearing a black polyester blazer in 40°C heat.) You will be required to pay a small official surcharge. The same can be done if you want to upgrade from 2nd class to AC.

The Indian Railways website (www.irctc.co.in) now offers a service for e-tickets. When nothing goes wrong—slow connections, power cuts, international credit cards not being accepted (most aren't, but some, like Citibank, are)—purchasing these tickets is convenient and cancelling the tickets is easy. First-time users need to register to login, for which you need to provide an Indian address.

Travel Agents

Sometimes it is worth paying the Rs 40 service charge rather than schlepping to the station, waiting in the mile-long queue, elbowing your way to the front while defending your spot from line-cutters, only to find that the train is full. If using travel agents, specify that if there is a waiting list of more than 15 or so, you don't want the ticket, or give them a few options, in order of preference. Don't forget to thor-

Tourist Booking Office

In the New Delhi Railway Station there is a special Tourist Reservation Office on the second floor that offers efficient and generally friendly service. Beware of cunning touts hanging around the train station, who will tell you that the tourist office is closed and that they know an "authorized agent" across the road.

oughly check your ticket once you get it—a traveller once bought a ticket through an agent, and when she got on the train, someone was sitting in her seat. Upon checking her ticket, she found that the agent had booked her for the wrong month.

You will often find big groups travelling together that seem to occupy the entire bogey: soccer teams, military troops, families en route to a wedding. If you're in luck and it's a family, they have probably brought more than enough food for the entire car, and according to traditional Indian hospitality, you can look forward to plenty of *puris* and dry curries, mango pickle, sweets and chillies. In cases like these, it's good to have something to offer in return, even just a packet of biscuits to pass around.

Each travel class offers a distinct cultural experience. Some travellers may snub anything seeming 'upper class' because it is not the 'real India.' But upper class India is still a reality, and as foreigners, we are lucky to have easy access to the diversity of India's people. We have no fixed rules about which class we travel in. If we are feeling fine, we will go for the second class (rarely in 'general', unless for very short trips). However, if we are sick, particularly vulnerable, or following a retreat, or, if we know that a specific train line is unusually crowded, then we may travel in the AC class.

Once, we were crossing the country from Gorakhpur to Igatpuri during the most auspicious bathing day of the *Kumbha Mela* in Nasik (the last stop before Igatpuri). Anticipating the crowds, we had rightly decided to get an AC ticket. Indeed, when we casually strolled out of our comfortable bogey to stretch our legs on the platform, we stared in disbelief at the second-class cars overflowing with bodies, faces crushed against the windows and limbs dangling between the bars. When the train arrived in Nasik, it literally bounced up a couple of feet, freed from the weight of thousands of eager pilgrims.

If you're travelling second class, it's good to bring a sheet to cover the berth, and in the winter, a thick blanket or sleeping bag. If your stomach doesn't tolerate fried spicy foods, you may want to bring snacks with you; fruits, nuts, and biscuits travel well. Train *thālis* are usually spicy and cold (and the hygiene often leaves something to be desired).

Stations

Train stations aren't as intimidating as they seem. Once you get inside the station, major cities will have electronic boards indicating the number of the platform from which your train departs. If there is no board, ask at least three *koolies* (the porters in the red shirts) where to go, and follow the most popular answer. You can also ask them the location on the platform where your particular bogey will pull up.

The following story inspires us to have confidence in the honesty of the railway workers:

> *My wife and I arrived late into Bombay from the north. We planned to connect with a midnight train to Goa. As we got down on the platform we saw the Saraswati Express steaming up on a nearby track and realized we had to get our onward tickets immediately. All the ticket wickets had long lines and I didn't know where to start.*
>
> *Some red-shirted porters approached us. (My first thought was: these guys are going to cost me.)*
>
> — *Yes, Sir...Where are you going?*
>
> — *Margao.*
>
> — *I can get your tickets for you...40 rupees each.*
>
> *I cringed; but the younger porter pointed to the eldest's brass badge and assured me all was on the up-and-up. I gave him 80 rupees and about 2 minutes later he stood before me smiling with 2 tickets to Margao.*
>
> — *Now, Sir...How about reservations? 100 rupees for the two second-class berths and bags on board...complete and fixed.*
>
> — *Go ahead. (I now had full confidence in him.)*
>
> *In 10 minutes we were in our seats, thinking we had spent our money well.*
>
> – Bill Hamilton

Cancellations

You can cancel a confirmed ticket up to two days before departure and get a full refund minus a small fee. If less than a day, you lose 25%, and less than 4 hours, you lose 50%.

You don't have to pay a fee to cancel wait-list or RAC tickets, provided you do it either within three hours after the train's departure, or two hours after the reservation office has opened, whichever is later.

Buses

To travel from one town to the next, there are roughly two kinds of buses: state buses and private buses. The privately-run lines offer different degrees of comfort, such as the regular, deluxe and sleeper buses. The regular buses are rusty, clunky mechanical miracles; it's amazing how long Indian mechanics can keep a vehicle alive. The deluxe and sleeper buses are definitely more comfortable but despite the name, it is almost impossible to sleep. The main difference between the state-run and private buses is that the private ones tend to want to maximize the number of passengers, so they stop for everyone and anyone, and it can get quite cramped, whereas the state-run bus driver's main concern is to be on schedule.

For longer trips, you should consider taking the train if you have the choice. Buses are good for shorter trips (3 to 6 hours), as they are regular and quite easy to board. You can buy tickets at the terminal, or on the bus itself. It's not necessary to book in advance like the train, although if you want a guaranteed seat it is best to do so. The driver is in control of the steering wheel and the altar on the dashboard, but the conductor is the one running the show. He is easily recognizable as the guy with the whistle and the black purse full of change, hanging out the door yelling instructions to the driver or the name of the destination. He is responsible for collecting the tickets and money, as well as telling the driver when to stop to drop off or pick up passengers.

Bus survival tips:

- You're at the terminal, the bus is about to leave, there is no assigned seating. Stand near the door and clamour in as soon as it cracks open, otherwise you might be left standing.

- Try to bring your luggage with you on the bus. If they insist that you put it on the roof luggage rack, go up with them and lock your bags. In monsoon, make sure they are covered with a tarp. It's best to keep valuables in a small hand/shoulder bag/backpack that you can always keep on your lap.

- If your gear is on the roof, keep an eye on it during rest breaks.

- Sitting up front next to the driver will give you a better view, but once he starts passing fast trucks in a blind curve, along with his incessant honking, and the 'private AC' heat from the motor next to him, you might reconsider that empty backseat next to the mother with the howling baby.

- We have found that wearing earplugs considerably reduces the stress of road travel.

- Go to the toilet before getting on.

- If you have to get off for a pee-break or to be sick, ask the conductor with your best pitiful face. When you dart off, he will inevitably make some wisecrack about foreigners' weak bladders, but your relief will be worth it. (At night, make sure you're not in the headlights to add to the spectacle!)

- Beware of suspiciously refreshing liquid coming in from the windows; someone sitting in front may be sick.

- When you board the bus, note some outstanding feature like a fluorescent pink luggage rack, so that you can easily recognize it after a *chai* stop.

- If you smile and make yourself noticed by the driver and conductor, they are less likely to leave you behind after a break.

- At night, sit on the left side of the bus to avoid the bright headlights of oncoming traffic. A fact about night road travel: don't try to transfer your idea from back home that there is less traffic at night. In India, tolls are cheaper at night than in the day, and as a result, the roads are full of 'Goods Carriers' driving at breakneck speed and honking more than usual (if that's possible).

- Always bring water with you. You'll find snacks like biscuits, fruits, nuts, cold drinks, and *chai* at stops. Vendors will sometimes even board the bus for a few stops to sell their goods.

City Buses

Some foreigners, especially those staying in one place for a long time, really get into the local bus systems. A few rupees can take you a long way. The big cities offer elaborate public transportation, sometimes with reduced-pollution vehicles too. However, if you're in town for only a few days and you have many things to do or see, it is probably easier and less time-consuming to take a rickshaw or taxi.

Taxis

Taxis are easily recognizable as the black and yellow *Ambassador* cars (the ones that look like they just came out of the '50s) that you find in every town or city. Some cities, like Mumbai for example, don't allow rickshaws into the inner city, so you'll have to resort to the taxi service, which is slightly more expensive. Taxi drivers don't expect to be tipped. Taxis usually have meters and the driver carries a conversion chart to determine the correct price. However, drivers often refuse to use the meters and insist on determining a price that will be leagues higher than what you would pay on the meter. If you find yourself in this situation, it's a good idea to ask a knowledgeable local person about approximate fares. It's also better to set a price before getting in, and make sure it covers luggage and everyone in the vehicle. We once agreed on Rs 350 from the Mumbai airport to the Fort area, when half-way there, the driver said, "Three-fifty for you, and three-fifty for you!" Obviously, we ignored his constant pestering and when we safely arrived at our destination, gave him the three-fifty that we initially agreed on.

In the airports, there are usually booths where you can book a pre-paid taxi. These are handy, especially if you don't know how much the price should be, or don't feel like haggling with the driver.

Auto Rickshaws

The auto rickshaw is the common people's transport for short to medium distances. It is sometimes called an 'auto', tempo', or 'three-wheeler'. It drives like a scooter, with one front wheel and a backseat with two wheels, the whole covered with a metal frame.

Without luggage, four can fit comfortably, three in the back and one with the driver (although sitting in front with the driver is technically illegal but rarely enforced).

Rickshaws are cheap and readily available, although they are noisy and polluting. You can get private or shared rickshaws, but if you're going to a specific place, it may not be worth it to wait for another passenger. It's good to always carry small change as drivers rarely do (or pretend not to).

If you're not sure what the regular price is, just ask a few locals to get an idea. Try bargaining with several drivers to get an idea of how much the fare should be. A typical conversation with a prospective driver goes like this:

You're walking out of the railway station with your heavy backpack. A thin man with a moustache approaches you in a hasty manner:

— Hello madam, where going?

— How much to Krishna Guest House?

— 100 rupees only madam.

— Oh, no, no. 40.

— *Aray baba*, No madam. Too much far. (You keep walking silently as other drivers try to get your attention.)

— *Oi!* OK, OK, 80 rupees madam.

— 50.

— *Okay-ji*, 60 madam, last price.

— *Thik, chelo!* (OK, lets go!)

Cycle Rickshaws

Cycle rickshaws are good for short, flat distances. Incredibly, it seems that cycle rickshaw makers have not yet discovered the benefits of multi-gears. On hills, the poor driver often has to get out and push the lot; he may even ask you to get out. Try not to feel guilty. These guys are in good shape, and this may be their only way to make a living.

Hand-pulled Rickshaws

Only Kolkata (Calcutta) still has hand-pulled rickshaws. These fellows often don't know the place where you want to go. We once asked to be taken to the *Tagore House*—the house where Rabindranath Tagore was born and died, a well-known site in the city—and the driver, not knowing where it was, took a detour through one of Kolkata's poorest slums. We got lost again on the way back with another *rickshaw-wallah*, even though we asked for a major intersection!

Tempos (or Tuk-tuks)

Tempos are large shared rickshaws that regularly shuttle back and forth to specific *chowks* (mini-terminals), usually from downtown to the suburbs and back. These are quick, cheap, and easy—once you figure out their routes.

Rented Cars

When you rent a car in India there is a wide variety of models to choose from, depending on the number of people and where you want to go. The rental mercifully includes a driver.

If you're going city-driving, small cars are adequate and you might want to get air-conditioning to filter out the fumes.

If you are a small group going to the back-country or on particularly rough roads, you will want a jeep or van.

Prices vary widely, but are always higher when the price of petrol is soaring. Shop around, and make sure to meet the driver. If you're hiring a car and driver for a few days, see to it that the driver knows a minimum of English and that you feel comfortable with him; a sour driver can really spoil your trip. For longer trips, it is also a good idea to check the condition of the tires before setting off. Our friend once found a huge hole in one of the tires during a *chai* break, yet still the driver was reluctant to change it.

Although most drivers know where they are going it is always good to have a little extra help. If you plan on visiting lesser known sites and you happen to have an iPad or some other tablet, you may want to consider downloading a GPS application. Despite not having some of the newer roads when we used it on our last three-week *yatra*, **Navigon GPS India** proved, on most occasions, to be a good navigation tool, providing reliable information regarding times and distances.

The most prominent feature of the Indian roads is the noise: horns blast continuously, making, at times, a tremendous racket. Usually, this is by no means due to ill-tempered drivers and aggression; rather it's an accepted and even encouraged aspect of driving behaviour. Traffic is chaotic, to say the least, with lanes only nominal, suggested routes for travel. In practice, vehicles go every which way, crossing lanes and swerving wildly to avoid slow movers and pedestrians, who, if they want to cross, must often use the technique of slowly stepping out in front of traffic to make it stop bit by bit. So using horns is seen as a safety measure, so much so that buses and trucks and auto rickshaws often have the words 'Horn Please' delicately painted on the back of the vehicle. Perhaps needless to say, Indian traffic statistics are pretty grim in terms of accidents and fatalities. (But don't worry, I only ride with the SAFE drivers…)

– Peter Buchanan

Airplanes
It pays to know your schedule ahead of time; if you book a month in advance, you can save about 20% on airfare with Indian Airlines and Jet Airways. If you're under 30, you get the 25% youth discount on economy class with Indian Airlines. Alas, you can't combine both discounts. Some airlines have a two-tiered price ladder—foreigners officially paying a higher price than Indians. Fancy hotels and travel agents can book the flight for you. Check the airlines' websites for the latest schemes:

- Indian Airlines: www.indian-airlines.nic.in
- Jet Airways: www.jetairways.com
- SpiceJet: www.spicejet.com
- Kingfisher Airlines: www.flykingfisher.com

The last two are two of the budget airlines which have recently begun operating in India. After years of expensive domestic flights, it seems that the days of discounted air travel have finally arrived in India. Check out these last two for discounted fares. Still, for reliability and safety, Jet Airways and Indian Airlines are hard to beat.

Hitch-Hiking
Stopping a ride for free is not so common in India, but you see many people standing on the side of the road with bundles and children waving down passing trucks, rickshaws, and buses, for which they will give a few rupees to the driver. In India, the 'thumbs up' signal means you're cool; it won't get you a ride. To stop a vehicle, wave your arm with the palm face down. For male travellers, stopping motorbikes, cars, bicycles, or bullock carts in smaller towns and villages can be quite effective. Almost all drivers are willing to give a ride further along, sometimes even going out of their way to drop you off. This is not recommended for solo female travellers, however.

Although travelling by a trundling bullock cart piled high with hay is certainly romantic, it's not ideal for covering any reasonable distance. If point A to B is a longer journey, try catching a ride with one of the bigger Tata lorries, which you can usually identify by the Sikh spear symbols located above the windshield. These thundering vehicles, owned by Sikh businesses that have cornered most of the long-distance transport market, don't travel much faster than 70 km/hour but the drivers travel non-stop, only taking short breaks for meals at their favourite *dhabas*. The drivers, adept at anything mechanical, are usually friendly and will certainly offer you an interesting perspective on Indian life.

Bicycles
If you plan to stay in one place for an extended period of time, it might be worth it to rent (or buy) a bicycle. When cycling through town at a leisurely pace, you are too fast for the persistent vendors and touts, and yet slow enough to appreciate the scenery. It can also reduce your costs of hiring rickshaws. Having your own transportation makes you feel more independent and less 'touristy'.

For the athletic and adventurous, cycling through India can be a great way to get around. In this case, it is better to bring your bike with you from home, and to have a few mechanical skills up your sleeve. For more information about biking through India, see: www.mrpumpy.net

Motorcycles

The following section on motorcycles was written by Indophile and aficionado of roaring Enfield engines, Sierra Laflamme:

Travelling by motorcycle can be one of the most exciting and adventurous ways to see India. Apart from the freedom to be able to just saddle up at a moment's notice and drive off to wherever the whimsy takes you, the ability to explore remote corners of the country that are not frequented by public transport, and the exhilarating feeling of the road slipping away beneath your feet and the wind in your face, foreign tourists travelling India by motorcycle almost always report stories of warm welcomes and flat-out amazement on the part of the local people with whom they come into contact. And come into contact with them you will! Motorcycle travel is fraught with breakdowns, washed-out roads, wrong turns leading you hundreds of kilometres into the wilderness, all of which necessarily put you into the helpful and gracious care of local people. Even when things are going smoothly, the crowds of children running and shouting in glee behind you and the curious men who approach you at every tea stop will ensure that you are always the centre of attention—which can be both a blessing and a curse! If it is solitude you seek, never fear, for hours and days spent winding gently along deserted mountain roads, with nothing but a carpet of rhododendron petals covering the road for company, will give you all the time in the world for contemplation. Motorcycle travel really opens up whole new ways of seeing and living in India.

Bear in mind that the motorcycle adventure is not one that should be embarked upon without due consideration. Driving conditions can be anything from challenging to dangerous: unmarked speedbumps; potholes the size of elephants; crazy, weaving, over-burdened cyclists; livestock of every stripe; small children, and motorists of dubious levels of sanity and sobriety coming at you from all directions, some travelling at an old man's walking pace, some at mach 9. Traffic within the major cities can be so mind-boggling that you might reasonably wonder if you have died and gone straight to hell. And whole days spent waiting at some smoky, oily, noisy crossroads while someone tries to machine you a part to fix your latest breakdown, can try even the most patient of travellers. There are things that you can do to mitigate these and other adversities:

*   Breathe. Cultivate patience. And above all, learn to see the traffic, the breakdowns, and the days that didn't go according to plan as a part of the journey. When you see yourself getting short with a mechanic or someone trying to give you directions, take a step back and you will undoubtedly see how hilarious the whole situation must be from an outsider's point of view; more often than not, you'll start to see the humour in it, too.

*   Don't get yourself locked-in to tight schedules. Always allow an extra day or two in a trip to accommodate the unforeseen situations that may arise.

*   Try not to do many miles in one day. Just concentrating on the obstacles

ahead takes an amazing amount of energy, and can be exhausting. An exhausted driver is one more likely to get lost or get into an accident, and much less likely to enjoy the drive. Plan to average no more than 50 km/hour on major divided highways, 30 km on other regular roads, and 15 km on unpaved or heavily damaged small roads—and less than that if you are a new driver.

- Whenever possible, do not drive at night. Your headlight, if you're driving an Indian motorcycle, will be very weak, and the road will be full of unmarked and unlit obstacles, from animals to vehicles whose owners think that using the headlights will shorten the battery's life. Night driving is slow, stressful, and very dangerous. Plan to arrive at your destination with a few daylight hours to spare, and don't scoff at the idea of spending a night sleeping on a string bed at a road-side *chai* shop rather than continuing your journey into the night.

- Outfit your bike with good luggage carriers, roll bars, a loud horn, and lockable fuel cap. Make sure your luggage is easily split into two even-weighted bags, one for either side of the bike—one big backpack strapped to the seat will make you top heavy and skittish. And carry an assortment of basic spare parts and tools—a complete set if you have brought your motorcycle from another country. If you puncture a tire, there are *puncture wallahs* and mechanics everywhere. Limp your bike along or remove the wheel and carry it until you find one. In the worst case scenario, it is not hard to find a small truck willing to take you and your bike to the next town.

- Keep on top of general maintenance. Indian parts or oils can be of a lesser quality than you might be used to, and should be checked and replaced frequently. And the rough roads will often rattle nuts and bolts right off as you drive—make a habit of tightening all your nuts every few days. Keep your bike more or less clean—it's easier to spot problems that are about to happen when they're not covered by five inches of mud and grease.

- Check your directions frequently. Indian roads can be an unmarked spider's web, and it is very easy to get lost. In rural areas it is often advisable to stop at every intersection and ask! And keep in mind that two people may have two different ideas about which is the best road to take to get to any one place.

- Stay humble. Remember that private vehicle ownership, and the ability to pay for gas, is the privilege of very few in India, and that your choice of mode of travel will single you out immediately as someone who, by local standards, is rich. Keeping your bike clean and in good running order shows people around you that you do not take these riches for granted, and your humble bearing will show them that they have not gone to your head. And when in doubt about the local protocol regarding parking, line-ups at fuel pumps, running noise, or anything else, just stop, turn off your engine, look around, and ask. People will be more than happy to explain to you the way things are done in their place.

There are two main types of motorcycle available in India—the old British-style Enfields, and the smaller Japanese models. Enfields are most travellers' bike of choice—they have bigger engines, more carrying capacity, are much more comfortable to drive, and hold the road well. The Japanese bikes have the advantage of being lighter (easier to carry over streams or load into trains), cheaper to buy, rent and repair, and have a much higher fuel efficiency. All of these motorcycles can be bought new or second-hand.

Buying new is easier if you want to have legal ownership papers, and you can guarantee that no one has used an old beedie to replace a worn valve shaft; however, the cost of buying new can be prohibitive, and the time-consuming running-in period of a new engine can be frustrating. Older bikes are much more casual to buy and sell, but the odds of getting ownership papers transferred to your name are next to none—though this will not stop you from being able to insure and drive the bike legally. Renting is a good option for shorter trips (under two months), and can be done from bike mechanics in the major tourist hubs—Delhi, Mumbai, Dharamshala, Goa, Pushkar, Bangalore, to name a few—just ask around. You will most likely be asked to leave some cash, a plane ticket, or passport as a refundable deposit. Some of the larger bike rental outfits will even organize group tours, with guides and even follow-vehicles with a mechanic and spare parts. Keep in mind that, unless you have rented your bike as part of a big group tour, you are responsible for its upkeep and safe return to its owner. Regardless of whether you buy or rent, you will need an international driving permit and a year's local insurance to operate a motorcycle legally in India.

Though there are far too many motorcycle salesmen, repair shops, rental spots, and parts dealers in India to list here, one stands out as having offered consistently reliable, friendly, knowledgeable and fair service to foreign Enfield drivers throughout the years: Lalli Singh, at Inder Motors, Karol Bagh, New Delhi, phone: [+91] (011) 2572 8579. From repairs to sales to rentals to full-fledged tours, Lalli will be a fountain of helpful advice, top-notch service, and hard-to-find professionalism.

It would take more pages than this book has to explain every in and out of buying, renting, owning and maintaining a motorcycle in India, but even if we had the room, these tips would not compare to the advice of fellow drivers and mechanics in India. Make sure to keep up-to-date on all the changes in local road conditions, civil unrest, and maintenance, by spending time talking to others as passionate about motorcycle driving as you. Keep your ears, eyes and heart open, and enjoy the dream of driving on Indian roads!

Finding your way

Lost in a big city? In India, it's very easy to spend hours looking for a place that is just right around the corner. If you randomly ask passers by, you may find yourself getting even more confused. The answer to: "Is Prince of Wales Museum this way?" will invariably be "Yes." Often, locals won't admit that they don't understand your question. Ask several people along the way to make sure you're heading in the right direction. Don't point to your destination, but phrase your question strategically: "Where is Prince of Wales Museum?" One old Indian man told us to "Always ask a gentleman. You can recognize him by his shiny, polished shoes."

Always ask for landmarks. Drivers often have no idea of any street names apart from the major arteries. Your local friends often live on tiny obscure streets that are difficult to find, especially at night.

Don't be afraid to be adventurous; you will often find that a quaint alley with children playing cricket, women winnowing rice, and girls checking each other's heads for nits, runs parallel to the main road full of noisy horns and toxic fumes.

Baggage
Always label your luggage, and include a label inside, in case it is ever lost.

It's good to have a cover for your pack to protect it from dirty floors and motor-oil-leaking stowage compartments. You should get these at home, or perhaps have one tailored with rough fabric in India.

The Conscientious Meditator

Continuity of mindfulness is a quality that every meditator tries to cultivate as much as possible. Since a wise person knows how every mental, verbal or physical action has an impact on the world around, we should try to exercise proper judgement in everything we do. Although we cannot control the effects of these actions, we can certainly control our intentions in even the simplest deed, from saving our banana peels for the cow next door, to avoiding setting up conditions that may tempt someone to break their *sīla*.

The Environment
India has always been a throwaway culture. Banana-leaf plates and terracotta *chai* cups were meant to be used once, and then chucked out the window, where they would be eaten by the cows, or disintegrate. These products were good in that they were hygienic and provided work for rural artisans. Unfortunately, these organic products are being replaced by industrial plastic. The commodities have changed, but the habits have not. This results in the mountains of plastic rubbish that you see along the roads, and clogging rivers and gullies.

Only a few years ago, most shops would wrap up your *samosas*, alarm clock, or oranges in nifty packets made from yesterday's newspaper. Today, every vendor takes pride in handing you your goods in a thin plastic bag. One way travellers can make a difference is by limiting their use of plastic.

- Carry your own reusable cloth bag for shopping.
- Tell the vendor that you don't need a plastic bag for your biscuits.
- Buy yourself a cup and use it for tea in the trains. (This may also prevent you from getting sick from the street *chai-wallahs*, as they usually just rinse out used cups with questionable water.)
- Buy food in bulk instead of pre-packaged, and bring your own Ziploc® bags (from home) to store it.
- Drink cold drinks from glass bottles instead of plastic.
- And, most importantly: PROCESS YOUR OWN WATER (see the **Health** section). If you can't do this on your own, encourage the local restaurants and guest houses to provide this service.
- Conserve electricity.
- Give up toilet paper. Go Indian style!

Shopping
Unless we are in a meditation centre where we can go for weeks on end without touching money, the commercial aspect of life is a daily reality we have to face.

Whether it is for shampoo or an expensive carpet, the way we spend our rupees has an impact on the local community.

An excellent way to support the grassroots local artisans is to shop at cooperatives, such as the Khadi Bhavans, the Aurobindo ashrams, SEWA (the Self-Employed Women's Association in Gujarat) or the Tibetan Refugee Associations (wherever there is a large Tibetan population, such as Bodhgayā and Dharamsala).

Khadi

Khadi means hand-spun and hand-woven natural textiles (cotton, silk and wool), where the entire process, from picking the cotton or shaving the sheep, to dying the fabric, is performed in a non-violent way. Khadi-makers also say that because of their unique weaving technique, khadi is the coolest and most comfortable fabric (although it may initially be quite rough, after a few vigorous washings it will become as soft as baby clothes).

Gandhi started the khadi movement as a way of boycotting British textiles and making India self-sufficient. He encouraged every Indian to spin cotton a couple of hours every day as a form of protest as well as a meditation. Gandhi considered wearing khadi a moral duty, and even that it had beneficial psychological and spiritual effects on the person who wore it.

You can find khadi shops in almost every town, although the big cities usually have a much wider selection. In Mumbai and Delhi, the *khadi bhavans* have ready-made clothes as well as uncut fabrics, and fabulous shawls. (If you buy fabric and want to have it stitched, make sure you find a reliable tailor, because once you've spent the money on expensive raw silk, it's a shame to have it ruined by a bad cut or sloppy job.)

In most khadi shops you can also find village industry products, which are all produced in a non-violent way. You will find honey, jams, pickles and chutneys, woven baskets, handmade paper, pottery, oils, shampoo, incense, soap and leather products made from animals that have died natural deaths.

In a country where the mechanized industries have put thousands of people out of work, encouraging the local artisans has a concrete effect. In 2004, the khadi movement employed 860 thousand people, and the village industries over 6 million.

Non-Violent Silk

Silk is the fibre that makes up the cocoon of the silkworm. The making of conventional silk is a brutal process. As the worms damage the cocoons when they hatch, the idea is to kill them before they reach maturity, by boiling, micro-waving, or baking the cocoons. One conventional silk sari results in about 50 000 dead silkworms. In khadi silk however, the adult moths are allowed to emerge, and the discarded cocoons are used to spin silk.

You also get a break from haggling, as all prices are fixed. Beginning on Gandhi's birthday, October 3rd, to the end of January, the khadi shops offer reduced rates on textiles.

An alternative to Khadi cooperative shops is Fab India, which can be found in major cities throughout India. They have high quality Khadi clothes at prices only slightly above that of the Khadi Bhavans. These franchise stores also sell a range of textiles for the home, as well as other natural consumable products.

Etiquette around Monks & Nuns

The following etiquette should be practised in the company of monks and nuns:

• Address monks as "Bhante" (Venerable Sir).
• Address nuns as "Ayya" (Honourable One).
• Stand up to welcome a member of the Saṅgha.
• Practise noble speech.
• Refrain from all physical contact and be mindful that a monk or nun should never be alone with a person of the opposite sex.

Saṅgha Dāna

After a 10-day course in Bodhgayā, a small group of meditators decided to give *Saṅgha Dāna* (a donation to the community of monks) at a local monastery. The head monk gave us a short, yet very inspiring, Dhamma talk beforehand. He said,

By giving Saṅgha Dāna, even though there are only six monks here, you are giving to the Saṅgha as a whole; to the Saṅgha of the present, and the Saṅgha of the past. Giving to the Saṅgha is like giving to the Buddha, and so, your mind becomes full of joy at making this offering.

Here are eight qualities of a good *Saṅgha Dāna*:

1. Giving something clean, pure, and attractive
2. Giving choice materials of excellent quality
3. Giving at appropriate times
4. Giving what is suitable for and acceptable to the recipient
5. Giving after careful preparation
6. Giving according to one's ability in a constant manner
7. Giving with a pure, calm mind
8. Feeling glad after giving

During a *Saṅgha Dāna* for 250 *bhikkhus* in Bodhgayā, S.N. Goenka explained two important reasons why we should support the noble community:

Firstly, the bhikkhus are people who have renounced the household-er's life, and it is the duty—the responsibility—of those of us who have a household, to provide for their physical requirements. The second reason is gratitude. We are certainly grateful for the Buddha's teaching when we gain so much from the practice of Vipassana. We should therefore be grateful to the Bhikkhu-Saṅgha because they have preserved the Buddha's teaching up to the present day so that we could receive it. In several of India's neighbouring countries, the theoretical teaching, the words of the Buddha, were preserved. In one country, Myanmar, they also maintained the purity of the practical teaching that we have learned, and for this we owe them great respect and gratitude.

The Buddha once told Ānanda, "Ānanda, in times to come, there will appear vile *bhikkhus*, devoid of morality, who are *bhikkhus* only in name, who will wear their robes around their necks. With the intention of giving to the Saṅgha, offerings will be made to these immoral *bhikkhus*. Even when offered in this manner, a *Saṅgha Dāna*, an offering meant for the whole Saṅgha, I declare, will bring innumerable, inestimable benefits."[2]

If the offering is given with a pure mind, it is blameless. Without judging the recipient, whether he or she is a *sāmaṇera* or a *bhikkhu*, learned or unlearned, wise or foolish; if you keep in mind the Saṅgha as a whole, the *dāna* will truly be a noble offering.

On one occasion, Mahāpajāpatī Gotami, the Buddha's aunt and foster-mother, visited the Buddha at Nigrodhārāma. Handing him a roll of cloth, she said, "Please accept this cloth my son. I spun it myself especially for you." The Buddha gratefully replied, "Please donate it to the community of *bhikkhus*. They will redistribute it according to need." Seeing that she felt slightly hurt, he explained, "There is no difference between making an offering to the Buddha or the Saṅgha. Maintaining an attitude of non-differentiation will inspire later generations to show respect and gratitude to the Saṅgha. This will help the Dhamma last longer." The Buddha continued,

Giving gifts to anyone brings benefit; however the merits are greater in some cases than others. For example, giving food to a hungry animal is meritorious, but giving food to a hungry person is even more so. Similarly, giving food to a hungry person walking along the path of purification is more worthy than giving to a hungry immoral person. Because the fruits of the offering ascend higher and higher according to the integrity of that person, offering something to a fully enlightened being is the most meritorious. Since offering to the Buddha and offering to the Saṅgha is synonymous, giving something to any member of the Saṅgha is just as meritorious as giving something to the Buddha.[3]

Proper etiquette for a *Saṅgha Dāna* includes the following:

- Both women and men can give.
- The donor should be dressed appropriately (no shorts or sleeveless shirts).
- Both the donor and the recipient should be barefoot.
- The donor should give with both hands.

Removing Shoes

It is considered respectful to remove your shoes while entering any temple or mausoleum, and even private homes.

- If you are sitting, do not point your feet towards the monks and nuns. It is considered more polite to sit on your heels than to sit cross-legged.
- It is best to avoid giving money; monks and novices should not touch money. If necessary, money may be given in an envelope, so the *bhikkhu* cannot see the amount (you can also give a check, made out to the monastery, of course). The donee will then give it to the monastery.
- The donor should give with a mind full of surrender, "I take refuge in the Saṅgha" and *mettā*, "May this offering help you progress on the path of *Dhamma*."

If you are giving food, it's best to ask the monk or nun in charge about how to offer the food, as etiquette varies from one monastery to another. Once you have given, say, a bowl of curry, do not touch it until they have finished eating. If you accidentally touch it, they will assume that you have taken it back and they cannot serve themselves until you re-offer it.

Some traditions are strict about monks receiving gifts directly from a woman's hands. For example, Thai monks carry a "receiving cloth" that they place on the table or floor in front of them on which you can place the gift. If you are not sure what to do, you can always ask, "Bhante, what is the proper way for me to give you this book (or apple or toothbrush, etc.)?"

Piṇḍapāta

Piṇḍapāta is the practice of going out on alms rounds. Some monks undertake the *dhutaṅga* (ascetic practice) of eating only food collected on alms rounds.

There was a German monk in Bodhgayā who would go on alms round at the temple every morning. He was very serious, walking slowly with eyes downcast. While placing some bananas in his large bowl, we noticed that his bowl contained only bananas and cheap biscuits. Surely he could not survive on this alone! So we started making individual packets of nuts and raisins, and sometimes offered cooked food that we bought at a nearby restaurant.

For more detailed information on etiquette around monks and nuns, see *The Bhikkhus' Rules: A Guide for Laypeople* by Bhikkhu Ariyesako. Also available on-line at http://accesstoinsight.org/lib/authors/ariyesako/layguide.html

Other Dāna

Sumedha the Wise (the Buddha in a past life, when he vowed to become a *bodhisatta*) knew very well the virtues of *dāna*. When his wealthy parents passed away, they left him a great inheritance. While he was sitting cross-legged on the upper terrace of his mansion, he thought, "Although very rich, all my ancestors were unable to take a single coin with them when they passed away; I should find a way to bring this wealth with me after death…" He then went into the town and, while beating a big drum, proclaimed, "Those who want my riches can come and take them!"

By giving away his wealth, Sumedha was developing his *pāramī*—the only things that accompany us after death. Indeed, *dāna* is one of the ten *pāramī* that we accumulate along the spiritual path. Generosity makes the mind and heart pliable; this is why the Buddha taught that it is the first *pāramī* to develop.

Even after spending many years in India, the plight of the Indian beggar never leaves us indifferent. Seeing the world's most impoverished people with their earthy bodies covered in dirt, soot, and dung is one of the most difficult things to witness. Some of these beggars may be part of a ruthless begging syndicate that kidnaps children and then maims them in order to evoke greater sympathy (thus, greater rupees) from passers-by. Others may be innocent village children who have discovered that it is easier to get money by sticking out their palms than from hard work. Some might be pick-pockets in the guise of beggars. Others are genuine and completely unable to do anything else except beg.

Every time we see an outstretched palm (or stump) all we want to do is empty our pockets. But the reality is that we can't give to every single beggar; or we'll end up in the streets with them. So, what we have found works best for us, is, rather than dishing out money in the streets, we buy fruits and distribute them. Usually the beggars graciously take the food, but in some cases they don't (a banana isn't going to pay for their bottle of whiskey).

If you feel like giving, you can devise a system for yourself, such as, "I will only give to old women," or "I will only give 30 rupees a day," or "I will only give to people who work and don't get paid, like the boys who sweep the floors on the trains," or "I will only give to handicapped people who cannot work." One woman we met in Kolkata would choose a different street kid every evening and bring the boy or girl to a restaurant for a glass of warm milk and peanut-butter toast. The owners were not too fond of these patrons, but since she was paying the bill, they couldn't say much. As one friend who couldn't resist giving handouts said, "I'm investing in a long term karmic insurance plan."

Mother's Milk

Many tourists have helped out mothers and their children by buying them powdered milk or other baby products. What these generous folk don't know is that often, after they have dished out several hundred rupees at the general store and received numerous words of praise and awe, the woman waits for the tourist to be out of sight, then sells the goods right back to the merchant and splits the profits with him.

Tolerance

During your travels in India, especially while on pilgrimage, you will come across many people with different views and practices. It is helpful to keep an open mind and guard yourself against judgements and prejudices. Unfortunately, we have met too many 'Vipassana Dogmatists' who look down on other traditions and practices. Of course, when you find something good that works for you, you want to share it with others. But attachment to views is one of the biggest bondages, and to have contempt for another spiritual practice that may be benefiting someone is not inspiring to that person.

The Buddha warns us against this kind of dogmatism:

> *The person abiding by a certain dogmatic view, considering it to be the highest in the world, claims: "This is the most excellent," and disparages different views as being inferior. As a result, he is not free from disputes. When he sees personal advantages from the things that he has seen, heard, cognized, or from rule or rite, he clings passionately to that alone and sees everything else as inferior.*
>
> *The wise person, on the other hand, does not engender dogmatic views in the world... And therefore, does not consider himself as superior, inferior, or equal. He has abandoned the notion of self and is free from clinging. He neither depends on knowledge nor does he take sides in the midst of controversy.*[4]

Language

Although English is one of India's 16 official languages and is quite commonly spoken, speaking *thodi thodi Hindi* (little little Hindi) will be greatly appreciated by your friends, and will help when looking for a room, shopping in the market, and ordering a meal. It may also save you money. (We once paid the entrance fee for locals, Rs 5, instead of the Rs 100 foreigners' fee, just because we made the effort to speak a little Hindi!)

Indian languages are divided into two families: the Indo-Aryan languages of the north, and the Dravidian languages of the south. English is more widely spoken in southern India than in the north. Northern languages are descendants of Sanskrit, which is considered a sister-language to Latin. They are all closely related to Hindi, so, having a few Hindi words under your belt should be enough to be understood.

Don't be afraid to try; only by making mistakes do we learn. It can be frustrating at times to be unable to communicate intelligently, but it's only by talking, even in a rudimentary way, that your tongue will soften up and your vocabulary increase. A mistake is better than silence. If you're stuck, try using the English word; it may be understood. Expose yourself to the language; your ear will gradually catch the recurring words and the spaces between them. If you hear a Hindi word over and over, ask an Indian friend what it means; this word will stick in your head and become an anchor for you.

The best place to start is at the restaurant. Study the menu carefully; it usually has the Hindi names (in Roman script) with an English translation. Much of Indian life revolves around food; knowing your vegetables and favourite dishes will prepare you for the inevitable question: "Do you like Indian food?" This question is not trivial; you could seriously offend someone with a blunt "No." If you don't like the spicy yogurt and chickpea dish, they don't have to know. Instead, list the dishes that you do like: *alu gobhi, masala dosa, malai kofta*—they will be impressed with your pan-India gourmet tastes.

If volunteering at a Vipassana centre in S.N. Goenka's tradition, you can offer to play the Hindi discourse. Goenka-ji's Hindi is very proper and formal, as well as poetic, thus exposing you to a great vocabulary.

Greetings
The traditional Hindu greeting is *Namaste* or *Namaskar*, which you say with folded hands. It means: "I bow to the light in you."

Muslims greet each other with *"Salām alekum"* which means "Peace be with you." You can reply with the same, or *"Wālekum as salām."*

Please & Thank You
When the bus conductor says "Give ticket," he is not trying to be rude. 'Please' is simply not used in Indian languages. It is not that these languages lack politeness; only that courtesy is implied in the verb, or in a term of endearment. These meanings get lost in translation, making it seem rude and rough. You can continue to use 'please,' as most Indians will understand it.

Similarly, *dhanyavād* (thank you) is not used except in movies and the evening news. However, since most of us have a compulsion to acknowledge every service given to us, *dhanyavād* is good (or *shukriya* if you're in a Muslim area) and the waiter or ticket collector will find it charming.

Ji
Ji is a term of endearment and respect that is placed at the end of the name: Gandhi-ji, Munindra-ji, Mata-ji. Always use it to address someone older than yourself, or to whom you want to convey respect. It can also be used alone to mean 'Yes.'

Ben & Bhai
Ben means sister, as does *didi*, thus Shanti-*ben*, Nena-*didi*. *Bhai* means brother: Sudhir-*bhai*, Jayesh-*bhai*. First names without suffixes are used in intimate relationships. While addressing someone your age, *bhai* and *ben* will do. If addressing an elder, *-ji*, or *Uncle* or *Aunty* (in English) is appropriate.

A Few Words

Below are a few common words and expressions that may be useful. We have tried to keep it simple; it's easier to say *"Nahi samasta"*—I don't understand, (or *"nahi samastī"* if you're female)—than the grammatically-correct *"meri samajh me nahi āyā."* This list is just meant to get you started.

Basic Pronouns:

Maiñ............I		*Méra*............My	
Ham............We		*Hamara*........Our	
Āp................You		*Āpka*............Your	
Yé................S/he; They (near)		*Īnkā*.............His/Hers; They (near)	
Woh..............S/he; They (far)		*Ūnkā*............His/Hers; They (far)	

Useful Interrogatives:

Kaun?..........Who?....................*Yé bhikshu kaun haiñ?*.....Who is that monk?
Kyā?............What?.................*Āpka nām kyā hai?*...........What's your name?
Kab?............When? ....*Bus kab chalégī?*..............When will the bus leave?
Kahāñ?........Where?...............*Mandir kahāñ hai?*...........Where is the temple?
Kaise...........How? ....*Āp kaise hai?*....................How are you?
Kitnā hai? How much? ....*Santarā kitnā hai?*............How much is the orange?
Kitné?.........How many? ....*Āp kitné bhāī hai?*...........How many brothers do you have?
Kaun sé?.....Which?...............*Mumbai kaun sé bus jātī hai?* Which bus goes to Mumbai?
Kyoñ?.........Why?.................*Rickshaw kyoñ rokhnā* ....Why did the rickshaw stop?

Very Simplified Expressions & Questions:

Acchā....................Good; Right; I understand		*Dāhinā karo*..............Turn right	
Thīk hai.................OK; Fine		*Bāéñ karo*..................Turn left	
Nahīm....................No; Don't		*Kitné bajé haiñ?*.........What time is it?	
Chélo....................Let's go		*Jaldi!*..........................Hurry; Early	
Jāo!......................Go away!		*Dhīre dhīre*................Slow down	
Aīyé; ao...............Come		*Mujhé chai chāhiyé*.....I want tea	
Yah kyā hai?.........What's this?		*Kamrā hai?*................Do you have a room?	
Dékho...................Show me			
Kahañ ja ra hai?.......Where are you going?		*Kucch bhī chalégā*......Anything will do	
Kitné dér hai?.............How long will it take?		*Dekkhengé*.................Let's see; maybe	
Kitnā dūr hai?.............How far?		*Méra pét kharāb hai*...My stomach is upset	

Family Members:

Pitājī....................Father
Mātājī....................Mother
Bhaīyā; Bhāī..........Brother
Behn; Dīdī.............Sister
Béṭā.......................Son
Béṭī.......................Daughter
Pati.......................Husband
Bībī.......................Wife

Food:

Khāna....................Food; Meal
Garam....................Hot
Ṭhanḍa...................Cold
Aur........................More, also and
Bas........................Enough
Pānī.......................Water
Garam Pānī............Hot Water
Ublā Pānī...............Boiled Water
Chāwal..................Rice
Shākāhārī; Veg.......Vegetarian
Gosht;Non-Veg.......Meat
Anḍā......................Eggs
Thoṛa....................Little
Bahut.....................A lot, many,
                            too much
Binā......................Without
Nashta...................Breakfast,
                            also snack
Namak...................Salt
Mirch.....................Pepper
Adrak....................Ginger

Location:

Nīche....................Down; Below
Upār......................Up
Pīche....................Behind
Aggé.....................Front; Ahead
Ghar......................House
Meiñ.....................In
Par........................On
Ko.........................To

Bhūkh Lagi............Hungry
Pyās Lagi...............Thirsty
Dahī......................Curd
Dūdh.....................Milk
Ghī.......................Clarified Butter
Phal......................Fruit
Kehlā....................Banana
Papītā...................Papaya
Santarā.................Orange
Mosambi...............Sweetlime
Nīmbū..................Lemon
Nāriyal..................Coconut
Ām........................Mango
Khajūr...................Dates
Angūr....................Grapes
Anār......................Pomegranate
Tarbūjā.................Watermelon
Bādām..................Almonds
Kājū.....................Cashew
Mūngphalī.............Peanuts

(See also Food: What You'll Eat.)

Numbers:

Ek.........................One
Do.........................Two
Tīn........................Three
Chār......................Four
Pānch....................Five
Che.......................Six
Sāt........................Seven
Āt.........................Eight
Nau.......................Nine
Das.......................Ten
Gyārā....................Eleven
Bārā......................Twelve
Terā......................Thirteen

Chaudā.................Fourteen
Pandrā..................Fifteen
Solā......................Sixteen
Satrā.....................Seventeen
Attharā.................Eighteen
Unnīss..................Nineteen
Bīs.......................Nineteen
Ikkīs....................Twenty-one
bāīs.....................Twenty-two
tēīs......................Twenty-three
chaubīs................Twenty-four
paccīs..................Twenty-five

Numbers (continued):

chabbī ....Twenty-six
sattāīs ....Twenty-seven
aṭṭhāīs ....Twenty-eight
unatīs ....Twenty-nine
tīs ....Thirty
ikatīs ....Thirty-one
battīs ....Thirty-two
taiṃtīs ....Thirty-three
cauṃtīs ....Thirty-four
paiṃtīs ....Thirty-five
chattīs ....Thirty-six
saiṃtīs ....Thirty-seven
aṛatīs ....Thirty-eight
unatālīs ....Thirty-nine
cālīs ....Forty
pacās ....Fifty
sāṭh ....Sixty
sattar ....Seventy
assī ....Eighty
nabbē ....Ninety
Ek so ....One Hundred
Do so ....Two Hundred
Ek hazar ....One Thousand
Lakh ....One Hundred
                          Thousand
Crore ....Ten Million

Pehlā ....First
Dūsrā ....Second
Tīsrā ....Third
Chauthā ....Fourth
Pañchwān ....Fifth
Chhaṭhā ....Sixth
Sātvāñ ....Seventh
Ātvāñ ....Eighth

*(From here onwards, add
the suffix -vāñ to the number.)*

Indian Standard Time	**Time:**
When someone makes an appointment with you, you should assume that it is IST—Indian Standard Time—meaning that they can be anywhere from half an hour to three hours late.	*Āj*................Today
	Kal................Yesterday, or tomorrow!
	Shām................Evening
	Rāt................Night
	Din................Day
— *You will get them tomorrow.*	*Hafta*................Week
— *What's tomorrow?*	*Mahina*................Month
— *Not today.*	*Sāl*................Year
	Bād mein................Later
	Ke bād................After
	Pehela................Before
	Abhī................Now
	Minaṭ................Minute
	Ganṭā................Hour

Lonely Planet puts out a nifty pocket-sized Hindi/Urdu phrasebook with enough vocabulary and practical phrases to give you a firm footing.

Mussoorie, a small town in the Himālayan foothills not far from Dehra Dun and Rishikesh, has a reputed language school (plainly known as the "Mussoorie Language School"). You can also find Hindi Teachers in most tourist places.

Learning Pāli
The Vipassana Research Institute at Dhamma Giri offers an 3-month Pāli Study Programme to serious old students. Its goal is to provide students with a working knowledge of Pāli—three months are not enough to become a scholar. Every second year, the institute plans to have an advanced course for students who have already completed the beginner level. Contact the institute to find out about the schedule.

The daily schedule varies, but in general the student has 2 hours of classes everyday, a minimum of 3 hours of meditation, 3-4 hours of volunteer service, and the remaining time is for self-study, laundry, rest, etc. For more information about VRI's Pāli Programme, see the VRI website www.vri.dhamma.org or contact info@giri.dhamma.org

Once in a while, Pāli workshops are organized for old students at different locations in India, as well as in other countries. There are no fixed times; the usual way to find out is through the Vipassana grapevine.

Money

In every commercial exchange, one of India's greatest ascetics, Mahatma Gandhi, will be there smiling at you from every bill, reminding you of the value of simple living. India's currency, the rupee, is made up of 100 paise, the smallest coin being 50 paise.

"Hallo, Change Money?"

You can exchange money in banks, money changer offices, travel agents, and some upper-scale hotels, as well as fancy department stores. The Mumbai and Delhi airports have 24-hour **State Bank of India** currency exchange counters. Check the rates; banks are usually better for travellers' cheques (TCs). American Express also has decent rates. US cash and UK sterling are accepted anywhere (It's good to keep some US cash on hand for emergencies). Remember, you need to show your passport whenever you change money. Some places may charge commission for foreign exchange but the fee is usually nominal. Always double-check the amount when you change money. And don't accept ratty or torn bills; you may have trouble using them in the market.

You can change TCs in big cities and tourist hot spots; American Express and Thomas Cook are the most widely accepted brands. In smaller towns, they may not accept travellers' cheques in denominations other than the US dollar, British pound or Euro. (Most meditation centres will accept donations only in Indian rupees or US dollars.)

If you desperately need to change cash in a village or small town and there are no banks around, find the gold merchant. If he can't do it he'll know who can.

ATMs

All airports have ATMs that accept international bank and credit cards and cash machines are becoming increasingly widespread in India. Don't get too excited when you see one though, as they often only take local cards. In the big cities, even if the sign says 'Cirrus' or 'Plus' we have found that it is hit or miss. The banks in India that generally accept foreign cards include Citibank, HDFC, ICICI, UTI, HSBC, the Punjab National Bank, and the State Bank of India. You should be aware that these banks usually charge high international transaction fees, so it might be wise to make larger transactions less often. Note that while some ATMs snatch back your money if you don't grab it within 30 seconds or so, other machines take longer than 30 seconds to release the cash—so don't panic if the money doesn't instantly appear. Make sure you get a PIN number for your credit card, as these usually work when your bank card doesn't. As a last resort, some bigger banks will give you a cash advance on your credit card (which can be a long process: waiting in line to see the clerk who gives you a token for another clerk, and so on).

Credit Cards

Credit cards are accepted in middle- and upper-scale hotels and shops. It is profitable to use credit cards for big purchases, as the credit card companies usually give the official exchange rate of the day, as opposed to taking a small cut on the rate as money changers do.

Have You Run Out of Cash?

Did you spend your last rupees on a fabulous Kashmiri carpet? There are now Western Union money transfers in most tourist centres. Thomas Cook also offers a moneygram service, but both these options are very costly.

On-line Banking

This is where the internet comes in really handy. Most banks in the West now have Internet banking systems. You can easily pay your phone or electricity bills, and transfer money onto your credit cards. Make sure you sort out the logistics before you leave, like getting a username and password, entering your utility bill numbers, and becoming familiar with the site. These websites usually have a minimum browser requirement, for safety reasons, which we have sometimes downloaded in internet cafés. For safety, always empty the 'cache memory' when you're done.

Cost of Living

You can live very frugally in India, or you can live like royalty; some of the fancy hotels in big cities go for US$500 a night. The minimum amount of money needed per day for the shoestring traveller, excluding travel, is about US$10 for one person, or US$15 for a couple.

Communications

Telephone

While private home phones are still considered a luxury in India, mobile phones have become accessible throughout the country.

However, the public telephone is still the norm in India. These are easily recognizable by their bright yellow signboards with STD, ISD, PCO painted in black, and can be found throughout India. They sometimes have private plexiglass booths, but your conversation is usually open to anyone wanting to eavesdrop.

The price of the call is shown on a digital meter, usually above the phone. The price of long distance calls has gone down recently, so ask beforehand about the rate to your country; sometimes the meter has not been rectified and the shop owners continue to collect the same amount from unsuspecting tourists. Calls to the USA and Canada, for example, vary from 8 to 13 rupees per minute.

These booths may offer a 'call back' service for a nominal fee (Rs 3–5 per minute). Make sure you give your loved ones the exact access code from their country, or you may end up waiting for a long time.

Many of these public phone booths also have fax machines. The rates for sending a fax are the same as the phone call per minute.

Public Telephones

STD:	Subscriber Trunk Dialling: Domestic Long Distance
ISD:	International Subscriber Dialling: International Long Distance
PCO:	Public Call Office

Internet

Computer technology is one of the fastest growing industries in India. You can now find internet cafés (that don't necessarily serve coffee) at almost every corner in most medium-sized towns. Unless you're in a big city, however, the connection can be painfully slow. Morning is the best time, and evening should be avoided altogether. Rates vary from Rs 20 to Rs 40 per hour. More than that is too much, especially if it takes 5 minutes for your page to download. One way to avoid getting frustrated is to have a magazine article next to you to read while the page materializes (or you can use these moments to observe your impatience sensations!). Alternately, try working with two pages at once: you write one e-mail while the browser is searching for another page. If you aren't in a rush, you can also ask to check the speed before you commit.

The Head Wobble

You're walking through the bazaar, with your camera around your neck, amazed at the colours. You walk up to a tika vendor and point to your camera, asking if you can take his photo. He wobbles his head. You take this as a no. The next person does the same, and so does the next. You start wondering what you have done wrong or whether there is a taboo against photography in market places. And they are wondering why you ask them to photograph them and then don't.

A head wobble means anything from 'Yes' to 'I understand', although some may wobble even when they don't understand.

If you're writing a long letter, first write it in a word document and save it as you go, instead of writing directly into your on-line account; too many witty tales have been lost in cyber space because of untimely blackouts.

I-way internet cafés can be found in major cities, and often have fast connections at decent prices. You can also make international calls there over the internet. They're cheap, although the sound quality isn't always as good as a regular phone line.

Going on retreat? You may want to use the auto-reply option in your e-mail program so that people trying to contact you don't begin to think you are snubbing them.

If you are travelling with your own laptop you may want to consider purchasing a USB modem device from any cell phone company such as Vodafone or Airtel. 3G model iPads and similar tablets have an internal SIM card like an iPhone. Most cell phone companies can sell you a data plan.

Post

It's relatively easy to find the post office: just ask around. The Indian postal service is usually reliable for sending letters; however, if you're sending anything of any value, then consider sending it by registered mail—it's a cheap way to discourage potential tampering.

Parcels

Most packages that we have sent home have made it safely, although not always in the quoted time. One friend sent a parcel to himself, and received it in France one year later! Other friends never got their box of beautiful hand-knit woollen sweaters. When you're sending a package, it's simply implied that a small risk is involved. If you're highly attached to the item, it may be better to lug it around. (We suggest you reserve shopping for the few days before your return flight.)

Sending a parcel can be a day-long mission, but it doesn't have to be. Before going to the post office, go to a tailor that does 'parcel packaging'—you can usually find one near a post office. He will stitch your parcel up in cheap cloth and put red wax on the seams in an old-fashioned manner. The good tailor will have a black marker with which you can write the receiver's address, as well as a return address. Remember that many post offices only deal with packages in the morning, so we suggest you get there first thing.

Money Order
This service is usually offered only in the morning. You fill out a form and pay the amount you want to send plus a small service fee. The slip goes directly to the recipient in another Indian town, who can collect the cash at the closest post office.

Poste Restante
This service has become obsolete since the spread of e-mail. If you're one of those 'anti-computer' types, however, the poste restante system is still available. Even better, if you know that you'll be sitting or serving at a centre, you can have mail sent there. Make sure the sender specifies which course(s) you're attending.

Warning: Don't send any electronic equipment by post, and don't have any sent to you in India. A friend asked his father to mail him his laptop. When it arrived, the Indian Customs required him to pay *two and a half times* its value in duty. When he asked if he could return it home, they said "yes," but he still had to pay the duty!

Business Hours

Although shops, post offices, and government offices are usually open from 10 a.m. to 5 p.m. Monday to Friday, the best time to do any official business is between 10 a.m. and 12 a.m., because sometimes they will not provide certain services after lunch, like sending a parcel in a post office, for example. Banks are open 10 a.m. to 2 p.m., Monday to Friday. Some businesses are open "half-days" on Saturday mornings, and on holidays, which, in India, can mean every other day. Some offices and businesses close for lunch; others may close up shop to watch a cricket match. The bazaars are usually open in the evenings until about 8 p.m. The best thing to do is ask a local what time things open and close.

Shopping

The market is the heart of any Indian town. Not only is it a place for commercial exchanges, but it acts as a community centre where old men chew *paan* and reminisce of the good old days, womenfolk compare bangles and gossip, children run after street dogs, and cows wander from stall to stall as if on alms rounds. You'll find all kinds of shops: roadside hole-in-the-wall shops, big city department stores, shops in the backs of trucks, shops on wheels, shops on sticks, even shops in inverted umbrellas.

Unfortunately, most of the traditional hand-made goods have been replaced with ugly industrial plastic. It's now more difficult (and more expensive) to find true craftsmanship.

Haggling
Whether you're looking for carrots or Kashmiri carpets, it's always a good idea to check the competition before settling on an item and committing to a bargaining match. It's even better if you know a local person who can guide you around the local economy.

> — You're lying !
> — No Ma'am. I am doing good business!
>
> – Kashmiri carpet vendor

Indians love haggling: they can spend an entire afternoon perusing shop after shop, arguing over a few rupees, only to return to the first to strike a deal. Bargaining is usually expected, and once you learn the ropes, the merchants will respect you for it; they may even invite you in for tea and a meeting with their mother. It's a friendly ping pong match where the goal is for both parties to settle on a mutually fair price. It's not uncommon for vendors in tourist areas to double—or triple—the price in the hopes of catching an unsuspecting tourist. It's usually safe to start your offer at half of the asking price and work your way up. If the vendor immediately accepts your first offer, you're probably paying too much, but it's too late. If you have absolutely no idea of the value, you can try being vague, by signalling your interest without giving a figure: "Hmm, very nice, but I can't afford it…" will probably bring the price down.

When dealing directly with artisans or independent vendors remember the intricate work and specialized craftsmanship that created your souvenir. Settle on a price that's fair, even if it's a few rupees higher than what you had in mind.

Indian vendors are usually superstitious about the first and last customer of the day, and you can usually get great prices early morning or just before closing.

Bartering
There was a time when Levis® jeans or European perfume could be traded for great local wares, but as western commodities inundate India's markets, vendors are no longer interested in exchange and only want rupees.

Local Souvenirs
Tired of the same old plastic *malas* and tacky t-shirts? Try shopping in the local markets for your souvenirs. Bangles, *saris*, incense, *bindis*, cardamom, stainless steel plates or tiffins make for original (and inexpensive) gifts, as well as a great story.

Shopping Tips
- Bring small change with you to the vegetable market.
- Don't accept torn bills; you'll have a hard time getting rid of them in turn.

- Bring cloth carry-all bags; say no to plastic.
- Big-city department stores have western goods at almost-western prices.

Electricity

Theoretically, electricity in India is the same as in Europe: 230-240 volts, 50 Hz, alternating current. In reality though, the voltage often fluctuates, so all appliances like fridges, computers, or TVs should be plugged in to a voltage stabilizer. A spike guard, available at any electronics shop, has a fuse on it that will blow if the power spikes. Investing in this Rs 50 gadget is much better than frying your laptop.

Blackouts are frequent so keep torches, candles and matches handy. In some places, there are planned power-cuts called 'load shedding.' Find out locally when they are, so that you don't make a trip to town to check your e-mail and then find out that the power is cut for 3 hours.

Laundry

> *If you beat your clothes, the dirt will run away.*
>
> – Himāchali Villager

You see them at the river banks, thrashing the clothes—*shlop, whack, shlop*—as though exorcizing demons. They are the *dhobi-wallahs*: people who do laundry. You can give them your dirty clothes in the morning, and they usually come back that same evening, crisply ironed. They may also return a different color, or with missing buttons or drawstrings. This is the risk you are prepared to take for the low cost of about 10 rupees per piece. Remember that ladies' underwear is a discreet item in India; you don't give it to the *dhobi-wallah*, and you don't hang it outside after washing it, but in your room or bathroom.

The *dhobi-seva* in established meditation centres like Dhamma Giri is incredibly efficient, and cheap (around Rs 5 per piece). But why do your whites come back with a bluish tint? They put a drop of indigo in the white load to keep it from turning yellow! If you don't know whether or not you can trust the laundry service, first send an article that you're not attached to, like a towel. Keep in mind, however, that there's always a risk.

While travelling, we do our laundry by hand and our motto is: "If it doesn't smell bad, it's clean." With that said, we have also noticed that Indian people, generally, place a strong emphasis on personal hygiene and appearance, and usually equate the outward image they present to the world with their social status. A foreign tourist in India will always be perceived as rich even if that is far from the truth, and a rich person travelling in dirty, torn, creased, or ill-fitting clothes really challenges traditional ideas of propriety, and can sometimes be taken as an affront to the local value system. You will be surprised how much smoother your travels can be when you make that extra effort to wear clean clothes without holes, to put on shoes or sandals that get an occasional polish, and to keep your hair (and beard) neat.

Toilets & Bathrooms

There are two kinds of toilets in India, the 'Western' style: the classic sit-down, flush toilet, and the 'Indian' style: a hole in the floor with a place for the feet on either side, over which you squat. Some seasoned travellers come to prefer the Indian toilets as they are more hygienic and offer a better evacuating position.

Indians use water, not toilet paper. They actually find the use of toilet paper quite disgusting. One Indian friend used this argument: "If you had excrement on your face, would you wipe it off with paper or wash it with water?"

There is usually a tap, bucket, and jug next to the toilet. Everyone develops their own washing technique, but use your right hand to pour the water, and your left to wash yourself. Always wash your hands with soap afterwards; if soap is not available, alcohol-based solutions like 'Pure Hands' are convenient.

Women often complain that they stay wet after using water. A simple solution is to carry a small hand-towel to use for drying oneself.

Be careful not to drop anything down the toilet! Tales abound of dropped keys, sunglasses, even passports that had to be retrieved from the mysterious ceramic hole.

Pointing your pinky in the air is the sign that you have to pee.

Most Indians don't know the luxury of a gushing hot shower. They usually fill up a bucket of hot water, squat, use a jug to wet themselves, lather, and rinse. The process is completed with incredible efficiency.

You may have to bucket-bathe in some guest houses and meditation centres. In the winter, most guest houses will provide hot water on demand. Or there may be a geiser (hot water tank) that you have to switch on, which takes about 30 minutes to heat. If there's no heating system, you can always leave a full bucket in the sun for a few hours.

Warnings

India is a safe country overall. You will, however, inevitably hear some disturbing stories. Remember that although these incidents are rare, they are the stories people love to tell. So try to keep that in mind when a new acquaintance tells you about their friend's brother who ate a biscuit on the train and woke up in the hospital with all his belongings stolen.

Almost every day in an Indian newspaper you can find at least one Bihar horror story of theft, murder or corruption. Whether the stories are accurate or not, they have imprinted a collective paranoia on the minds of the Indian population. When we tell our Indian friends that we are going on pilgrimage, the common responses are, "Very good that you will experience the vibrations of these places, but don't bring anything of value, never travel at night, and don't trust anybody!"

Our first time travelling in Bihar, however, proved to us that most of these fears are all based on media-constructed fairytales. Yes, it's true the government is corrupt, the towns are dirty, and the majority of Biharis are poor and uneducated, but most of these people are also warm, helpful, and welcoming. There are also some conflict zones, such as Kashmir bordering Pakistan, and Nagaland and Manipur in the north-east. It is better to check the political situation before entering a sensitive area.

Having said this, India is not a predictable exotic amusement park. Accidents happen, so being vigilant is important. While travelling on buses and trains, always wear your money-belt under your clothes, just to be safe.

I had recently been thinking to myself, "It's been almost two years and I haven't lost my wallet or been pickpocketed."

I was on the New Delhi-Howrah Express when we were just pulling in to Calcutta. I had just met a couple who were also going to Thailand like I had planned, and would show me around and where to stay and get the cheapest flight. Waiting for the long stop, moving 5 kmph for what seemed like an afternoon, I lay on a top bunk with my most precious bag under my head as a pillow. I was beginning to daydream a bit when an Indian man tapped me to let me know we were stopped and it was time to get off. I quickly got up and gathered my three big loads—one overloaded backpack, a 30 lb brass gong from Myanmar, and a miscellaneous bag of books and other gifts to bring home. Needless to say, I was burdened by my baggage, but convinced myself it was going to be worthwhile to bring it all home. I followed my new travel mates onto an empty bus heading to the Sudder Street area. A minute or two went by and I started thinking of my passport and wallet and... MY BAG! I LEFT IT ON THE TRAIN!... My heart stopped and I blankly looked at my friends after spontaneously exclaiming a single 'harsh' word. It was the thing that so may people talk about as being the worst thing to happen in a foreign country: loosing your wallet and passport (although it can always be worse). I decided I had to at least make the effort of recovering it even though by now I knew India well enough to know that unattended baggage anywhere remotely near a train station might as well be dāna to the locals. I really didn't want to hobble back to the station with all my bags being as tired as I was. But I had to try. As I suspected, the train had been scoured clean by all the homeless kids and porters that board the train before it comes to a halt.

It was incredibly hot and humid, and the buses were very crowded. I had to squish up against other sweaty bodies, hunched over, as the *buses were often shorter than my 6'5" long body. The Canadian consulate rep was only able to give me a few hundred rupees, probably just over US$5. This had to give me food and accommodation for at least a couple of nights, so I had to really budget (which actually isn't all that hard in India). I was reminding myself of how the worst thing wasn't so bad after all, and how all of those things, my pictures, my journal, money, ID, addresses and notes, were all ultimately immaterial, and hey, I was still breathing. I was actually quite happy with myself at keeping it 'together.' As the day turned to night I was still travelling amongst the hoards of humanity—pushing, dirty, noisy, hungry, thirsty—physically drained almost to the limit, when I found out I'm on the wrong bus. The straps and bag handles felt like wire cheese cutters on my shoulders and hands.*

I found myself on a busy side street feeling discouraged and unable to think. I finally decided to give into one of the many persistent rickshaw drivers yelling "Hello sir, sir, sir" and get a ride. He spoke no English and I thought we had settled on a price of 5 or 10 rupees to take me to the Salvation Army. I put all my bags on the rickshaw, and to my surprise it was only right around the corner from where I had given up walking. Sure enough, the driver was insisting on something like 50 rupees. My patience was at an all time minimum. After a brief argument and a settlement I was ready to collapse. Finally I was here. I was just signing in to the typical log book when I was asked to confront the 'Captain' to explain why I didn't have a passport. I was barely allowed to finish my sentence when I was met with cold words of rejection: "I don't care where you stay, but without a passport, you are not staying here." I tried to explain my situation, my day, in more detail only to be cut off by admonishments like "You should be more careful with your belongings." All I wanted was a mattress and a cold shower. Very strong sensations were arising in me as I tried to reason with the man, but he only further kept shooing me off coldly as if I was a little fly bothering him, without the slightest desire to listen. I could just barely contain myself and I think tears must have welled up along with a great concoction of emotion towards this 'Captain of Salvation.' He was at least kind enough to let me leave my bags of burden there while I sought out another place and made a desperate phone call. But of course every other rest house was the same: "No Passport = No Bed." Thankfully, I had the consulate rep's cell number and he managed to convince the Captain to let me stay the night. The Captain brought me up to his office and proudly explained how as God's servants they were there to always lend a helping hand. Assuming I was a regular churchgoer and a good Christian, he shook my hand and I said "Namaste." He frowned and said to me uncomfortably, "We don't say that in here."

An old dirty mattress never felt so good in my life as it did that night.

— Michael Pancoe

Volunteer Work

There are loads of opportunities for volunteer work in India. A friend worked on a 'Pedal Power' project that was making electric generators powered by bicycles. Others have helped with the Mother Teresa sisters in the streets of Kolkata. Others have taught English to Tibetan refugees in Dharamsala. Whatever skill you possess is useful—you can proofread a pamphlet, make a poster or help organize an event.

In many tourist areas, you will see ads in tourist restaurants for volunteer work. Ask around.

Last but not least, giving service in a Vipassana centre is always a rewarding experience. See the **Dhamma Service** section below.

Dhamma Centres

Communication before arriving: It's best to contact the centre or centre's city office to let them know of your plans instead of showing up unexpectedly. If whoever answers the phone does not speak English, ask someone nearby who does to translate for you (speaking broken Hindi is easier face-to-face than it is over the telephone).

Keep in mind that centres are not meant to be used as guest houses, but as places to sit and serve. However, the Middle Land centres are sometimes the exception to this rule, and will allow old students of S.N. Goenka who are on pilgrimage to spend a night or two if space permits.

Facilities: As every Vipassana centre fends for itself, you will find that the level of comfort varies widely from one to the other. Centres near big cities for example, will often receive more *dāna* than rural centres, and consequently, the facilities may be more comfortable. All meditation centres, however, provide the basic minimum of a bed, mattress, pillow, bedding, mosquito net, toilets, hot bucket baths, as well as simple vegetarian food. In some centres you will sleep in a dorm with 10 other students, while in others you may have a private room with an attached bathroom. Some will encourage (or oblige) you to use the laundry service; others will say "self-service is the best service."

Food: The food in centres is a reflection of local traditional cooking: Gujarati millet chapattis at Dhamma Sindhu; fried noodles for breakfast in Nepal, and sweet *khīr* (rice pudding) in Bodhgayā. The food is generally clean, and the water is usually filtered with Aquaguard systems, or boiled.

Dress: Simple, modest, and comfortable clothing is essential. Follow the usual dress code of covering shoulders and legs (both for men and women), but be warned that an item that is appropriate in the West may not be in India. If unsure, ask a senior meditator.

Your overall appearance should be neat. Indians pride themselves on personal cleanliness: "Cleanliness is next to Godliness!" is a common slogan and you should make an effort to abide by it.

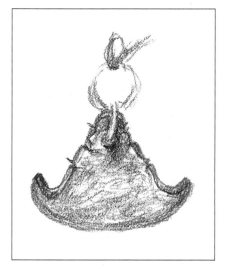

Segregation: It is very important for men and women to respect the segregation guidelines while at a Dhamma centre. Although volunteers of the opposite sex are allowed to communicate about work-related matters and married couples are usually allowed to briefly meet in a public place to discuss their business, casual chit-chat between Dhamma workers of the opposite sex is not approved.

Dhamma Service: The Dhamma *sevaks* and *sevikas* are invaluable parts of the Dhamma machinery that supports the meditators looking inside. As a foreigner, however, you may find that your duties are limited by the language barrier; you may be asked simply to ring a small bell, sit in the meditation hall with open eyes, or play foreign language discourses. Try not to feel useless or unimportant. As Goenka-ji says, "The best service you can do is to meditate."

If you're really bored, however, enquire if the kitchen needs help, or take a look at the garden: does it need weeding? Or maybe you have some computer skills and can help the management update old signs. There's always a toilet needing cleaning or a path needing sweeping.

Remember that you are a guest in this country. Locals have their own way of doing things, and customs and habits should be respected. Foreigners should be especially sensitive about telling people how to do this or that. It's not uncommon for foreign servers to impose their way of thinking on the local centre management: "That's not an efficient way of doing it. In the West we do it like this…" But we are not in the West. Unless it is something that you feel is completely 'anti-Dhamma,' most of the time it is better to just adapt yourself to the situation and see it as an opportunity to dissolve the ego.

Suggested Itineraries
for a Dhamma Yatra

If you are considering going on a pilgrimage (*yatra*) to the sacred Dhamma places in the Middle Land, we suggest one of two itineraries, both round-trip routes from Delhi. The first route is for those of you who want to go only to the main destinations, while the second is for the more enthusiastic *yatri* (pilgrim) wanting to meditate off the beaten track.

The **first route** for a *yatra*, which will require a minimum of two weeks by private vehicle and three weeks by public transport, looks something like this: Delhi to Vārāṇasī & Sārnāth, to Bodhgayā, to Rajgir & Nalanda, to Patna, to Vaishali, to Kushinagar, to Lumbinī, to Kapilavatthu, to Shravasti, and back to Delhi.

The **second route** includes all the places mentioned in the Middle Land section, and requires at least 6 weeks by private vehicle and 8 weeks by public transport.

The suggested durations will enable you to explore and meditate in these places for a few days, without the frustrating rush of trying to see too much in too little time. You can, of course, leave out any of the places according to your interest or time constraints.

There are also several tour operators who offer pilgrimage packages, taking care of all your travel, food and accommodation needs. While it can be argued that this sort of packaged tour reduces the opportunities for spontaneity and adventure, this method of travel enables pilgrims to focus on experience and Dhamma practice without all the logistical headaches, and may be best for those with limited time to plan or travel.

As always, word-of-mouth is the best way to go about deciding what's best for you. Some travellers have recommended tours from www.buddhapath.com, www. buddhapilgrimage.com and www.buddhist-pilgrimage.com. Visit their websites for prices and dates. The Indian Railway Catering and Tourism Corporation (www. irctc.co.in) offers a luxurious, all-inclusive 8-day pilgrimage to the main holy sites (Lumbinī, Bodhgayā, Sārnāth, Shravasti, Rajgir and Kushinagar). Pilgrims travel on the *Mahaparinirvana Express*—an air-conditioned train specially reserved for the pilgrimage—access the sites by road in air-conditioned jeeps and buses, and stay in high-end hotels (www.railtourismindia.com/buddha).

I have to admit I was very sceptical of the 'merit' of visiting a place. I thought, "What is all this hokey-pokey talk about vibrations that are 2 500 years old?" I am very grateful that in spite of my stubbornness and doubt, I signed up for the yatra with Goenka-ji and experienced it for myself. It was so wonderful, filling me with so much inspiration to keep walking the path.

– American Pilgrim

The Middle Land
(*Majjhima Desa*)

Dhamma Art, Architecture & History

Stūpas (Pagodas, Cetiyas, Chortens)

The burial mounds known as stūpas are the most notable of all monuments honouring the Buddha and are found throughout the Middle Land. The definition of stūpa is a 'heap,' and most of the original structures during the Buddha's lifetime were mounds of earth placed over the relics of saints or royalty, topped with a wooden umbrella. From the 3rd century onwards, stūpas developed into beautiful and elaborate structures symbolizing the glory of the Buddha and his teaching.

Some experts say that stūpas were designed to look like an inverted bodhi leaf, while others claim that the stūpas represent the Buddha's begging bowl turned over and his walking stick protruding from it. The common Indian stūpa is built in five sections which symbolize the five elements of the cosmos: the base (*medhi*) symbolizes the earth, the dome (*aṇḍa*) symbolizes water, a platform that sits on top of the dome (*harmika*) symbolizes wind, a shaft (*yashṭi*) protruding from the platform symbolizes fire, and an umbrella (*chātravali*) crowning the structure symbolizes space. These stūpas were often encircled by a railing (*vedika*) with a gateway (*toraṇa*). South Asian stūpas, referred to as pagodas, are usually topped with a spire, and East Asian stūpas are usually crowned with curved and tiered eaves.[5] Most of the stūpas we see in the Middle Land today are not original, but comprise several layers built one on top of the other over the centuries. In Asia it's considered sacrilegious to open or demolish an existing stūpa, monastery or temple, so what we see today is the latest renovation or reconstruction. Remember that you should always walk around a stūpa in a clockwise direction, keeping it to your right.

You will often notice clusters of miniature stūpas surrounding the primary ones. These are votive stūpas built by devotees before the 13th century who had taken some personal vow and were striving to develop their religious merit. These stūpas usually contain small statues of the Buddha, copies of Dhamma texts and/or clay tablets inscribed with the Buddha's words.

The Buddha said that there are four classes of people worthy of a stūpa. They are: Buddhas (*sammāsambuddhas*), solitary Buddhas (*paccekabuddhas*)[6], enlightened disciples (*arahants*), and wheel-turning monarchs (*dhammacakkavatin*). There are generally three types of stūpas erected in honour of these beings: stūpas that enshrine corporeal relics (*sarīradhātu cetiya*), stūpas commemorating events associated with the above four personages (*uddissa cetiya*), and stūpas containing the person's personal objects such as robes, bowls, or a walking stick (*paribhoga cetiya*). Bodhi trees are also referred to as a *paribhoga cetiya*.[7]

The Buddha stressed the importance of paying homage to those who are worthy of veneration:

Paying homage to those who are worthy:
To Buddhas or their disciples
Who have defeated desire and crossed the stream of grief and
lamentation,
Paying homage to them will lead to emancipation and fearlessness.
These merits cannot be measured.[8]

Laying flowers, lighting incense, or bowing to stūpas are not acts required of visitors, but they are traditional Asian ways of expressing gratitude and respect to what the stūpa represents. For example, when a meditator bows in front of the Bodhi Tree in Bodhgayā s/he is not bowing to the tree itself, but to what the tree represents: Awakening. Sayagyi U Ba Khin taught his students that when bowing three times in front of a stūpa or Buddha image, the first time should be with the observation of sensations with *anicca* at the top of the head. The second time should be with the understanding of *dukkha*, and the third time with *anattā*. As Sayagyi said, "reverence expressed in this manner is the proper reverence; otherwise it is merely an empty ritual."[9]

Temples & Monasteries

Other ruins usually found in the vicinity of stūpas include those of temples and monasteries (*vihāra, saṅghārāma*), most of which were probably first constructed around the time of King Asoka (3rd century BCE). They continued to be active until approximately the 13th century CE, when they were either destroyed or abandoned during the Turkish conquests or by later Brahmanical opposition.

The first *bhikkhus* were nomadic, staying in forests, mountain dwellings, and parks maintained by wealthy benefactors. As more people joined the Saṅgha, the Buddha permitted *bhikkhus* to stay in more permanent structures that were donated by lay devotees. For many *bhikkhus*, the lifestyle of renunciation changed from "wandering alone like a rhinoceros" to "living together in friendliness and harmony, like milk and water mixed, looking upon each other with the eye of affection."[10]

Statues of the Buddha

For the first 500 years of the Buddha's teaching, there were no statues of the Buddha. Instead, bodhi trees, stūpas, empty chairs, wheels, or pairs of footprints were used to represent him. The first statues were produced during the Kusana period (2nd century BCE to 3rd century CE), whose culture was heavily influenced by the Greeks. Talented artists expressed their dedication by producing magnificent stone and metal statues portraying the Buddha's wisdom and compassion, which, in turn, became objects of devotion.

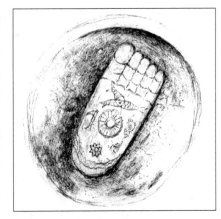

Images of the Buddha usually portray him sitting in the lotus posture, standing, or lying down (usually symbolizing his passing away). Sculptures of the Buddha sitting on a chair are not of our present Buddha, Siddhattha Gotama, but of Matteyya (or, *Maitreya* in Sanskrit), the next Buddha. Most of these figures have a halo behind the head and also bear some of the 32 marks of a great being (*mahāpurisa lakkhana*), such as a lump on top of the head (*unhisa*), spoked wheel imprints on the palms of the hands and the soles of the feet, and a mark between the eyebrows (*unna*). The elongated earlobes are probably a result of the Sakyan custom of wearing heavy earrings, which the Buddha would have done before his renunciation. The Buddha's hands are always placed in one of the five gestures (*mūdra*): the meditation pose (*dhyānamūdra*) has his hands resting in his lap; the teaching gesture (*dhammacakkamūdra*) shows both hands raised in front of the chest turning a wheel; the sign of imparting fearlessness and *mettā* (*abhayamūdra*) portrays him with his right palm facing outwards; when he has his left palm out with his fingers pointing down, he is in the position of bestowing blessings (*varadamūdra*), and the earth-touching gesture (*bhumisparsamūdra*) shows the left hand in the lap and the right hand touching the ground, asking the earth to bear witness to his great victory over Māra, the source of immorality. Sometimes, at the sides of these statues, small figures of devotees are depicted with their palms joined together (*añjalimūdra*).

Dhamma Asoka: His Pillars & Policies

The great Indian Emperor Asoka was crowned around 270 BCE as the third emperor in the Mauryan lineage, which was established about fifty years earlier by his grandfather Chandragupta Maurya. After inheriting the throne from his father Bindusāra, Asoka briefly continued his family's military campaigns, conquering most of the Indian subcontinent, with the exception of its southernmost tip and the area of modern Bangladesh and Assam. One of his expansionist campaigns led to the bloody battle in Kalinga, where thousands of people were massacred. The horrors of this battle weighed heavily on his conscience, and out of remorse he decided to discontinue his violent policies. Eight years into his reign, Asoka encountered the Dhamma, and as his heart softened, his entire life and manner of governing changed dramatically.

After learning the Dhamma, Asoka renounced all force, forbade hunting for pleasure, promoted principles of morality and meditation, adopted a policy of religious tolerance, and worked for the general well-being of his people. Public welfare schemes were set up to build hospitals, cultivate medicinal plants, construct inns for travellers, dig wells, plant trees and create schools. Asoka was known to maintain a fatherly principle in government administration, as is seen in the Dauli rock edict that reads, "All men are my children and just as I desire for my children that they may enjoy every kind of prosperity and happiness, so also do I desire the same for all men." He instructed his officers to care for their citizens "as the skillful nurse is eager to care for the happiness of a child." He encouraged his officials to cultivate love and compassion and to eradicate anger, jealousy, pride, stress and laziness. These guidelines were especially important in dealing with criminals, to whom he gave milder punishments than before, chances for rehabilitation, and release on the grounds of old age and sickness. When Asoka travelled around his empire, rather than hunting and engaging in leisure activities, he would meet his people and help solve their problems. In this way, he wrote that his victories were "conquests of right and not might."

Asoka also forbade animal sacrifices in his kingdom and stopped the slaughter of animals for the royal kitchen under the principle of non-violence, which was made widespread through edicts containing messages like "Not to injure living beings is good." It's also possible that vegetarianism first became widespread in India during his rule. Asoka's decrees are said to be the oldest surviving Indian documents, and he also takes credit for the reintroduction of writing in India after nearly 1 500 years of widespread illiteracy.

Much of our knowledge about Asoka's reign comes to us in the form of edicts carved on stones, cave walls and fine polished sandstone pillars, which he placed throughout his empire, including at the sacred Dhamma *yatra* sites. In addition to revealing ancient India's aesthetic glory, the 15 m tall pillars also exemplify technical genius, exhibited by their strength and durability after centuries of exposure to the elements. These masterpieces, built in quarries near Vārāṇasī, were carried to their destinations, in some cases thousands of kilometres away. Although most of the remaining pillars have been broken due to religious and political prejudice, some still have their original crown of animals—the lion, elephant, or bull—symbolizing nobility. Asoka also built and reconstructed stūpas throughout his land. He opened seven of the eight original stūpas that had held the Buddha's relics,[11] and he divided these seven portions into "84 000,"[12] which he enshrined in stūpas throughout his empire.

Although a layperson, this righteous ruler tried to assist in mending a schism that led to the development of the *Sthaviravāda* (the predecessor to Theravāda) and the *Mahāsaṅghika* (the predecessor to Mahāyāna) sects. While Asoka seems to have supported both groups, his religious missions spread the Sthaviravāda teachings. His proclamations illustrate his concern for the unity and well-being of the Saṅgha. In the middle of the 3rd century BCE, Asoka sponsored the nine-month Third Council of 1 000 monks presided over by the *arahant* Moggaliputta Tissa, in an effort to standardize the canon and purify the Saṅgha of divisive elements. In one edict illustrating his desire for a unified Saṅgha, he wrote: "No one is to cause dissension in the Order. Whoever creates a schism in the Order…is to be put in a place not inhabited by monks or nuns. For it is my wish that the Order should remain united and endure for long." During this council, the *Kathāvatthu* ("The Points of Controversy") was added to the Abhidhamma Piṭaka.

In addition to his support for the Saṅgha, Asoka built facilities for other religious traditions. One decree says, "All sects deserve reverence for some reason or another. By thus acting a man exalts his own sect and at the same time does service to the other sects." This volition to serve all his subjects arises from having purified his mind. In one edict, he acknowledged that this was possible because of two things: one was the rule of law and order in his kingdom (*dhammaniyamani*); the other was the practice of meditation (*nijhatiya*), the practical aspect of the Dhamma.

After the Third Council, Asoka dispatched missions of awakened *bhikkhus* throughout India and to Nepal, Afghanistan, Syria, Egypt, Greece, Sri Lanka, Myanmar and Thailand to spread the Dhamma. Two of the most important of these missions were to Myanmar and Sri Lanka. The *arahants* Sona and Uttara Theras were sent to Suvanna Bhumi (modern day Myanmar), where they taught both the theoretical (*pariyatti*) and practical (*paṭipatti*) aspects of the Dhamma. From that point onwards, a lineage of *bhikkhus* has kept both aspects alive, and they remain today. The *Mahāvaṃsa*, a Sri Lankan chronicle, tells the story of how the Dhamma was introduced to Sri Lanka around 247 BCE by Asoka's children, the *arahants* Mahinda and Saṅghamitta. They gave King Devanampiya (r. 250-210 BCE) a cutting from the original Bodhi Tree in Bodhgayā, which he planted in Anuradhapura, where a descendant of that tree lives today. Around 29 BCE, the Fourth Council was held in Sri Lanka and the Dhamma was written down in the Pāli language (and Sinhalese script) for the first time after centuries of oral transmission. The fact that we have any knowledge at all of the Buddha's original teachings is entirely due to the remarkable dedication of the Myanmar and Sri Lankan scholars and meditators.

Asoka died around 230 BCE, leaving behind a strong legacy for future rulers to follow. In the end, not only did he have a strong influence on the propagation of the Dhamma, but the Dhamma had a great impact on his character and method of rule.

The Dhamma's Decline in India

As Asoka's successors were not able to maintain the same high standard of rule, the Mauryan imperial order lasted only another 50 years before it was replaced in the south by several smaller kingdoms and in the north by the Sungha dynasty, whose rule began the slow persecution and devolution of the Dhamma and the rise of Vedic Brahmanism. However, after the fall of the Sunghas, a series of invaders that included the Greeks, Scythians and Parthians, all seemed to have treated the Buddha's teachings with respect. Indeed, the Greek King Menander (or Milinda, c. 150 BCE) even adopted the teachings himself.[13] The Dhamma continued to thrive in India, albeit on more equal terms with other yogic sects and Vedic Brahmanism, until the next great phase of expansion under the Kushan dynasty. The Kushan emperor Kanishka (r. 78-123 CE) was known as the Mahāyāna equivalent of Asoka, and is credited with the upsurge and spread of Mahāyāna teachings in India, Central Asia and China. While Kanishka did show a predisposition to religious tolerance, he never adopted a policy of non-violence, and his rule saw a number of bloody massacres. Although he seems to have favoured the Mahāyāna, he also supported other lineages in the Buddha's tradition. During Kanishka's reign and for the next several hundred years, *bhikkhus* began paying more attention to philosophical scholasticism, which was marked by the founding of the great monastic universities Nāḷandā, Taxilā (*Takkasilā*) and Vikramaśila.

At this time, a number of cultural interpretations of the Buddha's teaching were also adopted, factors contributing to the eventual decline of the original Dhamma in India. As meditation practice moved into the background, the trend of venerating and mythologizing the Buddha increased. Changes in ways of representing and relating to the Buddha manifested themselves in sophisticated artistic expression and merit-making activities, resulting in the rise of ritual and devotional worship (*bhakti*). These changes contributed to not only the blurring of distinction between the Buddha's tradition and Hindu Vedantic practices, but also to the alteration of the Buddha's teaching from a universal, non-sectarian way of life, to a particular, sectarian, religious system.[14] The intermingling of Mahāyāna Buddhist and Hindu philosophies and practices made it very difficult for the untrained eye to distinguish between the two traditions, especially because of the increase of metaphysical speculation and deification in the new 'Buddhism.' However, whereas Hinduism established itself among the masses, Buddhism retreated into monasteries and universities, becoming a religion of elite specialists. These practitioners of the new Buddhism lost touch with the popular culture and ceased to proselytize; instead turning inwards to subtle philosophical debate and ritual. Despite the decline of the Buddha's original message over the next centuries, the evolved religion of Buddhism continued to flourish beyond the Gupta period (320-500 CE), especially since Buddhist monks were considered the greatest scholars of the time in not only the field of philosophy, but also astronomy, logic, grammar and medicine.

In the seventh century, the advent of Tantric, or esoteric, magic-oriented Buddhism gained popularity as monks became dissatisfied with the arid scholasticism that characterized Indian Buddhism at this time. However, secret Tantric ritualism didn't help the Saṅgha make contact with popular culture, either. Both scholasticism and esotericism spelt disaster for the long-term sustainability of the Saṅgha in India. Monks forgot about the lifestyle of the wandering mendicant that connected the Saṅgha to the ordinary people who supported them. As the Saṅgha's popular base declined, donors lost interest in financing both the expensive monastic institutions and the secluded monks practising things that nobody could understand. By the eighth century, the end of the Dhamma in India was in view and an exodus of foresighted monks went to East and South East Asia. These practitioners perceived that the Dhamma's future lay beyond the land of its birth.

The final blows for the surviving Indian Saṅgha were in the twelfth and thirteenth centuries, when Turkish Muslims invaded India. They persecuted all Buddhists, massacred the distinctively dressed monks, and destroyed Buddhist monasteries, temples, stūpas, universities and libraries. Whatever was not destroyed was eventually taken over by nature or later converted into Hindu temples. For the 600 years during the Islamic dynastic rule of northern India, pilgrims were prohibited from visiting their sacred places. It was only after the British colonial administration took control of India in the 19th century that pilgrims were once again free to visit the old sacred sites, which were rediscovered, restored, and preserved by British and Burmese authorities.

The Rediscovery of Dhamma Culture & Practice in India

While visiting the sacred places and their ancient monuments, it's important to remember the people who rediscovered them after they had been lost to nature and time. Most of what we see today is a result of the pioneering efforts made by 19th century European Orientalists such as Charles Wilkins, William Jones, Francis Buchanan, James Prinsep, Alexander Cunningham, Archibald Carlleyle, James

Fergusson, Lawrence Wadell and others who dedicated all their spare time—on top of their busy colonial administrative duties—to learning Indian languages, deciphering ancient inscriptions, and searching for ruins connected with the Buddha's life and times. These Orientalists had a deep passion for uncovering India's ancient history and culture, and the Buddha's contribution to Indian civilization. While pursuing their hobby, they put their lives in danger, facing disease, banditry, uncooperative locals and terrible travel conditions. However, through their love of learning, uncanny guesswork, and with the help of old Chinese travelogues, these adventurers overcame their obstacles and located, excavated, and explained most of the *yatra* sites that we see today.

The Dhamma's practical aspect of mental purification, however, returned to India only in the latter half of the 20th century. In 1954 the social reformer and human rights advocate Dr. Bhimrao Ramji Ambedkar publicly took refuge in the Triple Gem and Five Precepts with a half million low-caste Indians, preaching that anyone who did so would help India rid itself of corruption and oppression. After the Tibetan spiritual leader-in-exile His Holiness the 14th Dalai Lama arrived in India in 1959, people from all around the world flocked to see him and learn about the Buddha's teachings on compassion and forgiveness. When the Myanmar-born Indian S.N. Goenka returned to India ten years later, the gateway to liberation swung open as he taught one 10-day Vipassana course after another. Since then, the Dhamma teachings of ethical integrity, concentration, wisdom and love have flourished throughout the land of its birth and beyond.

A Note on ASI

In 2000, the Archaeological Survey of India (ASI) decided to charge entry fees to all the archaeological sites it runs, including sacred Buddhist sites. While Indian vistors are required to pay Rs 5 or Rs 10, foreigners must pay between Rs 100 and Rs 250, depending on the site.

If you find yourself discouraged by this policy, the first thing to do is check your equanimity and then, if possible, practise *mettā*; there is no point aggravating the situation and hampering your short time there. The next step is to write a polite letter detailing your issue, which might include the inappropriateness of charging pilgrims to enter sacred places. Public pressure from concerned travellers may help to encourage a change in policy. Should you wish to send copies of your letter to the Prime Minister of India and/or the Minister of Tourism, the addresses are also provided below.

The Director
Office of the Director General
Archaeological Survey of India
11 Janpath
New Delhi–110 011
India
Tel: +91 (0)11-23015428
Fax: +91 (0)11-23015428
E-mail: asi@del3.vsnl.net.in

The Prime Minister's Office
South Block, Raisina Hill
New Delhi–110 011
India
Tel: +91 (0)11-3012312
Fax: +91 (0)11-3019545
         +91 (0)11-3016857
Website: http://pmindia.nic.in/
         writetous.htm

Minister of Tourism
#501, 5th Floor, C-Wing,
Shastry Bhavan
Dr. Rajendra Prasad Road
New Delhi–110 001
India
Tel: +91 (0)11-4610350
E-mail: akumar@parlis.nic.in
Website: www.anaanth.org

The Middle Land: Uttar Pradesh, Bihar & South Nepal

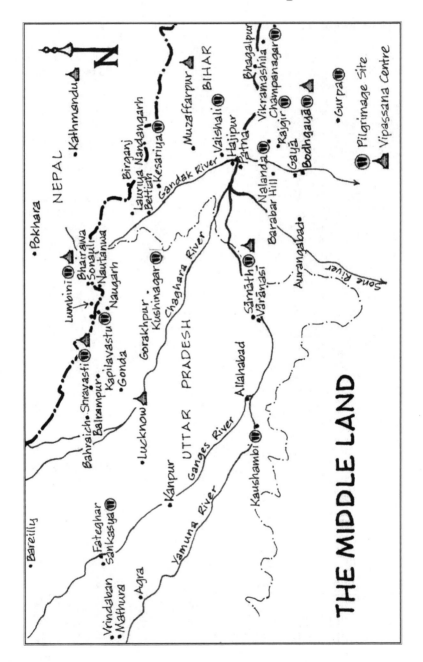

While 800 meditators were sitting a 1-day course on the train from Mumbai to the Middle Land, Goenka-ji said:

This pilgrimage should not be taken as a blind rite or ritual—not by the present generation and not by future generations. There is no blind belief involved in this. It is a positive and wholesome meditation while we are moving...visiting all the important places of the Enlightened One. Seeing where he was born, where he became Enlightened, and where, throughout his life, he continued to guide people in Dhamma, we shall take advantage of the wonderful vibrations of this land, the wonderful land of India, the country of origin of pure Dhamma. May we all work seriously!

During the Buddha's time, India was known as the "Island of Rose-Apples" (*Jambudīpa*) and the area where the Buddha meditated, travelled, and taught was referred to as the Middle Land (*Majjhima Desa*), which roughly corresponds to the modern Indian states of Uttar Pradesh and Bihar, and the Terai lowlands of southern Nepal. Despite being one of India's most impoverished areas today, at one time the region was one of the greatest centres of human civilization. Not only was it home to some of India's most glorious empires, but it was also the spiritual nerve centre and birthplace of the Dhamma.

I've always been fairly skeptical about, well, everything. This means that, with only circumstantial evidence, I've been a little tentative about my acceptance of the idea that Dhamma vibrations (anti-craving, anti-aversion, anti-ignorance) truly exist and have an effect. But on this trip I've definitely experienced distinct differences in meditation and the general atmosphere at the Buddha places, as opposed to other parts of India or at home. My awareness has often been better, and meditation has sometimes been more difficult but ultimately more fruitful. So, I'm more confident in saying that Dhamma vibrations are real and can have a strong effect. The tradition says that this kind of incremental acceptance is perfectly fine, because as much as you experience directly, that much you should accept. No dogma.

– Peter Buchanan

The concept of pilgrimage started in the Mahāparinibbāna Sutta where Buddha mentioned the four places a devotee should visit: the place where he was born [Lumbinī], the place where he got Enlightenment [Bodhgayā], the place where he first taught the Dhamma [Sārnāth], and then the place where he passed away [Kushinagar]. Referring to pilgrimage, the Buddha used the word cetiya-carika, travelling to a cetiya, a pagoda. A cetiya, pagoda, or thūpa, is said to be prepared so that a devotee could have a place to visit and pay respect. But, I feel that a cetiya is also a place where a person goes to apply his consciousness to Dhamma. He doesn't merely prostrate there, but meditates there. When one meditates at a cetiya he acquires wonderful merit, and this becomes a guiding force for him to travel on the path of spirituality.

In addition to the four places which Buddha mentioned, four more places were later added by the Pāli commentators to the list [Shravasti, Rajgir, Sankasya, and Vaishali]. So, from four it became eight, and, with time, pilgrims began visiting the entire area of Magadha, also called the Middle Land, Majjhima Desa. The whole process of pilgrimage became bigger and bigger because pilgrims wanted to visit every place connected to the Buddha, to the Dhamma, and to the chief disciples like Sāriputta, Mahāmoggāllana, Mahākassapa. By the seventh century when the Chinese pilgrim Xuan Zang arrived, there was a monastery every three kilometers! So people were coming—and continue to come—to earn merits and receive the Dhamma.

-                            – Dr. Ravindra Panth, Nava Nāḷandā Mahāvihāra

Lumbinī

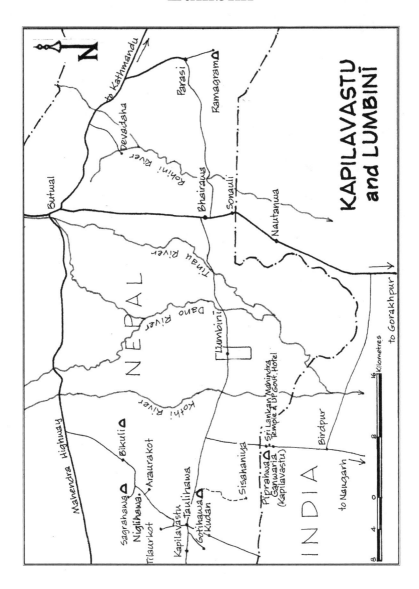

Birth of the Bodhisatta

"Let's stop for a rest over there," Queen Māyā said to one of her attendants, pointing to an inviting grove of sāla trees nearby. "All this traveling is making me exhausted and the horses must feel the same."

The journey from Kapilavatthu to her parents' home in Devadaha in the country of Koliya was long, and the hot summer sun wasn't making it any easier. The forest's fragrant flowers and warbling birds enticed the pregnant Queen, who was as beautiful as a rose and pure in mind as a lotus. Cooling off in the shade of a huge *sālā* tree, she remembered a dream she had had ten months before, in which a magnificent six-tusked white elephant holding a brilliant pink lotus flower in its trunk had entered her womb. While lost in her reverie, she was suddenly pulled back to the present moment by the most extraordinary labour sensations.

Astounded, yet totally at ease, she grabbed on to a low branch of the mighty tree. Her side began to widen and open, forming the most unusual birth canal. Quickly and painlessly, out came the most radiant being she had ever seen.[15]

And so it was on the full moon day of Vesākha (month of April-May) sometime between 623 BCE and 563 BCE[16] that Prince Siddhattha Gotama, the Buddha-to-be, was born in a forest grove in Lumbinī. When the baby was born, a great earthquake shook[17] and a magnificent light shone throughout the universe. At that moment the sick were cured, prisoners were freed, and peace prevailed everywhere. A shower of heavenly flowers and melodious celestial sounds rang through the air. Two jets of water, one cool, one warm, fell from the sky, bathing the mother and child, even though they had not been smeared by any blood or mucus. The miracle child took seven steps and proclaimed: "I am born for Enlightenment for the good of the world; this is my last birth in the world of phenomena."

Witnessing the great omens, a local sage named Asita went to the top of Mount Meru in the Tusita Heaven where there was a gathering of devas in a joyous mood. "Friends, what is the meaning of all this excitement? What wonderful thing has happened for all this rejoicing?" The merry devas answered,

In the village Lumbinī in the Sakyan country,
A great being, a precious jewel, set on Buddhahood
Has been born for the welfare and happiness of the world!

Because of that we are extravagantly gay.

The perfect being, the pinnacle of humanity, the lord of all creatures;
With the roar of a lion, the monarch of all beasts,
Will turn the Wheel of Truth in the Grove of the Ancient Seers.[18]

On the same day of the Bodhisatta's birth, a few others were born who would later play major roles in the future Buddha's life: Ānanda, Siddhattha's cousin and future attendant of twenty-five years; Devadatta, his cousin and rival; Channa, the charioteer who explained to the prince the meaning of the Four Great Signs and who helped him escape from the palace on the eve of his Great Renunciation; and Kanthaka, his horse;

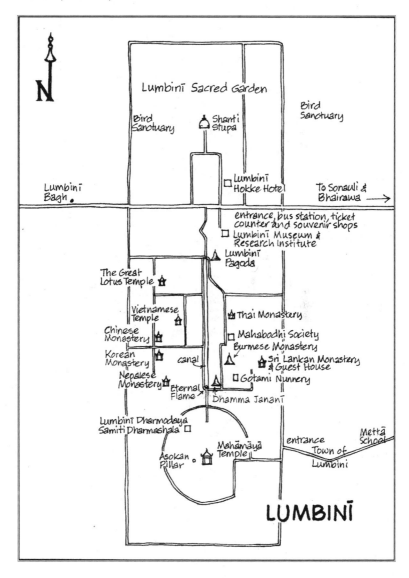

Site-Sitting

A nice way to spend your days in Lumbinī is to go temple-hopping by foot, bike or rickshaw. The sacred garden is a peaceful haven, free from the noise and commotion at other religious sites in India and Nepal. The atmosphere, as S.N. Goenka says, is "charged with the vibrations of purity, the vibrations of the Himālaya." Innumerable beings have been meditating in the place where the Bodhisatta took his last birth. Go and take part!

Lumbinī Sacred Garden

The **Mahāmāyā Temple** is said to have been built over the exact spot where Siddhattha was born, which, according to the Nepal Department of Archaeology, is the encased stone slab with a semblance of a rather large baby's footprint on it. The marker stone predates Asoka's visit to Lumbinī, but archaeologists tell us that the platform that it rests on was placed by the great emperor in the 3rd centure BCE. Above the stone is a damaged nativity sculpture from the 4th century CE depicting Queen Māyā holding a branch of the *sālā* tree just after giving birth to Siddhattha, who is standing upright on a lotus pedestal. Her sister Mahāpajāpatī is supporting her while the gods Brahma and Indra bestow blessings. For centuries, locals have worshipped, and continue to worship, this statue as Mahādevi, a Hindu goddess. Surrounding the Mahāmāyā Temple are ruins of temples, monasteries, and votive stūpas, which sprang up just after King Asoka and lasted until the 10th century. The monuments are decorated with butter-lamps and sticks of incense—outward signs of pilgrims' devotion.

Lumbinī's oldest and most important monument is the **Asokan pillar**, which was erected 20 years after Asoka's coronation. The pillar's Brahmi inscription marks this site as the Buddha's birthplace. Although the crown is no longer present, Xuan Zang (7th century) tells us that the pillar was crowned with a horse—a symbol of nobility, and perhaps representing Kantaka, Siddhattha's companion. In the 14th century, the Nepalese prince Ripu Malla engraved the Tibetan mantra *Om mani padme hum*—'Praise to the Jewel in the Lotus' (i.e., the Dhamma). Re-discovered in 1896 by the German archaeologist Dr. Führer, the pillar confirmed Lumbinī's location, which had been forgotten for more than 700 years. When the weather is right, meditating on the lawn by the pillar can be very pleasant, as the silence is broken only by the Tibetan prayer flags flickering in the wind, or a group of pilgrims arriving to worship. Twenty paces from the pillar is the spring fed rectangular **pond** where Queen Māyā is said to have bathed before giving birth to Siddhattha. In 1939 the pond was remodelled with the brick embankment seen today.

The sacred garden is also an ideal place to reflect on the vast empathy the Bodhisatta developed life after life, experiencing the world from every possible angle and practising selflessness by giving away his material possessions, by generating forgiveness and compassion, and even by forfeiting his own life. Whether he was a king, a merchant, a farmer, a rabbit or a monkey, the Bodhisatta strove towards perfection all alone, without the support of the Dhamma teachings or the company of a Saṅgha. Only after his life as King Vessantara, in which he equanimously gave up his wealth and family, was he prepared for his very last birth in this garden.

While King Asoka exempted pilgrims from all religious taxes, the current administration does not. Pilgrims are required to pay an entrance fee, but fortunately the entry ticket is valid for three days. The sacred garden is open from dusk until dawn.

Dhamma Jananī, Lumbinī Vipassana Centre

Amidst fantastic temples and lush gardens is this humble, yet very strong, Vipassana meditation centre. Everyone who sits at Dhamma Jananī ('Birthplace of Dhamma') raves about how great the quiet, 3-acre centre is for its support in the process of eliminating deep-rooted *saṅkhāra*.

Dhamma Jananī is located on the first property after the eternal peace flame in the Theravāda monastic zone. Ten-day courses are offered every month from the 15th to the 26th, and old-students who have completed at least three 10-day courses are always welcome to come for self-courses. With the Burmese Temple and Gotami Nunnery as the centre's sole neighbours, the only external sounds are those of sympathetic Buddhist pilgrims.

To get to the centre, cycle rickshaws are available from the bus stand just outside the gateway to the Lumbinī Zone; otherwise it's a 20-minute walk to the centre.

Contact:
Dhamma Jananī, Lumbinī Vipassana Centre
near Lumbinī Peace Flame, Rupandehi
Lumbinī Zone, Nepal
Tel: [+977] (0)71-580282, [977] 98069-95464, and [977] 97470-11497
E-mail: info@janani.dhamma.org
Website: www.janani.dhamma.org

Modern Temples & Monasteries
As in most of the sacred places in the Middle Land, more than forty temples from every Buddhist country have been built in recent decades to honour the Buddha, Dhamma and Saṅgha. The first modern temple, located just opposite the Mahāmāyā Temple, was established by the Nepalese Theravāda community in 1956. The construction of this temple marked the beginning of Lumbinī as a pilgrimage site, transforming the village from a jungle thicket into a beautiful garden worthy of its sanctity. The temple is worth visiting for its historical importance, as well as its artistically carved woodwork in the doorways and window frames, beautiful statues donated from many Asian countries, colourful murals depicting the Law of Dependent Origination, scenes from the Buddha's life and an interesting caption of the major Hindu gods welcoming the Buddha.

At the end of the 2 km-long canal and tree-lined avenue that begins at the eternal peace flame, stands the immense Japanese Shanti Stūpa containing Buddha relics, making it a great place for meditation. On a clear day this tranquil stūpa, surrounded by a crane sanctuary, has a fine view of the distant Himālayan Annapurna mountain range.

Museum & Research Institute
The Research Institute has a dusty collection of Dhamma literature, and the museum contains artefacts found in the area and photographs of other places connected with the Buddha's life and teaching. They're both open from 10:00 a.m. to 4:00 p.m. every day except Mondays.

Sleeping & Eating

Most of the monasteries in the 10 km² forested Lumbinī Peace Zone offer room and board to pilgrims. The newer establishments (2-3 km from the Sacred Garden) such as the **Nepalese Mahayana Monastery**, the **Korean Monastery**, the **Sri Lankan Monastery & Guest House**, the **Mahābodhi Society**, and the **Thai Monastery** tend to be a bit more comfortable than some of the older institutions, although they also suffer from mosquito infestation and sporadic electricity. The **Shanti Guest House** in Mahiliwar, on the outskirts of Lumbinī, offers simple, yet comfortable rooms on a donation basis to meditators. Biraj Singh, the owner, also runs a tea stall, a delicious home-style vegetarian restaurant, and souvenir stand near the Lumbini Sacred Garden. If you want to be closer to the Sacred Garden and Vipassana centre, it's best to stay either at the **Lumbini Dharmodaya Samiti Dharmashala** next to the Sacred Garden or at the **Gotami Nunnery** (open to men as well) across from Dhamma Jananī. The **Burmese Monastery** is first class. If you want to stay there and are a not a Myanmar citizen, however, then you need to get written permission in advance from the Myanmar embassy in Kathmandu. There are also a few budget hotels just before the main entrance to the 'Peace Zone,' but these are far less appealing as they're in the noisy market area. The luxurious and expensive **Lumbini Hokke Hotel** is near the Japanese Stūpa. If food is not available where you are staying, you can get a bite to eat at one of the restaurants or local food stalls (*dhabas*) around the parking lot of the Sacred Garden.

Pilgrims who only have time for a one-day visit to Lumbinī and want to get an early start back to India the next morning, often end up spending the night in an unattractive hotel in Sonauli, the noisy border town. This is usually unnecessary. Lumbinī is close enough to the border and it's easy to catch an early 45-minute bus ride or 30-minute taxi to Sonauli or Bhairawa, which is just a 10-minute drive from Sonauli. If you're in a situation where you absolutely need to spend the night in Sonauli, the Nepalese side of the border is slightly less noisy than the Indian side.

Coming & Going

To get to Lumbinī from India, go to the Sonauli border crossing via Vārāṇasī (413 km, 9 hours by bus, 6 hours by taxi) or Gorakhpur (123 km, 3 hours by bus or 2 hours by private/shared jeep-taxi). **Buses** from Gorakhpur leave about every half hour. Shared **jeep-taxis** leave from the train station in the morning. Whichever vehicle you take, you'll get dropped off 1 km before the border. If you have lots of luggage or are feeling too tired to walk, **rickshaws** will help relieve you of your burden.

Once at the border, non-Indian citizens need to 'check-out' at the Indian Immigration booth about 100 m before the border and then 'check-in' at the Nepalese Immigration booth immediately after the archway. The border is open 24 hours, but you may need to wake someone up if you arrive in the middle of the night. Fifteen-day multiple-entry Nepalese visas can be bought at the border for $US 25, 30-day visas for $40, and 90-day visas for $100 (US cash only, no rupees), with a passport-size photo. Three-day pilgrim visas are free only for members of the South Asian Association for Regional Cooperation.

Once you have your visa and stamps, you can catch one of the old beat-up Japanese mini-buses or a shared jeep to the Siddhartha Bus Stand in Bhairawa 10 minutes away (they leave every ten minutes from the end of the strip of shops and restaurants). Then get on the next **bus** to Lumbinī (27 km), which takes about one hour. Alternately, you can hire one of these **jeeps** to take you all the way to Lumbinī. For those who prefer to travel by **air**, irregular flights also fly to Bhairawa from Kathmandu and Vārāṇasī. The airport is 13 km from town.

Excursions

Rohinī River

During the Buddha's life, the Rohinī River divided the Sakyan and Koliyan territories. One hot and rainless summer, many of the crops began to shrivel up. Farmers from both republics wanted to divert the river's flow to provide enough water for their crops. However, it became apparent that there wouldn't be enough for everyone. Bitterness developed, leading to insults, then punches, and eventually to the brink of war, by which point most of the people holding weapons didn't even know why they were risking their lives.

Fortunately, the Buddha arrived at the scene and prevented what was to be massive bloodshed. When both armies saw him, they immediately threw down their weapons and reverently bowed down to their great kinsman. With utter compassion, he scolded them: "Human life is infinitely more valuable than a little bit of water! Give up your greed and hatred, and live with brotherly love and contentment." The Buddha continued:

It is a blessing to live among those who hate,
And not hate anyone;
Let us live among those who hate,
And be without hatred.

It is a blessing to live among those who are ailing,
And be without ailments;
Let us live among those who are ailing,
And be without ailments.

It is a blessing to live among those who are yearning
for sensual pleasures,
And not be yearning for such things;

*Let us live among those who are yearning for sensual pleasures,
And be without yearning.*

With their heads hung low in shame, both armies fell into a guilty silence and went home. Shortly after, 250 young men from each side became *bhikkhus*, and eventually attained full liberation.[19]

The Rohinī is the second river east of Bhairawa on the road to Parasi, but the exact location of this dramatic event has not been identified. If time permits, go and sit on the Rohinī's sandy bank and contemplate the Buddha's love for his clansmen and his courageous efforts to prevent war and promote peace, friendship and reconciliation.

Nepalese Kapilavatthu & Surrounding Areas

The capital of the Sakyans and the home of Prince Siddhattha is a peaceful place to visit, as described in the next section.

Kapilavastu (*Kapilavatthu*)

Prince Siddhattha's First 29 Years

After the extraordinary birth, Queen Māyā and her newborn returned home to her husband, King Suddhodana, in Kapilavatthu. Delighted beyond words, the beaming king's love for his little prince was boundless.

The sage Asita went to the palace to inspect the boy, who shined like a polished gold coin. Āsita was famed not only for his spiritual knowledge, but also for his skill in interpreting signs. Examining the baby's glowing and beautiful body, Āsita immediately recognized the 32 special marks of a great man (*mahāpurisa*): level-treaded feet; wheel marks with a thousand spokes on the soles of the feet; projecting heels; long fingers and toes; soft and tender hands and feet; net-like hands and feet; arched feet; antelope limbs; hands that can reach to the knees without bending; male organs enclosed in a sheath; golden complexion; delicate skin; one hair from every pore; body hairs growing upwards; upright limbs; seven convex surfaces; lion chest; full shoulders; height is the length of his arms; well-rounded bust; superior delicacy of taste; lion jaw; forty teeth; even teeth; teeth without gaps; very white teeth; very long tongue; Brahma-like voice similar to a *karavika* bird; deep blue eyes; cow-like eye lashes; white tuft between the eyebrows and protuberance on the crown of the head like a royal turban.[20]

Seeing these special marks on the child, Āsita first expressed overwhelming joy, followed by a great show of lamentation. Alarmed at the sage's tears, the parents asked, "Is our baby in danger?"

"No," he answered, calming their worries. "This child will never be harmed. My happiness came at seeing that a great being has descended upon the earth and will bring salvation to the suffering world. My grief, however, comes from knowing that I will not live to see the day when the child's latent abilities come forth. Your boy is destined for supreme greatness: either as a universal monarch (*cakkavatin*) or as a spiritual saviour of humankind!"

When the royal parents heard the sage's prediction, although they felt pity at Āsita's dilemma, their hearts rejoiced. Five days later, the court priests performed the boy's name-giving ceremony. Measuring their astrological calculations, they proudly declared the infant's name: Siddhattha—he who accomplishes his goal.

All the priests, hoping to get a fine reward, professed that the boy will someday become the greatest king of all time. Kondañña, however,

one of the court priests who would later become the first disciple of
the Buddha to attain emancipation in Sārnāth, warned the king, "If
the boy ever comes in contact with human suffering, his compassion
will lead him to abandon the princely life and embark on a quest for
spiritual release. He will become the world's saviour, not its ruler."
The king did not like these words. He wanted his son to be a ruler,
not a monk. He convinced himself that Kondañña's prophecy must
surely be mistaken. Clinging to this hope, King Suddhodana forgot
about the wise priest's words.

Seven days after Siddhattha's birth, Queen Māyā died unexpectedly.[21] Mahāpajāpatī, the queen's younger sister, became both the
new queen and Siddhattha's foster mother—nurturing and nursing
the infant as if he were her own. As the boy grew up, he rarely took
part in the childish games and pranks common for his age. Rather,
the young Siddhattha preferred wandering alone in the royal gardens
and contemplating the wonders of nature under large trees. Watching this unfold, King Suddhodana became nervous and feared that
Kondañña's prophecy might come true. Determined to shield his son
from any contact with the sufferings of the outside world, Suddhodana tried his best to divert Siddhattha's attention to worldly pleasures. He built three pleasure palaces for Siddhattha, one for each
Indian season: winter, summer and monsoon. Siddhattha lived out
his entire youth in these palaces, where he quickly gained proficien-
cy in all the arts of the day—intellectual, military and artistic. He
wore the finest garments, ate the choicest foods, was entertained by
the most talented minstrels and enjoyed a large company of concu-
bines. At the age of sixteen he married the beautiful Koliyan princess
Yasodharā. Throughout his youth Siddhattha lived a life of luxury
and ease, sheltered from witnessing disease, old age, death, or any
form of suffering.

In his twenties, Siddhattha grew discontented with his pleasure palaces and set his heart on an excursion beyond the royal boundaries
to see what life was like outside. King Suddhodana, thinking that his
son was tied to the worldly life for good, granted his son permission
to visit the outside world.

On four successive excursions outside the palace, accompanied by his
loyal attendant Channa, Siddhattha experienced the world in ways he
never expected. For the first time in his life, the prince encountered
the sight of an old person, a diseased person, a corpse, and finally a
radiantly serene mendicant. The first three sights shattered Siddhattha's sense of privilege. They forced him to acknowledge that such
painful and undignified conditions awaited him and Yasodharā—as
surely as they awaited all other creatures. Years later, he recounted to
a group of *bhikkhus*:

*Whilst I had such power and good fortune, yet I thought: "When
an untaught ordinary man, who is subject to ageing...to sickness...
to death, not safe from ageing...from sickness...from death, sees
another who is ageing...sick...dead, he is shocked, humiliated and
disgusted; for he forgets that he himself is no exception. But I too
am subject to ageing...to sickness...to death, not safe from ageing...
from sickness...from death, and so it cannot befit me to be shocked,
humiliated and disgusted on seeing another who is aged...sick...
dead." When I considered this, the vanity of youth...health...and
life entirely left me.*

The fourth sight, the encounter with the holy wanderer, sowed a seed
in Siddhattha's mind: the only way to find an end to suffering was
to abandon the householder's life and become a wandering ascetic of the forest. The final incident that seems to have concretized
Siddhattha's decision to leave his family was the birth of his son
Rāhula, whose name literally means 'fetter.' Although he had immense love for the baby, Siddhattha believed his son would shackle
him to a way of life that would prevent him from finding the truth.
Siddhattha was convinced that it was his attachment to things and
people that bound him to an existence of pain and sorrow. Thus, on
the full moon of *Āsāḷha*, at the age of 29, Siddhattha, with tears in his
eyes and a heavy heart, secretly left his family and took to the road,
vowing only to return after successfully completing his quest—total
freedom. This mission, or Great Renunciation (*Mahābhinikkamana*),
was not one of escape, but of compassion: Siddhattha believed that
if he could solve the riddles of misery, he could then share the liberating solutions with all of humanity. With this in mind he snuck
out of the palace with the help of Channa and his horse Kanthaka.
Once he was at a safe distance from the city limits, Siddhattha cut
his wavy black hair, switched his fine royal clothes for the simple
earth-coloured robes of a wanderer, and headed for the forest alone.[22]

The Buddha's Return to the Sakyans

Within the first year of Siddhattha's Awakening, his name was famous all over the Middle Land. King Suddhodana had not seen his
son for seven years and sent word requesting that he return. Knowing
that his father longed to see him, Siddhattha—the Buddha—agreed
to return to his homeland.

"There he is!" Suddhodana rejoiced as he saw his son walking in the
distance with a retinue of enlightened disciples. The king jumped
onto his horse and rode out to meet him. As he got closer to his son,
he was able to recognize certain physical features, but even before
uttering a word he felt an incredible distance between them, for this
noble sage was no longer his little prince, but a great sage. He gazed
into Siddhattha's clear eyes feeling as happy as the day his son was

born, yet at the same time he felt sad: his last hopes that Siddhattha would ascend the throne were shattered. The Buddha broke the
silence: "I know the king's heart is full of love and that for his son's
sake, he feels deep regret. But let these ties of love that bind him to
his son be spread out with equal kindness to all his fellow beings.
Doing this, he will receive something much greater than his son, as
the peace of liberation will enter his heart."

Knowing his son spoke the truth, he clasped his hands in reverence
and left his son to rest in the park after his long journey.

The next morning, the king
prepared a huge feast, assuming that his son and the other
monks would come to the palace for their meal. However,
the king did not specifically invite them to come, so the *bhikkhus* went on their usual alms
rounds in the streets. When
the king heard of this, he was
ashamed and ran out to his son.
"Why do you disgrace me like
this? It is not the custom of our
royal Sakyan lineage to beg in
the streets for food," he said
scornfully.

"But father, that is your lineage," the Buddha calmly replied. "I am
from the lineage of Buddhas, and begging for food is our custom."
Allowing his father to digest this striking statement, the Buddha continued in verse,

Awake! Be not heedless.
Practise the Dhamma scrupulously.
He who embarks upon the path of Truth,
Lives happily in this world and the next.

Practise the Dhamma that is wholesome.
Abstain from what is unwholesome.
One who practises the Dhamma,
Lives happily in this world and the next.

Hearing these sagely words, Suddhodana trembled with joy, realizing
the benefits of his son's renunciation, thus becoming a *sotāpanna.* [23]

The Buddha then went with Suddhodana to visit the rest of the family. Entering the front gate, all his relatives came rushing out to greet
him except Yasodharā. She still felt terrible grief from his having left

her and could not bear to see him. After being reunited with all his close relatives, the Buddha, accompanied by Sāriputta, went up to Yasodharā's room where they found her on the floor weeping. From the time Siddhattha left to live the life of a recluse, Yasodharā painfully gave her husband her wholehearted support, even though it was impossible for her to be with Siddhattha during his struggles.

With kind eyes, the Buddha said to her, "Only someone with great virtue was able to play your role in the awakening of Buddhahood. For countless lives you have been assisting me in my quest. Without your purity and devotion, my mission would never have been accomplished. You are weeping now, but have trust in me; your noble attitude will be a soothing balm to transform your sorrow to joy." Yasodharā understood the Buddha's words, stopped crying, and bowed down to him in reverence.

Later, while the Buddha was sitting with the king telling him about his adventure, Yasodharā and Rāhula were standing by the upstairs bedroom window. Pointing at the Buddha, she said, "Do you see that holy man in the earth-coloured robes with your grandfather?" Rāhula nodded.

"He is your father. Go and ask him for your inheritance." Rāhula ran downstairs to the Buddha. Without any fear or hesitation, he affectionately looked up to the Buddha's face and said, "Father!"

The Buddha looked at him with loving eyes and stroked the boy's head. Saying nothing, the Buddha smiled, took the boy's hand, and left the palace. The contented little Rāhula walked with him in silence all the way to where the *bhikkhus* were camped. The child broke the silence and asked, "Father, my mother said I should ask you for my inheritance. Can you show it to me?"

Beaming with love, the Buddha turned to Sāriputta who was standing nearby, "My son wants his inheritance, please give it to him." Understanding his teacher's words, Sāriputta shaved the boy's head, dressed him in a robe made from rags, and then ordained him as a novice monk (*sāmaṇera*). After eleven years of practising the Dhamma, Rāhula became an *arahant*.

When the news of Rāhula's ordination spread to the palace, King Suddhodana was deeply wounded. First he had lost his son Siddhattha, who in turn influenced his half-brother Nanda, as well as several Sakyan cousins. Now, he had lost his grandson and final heir to the throne. He went to the Buddha and requested that children should only be admitted into the order with the consent of their parents. The Buddha comforted the distressed king by speaking about the truths of *anicca* and *anattā*, and explained that the life of a *bhikkhu* is highly beneficial for realizing these truths. Nonetheless, the Buddha agreed with his father's request.[24]

The Kapilavatthu Debate

Since the mid-19ᵗʰ century, Orientalist scholars have debated the location of Kapilavatthu. Most Nepalese believe it to be 32 km north-west of Lumbinī in Tilaurakot, where the ruins of a palace stand. Most Indians, on the other hand, think that Kapilavatthu is in India at the collection of ruins in the villages of Ganwaria and Piprawaha, south-west of Lumbinī. In the late 19ᵗʰ century William Peppe, a British landlord, found two caskets containing gold ornaments and fragments of charred bones of the Buddha in a stūpa at the Indian ruins (the relics are now in the National Museum in New Delhi), and in the 1970s some seals were unearthed here bearing the inscriptions "*Kapilavastu*" and "*Kapilavatthu Bhikkhu Saṅgha*."

The two Kapilavatthus are only 50 km apart, but each nation stands to win a good deal in having its claim verified, especially with all the religious tourism it might eventually bring. It's worthwhile for pilgrims to visit and meditate in both sites: both could plausibly be related to the Sakyan capital.

Nepalese Kapilavatthu & Surrounding Sites: Site-Sitting

Pilgrims visiting the following places will see nothing more than an area of brick ruins associated with the Sakyan kingdom. But, these rarely visited and picturesque places surrounded by forests, farms, and traditional village hamlets (probably not too different from those of the Buddha's time) are worth the trip.

Taulihawa

It's claimed that this town is the area where King Suddhodana met Siddhattha for the first time after his son's enlightenment. After their conversation, the king began to comprehend the depths of the Buddha's teaching and became a *sotāpanna*. There is no marker identifying the location of this historic event.

Tilaurakot

The once flourishing city of Kapilavatthu is now little more than a pile of brick remnants said by local guides to be those of the royal palace in which young Siddhattha grew up. These bricks, however, date mostly from the Kusana period (2ⁿᵈ century BCE to 3ʳᵈ century CE), although some pottery has been found dating back to the 7th century BCE. The present ruins may have been commemorative buildings rather than original Sakyan structures. The ruin of the palace's east gate is a terrific spot to meditate and reflect on the enormity of Siddhattha's great renunciation (see p.99-101).

Three stūpas whose layers date from the 4th century BCE to the 1st century BCE can be found beyond the east gate. To get to them you will need to either hop the park's fence or climb under where there is a large enough opening; otherwise you will need to drive from the archeological park's entrance, but this is quite a long detour. The first monument, which is visible from the east gate ruins, is referred to as the Kanthaka Stūpa. This grassy knoll is said to mark the spot where Siddhattha's horse, Kanthaka, died upon returning to the palace without his master who had just renounced the world. The other stūpas, in the village of Dhamnihawa, are believed to have been built over the mortal remains of King Suddhodana and Queen Māyā. Once you have gotten beyond the fence then walk north (to your left) along the narrow road for about ten minutes. After you pass a small Hindu temple with a Buddha statue and an elephant statue on your right, you will soon come to the two stūpas on your left.

Niglihawa
Niglihawa is believed to be the place of birth and enlightenment of the Buddha Koṇāgamana (*Kanakamuni*, in Sanskrit), the second Buddha of this era. On the west bank of the village water tank are two broken pieces of an Asokan pillar. Its Brahmi inscription also mentions a stūpa, but no traces of it are found today. The pillar was later inscribed with a Tibetan mantra and images of cranes—ancient forms of graffiti! It's possible that the pillar was moved from its original location.

> *Glory to Kakusandha,*
> *Victory over Māra's army.*
> *Glory to Koṇāgamana,*
> *The complete and perfect Brahmin.*
> *Glory to Kassapa,*
> *Liberated in every way.*
> *Glory to the Sakya's radiant son,*
> *Teacher of the Dhamma*
> *That transcends all dissatisfaction.*
> *And all those who are free from this world,*
> *Seeing to the heart of things,*
> *They who are gentle in speech,*
> *Filled with might and wisdom.*
> *To the one who assists both gods and men,*
> *Praise to Gotama,*
> *Trained in wisdom and conduct,*
> *Mighty and resourceful too.*
>
> *- Āṭānāṭiya Sutta*[25]

Aurorakat

Aurorakot is said to be the place where Buddha Koṇāgamana grew up as a child. Today we can see parts of the palace's ancient rectangular fortification wall, protecting contemporary cricket players and goat herders.

Sagarhawa

Wishing to marry into the clan of the Sakyans, King Pasenadi of Kosala sent some emissaries to Kapilavatthu with a request for the hand of one of the Sakyan princesses. The Sakyans were repulsed by the idea of inter-caste marriage; however, they did not want to offend King Pasenadi either, as his kingdom was becoming increasingly powerful. So, the Sakyan princes sent a slave-girl posing as a princess to marry the Kosalan king. Very pleased with his gorgeous new wife, King Pasenadi made her one of his chief queens and soon after she gave birth to a son, Viṭaṭūbha. While growing up, the prince wanted very much to visit his mother's homeland, but was never given permission in fear that he would find out the truth. When the prince was 16 years old, he refused to take no for an answer.

Arriving at the Sakyan palace, Viṭaṭūbha was received with hospitality. However, the Sakyan elders hid all the Sakyan princes who were younger than Viṭaṭūbha so that they would not have to bow down to someone royally unworthy. Viṭaṭūbha enjoyed his visit and the Sakyan elders were pleased with their cunning. While Viṭaṭūbha and his entourage were on their way home, they stopped in a village just on the inside of the Sakyan border. One of Viṭaṭūbha's guardians overheard a servant talking about Viṭaṭūbha's true mother. When the prince was told the truth, he went into a rage and vowed that one day he would kill the entire Sakyan clan.

A few years later, Viṭaṭūbha became king and immediately waged war on the Sakyans. The Buddha was able to cool down the fuming king on three separate occasions, but eventually Viṭaṭūbha's anger was so deep that not even the Buddha was able to talk him out of it.

Surrounded by his powerful army, the king marched into the Sakyan territory and massacred almost the entire clan. On their way home, Viṭaṭūbha and his army camped on the bank of the Aciravati River. That night, a heavy rain fell and caused a great flood, drowning them all.

Hearing about these two tragic incidents, the Buddha explained to the *bhikkhus* that the Sakyan princes were collectively paying back a karmic debt from a previous existence when they had intentionally poisoned a neighbour's river to kill all the fish. Then, referring to the fate of Viṭaṭūbha and his army, the Buddha said, "Just as a great flood sweeps away all the villagers in a sleeping village; death carries away all the creatures hankering after sensual pleasures."[26]

King Asoka placed a pillar here in memory of the catastrophic event but it is no longer seen today. Now there is a rectangular tank known as Lambusagar that is said to mark the spot of the massacre. Be aware that there is no sign marking this site.

Bikuli

A stūpa in this nearby village marks the spot where the seven-year-old Siddhattha meditated for the first time during his father's ploughing ceremony. While his father was performing the annual farming ritual in the scorching heat, the Bodhisatta found refuge under the cool shade of a rose-apple tree and naturally began observing the flow of his breath, leading him into the first *jhāna*.

Nigrodha's Park (*Nigrodhārāma*), Kudan

During his first visit back to his homeland, the Buddha and the community of *bhikkhus* spent nearly six months in Kapilavatthu. News of the prince's return spread rapidly throughout the country, confirmed by the large number of serene disciples begging every morning for their food. Most of the Sakyan people were inspired by the *bhikkhus*' presence and eager to learn the Dhamma. The great Nigrodhārāma Monastery was established and 500 young Sakyan men, inspired by their clansman's teachings, renounced the worldly life and donned the earth-coloured robes.

One day, the Sakyan prince Mahanama visited the Buddha and asked him, "Venerable sir, how does one practice as lay disciple?"

"Mahanama, if a person takes refuge in the Buddha, Dhamma, and Sangha, then Mahanama, he is a lay disciple," replied the Buddha.

"Then, Venerable sir, how does a lay disciple practice virtue?"

"If a lay disciple abstains from harming living beings, abstains from stealing, abstains from sexual misconduct, abstains from wrong speech, and abstains from intoxicants that causes heedlessness, then Mahanama, a lay disciple practices virtue."

"Then, Venerable sir, how is a lay disciple engaged only in his own welfare, but not in the welfare of others?"

"Mahanama, if a lay disciple possesses faith and virtue, but does not rouse faith and virtue in others, then he is engaged only in his own welfare, not in the welfare of others. If a lay disciple desires and enjoys discussions with other meditators, but does not rouse this desire and enjoyment in others, then he is engaged only in his own welfare, not in the welfare of others. If a lay disciple desires and enjoys receiving Dhamma instructions, but does not rouse this desire and enjoyment in others, then he is engaged only in his own welfare, not in the welfare of others. If a lay disciple mindfully practices the Dhamma, but does not rouse others to mindfully practice the Dhamma, then he is engaged only in his own welfare, not in the welfare of others. If a lay disciple understands the Dhamma's meaning and benefits, but does not rouse others to understand the Dhamma's meaning and benefits, then he is engaged only in his own welfare, not in the welfare of others."

"Then, Venerable sir, how is a lay disciple engaged in both his own welfare and in the welfare of others?"

"Mahanama, if a lay disciple possesses faith and virtue and rouses faith and virtue in others then he is engaged in both his own welfare and in the welfare of others. If a lay disciple desires and enjoys discussions with other meditators and rouses this desire and enjoyment in others, then he is engaged in both his own welfare and in the welfare of others. If a lay disciple desires and enjoys receiving Dhamma instructions and rouses this desire and enjoyment in others, then he is engaged in both his own welfare and in the welfare of others. If a lay disciple mindfully practices the Dhamma and rouses others to mindfully practice the Dhamma, then he is engaged in both his own welfare and in the welfare of others. If a lay disciple understands the Dhamma's meaning and benefits and rouses others to understand the Dhamma's meaning and benefits, then he is engaged in both his own welfare and in the welfare of others."

Mahanama understood these important lessons concerning practice and relationship with others. Soon enough, with dedicated mindfulness, he too awakened to the true Dhamma.[27]

One day, six of the Buddha's cousins—Bhaddiya, Anuruddha, Ānanda, Bhagu, Kimbila and Devadatta—set out to meet him set out to meet him at Nighrodha's Park.. They all desired to go forth into the homeless life because the householder's life now seemed unbearable to them. Upāli, the royal barber, travelled with them. Reaching the forest, the princes took off all their fancy jewelry and fine clothes and gave them to Upāli, saying, "Take all these things; you will get enough money from them for the rest of your life. We no longer have any need for them. We are all going to follow Siddhattha on the path of renunciation." Taking the bundle of expensive adornments, Upāli started thinking, "The Sakyans are a fierce and tempered people. When they see me with all these riches, they will think that I murdered the princes." Upāli threw the jewels and garments in a tree and caught up with the princes saying, "If the renunciate's life is fitting for my masters, it is certainly fitting for me!" They happily agreed and decided that Upāli should be ordained first; being his juniors, they would have to salute him, which would help dissolve their strong Sakyan egos.[28]

The Nigrodhārāma was also well known for being the location where little Rāhula, the Buddha's son, received his ordination and spent much of his formative years learning the Dhamma and discipline. It is also believed that this park was where Mahāpajāpatī, the Buddha's foster mother and aunt, offered her kin a robe, signifying her approval of Siddhattha's way of life. The two stūpas amongst the numerous mango and banyan trees that we see today are believed to commemorate these events.

Gotihawa

Early Theravāda commentaries explain that five Buddhas will arise in the present era. Siddhattha Gotama was the fourth and Mateyya (*Maitreya*, in Sanskrit) will be the fifth. Buddha Kakusandha (*Krakucchanda*, in Sanskrit) was the first. Locals claim that the village of Gotihawa was Buddha Kakusandha's birthplace. This information is based on a stump of an Asokan pillar that they say was erected in his honour. However, there is no inscription on the pillar or any other evidence to back this claim. There are some ruins of a stūpa near the village boundaries.

Rāmāgrāma Stūpa

Of the eight original stūpas that held the Buddha's relics after his *parinibbāna*, Ramagrama is the only one that King Asoka left untouched. Legend has it that when Asoka came to open the stūpa, a protective spirit (*nāga*) warned him not to, and the king humbly obeyed.

Devdaha

Devdaha was Queen Māyā's hometown and the capital of the Koliyan territory. Today, however, all you will see is a magnificently tall tree. Locals say that birds never make nests here.

Devdaha is best remembered as the place where the Buddha refuted the Nigaṇṭha (Jain) belief that whatever a person experiences, whether pleasant or unpleasant, is a result of some past deed. The Buddha taught that our present experiences may be connected to the past, but are also connected to the present.

According to the Nigaṇṭhas, the goal of the spiritual life is to purify the soul. To do this, the renunciate must follow a strict and painful ascetic regime that will burn away all past deeds and prevent the performance of any present karmic deeds. By exerting oneself in this way, no future consequences could possibly arise, suffering will come to an end, and the soul will be free.

The Buddha rejected this doctrine by explaining that since the intense pain felt by a Nigaṇṭha ascetic is only felt during the time of extreme austerities and not at other times, the painful experience is not a result of the past, but an association of the present.

The Buddha concluded his exposition encouraging his students to always be mindful of a middle path by neither allowing suffering to overwhelm them nor pleasures to infatuate them. All the meditators who heard the Buddha's clarification on action felt satisfied, delighted, and energized to strive correctly for liberation.[29]

Sleeping & Eating

Besides the few dingy rooms in Taulihawa, there aren't any obvious accommodation options in any of these areas. It's best to make a day-trip or two from Lumbinī. Bring your own food and have a picnic somewhere along the way to avoid spending your limited time and energy trying to find a decent restaurant and then waiting for your meal (which can take a while if the food is being freshly prepared).

Coming & Going

If you aren't already travelling with your own vehicle and you want to visit all or most of these places in one day then we suggest that you hire a **jeep** in Lumbinī or Bhairawa. If you cannot afford a jeep or you just feel like travelling on **buses** and don't necessarily care to soak in each and every site, you can catch a direct bus to Taulihawa from Lumbinī (27 km) or Bhairawa (50 km). Ask locals for bus timings as they're always changing. From Taulihawa, rent an **auto-rickshaw** to take you to Tilaurakot (6 km northwest), then Niglihawa (5 km further), then Gotihawa (15 km back south), and then Kudan (3 km east). You'll have to travel quickly to visit all the sites and catch a bus back to Lumbinī the same day. Some of these places are difficult to find. You may want to consider hiring a guide at the archeological park at Tilaurakot to accompany you to the various sites in the region.

To get to Rāmāgrāma from Lumbinī, take a bus to Bhairawa (22 km), another bus to Butwol (22 km), and then a bus to Parasi (29 km), where you can hire a jeep to take you to Rāmāgrāma (6 km). If you have your own vehicle and want to go to this rarely visited and very tranquil grass covered mound, go directly to Parasi from Bhairawa and then follow the signs to the stūpa. To get to Devadaha, go to Butwol and then take a bus or jeep to Devadaha (12 km).

After a Vipassana course in Kathmandu we stayed in Lumbinī for a week. Following an early-morning sitting at the pillar, we met our Nepalese friend Bisu who was coming from Dhamma Giri. "Hey, I'm going to visit Kapilavatthu, do you want to come along?" he asked. "Sure," we said, knowing very well that our planned day of rest would be replaced with an exhausting full-day trip (even though it's just 33 km).

We hopped onto the crowded bus, squatting at the front where seats should have been. The other passengers enjoyed ogling us; it's rare that foreigners visit these parts, especially dressed like locals. When we got to Taulihawa, Bisu borrowed a friend's bike and we got a cycle rickshaw to take us the few kilometres to Tilaurkot.

Greeting us at the ruins was a small girl of about seven or eight sucking on a ripe mango that had just fallen near her grandfather's hut, a makeshift frame of sticks covered with some old cloth, probably not too different from huts in the Buddha's time.

Although only partially unearthed, the ruins could plausibly have been a royal palace. Walking around in silence and sitting for a few minutes at the eastern gate where Siddhattha escaped in the middle of the night on his horse Kantaka, made the story come alive for us.

On our way back we were welcomed by Bisu's meditator friend who offered us refreshments, the comfort of his mud-brick cottage, and a meditation with his wife and nephew. We all appreciated the bonding power of the Dhamma.

After buying a bag full of ripe mangoes, we headed to the bus stand and saw that the last bus was full. Our local Dhamma brother arranged with the driver to let us ride on the roof, and so, with a spectacular sunset and fresh breeze after a scorching day, we headed back to Lumbinī, local style.

- MD & KG

Indian Kapilavatthu: Site-Sitting

Piprahwa

Piprahwa may have been the site of one of the monasteries where the Buddha and Saṅgha lived, meditated, and taught the Dhamma. The quiet and shady mango grove beside the ruins makes an excellent place for a picnic and meditation.

The most important monument here is the **Sakyan Stūpa**, which is made up of three layers built at different times; the first dates back to the 5th century BCE. Each layer contained a chamber-room that housed one or two relic caskets (five caskets were found altogether and the caskets and relics are now housed in the National Museum in New Delhi.). Today we only see the third layer. It is interesting to note that when the earliest stūpa was found, there was no indication of it having been opened. This suggests that the story about King Asoka opening seven of the eight original stūpas built to house the Buddha's relics (with the exception of Rāmāgāma) may not be entirely correct. Perhaps, as Venerable Dhammika suggests, he did not open this stūpa out of respect for the Sakyans.[30]

The other ruins consist of monasteries, a votive stūpa, and what was possibly a public hall. The ruin of a large **Eastern Monastery** was where a Kusana period (2nd century BCE to 3rd century CE) seal was found with the words "*Kapilavatthu Bhikkhu Saṅgha*," proving that this site was connected with the Buddha's hometown.

Ganwaria

Ganwaria is about one kilometre south of Piprahwa. It was probably the actual town of Kapilavatthu. Today, all we can see is a collection of ruins that may have been a monastery and some public buildings. The rest remains a mystery, as most of the structures were probably made of mud and timber and have gone back to the earth without a trace.

Sleeping & Eating

Although most people just visit for the day en route to Shravasti, pilgrims can sleep and eat at the **Sri Lankan Mahinda Temple**.

Coming & Going

To get to Indian Kapilavatthu, take a **train** or **bus** to the small town of Naugarh, and then another bus, **taxi**, or **auto-rickshaw** to Kapilavatthu. From Naugarh, you can catch a train to Balrampur or Jharkund (if going to Shravasti) or Gorakhpur (if going to Kushinagar). Ask a local for train timings. Those with limited time and a few extra rupees to spend can get a taxi from Sonauli (70 km), Gorakhpur (97 km) or Kushinagar (148 km) to Kapilavatthu, where you can spend a couple of hours exploring inside and out, and then continue onwards to Shravasti (147 km).

For those of you travelling by taxi it may seem tempting to avoid driving all the way to Sonauli to cross the border when there is a short-cut road between Lumbinī and the Indian Kapilavatthu that is hardly ever patrolled. If you do decide to go the faster way and do get caught by a border patrol on either side, expect to pay a hefty fine.

Bodhgayā (*Buddhagayā, Uruvelā*)

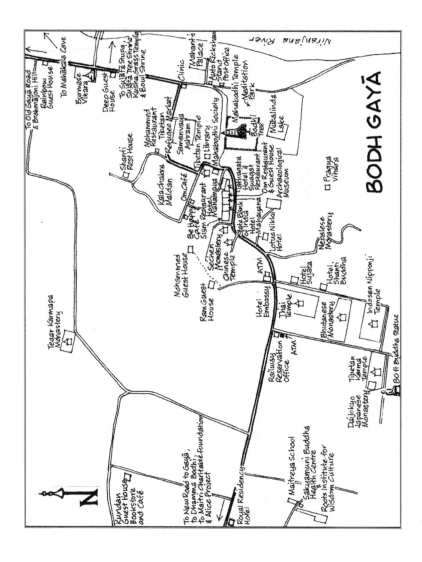

The Great Awakening

For six years Siddhattha wandered throughout the Indian plains in search of Truth. He explored the spiritual path with many ascetics, including Āḷāra Kālāma and Uddaka Rāmaputta, with whom he practiced the seventh and eighth jhānas, respectively. These deep absorption meditations made his mind calm and tranquil, but he was still not satisfied as he saw that latent defilements remained deep inside his mind. Siddhattha moved on in search of a better system, and came across a band of five ascetics near Uruvelā[31] who earlier had been wealthy residents of Kapilavatthu and who followed Siddhattha into the homeless life. The group were living austere lives by guarding their senses, subduing their passions, and practising severe mortifications of the body. Admiring their earnestness, the Bodhisatta joined them and quickly surpassed them all in the severity of his practices.

Years of self-torture had reduced Siddhattha's body to a battered skeleton, yet, total purification of the mind still seemed far away. He was tired, hungry, and on the verge of death. One afternoon, while bathing in the Nirañjanā River, Siddhattha collapsed from utter weakness. He slowly moved towards a tree branch leaning over the surface of the water and dragged himself towards the bank, where he collapsed again. He asked himself whether this extreme lifestyle actually led to liberation. The cool breeze gently caressing his skin felt good and eased his mind. He began to see the connection between mind and body.

The broken Siddhattha sat by the gently flowing river, which reminded him of his easy childhood days. He remembered the day he accompanied his father to the annual ploughing festival. The sun was

scorchingly hot and he sought refuge under the cool shade of a rose-apple tree, where he sat cross-legged. Young Siddhattha naturally began observing the flow of his breath and soon entered the first *jhāna*. Recalling how good he felt that day 28 years earlier, it occurred to him that perhaps the way to liberation was through natural, detached observation, and not through self-mortification.

Siddhattha decided it was time to take a new course of action, starting with regaining his health by eating food again. He went to a nearby shrine in the small village Senāni near Uruvelā and sat under a tree, figuring that sooner or later, someone was bound to come with an offering and perhaps give him some food. It was common practice then (and still is today) for people to worship at shrines in hopes of having their desires fulfilled. Indeed, a woman named Sujātā came with an offering of rice pudding (khīr), and offered it to Siddhattha, thinking that he was a tree deity. His lips quivered and his mouth and throat moistened from the sweet *khīr*; it had been so long since he had eaten anything so rich and nourishing. Slowly consuming the dish, he became confident that this was the right move on his journey. When his companions saw him eating food and speaking to a young woman, they abandoned him in disgust thinking that he had given up the struggle and reverted to a life of luxury.

Seeing them leave him so easily, Siddhattha felt sorry for their lack of confidence and misunderstanding. Re-energized by his new insights and with a renewed determination to accomplish his mission, Siddhattha did not worry about being alone. He walked along the clear-flowing Nirañjanā River[32] and placed his bowl on it, solemnly declaring, "If this bowl floats upstream, I will become enlightened." The bowl floated upstream.[33]

Following the smooth silver sand of the riverbank, he entered into a grove of trees. The inspired Bodhisatta spotted the awe-evoking Bodhi Tree that would soon shelter his monumental accomplishment. The moon was full and a soft breeze rustled the leaves in the forest.

Thousands of insects chirped, as if encouraging him in his quest. Siddhattha, bent on attaining his goal, sat down at the foot of the majestic tree and vowed to himself, "Here on this seat my body may shrivel up, my skin, my bones, my flesh may dissolve, but I will not move from this very seat until I attain enlightenment." He gently closed his eyes and turned his awareness inwards.

Māra, the enemy of truth, approached the Bodhisatta with his three beautiful daughters and an army of demons. He tried to instill fear by darkening the sky and raising vicious thunder and rainstorms. He commanded his army to attack the Bodhisatta with scenes of anger and hatred, and ordered his daughters to tempt him with lust. Fearless and without budging, Siddhattha remained calm, collected, and unperturbed. He knew nothing in the world could harm him. Real-

izing his defeat, Māra fled away in disgust. The dark clouds rolled back to reveal the bright moon and heavenly flowers fell from the sky in victory.

Fortified by lifetimes of *pāramī*, the Bodhisatta's mind gradually became finer and finer, travelling from extreme bliss to deep equanimity, never yielding to the pleasant feelings—he took each moment as it was.

During the first part of the night, Siddhattha gained the knowledge of all his past lives (*pubbenivāsānussati ñāṇa*). Through the middle part of the night, he acquired the knowledge of divine sight (*dibbacakkhu ñāṇa*). Siddhattha saw the lives of all beings of the universe and how they passed away and reappeared according to their actions. During the last part of the night, he developed the knowledge of the chain of cause and effect that conditions the universe (*paṭiccasamuppāda ñāṇa*). By his experience, he saw that whatever arises has a cause. If the cause is eradicated, then there is no resulting effect. By removing all the causes of suffering, suffering cannot arise. This simple yet profound realization enabled him to completely destroy the last traces of craving, aversion and ignorance. He joyfully uttered:

Aneka jāti saṃsāraṃ,
Sandhāvissaṃ anibbisaṃ;
Gahakāraṃ gavesanto,
Dukkhā jāti punappunaṃ.

Gahakāraka diṭṭhosi,
Puna gehaṃ na kāhasi;

Sabbā te phāsukā bhaggā,
Gahakūṭaṃ visaṅkhitaṃ;
Visaṅkhāragataṃ cittaṃ,
Taṇhānaṃ khayamajjhagā.

For countless births I travelled through this cycle,
Seeking in vain the builder of this house;
In my search over and over,
I took new birth, new suffering.

O house-builder, now I have seen you,
You cannot make a new house for me;
All your rafters are broken,
The ridgepole is shattered;
The mind is freed from all past conditionings,
And has no more craving for the future.

Free from the prison of ignorance that had confined him for countless lifetimes, the Buddha blissfully spent the next seven weeks in the vicinity of the Bodhi Tree enjoying the fruits of his attainment and reflecting on the implications of what he had discovered.[34]

While sitting under the Bodhi Tree, the Buddha understood that the ignorant mind—the mind that does not understand the universal traits of impermanence, suffering, and selflessness—is dependent on blind, habitual patterns of reaction. These reactions condition a flow of consciousness that operates in terms of mind and body, which is responsible for the six senses that allow a person to experience the outside world. This contact stimulates various sensations—pleasant, unpleasant or neutral. Reacting to one of these types of sensations brings about craving, aversion or ignorance. These negative attitudes linger on and eventually become deep-rooted attachments. These attachments push along the process of becoming, in which one's obsessive self-interests continue to develop and new personal self-images are born (in every moment of this life and in to the next). With birth, the sorrows and stresses of life arise, which then become another condition for ignorance, and the cycle continues.

The Buddha also analysed the chain in terms of cessation of its factors, showing how the entire world of suffering can be stopped. He realized that when the mind truly understands the way things are, its habitual reactions cease, and in turn, the flow of consciousness also ceases. When there is no flow of consciousness, there is no mind and body, and no senses with which to experience the world. Neither sensations nor the afflictive attitudes that result from the sensations continue to arise and impress themselves on the mind. The meditator is freed from all attachments.

Siddhattha recognized the link of sensation as the point at which to break the chain of suffering. When one understands how craving is conditioned by pleasant sensations, how aversion is conditioned by unpleasant sensations, and how ignorance is conditioned by neutral sensations, attachment cannot arise.

The Chain of Dependent Origination
(paṭicca-samuppāda)

With the base of ignorance (avijjā), reaction (saṅkhāra) arises;
with the base of reaction (saṅkhāra), consciousness (viññāṇa) arises;
with the base of consciousness (viññāṇa), mind and body (nāma-rūpa)
arises;
with the base of mind and body (nāma-rūpa), the six senses (saḷāyatana)
arise;
with the base of the six senses (saḷāyatana), contact (phassa) arises;
with the base of contact (phassa), sensation (vedanā) arises;
with the base of sensation (vedanā), craving (taṇhā) arises;
with the base of craving (taṇhā), attachment (upādāna) arises;
with the base of attachment (upādāna), process of becoming (bhava) arises;
with the base of the process of becoming (bhava), birth (jāti) arises;
with the base of birth (jāti), ageing (jarā) and death (maraṇa) arise, to-
gether with sorrow (soka), lamentation (paridev), physical pains and mental
anguish (dukkha-domanassupāyāsā).

Thus arises this entire mass of suffering (*evametassa kevalassa dukkhakkhadhassa samudayo hoti*).

By observing this process with equanimity, the mind stops reacting blindly to outside stimulation. A transformation in attitude then occurs, and the sensations no longer give rise to negative reactions; they lead instead to the wisdom of impermanence. All selfish intentions and accumulated mental conditionings are then dissolved, and nothing is left to reinforce the ego or push it in to another birth. In this way, old age, sickness, death, and all the other miseries of life cease to be causes of unhappiness, and only a sense of peace, love and happiness remains.

He pointed to a tree surrounded by a heavy, carved stone railing and a curious mixture of reverent pilgrims and gawking sightseers. We stood off to the side. I wondered if I was supposed to say anything. Nice tree. Big deal. Its bark was dry and blotchy, its limbs kind of droopy. Like an old, retired man whiling away his empty time on a park bench. I was ready to leave. Instead, we sat down on a flat stone surface in a corner of the courtyard. I noticed after a moment that Bill's eyes were closed and his hands folded loosely in his lap. I did the same.

Almost immediately, that new-found sensor, which for a lack of better understanding I referred to as my 'body,' came alive. I felt a surge of power flowing through me. My back straightened up and my head and shoulders pulled into line. I felt my chest drawn forward in the direction of that tree. An enormous calm enveloped me. All the noise

The Reverse Order of the Chain of Dependent Origination
(*paṭiloma-paṭicca-samuppāda*)

With the complete eradication and cessation of ignorance (avijjā), reaction (saṅkhāra) ceases;

with the cessation of reaction (saṅkhāra), consciousness (viññāṇa) ceases;

with the cessation of consciousness (viññāṇa), mind and body (nāma-rūpa) cease;

with the cessation of mind and body (nāma-rūpa), the six senses (saḷāyatana) cease;

with the cessation of the six senses (saḷāyatana), contact (phassa) ceases;

with the cessation of contact (phassa), sensation (vedanā) ceases;

with the cessation of sensation (vedanā), craving (taṇhā) ceases;

with the cessation of craving (taṇhā), attachment (upādāna) ceases;

with the cessation of attachment (upādāna), the process of becoming (bhava) ceases;

with the cessation of the process of becoming (bhava), birth (jāti) ceases;

with the cessation of birth (jāti), ageing (jarā) and death (maraṇa) cease, together with the sorrow (soka), lamentation (paridev), physical and mental suffering and tribulations (dukkha-domanassupāyāsā).

Thus the entire mass of suffering ceases (*evametassa kevalassa dukkhakkhandhassa nirodho hotī*).

and humming activity receded to a faint background whisper. I in- *tuitively felt some inkling, some tiny hint of what transpired in this spot twenty-five centuries ago, was still going on. Right now. My mind rushed first for explanation, then for phrases of description like 'vibrations' and 'sanctified ground.' But the words were babbling. I relaxed into awe. Place and time lost their meaning. Where I was experiencing this and when had no relevance.*

My body told me it was so. It told me that the world can whir and hum and crank on with its noisy business, and yet the stillness is there. The peace is within. Prostrations and chanting and suppli- cation and prayer clogged the air and yet the cool, empty space beneath that tree remained untouched. The Buddha still sat there, as he did twenty-five centuries ago, with eyes closed and attention turned inward. And even though he was alone then, in silence, still the outside world confronted him. His own desires for that world, his senses, and the machinery of his mind assaulted him with a thousand prostrations and supplications and prayers for his attention. And he continued to turn inward, deeper and deeper within.

I was just on the edge, the most distant approach to that space within, standing before an unknown universe of infinite possibility. To go further I could carry nothing with me, no baggage of the outer world. These past weeks had been a reluctant, painful process of giving up that baggage. But I'd done it. And so forfeited my right to travel out there. I would be blown out if I tried. That kind of tourism was dead for me.

We seemed to open our eyes together. I shook my head slowly in amazement. Few words came out. As my mind started rolling again, though, it wanted to know...how, what had I felt? Where had I been?

— Eric Lerner, *Journey of Insight Meditation*

Bodhgayā is much more of a working Buddhist centre than the other pilgrimage places. It is the major focus of ritual activities for all Buddhist sects, and at the time we were there, there were more Tibetans than any other single group. The Tibetans always come down from the Himālaya to Bodhgayā during the winter months, but last week was especially thick with Tibetans who came to participate in the Janang Monlam Chenmo, a massive prayer festival. I had decided, before I knew about the festival, that I wanted to meditate for a four-day self-retreat in Bodhgayā, and being somewhat stubborn when I have a plan in mind, I didn't abandon the idea. Hundreds of monks surrounded an elaborate altar near the Bodhi Tree, just a few feet from where I wanted to sit, and three or four of them led the others in chanting, amplified through a very healthy PA system.

Meanwhile, monks and lay people from various countries sat in the meditation space under the tree doing their own chants, sometimes in large loud groups led by monks with megaphones, sometimes individually. Others circumambulated the temple, always in the prescribed clockwise direction. Some of the Tibetans circumambulated the temple through the act of prostration, in which practitioners go from vertical to face-down horizontal. Prostrations are physically demanding, especially for some of the devout older people who are not in the best health. Many of the Tibetans have special prostration boards: long wooden boards that can be padded with cushions and which allow the hands, often fitted with small cloth-covered blocks, to easily slide as practitioners extend into the horizontal position.

During my self-retreat, I had to deal with a lot of my own aversion to all of this distracting activity. Had I been less stubborn, I might have given up, but as it is I'm very happy I finished my retreat, as it helped me improve my tolerance. I learned to respect and value other people's rights to practise their religious traditions. One can see this with the Tibetans, who seem to have a very strong group identity based on religion, which has allowed them to weather hard-

*ship, cruelty, and exile for decades, all with dignity, self-respect, and
compassion towards those who have harmed them.*

– Peter Buchanan

Site-Sitting

Mahābodhi Temple Compound

The world awoke to Bodhgayā's plight after Sir Edwin Arnold published his epic
poem *The Light of Asia* in 1875, along with a heartfelt newspaper article describing
the pathetic disregard that had befallen the most sacred Buddhist site. The poem's
sympathetic portrayal of the Buddha's life and teaching showed that the Dhamma
was not gloomy and pessimistic—as described by early Western academics and
Christian missionaries—but a sophisticated and ethical way of life. Inspired by the
poet's words, Anagarika Dharmapala, a Sri Lankan Buddhist, dedicated his life to
the revival of the Buddha's teachings and to the restoration of Bodhgayā and the
Mahābodhi Temple.[35]

The Mahābodhi Temple, like most North Indian monastic complexes, ceased to
be active in the 13th century due to the Turkish invasions, ever-decreasing lack of
royal patronage, and the decline of Dhamma practice in its native land. However,
since the late 19th century, when Burmese officials and British surveyors began
their task of "rediscovering" Bodhgayā's landscape, the town has slowly transformed from a deserted and neglected ghost town into a thriving international
pilgrimage centre. On any given day at the Mahābodhi Temple, you'll find royalty
and paupers, scholars and practitioners, monks, nuns, and spiritually interested
tourists from all over the world who come to meditate, pray, discuss the Dhamma
or just to socialize. This cultural variety makes Bodhgayā a true mirror of the universal aspect of the Buddha's teaching.

Strolling around the temple gardens, it's easy to feel the devotion of pilgrims of
old, expressed through richly decorated stūpas and graceful sculptures. This el-
egance continues to inspire pilgrims today as international devotees build modern
temples and monasteries representative of their countries. Whether they are from
Myanmar, Thailand, Taiwan, Tibet or Japan, each temple is a living symbol of
their faith in the Dhamma.

Buddha Pada Temple

Descending the marble stairs leading to the temple and passing through the intricate stone archway with two statues of kneeling Burmese devotees at its base,
you're welcomed by the Buddha Pada Temple's large round stone with carved
footprints. In ancient times, before the advent of Buddha statues, carved footprints
were often used to represent the Buddha.

Adjacent to the Buddha Pada Temple is a row of small shrine-rooms containing
Buddha, Bodhisatta, and Hindu images. These shrines were built at a time when
Bodhgayā was practically forgotten by the Buddhist world and taken over by a
Shaivite sect. Sometime during the 17th century, a Hindu *Mahant* (priest) and his
group of Shaivite *sannyāsins* moved into the deserted temple. They continue wor-
shipping at the temple to this day. Shaivite priests often try to reel in pilgrims and

tourists for a costly *pūjā* or donation. If they ask you for money after you look at the statues, only give if you want to, not because you feel obliged.

Shortly after the arrival of the Shaivites, the temple and Bodhi Tree were assimilated into the Hindu Vaishnava pilgrimage network as one of the forty-five sites (*vedis*) for the ritual of *Gayā-shrāddha*, which can be observed when thousands of Hindu pilgrims pour into Bodhgayā during the two weeks leading up to the full moon in October.

Mahābodhi Temple

Sitting here—at the most important monument honouring what Buddhists consider to be the highest spiritual attainment of any human being—is a moving experience that any sincere meditator visiting India should not miss. Silently walking around the 53 m high pyramidal tower, feeling its vibrant power and exploring the various niches and alcoves containing images of the Buddhas and *bodhisattas*, are all ways of joining in the temple's joyous celebration of peace.

The details of who built the present temple—and when—are a bit of a mystery. The first substantial temple may have been built by Asoka. However, the magnificent sandstone temple that we see today, crowned by a pointed spire and flanked by four corner steeples, was initially constructed after the 4ᵗʰ century, and the structure has since undergone many renovation and restoration projects organized by foreign Buddhist monks and rulers, especially the Burmese in the 11ᵗʰ and 15ᵗʰ centuries. Most of the architecture around the main temple and the ornate sculptures on the temple were carved in the Pala and Sena periods (8ᵗʰ to 12ᵗʰ centuries), funded by patrons from Ceylon (Sri Lanka), India, China, Korea and Central Asia.

Bodhi Tree

Behind the Temple is the celebrated Bodhi Tree—a descendent of the original Bodhi Tree that travelled many kilometres before being brought back to Bodhgayā. When the *arahant* nun Saṅghamitta (King Asoka's daughter) went to Sri Lanka, she took a branch of the original sacred tree with her and planted it in the ancient capital Anuradhapura.

In the 19th century, a branch from the Sri Lankan tree was brought back to Bodhgayā and planted behind the temple to replace the decaying bodhi tree there. The Sri Lankan Bodhi Tree continues to flourish and is the oldest documented tree in the world.

> *The Bodhi Tree,*
> *thenceforward in all years*
> *Never to fade, and ever to be kept*
> *In homage of the world,*
> *beneath whose leaves*
> *It was ordained that truth*
> *should come to Buddh.*
>
> – Sir Edwin Arnold, *Light of Asia*

The Diamond Throne (*vajrāsana*) under the Bodhi Tree —the polished sandstone slab decorated with triangles, a Mauryan-style palmette and wild goose frieze—is believed to mark the exact spot where the Buddha sat when "vision arose, knowledge arose, wisdom arose, understanding arose, light arose." For the next seven days, the Buddha remained sitting on the "Victory Throne" (*Aparajita*), "experiencing the joy of liberation."

Most scholars acknowledge that the stone was probably put there by King Asoka and is the oldest monument in Bodhgayā. Because they are migratory birds, the wild geese are thought to represent detachment.

Legend says that during Asoka's tyrant days, before encountering the Dhamma, he ruthlessly had the tree cut down to annoy the local monks, who seemed unaffected by his cruel behaviour. However, through some miracle or freak of nature, the Bodhi Tree spontaneously sprouted up again. Later, after his conversion to the Buddha's way of life, Asoka became very devoted to the Bodhi Tree and spent much time meditating at its roots. His queen, jealous of her new rival, had the tree cut down in order to lure him back to her, but to her surprise, it sprang up yet again!

While sitting under the Bodhi Tree, whose *nibbānic* tranquility casts a peaceful calm upon its visitors, you'll find it easy to tune out external distractions and turn inwards to the reality of impermanence. Many meditators have found that meditating here as much as possible is highly beneficial to their daily practice of working to purify the mind.

At the end of the group-sitting under the Bodhi Tree, Goenka-ji began chanting the beautiful words, "Ananta pūṇyamayī, ananta guṇamayī, Buddha kī nirvāṇa-dhātu, dharama-dhātu, bodhi-dhātu!"

("The Buddha's vibrations of Nibbāna, Dhamma, and Enlightenment are a source of endless merit, of endless benefit!") I was filled with joy, with overflowing happiness, with love for all beings, with blissful gratitude for the teaching of Dhamma and for being on yatra with a thousand Vipassana meditators and Goenka-ji. The words came across alive and strong, blessing anyone else who happened to be around the Mahābodhi Temple that evening. Then I remembered to stop reminiscing and start meditating!

– Canadian Dhamma Pilgrim

Unblinking Shrine (*Animisa Cetiya*)
The Buddha spent his first week sitting under the Bodhi Tree enjoying the fruits of his discovery (without budging!). He then got up, walked a few paces north-east of the tree, and found a spot where he stood gazing at the tree unblinkingly for another week, out of gratitude for the tree having sheltered him during his quest. The shrine at this spot, a white mini replica of the Mahābodhi Temple, marks this event.[36]

The small knoll where the shrine rests is a nice vantage point from which to admire all the dedicated pilgrims circumambulating the temple. It's also a great place to meditate and cultivate gratitude for everything the Buddha accomplished while under the Bodhi Tree.

Jewel Promenade Shrine (*Ratanacaṅkama Cetiya*)
The Buddha spent his third week after enlightenment mindfully walking up and down the jeweled promenade (*ratanācaṅkama*), said to have been bestowed to him by some devas and brāhmas. The shrine, perpendicular to the Bodhi Tree, originally consisted of a long brick platform with a row of eleven pillars on either side supporting a roof. Today, the platform is encased in stone, and only the lotus-shape base of one row of pillars is visible. The other row is said to be under the present temple.

Walking up and down here after a long session of sitting under the Tree is an excellent place to maintain *sampajañña*: "While walking, the meditator thoroughly understands with the wisdom of impermanence, 'I am walking.'"

Jewel House Shrine (*Ratanāghara Cetiya*)
The Buddha's fourth week after experiencing *nibbāna* took place in the Jewel House, also said to have been built by some *devas* and *brahmas*. Although there is no record of where this house actually stood, the commemorative panel is located in the north-west corner of the temple grounds. Legend says that while the Buddha spent the week reflecting deeply upon the Abhidhamma—the teachings on the psychology of the mind—blue-, yellow-, red-, white- and orange-coloured rays emanated from his body. Today's small roofless shrine

is a good place to contemplate with *anicca* the manifold mental states that we continuously experience, and how we mistakenly attach ourselves to them.

Ajapāla Commemorative Pillar

The Buddha spent his fifth week sitting under the "Goatherd's Banyan Tree" (*Ajapāla*), some distance east of the Bodhi Tree, enjoying the fruits of enlightenment (*phalasamāpatti*). This spot, perhaps near the Sujātā Temple across the river, is where the Buddha first had contact with another human being after his Enlightenment.[37] The Buddha explained to an arrogant brahmin the real qualities of a brahmin, which are found in wholesome actions of body, speech, and mind—not in one's birth, or knowledge of the Vedic scriptures:

> *The brahmin who is rid of evil things,*
> *Not haughty, undefiled and self-controlled,*
> *Perfect in Knowledge and living the Holy Life,*
> *Can rightly employ the word 'brahmin.'*[38]

Mucalinda Lake

In his sixth week after Enlightenment, the Buddha meditated by Mucalinda Lake, and untimely rain fell during the entire seven days. Calinda, a powerful divine serpent (*nāga*), coiled himself around the Buddha and opened his hood over the Buddha's head, shielding him from rain, wind and insects. Imagining this fantastic event, the Buddha's words come to mind, "One who protects the Dhamma is protected by the Dhamma."

Behind the Asokan pillar, the small man-made lake—filled with water lilies, lotus flowers, and over-fed catfish—is said to mark the spot of this occurrence. However, local *bhikkhus* say that the real Mucalinda Lake is not what we see in the temple complex, but is actually a pond in Muchalin Village, located south of the Mahābodhi Temple. To get to the pond from the temple, turn right on the Gayā Road from the steps leaving the plaza and walk, bike, or drive for about two kilometres. After passing a small concrete bridge and a few tombs of Hindu saints located in front of a vegetable plot on the right-hand side of the road, turn right onto a narrow dirt road. The shallow and muddy pond on your left, surrounded by garbage and cows, is the pond.

Rājāyatana Commemorative Pillar

The seventh week after his Awakening, the Buddha sat under the Rājāyatana tree, south of the Bodhi Tree, feeling the pleasure of deliverance. Although there is a commemorative pillar for this tree at the foot of the temple precinct's stairs; the actual site has not been found.

During the entire seven weeks following his enlightenment, the Buddha did not eat, wash, drink, sleep or even lie down. At the end of the seventh week, Tapussa and Bhallika, travelling merchant brothers from Ukkala[39] were passing by. Seeing the Buddha's radiance, the brothers approached him respectfully and offered rice cakes and honey balls. The Buddha accepted the food and spoke to them about the road to salvation. Tapussa and Bhallika, delighted, bowed in reverence and became the first people to take refuge in the Buddha and Dhamma. They asked the

Buddha for some relic of his, and he gave them eight strands of hair,[40] which are now enshrined at the Shwedagon Pagoda in Yangon, Myanmar.

Shortly after eating his first meal, the Buddha had doubts about people's abilities to understand the Dhamma, which he said to himself was, "profound, difficult to see and understand, peaceful and sublime, unattainable by mere reasoning, subtle, to be experienced by the wise." Māra, knowing these thoughts, came to the Buddha and said, "O Holy One, you have attained the highest bliss. It is now time for you to enter final *nibbāna*." Brahma Sahampati, however, hearing Māra's wicked plea, quickly descended from his heaven, saying, "Let the Blessed One teach the Dhamma, let the Sublime One teach the Dhamma. There are beings with little dust in their eyes. If they do not hear the Dhamma, they will worsen; while if they do, they will prosper."[41]

The Buddha beamed with a compassionate smile. He turned to Māra and said that he would not pass away until an enlightened Saṅgha of *bhikkhus*, *bhikkhunīs*, *upāsakās* and *upāsikās* was firmly established. Some traditions maintain that it was only after the Buddha agreed to the brahma's request, that he really became a *sammāsambuddha*.

Meditating under the banyan tree or by one of the many shrines here is conducive to developing gratitude to both this brahma and to the Buddha for sharing his experience with humanity, giving countless beings the opportunity to come out of their self-created misery.

Wrapped in my shawl, rucksack packed with the bare essentials—toiletries, a change of clothes, sitting cushion, and a mosquito net—slung over my shoulder, I set out from Dhamma Giri through the gate with its hand-painted blessing: "May You Grow In Dhamma." It was around 11 p.m. on an evening in February, and unusually cold for Igatpuri.

I had just finished sitting a 45-day Vipassana course, and was on my way to Bodhgayā to meet a few friends with whom I would meditate under the Bodhi Tree for about 10 days. This would be my second pilgrimage to Bodhgayā; the first was a few years earlier during the month of May: the hottest time of year.

My only concern was the train journey. There had been a mix up getting my tickets, so I had no confirmed seat. Approximately 30 hours on the Howrah Mail was a little daunting for me to imagine after my long course. Indian trains are tough in ordinary circumstances, but without a seat and also on a major holiday…but what could be done? I was going to Bodhgayā—my favourite place in the world, and I had already made plans to meet my friends. So seat or no seat, I was off.

Igatpuri is just a few stops from Mumbai, where the Howrah Mail begins its journey, so it's usually not full by the time it arrives in Igatpuri. When the train screeched to a stop and I got on board I was in for a big surprise. One bogie in 3-tier class on an Indian train has nine compartments with eight seats in each compartment. That's 72 people. Usually, there will be a few extra passengers here and there, but tonight was different. I quickly lost all hope of getting a seat. There must have been more than 200 people stuffed into each bogie! Even finding space near the toilets in between the cars was hard.

The train slowly pulled away from the station and headed into the night. I was still squeezing my way through bodies with my small pack, looking for a place to squat down. I finally found a spot between a door and the sink outside the toilet. I hunkered down on my heels and started practising Vipassana and contemplated the huge significance of where I was going.

The journey was long. Occasionally one passenger would beckon me over to sit on the edge of his seat. Normally, in the berth where he was sitting, there would have been two passengers, one on the upper bunk and one on the lower during the night. During the day both occupants would share the bottom. On this journey, however, there were between five and seven people on the bottom bunk alone, and another four on the top. This was during the day. At night the numbers decreased slightly as people would spread some newspaper on the floor to lie down on and go to sleep. These passengers would occasionally take interest in me and squeeze over to interrogate me about the U.S., foreign politics, or some other inconsequential chatter. Nevertheless it gave me the chance to rest my legs and backside for a few minutes. As soon as it was time to lie down or eat, however, their interest in me faded, and the precious little corner lost. We finally pulled into Gayā at 4 a.m.

I got down from the train, my body aching and stomach hungry. I hadn't slept in over two days, but felt all right. People recommended that I not travel from Gayā to Bodhgayā in the dark, so I thought I'd wait in the station for a few hours until daylight. The station was packed with sleeping people sprawled all over the floors. I negotiated my way through the bodies and suddenly found myself with a rickshaw driver asking, "Buddhagayā? Buddhagayā?"

"It's dark," I replied, "Not safe?"

"No, no. Safe." he said. By this time he already had me out of the station and next to his over-sized rickshaw, which had two other passengers in it. Both looked like farmers, weathered and honest in appearance.

I climbed in and wrapped my shawl tight around me as the rickshaw rumbled through the fogged-in streets of Gayā. It was wet and cold. The mist and fog engulfed every open space. As we neared the outskirts of Gayā I felt the strong Dhamma vibrations. My body and mind sunk into a deep calmness, a deep peace.

This was Bodhgayā, the place where the greatest human ever achieved the perfect state of peace and became fully liberated. Rid-

ing through the night, aware of the Dhamma vibrating throughout my body, it amazed me, how after such a dreadful train-ride, being hungry and tired for so long, I was suddenly totally awake, totally aware and rejuvenated. The glory of Dhamma!

We pulled into Bodhgayā and I went directly to the Mahābodhi Temple to meditate for a few hours until light. Once daylight came I found my friends. We went to get permission to stay at the Mahābodhi compound through the night for the next eight nights.

We meditated with a couple of forest monks from Thailand every night. Other pilgrims would come meditate at night as well. During the days I would rest, meditate, and discuss the Dhamma with some of the monks. We took our meals in silence. The experience was great, a true pilgrimage. At times difficult, at other times very ordinary, all the while a unique opportunity to grow in Dhamma and express gratitude to the Buddha for giving us this wonderful path.

– Brett Morris

Meditation Park
For a nominal fee, meditators can escape the hullabaloo surrounding the temple and meditate in a pleasant and relatively quiet park between 6:00am and 6:00pm. The park is located at the southeast corner of the Temple compound (near the toilet block).

All-Night Meditation at the Mahābodhi Temple
Meditating throughout the night at the temple is an excellent way to maximize your stay in Bodhgayā. Sitting under the silent stars after the distracting masses have left, you will find that the accentuated spiritual mood is a real blessing.

If you want to sit all night at the temple (9:00pm to 4:00am), you need to get prior written permission from the Temple Management Committee Office, located near the entrance to the plaza. Don't forget to bring a photocopy of your passport/identity card and the Rs.100 entrance fee. Permission is usually granted except during the crowded months of December and January. Be sure to bring appropriate clothing to protect against weather and mosquitoes.

Library
The library, next door to the Temple Management Committee Office located near the entrance to the plaza, has a small, disorderly collection of Buddhist books in English and Hindi. You can't take books out of the library, but you can read them there or have them photocopied. This is also a safe place to keep your bicycle while meditating at the temple.

The Mahant's Palace
Near the post office and rickshaw stand on Old Gayā Road is an unmarked gateway with large, black wooden doors that lead to the Mahant's palace courtyard, usually crowded with cows, goats, chickens and dogs. Although the Hindu precinct is

most notable for the first Mahant's tomb (*samādhi*) covered with his tiger-skin rug, the palace's inner courtyard has a gallery containing many beautiful carvings of the Buddha and *bodhisattas*. Unfortunately, these ancient statues are not properly cared for, shown by the careless paint stains found on many of the 2000-year-old images.

Archaeological Museum
The museum has a small collection of mislabelled sculptures (and many statues without heads) found around Bodhgayā, including pieces of the Mahābodhi Temple's original intricately carved stone railing. The museum is open from 10:00 a.m. to 5:00 p.m. and closed on Fridays.

Kusha Grass Temple
This small shrine is said to mark the spot where an old buffalo herder offered Siddhattha a bundle of grass to use as a cushion just before his enlightenment.

Nodding Off

At the beginning of his first retreat, Moggallāna kept nodding off during meditation. The Buddha visited the *bhikkhu* and taught him eight ways to fight drowsiness, from the subtlest to the coarsest:

1. Pay no attention to thoughts that cause drowsiness. If that does not work,
2. Reflect on the teachings. If that does not work,
3. Repeat the teachings out loud. If that does not work,
4. Pull your earlobes and rub your limbs. If that does not work,
5. Get up from your seat, splash water on your face, look around in all directions and up at the constellation of stars. If that does not work,
6. Pay attention to the perception of light, making the mind full of brightness. If that does not work,
7. Walk up and down mindfully. If that does not work,
8. Lie down lion-like on the right side, placing one foot on the other, keeping in mind the thought of rising as soon as you wake.

The Buddha reminded him that while doing these practices, one should constantly remember the unworthiness of attachment and the importance of cultivating an understanding of impermanence, dispassion and renunciation. With the help of these suggestions, Moggallāna continued his practice and after seven days, became fully liberated from the taints of existence.

A, 7:58

By foot, cycle, horse-cart or car, cross the Nirañjanā River's bridge near the Burmese Vihāra, and then make your first right. The shrine is about half a kilometre down the rocky road.

Sujātā Stūpa, Sujātā Tree Shrine, Bowl Shrine
There are three stories behind the Sujātā Stūpa. The first and more popular is that it marks the spot of the home of Sujātā, the girl who fed the Bodhisatta rice pudding before his Awakening. The second, according to the Chinese pilgrim Xuan Zang (pronounced Shwandzaang), is associated with the site where the Buddha lived in a past life as the 'perfumed elephant' (*gandhahasti*), with a sweet odour and the strength of ten ordinary elephants. The perfumed elephant's mother was blind, so everyday he fed and bathed his mother with filial care. One day the king saw the magnificent creature and captured him. The king offered him the finest foods, but the elephant refused to eat. The king asked the elephant why he wasn't eating, and he replied, "My mother is blind and hasn't eaten or had anything to drink for days. How can I eat when she suffers?" The king felt pity for the elephant and set him free.

The third story, according to some villagers, is that the stūpa marks the site of the Ajapāla Tree where the Buddha spent his fifth week after Awakening. While interesting, this story does not have any archaeological or historical evidence to support the claim.

To reach the stūpa, cross the Nirañjanā River's bridge near the Burmese Vihāra and continue going straight. There are signs leading the way. To get to the shrine, follow the footpath behind the stūpa through the paddy fields for about 1 km to the Hindu temple in the village of Bakraur. Behind the temple is the tree shrine believed to mark the spot where Sujātā offered rice pudding to the Bodhisatta.

About 100 metres behind the Sujātā Tree Shrine on the bank of the Mohane River is a small shrine with a brightly painted Burmese-style standing Buddha statue and an aquatic serpent king (*nāga-rāja*), claimed to be where the Bodhisatta's bowl floated upstream after he put it in the river, solemnly declaring, "If this bowl floats upstream, I will become Enlightened."

It is interesting to note that the story takes place on the bank of the Nirañjanā River, not the Mohane River. When asked why the shrine was built on the Mohane if the event didn't occur there, U Nyaneinda, the abbot of the Burmese Vihāra who donated the shrine in 1993, responded that no one who owned land on the Nirañjanā was willing to let him build a shrine there. The man who gave him land to build the Bowl Shrine saw how popular the Sujātā site was and hoped that this shrine would also be popular. What's more important than the exact location, the Burmese *bhikkhu* felt, is that pilgrims have more places to visit, and that locals learn the stories of the Buddha's life and generate respect for him.[42]

Dhamma Bodhi, Bodhgayā International Vipassana Meditation Centre
A powerful meditation centre located in the 'Navel of the Universe,' Dhamma Bodhi ('Awakening of Dhamma') is a place sincere Vipassana meditators shouldn't miss. About 4 km away from town and surrounded by stretches of fertile paddy

fields and a nearby university campus, the rural calm of Dhamma Bodhi is an ideal setting for the serious eradication of impurities.

During a one-day course at Dhamma Bodhi, S.N. Goenka told the meditators:

> *In a wonderful place like this, where an enlightened person meditated and realized this wonderful Truth, the vibrations of the entire atmosphere were charged with his love and compassion. These vibrations are still here and we benefit from them by meditating at this place. When 10-day courses are held here in Bodhgayā, people realize a great benefit. In five or ten courses elsewhere they might not get the benefits they would get from one course in this place. This is one reason why we want a good meditation centre to be developed in Bodhgayā. But it is only if you meditate that you benefit from coming here.*

The 18-acre centre, with its three Dhamma halls, Burmese-style pagoda, fruit trees and well-kept vegetable gardens, can accommodate about 90 students in single and double rooms, mostly with attached bathrooms. From November to March, Dhamma Bodhi attracts foreigners from all over the world who come to put the Buddha's teachings into practice—so registering in advance is recommended. Courses attract fewer students during the off-season when hot weather and mosquitoes present greater challenges (perhaps all the more reason to visit at this time!). Ten-day courses start the 1st and 16th of every month. Meditators and servers, short- or long-term, are always welcome. Servers, in particular, are often in short supply, and many have reported that the strong atmosphere of Dhamma Bodhi offers unique, though ultimately rewarding, challenges to one's equanimity.

Travel to and from the centre is not difficult as there are plenty of taxis, cycle rickshaws, and auto-rickshaws available from Bodhgayā. For the mellow and adventurous, try walking the meandering path, through the mud-hut hamlets and paddy fields, that runs parallel to the main road.

Contact:
Dhamma Bodhi
Bodhgayā International Vipassana Meditation Centre
Gayā–Dobhi Road, near Magadha University
Bodhgayā–824234, Bihar
Tel: [+91] (0)631-2200437; 94716 03531; 99559 11556
E-mail: info@bodhi.dhamma.org
Website: www.bodhi.dhamma.org

> *We ended our yatra by giving volunteer service on a 10-day course at Dhamma Bodhi. It was one of our best experiences serving. The students were marvellous and very serious. About seventy percent were foreigners of all different nationalities and all had some interest in Buddhism. There were a few new students from Patna who had hardly even heard of the Buddha and knew nothing about Bodhgayā, but nevertheless they were still very keen. There's something about*

the place that makes the understanding of anicca so sharp. We just felt like meditating all the time. The accommodations had been upgraded since the last time we visited, and the centre felt like a deva-realm with its well-tended gardens, beautiful meditation hall and spectacular pagoda.

– Chris & Kerry Waters

Volunteer Work in Bodhgayā

From the days of Emperor Asoka in the 3rd century BCE, until its desecration by pillaging Turks in the 13th century CE, Bodhgayā was something of a spiritual colony decorated with monasteries and meditation centres, where the pious spent their days in meditation and social service. Today there is a revival of this way of life, seen not only in all the meditation and philosophy courses being offered, but in social projects such as free clinics, education and vocational training offered by religious institutions, NGOs and private individuals.

If you are interested in donating money or lending a hand to these social projects, the best way to get the latest information is through word-of-mouth. Beware of the many '*welfare-wallahs*' who besiege pilgrims and tourists to sponsor their charitable projects. Unfortunately most people who approach you in the streets are more interested in filling their pockets with your rupees than helping out the needy. Some good places to start are the health projects at the **Root Institute**, (www.rootinstitute.com) and the **Maitri Charitable Foundation** (www.maitri.org), or at the schools **Alice Project** (www.aliceproject.org), **Maitreya Universal Education Project** (www.maitreyaeducation.org), and **Pragya Vihar** (www.pragyavihar.org).

Sleeping & Eating

Like most of the places along the Dhamma pilgrim's circuit, Bodhgayā is filled with modern Buddhist temples in their cultures' traditional styles, giving the simple Bihari town a global flavour. Most of these temples have accommodations for pilgrims, but have unfortunately lost the pure donation system. If you are on a tight budget, try the **Burmese** or **Nepalese** monastaries. Otherwise prepare to pay between 250 and 500 rupees per night at the others. Popular choices include **Sechen, Bhutanese, Tergar International, Japanese Daijokyo, Root Institute**, and **Sri Lankan Mahābodhi**. Most of these monasteries are in the vicinity of the Mahābodhi Temple or near the Great Buddha sandstone statue (*assi feet Buddha*), about 1 km outside of town.

There is no shortage of budget and mid-range guest houses and hotels, most of which are of similar quality. Try your luck around the Burmese Monastery (**Deep Guest House, Rainbow Guest House**), across the playing field near the Kalachakra Maidan (**Shanti Guest House**), near the Mahābodhi Society (**Om Guest House, Hotel Mahamaya, Jeevak Hotel**) or in the villages opposite the Royal

Thai Temple (**Mohammed Guest House, Ram Guest House, Kundan Guest House, Bookstore, & Café**). For those who like their creature comforts, the **Mahayana Hotel, Hotel Sujata, Tathagatha Hotel, Royal Residency** or **Lotus Nikko** hotels are for you. Wherever you stay, the rates usually go up 20-50% during the winter months.

Restaurants are scattered throughout town, and all serve pretty much the same Tibetan, Indian, and Western-style dishes. Most Western budget travellers like **Mohammed's** and **The Olive**, while finer diners tend to go to **Sujata, Swagat,** or **Siam** (for Thai food). The **Tibet Om Café** (and Bakery) in the Pilgrim's House near the Kalachakra grounds is another favourite of long-term vegetarian Bodhgayā residents on a budget, and features a small Tibetan handicrafts store inside. Just in front of the Vietnamese Temple is the **Be Happy Café**, famous for its vegetarian pizzas, desserts, breads, and espresso. You can also refill your water bottles there with UV filtered water. **Bowl of Compassion** is also a popular choice for local and international cuisine. A portion of their profits from the "compassion meals" helps eradicate local poverty. Ask around for other current favourites. In the tourist season, vendors line up along Temple Road selling cheap food, hand-made woollens, Bodhgayā *bhikkhu* bags, painted Bodhi leaves and all sorts of meditation paraphernalia. Near the Kalachakra grounds and Tibetan Refugee Market, a string of several popular seasonal Tibetan tent restaurants also opens up during this time.

Coming & Going

Bodhgayā is approximately 12 km south of Gayā, where you can find the nearest major bus stand, airport and railway station. From the Gayā railway station, there is no shortage of rickshaws and taxis to Bodhgayā.

From Gayā, **buses** to Rajgir (70 km, 2.5 hours) leave from Gaurakshani bus stand and buses to Patna (92 km, 3.5 hours) and other major towns in Bihar leave from Gandhi Maidan bus stand. Every morning, the Tourist Development Corporation offers daily deluxe buses to Patna from Gandhi Maidan.

If coming by **train**, Gayā is a major junction between Delhi, Vārāṇasī and Kolkata (Calcutta). Some important connections that stop in Gayā:

- Howrah Rajdhani Express 2301/2302 (New Delhi-Howrah/Kolkata via Mughal Sarai)
- Bhubaneshwar Rajdhani Express 2421/2422 (New Delhi-Bhubaneshwar)
- Poorva Express 2381/2382 (New Delhi-Howrah/Kolkata via Vārāṇasī)
- Kalka Mail 2311/2312 (Howrah/Kolkata-Kalka via Mughal Sarai)
- Jodhpur Howrah Express 2307/2308 (Jodhpur-Howrah/Kolkata via Jaipur)
- Doon Express 3009/3010 (Dehra Dun-Howrah/Kolkata via Vārāṇasī)
- Chanbal Express 1159/1160 (Howrah/Kolkata-Gwalior)
- Howrah Mumbai Mail 3003/3004 (Howrah/Kolkata-Mumbai via Mughal Sarai and via Igatpuri)

If you need to book a train ticket while in Bodhgayā, go to the computerized railway reservation office at the corner of Great Buddha Statue Road.

We are always told by our non-Bihari friends not to travel the Gayā-Bodhgayā road between sunset and sunrise, and that if we do arrive in Gayā after dark, then it is absolutely essential that we spend the night in a spartan, over-priced hotel there. Although it's true that there were a few instances of highway robbery in the 1990s, these warnings are generally derived from a source of paranoia or misinformation. Nevertheless, if your train leaves or arrives in the middle of the night, the railway station has passable rooms. **Ajatsatru Hotel**, opposite Gayā's train station, is a decent place to have a meal and relax while waiting to depart on a late train.

The newly built Gayā airport (8 km) has international flights to/from Thailand, Myanmar and Bhutan, with other available domestic and international routes expected soon.

We thought we were being smart. We bought tickets for the Purushottam Express, the fastest morning train out of Mughal Sarai bound for Gayā—a quick and easy two-and-a-half-hour journey, which would allow us to have most of the day to get settled and wander around Bodhgayā.

We got to the station an hour early, enough time to drink some chai and eat fresh puris with apples and cinnamon. A train pulled in, it started raining. We asked a ticket collector if this was our train. "Oh no, it is not; but this train is also going to Gayā itself, get on!" he said, with urgency in his voice. As we hurriedly hauled our luggage onto the bogie and saw the empty wooden-plank seats and peanut-shelled floor, we suddenly got a strange "this-is-a-mistake" feeling. The train has not yet pulled out...there is still time to get off...we... stayed.

It's a passenger train. These (extremely) slow trains stop at every station and always give priority to the long distance express trains. The train is constantly delayed and the journey to Gayā ends up taking nine hours, way longer than if we would have waited for our original train. We wanted to get there before dark because we had been told that the rickshaws don't drive the Bodhgayā road at night due to potential bandits. We finally arrived and as we exited the station, we were swarmed with drivers wanting their last fare of the day. We chose the driver with the nicest smile and cheapest fare, and quickly got to the Tibetan Monastery near the Mahābodhi Temple, where we found a room and dropped off our luggage.

The sun has just set; we are weary and hungry. "Do we sit first or eat first?" we asked ourselves. "We're in Bodhgayā, let's sit."

We crossed the street to the Mahābodhi Temple, checked-in our shoes, and made our way down the stairs—the damp stone felt cold on our bare feet. It was drizzling and the droplets cast a magical glow as they fell through the shafts of light illuminating the temple, like a misty, protective aura. The nights were cool following monsoon and we decided to meditate in the temple's inner chamber. The small room was already packed with a mix of Indian and Thai monks sitting at the very front, and lay-devotees behind them. As we squeezed into a spot, the monks began to chant in Pāli. We sat there for an hour or so as the echoing sound-vibrations flooded our entire bodies. Equanimity pervaded the area, and it was naturally easy to observe the changing reality from moment to moment—whether experiencing serene one-pointedness or itchy irritating sensations caused by biting mosquitoes. Nothing else mattered anymore: no trains, no delays, no peddlers; just us, in the exact spot where Prince Siddhattha conquered all internal turmoil and gained peace, wisdom and compassion.

Elated and refreshed, we joined a group of pilgrims in circumambulating the temple, then headed out to have a quick bite before collapsing on our beds.

– MD & KG

Excursions

Mahākala Cave, Dhungeswari Mountain (*Pragbodhi*)

"You are emaciated from fasting, and are on the verge of death. What good is all this exertion? You should live and do good works," Māra said to the exhausted Bodhisatta, hoping that he would quit his mission. "Be quiet, you wicked being. Why have you come here, Evil One, friend of negligence? I do not need your merits…If my mind becomes tranquil, I don't care if the body wastes away. Death in battle is better than a life with defeat," Siddhattha gasped. Māra, sulking, shrank away.

During the six years between his Great Renunciation and Enlightenment, the Bodhisatta first stayed a short while near Rājagaha, where he mastered the *jhānas* under the tutelage of Āḷāra Kālāma and Uddaka Rāmaputta. After leaving these teachers, it is believed that Siddhattha spent much of his time in the Mahākala Cave on Pragbodhi Mountain, where he practised extreme austerities such as: clenching his teeth while pressing his tongue against the roof of his mouth as hard as he could; holding his breath; fasting or taking minimal amounts of food (such as one grain of rice or one kola fruit nut per day). Some of his other practices included eating cow or human dung, or only wild foods; wandering naked or wearing refuse rags or tree bark; pulling out his hair; standing or squatting continuously; sleeping on a mattress of spikes; not bathing, letting dust and dirt accumulate until it just flaked off; sleeping outside in all seasons in forests or charnel grounds; and keeping himself so isolated that if he heard or saw people coming, he would run away. After years of these tortures, the Bodhisatta was completely worn out. He examined his practices honestly and saw that it just wasn't giving him the results he had expected. His lack of success was because of ill-founded views based on pride and attachment. Years later, the Buddha narrated to some *bhikkhus*,

My body reached a state of extreme emaciation. Because of eating so little my limbs became like the joined segments of vine-stems... my backside became like a camel's hoof...the projections on my spine stood forth like corded beads...my ribs jutted out as gaunt as the crazy rafters of an old roofless barn...the gleam of my eyes sunk far down in their sockets like the gleam of water sunk far down in a deep well...my scalp shrivelled and withered as a green gourd shrivels and withers in the wind and sun...the skin of my belly touched my backbone, too...if I urinated or evacuated my bowels, I fell over on my face there. If I tried to ease my body by rubbing my limbs with my hands, the hair, rotted at its roots, fell away from my body as I rubbed. But by those observances, the practise of difficult feats, I did not gain the noble understanding that leads the meditator to the complete exhaustion of suffering.[43]

To get to Dhungeshwari Mountain, it's possible to hire a vehicle to drive you all the way to the foot of the mountain itself, about 30 minutes from Bodhgayā. Other options are to take a private or shared rickshaw or tonga from the Mahant's Palace along the Old Gayā Road to the village of Khiryama (6 km), marked by two large yellow circular water tanks on the river bank and a sign that says Khiryama. Walk across the dry riverbed (not possible during monsoon season) and then go through the villages and paddy fields towards the mountain, about a one-hour walk from the river. Our favourite way to go, however, is by bicycle (which you can rent in Bodhgayā): it takes a little over an hour. If you feel lost, just ask for Khiryama first, and then Dhungeshwari; all the villagers know where it is. You can also walk or bike from Sujātā Village along the river; by this route the journey takes a little over 3 hours on foot or 1.5 hours by bike.

To get to the Mahākala Cave on Dhugeshwari Mountain, hike for about 20 minutes upwards on the path until you reach the Mahākala Temple, run by charming and hospitable Tibetan monks and a local caretaker. Palanquins are available for those suffering from *jarā*, *byādhi*, and *thinamiddha*. Just above the temple is the dark cave, with its Christmas lights, low oxygen, and rough statue of the emaciated Bodhisatta. Sitting at his feet and looking into his sunken eyes, many have felt waves of gratitude swell up in the mind, perceiving that, "He did this for me, for all of us..."

If you have the energy, the steep 15-minute climb to the mountain top is worth the spectacular views that Dhugeshwari commands over the landscape, surmounted by hovering vultures in search of their lunch. Meditating on this rugged and bare mountain can help us appreciate the hardships that the Bodhisatta faced in this wild setting.

Brahmājoni Hill (Gayāsīsa)

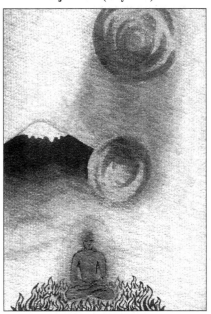

After setting in motion the Wheel of Dhamma in Sārnāth, the Buddha returned to Gayā and taught the Dhamma to the eminent Kassapa brothers— Uruvelā, Nadi, and Gayā—and their one thousand disciples. Uruvelā Kassapa, a matted-haired fire worshipper, was considered to be one of the foremost spiritual authorities at the time. Knowing the mendicant's mind and how to communicate effectively with it, the Buddha skilfully performed a series of super-normal feats such as reading Uruvelā Kassapa's mind, splitting five-hundred logs in an instant, remaining unharmed during a great flood, and taming a fierce and powerful *nāga*. In this way, the Buddha was able to show the Kassapa brothers and their disciples that arahantship could neither be attained through fire-worship, nor from indulging in the fame and fortune from performing sacrifices.

Highly impressed with the Buddha's words and deeds, the entire group of matted-haired fire-worshippers shaved their heads and joined the Buddha's community as *bhikkhus*. A few days later, the Buddha summoned the *bhikkhus* to the plateau of Gayāsīsa Mountain, where he delivered his third teaching, the Fire Sermon:

Bhikkhus, all things are on fire. What is on fire? The six sense organs—eyes, ears, nose, tongue, body and mind—are all on fire. The six sense objects—sights, sounds, smells, tastes, sensations and mental objects—are all on fire. The six consciousnesses—sight, hearing, smell, taste, feeling and thought—are all on fire. The six contacts between the sense organs and the sense objects are all on fire. All these sensual experiences are on fire, whether pleasant, unpleasant or neutral. They are burning from the flames of craving, aversion, and ignorance. They are burning from the flames of birth, old age, sickness, and death, and from the flames of sorrow, lamentation, pain, grief and despair.

Bhikkhus, when noble followers understand the truth, they grow disenchanted with the six sense organs, six sense objects, six consciousnesses, six contacts and six sensual experiences.

When they grow disenchanted, craving fades away. With the fading of craving, they are liberated. When liberated, there is knowledge that they are liberated. They understand: "Birth is exhausted, the holy life has been lived, what was to be done is done, there is no more of this to come."

By the end of the sermon, the hearts of the one-thousand ascetics were gladdened and they all achieved arahantship: total liberation from clinging to the taints of existence. [44]

As the Buddha stood on the mountain and looked down at the hoards of people performing their ritual baths in the Phalgu River, hoping that all their past evils would be washed away, he said to those around him:

Not by water is one made pure,
Though many people may bathe here.
But one in whom there is Truth,
He is pure, he is a brahmin.

After training the Kassapa brothers and their one thousand followers, the Buddha left Gayā never to return, having seen that the citizens there clung tightly to their religious rites and rituals, making it impossible for them to understand his message. [45]

Years later while in Sāvatthī, the Buddha was asked by a Vedic priest if bathing in holy rivers, such as the Phalgu in Gayā, really did wash away past sins and provide liberation. The Buddha responded,

A fool may bathe in these rivers forever
Yet he will never purify his evil deeds...
One pure in heart has everything...
And brings his virtue to perfection.
It is inside yourself, brahmin, that you should bathe,
To make yourself a refuge for all beings.

If you speak no lies,
Do not harm any living beings,

And do not steal;
You will be confident and eliminate hatred.
Then what need is there in going to Gayā?
For any water-well will be your Gayā.[46]

After creating a schism in the Saṅgha during the last years of the Buddha's life, Devadatta brought his five-hundred followers to Gayāsīsa. Out of compassion for the misguided monks, the Buddha sent Sāriputta and Moggallāna to Gayāsīsa to set them straight. When Devadatta saw the Chief Disciples coming, he was elated, believing that they were also coming to join him. Devadatta joined his palms together and asked Sāriputta to give a discourse to the monks, as he was feeling tired after eating a large meal.

While Devadatta's eyes grew heavy and he fell into a deep sleep, Sāriputta gave a profound and heartfelt discourse on the Four Noble Truths. The group of *bhikkhus* listened as if spellbound by the elder's words, and almost all of them, except for a few of Devadatta's loyal followers, became *sotāpannas*.

When the discourse was over, the group followed the two elders back to the true Master. Opening his eyes and wiping the drool from the side of his lips, Devadatta suddenly realized what had happened. He instantly fell ill and blood gushed out from his mouth.[47]

To get to Brahmājoni, hire a private vehicle or jump into a shared rickshaw on Old Gayā Road and tell the driver to let you off at the road leading to Brahmājoni (just before entering Gayā city, opposite the new bridge). You can then walk the remaining ten minutes to the hill. From the base of the hill, follow the steep steps for about 15 minutes. After passing through a small gateway full of people wanting money, turn left onto the rough path; there is an unclear sign indicating the way.

Going back to the main steps, you can climb to the top where there are shrines to some Hindu folk gods and goddesses. Locals believe that if you crawl into the small natural fissure—said to symbolize the divine womb—you will never experience rebirth again.

Surji/Suraj Kund
This water tank is a popular place for sun-worshipping Hindus to come for their ritual ablutions, especially during the light-half fortnight of *Chaitra* (March-April), and *Kartika* (October-November). The tank is also said to mark the spot where Sūciloma, a spikey-haired demon (*yakkha*), threatened to rip the Buddha's heart out and fling him across the river if he failed to answer certain questions: "From where do passion and hatred spring? From where do discontentment, attachment, and fear spring? From where do evil thoughts arise and harass the mind as boys do a crow?" The Buddha, not intimidated by the nasty Sūciloma, calmly replied,

Passion and hatred spring from egoism,
And so does discontentment, attachment, and fear.
Evil thoughts, too, arise from egoism,
And harass the mind as boys do a crow...

Listen, yakkha, those who know the source, overcome these.
They cross the flood which has never been crossed,
And are never reborn again.

Sūciloma, delighted at the Buddha's reply, bowed his head in reverence and vowed to always protect the Buddha, Dhamma and Saṅgha.[48]

Suraj Kund is about 100 metres just before and to the left of the famous Vishnupad Temple in Gayā. Near the ghat amongst a few sculptures are some old Buddhist stūpas.

Kukkutapadagiri (also known as Gurupadagiri), Gurpa Village

Knowing that the end of his life was drawing near, the resilient Mahākassapa set out for his favourite mountain resort, the Kukkutapadagiri (Cock's Foot Mountain). While threading his way to the top of this remote and rocky triple-peaked mountain, Mahākassapa's path was blocked by gigantic boulders. The austere and stern monk struck them with his staff and the rocks opened up to let him pass. The *bhikkhu* then climbed up to the summit, found a nice cave for meditating, and entered into a deep trance. The rocks closed up around him and he was never seen again. Legend narrates that when Mateyya, the next Buddha, appears in the world to re-introduce the Dhamma, he will find this mountain, awaken Mahākassappa and take his robe (which was given to him by the Buddha when they first met near Nālandā).

The adventure to Kukkutapadagiri is only for the stout-of-heart who are in good shape. To get there, you have two options: car or train (no buses available). If you choose the much easier way and go by car, take Fatipur Road (or 'Fatipur Pothole') via Gayā until you reach the railway station at Gurpa Village (43 km, about two hours from Bodhgayā).

If you choose to go by train from Gayā, try the Gayā Dhanvad Passenger (around 5:00 a.m.), Jammu Tawi Express (around 6:00 a.m.) or Jammu Tawi Express (around 11:30 a.m., not recommended). Each takes about an hour or so. To get back, you can catch the Asansol Vārāṇasī (around 1:00 p.m.), the Gayā Dhanvad Passenger (around 7:00 p.m.) or the Jammu Tawi Express (around 8:00 p.m.).

Once you arrive at Gurpa Village, cross the railway line and walk about 1 km along one of the footpaths leading to the foot of the mountain. Then climb the steep and strenuous trail for about 45 minutes until it ends at the base of a cliff, where there is a huge narrow crack. Enter the crack (perhaps where Mahākassapa struck the rocks?) and proceed upwards (don't forget your torch!) until you exit the crack. Keep climbing for a few metres. On your right you'll find a spacious cave with a painting of a cock's foot at its entrance. The cave opens to a ledge commanding breathtaking views, and has a small water tank containing dark limpid water believed to have healing properties. Mahākassapa, and other rugged *bhikkhus* such as Asanga and Sanarastika are said to have lived and meditated here. Scrambling above the cave you will reach the summit, decorated with some Buddhist antiquities, a couple of simple Hindu shrines and a shrine housing a set of footprints representing Mahākassapa.

Barābar, Nāgārjuni, & Kauwa Dol Hills

These ancient, boulder-strewn hills were once a popular setting for *bhikkhus* and wandering ascetics. It is easy to imagine the contemplative yogis meditating in these old hills and thick forests in the days before the terrain was domesticated by village life and agriculture.

Barābar Hill

The man-made caves of Barābar and Nāgārjuni are wonderful examples of early cave architecture (which reached its apex with the cave temples at Ajaṇṭā and Ellora). In the twelfth year after his coronation, King Asoka had a stūpa built on top of Barābar Hill to commemorate the spot where the Buddha enjoyed meditating throughout the night. Asoka also ordered the Barābar caves to be cut out for the Ājīvakas, a sect founded at the time of the Buddha by Makkhali Gosala, which faded into history not long after the Mauryan era. These offerings demonstrate Asoka's tolerance and support of spiritual traditions other than the Buddha's.

Walking up the steps for about five minutes, you will find the large Karna Cave on your left. Continuing up the path and around the bend, you will reach the Sudama Cave and Lomas Rishi Cave, with its semicircular doorway decorated with elegant carvings. The interiors of the Sudama and Karna caves consist of long barrel-like halls with chambers attached, and bear Brahmi inscriptions indicating who built them, for whom they were built, and when they were built. The interior walls have a remarkable glass-like polish, characteristic of Mauryan work. These caves are excellent for exploring, meditating, and chanting.

Heading back down towards the Karna Cave and taking the path on the left, you will come to the simple Vishwa Ghopri Cave. Follow the path around the cave and down the steps carved in the rocks, and you will reach the bottom.

The tiny **Nāgārjuna Museum**, located at the foot of the hill, has a handful of broken Hindu and Buddhist statues and a nice model of the area.

Nāgārjuni Hill

King Dasaratha, Asoka's grandson, emulated his grandfather's generosity to spiritual seekers by commissioning the carving of the large Gopika Cave on Nāgārjuni Hill. The cave resembles the others with the added bonus that to reach it requires a peaceful 2 km walk through the paddy fields from Barābar.

Kauwa Dol (Kuri Sarai)

This rocky hill was once inhabited by the Bengali Buddhist saint Śilabhadra and his disciples. At the foot of the hill beyond the village of Kurissara are several fabulous Hindu and Buddhist carvings on the rocks. The village's glory is an impressive 8-foot-tall black-stone Buddha statue in the earth-touching posture. Judging by some partially unearthed stone pillars and blocks, further excavations would likely reveal much more Dhamma history. Aside from the hundreds of villagers who will be fascinated by your presence, the place is very calm and peaceful, and it's easy to see why *bhikkhus* preferred it as a place for practice.

To get to these hills from Gayā, you can take a crowded direct bus to Barabar (42 km), or to Bela (30 km) and then to Barabar (15 km) or Kurissara (9 km). If you plan on making a daytrip by bus, then you will probably need to skip out on Kauwa Dol. Your other, more comfortable option is to hire a taxi for the day.

If you feel like staying overnight, there is a government rest house in Barabar. There is a small *dhaba* outside the museum, but you might also want to consider bringing some of your own food.

Sārnāth (*Isipatana*)

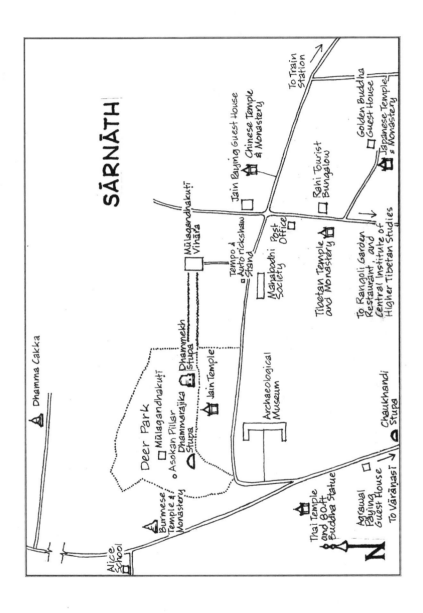

Turning the Wheel of Dhamma

After tasting the nectar of liberation and developing infinite compassion in his heart, the Buddha felt he wanted to share his discovery with the world. The first people to come to his mind were his former teachers, Āḷāra Kālāma and Uddaka Rāmaputta. He knew that if anyone could understand his message, it would be those two. Using his psychic abilities to find their whereabouts, the Buddha saw that they had both recently passed away. Next, then, in his mind was the group of five ascetics (*pañca-vaggiya*): Kondañña, Bhaddiya, Vappa, Assaji, and Mahānāma. Rather than dwelling on the fact that they had abandoned him, the Buddha only thought about how they had helped him during his intense and difficult training. Through the power of his divine eye, the Buddha saw that they were living in Isipatana at the Deer Park (*Migadāya*),[49] a royally protected area for animals to graze without fear and for religious mendicants to meditate without disturbance. On his way to Isipatana, the Buddha met a few individuals, such as the ascetic Ājīvaka Upaka, who recognized by the Buddha's clear and radiant appearance that he was no ordinary person. None of these people, however, was curious or competent enough to comprehend the Dhamma at the time. Nonetheless, these meetings did plant seeds that would sprout when these fortunate beings encountered the Dhamma in the future; they would become attracted to it, practise it, and realize the ultimate truth.[50]

On the full moon day of *Āsāḷha* (June-July), the Buddha reached Isipatana. Seeing him approach in the distance, the *pañca-vaggiya* made an agreement among themselves to let the Buddha sit with them as a fellow Sakya clansman, but not to greet him with folded-hands or take his robe and bowl, as was the custom amongst recluses. In their minds, Siddhattha had abandoned the holy life and reverted back to a life of luxury. However, as the radiant Buddha came closer and closer to their circle, each of them forgot their pledge. They stood up to meet him, took his robe and bowl, and prepared water to wash his feet.

The Buddha told his friends of his experience at Bodhgayā, and promised that if they practised in the same way, they too would attain emancipation. Initially, they doubted his claim. The Buddha counter-questioned them: "You are my Sakyan clansmen, you know me well, have you ever known me to lie?" They admitted that they had not, and agreed to listen to what he had to say.

With complete spiritual authority, the Buddha began his famous first discourse, 'Setting the Wheel of Dhamma in Motion' (*Dhammacakkapavattana Sutta*). His voice was filled with confidence and his manner was serene. Everything he said was based on his direct experience alone, not on any scriptures or hearsay.

Bhikkhus, those walking on the path of purification should avoid two extremes: self-indulgence and self-affliction. Plunging into sensual pleasures makes one lazy; depriving the body of its basic needs wastes one's energy. Both these extremes lead to failure. Therefore, bhikkhus, you must walk along a middle path.

Bhikkhus, there are four noble truths: the existence of suffering, the arising of suffering, the cessation of suffering, and the path leading to the cessation of suffering...

Now this, bhikkhus, is the noble truth of suffering: birth is suffering, ageing is suffering, sickness is suffering, death is suffering; sorrow, lamentation, pain, grief and despair are suffering; association with the unpleasant is suffering, separation from the pleasant is suffering, not getting what one wants is suffering—in short, clinging to the five aggregates[51] is suffering.

And this, bhikkhus, is the noble truth of the arising of suffering: craving—accompanied by over-indulgence, lust, and relishing—produces renewal of being. In other words, the arising of suffering is craving for sensual pleasures, craving for being, and craving for non-being.[52]

And this, bhikkhus, is the noble truth of the cessation of suffering: suffering fades, stops, and no longer remains when that same craving is renounced, relinquished, let go of, and rejected.

And this, bhikkhus, is the noble truth of the method of practice leading to the cessation of suffering: it is precisely the Noble Eightfold Path—right view, right thoughts, right speech, right action, right livelihood, right effort, right awareness, and right concentration.[53]

By the end of this profound, world-transforming discourse, Kondañ-ña, the oldest of the five in years and in wisdom, grasped the meaning of the Buddha's words and attained the first stage of enlightenment (*sotāpanna*). Love, compassion, goodwill and peace reigned within the old meditator's heart.

Shortly after illuminating these truths in the *Dhammacakkapavattana Sutta*, the Buddha further nourished the five *bhikkhus* with a second discourse, the *Anattalakkhana Sutta*. In this teaching, the Buddha explained that the way we conventionally perceive the five aggregates of mind and body as a permanent self is a delusion, and this error of perception creates a false sense of control and ownership. The existential miseries of old age, sickness, and death come whether we like it or not. No "I" can ever change this fact of life. Since these aggregates are impermanent, it is neither logical nor plausible to consider them as one's own property. Doing so only results in misery.

The Buddha questioned them, "Is material form...sensation...perception...formative reaction...consciousness...permanent or impermanent?"

"Impermanent, Master," they responded.

"Is that which is impermanent pleasant or unpleasant?"

"Unpleasant, Master."

"So, is it fitting to regard what is impermanent, unpleasant, and subject to change as: 'This is mine, this is what I am, this is myself'?"

"No, Master..."

"Therefore, *bhikkhus*, any material form...sensation...perception... formative reaction...consciousness, whether past, future, or present; internal or external; coarse or fine; inferior or superior; or far or near, should all be regarded as it actually is by properly understanding: 'This is not mine, this is not what I am, this is not myself.'"[54]

Following his advice, all five *bhikkhus* let go of the illusory "I" and became fully enlightened beings (*arahants*). The Buddha did not awaken them by any magic or miracle; all he did was give guidance along the way. The realization came from the meditators themselves.

The first two discourses given in the Deer Park mark the beginning of the Sangha, and because the Buddha and his five disciples found the park's protective atmosphere very conducive to meditation, they decided to spend the rainy season there.

One morning, a depressed young merchant named Yasa stumbled into the park. Yasa had run away from his luxurious yet suffocating life in Vārānasī and come in search of inner peace. Wandering into the park, muttering to himself about the ills of the world, he found the Buddha sitting serenely on a rock. "Who are you, sir?" Yasa inquired,

Four Noble Truths

The Buddha taught that acknowledging the inevitable truth of suffering is the first step on the path towards recovery from self-created human misery. Each of us faces different levels of suffering. On the surface level of reality, birth, old-age, sickness, and death are all undesirable situations that are unavoidable. So are changes in circumstances, such as becoming involved with things that we would rather avoid, being separated from the people and things we love, and failing to achieve our goals. We also suffer from the attachments we develop to our views, beliefs, rituals, people and material objects, usually associating these things with our identity and assuming them to be the basis for our happiness.

At a deeper level, the Buddha taught that these objects of attachment are actually secondary. The real attachment is towards this 'I,' 'Me,' and 'Mine,' which is in actuality nothing but a rapidly changing process of mental and physical aggregates. Attaching oneself to what is ungraspable and impermanent is the real cause of human misery.

It often appears that the causes of our suffering arise because of external circumstances. The Buddha's second noble truth, however, shows that the real causes of our suffering are entirely inside of us. These causes are found in our greedy cravings for sensual pleasures, in our fear and aversion towards unpleasant situations, and in the ignorance of our deeply conditioned, reactionary mental habit patterns. As long as we remain unaware of this process, these causes continue to multiply our attachments, thus multiplying our suffering.

The third noble truth shows the flip side of the second. If we remove the causes of our suffering, then there will be no distressing effects to bother us. We actually have control over how much we suffer. As Ian McCrorie wrote in *The Moon Appears When the Water is Still*, "Pain visits all, but suffering comes not to those who welcome its arrival."

The Buddha's fourth noble truth, which he discovered, followed, and taught, is the universal eight-part training for the eradication of the causes of suffering: craving, aversion and ignorance. This path consists of right view, right thought, right speech, right action, right livelihood, right effort, right awareness and right concentration.

Right view (*sammā diṭṭhi*) is not merely adhering to some dogmatic principle or ideology, but is a rational and experiential understanding of the laws of nature, which are characterized by three inter-related characteristics (*ti-lakkhaṇa*): anicca, dukkha, and *anattā*.

Anicca, the impermanent nature of all phenomena, is the Buddha's guiding thread in his teaching of human liberation. This is not merely an intellectual concept, but, as Paul Fleischman elucidates, a "word-indicator that points to a fact of reality: the ceaseless transformation of all material in the universe...Every 'thing' is really an 'event'. Even a stone is a form of river, and a mountain is only a slow wave."[55] The individual person, too, is born and eventually dies, changing from moment to moment throughout a fleeting life. Nothing remains unchanged.

Dukkha is the nature of suffering resulting from the inherent dissatisfaction we all experience when faced with an ever-changing reality. As human beings, we are constantly involved with unwanted situations and become frustrated when we are separated from—or fail to get—the objects of our delight. Because of our inherent disposition towards 'I,' 'Me,' and 'Mine,' we long for permanence, comprehensibility and control, yet are continually confounded with an impermanent, fluxing and flowing world. When we rely on anything other than our own spiritual development for our well-being, we are bound to become unhappy.

Anattā, or substancelessness, is the understanding that there is no abiding separate self, soul or individual entity. All things are interdependent on one another; nothing can exist independently from anything else. A tree can only exist in relation to the soil that nourishes its roots, the sky that provides it oxygen to breathe, and the sun that gives it energy to grow. Without these supportive elements, a tree cannot exist. When we attempt to anchor ourselves in external things that inevitably change, including our own self-concepts, we fail to achieve any real stability, security or peace.

Right thoughts (*sammā saṅkappa*) are those focussed on, and conducive to, mental purification, such as generosity, ethical integrity, renunciation, compassion, nonviolence, tolerance and so forth. Cultivating these types of thoughts is essential for anyone walking on the path of liberation.

Right speech (*sammā vācā*) means avoiding telling lies, generating schisms amongst friends, backbiting, slander, harsh words and idle and frivolous gossip. The Buddha taught that one who engages in right speech is one who "speaks the truth…is trustworthy, dependable, straightforward with others…reconciles quarrelling, rejoices and creates harmony with pleasant words…is courteous…speaks at the proper time, according to the facts and to what is helpful…"[56]

The Buddha taught his students to avoid sectarian definitions of piety and sin. He preached that **right action** (*sammā kammanta*) consists of any action that contributes towards the peace and harmony of oneself and others. On the other hand, any action that disturbs the peace and harmony of oneself and others is unwholesome. Likewise, **right livelihood** (*sammā ājīva*) encourages peace and concord and discourages the breaching of a person's moral conduct. The Buddha often provided general guidelines to his students when it came to employment (i.e. avoid trades dealing with weapons, slaves, intoxicants, poison and breeding animals for slaughter), but rarely gave details about how to go about one's trade. In this way, his students had to make their own decisions based on their personal experience, rather than relying on his guidance for every little detail in their lives. The Buddha taught that by practising the Dhamma, the illusory ego dissolves and our interdependent and selfless nature manifests itself. Qualities of love, compassion, and non-violence develop naturally, and our ability to make responsible decisions improves, resulting in a life of greater personal, social, and ecological harmony.

There are four **right efforts** (*sammā vāyāma*) that a meditator needs to practice: (i) prevent unhealthy mental states from arising, (ii) abandon unhealthy states that are already present, (iii) generate healthy mental states, and, (iv) maintain the healthy states that are already there. Since the Dhamma path requires a lifetime of sustained practice, right effort also includes developing patience, calmness and acceptance with all our personal shortcomings and the difficulties that we encounter along the way.

Right awareness (*sammā sati*) is paying attention to whatever is happening in the present moment as it is (*not* as we would like it to be). Developing a single-pointed mind, free from sensual or material gratification is **right concentration** (*sammā samādhi*).

When the Buddha's Noble Eightfold Path is practised properly, it "produces vision, produces knowledge and leads to peace, to penetrative insight, to self-awakening, to *nibbāna*."

momentarily forgetting his own anxieties. "I have never seen anyone looking as serene and worry-free as you."

"Sit, friend, let's talk. Nothing in this world is worth getting worked-up over," the Buddha answered, in a clear and soothing manner that helped Yasa relax. The Buddha then skilfully counselled Yasa with the progressive Dhamma instructions on: (i) the benefits of charity, (ii) ethics as the foundation for liberation, (iii) the harmfulness of over-indulging in sensual pleasures, (iv) the futility of conceit, and (v) the bliss of renunciation. These discussions soothed Yasa's mind, making him receptive to the subtleties of the Four Noble Truths. Penetrating directly into the heart of the Buddha's words, Yasa, through his own understanding, freed himself from all his sorrows and became the Buddha's sixth enlightened disciple.

That afternoon, Yasa's father, a wealthy and reputable merchant, unaccustomed to wandering in a forest, met the Buddha while searching frantically for his son.

"Sir, have you seen my son Yasa wandering about? I found his shoes at the entrance to the forest, so he must be somewhere around here..." the merchant asked, with a tinge of hope in his voice.

"Do not worry," the Buddha answered, "Yasa will come shortly. He is meditating in one of the nearby huts."

As with Yasa, the Buddha's presence calmed the old man down. The Buddha explained to him why Yasa had run away, and how he had now resolved his personal problems. The Buddha then taught Yasa's father the same progressive instructions and the Four Noble Truths. Yasa's father listened attentively and found solace in the Dhamma. Delighted at hearing and experiencing such wisdom, Yasa's father tasted the fruits of sotāpannahood and became the first person to take refuge in the Triple Gem—the Buddha, Dhamma, and Saṅgha.

Soon after, Yasa arrived and joined them. Yasa's father was very pleased to see his son so happy, clad in a *bhikkhu's* robe with a shaved head and sparkling eyes. He bowed to his son and invited the Buddha and Saṅgha to his home for the next day's meal.

The following day, the Buddha and his six disciples walked to Yasa's family home for their alms. "What have you done to yourself, you foolish boy?" Yasa's mother and his wife both cried out in horror and disapproval when they saw that he had become a *bhikkhu*. The Buddha, however, as he had done with Yasa and his father, soothed the apprehensive women with the progressive Dhamma instructions and the teaching of the Four Noble Truths. Comprehending the depth of the Buddha's words, both the women felt as if a gateway of happiness had opened in their hearts, and each became a *sotāpanna*. With joined palms, they bowed in sincere reverence to the Buddha and Saṅgha and became the first women to take refuge in the Triple Gem.

Word of Yasa and his family's spiritual transformation began to spread around Vārāṇasī. Fifty-four of Yasa's friends, all the sons of wealthy merchants, discussed the unusual events among themselves, saying "Yasa is surely an intelligent fellow who always carefully considers his actions. His teacher must really be extraordinary. Let's go visit them at the Deer Park." The group went to the Deer Park, met the Buddha, received the progressive Dhamma instructions and Four Noble Truths, and experienced the unshakable peace of arahantship.

By the end of the Buddha's first rainy season (*vassā*) after Enlightenment, there were sixty enlightened *bhikkhus* in the world. To these shining examples of the Dhamma, the Buddha exhorted,

Go now and wander, bhikkhus, for the good of many, for the happiness of many. Shower the world with compassion, for the welfare, good, and happiness of both gods and men. Let no two of you go in the same direction. Teach the Dhamma which is beneficial in the beginning, beneficial in the middle and beneficial in the end. Explain both the letter and the spirit of the holy life, completely fulfilled and perfectly pure.[57]

From that point onwards, the Dhamma started spreading throughout India and the world.

Site-Sitting

Deer Park

Scattered throughout the park are ruins of various stūpas, temples, shrines and monasteries first built by King Asoka during the Mauryan era (4th to 2nd century BCE), and later renovated and reconstructed by various royal patrons of the Gupta (4th to 7th century CE) and Pala (8th to 12th century CE) dynasties. After its destruction in 1194 by the Islamic invader Qutbuddin Aik, Sārnāth was lost for the next 640 years, until Alexander Cunningham and his team of archaeologists discovered the ruins, opening a forgotten door to India's past splendour.

Exploring the ruins and meditating for an entire day in the park is well-worth paying the entrance fee. If you are really strapped for cash and can't afford to part with your rupees, then you can always meditate on the other side of the fence at the peaceful Burmese Temple or crowded Jain Temple. The Deer Park is generally busier on weekends and holidays when Vārāṇasī urbanites use the park as a picnic spot.

Dhammekh Stūpa

In the eastern corner of the park stands the gigantic, yet somewhat dilapidated, 33-metre-high Dhammekh Stūpa (Sanskrit: *Dharmekh*). The original stūpa, built by Asoka, was later enlarged by royal sympathizers. The stūpa's remaining façade features intricately-carved stonework of animals and floral patterns, providing some indication of its past grandeur. Some of the smaller votive stūpas nearby may give a clearer image of what the original Dhammekh Stūpa might have looked like.

The name of the stūpa, Dhammekh, translates as 'one Dhamma', referring to the Buddha's teaching that there is only one path of the Dhamma—*sīla*, *samādhi* and *paññā*. This popular monument attracts pilgrims, tourists, vendors and merchants, and meditating here can help strengthen our practice of these three trainings.

Dhammarājika Stūpa Foundation
Just after the main entrance is the foundation of the once great Dhammarājika Stūpa (Sanskrit: *Dharmarājika*). The Archaeological Survey of India claims that this ruin marks the site of the second discourse, while the Dhammekh Stūpa marks the spot of the first. Other scholars, however, argue that the close proximity of the main shrine and Asokan pillar to the Dhammarājika Stūpa, and the fact that the Buddha's relics[58] were found in the Dhammarājika Stūpa and not in the Dhammekh Stūpa, indicates that it must have been the site of the first discourse, and that the Dhammekh Stūpa marks the site of the second.[59]

In any case, the whole debate is of little concern for the Dhamma pilgrim. The entire park is a peaceful place suitable for meditation, and when meditating anywhere, whether at these stūpas or in our own homes, it's most important to practise the Four Noble Truths with an understanding of *anicca*, *dukkha*, and *anattā*; to observe the reality of the present moment as it is, with awareness and equanimity.

Mūlagandhakuṭi (Fragrant Hut)
This shrine, now in ruins, was built over the site of the hut where the Buddha slept and meditated. This spot, being a little more secluded than the others, is perhaps a more conducive setting to undisturbed meditation.

Asokan Railing
South of the Mūlagandhakuṭi is a stone railing that was part of the Dhammarājika Stūpa. Its fine polishing and single-block Chunar sandstone carving is representative of classic Mauryan stonework.

Asokan Pillar
The broken shaft and damaged four-lion crown (now in the museum) of this once tall and mighty pillar not only symbolizes the pomp and glory of ancient India, but also hints at the vicinity of where the Buddha began his forty-five year teaching career and first established the Saṅgha of sixty arahants.

The pillar's inscription points out the necessity of keeping the Saṅgha unified, and was probably issued by King Asoka sometime after the Third Council, which was held in order to settle some discrepancies and rid the order of undisciplined monks. In 326 BCE, Asoka sponsored the nine-month long council in Patna where 1 000 *bhikkhus*, presided over by the arahant Moggaliputta Tissa, standardized the Pāli canon, added the section 'The Points of Controversy' (*Kathāvatthu*) to the Abhidhamma Piṭaka, and removed divisive elements that had crept into the Saṅgha. The present edict illustrates Asoka's desire for a unified Saṅgha. He engraved, "No one is to cause dissension in the Order. Whoever creates a schism in the Order…is to be put in a place not inhabited by monks or nuns. For it is my wish that the Order should remain united and endure for long." Those *bhikkhus* whose views differed from that of the elder Moggaliputta Tissa, however, went on to develop their own separate institutions whose lineages exist to this day in various evolved forms.

Sitting in this quiet spot, away from the traffic of the park, is a great place to reflect upon the magnitude of Asoka's unswerving devotion to the Dhamma, and all his hard work in striving to create ideal social, political and spiritual conditions for his empire.

Chaukhandi Stūpa

About 1 km from the Deer Park and archaeological museum, towards Vārāṇasī, is an octagonal tower sitting on top of a crumbling stūpa. The tower was built in 1588 by the Mughal Emperor Akbar in memory of his father Humayan. The stūpa, partly covered with vegetation, is believed to mark the spot where the Buddha first encountered his five companions and convinced them that he had truly become a self-taught, fully enlightened being.[60] No relics were found in the stūpa, but the sculptures around it suggest that it dates from around the fifth century.

Mūlagandhakuṭi Vihāra

This temple compound, just east of the Deer Park, was constructed in 1922 by the Buddhist revivalist Anagarika Dharmapala. Practitioners and sympathizers from all over the world have donated their time and money to the temple, indicating the trans-cultural appeal of the Buddha's teachings.

Every evening in the Mūlagandhakuṭi Vihāra, local *bhikkhus* chant, in unison, the *Dhammacakkapavatthana Sutta*, the Buddha's first discourse on the Middle Path and Four Noble Truths. The *sutta* is chanted in Tibetan from 4:30-5:00pm and in Pāli from 6:00-7:00pm. Many practitioners find it wonderful to meditate at this time, as the echoing vibrations of the Buddha's profound words fill the temple and the body and mind. (It's also a good opportunity to test your understanding of Pāli!) The temple also contains bone relics of the Buddha, which are believed to support a favourable atmosphere for meditation. The relics are kept behind the Buddha statue. If asked, the attendant monk will sometimes let meditators sit behind the statue closer to the relics and away from crowds.[61] Every year the temple celebrates its anniversary on *Karthika Purnima*, the full moon day in the month of November, by parading the relics around town.

Inside the temple, Japanese artist Kosetsu Nosu painted an exquisite mural depicting scenes from the Buddha's life. Nosu came on assignment from the imperial government of Japan at the request of the Mahābodhi Society, and the paintings were opened to the public in 1936.

The South Wall:

1. The Bodhisatta in the Tusita heaven waiting to be reborn.
2. Queen Māyā's auspicious dream of the Bodhisatta's conception.
3. Prince Siddhattha's birth under a *sālā* tree in Lumbinī.
4. The seven-year-old prince meditating while his father performs the annual ploughing ritual.
5. The 'Four Sights' that prompted Siddhattha to renounce the householder's life in search of liberation.

6. Siddhattha taking a last look at Yasodharā and Rāhula before sneaking out of the palace.

The West Wall:

7. Riding on his horse Kanthaka and accompanied by his attendant Channa, the Bodhisatta escapes into the night.

8. Receiving instructions from his meditation teachers, Āḷāra Kālāma and Uddaka Rāmaputta.

9. Weakened by years of extreme self-torture, the Bodhisatta accepts food from Sujātā while the five ascetics look on with disapproval.

10. Māra and his army attacking the Bodhisatta.

11. The Buddha being greeted by the five ascetics as he arrives in Sārnāth to teach them the Dhamma.

12. The Buddha teaching the Dhamma to King Bimbisāra.

13. Anāthapiṇḍika purchasing the royal park from Prince Jeta.

The East Wall:

14. The Buddha and Ānanda tending to a sick monk who had been neglected by his fellow *bhikkhus*.

15. The Buddha mediating a dispute between the Sakyans and the Koliyans who are about to go to war over the water in the Rohini River.

16. The Buddha returning to Kapilavatthu for the first time after his Awakening

17. The Buddha on his deathbed while Bhikkhu Anuruddha urges the other *bhikkhus* not to cry over something that is impermanent. On the Buddha's right is the wandering ascetic Subhadda who became the Buddha's last enlightened disciple before his *parinibbāna*.

18. The Buddha teaching the Abhidhamma to his mother in the Tāvatimsa Heaven.

19. The Buddha converting Aṅgulimāla from a murderer into a saint.

20. Devadatta and Ajātasattu scheming to kill the Buddha and King Bimbisāra.

21. Ānanda asks a low-caste girl to give him some water, illustrating the Buddha's rejection of racism and casteism.

Walking clockwise around the temple, you will notice a small monument marking the spot where Anagarika Dharmapala was cremated, and behind that is a small deer petting zoo. On the east side of the temple are larger-than-life-sized statues of the Buddha and the *pañca-vaggiya* sitting under a bodhi tree (which is a descendant of a sapling from the original Bodhi Tree). Surrounding the tree are images of the twenty-seven previous Buddhas, as well as marble plates where the *Dhammacakkapavatthana Sutta* is inscribed in different scripts with their translations. The quietest time to meditate here is at sunrise when the gates first open.

Archaeological Museum

One of the more impressive archaeological museums along the pilgrim's circuit, the small Sārnāth museum displays a fine collection of more than 2 500 pieces of art. The most famous piece is the colossal lion capital that originally crowned the

Asokan pillar in the Deer Park and which today is India's national emblem. The capital consists of four lions sitting back to back with their paws resting on four Dhamma wheels. The majestic animals are representative of the Buddha's 'lion's roar'—the valiant proclamation of the Dhamma to the four cardinal directions. Below the lions and between the Dhamma wheels are images of a bull, horse, lion and bull-elephant, each an ancient Indian symbol of nobility and enlightenment. One could hardly envision a more suitable symbol for the place where the Dhamma was proclaimed to the world for the first time.

The museum also houses many other images of the Buddha displaying his different hand symbols (*mūdra*): teaching (*dhammacakkamūdra*); meditation (*dhyanamūdra*); earth-bearing witness (*bhumisparsamūdra*); protection (*abhayamūdra*), and gift-bestowing (*varadamūdra*). These images are sometimes flanked by images of *bodhisattas*. Dhamma wheels and two deer are sometimes present, symbolizing the Turning of the Wheel of the Law in the Deer Park. The deer also represent the Buddha's teaching that the mind should have the quality of a deer (*migabhūtena cetasā*)—"gentle, alert, and quick to notice danger."[62] Other works include panels of the Buddha's life, sculptures of *bodhisattas*, Brahminical deities, mythical animals, parasols, pottery and royal inscriptions. The museum is open from 10:00 a.m. to 5:00 p.m. every day except Fridays. There is a nominal entrance fee.

Dhamma Cakka, Sārnāth Vipassana Centre

Surrounded by paddy fields and village hamlets, Dhamma Cakka ('Wheel of Dhamma') maintains an air of rural tranquility. The well-built centre has a capacity for approximately 40 meditators to reside in comfortable single or double rooms, and meditate in a charming octagonal Dhamma hall. Lovely flower and vegetable gardens dotted with young trees line the walking areas and provide a supportive ambience for serious practice of the Noble Eightfold Path.

Ten-day courses are held every month from the 3rd–14th and the 18th–29th. It is a unique opportunity to meditate or serve in this atmospheric setting, so close to where the Buddha delivered his first two discourses illuminating the way to *nibbāna*. The tight-knit local community of meditators welcomes fellow travellers on the path of purification.

If coming from Vārānasī , you can take a taxi or rickshaw directly to the centre. If coming from Sārnāth, you can take an auto or cycle rickshaw, or you can walk. Go past the Burmese Temple for about 4 km and then turn right at the green sign reading 'Dhamma Cakka Vipassana Centre' and continue for another kilometre.

Contact:
Dhamma Cakka, Vipassana Sadhana Kendra
Khargipur Village
Sārnāth, Uttar Pradesh
Tel: [+91] (0)542-3208168
E-mail: info@cakka.dhamma.org
Website: www.cakka.dhamma.org

Sleeping & Eating

Many of the temples and monasteries that surround the Deer Park offer simple lodging. You can try your luck at the **Burmese Temple, Chinese Temple, Japanese Temple, Tibetan Temple** (across from the Central Institute of Higher Tibetan Studies) and **Vajravidya** (behind the Deer Park), and **Jain Dharamshala**. Some of these manage to survive off the 'pay-as-you-like' system, while others request a nominal 'suggested donation'. Budget and mid-range options include the **Jain Paying Guest House, Agrawal Paying Guest House, Mrigdava Hotel & Tourist Info Centre, Golden Buddha Guest House**, and **Mahabodhi Guest House**. If you can't get food at your accommodation, there are a few restaurants and food stalls around the park.

Coming & Going

From the Vārāṇasī (12 km) and Mughal Sarai (15 km) train stations, there are a stream of **buses, taxis, auto rickshaws** and **shared tuk-tuks**. If coming by bus from Sonauli (about 9 hours), tell the driver to drop you off at the Sārnāth bus stand rather than going all the way to Vārāṇasī and then doubling back. A few local **trains** stop at the Sārnāth station, just outside of town.

If you don't mind the blistering summer heat or the sticky humidity of monsoon season (depending on the year), then it is worthwhile to visit Sārnāth during the full moon of *Āsāḷha* (June-July), the day commemorating the Buddha's first discourse.

After a gruelling night without a fan (no electricity!) marked by clammy sweat and mosquitoes, we started our morning by meditating in the main temple and listening to the monks chant the homage to the Triple Gem and the Dhammacakkapavatthana Sutta. Feeling recharged, we went to the Deer Park for a one-day self-course.

> *As rainwater falls outside*
> *Cleansing trees and grass;*
> *The water of wisdom falls inside*
> *Cleansing body and mind.*
>
> *– S.N. Goenka*

Taking advantage of the shade provided by colossal amla and banyan trees, we sat happily, observing the constant stream of sensations arising from both our mental contents as well as from contact with curious children (and adults) wanting to know our names and country; obnoxious post-card, statuette and ice-cream vendors, and the stares and giggles of Sunday picnickers from Vārāṇasī. "Sit-hopping" from tree to monument and monument to tree, we felt a calmness persisting throughout the day, arising from a blend of the uniqueness of the place and the intense heat.

*Facing what would have been the Buddha's hut, we closed our day
with the practice of mettā. Suddenly, while sharing our merits with
all beings, the skies released a heavy downpour of cooling rain—a
final cleanse that left us drenched, but fresh and content—a perfect
ending to our celebration of the Dhammacakkapavattaa.*

— MD & KG

Excursions

Vārāṇasī (*Benares, Kashi*)

Although Vārāṇasī was never an important city in Buddhist history, for the devout Hindu it is considered to be the oldest inhabited and most sacred city in India. Every year countless believers from all over the Indian subcontinent, particularly those nearing death, fulfill a lifelong desire by coming to the Ganges River in Vārāṇasī, the city of Shiva, for a ritual bath that is believed to cleanse all past sins and guarantee the soul swift passage to salvation.

For the Dhamma pilgrim, Vārāṇasī is primarily important as a connecting link for business and travel routes. However, this commercial and cultural centre is an interesting stop-over in its own right, and an excellent place to explore Indian arts and culture. You'll see many advertisements around the old city for yoga, music, dance, ayurveda, cooking and language lessons: either short- or long-term. It's easy to find lodging somewhere along the *ghats* (riverside bathing steps) and pursue your lessons at whatever pace suits you. This captivating city is also well known for its remarkable Indian classical music concerts, both announced and impromptu.

Vārāṇasī is situated along the cresent-shaped western bank of the Ganges, where the ghats run for some seven kilometres. Extending from the ghats inland is Vārāṇasī 's Old City, a tangled maze of narrow alleys where the best way to avoid getting lost is to travel along the riverbank, following the continuous series of ghats. The more modern extension of Vārāṇasī is further west, between the Old City and the train station. Most of Vārāṇasī's luxury hotels and restaurants can be found in the Cantonment area, just north-west of the train station. Cremating the dead on open fires, a custom since ancient times, is primarily conducted at two ghats, Manikarnika to the north, and Harish Chandra to the south. The areas around these ghats are often choked with smoke and crowded with funeral processions, so it is advisable to stay elsewhere. Dasaswamedh, the city's main ghat, is located roughly halfway between the two cremation ghats.

Vārāṇasī's Old City is ideal for catching the sunrise over the Ganges, wandering through the labyrinth of medieval lanes, observing the living spirituality of Hinduism, avoiding speeding bicycles and pooping cows, and relaxing on one of the countless rooftops, watching as the Ganges mirrors our constantly flowing lives. Enjoying a boat ride or walking along the ancient ghats is also a great way to get a glimpse of Vārāṇasī culture, especially at dawn when the river is bathed in a magical light. Moving from one ghat to the next and passing ancient temples, rustic palaces, historic fortresses penetrated by modern guest houses and busy tea-stalls, you will find yourself amidst the life of the city: people bathing, doing their laundry, swimming, washing their buffaloes, offering massages and boat rides ("Hallo, boat?"), selling trinkets, reading palms, praying, doing yoga, playing cricket, cremating their loved ones or simply getting a shave. Vārāṇasī 's dramas are infinite.

For shoppers, Dasaswamedh Road (leading to Dasaswamedh Ghat, or just 'main ghat'), Godaulia (the area bordering the old city), Golghar (market near the main post-office) and the Cottage Industry showrooms in the Cantonment offer Vārāṇasī's rich selection of silk fabrics and perfumes (also popular during the Buddha's time), beautiful handwoven Indian rugs, brass and silver antiques, wooden handicrafts and musical instruments. Beware of the *come-have-some-tea-wallahs* who charm you into their shops and then pressure you to buy whatever they are selling.

Besides the bazaars and the two-hundred-plus temples, other places of interest are the Sanskrit University, whose library possesses the world's largest collection of Sanskrit literature, and Benares Hindu University's (BHU) Bharat Kala Bhavan, which has a fine exhibition of Hindu, Buddhist and Jain sculptures and paintings. They are both open from 10:30 a.m. to 5 p.m. (7 a.m. to 12:30 p.m. in the summer), and closed on Sundays.

We stayed within the mazeway of Vārāṇasī 's Old City for more than a week, and became fairly well oriented within a short radius around our slouching old guest house, where we paid about three dollars a night for a passable and quiet room. But if we ventured further into the Old City, or tried to re-enter along some other route, we would inevitably become bewilderingly and absurdly lost, so much so that it's now quite easy to imagine people arriving one day and remaining lost for a lifetime, absorbed by the enveloping city. This is precisely what I suspect has happened to a great many of the supposed holy men who wander there, half-naked and smiling oblivions through a penumbra of hashish smoke.

Like the ghats, the buildings of the Old City descend steeply and stepwise to the Ganges: haphazard and historied, their vari-coloured stories like layers of sediment, the buildings there interlock in an incidental multi-dimensional jigsaw where windows look upon walls, doorways gasp in stairless air, and the roofs of some form the terraces of others. On our first night in Vārāṇasī we watched, from one such vantage, as a lone woman performed puja in the gathering dusk. By the erratic light of ghee butter candles arranged in a sort of mandala along her crumbling brick-and-mortar balcony, the woman made a complex series of offerings and prayers to the goddess Ganga, sprinkling flowers and oil, scattering spices and turning to bow in the four directions, her movements so practised as to seem casual, like cooking a familiar dish.

As with other Indian gestures, this nonchalance initially appeared to be perfunctory, even dismissive, but as we watched it became evident that this solitary ritual was a kind of meditation. Through a series of focused and repetitive acts this woman was gracefully steadying and centering herself within the coordinates of known space, making explicit an awareness of her place in the present moment, and giving thanks. Simply observing this private day's-end peace, we found ourselves calmed as well, and introduced, for the first time, to the living heart of the ancient city by the river.

Things were perhaps unusually quiet for tourism and it's accompanying hassles while we were there in the Old City because the river boatmen were on strike in protest of a new tax imposition. Fortunately, the strike ended just before we were to leave, and on the morning of our last day we were graced with a dawn boat ride on the Ganges—the strange city shimmering and seemingly orderly, its mythical power fully apparent when seen from that vantage in the diffused light of sunrise, where fading fog blends imperceptibly with the smoke and ash of burning bodies along the cremation ghats, shrouding the forms of morning bathers and those washing their clothes in the sacred waters; scores of ancient stone temples leaning in as if to look on approvingly.

We took pains to avoid those waters, however; the holy Ganges is filthy. Most of Vārāṇasī's sewage is discharged, untreated, directly into the river, and the water there is actually septic, meaning that no dissolved oxygen exists. Ever since visiting the first derelict, mud-splattered shrines of Kathmandu, we have struggled to understand this apparent disconnect between religious veneration and actual care and concern; between ritual purity and hygienic cleanliness. Though a distance between articulated values and embodied experience is to be found everywhere, in every tradition, India is often a land of incredible extremes, and this distance was continually reiterated for us as we followed her pilgrims' paths further...

– Austin Pick

Vārāṇasī: Sleeping & Eating

The Old City and the Cantonment are the two main tourist areas, full of hotels, restaurants, internet cafés, travel agents and money-changers. Wherever you plan on staying, be firm when giving instructions to the *rickshaw-wallah*; since they usually get a commission, they can be very persistent in wanting to take you to their hotel. Don't listen to any nonsense that your choice of hotel is full, closed, flooded or burnt down. For places in the Old City, it's easiest to just tell the driver to take you to Dasaswamedh Ghat (main ghat) and then walk to the hotel from there along the river. Many hotels now offer pickup service from the train station, so ask about that if you book ahead. Vārāṇasī has a reputation for tourist scams and swindles, so take care not to trust everyone, keep an eye and a hand on your belongings at all times, and inform yourself by talking with other travellers.

The more comfortable hotels are in the quiet, colonial Cantonment area behind the railway station. Some mid-range choices are the **Hotel Surya** on The Mall and hotels **India**, **Vaibhav**, and **Temples Town** on Patel Nagar. Luxurious choices on The Mall include the **Hotel Varanasi Ashok** and **Hotel Ideal Palace**. The two five-star hotels are the **Taj Ganges** on Nadesar Palace and **Hotel Clarks** on The Mall. All the hotels in this area have restaurants.

The Old City is packed with alcohol-free restaurants, and budget and mid-range guest houses abound. Those along the ghats often have rooftop terraces offering fantastic views of river life. Amongst the innumerable guest houses, a few recommended include **Alka Hotel and Vegetarian Restaurant** (Meer Ghat), **Ganpathi Guest House** (Meer Ghat), **Vishnu Rest House** (Panday Ghat), **Shiva Guest House** (Munshi Ghat), **Shanti Guest House** (Manikarnika Ghat) and **Scindhia Guest House** (Scindhia Ghat). Cheaper places can be found within the avenues of the Old City itself. If you plan on staying a little longer, Assi Ghat, not far from Benares Hindu University, has some good choices such as the **Sahi River View Guest House** (budget and mid-range), **Hotel Haifa** (mid-range), and **Palace on the Ganga** (luxury). Bargaining for hotel rates will usually save you some rupees, especially during the hot season when there are fewer tourists.

Aside from those in the hotels, Vārāṇasī has some other restaurants worth mentioning. **Ganga Fuji Restaurant** (not to be confused with Ganga Hotel) offers excellent Indian food and free live Indian classical music every evening from 7:30 p.m. Nearby, around the corner from Golden Lodge, **Megu Café** is not to be missed for authentic Japanese food. **I:ba**, off Shivala Road in the vicinity of Harish Chandra Ghat, features modern décor and a menu to match, with Thai, Japanese, and Indian dishes. **Brown Bread Bakery**, **Dolphin Restaurant**, **Lotus Lounge** and **Bread of Life Bakery** are all long-standing popular choices. Directions are notoriously difficult in Vārāṇasī 's Old City, so ask around.

If you need to catch a train early in the morning, you may want to consider staying in one of the hotels across the street from the train station on Parade Kothi, rather than coming all the way from the Old City. **The Tourist Bungalow** and **Hotel Plaza Inn** are decent mid-range choices, and there are also several basic budget hotels from which to choose.

Vārāṇasī: Coming & Going

Vārāṇasī has two **train** stations, Vārāṇasī Junction Train Station to the west, and Kashi Train Station to the north. All references in this book refer to Vārāṇasī Junction, which is the city's main train station. Vārāṇasī is a major stop on the Delhi-Kolkata rail line, and trains arriving and departing here also service many of India's other major cities. For those travelling to Kushinagar, there are regular trains north to nearby Gorakhpur. For those travelling to or from Nepal, it is possible to take a narrow-gauge train between Gorakhpur and Nautanwa, 5 kilometres from Sonauli at the border. See the

Kathmandu/Nepal section in the 'Beyond the Middle Land' section for more information.

To and from Sārnāth there is a regular stream of **city buses**, **tuk-tuks**, and shared and private **rickshaws** and **taxis**, many of which arrive and depart in the vicinity of bus and train stations in Vārāṇasī. Regular buses bound for Sārnāth can usually be found just outside the main train station.

The main bus stand is near the train station. Private, faster buses are usually lined up right near the station's entrance. **Buses** head to most towns in Uttar Pradesh and major towns in Bihar such as Patna and Gayā. If you are heading to Nepal, there are regular buses available to the border town Sonauli. It is best to avoid travel agents trying to sell you bus tickets going directly to Kathmandu or Pokhara. These package deals usually involve changing buses and sometimes spending the night in a dingy hotel in the noisy town. It's less complicated to arrange each stage of your journey as you go. See the Kathmandu/Nepal section in the 'Beyond hte Middle Land' section for more information.

Vārāṇasī and Mughal Sarai (16 km from Vārāṇasī) are both well connected by **train** to major cities all over India. The Tourist Reservation Office in Vārāṇasī Junction Railway Station is a haven for weary travellers, and you can make reservations there, but expect to wait in line for some time.

Some important rail connections from Vārāṇasī:

- Kashi Vishwanath Express 4257/4258 (New Delhi-Vārāṇasī)
- Poorva Express 2381/2382 (Howrah/Kolkata-New Delhi)
- Mahanagri Express 1094/1095 (Mumbai-Vārāṇasī)
- Kurla Vārāṇasī Express 1065/1066 (Kurla/Mumbai-Vārāṇasī)
- Ganga Kaveri Express 6039/6040 (Chennai-Vārāṇasī)
- Pune Vārāṇasī Express 1031/1032 (Pune-Vārāṇasī)
- Secunderbad Vārāṇasī Express 7092/7091 (Secunderbad/Hyderabad-Vārāṇasī)
- Doon Express 3010/3011 (Dehra Dun-Howrah/Kolkata)
- Intercity Express 5104/5105 (Gorakhpur-Vārāṇasī)
- Varuna Express 4227/4228 (Lucknow-Vārāṇasī)
- Farrakka Express 3484/3485 (Patna-Vārāṇasī)

The Gateway

Kashi, Benares—
Gateway to our upcoming five-week pilgrimage,
To the sacred places related to the life and
teaching
Of our Exalted Buddha, Siddhattha Gotama.

Varanasi—a Hindu holy land,
Where the Ganga ghats and narrow lanes
Have been trod upon by innumerable saints
and sages
For innumerable centuries.

No doubt,
That the Buddha too
Walked along these shores of Ganga Dev.

Sauntering through the backlanes and
streets of the old city,
Feeling activity behind these ancient portals.
The mysteries are a symbol,
A prelude to the infinite mysteries
that lie before us,
On our upcoming journey.

Now we sit at the rooftop restaurant
of our guest house,
Digesting our meal, digesting what
lies ahead of us.

Watching the Ganga flow
Littered with Durga murtis
From last night's festivities
Glittering in the rising sun's rays.

Smoke from the burning ghats wafts
through the air;
A reminder of the impermanence of life—
The decaying nature of these
utterly difficult bodies to maintain.

O, Arupa Brahmas,
How lucky you are.
I (partially) envy you.

Watching the monkeys amock,
Listening to the rattling of the temple bells,
Smelling the flesh of bodies and the pollution
of civilization,
Tasting the Ganga chai,
Feeling my delicate stomach—
Reminding me of how temporary
and unsatisfactory
All these sense objects really are.
A perfect reflection to commence with
Before embarking on the trail of
the Buddha's footsteps.

– KG

Some rail connections from Mughal Sarai:

- Patna-Rajdhani Express 2309/2310 (Patna-New Delhi)
- Howrah Rajdhani Express 2301/2302 (Howrah/Kolkata-New Delhi)
- Neelachal Express 8475/8476 (Puri-New Delhi via Mughal Sarai)

Vārāṇasī is connected by **air** to Mumbai, New Delhi, Lucknow, Agra, Khajuraho, and Kathmandu. Flights (and trains) to and from Vārāṇasī are often delayed during the winter due to fog, so it is advisable to check if your transport is on schedule. Waiting around in the airport or train station is never fun, especially when you could be wandering around the ghats. The airport in Babatpur is 22 km from the train station area and 26 km from Godaulia (city centre).

Rajgir (*Rājagaha*)

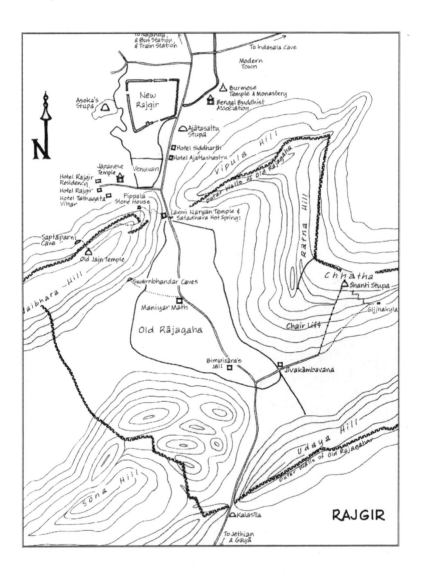

Tales from Rājagaha

Shortly after shaving off his hair and donning the earth-coloured mendicant's robe for the first time, Siddhattha walked 600 kilometres from Kapilavatthu to Rājagaha, hoping to find a teacher amongst the numerous ascetics that congregated in the forests and mountains surrounding the city. One morning, King Bimbisāra saw Siddhattha walking through the town slowly on his alms round, dignified as a lion passing through a jungle. The king was immediately attracted by Siddhattha's nobility. Discovering that Siddhattha was staying in a cave on the east side of Paṇḍava Mountain, Bimbisāra went to go see him.

After a few minutes of pleasant conversation, the king learned that Siddhattha came from a royal family, and offered him a high position in his court. "Recluse, your hands seem fit to grasp the reigns of an empire, not a begging bowl. Come join me in ruling the country. Despise not wealth and power, but enjoy them with wisdom and discretion," said the king to Siddhattha. The Bodhisatta looked into the king's eyes and politely replied,

"Thank you for your generosity and prudent words, but I have severed all ties to search for deliverance—the highest treasure of all. Just as a rabbit rescued from the serpent's mouth would not jump back into it to be devoured, I cannot return to the world of illusion. If you really do feel affection towards me, then please do not try to entangle me with new duties and responsibilities."

The king was disappointed, but understood Siddhattha's refusal. "May you find what you seek, and after finding it, come back and show me the way," the king said to the mendicant. Siddhattha replied, "I promise your highness, thank you."[63]

Disenchanted with the sensual pursuits of worldly life, two friends named Upatissa and Kolita began their search for a path of liberation. They first studied under the tutelage of the well-known sceptic philosopher Sañjaya Belaṭṭhaputta, but after some time became dissatisfied with his teachings and decided to search elsewhere. Wandering the country, they met different teachers, ascetics and philosophers, yet none were able to quench their spiritual thirst. Upatissa and Kolita made a pact that if one of them found the way, he should immediately inform the other.

One morning, after returning to Rājagaha, Upatissa spotted the Venerable Assaji—one of the Buddha's five original ascetic companions—on his alms round. Upatissa was impressed by the *bhikkhu's* noble composure as he moved quietly in the streets.

After Assaji had finished his meal in a nearby park, Upatissa approached him and asked, "Sir, I admire your way. I feel that you have attained truth. Tell me, who is your teacher and what is his philosophy?"

"You should ask him yourself, he is able to quench your thirst better than I can. He is staying nearby in the Veḷuvana," Assaji replied in a soft and humble manner. But when Upatissa insisted on hearing a few words, the elder said, "In short, the Great Monk has shown the cause of all causally-arisen things, and what brings their cessation."

Hearing this profound statement (and having lifetimes of pāramī to back him up), Upatissa immediately entered the stream of liberation. He then rushed off to Kolita and repeated Assaji's stanza, which had the same illuminating effect. Elated, Kolita wanted to go see the Buddha straight away, but Upatissa, out of respect for their former teacher, first wanted to inform Sañjaya of their discovery and see if he wanted to join them. Hearing their story, Sañjaya refused their offer and tried to convince them to stay with him as co-teachers, but their resolution was unshakable. Word of Upatissa and Kolita's transformation spread like wild-fire around Sañjaya's community, and most of Sañjaya's students followed the "excellent pair" to meet the Buddha.

Upatissa and Kolita met the Buddha at the Veḷuvana monastery, and soon joined the order of *bhikkhus*. From then onwards they were known as Sāriputta and Moggallāna. Moggallāna went to meditate in the Deer Park at Bhesakala Grove[64] near Kallavālaputta Village and attained arahantship after seven days of continuous and proper practice. Sāriputta meditated in the Boar's Cave below Vulture's Peak, and after fourteen days he realized arahantship while listening to the Buddha give a discourse to his own nephew. On that day, the Buddha appointed Sāriputta and Moggallāna as his two Chief Disciples (*mahā aggasāvaka*).[65]

Shortly after the Buddha's arrival in Rājagaha, many young men became *bhikkhus*. While many of Rājagaha's citizens were happy to have the Saṅgha practising the Dhamma around their city, others were not. They accused the Buddha of being a home-wrecker and a brainwasher.

When the Buddha heard about the Saṅgha's bad press, he told the *bhikkhus* not to worry, as these misunderstandings would soon lose their strength and be forgotten. "If people revile you," he said, "tell them that the Buddha leads people on to the path of truth. Who can condemn morality, concentration, and wisdom?" The *bhikkhus* followed the Buddha's instructions, and within a week, the murmurings came to an end. The Buddha then proclaimed,

Abstain from all unwholesome actions,
Perform wholesome ones,
Purify the mind—
This is the teaching of the Buddhas.[66]

Sudatta was a wealthy merchant and philanthropist from Sāvatthī, and was well known for his generosity towards the poor. His charitable efforts were so great that the people of Sāvatthī always referred to him as Anāthapiṇḍika—one who cares for the hungry and homeless.

One day, while staying at his sister and brother-in-law's house in Rājagaha during a business trip, Anāthapiṇḍika was surprised that his relatives all but ignored him because they were preoccupied with arranging an upcoming feast. He was amazed at the amount of unusual activity. "Is some important official or king coming for a visit?" he asked. "No, much better," his brother-in-law replied. "The Buddha is coming for alms tomorrow with a retinue of disciples."

Simply hearing the word 'Buddha' filled Anāthapiṇḍika with great joy, and the word kept ringing in his mind, "Buddha, Buddha, Buddha…" He wanted to go and meet this 'Buddha' right away, but was told he would have to wait until the following morning at the appropriate time.

That night, Anāthapiṇḍika was so excited at the possibility of meeting a fully enlightened being that he was unable to sleep. He got out of bed three times thinking it was dawn, but each time found that the sky was still dark. Unable to wait any longer, he got dressed and set off for the Bamboo Grove. The air was chilly and he was unaccustomed to walking in the darkness. Fear crept in and he considered turning back. However, a benevolent and invisible *yakkha*, or nature spirit, shone a bright light on the path to help him see, and encouraged him by saying, "Hundreds of animals adorned with jewels are not worth one-sixteenth of you taking even one step forward on this path. Keep going. Don't turn back!"

Thus heartened, Anāthapiṇḍika kept walking, and his sceptical mind began to churn with doubt. "How do I know if he is really a Buddha? Perhaps he is a charlatan like all the other so called 'bhagwans.' If he really is the Buddha, then he will address me by my given name, Sudatta, which nobody knows except my family."

Knowing what was occurring in the merchant's mind, the Buddha left the monastery early and went out to greet him.

"Sudatta, there is nothing to worry about," the Buddha said to the anxious merchant. Thrilled, Anāthapiṇḍika threw himself at the Buddha's feet. Feeling flushed, not knowing what to say to an enlightened person, Sudatta blurted out, "Did the Blessed One sleep well?" The Buddha, with a gentle smile, replied,

A true brahmin always sleeps well—
He who has attained nibbāna,
Does not cling to sensual desires, and
Is cooled without acquisitions.

Having rejected all attachments,
There is no conflict in his heart.
He who is at peace sleeps in ease,
For peace is established in his mind.

Although pleased to hear such inspiring words, Anāthapiṇḍika still had doubts about his own ability, as a layperson, to practise the Dhamma. "Must I give up my wealth, my home, and my business enterprises, and live the life of a *bhikkhu* in order to attain *nibbāna*?" he asked.

"Liberation is attainable by anyone who walks on the Noble Eightfold Path." the Buddha explained. "Whoever clings to his wealth, should cast it away before his heart is poisoned by it; but whoever does not cling to his wealth and uses it rightly is a blessing to his community. It is not life, wealth, or power that enslaves man, but the clinging to them...You must be like the lotus flower growing in the mud, but at the same time, unsmeared by it."

Glimpsing the depth of the Buddha's teaching, Anāthapiṇḍika let go of his doubts and entered the cool stream of liberation. Anāthapiṇḍika felt so fortunate to have met the Buddha. He invited him to his brother-in-law's house for the next day's meal, during which he implored the Buddha to come to Sāvatthī, the largest city at the time. He told the Buddha that many people there were ready for the Dhamma and that he would find a suitable place for the Saṅgha to reside. Seeing the merchant's sincerity, the Buddha agreed. [67]

Every morning, Sirimā, a very beautiful courtesan devoted to the Saṅgha, offered alms-food to eight *bhikkhus*. One morning, one of these *bhikkhus* mentioned to another *bhikkhu* how attractive Sirimā was. Without even seeing her, this *bhikkhu* became infatuated with her. The next morning, he went with the others to Sirimā's house to see her for himself. The *bhikkhu* was so excited that he could barely hide his attraction. That morning, Sirimā was not feeling well, but she still came to pay her respects while her servants fed the *bhikkhus*. Seeing her, the *bhikkhu's* heart began to beat fast and sweat poured down his face. Even though Sirimā was ill with bloodshot eyes and pale skin, the *bhikkhu* was still full of lust.

That night Sirimā died, and her body was taken to the cremation grounds. The Buddha told the attendants to keep the corpse for three days before cremating it, and to have it protected from crows and vultures. On the morning of the cremation, the Buddha took a group of *bhikkhus*, including the young and lustful one, to the cremation grounds to examine Sirimā's corpse, which had become bloated and infested with maggots. Instructing the *bhikkhus* to meditate on the decaying and filthy nature of the human body, the Buddha commented,

Look at this illusory human image,
A structure of repulsive flesh and bones.
Liable to constant illness, full of countless hankerings,
Nothing here is permanent or stable.

While gazing at the decaying body with insight, the young *bhikkhu* realized his foolishness, let go of his lust, and attained sotāpanna-hood.[68]

A woodcutter went into the woods with his son to cut some firewood. He left his oxen unyoked and they wandered off. Discovering that his animals were missing, the woodcutter went to look for them, leaving his son alone with the cart of firewood. Later, two malicious *yakkhas* came to frighten the boy, but when they heard him reciting inspiring homages to the Buddha, they had a change of heart. Seeing that the boy had no food, the compassionate *yakkhas* flew to the royal kitchen and stole some food. They left a note explaining that the missing food was for a lost boy in the woods who was a devotee of the Buddha.

When the king was told about this unusual event, he went to the Buddha asking how to protect oneself against evil and danger. The Buddha replied that there are six ways:

1. Reflecting on the unique qualities of the Buddha
2. Reflecting on the unique qualities of the Dhamma

3. Reflecting on the unique qualities of the Saṅgha
4. Practising mindfulness of the body
5. Cultivating a non-violent mind
6. Developing concentration[69]

Sāriputta went to visit the Brahmin priest Dhānañjāni, who was notorious for his dishonesty and unloyalty.

"Brahmin, why do you maintain such unvirtuous conduct in the guise of a holy man?" the elder asked.

"Bhante, I need to compromise my morality to support my family and employees, to maintain certain social obligations, and to have enough money to perform the elaborate Vedic rites and rituals," replied Dhānañjāni the swindler, with a mix of confidence and guilt in his voice.

"If you truly cared about all these things," Sāriputta said, "then you should practise morality at all times. If your moral foundation is weak, then everything you build in your life for you and your loved ones will crumble into misery. Cultivating morality is always beneficial; cultivating immorality is always harmful." Dhānañjāni was speechless. He knew that everything Sāriputta said was true. Sāriputta smiled at the brahmin, got up from his seat, and returned to the Veḷuvana.

Some days later, Sāriputta went back to see Dhānañjāni. When he arrived at the house, he found the priest deathly ill. Dhānañjāni, barely able to speak, whispered to Sāriputta that he appreciated the words of wisdom that he had received the other day. He told the *bhikkhu* that he had started to change his ways and sought forgiveness from all those he had harmed in the past. Sāriputta sat next to Dhānañjāni and taught him how to fill his mind with loving-kindness, compassion, appreciative-joy and equanimity, and to then spread those exalted feelings throughout the world. Doing as instructed, Dhānañjāni practised the sublime meditation of *mettā* for a few minutes before passing away. All those around noticed that the priest had died happily, with a bright smile on his face.[70]

Towards the final years of the Buddha's life, Devadatta, the Buddha's envious, arrogant and ambitious cousin, conspired against him. By performing impressive feats of supernatural power, Devadatta won the alliance of Ajātasattu, King Bimbisāra's foolish son. Devadatta was convinced that this new friendship with the prince would help him gain control of the Saṅgha.

Devadatta then went to Veḷuvana while the Buddha was giving a discourse to the king and a large assembly of ministers. At the end of the talk, Devadatta stood up and said: "The Tathāgata is now advanced in years and his health is no longer what it was. The task of leading the Saṅgha is a heavy burden for him; perhaps he should retire peacefully and let me serve as leader of the Saṅgha."

The Buddha looked directly into Devadatta's eyes. "Enough Devadatta, there are several senior *bhikkhus* more capable than you to lead the Saṅgha, and I have not asked any of them to do so. Why do you think I would even consider you for such a delicate task?"

Turning red with embarrassment, Devadatta sat down, realizing that the Buddha's harshness in front of the king meant that he would never be the one to take power over the Saṅgha. At that moment, Devadatta's tremendous greed caused him to lose all the supernatural powers he had acquired from his intensive meditation practice.

Humiliated, Devadatta plotted to murder the Buddha. He convinced Ajātasattu to assassinate King Bimbisāra and usurp the throne, and to help him kill the Buddha so that he could rule over the Saṅgha. The gullible prince agreed.

That evening, Ajātasattu planned to kill his father. Just as he was sneaking into his father's bedroom with a concealed knife, the imperial guards caught him.

"Son, why were you entering my chamber with a knife?" the King asked his son.

"I was going to kill you, father," Ajātasattu answered, trembling and unable to conceal his intentions.

"But why?" the king asked, surprised that his son could ever dream of such a heinous act.

"I want to rule the kingdom myself," Ajātasattu said, his eyes lowered in embarrassment.

"If you want the throne, son, it is yours. There is no need to kill me. I am old and am not interested in ruling anymore," Bimbisāra said, after a long uncomfortable silence.

Now as king, Ajātasattu supplied Devadatta with a team of sixteen assassins to kill the Buddha. When the time came, however, none of the assassins was able to complete his mission. Every time a team of two approached the Buddha, they were showered with loving-kindness and compassion, received a short discourse, and then became *sotāpannas*.

Frustrated, Devadatta decided to take matters into his own hands. While the Buddha was climbing up Vulture's Peak, Devadatta, sitting on top of the mountain, hurled a large boulder down at him. By a stroke of good fortune, the boulder crashed into another large rock just before reaching the Buddha. The impact of the collision, however, sent a small splinter flying out, which pierced the Buddha's foot. Blood gushed from the cut, staining his robe.[71] Devadatta ran away before being caught.

A few days later, Devadatta tried to kill the Buddha for a third time by bribing a royal elephant keeper to intoxify the infamously violent elephant Nāḷagiri. The mad elephant was then set loose in the streets of Rājagaha while the Buddha was on alms rounds. Everyone in the streets started panicking, screaming and running wildly for cover. Seeing the Buddha—the only person in sight—the drunken Nāḷagiri raised its trunk, lifted its front legs, let out a mighty cry, and then charged at him with full force. The fearless Buddha did not budge, but calmly generated mettā towards the elephant, who came to a sudden halt. Deeply moved, Nāḷagiri kneeled down on all fours as if to bow down at the Buddha's feet. The Buddha lovingly stroked its head and then led the obedient elephant by the trunk back to the royal stable as the entire city rejoiced.

After his three foiled attempts at the Buddha's life, Devadatta tried another tactic. He went to Vulture's Peak, where the Buddha was giv-

ing a discourse to an assembly of *bhikkhus*, and demanded that five new rules be added to the monastic code of discipline, arguing that the current regulations were too lenient.

"First, monks should only live in forests; not in towns or villages," Devadatta said. "Second, monks should only eat food collected from alms rounds and should never accept invitations to eat in a lay-person's home. Third, monks should only wear robes made from rags gathered from rubbish heaps, not robes given by the laity. Fourth, monks should only sleep at the foot of trees, not indoors. Fifth, monks should only eat vegetarian food."

"Devadatta," the Buddha calmly said, "severe rules will not lead *bhikkhus* onto the middle path. If a *bhikkhu* wants to keep more stringent rules, he may, but these rules will not be made compulsory."

Devadatta's mouth turned up in a self-satisfied smile. He openly accused the Buddha, and the *bhikkhus* who did not share his own view, of living a luxurious life—not the life of a true monk. Devadatta, followed by 500 deluded young *bhikkhus*, went to Gayāsīsa and set up a new community.

Shortly after the split, Sāriputta and Moggallāna, the Buddha's two chief disciples, went to Gayāsīsa and won back the hearts of the misguided monks by giving them a profound discourse, which resulted in all the *bhikkhus*—except for a few of Devadatta's close friends—becoming *sotāpannas* and returning to their true master. When Devadatta woke up and realized what happened, he instantly fell ill and blood gushed from his mouth.

When the group returned to Rājagaha, the Buddha explained, "*Bhikkhus*, Devadatta was obsessed with eight types of unwholesome thoughts. Which eight? Gain and lack of gain; fame and lack of fame; honour and lack of honour; evil wishes and evil friends. When you see these types of thoughts arise in the mind, you must overcome them."[72]

After a 10-day course at Dhamma Bodhi, a group of us decided to hire a Tata Sumo and head off to Rajgir for a day-trip. The drive was quite fast on the newly-paved road, and when we pulled up to the hot springs, it was still early morning. We decided that a group sitting in the Sattapanni Cave would be a good way to start the day.

We manoeuvred through the crowd of dripping pilgrims and splashed our faces with hot water, then reached the cave after a half-hour hike. We'd come prepared with flashlights and candles, so explored the different entrances and found a chamber where we could all sit.

Immediately after closing our eyes, the sound of flapping wings, along with the sensation of air moving around our heads, alerted us to the fact that we had disturbed the resident bats, which were now flying around in circles wondering who the new guests were. Waves of fear flooded my mind with images of bats getting tangled in my hair, bats biting my neck, and my having to run off to a hospital for rabies shots. Constantly reminding myself of where I was and remembering anicca helped me to calm down the mind, and the bats seemed to leave us alone after a short while.

Just as silence started to envelop us, however, a local 'guide' brought in a group of Korean Buddhists, who seemed bewildered not only by the cave's darkness, but also by the presence of a group of young Westerners meditating. The guide pointed to a rock that he called a shrine, instructing the naïve pilgrims to bow down and leave money—money he then pocketed as soon as they'd turned their backs. Witnessing this extortion (I couldn't resist the temptation to peek every now and again), waves of disgust, frustration, and compassion surged through my mind, but as before, my equanimity prevailed and these recognized emotions slowly dried up.

When we later met the Korean group, some of them came up to us and took our hands. They said they'd never seen people, especially Westerners, meditate so seriously. After giving them some information about Vipassana courses, we exchanged blessings and carried on our separate ways. My mind laughs, feeling that nothing happens without reason.

Moving on, we stopped at the ruins of Jīvaka's mango grove for a picnic of Tibetan bread, peanut butter, dates and fruits. We then headed up to the Japanese Shanti Stūpa, which contains relics of the Buddha. Our idea was to sit there for a little while, but it was so crowded with Indian tourists—who seemed more interested in the rope-way up than in the actual stūpa—that we decided to go straight to Vulture's Peak for a sitting in Ānanda's cave, which is blessed by its nibbānic vibrations, relative isolation and refreshing coolness.

Sitting in the cave, we appreciated the tranquillity of the sacred mountain, the sounds of nature and our knowledge that all the tourists were off in the distance. While we were meditating, however, a group of considerate Burmese pilgrims came to quietly pay homage to the place where the Buddha's attendant awakened. We heard the ruffling of plastic and papers, which we ignored, figuring that it was only someone coming to offer flowers, money, or incense to the cave's shrine. A little while later, however, when we opened our eyes, we saw there, placed in front of each of us, a little caramel candy—a sweet ending to a sweet day.

– MD

Site-Sitting

Rājagaha, or 'royal residence', is one of India's oldest inhabited cities. During the Buddha's days it was the capital of the Magadha kingdom, renowned for its beauty and often praised for its delightful ponds, parks, meadows, forests and five surrounding mountains.[73] Today, as in the past, the town is a thriving religious centre visited not only by Buddhists, but also by Jains who come to pay tribute to the area where Mahāvira spent 14 rainy seasons, and Hindus who visit the ancient town referred to in the great literary scriptures of the Ramayana, Mahabharata, and the Puranas.

Rājagaha, often skipped by meditators, is an important place to visit along the pilgrim's path. The Buddha meditated here during his second, third, fourth, thirteenth and fifteenth rainy seasons after enlightenment, and, after Sāvatthī, delivered more discourses here than any other place. Seeing the ancient hills, decorated with stone stairways winding their way up to religious shrines, visitors may be touched by the feeling that intense spiritual work has taken place here.

Most of the sites around Rājagaha are scattered over a large area, so it's good to have a few days to absorb everything. If your time is limited, it is best to hire a horse-buggy or rickshaw for the day. Remember to make sure that the agreed-upon price includes 'waiting charges.' All the sites in Rajgir are free to visit, except for the Bamboo Grove.

Bamboo Grove (*Veḷuvana; Venuvan*)
This pleasant park, with its lotus pond, pavilions, flower gardens, walking paths and clusters of bamboo trees, is the site of the Saṅgha's first monastery. King Bimbisāra donated the garden as a sign of gratitude for having received the precious gift of the Dhamma. The loca-

tion was perfect for the Buddha's Order, "neither too far from the town, nor too near, suitable for coming and going, accessible to people at all times, unfrequented by day and quiet at night, undisturbed by voices—an atmosphere of aloofness."[74] It was at here where the Buddha instituted the 3-month rainy season retreat (*vassā*), requiring monks to stay in one place—partly so that they could meditate seriously, partly to prevent them from damaging crops and harming insects while walking through monsoon flooded fields. The Buddha spent his second, third, and fourth rainy seasons after his enlightenment at the Bamboo Grove, whose congenial grounds became the scene for many important discourses.

There are several areas of the park mentioned in the Pāli canon, such as 'The Squirrel's Feeding Place' (*Kālandakanivāpa*), 'The Peacock's Feeding Place' (*Moranivapa*), and the lotus pond (*Sumagadha*). The only identifiable place today, however, is the pond. Judging by the present size of the park, we can infer that in the Buddha's days the Veḷuvana was much larger. Across the stream behind the Veḷuvana is a striking Japanese temple; all of that land was probably a part of the Veḷuvana during the formative days of the Saṅgha. Take your time to mindfully wander around the peaceful gardens and meditate under the shade of the bamboo, in one of the pavilions by the pond, or at the shrine with the beautiful Thai Buddha statue.

Tales from the Veḷuvana

Every time the brahmin's wife sneezed, she would blurt out, "Namo tassa bhagavato arahato sammāsambuddhassa."[75] Fed up of hearing these words of veneration to the Buddha, the agitated brahmin went to the Buddha and asked him some tricky questions, hoping they would prove him worthless. "What do we have to kill to be able to live happily and peacefully?" the brahmin asked with an arrogant smirk on his face.

"Brahmin, in order to live happily and peacefully, one needs to kill hatred (*dosa*)," the Buddha calmly replied.

The brahmin was impressed with the Buddha's sharp wit and intelligence. He saw his own folly in getting angry, joined the Saṅgha, and after a few days of sincere practice, became an *arahant*.

When the brahmin's brother, Akkosaka Bhāradvāja, heard that his brother had joined the Saṅgha, he became furious. Many of his friends and relatives had left his sect to pursue the Buddha's universal path; his brother's conversion was the last straw. Fuming with rage, Akkosaka Bhāradvāja stomped to the Veḷuvana Monastery. Seeing the Buddha sitting under a bamboo tree, the brahmin approached him, hurling a string of insults. The Buddha just sat there calmly and quietly, remaining perfectly unperturbed. When the haughty brahmin ran out of steam, the Buddha questioned him, "Brahmin, do guests ever come to visit you?"

"Of course they do," Akkosaka rudely replied.

"Do you ever offer them food?"

"Certainly," he grumbled, wondering where these irrelevant questions were leading.

"Do they always accept all the food you offer?"

"No, not always."

"What do you do with the food not eaten by your guests?"

"We keep it. What do you think we do with it?"

"Similarly, Akkosaka, these abusive words are not accepted here; they must stay with you. If I reply with abuse to your abuse, then I join you for dinner. If I ignore your abuse, you sit at your dinner table alone."

Akkosaka Bhāradvāja was a highly intelligent man, having a thin veil of ignorance before his eyes. The Buddha's dignified composure and sagacious words tore that veil away. Akkosaka Bhāradvāja's mind became calm, and the Buddha explained to him that flaring up at someone who is already angry only makes the situation worse; therefore to calm a situation, you must be calm yourself. And to be calm, you must understand your mind and how to prevent it from being provoked. Deeply grasping what the Buddha meant, Akkosaka Bhāradvāja became an *arahant* and joined the Saṅgha.

Later that evening, a congregation of *bhikkhus* praised the Buddha for his ability to respond to Akkosaka Bhāradvāja without argument and pride.

"*Bhikkhus*, because I am patient and forbearing, and do no wrong to those who do me wrong, I have become a refuge to many," the Buddha explained to them, and then continued with a verse,

One possessing forgiveness,
Remaining calm under criticism, abuse and punishment,
And developing patience as one's army—
This person I call a brahmin."[76]

Some *bhikkhus* approached the Buddha and complained that one of their fellow *bhikkhus* ignored everyone else, extolling the virtues of being alone. The Buddha called that monk over to him.

"*Bhikkhu*, is it true that you always keep to yourself and avoid being in the company of other *bhikkhus*?" the Buddha inquired.

"Yes, Lord. You have instructed us to practise alone. So that is what I am doing," the *bhikkhu* answered.

"The proper way of living alone is not through avoidance. So how then should one live alone? What is past is left behind, what is future is relinquished, and any craving and aversion in the present is subdued. That is how a *bhikkhu* should live alone."[77]

The *bhikkhu* thanked the Buddha for revealing his mistake. He now had a better grasp of what it meant to truly live alone.

King Bimbisāra insisted that Queen Khemā visit the Buddha at the Veḷuvana Monastery. She had always resisted in the past because she had heard that the Buddha spoke disdainfully about giving too much importance to physical beauty, and she feared that he would criticize her for her vanity. After repeated requests by the king, she finally gave in.

When Queen Khemā arrived at the monastery, the Buddha was in the middle of expounding the Dhamma to a group of householders. Using his supernormal powers, the Buddha created an image of a gorgeous young woman that only the queen could see. The queen felt uneasy, as she had never seen a woman more beautiful than herself. Fixated on the illusion, the queen noticed that the woman's beauty slowly began to fade. She grew older and older, until she reached the point where she became a decrepit old woman. The queen was shocked and covered her eyes with her hands. Opening her fingers, Khemā took another peak and saw a corpse full of maggots. She felt like she was going to vomit, but she couldn't take her eyes off of the awful image. Within an instant, she was struck by a flash of insight and understood how foolish it was to pay so much attention to her body, which is subject to old age, illness, and decay. Khemā then tasted the fruits of sotāpannahood. The Buddha said to the queen,

Those infatuated with the fire of lust, fall into the current,
As the spider entangles itself into a self-spun web.
The wise, having curtailed the current,
Let go, and leave all sorrow behind.[78]

Deeply experiencing the Great Sage's words, Queen Khemā attained arahantship. In front of the entire crowd, the Buddha initiated her into the Saṅgha as a *bhikkhunī*, and appointed her the Chief of Female Disciples.

Bhikkhu Channa fell gravely ill and was feeling constant and unbearable pain. He felt like a burden on the other monks who had to look after him. Before their alms round, Sāriputta and Mahācunda went to see if Channa needed any food or medicine. Channa told the elders that since he had already attained arahantship and was free from all forms of aversion, it was not necessary for him to go on living. Sāriputta and Mahācunda tried to talk him out of it, but to no avail—that evening Channa slit his throat. As the blood gushed out, Channa was suddenly seized with a fear of death—indicating that he was not yet an *arahant* as he had thought. Realizing his terrible mistake, Channa immediately started practising Vipassana, observing the sensations as the blood poured out of his veins. Just as he was breathing in his last breath, Channa reached the stage of arahantship and died with a radiant smile on his face.[79]

Vaibhara Hill (*Vebhara Giri*) & Hot Springs (*Tapodārāma, now Satdhara*)
The Laxmi Narayan Temple at the foot of Vaibhara Hill was constructed around the source of Rajgir's famous sulphur hot springs. If you can ignore the stream of persistent Hindu priests offering costly prayers, you can imagine *bhikkhus* of long ago quietly and mindfully bathing here on a cold winter morning before going on alms round.

A Tale from Tapodārāma
After finishing his morning bath, the young and handsome Bhikkhu Samiddhi saw a female *deva* staring at him with lustful eyes.

"You are still so young, my love, you should be pursuing the pleasures of worldly life like most men your age. Don't reject the present moment to pursue what time will bring," she said in her sweet celestial voice, hoping that she could lure him away from the monastic life. The young monk, however, was firmly established in his practice. "I reject what time will bring to pursue the present moment," Samiddhi wisely retorted with a gentle smile, "Please go see the Buddha. He can clarify the Dhamma for you better than anyone else."

She hesitated at first, but the glow and confidence in the young *bhikkhu's* face convinced her to go. Straightaway she approached the Buddha,

"Your *bhikkhus* live in the wilderness peacefully and restrained, eating just one meal a day. How is it that their faces are so bright and serene?"

"They neither regret the past nor long for the future. They survive on the present. That is why their faces are so bright and serene."

With a gladdened heart, the *deva* bowed in reverence and departed with a determination to practise the Dhamma with diligence. A few mornings later, the *deva* went to the hot springs again and found Samiddhi as he was about to go for his alms. She asked him to teach her the Buddha's exposition on "one who has had a single excellent night." Samiddhi, however, was unable to do so. All day he struggled hard to remember this teaching, but could not. That evening, when Samiddhi saw the Buddha, he asked him to expound this teaching. The Buddha agreed,

Let not a person revive the past
Or on the future build his hopes;
For the past has been left behind
And the future has not been reached.

Instead with insight let him see
Each presently arisen state;
Let him know that and be sure of it,
Invincibly, unshakeably.

Today the effort must be made;
Tomorrow Death may come, who knows?
No bargain with mortality
Can keep him and his hordes away.

But one who dwells thus ardently,
Relentlessly, by day and night—
It is he, the Peaceful Sage has said,
Who has had a single excellent night.[80]

Pipphali Stone House

On the stone path beyond the Laxmi Narayan Temple is a small stone hut which is believed to have been built around the cave dwelling used by both the Buddha and his great disciple Mahākassapa. It is inspiring to imagine the venerable *bhikkhus* meditating here for days in concentrated serenity.

On one occasion when Mahākassapa fell gravely ill, the Buddha visited him here and fueled his spirits with a talk praising the marvels of the seven factors of awakening (*bojjhaṇgas*): awareness, analytical investigation, effort, rapture, tranquility, concentration, and equanimity. By the end of the discourse, Mahākassapa's heart was filled with gladness and his illness disappeared.[81]

Saptaparni Cave (*Sattapanni Cave*)

Although the Buddha stayed here a few times, the cave is most celebrated for being the venue of the First Council (*Paṭhama Dhamma-Saṅgīti*) after the Buddha's death (sometime between 543 and 483 BCE).

While Mahākassapa and his 500 disciples were on their way from Pāvā to Kusinārā, hoping to meet the Buddha before he died, they came across a wandering mendicant who informed them that the Buddha had already passed away. The unenlightened monks among them wept in despair, while the enlightened ones remained in solemn silence. Subhadda, an old and ignorant monk, exclaimed, "Enough, friends, do not be sad, do not lament. We are better off without him. We have been frustrated by him saying: 'This is allowed; this is not allowed.' But now, we shall do as we like and we shall not do as we do not like." Hearing this foolishness, the elder Mahākassapa then foresaw the necessity of organizing the Buddha's teaching and community in order to prevent erosion of the Buddha's work.

On the full moon of Āsāḷha, three months after the Buddha's passing, Mahākassapa summoned 500 senior awakened *bhikkhus* to compile and authenticate the Buddha's teaching, which would be handed down for posterity. King Ajātasattu sponsored the seven-month-long event and the *bhikkhus* were able to work without any difficulties or disturbances. During the council, Mahākassapa questioned the recently awakened Ānanda, who was gifted with an extraordinary memory, to recite the Sutta and Abhidhamma Piṭakas. The recitation included the Buddha's actual discourses, where they were given, and on whose account. Mahākassapa appointed Upāli, who was the recognized authority on monastic discipline (*vinaya*), to recite the code of conduct, as well as the circumstances that caused these rules to be formulated. When both Ānanda and Upāli had finished their recitations, the entire assembly repeated them together in order to show the unanimous acceptance of the compilation. From that time onwards, the Buddha's teachings were preserved in this fashion until the Fourth Council (*Catuttha Dhamma-Saṅgīti*) held in Sri Lanka in 29 BCE, when they were written down for the first time on palm leaves.[82]

To get to the cave, follow the path past the Pipphali stone hut up to the top of Vibhara Hill. Before the last Jain temple, turn right onto the path that leads down the side of the hill. If unsure, ask directions at one of the Jain temples along the way. If it seems that the forty-five minute hike will be too much, you can hire a palanquin at the bottom to carry you up. Make sure the porters know exactly where you want to go as there is no sign marking the cave; most porters are usually hired to bring their clients to the Jain temples on the mountain top. Few meditators visit this rocky and isolated area, but given the fact that it's one of the most important places in the history of Dhamma, the trek up is well worth the visit, and the views are magnificent. Don't forget your torch (flashlight)!

From the bird's-eye view atop the hill, the paddy fields below are reminiscent of the time when the Buddha suggested to Ānanda, while they were standing on a neighbouring mountain, that the *bhikkhus'* robes should be cut and sewn in a similar pattern, symbolizing the *bhikkhu* as a fertile field in which seeds of merit and virtue are sown to benefit present and future generations.[83] This symbolic tradition is still kept today.

Ajātasattu Stūpa
This pile of bricks, approximately one kilometre north of the Veḷuvana, is said to be the stūpa that Ajātasattu built to house his portion of the Buddha's relics.

Vulture's Peak (*Gijjhakūṭa*)
When not staying with the Saṅgha at Bamboo Grove, the Buddha retreated to this crag, whose natural silence made it an ideal place for serious meditation. Many of the Buddha's students, including Sāriputta and Ānanda, became *arahants* in one of the caves on this rocky hill.

There are two ways to get to the peak. The first option is to walk for 20 minutes beyond the jumble of stalls up the stairway, then make a right at the fork in the path. According to Xuan Zang, the first cave on your right is said to be where Ānanda attained enlightenment just before the First Council. The second cave on your right is said to be the Boar's Grotto, where Sāriputta became an *arahant*. Ānanda's cave is one of our favourite places to sit at Vulture's Peak. It is spacious and hidden by boulders from the main path. At the end of the main path you will come to a stairway that leads to the top of the mountain containing ancient ruins and a small contemporary shrine. To the left of the stairway you will find a tiny dirt path that leads to two caves said by locals to be frequented by the disciples Moggallāna and Mahākassapa (note, however, that Xuan Zang did not mention these two caves in his records).

The left-hand path at the fork leads you by way of a further 20-minute walk up to the Shanti Stūpa, built by the late Japanese monk Nichidatsu Fujī of the Nipponzan Myōhōji sect. It is believed by followers of this tradition that Vulture's Peak was the place where the Buddha preached the Lotus Sūtra, which is the primary text followed by Nichiren Buddhists. Other Mahāyana Buddhist traditions assert that the sūtras *Prajñāpāramitā, Sūrāngamasamādhi, Lalitavistra,* and *Bhardrakalpikā* were delivered here. The modern Shanti Stūpa contains Buddha relics and is surrounded by fantastic views of the countryside. Before reaching the top, you will notice a small path on your right that leads to a crumbling Asokan stūpa. The walk to this stūpa is another 20 minutes, so most pilgrims do not make the effort, but the 360° panoramic view is quite rewarding for those who do.

If walking isn't for you, then you might prefer the second option: taking the famous Rajgir rope-way up to the Shanti Stūpa, and then walking down to the Vulture's Peak.

Tales from Gijjhakūṭa

Two weeks after Sāriputta attained stream-entry and joined the Buddha's Saṅgha, his nephew Dīghanakha came to visit him and meet the Teacher who had compelled Sāriputta to take up this way of life. Climbing to the top of the mountain, Dīghanakha found his uncle and the Buddha meditating in the Boar's Grotto (*Sūkarakhatā*) just below the peak. Dīghanakha, radically sceptical about everything, eagerly wanted to debate with the Buddha and prove to his uncle the superiority of his intelligence. "Sir, I reject all views," Dīghanakha boasted to the Buddha. "Dīghanakha, proclaiming such a definitive statement is itself an inherent contradiction." The Buddha responded with calm and assurance:

He who truly rejects all views would not assert any position at all, including the one so arrogantly professed.

Clinging to any view, no matter how intelligent or rational it seems, only leads to harm and dispute with others. Therefore, the best thing a wise person must do is to abandon all views, without taking up new ones.

Understanding how foolish he had been, Dīghanakha admitted his folly and relinquished his former position, accepting the Buddha's articulation of unattachment. The Buddha then gave him instructions in Vipassana meditation,

*All experiences, Dīghanakha, are impermanent, conditioned,
dependently arisen, subject to decay, vanishing, fading away,
and ceasing.*

Carefully following the Buddha's instructions, Dīghanakha became a
sotāpanna. Sāriputta, who was listening to the entire discussion and
put the Buddha's words into practice, became an *arahant*.[84]

Shortly after his ordination, Soṇa, the son of a wealthy magistrate,
was vigorously practising walking meditation barefoot up and down
the mountain to the point where his feet were becoming badly
wounded. He had not achieved anything and considered returning
to the lay life. Knowing that during his lay life Soṇa had been an
excellent musician, the Buddha, regarding proper practice, gave him
a simile of a lute:

"Soṇa, if the strings are too taut, what will happen?"

"They will break, Sir," Soṇa replied.

"And what happens if they are too slack?"

"The lute will be out of tune. It won't play properly."

"Similarly, Soṇa, over-striving leads to agitation and discourage-
ment, and under-striving results in laziness. A good meditator knows
his limits and practises in a balanced way."

Soṇa understood how he was practising in the wrong way, tuned himself accordingly, and eventually became an *arahant*.[85]

When the Buddha turned 55 years old, he asked Ānanda to be his
permanent attendant. Ānanda told him that he would only comply if
the Buddha met his demands:

*The Buddha will never give me any of his own robes. The Buddha
will not share his alms with me. The Buddha will not let me sleep
in the same hut as him. The Buddha will not ask me to accompany
him to a lay-disciple's home for a meal if I have not been specifically invited, though if I am invited for a meal, the Buddha may also
come. The Buddha will allow me to judge in permitting or refusing
those people requesting interviews. The Buddha will let me ask him
to repeat teachings that I have not grasped. And finally, the Buddha
will let me attend every discourse, or if this is not possible, he will
repeat them to me again later on.*

The Buddha happily agreed to meet these pious demands, which would later prove to envious *bhikkhus* that Ānanda was not receiving any sort of special favours for being the Buddha's attendant.

While sitting on top of the mountain gazing at the forests below, the Buddha spoke to a group of *bhikkhus* who were sitting next to him:

Bhikkhus, just as a foolish man clips off the twigs and leaves of a tree, thinking they were the heartwood; so is a foolish bhikkhu who joins the Saṅgha hoping to acquire fame and honour.

Just as a foolish man cuts off the tree's outer bark, thinking it to be the heartwood; so is a foolish, self-righteous bhikkhu who delights in disparaging the mistakes of others.

Just as a foolish man removes the inner bark, mistaking it for the heartwood; so is a foolish bhikkhu who practises meditation solely for the purpose of developing strong concentration.

Just as a foolish man collects the sapwood, confusing it for the heartwood; so is a foolish bhikkhu who desires to attain psychic powers.

Just as a skilled man who finds the heartwood and knows that it's heartwood; so is a wise bhikkhu who enters the Saṅgha, practises properly for the sake of all beings, and attains liberation from the mental defilements.

After giving time for his students to absorb this thoughtful simile, the Buddha added,

Bhikkhus, this holy life does not have gain, honour, and fame for its own benefit; does not have the attainment of virtue for its own benefit; does not have the attainment of concentration for its own benefit, and does not have the attainment of divine sight for its own benefit. The goal of this holy life is the unshakeable deliverance of mind. This is its heartwood, this is its end.[86]

One night on top of this sacred mountain, King Vessavaṇa, the Great King of the North, accompanied by a great array of yakkhas, gandhabbas, and nāgas, visited the Buddha. The Great King and the Buddha recited the *Āṭānatiya Sutta* to arouse confidence in the meditators and help them remain secure, protected, untroubled and at ease. The sutta praises all the Buddhas of the past, present and future as embodiments of truth, virtue, and loving-kindness.[87]

Seeing the Buddha go on his alms round in the city, a brahmin named Vakkali became attracted to the Buddha's noble appearance and joined the Saṅgha just to be near him. As a *bhikkhu*, Vakkali always tried to be around the Buddha, but rarely fulfilled his community duties and never practised any meditation.

Watching Vakkali's misguided behaviour, the Buddha admonished him, "Vakkali, it is useless for you to always follow me around, staring at my face. You should go to a quiet place alone and practise meditation. Only those who see the Dhamma see me; those who do not see the Dhamma, do not see me. For your own benefit, you must leave my presence."

Overhearing the scolding, some of the more immature *bhikkhus* giggled. Vakkali was so humiliated that he wanted to kill himself. He ran up to the top of Gijjhakūṭa as fast as he could. Standing at the edge of the cliff and staring down into the valley below, he murmured, "This is what you get for being such a fool around the Buddha and his noble disciples." As he bent his knees and prepared to jump, the Buddha appeared, "Vakkali, come here!"

Vakkali was startled. His head hung low and he felt even more ashamed than before. They sat together for a few moments in silence. The Buddha's *mettā* and compassion put Vakkali at ease, and the Buddha taught him about the true meaning of devotion and how spiritual delight arises from the proper practise of Vipassana. When the Buddha finished giving his instructions, Vakkali forgot all about his grief, developed perfect understanding of *anicca*, and rejoiced in the bliss of arahantship.[88]

King Ajātasattu wanted to attack the Vajjains of Vesālī to expand his empire. He sent his minister Vassakāra to inform the Buddha of his intentions and ask for the Buddha's opinion of the plan. The Buddha turned to Ānanda, who was standing nearby, and asked him,

"Ānanda, do the Vajjains still hold frequent and well-attended meetings?"

"Yes, Lord, I have heard they do."

"Do they still assemble, adjourn and perform duties in concord?"

"Yes, Lord, I have heard they do."

"Do they still follow their traditional laws?"

"Yes, Lord, I have heard they do."

"Do they still honour and revere their elders?"

"Yes, Lord, I have heard they do."

"Do they still treat their women with respect?"

"Yes, Lord, I have heard they do."

"Do they still maintain religious shrines of all the traditions?"

"Yes, Lord, I have heard they do."

"Do they still protect and provide material requisites for renunciates?"

"Yes, Lord, I have heard they do."

After Ānanda confirmed these seven points, the Buddha told Vassakāra that as long as any group follows these guidelines, they would be prosperous and not decline. After Vassakāra left, the Buddha then gave seven points to Ānanda for the Saṅgha to follow in order to remain harmonious and prevent decline:

1. Hold frequent and well-attended meetings.
2. Assemble, adjourn and perform duties in concord.
3. Follow the training precepts.
4. Honour and venerate senior, experienced monks.
5. Subdue craving.
6. Esteem forest abodes.
7. Maintain mindfulness.[89]

Three days before the First Council, Mahākassapa told Ānanda that only *arahants* would be allowed to attend. Since Ānanda was only a *sotapānna*, he felt great pressure to attain *nibbāna*. Not only did he want to be present for this great historical event, but since he had heard and memorized every discourse given by the Buddha, it seemed only natural that he should attend.

Ānanda retired to his cave on Vulture's Peak and spent the entire time in strenuous meditation, getting nowhere. At dawn, just before the council, Ānanda gave up the struggle with a sigh and accepted that he was not an *arahant*. He decided to rest. As he lay down, aware of the reality of the present moment and not longing now for any goal, he attained enlightenment before his head reached his pillow. Ānanda went to the council and recited the *suttas* that preserve the teachings we continue to practise today.[90]

Bimbisāra's Jail

Shortly after Bimbisāra had handed the kingdom over to his son Ajātasattu, the new heir became paranoid that his father might try to reclaim it. Overwhelmed by fear and anxiety, he had Bimbisāra imprisoned without food, hoping that the old king would die quickly.

Bimbisāra's wife, Queen Vedehī, was the only permitted visitor and helped keep her husband alive by smuggling food in for him. After a few days the guards noticed that the king's health was not deteriorating. The next time the queen came to the jail the guards searched her and confiscated all the food that she had brought. Vedehī then started smearing a mixture of milk, honey, and flour all over her body for the king to lick off, but after a few days that ploy was also discovered and she was banned from visiting him altogether. Bimbisāra, however, was a *sotāpanna*, and it is said that he was able to keep himself alive by subsisting on his meditative powers. Also, from the window of his jail cell, Bimbisāra was able to see the Buddha meditating on Vulture's Peak. This sight filled him with a gladness and encouragement, which helped him survive. After a couple of weeks, Ajātasattu grew impatient and ordered his guards to slit his father's veins. The wise and compassionate Bimbisāra died without hatred or regret in his heart.

That same day, Ajātasattu's wife bore him a son, Prince Udayibhadda. Feeling great love for his child, Ajātasattu asked his mother whether his father had also loved him so.

"No father could have loved his son more." she said. "One time when you were a child, your father sucked on a boil that developed on your finger to help ease the pain. When the boil burst, he didn't even take your finger out of his mouth to spit out the pus, feeling that the disgusting sight might frighten you. This is how deeply your father loved you."

Ajātasattu realized his grave mistake, and tried to call off the orders to have his father killed, but it was too late: Bimbisāra had just died. Ajātasattu was full of remorse, and was long haunted by fears of being murdered for the throne. His fears were realized many years later when he was killed by the hand of his own son.[91]

Maniyar Math
Just down the road and opposite to Bimbisāra's Jail is a cylindrical brick structure decorated with stucco figures that was used as a cult shrine to worship the *Nāga* gods. Although there is no record of what Maniyar Math commemorates, locals say it marks the place where the Buddha taught the Dhamma to a *yakkha*.

Jīvaka's Mango Grove (*Jīvakāmbavana*)
One night a courtesan abandoned her child near the palace gate. The baby was found and brought to Prince Abhaya. Taking one look at the beautiful infant, the prince decided to raise it as if it were his own and named him Jīvaka Komārabhacca. When Jīvaka was older and showed a sharp intelligence and keen sense of learning, the prince sent the child to Taxilā (*Takkasilā*) in Northern India[92] to study medicine. Several years later, after mastering the art of healing, Jīvaka returned to Rājagaha and became the personal physician of both King

Bimbisāra and the Buddha. After receiving meditation instructions for the first time, Jīvaka became a *sotāpanna*.

One time when the aging Buddha was ill, Jīvaka thought that he could better care for his teacher if they lived closer to each other, and proposed that the Buddha stay in his mango grove. When the Buddha consented, Jīvaka built a small monastery and donated it to the Saṅgha.

The ruins of the Jīvakāmbavana are located about half a kilometre before the parking lot at the foot of Vulture's Peak. Although the area is surrounded by dense forest, the ruins themselves are exposed to the elements and to the road. If you plan on meditating here for more than a few minutes, it is best to go early in the morning before the heat becomes intense and before the tourist crowds rush to the Rajgir Rope-Way.

Tales from Jīvakāmbavana

Wondering what the precise guidelines on vegetarianism were, Jīvaka asked the Buddha to clarify his position. At the time, rumours had spread that the Buddha tolerated the killing of animals by his lay-disciples in order to feed the *bhikkhus*. The Buddha responded,

"Jīvaka, *bhikkhus* are not required to follow a vegetarian diet. However, there are three instances when they must refuse non-vegetarian food: if they see, hear, or suspect that the animal is slaughtered for the purpose of offering. Refusing this meal will help people understand that *bhikkhus* do not advocate animal slaughter. So, unless the animal is killed on the *bhikkhu's* behalf, he must accept whatever is given without generating feelings of craving or repulsion. In this way, proper *bhikkhus* humbly live in dependence on others, spending their time meditating and generating mettā for all beings."[93]

On the full moon of the month of *Komudi* (September-October), King Ajātasattu complained to his ministers that he could not sleep. As king, he had committed countless wrongs and was now plagued with guilt and fear.[94] When his ministers proposed that he visit some of the popular religious teachers in the area, the king replied that he had already been to them and had not been impressed by their empty words. Ajātasattu summoned Jīvaka, hoping to find some cure.

"Jīvaka, please help me with my problem. Is there anything you can recommend?" the king asked in desperation, clutching his aching head.

"Your Highness, I am only a healer of the body," the royal physician answered. "I have no cure for the king's mental afflictions. The Buddha, however, is the master healer of the mind. You should go and see him. He is currently staying in my mango grove."

The king was silent. He hesitated, thinking that the Buddha would refuse to see him because of the way he treated his father. Jīvaka convinced him otherwise. That night, they proceeded to Jīvaka's mango grove. Entering the premises, Ajātasattu was seized with fright, imagining that Jīvaka, conspiring to usurp the throne, had lured him into this solitary forest to kill him. The atmosphere was so silent that he couldn't believe 1 250 monks were meditating nearby. Jīvaka's gentle composure assured him, however, and he was convinced to proceed. When they reached the Dhamma hall and Ajātasattu saw the Buddha meditating amidst a huge assembly, all of the king's anxieties vanished.

After exchanging greetings, the king asked the Buddha about the fruits of the recluse's life, admitting that he was feeling dissatisfied with his worldly ambitions. The Buddha then proclaimed the benefits of following the spiritual path founded upon right view. He concretely explained the various ascending stages of the path, as well as enumerating the immediate benefits felt by the meditators, who are in time transformed from fickle worldlings into noble saints. The Buddha announced how it is "good in the beginning," through the sense of security and pleasure derived from moral conduct; "good in the middle," through the exalted bliss yielded from one-pointed concentration and restraint of the sense faculties, and "good in the end," as it culminates in the total cessation of suffering.

"Many people from different classes choose to live the lifestyle of renunciation and meditation, rather than the comfortable material life," the Buddha explained. "As opposed to the transient enjoyments of worldly life that are tied up with craving and clinging, with the life of renunciation, one can experience the highest rewards that are concrete, lasting, personal, and directly verifiable."

Feeling relieved from his stress, the king prostrated in reverence to the Buddha. "Respected Teacher, you have shown me the true value of the Dhamma. Thank you. Please accept me as a lay-disciple, as you accepted my parents in the past," the king said, as tears rolled down his cheeks. That night, Ajātassatu slept with a peaceful heart.[95]

Swarnbhandar Caves (*Sonabhandar Caves*)

There are two incongruent stories associated with these caves. The first story, told by local guides, says that these caves were originally the entrance to King Bimbisāra's treasury (*swarn* meaning gold and *bhandar* meaning treasury). Inside the cave on the left-hand side, you can see the shape of a door, which is said to lead to all of the king's hidden gold and to a path that leads all the way up to Sattapanni Cave, where the First Council was held. It is believed that only those with a pure mind, who can recite Mahākassapa's mantra inscribed on the wall, will be able to open the door.

The second, more scientific story claims that these caves were carved out in the 3rd century CE for Jain ascetics. The cave on the right has carved figures of Jain Tirthankaras and the Brahmi inscription at the left cave's entrance reads: "The Sage Vairadeva, of great lustre, the jewel amongst teachers, caused to be made for the purpose of attaining salvation and liberation two auspicious caves worthy of ascetics, in which were placed images of Noble Ones."[96]

Kālasilā

> At the foot of Isigili Mountain are the ruins of an old, unlabelled stūpa believed to mark the spot where Moggallāna was murdered by some thugs hired by the students of a sectarian teacher whom he had defeated in a debate. The thugs tried several times to kill him, but each time they came near his hut, Moggallāna used his supernormal powers to make himself invisible. By doing this, not only did he save his own life, but he compassionately prevented the thugs from committing the heinous crime of killing an *arahant*. After repeating this drama several times, Moggallāna's powers failed him. The thugs found him and beat him to death.
>
> That evening some *bhikkhus* questioned the Buddha as to why Moggallāna wasn't able to vanish on that last occasion. The Buddha explained to them that Moggallāna was at last paying off a karmic debt from lifetimes ago, when he had murdered his blind parents.[97]

Kālasilā is just beyond Rajgir's gateway and the massive crumbling walls of the old city, along the main road coming from Bodhgayā that runs through the narrow pass between Sona and Udaya Hills (approximately 1.5 km from the turnoff towards Vulture's Peak). Behind the stūpa is a small stream where villagers do their laundry and catch minnows. Between the turnoff and Kalasīla on the left-hand side of the road is a stone compound enclosing a large flat rock with deep ruts, the fossilized remains of the ancient road, traversed by countless chariots of the times.

Sleeping & Eating

For meditators visiting Rajgir, two favourite budget places to stay are the **Burmese Temple** and the **Bengal Buddhist Association**, which are next door to one another at the edge of modern Rajgir (ask rickshaw drivers to take you to the Burmese Temple for both places; they may not know the Bengal Buddhist Association). These two places are opposite the crumbling and partially-buried eastern wall of New Rājagaha, built by Ajātasattu after the capital was shifted from the protective mountains to the plains.[98] If you climb to the top of the fort walls, you can see locals performing their morning ablutions, young boys playing cricket and goats munching away on grass. Looking west, you can see a stūpa and pillar constructed by Asoka.

There are also a few inexpensive hotels such as **Hotel Siddharth** (both are not far from the Veluvana and the hot springs), and **Hotels Rajgir** and **Tathagata Vihar** (both near the Japanese Temple behind the Veḷuvana). **Hotel Gautam Vihar**, between the bus and train stations, has relatively clean budget rooms. The high-end Japanese **Centaur Hokke Hotel** is 3 km from the hot springs on the road coming from Gayā, and the upscale **Rajgir Residency** is not far from the Japanese Temple. For food, your options are limited. The **Hotel Tathagata Vihar** and **Hotel Siddharth** have restaurants; otherwise you can try your luck at one of the *dhabas* opposite the Veḷuvana or go to the market in town and buy fruits, veggies and biscuits to eat in your room. If your taste sense door desires soba noodles, vegetable teriyaki, and green tea then head over to the **Lotus Restuarant** at the Centaur Hokke Hotel.

Coming & Going

There are regular **buses** to Rajgir from Gayā (70 km, 2.5 hours), Patna (100 km, 3 hours), Nāḷandā (11 km, 30 minutes) and Bihar Sharif (25 km, 45 minutes). Travel agents can also arrange **taxis** from Bodhgayā (2 hours).

If you are going to, or coming from Patna there are a few **trains** that stop in Rajgir and Nāḷandā. There are no direct railway lines from Gayā. If you are coming from or going to Delhi or Kolkata your rail options are:

*   Magadha Vikramshila Express 2392/2391 (New Delhi-Bhagalpur)
*   Howrah Delhi Janata Express 3040/3039 (Howrah/Kolkata-Delhi)

Excursions

Sāriputta Parinirvāna Vatta

Knowing that he would soon pass away, Sāriputta wanted to return to his birthplace to teach the Dhamma to his mother, who resented the Buddha for turning all her sons into *bhikkhus*. When he reached his mother's house, Sāriputta was attacked by severe dysentery. While on his deathbed, a stream of *devas* and *brahmas*, including the Mahābrahma, who Sāriputta's mother worshipped, came to pay their last respects to the venerable *bhikkhu*. This astounded his mother. She thought to herself, "If the gods that I worship have come to worship my son, what must be the power of his teacher?" Her resistence dissipated and she became receptive as Sāriputta spoke to her about the power of the Dhamma. Listening attentively and putting the words into practice, she became a *sotāpanna*. In this way, Sāriputta at last repaid the debt of life to his mother.

After Sāriputta's death, Bhikkhu Cunda took Sāriputta's robe and bowl to the Buddha who was staying at the Jetavana Vihāra in Sāvatthī. Hearing the unfortunate news, Ānanda began to cry. The Buddha gently rebuked him saying that there was no need for tears. Sāriputta was a great man, but he had not taken the Dhamma away with him.

Ānanda, have I not already told you that there is separation, parting and division from all that is dear and beloved? How could it be that what is born, comes to being, formed, and subject to pass away, should not pass away? That is not possible. It is as if a main branch of a great tree standing firm and solid has fallen; so too, Sāriputta has attained Final Nibbanā in a great community that stands firm and solid…Therefore, Ānanda, each bhikkhu should make himself his island, himself and no other, his refuge; each bhikkhu should make the Dhamma his island, the Dhamma and no other, his refuge.[99]

Sāriputta, the Buddha's right-hand man, was venerated for his wisdom by all of the Buddha's disciples. The Pāli texts indicate that Sāriputta came into this world and passed out of it in the village of Nālaka (also referred to as Nāla and Nāḷagāmaka). While most Buddhists equate this site with Temple 3 at the ruins of the Nāḷandā Mahāvihāra (due to a text written by the 16th century Tibetan scholar Lama Tarantha who wrote about the place from more than 1000 km away), Faxian and Xuan Zang's descriptions of the stūpa placed by Asoka marking the site point somewhere near the present-day villages of Chaṇḍīmau and Naṇand, next to Giriyek Hill. Several Buddhist artefacts have been found in these villages and the remains of a cylindrical stūpa crown the hill. There is also neat cave, yet to be identified, in the middle of a sheer cliff halfway up the southern side of Giriyek Hill.

To pay tribute to the great "Marshall of Dhamma" (*Dhammasenāpati*), the Government of Bihar, Bodhgayā Temple Management Committee, Nava Nāḷandā Mahāviha and the local community are developing this region as the Sāriputta Parinirvāṇa Vaṭṭa. If you are in this region at the right time, consider joining the annual "Sāriputta World Peace Walk" that occurs in this zone every *Kārtika Pūrṇimā* (October-November full moon), the same time of year that the *Dhammasenāpati* was born and passed away. Check with one of the above organizations or visit http://nalanda-insatiableinoffering.blogspot.ca/ for the event's details.

To get to Giriyek Hill (30 minutes, 7 km from Rajgir) from Rajgir, take Giriyek Road, which runs along the north side of the mountain and the massive Bharut ammunition factory. The road is very smooth until the campus of the factory ends. From that point onwards the track becomes very bumpy, so going by motorbike or jeep may be the best way to travel. Depending on the season, you may be limited to how far you can go by vehicle. During or after the monsoon season a small lake will force you to walk through the village and grazing area for about 1.5 kilometres. During the dry season you'll be able to drive right up to the point before the start of the climb to the cave. Beyond this path is another path with a flight of stairs leading up to a cave known by locals as *Guvha Mandir*. A friendly old sadhu lives there with some of his disciples.

Indasāla Cave

On a few occasions, this remote cave had the honour of sheltering the Buddha while he meditated. The cave, however, is best known for being the scene of the famous dialogue between the Buddha and Sakka, king of the devas, during which the Buddha eloquently answered forty-two of the celestial being's questions concerning how sources of conflict arise, and how to eradicate these through the practice of deep meditation.[100] Most pilgrims erroneously associate the Indasāla Cave with the cave on Giriyek Hill. However, judging by the location's description in both the Pāli texts and Xuan Zang's travelogue, the Indasāla Cave at Giriyek is probably not the actual cave used by the Buddha. In 2007, Bhante Priyapal, a scholar-monk from the new Nālandā University, took our Indo-Franco-Canadian pilgrimage group to a mountain near Apsadh Village that seems to better conform to the written descriptions. The ancient sources say that north of Ambasandā village is Vediya Mountain, a solitary rocky hill with two peaks and a large cave facing south. Giriyek, by contrast, is not an isolated formation, but a mountain with a broad peak forming part of a mountain range.

Vediya Mountain, today referred to by locals as *Parvati Ki Pahar*, is an interesting place to visit if you have the time. The mountain is crowned with a modern temple, partly built with Gupta-period bricks left over from ancient monasteries and from the famous *Haṃsa Stūpa* that Venerable Xuan Zang tells us was built over the wild goose who offered his life to a hungry monk. In addition to the large and energetically vibrant cave, which looks out over paddy fields dotted with palm trees and could fit at least a dozen meditators, visitors can get a sense of the Dhamma activity that once took place here from nearby ruins of monasteries and stūpas. In the village at the base of the mountain are several Buddha images from the Pala period, the most prized being a life-sized faceless image housed in a shrine. Ancient Buddha sculptures have also been found in other nearby villages such as Ghosrawan and Tetrawan. The inhabitants now worship these as local deities and are very proud of them. One elder told how all the village men once fought off the District Magistrate's thugs, who came a few years back to steal their gods. According to Burmese legend, the soil and water on this mountain have medicinal properties that can cure digestive and respiratory diseases.

To get to the Indasāla Cave via Apsadh (45 minutes from Nālandā), you will need to rent a car or jeep in Rajgir if you don't have one already.

Looking for some fun and adventure off the beaten Buddhist track, we headed out (by a very slow and bumpy horse-cart) to the lonely Giriyek Mountain. After making our way up the steep rocky path to the Guvha Mandir (which we had read was the Indasala Cave), we were surprised to find a group of sadhus sitting outside the cave, chatting away about man, god and everything in between. They were very welcoming and showed us around the cave, which they were temporarily using as their dwelling for prayer and meditation.

After confirming and reconfirming that this actually was the Guvha Mandir, we told them that we wanted to meditate here for some time, to which they happily agreed. They asked if they could join us, to which, of course, we also happily agreed. After about 15 or 20 minutes of silence, the sadhus began chanting Sita Ram, Sita Ram followed by some devotional songs to Krishna. It seemed to us to be an

*encouragement and our meditation continued for another half-hour
or so.*

*When we got up from our seats, the sadhus offered us each a warm
cup of chai. We exchanged some limited words—our Buddha for their
Bhagwan, our anicca for their Om. It was all very warm and friendly.
Both sides appreciated the spontaneous cultural and spiritual exchange. We descended the mountain, smiling and waving goodbye
to our new friends. The ride back to Rajgir did not seem so bad (and
neither did the sensations of our surprise, when we later learned that
we completely missed out on the real Indasala Cave!).*

– John Geraets & Karen Weston

Palm Grove (*Laṭṭhivana, Yaṣṭivana*), Jethian Village

Seven years after he attained Buddhahood, Siddhattha fulfilled his
promise to King Bimbisāra by returning to Rājagaha to teach the
Dhamma. When the Buddha arrived at the city, accompanied by the
highly respected religious mendicants—the three Kassapa brothers
and their 1 000 fire-worshippers-turned-*bhikkhus*—the townspeople
were astounded. Walking in a silent procession with downcast eyes
and begging bowls in their hands, the *bhikkhus* collected sufficient
food and then proceeded to the Palm Grove (*Laṭṭhivana*) to eat and
meditate. Hearing about the large group of noble mendicants, King
Bimbisāra came rushing to the Palm Grove with a group of brahmins.

Seeing the congregation of solemn meditators, Bimbisāra and the
brahmins were unsure as to who was the leader—the young and unknown Siddhattha or the elder and famous Uruvelā Kassapa. Sensing
their confusion, Uruvelā Kassapa prostrated at the Buddha's feet and
acknowledged him as his teacher. Highly impressed by the elder's
act of reverence, King Bimbisāra requested the Buddha to give them
a teaching. The Buddha was glad to see his old friend again and to
have the opportunity to fulfil his promise by sharing what he had discovered under the Bodhi Tree. The Buddha then taught the king and
his ministers the progressive instructions on: (i) the benefits of charity, (ii) ethics as the foundation for liberation, (iii) the harmfulness
of over-indulging in sensual pleasures, (iv) the futility of conceit, (v)
the bliss of renunciation, and (vi) the Four Noble Truths.

The eyes of the listeners grew brighter by the moment as they absorbed the Buddha's inspiring words. Feeling their hearts open and
their doubts vanish, the entire audience entered the stream of liberation. "Most glorious is the Dhamma taught by the Tathāgata!"[101] the
king cried out. "He sets up what has been turned over; he reveals
what has been hidden; he points out the way to the lost wanderer; he
lights a lamp in the dark so that those with eyes may see." The elated
king then invited the entire Saṅgha to the royal courtyard for the next
day's meal, where he offered his pleasure park, the Bamboo Grove

(*Veḷuvana*), to the Saṅgha. The Buddha accepted the donation and it became the tradition's first monastery. From that point onwards *bhikkhus* were allowed to dwell in permanent monasteries.[102]

The most famous monk to stay at the Palm Grove since the Buddha's time was the 7th century Chinese pilgrim Xuan Zang who spent two years here studying with Jayasena, a great Buddhist saint. Xuan Zang referred to this site as the Yaṣṭivana Vihara, explaining that the name of the site was derived from a time when a man, who after measuring the Buddha's height with stick (*laṭṭhi*) made from a palm-type of wood, threw it into the ground. The stick took root and eventually spread, thus becoming Laṭṭhivana/Yaṣṭivana.

In front of the village water reservoir/lotus pond is a shrine with an impressive black Buddha statue. The shrine, built by the Japanese government and the All Kochi Young Buddhist Association, is located on top of a mound that was probably the remains of a stūpa that either indicated where the Buddha stayed while at Laṭṭhivana, or where Bimbisāra and the Buddha met. There is another Buddha statue near the local school. You can ask one of the friendly locals to show it to you.

Many caves in the vicinity of Rājagaha are mentioned in the Pāli canon, but have not been located. A cave now called Rajpind Cave, which is on the northern slope of Chandu Hill (3 km north-east of the village), was identified by Xuan Zang to be Kapotakandara Cave (The Pigeons' Cave) where the Buddha and Sāritputta sometimes went to meditate. As many pigeons still inhabit this particular cave today, we can wildly speculate that this is the same place.[103]

To get to Jethian Village from Rajgir, take the Gayā-Rajgir Road. If coming from the direction of Rajgir, turn right after the Rajgir Gateway onto the very bumpy 14 km road that runs along the southern side of the mountains. After entering the valley where Jethian is located, take the right-hand road at the fork until you get to the shrine. Another way to get to Jethian from Rajgir is by foot. If you are into trekking along ancient pilgrimage routes then go to the Forest Rest House near the Swarnbhandar Caves and follow the footpath that climbs up to the mountain ridge and continues for approximately 14 km all the way to Jethian. There is a clearly marked sign posted by the Government of Bihar. Alternately, you can begin the trek in Jethian and ask the very cooperative locals to show you to the start of the path, which also has a clearly marked sign placed by the Government of Bihar. Hiring a local to guide is advisable since it will ensure that you don't get lost and remain protected from potential encounters with dacoits. From Jethian/Rajgir, you can instruct your driver to pick you up in Rajgir/Jethian. Ask locals for directions to Rajpind Cave on Chandu Hill.

Ayer Pathri (Buddhavana)

About 10 km southwest of Jethian lays the small village of Ayer, which is at the base of a "Buddhavana" hill. It is believed that Lord Indra massaged the Buddha's body with sandal-wood oil while he was staying in the low cave on the steep side of this hill. At present, the cave's entrance is littered with the remains of ancient brick votive stūpas and Buddha sculptures. If you have the time to spare, catching the views from this site makes for a worthwhile visit.

Nālandā

Famous for its heritage as an international centre of education for more than 700 years, people often seem unaware of the fact that Nālandā was also a place of prosperity and spiritual importance during the days of the Buddha. While staying in Nālandā's vicinity, the Buddha usually resided in Ambalaṭṭhikā or at Pāvārikā's Mango Grove. Venerable Xuan Zang informs us that King Sakraditya (5th century CE) established the Nālandā Mahāvihāra at the site of Pāvārikā's Mango Grove.[104] The *Jātaka* stories relate to us that in one of his former lives, the Buddha was a very generous king who had his capital here, and thus gave rise to the name 'Nālandā,' which means 'insatiable in giving.'

Tales from Nālandā

While residing at the Ambalaṭṭhikā, the Buddha preached the famous discourse on the 'All-Embracing Net of Views' (*Brahmajāla Sutta*), which took place after he heard a dispute between the two wandering ascetics, Suppiya and Brahmadatta. Suppaya had criticized and ridiculed the Buddha's teachings, while Brahmadatta had praised them. That evening, the Buddha narrated the dispute to his students and taught them the importance of always maintaining an attitude of equanimity in the face of criticism or praise.

Bhikkhus, whenever you hear someone criticize the Buddha or Dhamma, do not yield to emotions of anger, irritation, or resentment, which will only act as a barrier to your spiritual progress.

Similarly, whenever you hear someone praise the Buddha or Dhamma, do not yield to emotions of happiness, satisfaction, or pride, which will also act as a barrier to your spiritual progress. Only with a balanced mind, should you correct mistaken statements or acknowledge true ones.

The Buddha then discussed how and why the sixty-two different types of philosophical, speculative views regarding the laws of nature arise, how they contain errors and create obstacles to proper practice, and how they are eradicated by perfectly practising the first factor of the Noble Eightfold Path—right view.

Bhikkhus, these erroneous views deny moral integrity and the laws of cause and effect, they are not verifiable, and they are submerged in the belief of a permanent, unchanging soul. Accepting any of these wrong views is to fall into a thicket of views, a wilderness of views, a scuffling of views, an agitation of views, a fetter of views. All these opinions lead the seeker away from emancipation and are attended with suffering, vexation and despair.

The Buddha then proceeded to reveal to his students the method of practising Vipassana, which cuts through the entangling net of views:

Bhikkhus, with regard to all of these ...they experience these sensations by repeated contact through the six sense doors; sensations condition craving; craving conditions clinging; clinging conditions self-perpetuation; self-perpetuation conditions birth; birth conditions aging and death, sorrow, lamentation, sadness and distress.

When a bhikkhu understands they really are the arising and passing away of the six bases of contact, their attraction and their peril and the deliverance from them, he knows that which goes beyond all these views.

The *bhikkhus* rejoiced at hearing such a profound discourse on how to remain safe from the net of harmful theories and dogmas in the world.[105]

Shortly after his ordination, the seven-year old Rāhula went with Sāriputta to live at the Ambalaṭṭhikā. The Buddha came to see how his son was faring as a *bhikkhu*, and taught him about the importance of maintaining *sīla*, especially by avoiding lying or exaggerating, as children are often prone to do. "Why do we use a mirror?" the Buddha asked. "To see our reflection, Lord," Rāhula replied.

Correct, Rāhula; and in the same way as a mirror naturally reflects the image in front of it, so does a bhikkhu with a strong sense of moral integrity review his physical, vocal and mental actions before, during and after their performance. With proper contemplation, the bhikkhu can better evaluate whether his actions are profitable or unprofitable, and then shape future actions accordingly. If a bhikkhu realizes that he has made a mistake, he should immediately confess his fault to a wise companion on the path of Dhamma. This will help prevent similar harmful situations from arising in the future.

Knowing that he had made such mistakes in the past, young Rāhula bowed to his father and made a strong resolution to be more careful with his speech in the future.[106]

Site-Sitting

Ruins of Nāḷandā/ Pāvārikā's Mango Grove
One of the Buddha's favorite places while in this region was the tranquil mango grove that belonged to the wealthy lay disciple, Pāvārikā. Some time after the Buddha's death, a major famine broke out and Nāḷandā's prosperity waned. The desolation remained until King Asoka visited in the 3rd century BCE and lent support that helped the sacred town flourish once again. Nāḷandā reached its peak

between the Gupta and Pala periods (4th to 7th centuries) with the establishment of the Nālandā Mahāvihāra.

This great university of international acclaim was famous for its religious, philosophical, linguistic, social and scientific fields of study. When the famous Chinese pilgrim Xuan Zang arrived in 635 CE to study and teach there for five years, the university was already thriving. In his vivid and detailed accounts, Xuan Zang relates that more than 8000 students from all over Asia attended the university, and that the teachers numbered over 1 000. Despite these numbers, admission was not easy: most applicants were rejected by the gatekeeper, who would pitch a series of difficult questions that required quick and accurate answers. Many of the great early Mahāyana Buddhist thinkers were products of Nālandā's demanding curriculum. The logicians Dinnaga and Dharmakirti, the poets Shantideva and Chandrakirti, and the philosophers Śantarakśita, Padmasambhava and Kamalasīla, were all alumni of this excellent institute. These innovative minds spent their time here meditating and developing their intellects, which would later have a profound impact on the world.

The university thrived well into the 9th century. By the 12th century, however, the glory of Nālandā had come to an end. The strength necessary to preserve unity at the university was ruined, lost in a series of sectarian disputes and the dominating influence of ritualistic Hinduism. Nālandā's final ruin arrived with the Islamic invasion when many buildings, including the great library that housed some nine million manuscripts, were destroyed. This raid virtually wiped Nālandā off the map, leaving little behind but a mass of rubble and a memory.[107]

Today, the 35-acre archaeological park contains a row of temple and monastery ruins. Exploring the ancient shrines, meditation cells, slab stones for beds, alcoves for books and courtyards, you may find it easy to imagine what daily life for the students was like. It's definitely worth hiring a guide to point out the details that easily elude the untrained eye, though each guide's knowledgability varies somewhat.

Temple Site 3/Gandhakuṭi

Kevaḍḍha, an eager and devoted lay-disciple, went to visit the Buddha at Pāvārikā's Mango Grove.

"Lord, if you would only display supernormal powers such as mind-reading, flying and walking on water, then all the local people would have greater confidence in the Buddha and the Dhamma," Kevaḍḍha said, hoping to convince the Buddha of his plan.

"Kevaḍḍha, performing such magic tricks to impress people is low and vulgar. It increases the meditator's ego and does not relieve people's suffering," the Buddha answered with a gentle smile and sharp look into his disciple's eyes. "The highest miracle," he continued, "is eliminating the taints plaguing the human mind. Only by this manner will the masses be genuinely attracted to the Dhamma."

Realizing that his own approach was juvenile, Kevaḍḍha smiled and bowed his head to the Buddha. He left the Buddha with a new determination to practise the Dhamma with proper awareness and equanimity. [108]

The Jain ascetic Tapassi visited the Buddha, arguing that actions of the body, not of the mind, were most liable for carrying out immoral deeds. Unable to sway the Buddha into accepting his view, Tapassi left the Buddha and went to the ashram of his guru, the Jain leader Nigaṇṭha Nātaputta. [109] Tapassi sarcastically narrated his conversation with the Buddha to his teacher and to Upāli Gahapati, an influential community leader and supporter of the Jain sect.

The next day, Upāli went to the Buddha to clarify why he proposed mental actions as more accountable than verbal or physical ones. The Buddha explained to him that the mind was the essential ingredient for all other actions. If any action lacked a mental volition, then additional kamma would not be produced. The Buddha then gave various similes to illustrate his point.

"Suppose, Upāli, a Nigaṇṭha practitioner is about to die of fever and needs a cold-water treatment, but refuses it on the grounds that using cold water is against his vows because it contained living beings. Are his actions pure according to Nigaṇṭha practice?" the Buddha questioned.

"Yes, Lord," Upāli replied.

'What if the Nigaṇṭha secretly longs for the treatment to relieve him of his pain? Are his actions still pure?"

"No, Lord."

"In this way, the Nigaṇṭha's refusal keeps his verbal and bodily behaviour pure; but his mental conduct is impure. Upon death, he would not be liberated from cyclical existence.

"Wonderful, Lord, can you give another simile?" Upāli asked.

The Buddha nodded and questioned him,

"Upāli, can a strong man, with a single swing of his sword, turn the entire town of Nālandā into one giant mass of flesh?"

"Not even 50 men could do such a thing." Upāli laughed.

"What about a recluse, who has mastered his mind and developed certain supernormal powers? Can he do it with one hateful mental action?"

"Certainly, Lord, a recluse with that level of concentration can accomplish almost anything he sets his mind to," he answered, understanding what the Buddha was getting at.

Upāli was impressed by the Buddha's clarity and wisdom. After hearing several different similes, Upāli clearly understood the Buddha's point that mental activities have greater consequences and greater power than verbal and bodily ones. Upāli told the Buddha that he was actually convinced after the first simile; he just really enjoyed the way the Buddha spoke and wanted to hear more.

After taking refuge in the Buddha, Dhamma and Saṅgha, Upāli was warned to investigate his decision thoroughly. The Buddha did not want him to become a disciple just because it seemed logical at that moment. This impressed Upāli even more and he took refuge in the triple gem for a second time. The Buddha then told Upāli that even though he was changing practices, he should continue giving alms to the Nigaṇṭha sect which, for years, had depended on his charity. Astounded by the Buddha's sense of compassion and generousity, Upāli announced his confidence in the triple gem for a third time.

Certain of Upāli's sincerity, the Buddha gave him the progressive Dhamma instructions on: (i) the benefits of charity, (ii) ethics being the foundation for liberation, (iii) the harmfulness of over-indulging in sensual pleasures, (iv) the futility of conceit, (v) the bliss of renunciation, and (vi) the Four Noble Truths. The spotless, immaculate vision of Dhamma arose in Upāli, and with a deep understanding of impermanence, he became one of the many *sotāpannas* in the world.[110]

As a result of an error written by the 16th century Tibetan scholar Lama Tarantha (who probably never had access to Xuan Zang's historical records and who wrote about Nāḷandā, despite never personally visiting the place), most visitors mistake this site to mark the location of where Sāriputta was born and passed away. However, according to Xuan Zang, this temple ruin actually marks the location of the 'fragrant' hut (*Gandhakuṭi*) that the Buddha occupied while staying at Pāvārikā's Mango Grove. Over the centuries, the building transformed from a simple hut to a moderate stūpa and then into a great temple. The surrounding votive stūpas indicate that this site was probably the most sacred at Nāḷandā, and UNESCO has declared the monument a World Heritage Site.

Archaeological Museum & Multimedia Museum
The museum has a fine assortment of bronze, stone and terracotta works found in the Nāḷandā area, mostly dating from the Pala period (8th to 12th century). One of the most impressive statues is the black stone carving of the Bodhisatta Avalokitesvara bestowing a blessing. There is also an interesting collection of coins, pottery, iron tools, seals and manuscripts. The museum is opposite the ruins and open everyday from 9 a.m. to 5 p.m.

The multimedia museum takes the viewer through a 45-minute 3D "virtual journey" of Nālandā's historical, religious and geographical legacy. If you don't mind some historical inaccuracy or exaggeration here and there, then you will certainly enjoy being entertained in the refreshing air-con theatre. The museum has a decent bookshop and is located approximately 100m from the ruins.

Nava Nālandā Mahāvihāra
In 1951, Bhikkhu Jagdish Kaśyap, backed by India's first president, Dr. Rajendra Prasad, founded the New Nālandā University, in hope of reviving the ancient seat of Buddhist learning. The present campus is situated on the bank of a peaceful lake, two kilometres from the ruins. Walking the campus grounds among monks and scholars, or pouring through the books and manuscripts in the quaint library, there is a timeless quality that seems to echo what the original university must have been like over a thousand years ago.

The New Nālandā University presently offers diploma and degree courses in Pāli, philosophy and ancient Indian culture. International workshops and seminars on Buddhism and Indian culture are hosted every year, and Buddhist scholars are welcome to stay and pursue their research.

Xuan Zang Memorial
This magnificent hall is a tribute to one of the greatest Buddhist pilgrims, Xuan Zang (pronounced Shwandzang), who travelled overland to India from China in the seventh century without a map. The beautiful murals in the hall are stylistic replicas of the frescos of Ajaṇṭā and represent a fusion of Chinese and Indian art. The paintings depict how the monk sustained himself with faith and determination while crossing the Taklamakan Desert and Himālayan Mountains. The tremendous hardships he bore from difficult travel, however, were rewarded by the 15 years of joy he experienced as a pilgrim in India. In his epic journal, Xuan Zang left behind fascinating accounts of Indian culture, history, and society that he observed during his visits to the sacred sites, and while teaching and learning at Nālandā.

On his journey homewards, the legendary pilgrim carried with him 657 Buddhist texts, which he later translated into Chinese. These works helped clarify some misunderstandings of the Dhamma by early Chinese scholars, and also helped later researchers discover many of the lost sacred sites connected to the Buddha's life.

The complex's large bell, donated by the Chinese government, contains an inscription of the *Heart Sūtra*, the famous Mahāyāna text that articulates the empty and insubstantial nature of all existence. Striking the magnificent bell with mindfulness and equanimity assists the meditator in understanding the distinguishing feature of the Buddha's teaching. The memorial is about 2 km beyond the university ruins and is open from 9:00 a.m. to 5:00 p.m. You can find a rickshaw or tonga to take you there. It is not advised to walk after dark.

Silao
Early one morning, a man woke up and noticed a poisonous snake slither over his wife's arm, down the bed, and then out the room. He woke her up and told her what happened. He expressed his feelings

to her about the transitory nature of life and the urgency in finding a teacher who could help him find the way out of suffering.

With the blessings of his wife, he shaved his head, sewed together a robe from discarded rags, and set out on the road for the life of a homeless wanderer. Then while resting at the Bahaputta Shrine in Sīlao Village between Rajāgaha and Nāḷandā, the man saw the Buddha approach and offered him his robe to sit on. The Buddha remarked how nice a cushion it made and the man, without hesitating, gave it to him. The Buddha accepted it with a smile and then offered his robe in return.

Receiving Dhamma instructions from the Buddha, the traveller realized and experienced the peace of an *arahant*. This man was the legendary Mahākassapa. He went off to live in the wild and was soon recognized as the master of ascetic practices and the Buddha's fourth ranking disciple (after Kondañña, Sāriputta and Moggallāna). For many Buddhist traditions, this famous exchange of robes symbolizes the transmission of the lineage of Teachers.

Silao is on the left-hand side of the road that runs about halfway from Rajgir to Nāḷandā. Go through the village for about 200 m until you reach the yellow and pink Mahadevasthan Temple, believed to be at the same spot as the Bahaputta Shrine where the Buddha and Mahākassapa first met. Beyond the Hindu deity you will see two Pala period (8th to 12th century) statues: one is a repaired standing black Buddha statue, the other is a piece of statue that depicts Mahākassapa offering his robe to the Buddha.

Silao is also famous for being the *khaja* capital of the world. Since the Buddha's time, people would travel far and wide to devour this Indian sweet. Adventurers of the palate will not be able to resist scoffing down a *khaja* or two. Best to track down the *khaja-wallah* least swarmed by flies!

Juafardīh (Kūlika)

At the time this book was written, excavations of an Asokan stūpa at Koḷitagāma (present day Juafardīh) were said to mark the site of Mahāmoggallāna's birth and *parinibbāna* site (he may have actually passed away here after being beaten up at the Kālasilā Vihāra). The Great Disciple (*Aggasāvaka*) was born and passed away during the new moon of November-December (*Agahana Amāvāsyā*). If you are in this region at this time, consider joining the annual *Mahāmoggallāna Patha Padakkhiṇā Padayātra*. Joining this walking pilgrimage with the local *bhikkhu Saṅgha* will certainly be an unforgettable experience! Check with the Nava Nāḷanda Mahāvihāra or visit http://nalanda-insatiableinoffering.blogspot.ca/ for the event's details.

Most drivers will not know how to get to this site (about 5 km from the Nāḷandā ruins) so best to ask a local around the ruins or university.

Sleeping & Eating

Although most travellers prefer to stay in Rajgir, Nāḷandā can be a pleasant place to stay if you have the time. Most pilgrims stay and eat at the **Thai Temple** behind the university or at the **Chinese Temple** near the entrance of the town, about 3 km from the ruins.

You can also try your luck at one of the **Jain** *dharamshalas* outside of Nāḷandā on the way to Pawapuri (5 km), the village where Mahāvira died and was cremated, and which now has a beautiful temple in the middle of a lake filled with lotus flowers. If you do visit Pawapuri, travel another 5 km to Ghosrawan, which has a 10 ft high shiny black stone Buddha statue and some ruins of a monastery. The temple in the neighbouring village of Tetrawan houses some ancient Buddha and Bodhisatta statues.

Coming & Going

You can reach Nāḷandā from Rajgir (15 km) by **bus, taxi** or **horse-cart**. There are regular buses that ply between Patna (90 km) and Gayā (85 km) that stop in Nāḷandā. Frequent buses leaving from Bihar Sharif (10 km) on their way to Gayā also stop in Nāḷandā.

Some **trains** stop in Nāḷandā, including the daily *Shramjeevi Express 2401/2402* travelling between Delhi and Patna.

We woke up early that morning hoping to get to Nāḷandā quickly and spend the day wandering around the ruins and visiting the museum. But by the time we'd meditated, eaten, replenished supplies in the baffling Rajgir market and haggled with horse-cart drivers to take us to the bus stand, it was already past noon. Nearing the bus stand, the driver began to make conversation in Hindi and broken English:

"Where going?" he asks.

"Nāḷandā," we say.

"I take," he answers with a confident grin. The three of us look at each other and are a bit puzzled...

"Kitneh? (how much?)"

"100 rupeya."

The price is cheap, but what if the road is really bad, or worse, busy with lorries pouring diesel exhaust fumes right into our faces? But we're adventurers, so we take a chance. "Tikeh (o.k.)," we reply with some reluctance.

The road is surprisingly smooth and peaceful. The horse's steady clip-clopping rhythm and the surrounding agricultural fields create a magical setting. The two-hour journey passes very serenely.

The serenity, however, is anicca. The closer we get to our destination, the more our driver gets impatient with the time. "Nālandā, o.k.?!" he says, wanting to drop us right there on the highway at the town's entrance, about two km from the ruins.

"Nahee, Nahee (no, no)...Nālandā Mahāvihāra (the ruins)...aur kamra chahiye! (and we want a room)." We plead with him to take us closer to the ruins where we read that we can find a guest house to drop our heavy bags. Unhappily, he complies. He can't resist our innocent tourist smiles and overly enthusiastic thumbs up.

Approaching the ruins, we ask him to take us just one more minute to our guidebook's recommended Burmese Monastery. Five very long minutes later, we check out the only accommodation in sight (the book's recommendation is non-existent), which was a run-down colonial bungalow with high ceilings and trimmings on the doorframes.

Despite the decency of the rooms, our sensations are telling us otherwise: we would be the only guests, the over-staffed employees stare at us in an eerie way, and it is highly over-priced. We politely decline the room and decide to keep looking. By this time, the horse is soaked with sweat and the driver is really agitated. To keep the peace, we get off at the ruins with our packs, pay him a little extra, and try to decide what to do next.

Now it's late afternoon, the ruins are closing soon (and we don't want to pay the high entrance fee for a short visit while lugging our bags around), our guidebook has the wrong information, and we're being swarmed by beggars, touts and would-be guides. Now we're the agitated ones and the whole world seems to be laughing at us.

Then we remember: when we were at Dhamma Giri, some friends told us to visit a certain meditator/scholar living and working at the new Nālandā University. Not knowing what else to do, we decide to try to meet him. When we get there however, we find that he is "out of station" and the security guard doesn't even want to let us on to the premises. Overhearing our situation, some young Indian bhikkhus fortunately take pity on us, convince the guard to let us in, and invite us to their quarters for tea.

Meanwhile, security notifies our scholar's assistant, who tracks us down to see what we want. We end up chatting with him for a while, and it just so happens that he has just finished his first 10-day Vipassana course for the institute's employees. He is sympathetic to our plight and not only offers us a room to stay in for as long as we want, but provides a private cook to prepare our meals and snacks as well, free of charge. That night, lying down in our comfortable beds after a delicious dinner, we realize another lesson in surrender and trust, and the silliness of getting agitated. After a good laugh at ourselves, we doze off into long and restful sleep.

– MD & KG

Patna (*Pāṭaliputta, Pāṭaligāma*)

The Importance of Ethics

Towards the end of his life, the Buddha went to visit Pāṭaligāma, a city on the Ganges in the modern day state of Bihar. He knew that many of the city's inhabitants had great respect for the Dhamma, and had a deep wish for him to bless their city with his presence. When Pāṭaligāma's citizens heard that the Buddha was coming, they built a new assembly hall and asked him to consecrate it.

Thousands of people gathered at the new hall and eagerly waited to hear the Dhamma directly from the Buddha. The Buddha told his audience,

Friends, carelessness with your sīla brings about five dangers. Which five? (i) You will lose your wealth through negligence; (ii) you will get a bad reputation; (iii) you will not possess self-confidence; (iv) you will die in a state of confusion, and (v) after death, you will be reborn in a woeful state.

And, friends; perfecting your sīla brings about five benefits: (i) you will acquire much wealth through diligence; (ii) you will get a good reputation; (iii) you will feel confident and secure; (iv) you will die with a clear mind, and (v) after death, you will be reborn in a happy state.[111]

The Buddha then set off to continue his journey towards Vesālī. The townsfolk came to see him off and in the Buddha's honour, named the gate through which he left "Gotama's Gate" (*Gotamudvara*)[112] and the ferry landing that he used to cross the river "Gotama Ferry Landing" (*Gotamatittha*).[113] After walking a short distance, the Buddha turned around to look at the city, and shared with Ānanda a prediction that it would grow into a great metropolis, but then fall into ruin caused by fire, floods and war (which in fact did happen).

Several years after the Buddha's death, King Ajātasattu moved his capital from Rājagaha to the humble Pāṭaligāma (Pāṭali Village), which blossomed into the prosperous Pāṭaliputta (Pāṭali City). This city remained a capital for almost 1 000 years and reached its apex during the Mauryan dynasty led first by Chandragupta and later his grandson, the benevolent Asoka.

After the Buddha's death, Ānanda visited Pāṭaligāma a few times and preached several discourses in the Rooster's Park (*Kukkutārāma*).[114] The lay-supporter Kukkutasetthi built a small monastery here, which years later was renovated and expanded by King Asoka and renamed Asoka's Park (*Asokārāma*).

Over the years, the Kukkutārāma/Asokārāma grew into a large monastic complex and was the setting of the nine-month long Third Council (*Tatiya Dhamma-Saṅgīti*) sponsored by King Asoka around 253 BCE. During this meeting convened by 1 000 learned *bhikkhus* under the guidance of Thera Moggaliputta Tissa, divisive elements that had crept into the Saṅgha were removed[115] and the Abhidhamma was finalized by adding the Kathāvatthu, the fifth of seven books of the Abhidhamma Piṭaka. Shortly after the council, King Asoka sent out nine groups of enlightened *dhammadūtas* (messengers of Dhamma) to propagate the Dhamma throughout India and neighbouring countries such as Sri Lanka and Myanmar.[116]

Site-Sitting

Situated on the south bank of the Ganges River, this crowded, dirty, and noisy state capital has lost all resemblance of its past glory. It's difficult to imagine that modern Patna was once the largest city in the world and the seat of India's greatest empire from the 6th century BCE to the 4th century CE. A series of fires, floods and wars eventually destroyed most of Pāṭaliputta, and all that now remains of the past are the ruins of a large pillared assembly hall at **Kumrahar Archaeological Park** (6 km from the railway station) and some fantastic art in the Patna Museum.

Pāṭaliputra Karuṇā Stūpa

The Pāṭaliputra Karuṇā Stūpa is in the middle of Buddha Smṛiti Udyan, a 20-acre park near the railway station that was established in 2010 by the Bihar government to commemorate the 2550th anniversary of the Buddha's *mahāparinibānna*. Buddha relics donated by governments and monastic officials from Thailand, Sri Lanka, Myanmar, Japan, South Korea and Tibet are currently enshrined in the stūpa's inner sanctum. You are allowed to meditate in the presence of the relics, and are also encouraged to practice in the meditation hall adjacent to the stūpa. In addition to the library and museum, the park also houses two young Bodhi trees, one a descendent from Bodhgāya and the other from Anurādhpura (which is a descendent from the original tree that the Buddha awakened under).

Patna Museum

This excellent, Rajput-fashioned museum was built by the British in 1917, and now houses a collection of poorly labelled Buddhist statues from the past 2 000 years. The museum's marvellous collection of stone and metal statues and paintings of the Buddha and *bodhisattas* demonstrates how the Dhamma has inspired beauty and creativity throughout the centuries. In addition to the artwork, the museum's most prized possession is a relic casket containing what is believed to be the portion of the Buddha's ashes obtained by the Licchavī rulers after the Buddha's passing. There is a hefty fee of Rs 500 to see the display, but many meditators feel it's worth paying, as the casket is kept in a quiet separate room, making it possible to meditate in the relic's presence without any outside disturbance.

The museum also exhibits a variety of stuffed animals, tribal artefacts and the longest and oldest fossilized tree in the world (16 m long and over 200 million years old!). The museum is open from 10:30 a.m. to 4:30 p.m. and closed on Mondays and public holidays. The basic entry fee is Rs 10 for Indians and Rs 250 for foreigners (the price has gone up since the anecdote below was written).

— *Five rupees. (So says the man in the khaki uniform.)*
— *Great. (We think, "So cheap.")*

As we enter the Patna Museum, a colonial building with pillars, arched doorways, and flaking plaster, we find ourselves trapped in a labyrinth of hallways and end up in a dusty and crowded exhibition of various stuffed animals. A giant tiger in the middle of the room eerily surveys what goes on in his small kingdom, while the local 'freak of nature,' a pair of Siamese baby goats, stares at us with plastic eyes.

We quickly move through to the next exhibit of faded Indian paintings, and then to a room without lights containing ancient Buddhist and Hindu statues. What we are really looking for, however, is the soapstone casket with the Buddha's relics found in Vesālī's Licchavī Stūpa. We go upstairs and ask a rifle-wielding guard. "100 rupees," he says with a blank look in his eyes. We are appalled. The mind starts churning:

— *One hundred rupees, I'm not paying 100 rupees.*
— *That's 300 rupees for three of us...we paid only 15 to get in to the museum...*
— *But what if it's worth it...*
— *But what if it's not; we'll have wasted 300 rupees!*
— *But we came all this way...*
— *It's really only a few dollars...*

We pay the guard. He fetches the keys to open the huge steel padlock keeping the sliding iron gates together. He turns on the lights; flecks of floating dust glimmer in the air. Behind a glass window, on a raised platform, sits a small soapstone casket, with its contents neatly laid out beside it: a copper coin, a shell, two glass beads and a small gold plate (the ashes are still inside the casket). We gaze silently at the casket for a few moments and then tell the guard we want to meditate for a while. He hesitates and we have to bargain with him by promising not to burn more holes in the already very tattered carpet.

After about 45 minutes of peaceful meditation, the guard clears his throat; our time is up; another group is waiting to come in. The three of us silently smile at each other, all knowing what the other is thinking: It's not every day that you get a private audience with the Buddha's remains.

– MD & KG

Sleeping & Eating

Patna is a good place to visit for a day. If you need to stay overnight there are several budget and mid-range hotels and restaurants near the railway station on Fraser Road (or tucked away in the lanes just off the main road). Budget travellers can try their luck at **Hotel Parker** or **Hotel Amar**. For those who can spend a bit more money for a much higher standard, check out **Satkar International, Rajasthan Hotel and Vegetarian Restaurant**, or **Hotel President**. The **Marwari Awas Griha Hotel and Restaurant** serves one of the best, all-you-can-eat vegetarian thālis. Patna's best luxury hotels are **Pataliputra Ashok** and **Maurya Patna**, which overlooks the park Gandhi Maidan. The park's landmark Golghar (a domed granary built by the British) offers good views of the surrounding city.

Coming & Going

As the busy capital of Bihar, Patna serves as a major transportation hub for the region. Patna has two **bus** stands: the New Main Bus Stand (Mithapur Bus Station, 2 km south of the train station) and the Gandhi Maidan Bus Stand (on the north side of Gandhi Maidan Park). From the New Main Bus Stand you can get private buses to most major towns in Bihar, as well as to Vārāṇasī, Kolkata, and Raxaul (Nepal border). There are several buses that travel between Patna and Rajgir (and pass through Nālandā). From the Gandhi Maidan Bus Stand, slower, cheaper government buses are also available.

Patna Junction Railway Station is connected by **rail** to most major cities in India. At the 1st-floor reservation office, ticket window No.7 is reserved for foreign tourists. Some convenient trains are:

- Shramjeevi Express 2401/2402 (New Delhi-Patna via Vārāṇasī and Nālandā)
- Patna Rajdhani Express 2309/2310 (New Delhi-Patna via Mughal Sarai)
- Howrah Rajdhani Express 2305/2306 (New Delhi-Howrah/Kolkata)
- Magadha Express 2392/2391 (New Delhi-Patna)
- Poorva Express 2304/2303 (New Delhi-Howrah/Kolkata via Vārāṇasī and Gayā)
- Patna-Kurla Express 3202/3201 (Kurla/Mumbai-Patna)

Patna is also connected by **air** to Mumbai, Delhi, Kolkata and Lucknow. The airport is 7 km west of downtown Patna, and accessible by rickshaw and taxi. Indian Airlines and Air Deccan both offer flights to and from Patna.

Excursions

Hajipur (*Ukkācelā*)

While taking a rest in Ukkācelā from their wanderings in the countryside, the Buddha spoke to his company of *bhikkhus*, making a comparison between a cowherd and a brahmin,

Bhikkhus, the foolish cowherd leads his cattle, during the rainy season, through a river at a spot where there is no ford for safe crossing. Because of his failure to properly examine both shores of the river, his cattle drown. The wise cowherd, on the other hand, understands the weather and knows where all the fords for safe crossing are located. His cattle do not perish in the river and continue living their happy cattle lives.

Similarly, an inattentive and unskilled brahmin who preaches to the ignorant leads his audience astray from the proper path of awakening. People who place their faith in him continue walking on the road of harm and suffering. The wise brahmin, on the other hand, properly teaches his disciples how to walk along the path of peace and happiness.

The Buddha then uttered,

Knowing directly the entire world,
The Awakened One who understands
Opens the door to the Deathless
By which nibbāna may be safely reached.

Now Māra's stream is dammed,
Its current blocked, its reeds removed;
Rejoice then, bhikkhus, mightily
And set your hearts where safety lies.[117]

Knowing that his life was closing in on him, Ānanda set off from Rajgir towards Vesālī. When the news reached King Ajātasattu, the king set off after him in order to pay his last respects. Meanwhile, when Vesālī's citizens had heard that Ānanda was coming to their land to die, they flocked to the banks of the Ganges to welcome him.

By the time Ajātasattu caught up with the old *bhikkhu*, Ānanda was already in a boat in the middle of the Ganges. Ānanda found himself in a dilemma: the king was imploring him to return to that bank while hordes of people were on the other bank pleading for him to come to them. Not wishing to offend either party and wanting to avoid the possibility of future conflict between the two groups, legend tells that Ānanda levitated up into the air and burst into a ball of flames. Half of his ashes fell on one side of the river and half on the other. Stūpas were built over the ashes on both sides.[118]

The Ganges' constantly changing course has long ago washed away the stūpa on the southern bank of the river, but the stūpa on the northern bank can still be seen today on the western edge of Hajipur, not far from the market gardens. Today's stūpa is a grassy mound crowned with a Hindu temple named Ramchaura Mandir.

Hajipur is 10 km across the Ganges from Patna, and the stūpa can easily be reached en route from Patna to Vaishali, especially if you are travelling in a private vehicle.

Champanagar (*Campā*)

According to legend, the city got its name from the numerous sweet-smelling campaka trees that grew around it. When visiting Campā, the Buddha would usually meditate and teach at Gaggara's Lotus Lake, which was probably located in the same area as the body of water known today as Sarovana Talarb.

One day Pessa the elephant driver and his friend Kandaraka the wandering ascetic went to visit the Buddha at Gaggara's Lotus Lake. Pessa was already a meditator and wanted his friend to also benefit from the Buddha's teaching. After giving them a short talk on the four foundations of mindfulness, the Buddha spoke to them about the four types of person who live in the world: a person who tortures himself, a person who tortures others, a person who tortures both himself and others, and a person who tortures neither himself nor others. Pessa, wanting to demonstrate his knowledge to his friend and to the Buddha, added "Sir, the first three types of people are like animals entangled in the world of craving for pleasure and repulsion from pain."

The Buddha nodded in agreement; Pessa felt satisfied. Pessa thanked the Buddha for his time and left with his friend, saying that he would like to stay longer but had a lot of things to do that day. After Pessa had left, the Buddha told the congregation of *bhikkhus* that the elephant driver was a wise man, but if he had stayed longer for a further explanation of these four types of people he would have attained the first stage of enlightenment.

The Buddha continued,

The first type of person is the ascetic who tortures his body, like
I had done before I discovered the Middle Path. The second type
of person depends on harming others for his livelihood, such as
murderers and thieves. The third type of person is the monarch who
oppresses his people or the brahmin who depends on ritual sacrifice
in hope of gaining material or spiritual rewards. The fourth type of
person is the arahant who has perfected sīla, samādhi, and paññā.
This person lives here and now—desireless, extinguished, cooled—
and abides in bliss.

Having heard this precious teaching, the *bhikkhus* were satisfied and inspired to continue their work on the path towards perfection.[119]

When the brahmin elder Soṇadaṇḍa heard that the Buddha was staying at Gaggara's Lotus Lake, he immediately went with his students to visit him. When he reached the lake and saw the Buddha with all his disciples and those who had come to hear his teachings, Soṇadaṇḍa became nervous that perhaps the Buddha would ask him a question that he was incapable of answering properly. If this happened, he would look foolish in front of all his students and those who hire him to perform the Vedic rituals. Being humiliated in public was something he felt he couldn't afford to risk.

The Buddha, sensing the brahmin's uneasiness, addressed him:

"Soṇadaṇḍa, how many qualities does a person need to have to be considered a true brahmin?" the Buddha asked, knowing that this question was within the old man's field of knowledge.

"Five," he replied with pride and relief. Wiping the sweat off his brow, he continued. "A true brahmin must be born into a pure brahmin family descending from seven generations; he must be well-versed in the Vedas; he must be handsome; he must be virtuous, and he must possess wisdom."

"Could one of these five qualities be omitted for someone to still be considered a true brahmin?" the Buddha inquired.

"Certainly, Gotama. If the man was ugly, but possessed the other four qualities, he would still be considered a true brahmin."

"Could one of these four qualities be omitted for someone to still be considered a true brahmin?"

"It is possible. If someone was not well-versed in the Vedas, but still possessed the other three qualities, he would still be considered to be a true brahmin." Several brahmins in the crowd began to feel ill at ease with Soṇadaṇḍa's comment.

"Could one of these three qualities be omitted for someone to still be considered a true brahmin?" the Buddha asked, continuing with his questioning.

"Yes, it is still possible. We could leave out descent. If a person possesses morality and wisdom, he could still be considered a true brahmin."

Hearing this, the crowd of brahmins went wild, shouting and accusing Soṇadaṇḍa of giving up his faith and adopting the Buddha's belief system. After a few moments of grumbling, the charismatic Soṇadaṇda lifted his hand and hushed the crowd,

"If my nephew Angaka had pure descent, knowledge of the Vedas, and a beautiful appearance, which you all know he has; but was a murderer, a thief, and a liar, which you all know he is not, would he still be considered a true brahmin? Of course not! But because he is virtuous and wise, we can truthfully declare that Angaka is a brahmin."

Although unhappy, the crowd was silent; they knew that their elder's words were correct. The Buddha broke the silence with a discourse on the fruits of cultivating *sīla*, *samādhi*, and *paññā*. The discourse delighted Soṇadaṇda's heart and he offered the next day's meal to the Buddha and Saṅgha.[120]

Champanagar is far off the pilgrimage route, but because it's a difficult place to reach, it is also free from the noisy touristic elements found at the other sites. To get to Champanagar, take a bus, train, or taxi from Patna to Bhagalpur (220 km). From Bhagalpur, take a taxi to Champanagar.

The journey to Champanagar is long and the area is one of the most dangerous in Bihar, so avoid travelling at night and be cautious at unofficial roadblocks. Other than having a friend from Bhagalpur to shelter you for the night, your best bet for accommodation is the dingy hotel across from the Bhagalpur railway station.

Vikramaśila
During the 8th through 11th centuries, Vikramaśila was recognized as one of the most prestigious monastic universities, comparable to Nāḷandā, and was a centre for the study of Tantrayāna, the last of the three phases of Indian Buddhism. Famous Tantric Buddhist masters such as Naropa and Atisa spent several years here practising and expounding their interpretations of the Buddha's teaching. One Tibetan source indicates that the monastery was made up of 108 temple buildings and a large courtyard, surrounded by a protective wall. At its peak the monastic school was home to more than a thousand students and teachers from around the world, and had a long-standing relationship with Tibet.

Take caution when travelling anywhere beyond the established tourist and pilgrimage routes; this part of Bihar is widely reputed to be one of the most dangerous regions in India. Vikramaśila is 50 km beyond Bhagalpur. Take a taxi from Bhagalpur to Kahalgong and then on to Patharaghat, where there is a magnificent hill with rock cut caves, Buddhist statues, and a fine view over the Ganges. From Patharaghat, continue for another 3 km to the ruins of Vikramaśila.

In addition to the stone remains of the monastery and meditation cells, are the impressive ruins of the main temple, flanked by shrines on each side. Visitors have told us that the Archaeological Survey of India has a makeshift museum containing several Buddhist statues; unfortunately, the place is often locked up and finding the person with the key is a challenge.

Pilgrims travelling to Vikramaśila will find accommodation in Bhagalpur.

Vaishali (*Vesālī*)

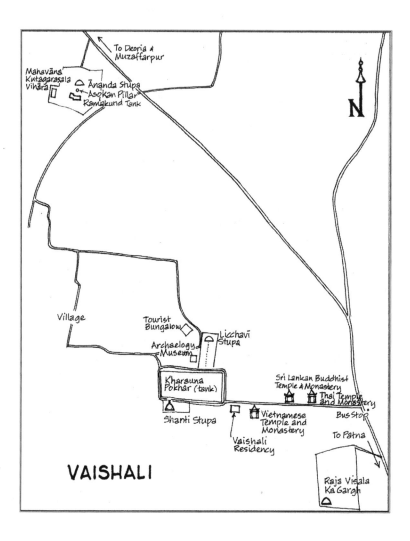

Now a collection of sleepy rural villages, Vesālī used to be one of the most prosperous and glamorous cities in the Middle Land. During the Buddha's time, the city was known for its creative arts, architectural wonders and enchanting parks and forests. Vesālī was so spectacular that the Buddha once compared the city to a celestial realm and the richly decorated Licchavī princes to celestial beings.

Vesālī was the capital of the Vajjian confederacy, reputed to be one of the first states in the world to adopt a democratic form of government, where leaders were elected from the aristocratic class. The confederacy consisted of eight tribes who all lived in harmony due to their strong practice of the Dhamma and their meticulous application of the Buddha's seven guidelines for preventing decline in government (see the section on Vulture's Peak for a list of the seven principles).

The people of Vesālī loved the Buddha and always offered him hospitality when he arrived. Feeling welcome, the Buddha spent his fifth and last rains retreats here. If he wasn't found meditating or teaching around the city's many different shrines, the Buddha spent his time at Ambapāli's Mango Grove or in the Great Forest (*Mahāvana*), which started at the city's outskirts and extended up the Himālayan foothills.

Tales from Vesālī

Five years after his Awakening, the Buddha walked to Vesālī from Rājagaha to teach the Dhamma while the city was suffering from a devastating drought, terrible famine and deadly plague. Seeing the misery that the people faced, the Buddha delivered the Jewel Discourse (*Ratana Sutta*), praising the inspiring qualities of the Triple Gem.

The Sublime One, knower of the sublime,
Showing the way to the sublime, offering the sublime,
Has expounded the incomparable Dhamma.
This is the precious jewel in the Buddha;
By this truth, may there be well-being...

Cessation, detachment, and deathlessness;
The well-established Sakyan sage
Attained these precious states.
Nothing compares to this Dhamma.
This is the precious Jewel in the Dhamma,
By this truth, may there be well-being...

Those with firm minds, free from craving,
Who apply themselves to the teaching of Gotama,
Having attained that which should be attained,
They plunge into nibbāna,
Enjoying the highest obtained peace.
This is the precious jewel in the Saṅgha,
By this truth, may there be well-being... [121]

Legend tells that as soon as he finished speaking, a loud burst of
thunder followed by a heavy rain fell on the city, purging it of its misfortunes. The Buddha then instructed Ānanda to walk around the city
and mindfully chant the *sutta*, which would help soothe the people's
minds and inspire them to practise the Dhamma.

Shortly after the Buddha's death, King Ajātasattu and his minister
Vassakāra drew up a devious plan for attacking the Vajjian confederacy. Knowing that the Licchavīs were sincere practitioners of the
Dhamma and followed the Buddha's seven guidelines for concord,
they understood that the only way to defeat them was by sabotaging
the republic's internal harmony.

Pretending to be a traitor to his king, Vassakāra joined the Licchavī
tribe and lived amongst them for three years. He gradually created
strife amongst the princes by lying to them and spreading false rumours. Eventually, the princes no longer trusted each other and the
confederacy fragmented. When the Magadhans attacked them, the
Licchavīs could not defend themselves. Vesālī's riches were plun-
dered, its independent political system destroyed, and the population
massacred.[122]

Sometime between 443 and 383 BCE, about 100 years after the First Council in Rājagaha, the Second Council (*Dutiya Dhamma-Saṅgīti*) was held at the
Vālukārāma Vihāra near Vesālī. The meeting of 700 *bhikkhus* was sponsored by
King Kālāsoka and presided over by the Bhikkhus Revata Thera and Yasa Saṅgiti
Thera. Monks from all over India attended the council, including Bhikkhu Sab-
bakamin from Kosambī, believed to be the oldest *bhikkhu* in the world and who, it
is said, once shared a room with Ānanda.

Different traditions maintain different accounts of why the council was called.
One version believes that the meeting was called because of a doctrinal dispute
concerning the status of the *arahant*. Certain monks argued that *arahants* were not
truly liberated from the fetters and were still subject to the temptations and passions of worldly existence. These monks dubbed themselves as the "Great Community" (*Mahāsaṅghika*), while the monks who continued to assert the purity of
the status of the *arahant* referred to themselves as the "Elders" (*Sthaviras*), so as
to identify themselves with what they believed to be the original teachings of the
Buddha.

Another account of the Second Council holds that the cause of the disagreement
was not doctrinal, but rather a dispute concerning certain breaches of the monastic
code of discipline. In this version, the Sthaviras refused to accept the changes of

certain *vinaya* rules by the Mahāsaṅghikas such as using salt to season food, drinking unfermented palm wine, and accepting gold and silver.

While the exact reason for calling the Second Council remains uncertain, what's certain is that the meeting resulted in a significant and far-reaching schism in the Saṅgha, one which has lasted to this day. The Mahāsaṅghika later evolved into the *Mahāyāna*, the "Great Vehicle," and the strongest surviving school of the Sthaviras became known as the *Theravāda*, or "Council of Elders."

Site-Sitting

Licchavī Stūpa

After the Buddha passed away in Kusinārā, his ashes were divided into eight portions that were distributed amongst the various regional kingdoms, where they were enshrined in what became known as the eight *mahāstūpas*. The stūpa at Vesālī was built by the Licchavī tribe to enshrine their portion of the remains. Some 300 years later Asoka excavated the stūpa and removed the majority of the relics, distributing them to other stūpas he'd built throughout his empire.

In 1958, the Licchavī Stūpa was opened by archaeologists, who found a small soap-stone casket containing burnt bone, a copper coin, a shell, two glass beads and a small gold plate. The archaeologists also found evidence of Asoka's earlier excavation. These treasures were taken to the Patna Museum, and can still be seen there today; all the pilgrim sees of the Licchavī Stūpa at the site is its foundation.

Shanti Stūpa

Towering over the village, the Nipponzan Myōhōji Shanti Stūpa graces Vesālī with its majestic beauty, and perhaps clues us into Vesālī's past splendour. Inaugurated in October 1996, the Stūpa was built by Nipponzan Myōhōji, a modern Japanese Buddhist order founded by Nichidatsu Fujī in 1917. Under Fujī's guidance, the organization has constructed Shanti Stūpas at sites throughout the world in order to promote the Buddhist vision of peace and harmony for all beings. The stūpa enshrines some of the Buddha's corporeal relics, and many meditators find that this helps create a tranquil atmosphere for meditation.

Archaeological Museum

Just north of the large water tank in the middle of the village is a small museum holding antiquities found in the area. The museum's stated hours claim that it should be open from 10 a.m. to 5 p.m. everyday except Fridays, although in our experience, this was not always the case.

The water tank is believed to be the *Abhiseka Puskarina*, the ceremonial place where Vajjian rulers were anointed at their coronation. Today it is the central meeting place for the village women to congregate and do their washing and socializing.

Raja Visala Ka Ghar (House of Vesālī's King)

Just off the main road coming from Patna is a large rectangular structure said to have been part of a Licchavī assembly hall. As centuries of regular flooding have left the city buried under numerous layers of silt, this is the only secular structure we have left of the ancient city. Nearby is a buried stūpa topped with the tomb of Sheikh Mohammad Qazin, a celebrated 15th century Sufi saint.

Looking out over the stark present-day landscape from the top of the mound, one gets a real sense of the incredible change that has occurred since the days when the Buddha described this place as a land of groves and gardens. Kingdoms have arisen and passed away, cultures have blossomed and withered, and religions have illuminated and brought darkness. And all that is left, and that will be left, is crumbled and buried under layers and layers of silt. Like so many of the ruins throughout the Middle Land, the few remains at Vesālī offer an education on the impermanence of all things.

Amvara Village

The village of Amvara, west of the Shanti Stūpa, is believed to be the spot where Ambapāli's Grove once stood. However, no archaeological ruins have been found to support this claim.

Ever since she was a child, Ambapāli had been considered the most beautiful girl in Vesālī. All the Licchavī princes wanted to marry her, and were always competing with each other for her attention. Realizing the impossibility of only one of them having her, the princes decided to make Ambapāli a lady of the court.[123]

The first time Ambapāli encountered the Buddha was while he was resting in her mango grove, shortly before his final rains retreat. She was surprised at how composed he was. Most men who looked at her either had eyes filled with lust or embarrassment. The Buddha was completely serene.

Seeing how much she suffered inside, the Buddha looked into her eyes with tenderness and said, "Ambapāli, beauty arises and passes away like all other phenomena. Fame and fortune are no different. Cherish all the moments left to you in this life. Do not lose yourself in the world of the senses." Hearing this precious teaching, she felt grateful and invited the Buddha and Sangha for the next day's meal.

A group of Licchavī princes stopped Ambapāli on her way home, and when they heard that she was going to serve the Buddha the next day, they tried bribing her with one hundred thousand pieces of money to give up her invitation to them. Ambapāli steadfastly refused, "Sirs, I would not hand over tomorrow's meal even if you gave me Vesālī with all its revenues." The next day, after the meal was finished, Ambapāli gifted her mango grove to the Sangha, which in time grew into a well-known monastery where many *bhikkhunīs* resided.[124]

Tales from Ambapāli's Grove

Later in life, Ambapāli ordained as a *bhikkhunī* and quickly attained arahantship. She composed a famous poem, which today, is one of the earliest known compositions by an Indian woman. Her poem

expressed the transiency of youthful beauty and the inevitability of
old age:

In youth, my hair was curled at the tips,
And black—like the colour of bees;
With age, it has turned to coarse hemp.

In youth, my hair was coiffed and fragrant—
Like a bouquet of perfumed flowers;
With age, it smells like musty animal fur.

In youth, my hair was styled with braids,
Ornamented with delicate pins, decorated with gold,
Splendidly thick and lush—
Like a well-tended grove;
With age, it balds and grows thin...

In youth, my teeth were beautiful—
Like white plantain buds;
With age, they have broken and yellowed.

In youth, my voice had a sweet, melodious tone—
Like a cuckoo bird singing in the jungle;
With age, it cracks and cackles...

In youth, my hands were delicate and splendid,
Always adorned with golden rings;
With age, they are like onions and potatoes.

In youth, my breasts were perfectly round, firm and high.
Now, with the drought of old age, they droop and dangle—
Like a pair of empty old water bags...

In youth, my feet were delicate—
Like soft cotton;
With age, they have shrivelled and cracked.

Then, this physical heap was gorgeous;
Now, it's a decrepit home of pains.
The truth of the Truth-Speaker's words never changes.[125]

During his last visit to Ambapāli's Grove on his way to Kusinārā, the
Buddha instructed the monks and nuns to diligently practise the four
foundations of awareness (*satipaṭṭhānas*):

Bhikkhus, a bhikkhu should dwell ardently aware with a constant
and thorough understanding of impermanence. And how should
a bhikkhu dwell ardently aware with a constant and thorough
understanding of impermanence? Here a bhikkhu dwells observing
the body in body, having removed craving and aversion towards the

world of mind and matter. He dwells observing sensations in sensa-
tions...mind in mind...mental contents in mental contents...

And how bhikkhus, does a bhikkhu dwell ardently aware with a
constant and thorough understanding of impermanence? Here a
bhikkhu is ardently aware with a constant and thorough under-
standing of impermanence while going forwards or backwards;
while looking straight ahead or sideways; while bending or stretch-
ing; while wearing the robes or carrying the bowl; while chewing,
drinking, eating, or tasting; while defecating or urinating; while
walking, standing, sitting, sleeping, waking, speaking or keeping
silent. In this way, a bhikkhu dwells ardently aware with a constant
and thorough understanding of impermanence: this is my instruc-
tion to you.[126]

Pinnacled Hall Monastery in the Great Forest
(*Mahāvana Kutagarasala Vihāra*)
The principle monastery in Vesālī was the Mahāvana Kutagarasala Vihāra, where the Buddha gave numerous important teachings. The site is perhaps most famous for hosting the legendary scene of the Buddha admitting women into the Saṅgha.

The archeological park containing the ruins of the Mahāvana Kutagarasala Vihāra is in the village of Kolhua. To get to the ruins, which are referred to by locals simply as Ānanda Stūpa, turn left at Vesāli's main gate towards Muzaffarpur. After about 3 km you will see a sign indicating the Ānanda Relic Stūpa and Asokan Pillar. Turn left and travel another kilometre until you reach the site. Alternately, if travelling by foot, bicycle, or rickshaw, you can take a longer, more scenic route through the village hamlets via the back road beginning at the Licchavī Stūpa. The villagers rarely see foreigners and will likely offer warm smiles and greetings. The archaeological park is open every day, and there is an entry fee.

Ānanda Relic Stūpa
The stūpa commemorates the Buddha's cousin and great attendant. When the stūpa was excavated in the late 1970s, small sheets of gold and semi-precious stones were found along with the stone relic casket containing Ānanda's mortal remains.

When meditating at this stūpa, practitioners may wish to reflect upon the selfless-service that Ānanda gave to the Buddha day and night for 25 years. The Buddha praised Ānanda's excellent qualities, at one time saying of him: "people are delighted when they see him, they are pleased when he speaks about the Dhamma, and they are disappointed when he is silent."[127]

Asokan Pillar
Locals claim that the stone pillar next to the Ānanda Stūpa was erected by King Asoka; some scholars, however, argue that this attribution is incorrect. The characteristic shaft of an Asokan pillar was slender and polished. This one, however, is thick, squat, and lacking polish. The lion capital is also unlike the other Asokan lion capitals found around India. Perhaps this pillar is pre-Asokan and was the prototype for his pillars.[128]

Ramakund

The water tank near the pillar is said to mark the legendary spot where a monkey once offered a bowl of honey to the Buddha. When the Buddha accepted the gift, the monkey was so happy that he leapt ecstatically from tree to tree. Carried away with enthusiasm, the monkey accidentally fell from a tall tree and died immediately. Later that evening, the Buddha told those who witnessed the tragic event that since the monkey's mind was joyous at the time of his death, he was reborn in one of the heavenly realms.

Tales from Mahāvana Kutagarasala Vihāra

Mahāpajāpati, the Buddha's aunt and foster mother, began to feel that palace life was stifling, and even a hindrance to her progress along her spiritual path. She very much wanted to join the Saṅgha, but the Buddha had already refused her request while he was staying at Nigroda's Park in Kapilavattu. Mahāpajāpati decided that she would try to convince the Buddha that she was serious and determined. She joined five hundred Sakyan princesses with similar sentiments, and together the women shaved their heads, donned the mendicant's robe, and walked barefoot from Kapilavatthu to Vesālī (about 430 km!) where the Buddha was staying. When they arrived at the gates of the Kutagarasala Vihāra, they were tired, dirty, their feet blistered and swollen. The women's wills, however, remained unshaken.

"What happened to you?" Ānanda cried out in disbelief. He had never seen any of these women even lift up a finger, yet now they looked like hardened mendicants.

"We wanted to show the Buddha that we are also capable of living the lives of renunciates. Please, Ānanda, speak to the Buddha on our behalf," Mahāpajāpati beseeched her nephew.

Ānanda was deeply moved by their devotion. He went to the Buddha and told him of everything the women had gone through. He asked, "Lord, is it possible for women to attain the fruits of stream-enterer, once-returner, never-returner, and *arahant*?"

"Yes, Ānanda, any woman who strives diligently on the path of Dhamma can attain any of these stages," the Buddha replied.

"Lord, can women attain the final goal more quickly if they renounce the world?" The Buddha nodded.

"Then please have compassion for them, Lord. Permit them to ordain into the Saṅgha."

He asked three times and finally after a long moment of silence, the Buddha consented on the condition that they follow certain rules that conformed to social customs of the time and which would help protect them from potential dangers. The women were delighted when Ānanda brought them the news. Living the lives of disciplined *bhikkhunīs*, they practised the Dhamma diligently, and in a short time tasted the fruits of *nibbāna*.[129]

"Lord, my memory is not very good. I cannot remember the 227 precepts for *bhikkhus*. What should I do?" Bhikkhu Vajjiputtaka complained to the Buddha.

Vajjiputtaka, do not worry about all these detailed guidelines. Simply maintain your practice of sīla, samādhi and paññā with perfect awareness and equanimity. That is all you need to do.

Understanding what the Buddha meant, Vajjiputtaka bowed and went to his hut to continue refining his practice of these three trainings. Within a short time, Vajjiputtaka became an *arahant*.[130]

Saccaka Aggivessana was a very clever and educated philosopher. Anyone who dared to confront him in a debate would shrink away in defeat shaking, shivering, trembling, and sweating under the armpits. One day, while impressing a group of 500 Licchavī princes with his oratory skills, Saccaka bragged that he could easily defeat the Buddha in a debate,

"Just as a strong man could drag around a long-haired ram by its coat, so too could I drag around the Buddha in a debate," he boasted. "And just as a strong brewer's mixer could take a straining cloth by the corners and shake and thump it about, so too could I shake and thump the Buddha about in a debate."

Saccaka's outrageous conceit aroused excitement in the princes. They urged him to prove himself and they all went to the Great Forest where the Buddha was meditating. After exchanging their greetings, Saccaka questioned him, "Sir, how do you discipline and instruct your disciples?"

"This is how I discipline my disciples, Aggivessana, and this is how my instruction is presented to my disciples: '*Bhikkhus*, material form is impermanent, sensation is impermanent, perception is impermanent, formative reactions are impermanent, consciousness is impermanent. *Bhikkhus*, material form is not self, sensation is not self, perception is not self, formative reactions are not self, consciousness is not self. All formations are impermanent; all things are not self.' That is the way I discipline my disciples, and that is how my instruction is presented to my disciples."

The arrogant Saccaka chuckled and looked around at the crowd hoping to get their support. He asserted, "Sir, you are greatly mistaken.

Each of the five aggregates *does* contain a self (*attā*), and each of these aggregates is responsible for producing meritorious or demeritorious actions." The Buddha then counter-questioned Saccaka,

"Tell me something, Aggivessana, is it possible to exercise total control over material form....sensations...perceptions...formative reactions...consciousness, saying 'let my material form...sensations... perceptions...formative reactions...consciousness be like this; let my material form...sensations...perceptions...formative reactions... consciousness not be like this?'"

Saccaka was speechless. The Buddha urged him to speak, telling him that he cannot come here and challenge him to a debate and then remain silent. With his head down, shoulders drooping, and sweat dripping profusely down his face, Saccaka gloomily responded, "Yes Sir, you are right. It is impossible to exert mastery over any of the aggregates. They can not be identified as 'mine,' 'I,' or 'my self.'"

The Buddha let a moment of silence pass so that Saccaka and all the princes could reflect on these truths. He then furthered his point,

Aggivessana, since all the aggregates are impermanent and not susceptible to perfect control, they naturally result in suffering. This is why all the noble disciples regard all experiences, whether past, future, or present, internal or external, coarse or fine, inferior or superior, far or near as they actually are: 'not mine, not I, not myself.'' Those who carry out the Tathāgata's instructions in this way live with satisfaction and are free from all doubts, fears and confusion that plague the human mind.

Saccaka, humbled by the defeat, apologized for his rude behaviour and invited the Buddha and Saṅgha for the next day's meal out of gratitude for the lesson he learned.[131]

A few days after his failure in refuting the Buddha's doctrine of *anattā*, Saccaka returned to the Buddha with some questions regarding meditation practices for developing awareness and concentration. The Buddha explained that no experience, pleasant or painful, will overwhelm anyone understanding the three characteristics of *anicca*, *dukkha* and *anattā*.

"How, Aggivessana, is one undeveloped in awareness and undeveloped in concentration? Here, Aggivessana, a pleasant sensation arises in an untaught ordinary person. Touched by that pleasant sensation, he lusts after the pleasure object. That pleasant sensation fades away, and then a painful sensation arises. Touched by that painful sensation, he sorrows, grieves, laments, weeps or beats his breast becoming distraught. When that pleasant sensation had arisen in him, it invaded his concentration and remained because his awareness was not developed. And when that painful sensation had arisen in him, it invaded his concentration and remained because his awareness was not developed. Anyone, Aggivessana, who reacts in this double manner, is undeveloped in awareness and undeveloped in concentration.

"And how, Aggivessana, is one developed in awareness and developed in concentration? Here, Aggivessana, a pleasant sensation arises in a well-taught noble disciple. Touched by that pleasant sensation, he does not lust after the pleasure object. That pleasant sensation eventually fades away, and a painful sensation arises. Touched by that painful sensation, he does not sorrow, grieve, lament, weep or beat his breast becoming distraught. When that pleasant sensation had arisen in him, it neither invaded his concentration nor remained because his awareness was developed. And when that painful sensation had arisen in him, it neither invaded his concentration nor remained because his awareness was developed. Anyone who reacts in this double manner is developed in awareness and developed in concentration."

The Buddha added that this practice not only applied to ordinary everyday sensations, but also to the most intense sensations. He gave examples of the terrible pains he felt during his period of extreme austerities and the most blissful sensations he experienced during his meditative attainments prior to his Awakening. The Buddha then continued with a simile,

Aggivessana, three men wish to ignite a fire and produce heat. The first man fails because he uses a wet piece of wood lying in the water. The second man also fails because he uses a wet piece of wood found on dry land. The third man, however, is successful. Why? Because he uses dry wood found on dry land.

The first person is like all the practitioners, no matter how earnest, who do not live withdrawn from sensual pleasures. The second person represents all those sincere practitioners who do stay away from sensual pleasures, but their minds still continue to lust after them. The third person symbolizes the practitioner who lives withdrawn from sensual pleasures and has abandoned all desires for them. Only this last person is truly capable of liberation.

Even though he felt satisfied with these lessons, Saccaka still felt an uncontrollable urge to refute some aspect of the Buddha's teaching or his community. Knowing that *arahants* laid their bodies down to rest, Saccaka accused the Buddha and his noble disciples of still abiding in delusion. The Buddha patiently retorted, "Aggivessana, even though arahants have eliminated sloth and torpor, they still need rest to dispel physical tiredness that is intrinsic to the human body.

Furthermore, abiding in delusion does not depend on whether one rests or not..." He continued:

A deluded person, Aggivessana, is one who has not abandoned the taints that defile, bring renewal of being, give trouble, ripen in suffering, and lead to future birth, old age, and death.

An undeluded person, Aggivessana, is one who has abandoned the taints that defile, bring renewal of being, give trouble, ripen in suffering, and lead to future birth, old age, and death...Just as a palm tree whose crown has been cut off is incapable of further growth, so too, the Tathāgata has abandoned the taints that defile.

Defeated again, Saccaka remained humble. He praised the Buddha for his skilled and gentle speech, even when spoken to in an offensive, angry, and bitter manner. Delighted by his encounters with the Buddha and the instructions he received, Saccaka left the Buddha in peace and never came back to bother him again.[132]

The Buddha spoke to the Licchavī prince Sunakkhatta about the importance of shedding the fetters associated with worldly things.

For those with minds intent on liberation, they should only ponder about liberation, talk about liberation, and associate with those also interested in liberation. When discussions concerning worldly things arise, they should not lend an ear to them or exert the mind in trying to understand them. Those who practise in this way will be just like a palm stump with its top cut off, incapable of growing again; so too, will all the fetters be cut off at their roots and no longer be subject to future arising.

Seeing that the prince needed a few more words, the Buddha gave him another short simile,

Sunakkhatta, just as a man who cherishes his life would not consciously drink poison or grab hold of a poisonous snake; so too, does a meditator practise restraint and avoid getting entangled by attachments.[133]

Sunakkhatta, pleased with the Buddha's encouraging words, returned to his palace and ardently practised the Dhamma.

At the end of his final rains retreat in Beluvagāmaka, a small village outside of Vesālī, the Buddha became severely ill. He bore the violent and deadly pains with perfect equanimity and awareness, never complaining for a moment. Although he was ready to die in the tiny village, the Buddha thought that it was inappropriate to pass away without giving a final address to the Saṅgha. Using his will power, the Buddha suppressed the sickness and continued with his daily routine of meditating and teaching. That evening, he mentioned to Ānanda that the path of Dhamma is like an open book, without any secrets or higher teachings.

The next morning after their alms round, the Buddha and Ānanda went to meditate at the Cāpāla Shrine. The Buddha, feeling his fragile and pain stricken body, realized that he had accomplished all that he had set out to do and relinquished his will to keep living. At that moment, thunder struck and a great earthquake shook throughout the universe. Ānanda opened his eyes, looked around to see what had happened, and asked the Buddha if he was alright.

"Ānanda, the Tathāgata has decided that he will pass away in three months time." Ānanda felt his body go numb and his head began to spin. He fell to his knees begging, "Please Lord, have pity on your disciples. Please, please, do not pass away yet. There is so much work left to be done.

The Buddha answered, "Enough, Ānanda, if you have faith in the Tathāgata, then you know his decisions are properly timed." After a long pause, the Buddha asked him to summon all the *bhikkhus* in the area to gather at the Kutagarasala.

That evening, before announcing his imminent passing, the Buddha advised the assembly of *bhikkhus* to follow his example and perfect the 37 Factors of Enlightenment (*bodhipakkhiya dhammas*),

Meditators, follow the Tathāgata's example so that the holy life may endure for a long time for the good of many, for the happiness of many. Shower the world with compassion, for the welfare, good, and happiness of both gods and men.

And how shall you follow the Tathāgata's example? By learning, practising, developing, and cultivating the Four Foundations of Awareness, the Four Right Efforts, and the Four Bases of Success, the Five Faculties, the Five Powers, the Seven Factors of Enlightenment, and the Noble Eightfold Path. Remember, meditators, all things are impermanent. Strive diligently to attain liberation. In three months, the Tathāgata will pass away.

The entire group of *bhikkhus* took the Dhamma teaching to heart. All were silent; they knew it would be the last time they saw their Master. After these final instructions, the Buddha left Vesālī and crossed through the villages of Bhaṇḍagāma, Hatthigama and Jambugama before stopping at Kessaputta.[134]

Sleeping & Eating

When we visited Vaishali there were not too many options for accommodating pilgrims. However, the government of Bihar has said that they will give land to Buddhist countries to construct more temples and monasteries. Until then, the best options are the **Vietnamese Mahāprajāpati Nunnery** (where periodic Vipassana courses are held), the **Sri Lankan Buddhist Temple**, and **Wat Thai Vaishali**, which are all clean and hospitable. The overpriced **Vaishali Residency** has superb rooms and delicious food, and the **Hotel Amrapali Vihar/Tourist Bungalow** near the Archaeological Museum has passable rooms and a dorm, but is only open from December to February. Accommodation at one of the Jain temples outside Vaishali is also possible. Many Jain followers come to Vaishali to worship at the birthplace of Mahāvira who was born and raised in the nearby village of Kaundupur around 599 BCE.

Coming & Going

Regular **buses** travel from Patna (56 km). However, be warned that what appears to be a short distance can actually be a long journey. Even when buses are marked 'Vaishali,' you still may have to change at other towns, depending on the mood of the driver and conductor. If your time is short, or you are leaving Patna in the afternoon, it's advisable to invest in a **taxi** to take you all the way. There are also buses to and from Muzaffarpur (36 km) for anyone interested in meditating at Dhamma Licchavī.

The closest **train** station to Vaishali is in Hajipur (35 km). The Vaishali Express 2554/2553 travels between Delhi and Barauni. Buses and tempos are available from Hajipur to Vaishali.

In Patna we were told that there was a one-hour direct bus to Vaishali. After a couple of unsuccessful attempts at finding the bus stand, we met a helpful man who brought us there. We asked the bus conductor,

— Vaishali?

— Yes, yes. Come, come.

— Direct?

— Yes, yes. Come, come.

— Where are you going?

— Yes. Come. (His arm moves as if he is sweeping air into the bus, in a way that threatens.) If you don't get on now, it will be too late.

So we get on and pay our fare.

An hour later, the bus reaches Hajipur—its final destination. Everyone gets off. When we ask the conductor what's up, he points to an-

other bus that he says is going to Vaishali. We unload our luggage, and verify that the new bus does in fact have "Vaishali" painted in big red letters on its front windshield.

After double and triple verifying with the conductor that this is a direct bus to Vaishali, we get on and pay our fare. During the endless halts to pick up and drop off other passengers, our neighbours strike up the usual conversation: "Which country?"

— Canada.

— Where going?

— Vaishali.

Hearing this, everyone makes an anxious face and begins to warn us about dacoits (thieves) on the road after dark. It seems everyone except us knows that this bus is stopping in Lalganj (15 km from Vaishali), and is not continuing on to Vaishali because the driver has decided it's not worth it for him to make the journey for three passengers (us!). Everyone has some piece of advice for us. While a middle-class gentleman proclaims, "Return to Patna or perish!" a kind woman offers to shelter us for the night in Lalgang. The offer is tempting, but we really wanted to get to Vaishali that evening. A young airforce soldier travelling to visit his family presents us with the best option, telling us he is going in our direction and will help us reach Vaishali.

The sun has set by the time we get off the bus. The shops are closing as we cross the small town's market street. We follow the airforce man through a couple of back alleys and find a crowded shared jeep-taxi that will pass by Vaishali. Somehow, we manage to squeeze ourselves into the back seat with our bags. As we start moving, though relatively comfortable, worry begins to creep in. Maybe we'll be robbed, or beaten up, or maybe even murdered! And if we do survive, we have no idea where we'll stay once we get to Vaishali. Vaishali is a tiny village in the middle of nowhere, and accommodations aren't mentioned in any of the available guidebooks written in the last 2 500 years.

Just as we find ourselves on the verge of succumbing to paranoia, our karmic insurance policy kicks in: the jeep's flickering headlights suddenly illuminate a sign that reads, "Sri Lankan Buddhist Monastery." All three of us shout at the driver to stop the vehicle, and quickly nudge our way out of the jeep. Two monks and a chaukidhar come out to greet us with friendly smiles. They offer us weary travellers a room with hot water for bathing, and the use of their kitchen. They have no idea how appreciative we are.

The next morning, after a good night's sleep, a refreshing bucket-bath, and a modest breakfast, we explored the tiny village of Vaishali,

*which the Buddha once compared to a deva world. Unlike the busy
capital it once was, the dirt-road village is now quiet. We walked
around the central, oblong-shaped water tank, visited by a flock of
Kingfishers, and then meditated at the Shanti Stūpa, where some
Buddha relics lie in the foundations.*

*While meditating, we could sense the quietness for miles around. Ris-
ing from this peaceful session, we were hungry and wondered where
we could find a place to eat. There are no markets or restaurants
in the off season, but walking down the stūpa's cool marble stairs,
we noticed some kind of celebration taking place. A dozen Japanese
monks were chanting in slow rhythm and beating on their drums, as
devotees sat quietly under a tent. A friendly man invited us to join, so
we sat down on the sidelines.*

*When the ceremony ended, the man invited us to help ourselves to
rice, dhal and vegetables from their vegetarian buffet. During the
delicious meal, we befriended a short Indian monk, and when we
asked him about the Ānanda Stūpa, he offered to guide us there,
though he'd never been there himself. So after filling our bellies,
we managed to find the only two cycle rickshaws in the village, and
headed out to the stūpa along narrow dirt roads lined with mud huts
with straw roofs. Villagers of all ages, who rarely see any foreigners
pass through (most people go via the highway), waved, smiled and
laughed, shouting out "Namaste" as we passed by. The scenery was
delightful and we reached the stūpa in good spirits.*

– MD & KG

Excursions

Kesariya (*Kessaputta*)

Dating back to the ninth century, this magnificent stūpa, possibly once the largest in the world, is rarely visited by pilgrims. Half excavated and half covered by
wild vegetation, this mountainous stūpa whose circumference is 425 m and height
30 m, is unlike others found around India. Its design resembles a pagoda that one
might come across in Myanmar, and is speculated to be a prototype of the massive
Borobudur Stūpa in Indonesia. All around the *mandala*-like, multi-terraced stūpa
are small niches enshrining crumbling life-sized Buddha statues with small spaces
in front of them for meditation and offerings.

Tales from Kessaputta

During his first visit to Kessaputta, the Buddha preached to the
Kāḷāma tribe his celebrated discourse concerning free inquiry and
careful scrutiny. The Kāḷāmas had heard numerous doctrinal tenets
from different sectarian teachers, and now wanted to know how they
could tell between one who speaks wisely and one who does not. The
Buddha replied,

Do not believe in what you have heard; do not believe in the tradi-tions because they have been handed down for generations; do not believe in anything because it is rumoured and spoken by many; do not believe merely because it is a written statement by some old sage; do not believe in speculations; do not believe something to be true that is based upon habits, and do not believe merely because it is the authority of your teachers and elders. Only after observation and analysis, when it agrees with reason and is conducive to the good and gain of one and all, then should you accept it and live up to it.

The Buddha then ended his discourse by instructing the Kālāmas with personal reflections on the four comforts of living a life free from ill will and animosity:

1. *If future rebirth exists, based on past and present blameless actions, then after death, I will get a good rebirth;*

2. *If rebirth and karma do not exist, then at least in this blameless life of mine, I live happily and am free from hostility, affliction and anxiety;*

3. *If evil comes to those who do evil, then evil will not come to me, be-cause I abstain from evil;*

4. *If no evil comes to those who do evil, it does not matter, because I am still living a happy and pure life.*[135]

After preaching his last sermon in Vesālī, the Buddha set out for Kusinārā. The devotional Licchavī princes followed the Buddha as he wandered through the countryside. When they reached Kessaput-ta, the Buddha told the princes of his approaching death. As a token of his gratitude to them, he handed them his alms-bowl[136] and then implored them to return to Vesālī. From that point onwards he wanted to walk to Kusinārā only with a retinue of *bhikkhus*. The princes la-mented with grief. They stubbornly refused to leave the side of their Master. Left without a choice, the Buddha used his psychic powers to create an illusory flood that separated them from him.[137]

Before leaving Kessaputta, the Licchavīs built a stūpa commemorat-ing the event and expressing their sorrow. The stūpa was later en-larged by King Asoka and subsequent rulers, especially during the Gupta period when it took on several additional layers and was em-bellished with hundreds of sculptures.

As it is very remote, the only way to get to Kesariya is by private vehicle. From Vaishali, you have two possible routes of travel, which will take approximately the same amount of time. The shorter, bumpier route via Chakia Road follows the Gandak River for about 55 km and then goes through the town of Sahib Ganj to Deuria Village, which is about 500 metres from the stūpa. The other option, longer but less bumpy is via the Muzaffarpur - Motihari Road where you'll need to turn off at Pipra and head towards Deuria. **Private taxis** from Patna are available for the long day trip. **Dhamma Licchavī, Vaishali Vipassana Centre**

This tranquil, 8.5-acre Vipassana centre in the middle of farmers' fields is about 12 km outside of the city of Muzzafarpur (36 km from Vaishali). Even though the centre's trustees and Dhamma workers are very hospitable to visiting meditators, courses here attract very few students, and are very small.

Ten-day courses are held the 15th to 26th of every month and one-day courses are held the first Sunday of every month. Foreign meditators are welcome to attend courses at this special Middle Land centre. Remembering the intense devotion of the Licchavīs, meditating in this out-of-the-way Vipassana centre may help support one's own devotion to the practice.

Contact:
Dhamma Licchavī,
Vaishali Vipassana Centre
Atardah (Lalitkunj)
Muzzafarpur–842002
Tel: [+91] (0)621-2243206/-2243407
Fax: [+91] (0)621-2247702

City Office:
c/o Rajkumar Goenka
Parijat, Marwari Bazar
Samastipur, Bihar
Tel: [+91] (0)621-243403/-243206
E-Mail: info@licchavi.dhamma.org
Website: www.licchavi.dhamma.org

Lauriya Nandangarh
Although this place has no direct association with the Buddha, the monuments here indicate that Dhamma activity was prevalent. Government excavations of the 20 vegetation-laden stūpas found fragments of charred human bones (most probably *arahant* relics), some earthen vessels and a golden human statue. The remains of another stūpa, one of the largest ever built in India, is found behind the local sugar mill about 1.5 km from the Asokan pillar. Other than a long strip of birch containing Dhamma words, nothing was found inside this stūpa. Archaeologists still do not know exactly what this massive structure commemorates.

During his reign, King Asoka constructed 40 pillars, but only a handful of these survive today. Many of them were knocked down during foreign invasions, some struck by lightning, some dragged (and damaged) to other sites, and a few, like the one at Sanchi, was smashed to provide stone for other building purposes. The Lauriya Nandagarh pillar is the only one that has remained undisturbed (besides the grafitti) at its original site, thus giving us a unique glimpse of how these majestic monuments once appeared.

Inscribed on the pillar are six of Asoka's edicts issued in 244 BCE. As they provide a unique insight into his tireless attempts to apply the principles of Dhamma to his government and society, they are worth quoting in full:

Beloved-of-the-Gods, King Piyadasi, speaks thus: This Dhamma edict was written twenty-six years after my coronation. Happiness in this world and the next is difficult to obtain without much love for the Dhamma, much self-examination, much respect, much fear (of evil), and much enthusiasm. But through my instruction this regard for Dhamma and love of Dhamma has grown day by day, and will continue to grow. And my officers of high, low and middle rank are practising and conforming to Dhamma, and are capable of inspiring others to do the same. Mahāmatras in border areas are doing the same. And these are my instructions: to protect with Dhamma, to make happiness through Dhamma and to guard with Dhamma.

Beloved-of-the-Gods, King Piyadasi, speaks thus: Dhamma is good, but what constitutes Dhamma? (It includes) little evil, much good, kindness, generosity, truthfulness and purity. I have given the gift of sight in various ways. To two-footed and four-footed beings, to birds and aquatic animals, I have given various things including the gift of life. And many other good deeds have been done by me. This Dhamma edict has been written so that people might follow it and it might endure for a long time. And the one who follows it properly will do something good.

Beloved-of-the-Gods, King Piyadasi, speaks thus: People see only their good deeds, saying, "I have done this good deed." But they do not see their evil deeds, saying, "I have done this evil deed" or "This is called evil." But this (tendency) is difficult to see. One should think like this: "It is these things that lead to evil, to violence, to cruelty, to anger, to pride and to jealousy. Let me not ruin myself with these things." And further, one should think: "This leads to happiness in this world and the next."

Beloved-of-the-Gods, King Piyadasi, speaks thus: My Rajjukas are working among the people, among many hundreds of thousands of people. The hearing of petitions and the administration of justice has been left to them so that they can do their duties confidently and fearlessly and so that they can work for the welfare, happiness and benefit of the people in the country. But they should remember what causes happiness and sorrow, and being themselves devoted to Dhamma, they should encourage the people in the country (to do the same), that they may attain happiness in this world and the next. These Rajjukas are eager to serve me. They also obey other officers who know my desires, who instruct the Rajjukas so that they can please me. Just as a person feels confident having entrusted his child to an expert nurse, thinking: "The nurse will keep my child well," even so, the Rajjukas have been appointed by me for the welfare and happiness of the people in the country.

The hearing of petitions and the administration of justice has been left to the Rajjukas so that they can do their duties unperturbed, fearlessly and confidently. It is my desire that there should be uniformity in law and uniformity in sentencing. I even go this far, to grant a three day stay for those in prison who have been tried and sentenced to death. During this time their relatives can make appeals to have the prisoners' lives spared. If there is none to appeal on their behalf, the prisoners can give gifts in orders to make merit for the next world, or observe fasts. Indeed it is my wish that in this way, even if a prisoner's time is limited, he can prepare for the next world, and that people's Dhamma practice, self-control and generosity may grow.

Beloved-of-the-Gods, King Piyadasi, speaks thus: Various animals are declared to be protected—parrots, mynas, aruna, ruddy geese, wild ducks, nandimukhas, gelatas, bats, queen ants, terrapins, boneless fish, vedareyaka, gangapuputaka, sankiya fish, tortoises, porcupines, squirrels, deer, bulls, okapinda, wild asses, wild pigeons, domestic pigeons and all four-footed creatures that are neither useful nor edible. Those nanny goats, ewes and sows which are with young or giving milk to their young are protected, and so are young ones less than six months old. Cocks are not to be caponised, husks hiding living beings are not to be burned and forests are not to be burned, either without reason or to kill creatures. One animal is not to be fed to another. On the three Caturmasis, the three days of Tisa and during the fourteenth and fifiteenth day of the uposatha, fish are protected and not to be sold. During these days, animals are not to be killed in the elephant reserves or the fish reserves either. On the eighth day of every fortnight, on the fourteenth and·fifiteenth, on Tisa, Punarvasu, the three Caturmasis and other auspicious days, bulls are not to be castrated, billy goats, rams, boars and other animals that are usually castrated are not to be castrated and horses and bullocks are not to be branded. In the twenty-six years since my coronation, prisoners have been given amnesty on twenty-five occasions.

Beloved-of-the-Gods, King Piyadasi, speaks thus: Twelve years after my coronation, I started to have Dhamma edicts written for the welfare and happiness of the people, and so that not transgressing them, they might grow in the Dhamma. Thinking: "How can the welfare and happiness of the people be secured?" I give attention to my relatives, to those dwelling near and those dwelling far, so I can lead them to happiness and then I act accordingly. I do the same for all groups. I have honoured all religions with various honours. But I consider it best to meet with people personally. This Dhamma edict was written twenty-six years after my coronation.[138]

Not far from Raxaul, the crowded town that borders Nepal, Lauriya Nandangarh is off the NH (National Highway) 28A coming from Bettiah (26 km), which is on the main road coming from Patna (190 km) via Motihari (the birthplace of George Orwell) and Muzzafarpur (110 km).

Today the monuments are surrounded by a festive assortment of vendors and stalls, so plenty of snacks are available. There is nowhere to stay, however, so you might want to consider visiting as a long day-trip from Muzzafarpur. If you are on your way to Nepal, then it's best to stay in Raxaul (**Hotel Ajanta**, on a side road near the bus stand is passable for one night). From Birganj, the town on the other side of the border, there are several buses a day to Pokhara (10 hours) and Kathmandu (12 hours). If possible, try to get on a bus that takes the scenic Tribhuvan Highway via Naubise for the Kathmandu trip.

Kaushambi (*Kosambī*)

The village of Kaushambi, situated 63 km south-west of Allahabad in Uttar Pradesh, was a major city in ancient times. After hearing the Buddha preach a sermon in Sāvatthī, three wealthy merchants from Kosambī invited him to teach the Dhamma in their city. They were so delighted when the Buddha agreed that each of the three built a monastery for the Saṅgha as a symbol of their devotion and gratitude. The three monastaries were known as *Ghositārāma*, *Kukkutārāma* and *Pavarika Ambavana*.[139] The Buddha visited Kosambī on many occasions, and spent four rainy seasons in and around the city: the 6th rainy season at Makula Mountain, the 8th at Suṃsumāragira, the 9th in Kosambī itself and the 10th nearby at Parileyya.

Tales from Kosambī

One hot afternoon, the Buddha was meditating in a shady grove of tall and beautiful simsapa trees, when a philosophically-minded *bhikkhu* approached him and asked for a complete description of the universe. The Buddha smiled, picked up a handful of leaves, and asked the young *bhikkhu*, "Which is more, my son, the number of leaves in my hand or the number of leaves on the trees in the forest?"

"The leaves that the Blessed One has picked up in his hand are few; those on the trees are many," replied the *bhikkhu*, wondering where this was leading.

In the same way, bhikkhu, the things that the Tathāgata knows by direct experience are many; the things that the Tathāgata has taught are few. Why has the Tathāgata not taught them? Because they do not bring benefit, they do not promote advancement in the holy life, and they do not lead to dispassion, to fading, to ceasing, to tranquility, to direct knowledge, to enlightenment, to nibbāna. That is why the Tathāgata has not taught them.

And what has the Tathāgata taught? This is suffering; this is the origin of suffering; this is the cessation of suffering; and this is the way leading to the cessation of suffering. And why has the Tathāgata taught them? Because they bring benefit, they promote advancement in the holy life, and they lead to dispassion, to fading, to ceasing, to tranquility, to direct knowledge, to enlightenment, to nibbāna.[140]

Understanding the futility of trying to figure out the inner-workings of the universe, the *bhikkhu* dropped his philosophical curiosity and assiduously began to practise the Four Noble Truths. Soon after, he experienced the peace of *nibbāna*.

At the request of his father, a seven-year-old boy was made a novice monk (*sāmaṇera*), and before having his head shaved, the boy was taught Vipassana. Then, while his preceptor, Bhikkhu Tissa, was shaving his head, the boy fixed his mind steadfastly on sensations as he'd been taught, with the understanding of impermanence, suffering, and no-self. Then and there, he attained arahantship.

After spending the rainy season in Kosambī, Tissa and his young pupil set out for Sāvatthī to meet the Buddha. On the way, they spent a night in a village monastery. Tissa soon fell asleep, but the boy sat up meditating all night. Early the next morning, unaware that the boy was sitting up in the dark, Tissa waved a palm-leaf fan to wake him, and accidentally hit the boy in the eye. Without a single complaint, the *sāmaṇera* covered his eye with one hand and ran off to fetch his teacher's morning bathing water. When he offered the water with only one hand, the elder scolded him, saying that he should always offer things with both hands. But when the boy removed his hand from his damaged eye to apologize, Tissa saw the wound and felt sorry and humiliated.

When they arrived in Sāvatthī, Tissa recounted to his friends what had happened along the way. He declared that the young *sāmaṇera* was the noblest person he had ever met. The Buddha, overhearing Tissa's words, remarked,

It is impossible for a Noble One to get angry.
Body, speech, and mind are calm and serene
In one who has found deliverance
By seeing things as they really are.[141]

Very impressed by the Buddha's noble character and striking appearance, a man offered his daughter, the young and beautiful Māgaṇḍiyā, to the Buddha in marriage. The Buddha refused the man's offer, remarking that he did not like to touch things that were full of filth, urine and excreta. Both of Māgaṇḍiyā's parents immediately understood the wisdom of the Buddha's message, and attained the third stage of liberation (*anāgāmi*). Māgaṇḍiyā, however, was highly insulted, and regarded the Buddha as her enemy from that point onward.

Soon after, King Udena saw the beautiful Māgaṇḍiyā and took her for his wife. Māgaṇḍiyā, now a queen, ordered her servants to follow the Buddha around and shout abusive words at him.

"Thief, fool, camel, donkey, one bound for Niraya Hell," the servants cried out when they saw the Buddha on his alms round.

"Lord, these people are ignorant. Let us leave Kosambī and go to another town where the citizens are more appreciative of the Saṅgha," Ānanda pleaded with the Buddha, tired of hearing such nonsense.

But the Buddha refused, saying, "This might occur in another town as well, Ānanda. It is not feasible to move away every time someone abuses us. It is better to solve a problem in the place where it arises. Like an elephant in a battlefield who withstands vicious attacks, we will patiently bear the abuses that come from the ignorant."

After a few more days of harassment, the group of abusers grew to be impressed by the Buddha's tolerance. Realizing their follies, they apologized, and a few of them even attained sotāpannahood.[142]

Unlike Queen Māgaṇḍiyā, Queen Sāmāvatī—King Udena's other wife—was ardently devoted to the Buddha. Sāmāvatī's faith infuriated Māgaṇḍiyā and she wanted to have Sāmāvatī thrown out of the palace. Māgaṇḍiyā often tried to convince the king that Sāmāvatī was disloyal and had plans to kill him.

One day, the scheming Māgaṇḍiyā put a poisonous snake into the king's lute and closed the hole with a bunch of flowers. That evening, when the king grabbed his instrument to play and removed the flowers from the hole, the snake jumped out, hissing and ready to attack.

"That demon," Udena cried out, now believing Māgaṇḍiyā's lies. In a vengeful rage, he grabbed his bow and arrows, rushed over to Sāmāvatī's chambers, and shot an arrow at her while she was meditating. Just as it was about to pierce her heart, the arrow abruptly dropped to the floor. Seeing this as an omen of Sāmāvatī's equanimity and good will, the king regained faith in her innocence. Begging forgiveness, he dropped to his knees and asked her to invite the Buddha and Saṅgha to the palace for alms-food.

This turn of events enraged Māgaṇḍiyā as never before. The next day, she ordered her servants to burn down Sāmāvatī's palace with all the maids inside. The building was soon ablaze, and realizing there was no escape, Sāmāvatī and her maids sat down and began to meditate. Thus, instead of panicking, they made best use of their final moments, and all of them attained the level of either *sakadāgāmi* or *anāgami*.

When the news of the fire spread, the king rushed over to the scene in tears, but it was too late: the queen and her maids had already perished. King Udena suspected that Māgaṇḍiyā was responsible for the fire, and deceptively remarked, "Whoever killed Sāmāvatī must have really loved me."

Delighted and ever eager for the King's favour, Māgaṇḍiyā immediately confessed. Udena stared blankly into her dark eyes for a long moment, and then turned his back on her, signalling his guards to seize her and throw her into the flaming building. Feeling suddenly alone in the world, King Udena walked away silently.

Later, when told about these incidents, the Buddha remarked,

Vigilance is the path to immortality;
Lack of vigilance is the path to death.
The vigilant do not die;
The unvigilant are already dead.[143]

Site-Sitting

Situated between the Ganges and Yamuna Rivers, the ruins at Kaushambi mark the site of the Vaṃsa kingdom's prosperous ancient capital. In addition to the ruins of a large fortress and a broken Asokan pillar, the remains of one of Kosambī's three monasteries can be found. Contemplating the Dhamma and meditating in this quiet, rural area is a pleasant getaway after spending time in noisy Allahabad.

Ghositārāma

Nearly half a kilometre south-east of a graffitied Asokan pillar are the ruins of the famous Ghositārāma monastery. Judging by the various layers exposed during excavations in 1951, archaeologists tell us that Ghositārāma was continually inhabited for about 1000 years, from the Buddha's time until the 5th century CE.[144]

Exploring the monastery ruins, you will find the Hariti Shrine, dedicated to the wild *yakkhini* Hariti. Hariti was infamous for devouring children. After the Buddha taught her the Dhamma, Hariti was transformed from a terrorizer of children into a protector of children.

Tales from Ghositārāma

Two elder *bhikkhus*, one an expert in the *Vinaya-Piṭika* and the other a teacher of the *Sutta-Piṭika*, had a misunderstanding over a minor disciplinary rule. The *Sutta* teacher left unused water in a vessel and said that since he was unaware that this was considered a minor offence, he was blameless. The *Vinaya* teacher disagreed. Unenlightened students of both teachers began bickering, backbiting, and insulting one another.

The Buddha tried three times to reconcile their minor differences by pointing out the futility of arguing and the value that each side has to the other. He reminded them of the dangers of becoming attached to one's own viewpoint, and the importance of listening to others. The two factions, however, had already become mired in their argument. These foolish *bhikkhus* refused to listen to the Master's judicious words and curtly asked him not to interfere. The Buddha showed his disapproval of these unruly and contentious *bhikkhus* by leaving Kosambī, departing with the following words,

"He abused me, he beat me,
He oppressed me, he robbed me!"
Hate is never alleviated in those
Who cherish such hostility.

"He abused me, he beat me,
He oppressed me, he robbed me!"
Hate is only alleviated in those
Who no longer cherish such hostility.

For in this world hatred is never
Alleviated by further acts of hatred;
It is alleviated by goodwill—
This is an ancient principle.

After leaving Kosambī, the Buddha travelled to Balakalonakara[145] where the *bhikkhus* Anuruddha, Nandiya and Kimbila were living together in perfect harmony. When the Buddha arrived, Anuruddha noticed him immediately. Instead of rushing to pay his master respects before the others, he called over his companions so that all three of them could share in the honour.

They told the Buddha that they lived as friendly and undisputing as milk and water. Viewing each other with kindly eyes, they practised *mettā* together. They amicably shared whatever alms they received, and equally divided the monastery's responsibilities. They meditated together in peace and quiet, and every five days they would discuss the Dhamma together.

Pleased with their living arrangements, which were an admirable contrast to the quarrelsome Kosambī *bhikkhus*, the Buddha went off to the jungle in Parileyya. There he found the silent company of an elephant and monkey, and remained for some time.

Meanwhile, back at Kosambī, the townsfolk had become disgusted with the ill-mannered behaviour of the local *bhikkhus* who'd driven the Buddha away. They withdrew all their support to these disruptive monks, forcing the *bhikkhus* to pass a difficult rainy season without proper nourishment. By the end of the rainy season, the hungry *bhikkhus* realized their mistakes and went to see the Buddha in Sāvatthī, where they settled their dispute and apologized for their behaviour. The Buddha told them,

As a deer in the wild, unfettered,
Forages wherever it wants;
The wise person, valuing freedom,
Walks alone like a rhinoceros in the woods.

If you can find trustworthy companions
Who are virtuous and dedicated;

Then walk with them content and mindful,
And overcome all dangerous obstacles.

But, if you cannot find trustworthy companions
Who are virtuous and dedicated;
Then as a king who leaves a vanquished kingdom,
Walk alone like a rhinoceros in the woods.

It is better to walk alone
Than to be in a fellowship of fools.
Walk alone, harm no one, and avoid conflict;
At ease like a lone rhinoceros in the woods.[146]

Prabhosa Hill (Mankula Hill)

The Buddha spent his 6th rainy season on this hill. Although the Pāli texts offer no indication of the hill's location, several scholars suppose that it must be Prabhosa Hill, the only high ground in the vicinity of Kosambī. The Buddha may have stayed in the cave there named 'Sita's Window', which has an inscription reading "the *arahants* of the Kaśyapa sect." Inscriptions and images found during recent excavations suggest that after the Buddha's time, Prabhosa Hill was mostly inhabited by Jain ascetics.[147]

The hilltop offers a sweeping view over the Yamuna River and the surrounding villages. The caves and rock shelters on the steeper, rockier north side of the hill are particularly interesting.

To get to Prabhosa, take the main road that leads from Kaushambi towards Allahabad. After about 1 km, take the road that branches to the left, and continue for about 10 km. Allow at least two extra hours for this side journey. This excursion is most easily made if you've hired a taxi for the day (see below). If you plan on making this trip, you may wish to inform your driver when negotiating the day's price, in order to avoid confusion later on.

Sleeping & Eating

There is only one guest house in the vicinity of Kaushambi, located a couple of kilometres before the main ruins. Most visitors stay in the holy Hindu city of Allahabad (38 km, see next section), and explore Kosambī as a full day trip.

Coming & Going

Buses bound for Chitrakut depart from the Leader Bus Stand in Allahabad, and stop in Kaushambi on the way. These buses are infrequent, so instead, consider hiring a **taxi** for the day from the train station in Allahabad. This will make your visit more comfortable and convenient.

Excursions

Allahabad

Allahabad, or Prayag, is a sacred Hindu city resting at the confluence (*saṅgam*) of India's three holiest rivers: the Ganga, the Yamuna, and the mythical Saraswati. The city is eulogized in the Vedic and Puranic literature as the symbolic centre of the universe and is also considered by Hindus to be one of the three bridges to heaven (the other two being Vārāṇasī and Gayā). People from all over India come to Allahabad throughout the year to bathe in the confluence or to take a breathtaking boat ride at sunrise or sunset. The saṅgam is 6 km east of the Allahabad Junction Train Station. Regular shared tempos go from the station to Daraganj Local Train Station, which is a short walk from the river.

Towering over the riverbank is the lofty Allahabad Fort, built in 1583 by the Mughal Emperor Akbar. Near the fort is an Asokan pillar that Akbar moved from Kosambī. Of the countless temples in the area, the underground Patalapuri Hindu Temple, accessible only through the fort, is legendary for its miraculous power to provide relief from the transmigratory cycle of *saṃsāra*.

Every 12 years, Allahabad hosts the Mahā Kumbha Mela,[148] the world's largest religious fair, when millions of devotees come for a ceremonial bath. At an exact moment determined by astrological calculations, the pilgrims charge into the water, hoping to eliminate their past evil *karmas* and gain release from *saṃsāra*. A smaller festival, the Magh Mela, is held in Allahabad every year from mid-January to mid-February, and the city is more crowded during this time. See www.kumbhamela.net for more information.

Historically-minded pilgrims will be interested in visiting the Allahabad Museum and the Archaeological Museum at the University of Allahabad's Department of Ancient History. Both these museums house antiquities found around Kosambī. They are located about 4 km north of the main train station, and are open daily from 10:00 a.m. to 4:00 p.m. (7:00 a.m. to 12:00 p.m. from May to June), closed on Wednesdays, Sundays, and holidays.

Most of the hotels are found in the Civil Lines area, just north of the Allahabad Junction Train Station (accessible via the station's back exit). Budget stays include a number of places along MG Marg, such as **Tourist Bungalow**, **Mayur Guest House**, or **Hotel Tepso**, and a few hotels on Dr. Katju Rd., such as **The Continental** and **Santosh Palace**. Expect 'city prices' at these budget places. Ultra-budget places can be found along Noorullah Rd., immediately behind the train station, but you'll typically get what you pay for. The retiring rooms at the train station are also an option. Mid-range choices include hotels **Samrat** (on MG Marg), **Allahabad Regency** (Tashkent Marg) and **Presidency** (on Sarojini Naidu Marg). For luxury, you can try **Hotel Yatrik** (on Sardar Patel Marg) or **Hotel Kanha Shyam** (off of MG Marg).

Along Sardar Patel and MG Margs, you can find several good restaurants to choose from, or you can be adventurous and eat at one of the many 'cheap and best' food stalls serving everything from South Indian snacks to Chinese-style chow meins.

Allahabad has two **bus** stations. The Leader Bus Stand, near the train station, serves buses to Delhi and Agra, as well as infrequent buses that stop in Kaushambi en route to Chitrakut (see previous section). From the Civil Lines Bus Stand behind the Tourist Bungalow on MG Marg, regular and deluxe buses leave for Vārāṇasī (3 hours), Lucknow (5 hours), Gorakhpur (10 hours) and Sonauli (13 hours).

Allahabad is also well connected by **train** to Vārāṇasī, Lucknow, Delhi and Kolkata.

Shravasti (*Sāvatthī*)

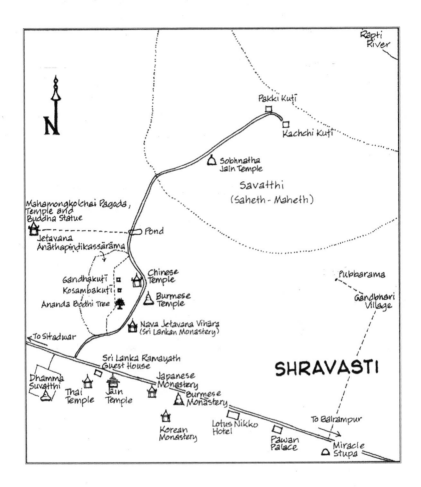

Sāvatthī, the capital of the Kosala Kingdom, was once the largest, wealthiest and most vibrant city in the Middle Land. The majority of Sāvatthī's citizens had immense devotion towards the Buddha, Dhamma and Saṅgha. During the 20th year after his Awakening, the Buddha decided that the city would make an excellent headquarters from which to teach the Dhamma. Meditators would know where to find the Buddha during the rainy season, and could make plans to come and receive instructions directly from him. From that time onwards, the Buddha spent every rains retreat (20th to 44th) in Sāvatthī except his last one, when he stayed in Vesālī.

Because the Buddha and many of his closest disciples spent much of their time here, Sāvatthī became the scene of many celebrated sermons, whether at Jetavana Vihāra, Pubbārāma Vihāra, Rajakārāma Vihāra or somewhere around the city.

Tales from Sāvatthī

Young Ahiṃsaka (one who practises non-violence) was the son of the head-priest in King Pasenadi's court. His father sent him to study at Taxilā, a renowned university, where he was favoured by his teacher. A group of jealous students wanted to ruin Ahiṃsaka's good name, and began to spread rumours that he was having an affair with the teacher's wife. At first, the teacher did not believe that his bright and courteous student could be capable of such a betrayal. But after being told the same lie a number of times, he began to believe the story, and vowed to take revenge on the boy.

In time the teacher became so angry that he wanted to kill his student. He knew that doing so would reflect badly on him; so he devised a plan even worse than murder. The teacher commanded Ahiṃsaka to kill 1000 people as an honorarium for his teachings. He instructed the young man to keep count by cutting off a finger from each victim, and then add it to a garland. Ahiṃsaka reluctantly agreed.

Having taken the awful vow, Ahiṃsaka went on a killing spree and within no time, the entire kingdom of Kosala feared him. People were afraid to walk alone, and would never go out at night. Nobody knew who this mysterious serial killer was. Everyone referred to him as Aṅgulimāla ('Garland of Fingers'). Whole platoons sent to arrest him perished by his sword. After several months of this madness Aṅgulimāla finally neared the goal, and needed only one more finger to complete his necklace. He was so anxious to finish this terrible task that he was ready to kill his own mother.

When the Buddha returned to Sāvatthī, just before the start of the rainy season, the first news he received was about this madman who had killed 999 people. Knowing that the murderer must be burdened by terrible suffering, the Compassionate One went forward to meet him. Walking slowly down an eerily quiet road, the Buddha crossed paths with shepherds and farmers who fearfully urged him to turn back. The Buddha simply expressed thanks for their concern and continued silently on his way.

Night was falling and the killer spotted what he thought would be his final prey: a solitary figure walking slowly through the forest. Following him from some distance, Aṅgulimāla stalked the Buddha. In the quickly fading light, the Buddha's pace gradually began to quicken, and the killer was unable to catch up with him. Aṅgulimāla eventually broke into a run, and his sweat ran freely, dripping into his sunken eyes as he became more and more enraged by the ease with which the tranquil *bhikkhu* evaded him. With each step he took, the Buddha seemed to be farther and farther away.

Seized by uncontrollable violence, Aṅgulimāla drew his sword and ran even faster. Then in frustrated desperation he shouted out, "Stop, monk! Stop!" The world came to a halt. The Buddha silently stopped, slowly turned, and said to him, "Aṅgulimāla, I have stopped; it is you who have not stopped."

Not understanding the significance of his words, the perplexed killer asked, "Why do you say that you have stopped, and I have not?"

I have stopped because I have given up violence towards all living beings and have established myself in universal love. But you have not given up violence and you have not yet established yourself in universal love. That is why you are the one who has not stopped.

Aṅgulimāla was startled. He had never encountered someone so serene, especially in his own terrifying presence. He flung his weapons into a nearby chasm and bowed in reverence at the Buddha's feet. With compassion and patience, the Buddha helped Aṅgulimāla understand what was really going on inside of himself. Metamorphosized by this insight, Aṅgulimāla became a *bhikkhu* and practised diligently, aware now of the consequences of his former acts.

Villagers frequently refused to help him during his alms rounds, and often pelted him with stones and beat him with sticks. Despite his apparent change, they still distrusted him and remained wounded by the suffering he'd once inflicted. Aṅgulimāla, however, chose not to react with anger and violence; he understood their actions, and saw that it was necessary to experience the fruits of his past evil deeds in this way. Through such diligent practice of compassion and empathy, Aṅgulimāla eventually became an *arahant*.[149]

Poṭṭhila was very conceited because he knew all the Buddha's teachings by heart. However, he rarely practised meditation and didn't attain any of the stages that he proudly spoke about in his lectures. The Buddha discerned Poṭṭhila's weakness and began addressing him as "Useless Poṭṭhila." Poṭṭhila was an intelligent man and understood that the Buddha did not approve of his lack of serious effort in meditation, and he resolved to better apply himself.

Poṭṭhila then went to a small forest monastery where thirty *bhikkhus* lived. He approached the senior-most *bhikkhu* and humbly requested him to be his mentor in meditation. The elder, wishing to humble him, asked him to go to the next senior *bhikkhu*, who in turn sent him on to the next. In this way, he was sent from one to the other until he came to a seven-year-old *sāmaṇera* who was an *arahant*. The young novice agreed, and instructed him in meditation. One afternoon, while Poṭṭhila was meditating in his room, the Buddha came to encourage him,

From meditation, wisdom arises;
Without meditation, wisdom does not arise.
Understanding how this branching path can lead to either gain
or loss,
The intelligent bhikkhu acts so that wisdom may arise.

Realizing the Buddha's words for himself, Poṭṭhila became an *arahant*.[150]

Tambadāṭhika served as the king's executioner for 55 years before retiring. One sunny morning, the old man went to bathe in the river. When he got there he saw Sāriputta meditating by the river. Tambadāṭhika thought to himself, "Throughout my life, I have been so busy executing thieves and murderers. I've never had the opportunity to meet with a *bhikkhu*." When Tambadāṭhika saw that Sāriputta had finished his session, he walked over to him and respectfully invited the *bhikkhu* to his home for a meal. Sāriputta accepted.

After finishing his food, Sāriputta spoke to Tambadāṭhika about the Dhamma, but the old man had trouble paying attention. His agitated mind kept wandering to thoughts of all the people he had killed during his career. Sāriputta sensed the old man's difficulty, and asked,

"Tambadāṭhika, did you kill all those criminals out of personal desire, or out of duty?"

"Honest Sir, it was my job to execute those people. I never had any desire to take their lives away."

"Then, my friend, don't worry about the past. You're not responsible for their deaths."

Tambadāṭhika was relieved. His mind calmed down, and he was able to listen attentively to Sāriputta's words. When the teaching was over, the old man was in great spirits. While walking home and appreciating life in a new way, a mad cow gored Tambadāṭhika in the stomach and he died on the spot.

That evening at the Jetavana Vihāra, a congregation of *bhikkhus* asked the Buddha what had happened to Tambadāṭhika. The Buddha explained, "*Bhikkhus*, even though Tambadāṭhika had committed murder throughout his life, he was reborn in the celestial Tusita realm. This good rebirth was a result of comprehending the Dhamma during Sāriputta's exposition."

"But Lord, how could such a person receive great reward after listening to the Dhamma just once?" a puzzled *bhikkhu* asked.

"The length of practice is of no consequence," the Buddha said, "for even one single moment of understanding can produce much benefit." He continued in verse,

Hearing a single word filled with meaning
Helping a person find peace;
Is better than a thousand words,
Empty of meaning.[151]

Uppalavaṇṇā was a gorgeous woman who refused marriage offers from Sāvatthī's richest men. Instead, she became a *bhikkhunī*, moved to the forest, and rapidly attained arahantship.

One day her cousin Nanda (not to be confused with the Buddha's half-brother) came to see her. Nanda had fallen in love with Uppalavaṇṇā before she became a *bhikkhunī*. Seeing her again, he went mad with lust and wanted to take her by force. Seeing the insanity in his eyes, Uppalavaṇṇā shouted at him, "You fool! Get away from me! Don't touch me!"

As an awakened *arahant*, she tried persuading him to leave her alone, not out of fear of rape or murder, but to prevent her cousin from committing a serious crime. Nanda, however, could not be stopped. After satisfying himself, he ran out of her hut, half ashamed. In his haste he tripped over a stone, soared through the air and landed in a pit of quicksand that swallowed him up.

When Uppalavaṇṇā reported the matter to the Buddha, he recited a verse,

So long as an evil deed does not mature,
The fool thinks his deed to be sweet as honey.
But, when his evil deed matures,
He falls into untold misery.

The Buddha sent a message to King Pasenadi, explaining the dangers that *bhikkhunīs* face while living alone in forests. The devoted king immediately constructed several new nunneries so that the *bhikkhunīs* could practise in peace.[152]

Adinnapubbaka was a stingy man who didn't care about anyone other than himself. When his son Maṭṭhakuṇḍali fell ill, he neglected to consult a doctor. Realizing that his son was about to die, Adinnapubbaka ordered his servants to move the boy from his bedroom to the veranda, so that visitors would not see all of the expensive things in his house.

That morning the Buddha passed by Adinnapubbaka's house while on his alms round and stopped to attend the boy with *mettā*. As a result, Maṭṭhakuṇḍali's heart was full of joy and devotion—the last emotions he experienced before dying.

Seeing his son die with a smile on his face in front of the Buddha like that, Adinnapubbaka felt deeply ashamed of his greed and negligence. He vowed to change his ways, and started by extending an invitation to the Buddha and some *bhikkhus* for the next day's meal. When they'd finished eating, the Buddha said to the grieving father:

"Adinnapubbaka, do not worry about your son's whereabouts. He has a fortunate *kamma* and was reborn in the Tāvatiṃsa heaven."

One of the *bhikkhus* was surprised by the Buddha's comment and inquired, "Lord, how could a person be reborn in a celestial world simply by mentally professing devotion to the Buddha, without having given charity or observing the precepts?" The Buddha replied in verse:

All phenomena of existence have mind as their precursor,
Mind as their supreme leader, and mind as their creator.
Speaking or behaving with a pure mind,
Happiness follows like a shadow.

Adinnapubbaka, and Maṭṭhakuṇḍali, who overheard the conversation from the Tāvatiṃsa heaven, both became *sotāpannas*. From then onwards, Adinnapubbaka donated most of his wealth to the Saṅgha and used his spare time for meditation and community service.[153]

One day while on a visit to a small monastery outside of Sāvatthī, Ānanda and the Buddha heard some painful groaning from one of the *bhikkhu's* huts. They entered the hut and found an emaciated *bhikkhu* with dysentery, lying on his mat in a puddle of excrement. Ānanda fetched some water and they bathed the sick *bhikkhu* and washed his robes. After nursing him with some medicine and *mettā*, the Buddha called for the other *bhikkhus*.

"*Bhikkhus*, when we leave our homes to practise the path of bhikkhu-hood we also leave the care of our families. If we don't take care of each other during times of illness, who will? If the Tathāgata fell ill would you take care of him?"

"Certainly, Lord," the *bhikkhus* responded.

"Then in the same way you would take care of the Tathāgata, you must take care of each other. Nursing any sick *bhikkhu* is the same as nursing the Tathāgata."

With joined palms, the *bhikkhus* exclaimed: "Sādhu, sādhu, sādhu!"

A poor couple had only one garment between them, so both could not leave the house at the same time. One evening, the husband went out and the wife stayed at home, naked. The man saw the Buddha preaching to a crowd and listened in on the teaching. Practising as the Buddha was instructing, the man's entire body became suffused with joy, and he felt an uncontrollable urge to offer his only garment to the Buddha. Thinking it over for a few minutes, he took his garment off, walked right up to the Buddha, bowed before him, and placed it at the Teacher's feet.

King Pasenadi was in the audience and witnessed the bizarre display of devotion. The poor man's faith and generosity pleased the king, and he offered the poor man a new expensive garment. Without even thinking for a moment, the naked man turned around and offered it to the Buddha. The surprised king then gave the man two pieces of cloth, and the man handed them right over to the Buddha. The king then gave three pieces, then four, then five, and each time, the man gave them to the Buddha. This game kept going on until King Pasenadi offered him thirty-two pieces of cloth. At this point, the poor man kept one piece for himself, another for his wife, and offered the remaining thirty pieces to the Buddha.

The next morning, King Pasenadi sent two large and expensive pieces of velvet cloth to the poor couple. The couple kept one as a canopy next to their house where they would offer alms to the Saṅgha, and donated the other to the Buddha to be used as a canopy next to his hut at the Jetavana Monastery. The next time the king went to see the Buddha he saw the velvet canopy and was delighted. King Pasenadi then sent the poor couple four elephants, four horses, four female servants, four male servants, four errand boys, the deeds of four villages, and four thousand pieces of money.

That evening, some disciples asked the Buddha, "Lord, how is it that a good deed done bears fruit immediately, as in the case of that poor man?" The Buddha smiled and replied,

Meditators, if he had offered his garment immediately after the first thought of giving arose, the king's reward would have been far greater. When you feel the urge to give charity, do it immediately. If you procrastinate, then you might not get the chance of doing the

*good deed at all, and you will not reap the good fruits that would
have come your way.*[154]

One morning, Koka the hunter passed a *bhikkhu* meditating in the
forest. That day Koka did not catch anything and superstitiously
blamed it on having seen the *bhikkhu*. On his way back, Koka saw
the *bhikkhu* again and set his pack of dogs on him. When the *bhikkhu*
swiftly climbed up a tree to escape the vicious dogs, his outer robe
slipped off and fell on Koka. The dogs, mistaking their master for the
bhikkhu, attacked and killed him. The *bhikkhu* felt terrible and went
to see the Buddha, who comforted him saying that he was not to
blame for this unfortunate event. The Buddha recited a verse,

Offending an innocent, pure and faultless person,
The evil rebounds at the fool;
Like fine dust thrown against the wind.[155]

Site-Sitting

Jeta's Grove Anāthapiṇḍika's Park (*Jetavana Anāthapiṇḍikārāma*)
This celebrated monastery was where the Buddha gave most of his discourses,
both to *bhikkhus* and lay people alike. The Jetavana was so popular that even after
the decline of Sāvatthī's glory, the monastery continued to be an important place
of Dhamma practice for many centuries.

Today's site, referred to as Saheth, is a collection of ruins surrounded by well-
maintained gardens. What we see today only represents a fraction of the Jetavana's
former glory. Most of the structural remains are still underground, awaiting further
excavation. Throughout the Jetavana complex, you will see ruins of monastaries,
temples and stūpas built over several centuries, commemorating the Buddha and
some of his well-known disciples.

Ānanda Bodhi Tree
Whenever the Buddha was away, visiting devotees often paid homage by leaving
flowers or incense in front of his residence.
Anāthapiṇḍika asked the Buddha whether this
was a correct practice or not. The Buddha replied that it would be better for people to pay
respects to a bodhi tree rather than his hut,
simply because a bodhi tree is a better symbol
of enlightenment than a building. The faithful
Anāthapiṇḍika immediately sent for a sapling
from the original Bodhi Tree in Bodhgayā and
brought it to the Jetavana in Sāvatthī. He gave
the sapling to the Buddha's attendant to plant,
hence the name "Ānanda Bodhi Tree."

The Jetavana Vihāra was abandoned for nearly a thousand years, and because there is no precise record of where Ānanda planted it, the tree that can be seen today is probably not the original.[156] Nonetheless, today's magnificent Ānanda Bodhi Tree is a worthwhile place to meditate, and serves as a powerful symbol of the Buddha's Awakening in the place where he spent the most time meditating and teaching the Dhamma.

Gandha Kuṭi

The most important site in the Jetavana complex is the ruin of temple #2, which marks the spot of 'The Fragrant Hut' (*Gandha Kuṭi*) where the Buddha used to meditate, exercise, meet students, and rest. Most of the dwelling places built for the Buddha were usually referred to as the *Gandha Kuṭi*, either because they retained the pleasant smell that emanated from his body, or because devotees used to come and offer perfumed flowers and incense at the door of his hut. Pilgrims still decorate these ruins with fragrant flowers, especially in the month of October when the rainy season comes to an end and *bhikkhus* are offered new sets of robes.

Kosamba Kuṭi

Just after the bodhi tree and before the *Gandha Kuṭi* are the ruins of the *Kosamba Kuṭi* (temple #3), the Buddha's second hut. In front of the *Kosamba Kuṭi* is a long brick platform that marks the area where the Buddha used to mindfully walk up and down in the evenings.

Tales from the Jetavana Anāthapiṇḍikārāma

After returning from his memorable trip to Rājagaha where he met the Buddha for the first time, Anāthapiṇḍika immediately began searching for a suitable place to accommodate the Saṅgha. The best place the wealthy merchant found was a pleasure grove owned by Prince Jeta.

"How much do you want for your pleasure grove, Sir," Anāthapiṇḍika asked.

"Sorry, it's not for sale," the prince replied with curt disinterest.

"Please, Sir, I must have it. I will meet any price you ask."

"Any price you say? Then I want as many gold pieces as it will take to cover the entire property. Not one piece less," the prince remarked, confident that this unrealistically high price would dissuade the insistent merchant.

To his astonishment, however, Anāthapiṇḍika agreed without hesitation, exclaiming, "The deal is done!" Before the prince could even argue, Anāthapiṇḍika immediately sent for his workers to come and spread gold coins across the land.

Prince Jeta was totally bewildered by this man's resolve, but Anāthapiṇḍika's determination and happiness began to win him over. Soon the prince also wanted to share in this great offering. Noticing that a small area was yet to be covered, Prince Jeta asked the merchant if he could donate that portion. Anāthapiṇḍika consented, not out of greed, but out of compassion. He felt that this act would later help the prince gain confidence in the Buddha and the Dhamma.

Anāthapiṇḍika spent a vast amount of his personal wealth in the construction of this monastery. He built large residential quarters and erected magnificent Dhamma halls, laid out beautiful terraces, put up store houses, levelled walkways, constructed bathhouses, excavated ponds and raised pavilions. In honour of the two men responsible for the birth of this amazing monastic complex, the site was named *Jetavana Anāthapiṇḍikārāma* (Jeta's Grove, Anāthapiṇḍika's Park).[157]

Anāthapiṇḍika asked the Buddha whether it was possible to practise the Dhamma without forsaking the worldly life. The Buddha replied that it was indeed possible, as long as one followed one's vocation in a righteous manner:

Not by shaving one's head does an undisciplined person
Who utters lies, become a renunciate.
How can one who is full of desire and greed be a renunciate?
One who subdues all evil—both small and great—
Is called a renunciate, because all evil has been overcome.[158]

In the first years of the Buddha's stay around Sāvatthī, large numbers of people took to the path of Dhamma. This frustrated many of the sectarian religious leaders, as it meant a decrease in devotees and donations. Eventually these leaders got together and devised a plan to damage the Buddha's reputation. They hired Sundarī, a beautiful and crafty woman, to spread rumours saying that she was sleeping with the Buddha.

After a few nights of Sundarī spreading her lies around town, the sectarians hired some drunken hooligans to rape and murder Sundarī and dump her body into a rubbish heap near the Jetavana Monastery. The next morning, the sectarians spread news about Sundarī's disappearance and reported the matter to the police, saying they suspected the Buddha had kidnapped her. The police searched the vicinity of the Jetavana and found Sundarī's body, but since there was no proof that it was the Buddha who committed the crime, they were unable to arrest him. Nonetheless, the sectarians paraded her corpse in the streets, shouting out accusations that the Buddha was a killer and a phony. The Buddha, unperturbed by these lies, told his students at the Jetavana:

Unguarded men provoke with words,
Like darts that fly against an elephant in battle.

But when harsh words are spoken to a bhikkhu,
They are endured with an unruffled mind.

After seven days of these false allegations, the local authorities caught the true criminals, who boasted of the deed at a tavern and were overheard by the police. The sectarians were forced to confess their guilt, and the Buddha's popularity only increased.[159]

Late one night a beautiful and splendorous *deva* visited the Buddha. After bowing before him with deep respect, she asked:

"Sir, many *devas* and men yearn for happiness and contemplate the means for achieving wellbeing. Could you please elucidate upon the greatest blessings?"

Pleased with the *deva's* earnest desire for proper practice, the Buddha smiled and uttered the famous *Maṅgala Suttaṃ*:

Avoiding association with fools,
Seeking association with the wise,
Honoring those who are worthy of honor—
This is the greatest blessing

Residing in a suitable place,
Enjoying one's earned merits,
Generating proper aspirations for oneself—
This is the greatest blessing.

Learning and developing skills,
Disciplining oneself,
Practising Right Speech—
This is the greatest blessing.

Supporting one's parents,
Caring for one's spouse and children,
Engaged in a transparent occupation—
This is the greatest blessing.

Practicing generosity and living virtuously,
Caring for one's dependents,
Being blameless in one's action—
This is the greatest blessing.

Abstaining from and shunning evil,
Refraining from intoxicants,
Vigilantly practising the Dhamma —
This is the greatest blessing.

Living with respect, humility,
Contentment and gratitude,

Listening to the Dhamma at the proper time —
This is the greatest blessing.

Accepting guidance and practising patience,
Meeting with saintly people,
Discussing the Dhamma at the proper time —
This is the greatest blessing.

Practising ardently and with self-restraint,
Perceiving the Noble Truths,
Experiencing nibbāna —
This is the greatest blessing.

Confronting the vicissitudes of life,
One's mind remains unruffled,
Sorrowless, stainless, secure —
This is the greatest blessing.

Having acted in this way,
One will be invincible and safe,
Wherever ones goes—
These are the greatest blessings.[160]

A man was distressed over the death of his son. Everyday he would go to the cemetery, crying out his son's name. One day he went to the Jetavana Vihāra, hoping to be consoled by the Buddha, who told him, "Death occurs everywhere. All beings that are born must die, including your son. Affection brings about sorrow, lamentation, pain, grief and despair." Failing to understand the Buddha's wisdom, the bereaved man became furious and stormed out of the monastery. The next day, he sent a message to the king and queen saying that the Buddha was a pessimist and that he preached that people shouldn't love each other.

King Pasenadi had not yet met the Buddha, and he was skeptical of this teacher who was said to be an enlightened master. The king asked his wife, who was already a devout Dhamma practitioner, if this accusation was correct,

"Is it true, Mallika, that this so-called Buddha of yours really is a pessimist?"

"My dear king, do you not love and cherish your daughter Vagiri?" the queen counter-questioned.

"Certainly," replied the king.

"And would you not be miserable if Vagiri died?"

The king was taken aback. He immediately understood how suffering existed within love, and began to feel slightly uneasy. His wife pointed out a profound truth, and he did not know how to get his head around it. Queen Mallika smiled gently. She knew that her husband's intellectual curiousity and puzzlement over this existential quandary would soon bring him to the Buddha, and that he would then taste the soothing relief of Dhamma.[161]

After eating a huge breakfast, King Pasenadi went to the Jetavana Monastery to listen to the Buddha give a discourse. Having overeaten, the king felt very drowsy and began to nod off. The Buddha scolded him:

The torpid, gluttonous, and slumberous man,
Rolls to and fro like a huge hog fattened by fodder;
That indolent and stupid fool
Continues wandering in ignorance again and again and again.

The king felt ashamed for his indulgent behaviour and apologized for visiting the Buddha in such a state. The Buddha advised him to take a little less food everyday until he reached the point where he was eating one sixteenth of the amount he was used to. The king did as he was told, and soon enough, he lost all his excess weight and felt much better about himself. Later, when King Pasenadi told the Buddha about how well his new diet was working, the Buddha replied:

Health is the greatest of gifts,
Contentment is the greatest of riches,
A trusted friend is the greatest relation,
And nibbāna is the greatest bliss.[162]

Refusing to believe that her baby had died, the grieving Kisāgotamī brought the tiny corpse to the Jetavana Vihāra hoping that the Buddha had a remedy for her child.

"Kisāgotamī, I can help you. Go to the city and bring back a handful of mustard seeds from a house where nobody has ever died," the Buddha instructed her.

She was delighted. She knew that if anyone could help her, it would be the Buddha. She went from house to house with the dead child.

"Do you have any mustard seeds, friend? The Buddha will use them in a ritual to revive my baby," she would say.

"Certainly, here you go," the people would say, handing her a bag of seeds.

"But, has anyone ever died in this household? The seeds won't work if there has been a death here."

Nobody was able to give her the seeds she needed. Eventually Kisāgotamī accepted the reality of death and cremated her child. She returned to the Buddha, who gave her a Dhamma talk on *anicca*, *dukkha* and *anattā*. Kisāgotamī attained sotāpannahood and joined the order of nuns.

Then one evening while she was lighting a lamp, Kisāgotamī noticed how the flames flare up and die out, and clearly perceived the arising and passing of beings. At that moment, she realized *nibbāna*.[163]

Nanda, the Buddha's younger half-brother, was dissatisfied with living the monastic life. Lustful thoughts constantly invaded his mind; every night he dreamt about his ex-fiancée and all the royal luxuries that he had left behind. The Buddha sensed Nanda's distracted mind and brought him to a celestial realm inhabited by 500 gorgeous, pink-footed nymphs.

"Nanda, succeed in your meditation practice and all these gorgeous celestial angels will fall madly in love with you and satisfy all your desires," the Buddha promised his younger sibling. Nanda couldn't believe his eyes, nor could he believe the Buddha's outrageous guarantee.

"Hmm, these nymphs make my ex-fiancée look like a mutilated she-monkey and the Buddha never lies." He resolved that from that point onwards he would practise with all his might.

When the other *bhikkhus* found out what happened, they were appalled by Nanda's ulterior motives for practising. Nanda was so embarassed he couldn't face anyone in the monastery. He sat alone in his room and practised Vipassana. Within a day, he attained arahantship and all his desires for acquiring the nymphs disappeared.

That evening, the Buddha commented to the Saṅgha,

Just as the monsoon rain pierces through the roof of an ill-thatched house,
So does lust enter an undisciplined mind.
Just as the monsoon rain cannot penetrate a well-thatched house,
So too, lust cannot enter a well-disciplined mind.[164]

One morning while on alms round with the Buddha and a group of *bhikkhus*, the 18-year-old Rāhula gazed at his father's body and thought, "my body is perfect just like my father's." Thinking such thoughts, the young man lost his mindfulness. The Buddha sensed that his son was off in dreamland, and gently reminded him to come back to the present moment. Rāhula felt embarrassed about his thoughts of self-admiration. He left the line of *bhikkhus* and sat down beneath a nearby tree to meditate.

That evening, Rāhula went to see the Buddha for some advice on how to give up his attachment to the body. The Buddha told him to reflect upon the body merely as material elements,

Rāhula, the parts of our bodies which are solid, such as hairs, bones, nails, teeth, skin, flesh, organs, feces, etc. are simply earth element. Understand these things as they are: "This is not mine, this is not what I am, this is not my self." Seeing the body with this wisdom, you will become disenchanted with the earth element.

Rāhula, the parts of our bodies which are fluid, such as bile, phlegm, pus, blood, sweat, tears, snot, urine, etc. are simply water element. Understand these things as they are: "This is not mine, this is not what I am, this is not my self." Seeing the body with this wisdom, you will become disenchanted with the water element.

Rāhula, the processes of our bodies which consume, digest, age, etc. are simply fire element. Understand these things as they are: "This is not mine, this is not what I am, this is not my self." Seeing the body with this wisdom, you will become disenchanted with the fire element.

Rāhula, the winds of our bodies which move in the abdomen, the bowels, the nostrils, etc. are simply air element. Understand these things as they are: "This is not mine, this is not what I am, this is not my self." Seeing the body with this wisdom, you will become disenchanted with the air element.

Rāhula, the spaces in our bodies such as the holes in our ears, nostrils, mouth, anus, etc. are simply space element. Understand these things as they are: "This is not mine, this is not what I am, this is not my self." Seeing the body with this wisdom, you will become disenchanted with the space element.

Rāhula took his father's words to heart. He knew the futility of developing attachment to things that were impermanent, unsatisfactory, and not self. The Buddha continued his instructions, telling the young *bhikkhu* to also liken his whole self to the elements.

Rāhula, try to be like the earth. By doing so, when agreeable or disagreeable contacts arise, they will not invade your mind and remain. Just as when people drop clean or dirty things, excrement or urine, spittle, pus or blood on to the earth, the earth is not ashamed, humiliated or disgusted.

Rāhula, try to be like water. By doing so, when agreeable or disagreeable contacts arise, they will not invade your mind and remain. Just as when people wash clean or dirty things, excrement or urine, spittle, pus or blood with water, the water is not ashamed, humiliated or disgusted.

Rāhula, try to be like fire. By doing so, when agreeable or disagreeable contacts arise, they will not invade your mind and remain. Just as fire burns away clean or dirty things, excrement or urine, spittle, pus or blood, the fire is not ashamed, humiliated or disgusted.

Rāhula, try to be like air. By doing so, when agreeable or disagreeable contacts arise, they will not invade your mind and remain. Just as when the air blows away clean and dirty things, excrement or urine, spittle, pus or blood, the air is not ashamed, humiliated or disgusted.

Rāhula, try to be like space. By doing so, when agreeable or disagreeable contacts arise, they will not invade your mind and remain. Just as space is not established anywhere, nothing will be able to invade your mind and remain.

Rāhula, practise loving-kindness to get rid of ill-will. Practise compassion to get rid of cruelty. Practise appreciative joy to get rid of apathy. Practise equanimity to get rid of resentment. Contemplate the repulsiveness of the body to get rid of lust. Be aware of impermanence to get rid of the conceit "I am." Observe the breath, for when that is maintained and developed, it brings great fruit and many blessings.

Rāhula was delighted with the teaching that his father had given him and was determined to practise the Dhamma with proper awareness, understanding, and equanimity.[165]

A couple of years later, shortly after Rāhula's twentieth birthday, he went for a walk with his father in the Blind Man's Grove, just outside the Jetavana Monastery. They sat down together under a tree and began meditating. The Buddha instructed him on the six sense doors, the six sense objects and the six contacts between the two, and how these eighteen elements are all impermanent, unsatisfactory, and not self.

Rāhula had heard these instructions innumerable times, but he had never tasted the subtle flavour of the Dhamma. This time, however, completely aware of his mind and body, the deeper meaning had become clear to him and the fruits of arahantship ripened. The story tells us that a thousand *devas*, who were meditating with them, also attained liberation.[166]

Sectarian philosophers were always quarrelling and wounding each other with verbal darts over whose speculative views were correct. "The universe is like this," one would profess. "No, the universe is not like that, it is like this!" another would proudly argue.

These debates usually began cordially, but almost always concluded in an angry shouting match. The Buddha instructed his students to avoid these useless debates, and told the story of a group of birth-blind men who each felt an elephant for the first time. Each one of them ran their fingers along the different parts of the elephant and guessed what they were feeling.

"Ah, these must be winnowing baskets," the first man said, taking hold of the ears.

"I think it is a post," a second man said, touching a foot.

"Close enough, but you're wrong. It's a plough pole," a third argued, holding the trunk.

"What? You must not be familiar around the kitchen. This is a mortar and pestle," another man claimed, grabbing the elephant's rump and tail.

"No, no, no. None of you know what you're talking about. It's a broom," an overly-confident man said, handling the tail's tuft.

"My friends, you're all crazy," the last man boasted, feeling the middle section, "All you're doing is touching the individual parts, not feeling the whole. What we really have here is a granary!"

These blind men, the Buddha explained, were just like the sectarian philosophers—arguing until their throats were dry. Each one of them only had a partial understanding of reality, a distorted picture of reality. By practising Vipassana with a humble and open mind, the meditator learns to see reality from all angles and refrains from making narrow minded judgements.[167]

Bhikkhu Mālukyāputta was dissatisfied with the Buddha's refusal to give definitive replies to the ten speculative metaphysical questions: (i) Is the world eternal? (ii) Is the world not eternal? (iii) Is the world finite? (iv) Is the world infinite? (v) Are the soul and body the same? (vi) Are the soul and body separate? (vii) After death, does the Tathāgata exist? (viii) Does the Tathāgata not exist? (ix) Does the Tathāgata both exist and not exist? (x) Does the Tathāgata neither exist nor not exist?

Pondering over these questions during his meditation, the monk became increasingly frustrated. He marched to the Buddha's hut, entered without knocking, and threatened to disrobe unless he was given clear answers. The Buddha looked at him sternly, "Mālukyāputta, did the Tathāgata ever promise to answer these questions when you went forth into the holy life?"

"No, Lord, you did not," Mālukyāputta replied, feeling uneasy for confronting the Buddha in such a bold manner.

"Then why do you make such demands again and again? You are like a man shot with a poisoned arrow who refuses to have it removed until he finds out the details of his assailant's caste, height, weight, village, and the type of bow, string, and arrowhead that he used. Such a man will surely die before getting all his answers to these questions."

Mālukyāputta was silent. After a few moments, which seemed like eons for Mālukyāputta, the Buddha continued:

The Tathāgata has left out these questions from the path because they do not belong to the fundamentals of the holy life, they do not lead to disenchantment, to dispassion, to cessation, to peace, to liberation. The Tathāgata's only concern is suffering and the way out of suffering. These speculative discussions have nothing to do with either.

Feeling ashamed of his arrogance, Mālukyāputta apologized and promised not to get involved with futile speculation and debate anymore. He returned to his hut to meditate, and shortly after tasted the fruits of *nibbāna*.[168]

A rival sect devised a plan to ruin the Buddha's reputation by instructing their beautiful devotee, Ciñcamādṇavikā, to spread false rumours about having sexual relations with the Buddha. Every night for a couple of weeks she would sleep by the Jetavana Vihāra, and in the morning tell people that she was sleeping with the Buddha in the *Gandha Kuṭi*. A few months later, Ciñca wrapped up her stomach with a round piece of wood, pretending to be pregnant, and went to the Jetavana while the Buddha was giving a discourse to a large assembly of *bhikkhus* and householders.

"You shameful recluse! All you do is preach, preach, and preach. Your words are empty," Ciñca shouted out, "First you got me pregnant and now you leave me all alone!"

The crowd was shocked. People looked around at one another in dismay; they could not believe what they were hearing. After a moment's pause, the Buddha replied, in a compassionate and non-accusational manner, "Sister, only you and I know the truth of the matter."

Sweat began to pour down Ciñca's forehead and her knees began to wobble. She had never been in the presence of such a powerful being before and she started to doubt her dishonest task. The crowd waited for her to respond, but she was unable to speak. She was so numb that she did not even feel the rat that had climbed up her leg. The rat gnawed on the rope and the wooden plank fell to the ground, exposing her fraud. Ciñca ran off as fast as she could. Some people ran after her, but the Buddha instructed them to let her go. Her karma will catch up with her, he said. As Ciñca was running, she tripped over a large rock, fell into a pit of quicksand, and drowned.[169]

After losing much personal wealth, Anāthapiṇḍika's main concern was not his own comfort and security, but that he would not be able to feed the Saṅgha as he had in the past. The Buddha consoled him,

Anāthapiṇḍika, whether you give simple or gourmet alms makes no difference. What is important is that you give with mindfulness and respect. Doing so, your mind will turn to the wholesome enjoyment of the five senses.

The Buddha provided Anāthapiṇḍika with a vivid outline of the relative degrees of merit that can be gained by performing different kinds of actions. He told the story of the brahmin Velāma (the Buddha in one of his former lives) who gave the finest alms to the local mendicants. None of these recipients, however, were worthy of such special offerings and the fruits of these wholesome actions were minimal. The Buddha explained,

Anāthapiṇḍika, the fruits of the offering are always greater when the recipient is a morally and spiritually developed being. Therefore, giving to a liberated person brings infinitely more fruit than giving to an ordinary worldling.

And even higher than an offering to a liberated being is taking refuge in the Triple Gem and keeping the five precepts. These are necessary foundations for good meditation practice.

And an even higher offering is developing concentration through the practice of ānāpāna and mettā-bhāvanā.

And the highest offering a person can make is developing a constant and thorough awareness of impermanence (sampajañña). This awareness removes all sensual desire, removes all desire for material existence, removes all desire for becoming, removes all ignorance, and uproots all conceit of "I am." Even a moment of insight into impermanence brings the greatest of all kammic results, as every one of these moments brings the meditator closer to liberation...[170]

Anāthapiṇḍika rejoiced at the Buddha's words, and letting go of his feelings of guilt, he became even more determined to maintain his *sampajañña* at all times.

Many of the *bhikkhus* wanted to spend as much time near the Buddha as possible. Bhikkhu Dhammārāma, however, was an exception. He always kept to himself so that he could remain focused on his practice. Dhammārāma tried to explain to his fellow *bhikkhus* that it was a distraction to be concerned with following the Buddha around.

A few ignorant *bhikkhus* could not understand this wise attitude and ran to the Buddha, saying that Dhammārāma did not feel any affection or reverence towards him.

The Buddha understood Dhammārāma's intention, however, and admonished the monks for acting foolishly. He encouraged them to follow their Dhamma-brother's admirable example, saying,

Offering flowers and incense—
You do not pay me homage.
Practising the Dhamma—
This is the real homage.

Dwelling and delighting in the practice
Following the discipline;
Never falling away from the true Dhamma.
This is the real homage.

Reassured that he was acting properly, Dhammārāma attained arahantship. The others saw their fellow *bhikkhu's* transformation, and vowed to practise as he did.[171]

A woman discovered that she was barren, so her husband took a second wife. She became so jealous that every time the second wife got pregnant she would slip her some poison that would cause the second wife to miscarry.

For many lives, the two women continued with their enmity towards each other. During the final drama, the first woman was reborn as an ogre (*yakkhini*) named Kāli, and the second woman became the wife of a rich merchant. Twice Kāli disguised herself as the second wife's friend, and devoured her children. The third time, the second wife recognized the yakkhini and ran with her baby to the Jetavana Vihāra. She found the Buddha and placed her baby at the Buddha's feet for protection. Kāli was stopped at the gates by the guardian *yakkha*s and *devas*. But with love and compassion, the Buddha invited Kāli inside to the monastery. He explained to both women how their long-standing rivalry had created so much suffering. They saw how hatred only caused more hatred, which could only be diffused by understanding and goodwill.

As a test, the Buddha told the mother to hand over her baby to the *yakkhini*, which she did reluctantly. The *yakkhini* was so overjoyed with unconditional love for the baby, the woman, and the Buddha that she became a *sotāpanna*. From that day onwards, she vowed to protect the mother and child. The Buddha smiled and said:

Hatred never appeases hatred;
Only through non-hatred is hatred appeased—
This is an ancient principle.[172]

The Buddha sent 500 *bhikkhus* to a forest grove to pursue their meditation practice. The forest *devas* who lived in the trees left for a few nights so that the monks could meditate in peace. After several days had passed and the monks only became more settled, it occurred to the *devas* that the *bhikkhus* would be staying there for some time. This made the *devas* unhappy, so they decided to frighten them away by making scary ghost-like sounds and flying around with headless bodies and bodiless heads. The *bhikkhus* were terrified, and fled back to the Jetavana Monastery. Exhausted and drenched in sweat, they told the Buddha about the horrible beings.

The Buddha comforted the *bhikkhus* and taught them the 'Discourse on Loving-Kindness' (*Karanīyamettā Sutta*):

Knowing where one's welfare lays,
And wishing to attain the Ultimate Peace,
One should be capable, straightforward, upright,
Soft-spoken, gentle, and humble.

One should be contented, easily supportable,
With few commitments and simple in living.
Senses calmed, discreet,
Prudent, and not be dependent on dear ones.

One should not commit even the slightest wrong,
Which the wise might condemn.
One should cultivate the thoughts:

May all beings be happy and secure,
May they be happy within themselves.

Whatever living beings there may be,
Excluding none, whether they are weak or strong,

Long or big, medium or small,
Fine or coarse.

Whether visible or invisible,
Dwelling far or near;
Born or coming to birth,
May all beings be happy.

Let no one deceive another,
Nor despise anyone anywhere.
Let no one get overwhelmed by anger or ill will,
Nor wish harm for another.

Just as a mother would risk her life,
To protect her only child;
Similarly, towards all beings,
Let a boundless mind be cultivated.

By cultivating a boundless mind,
Let thoughts of love pervade the entire universe;
Above, below and across,
Without any obstruction, hatred or enmity.

Whether standing, walking or sitting,
Or lying down, as long as one is awake;
This awareness should be practised,
This is the dwelling place of Brahmā.

Not succumbing to philosophical entanglements,
Becoming established in ethics and insight;
Having removed sensual craving,
Birth in the womb is never taken again.

After teaching the *bhikkhus* this heart-centred meditation, the Buddha instructed them to go back to the forest and recite the *sutta* while practising *mettā*. The *bhikkhus* did as they were told, and the forest *devas* were immediately calmed by the warm *mettā* vibrations. The *devas* then apologized and welcomed the monks to remain in the grove. The *bhikkhus* resumed their practise of Vipassana, and all quickly attained arahantship.[173]

A group of young *bhikkhus* went to visit the blind *arahant*, Bhikkhu Cakkhupāla. When they came to his hut, they saw many dead insects and inferred that the Cakkupāla had stepped on them and killed them. They reported the matter to the Buddha.

"Did you see Cakkhupāla killing the insects?" the Buddha inquired.

"No, Venerable Sir," the *bhikkhus* replied.

"Well, in the same way that you did not see him killing, he did not see those living insects. Without the intention of harming, karmic effects are not reaped, and since Cakkupāla is an *arahant*, he cannot kill anything on purpose. Just as a wheel follows its chariot, all phenomena have mind as their precursor."

The *bhikkhus* understood the importance of intention behind each action and attained arahantship.[174]

A young monk had serious doubts about continuing the difficult monastic life. One hot afternoon, while fanning his uncle, the *arahant* Saṅgharakkhita, his mind wandered into an imaginary conversation with himself,

"Maybe I should leave the Saṅgha.

"But how I will earn a living?

"I can sell my robes and buy a she-goat.

"Yes, she-goats breed quickly!

"Then I'll make enough money to get married to a beautiful wife.

"And she will give birth to a fine son.

"And then, when we have lots of money, we can take a vacation to visit uncle.

"But what happens if while riding in the cart, my idiotic wife drops the baby on the cart-track and the wheels drive over our son and kills him.

"I would beat that foolish woman with a goading-stick."

While lost in this strange fantasy, the nephew absent-mindedly struck his uncle's head with the fan. Saṅgharakkhita knew his nephews thoughts and joked, "I see why you beat your careless wife, but why do you beat an old man like me?" The young monk was so embarrassed that he ran away. Some other young *bhikkhus* saw the incident and chased after him, and when they caught him, they brought him to the Buddha. After hearing the young man's story, the Buddha said,

Controlling the wandering mind—
Solitary and substanceless—
Bhikkhus reside in the inner cavern of the heart,
Liberating themselves from the shackles of Māra.

The young *bhikkhu*, inspired by the Buddha's verse, became a *sotāpanna*.[175]

Pond
Behind the Jetavana Archaeological Park just off the road towards the city's ruins, there is a small bridge that stands over a pond which reminds us of the following story:

> While on his way to the city for his alms, the Buddha came upon a group of excited boys catching fish from a pond and beating them to death.
>
> "Children, if someone beat you, would it hurt?" the Buddha kindly asked.
>
> "Yes, Sir," the children answered.
>
> "Did you know that fish feel pain just as you do?"
>
> The children were ashamed and stared at the ground; they could not look the Buddha in the eye. He suggested to them that they should treat all beings in the same way that they wished to be treated, and then recited a verse:
>
> *If you don't want to suffer,*
> *Avoid harmful deeds:*
> *Both openly and in secret.*
> *If you harm others now, then later*
> *You too will surely suffer.*[176]
>
> The boys understood that tormenting other creatures was wrong. Empathizing with their fellow living beings, they became *sotāpannas*.

Ruins of Sāvatthī (Maheth)
North-west of the Jetavana ruins is the site of the ancient city, whose huge fortifications run about 5 km in a crescent shape. Only a few structures are discernable among the ruins. One is the ancient Sobhnatha Jain Temple, which marks the birthplace of Sambhavanatha, the third Jain Tirthankara. Two other structures are the **Pakki Kuṭi** and the **Kacchi Kuṭi**, stūpas commemorating Aṅgulimāla and Anāthapiṇḍika respectively.

Mahāṃongkolchai
This Thai lay Buddhist organization has created a tranquil meditative space open to the public. Ancient bricks from the Jetava Anāthapiṇḍikārāma dot the beautifully landscaped compound containing a meditation hall that can hold up to 10 000 people, an 80-foot tall Buddha Statue, and a pagoda modelled on Thailand's Phra Pathom Chedi (127 m high, second tallest in the world). All the work in this sacred space—from conception to construction—is performed by white-clothed volunteers following the Eight Precepts. Visitors are welcome everyday between 8:00am and 4:00pm and are asked to turn in their wallets, cameras and cell phones at the gate in order to maintain a contemplative atmosphere free from worldly distractions.

Miracle Stūpa

This stūpa marks the spot where the Buddha, at age 43, defeated the leaders of the six main religious sects by displaying the famous Twin Miracle (*yamaka pātihāriya*). Although the Buddha generally shunned exhibitions of miraculous powers, on this occasion he knew that the performance would result in the awakening of many beings.

The Buddha declared that on the full moon day of *Asālha* (July) he would perform the miracle under a mango tree. Hearing this forecast, some belligerent followers of other teachers cut down all the mango trees in the area. On the proposed day, a man named Ganda offered the Buddha a mango. When the Buddha finished eating the delicious fruit, he sowed the seed in the royal garden's ground, and a fully-grown mango tree instantly sprouted up.

The Buddha then leapt upon a thousand-petalled lotus that floated in the sky, and flames of fire and streams of water began to shoot out of his body simultaneously. The Buddha then transformed himself into a huge bull with a quivering hump, disappearing and reappearing in all four directions. And then, as a grande finale, he created multiple representations of himself and then ascended to the Tāvatiṃsa heaven, where he spent the rainy season teaching the Abhidhamma to a group of *devas*, including his mother who had been reborn there.

Unable to match their opponent's dazzling spectacle, the sectarian leaders left the scene depressed and defeated. Most of their students, however, realized that they had been following false gurus. Their minds (and the minds of millions of celestial beings who witnessed the extraordinary event) were softened, gladdened and pleased, which enabled them to open their hearts to the Dhamma and discover freedom within themselves.[177]

Eastern Monastery (*Pubbārāma, Purvarām*)

In the 31st year after the Buddha's Awakening, Visākha, the Buddha's foremost patroness, donated the Pubbārāma to the Saṅgha. Visākha was a great Dhamma practitioner and was often referred to as Mother Visākha, or Migāra's Mother (*Migāramātā*), because she gave Migāra, her father-in-law, his Dhamma birth.

Aside from the Jetavana, the Buddha gave more discourses here than any other place in Sāvatthī. The ruins of the Pubbārāma have yet to be excavated, but scholars say that the modern village of Gandbhari is the site of the Eastern Monastery (*Pubbārāma*). To get to the current site, follow the signs beginning across the road from the Miracle Stūpa. Follow the mud-brick lane through the small village for about a kilometre until you reach the Migāra Māttu Dharam Prasad Forest Monastery. Prior to the opening of this small monastery in 2008, the only thing that marked the site was a broken Asokan pillar which was worshipped by villagers as a Śiva lingam. Today's site is operated by Bhante Vimal, an Indian Vipassana meditator ordained in Sri Lanka. In 2013, no accommodations were available at the monastery but there was a meditation hall that could seat approximately 30 people. Meditators are always welcome to contribute to the site's revival by meditating in the hall and offering *dāna* for the monastery's development.

Tales from Pubbārāma

When Visākha was seven years old, she went with her grandfather, Meṇḍaka, to hear the Buddha teach the Dhamma. As a result, both of them attained sotāpannahood. When Visākha came of age, she married Puṇṇavaḍḍhana, the son of Migāra, a very rich man from Sāvatthī. Her new husband and father-in-law were disciples of a different teacher, and resented her devotion to the Buddha.

One day, while Migāra was eating his meal out of a golden bowl, a *bhikkhu* stopped for alms at the house. Migāra completely ignored the *bhikkhu*. Visākha was so ashamed that she said to the *bhikkhu*, "I am sorry, Venerable Sir, my father-in-law only eats leftovers."

Hearing this, Migāra went into a rage and told her to leave his house.

Visākha went to the town's council of elders and explained what had happened. They asked her why she spoke so rudely about her father-in-law, and she replied, "When I saw him completely ignoring the *bhikkhu* standing for alms-food, I thought to myself that he was not doing any meritorious deed in this life. All he was doing was eating the fruits of his past good deeds. This is why I said that he only eats leftovers."

The council decided that Visākha was not guilty, and that Migāra would have to give her permission to invite the Buddha and Saṅgha to the house for alms. Migāra reluctantly agreed, but refused to be present during the offering.

The next day, after Visākha finished serving the meal, the Buddha gave a short discourse on charity. Migāra, not wanting to be seen, was spying on them from behind a curtain. Hearing the Buddha's wise words, Migāra reflected on the truth of what he was saying and attained sotāpannahood. Migāra felt thankful to both the Buddha for helping him break through his veil of ignorance, and to Visākha, who was like a loving mother to him, even when he acted like a stubborn child.[178]

Visākha possessed a very valuable cloak studded with gems that her father had given her as a wedding present. One day, while Visākha was at the Jetavana she felt that her jewelled cloak was too heavy, so she took it off, wrapped it up in her shawl, and left it in a corner somewhere.

While Ānanda was walking around the monastery grounds, he found the precious garment and took it for safe keeping. When Visākha went to get her cloak, she was unable to find it. Rather than panic, she remembered the wisdom of *anicca* and stayed calm. Some *bhikkhus* approached her and told her that Ānanda had found it and kept it in a safe place for her. Grateful for Ānanda's kindness, she donated the expensive garment to him.

Ānanda, however, was a proper *bhikkhu* and did not accept the gift. Visākha then decided to put the cloak up for auction and donate the money to the monastery. The garment, however, was so expensive, that no one could afford to buy it. Finally, Visākha bought it from herself and used all the proceeds to build a monastery on the eastern side of the city. This monastery came to be known as Eastern Monastery (*Pubbārāma*).[179]

One of Visākha's grandchildren died from typhoid fever and she felt a deep loss in her life. She wanted to see the Buddha, even though it was pouring rain outside. When she arrived at the Pubbārāma, her clothes and her hair were soaking wet.

"Visākha, why have you come out to see me on such a miserable day?" the Buddha asked her.

"Lord, my dear grandson just died. I feel miserable," Visākha sobbed.

"Visākha, would you like to have as many children and grandchildren as there are people in Sāvatthī?" the Buddha inquired with a gentle smile.

"Certainly, Lord, nothing would make me happier." she said, with a feeble hope that the Buddha might be able to miraculously procure such a wish.

"Visākha, do you realize how many people die everyday in Sāvatthī? If you regarded all the people of Sāvatthī as you regard your own children and grandchildren, you would never stop weeping and mourning. Please, do not let the death of a child affect you so much. Sorrow and fear arise out of such personal affection."

Seeing that Visākha understood his difficult words, the Buddha continued with a verse,

Sorrow, lamentation, and
The diverse sufferings of the world
All depend on what is considered dear.
When these are absent, there's no more becoming.

The happy and the sorrowless
Cling to nothing dear in the world.
Desiring freedom from sorrow and lust,
Give up what is dear in the world.[180]

The Buddha gave a discourse to the brahmin Gaṇaka about the successive stages of training for a meditator.

1. Ethical integrity is developed and the senses are guarded from reacting blindly with craving and aversion.

2. Food is eaten in moderation, reflecting thus, "By this food, I shall remove the existing discomfort of hunger and shall prevent the arising of new discomfort from over-eating. I shall have just enough nourishment to maintain life and to lead a blameless life in good health."

3. Mindfulness is practised with vigilance at all times, whether walking, standing, sitting or lying down. This cleanses the mind of obstructions to spiritual development.

4. The constant and thorough awareness of impermanence (*sampajañña*) is cultivated every waking moment, while moving, eating, drinking, attending to the calls of nature, dressing, speaking, and so on.

5. Solitary living is taken up.

6. The five hindrances and three fetters[181] are abandoned.

7. The concentration exercises (*jhānas*) are mastered.

8. Arahantship is realized.

"Lord, your path is so clearly laid out. Why is it that so many people hear your teaching, but so few actually attain *nibbāna*?" Gaṇaka asked.

"Gaṇaka, suppose two men are given directions to travel from Sāvatthī to Rājagaha. The first man follows the directions properly and the second man does not, taking wrong turns here and there. Do you think that they will both reach Sāvatthī?"

"Of course not, Lord. Only the man who follows the directions properly will reach Sāvatthī."

"Similarly, Gaṇaka, some meditators follow the Tathāgata's instructions properly and reach the final goal; others disregard the instructions and keep wandering aimlessly in *saṃsāra*.

Listening to the simile, Gaṇaka understood that all the Buddha can do is show the way, nothing else. He thanked the Buddha profusely and vowed to follow the clear path of Dhamma until he reached the final goal.[182]

Nava Jetavana Vihāra (Sri Lankan Temple)

Across the road from the Jetavana Archaeological Park is the Sri Lankan Temple. The temple's shrine room walls are decorated with a beautiful mural depicting incidents from the Buddha's life (see below). Because the temple sits on part of the original Jetavana land, it can be a great place to spend a few meditative hours reflecting on the Buddha's precious teachings. You can meditate in the shrine room, or if it's not too hot, you can quietly sit on the roof, where it's possible to see the spots where both Devadatta and Ciñca were swallowed up by quicksand.

The mural depicts the following events:

1. Prince Siddhattha's royal life before Enlightenment in Kapilavatthu.

2. Temptations of Māra.

3. Setting the Wheel of Dhamma in Motion in Sārnāth.

4. The Buddha's passing in Kusinārā.

5. Anāthapiṇḍika meets the Buddha in Rājagaha.

6. Anāthapiṇḍika purchases the park from Prince Jeta.

7. Same as above.

8. Ānanda plants the Bodhi Tree in the Jetavana Monastery.

9. Visākha constructs the Pubbārāma Vihāra.

10. Ignorant *bhikkhus* reacting negatively to the blind *arahant* Bhikkhu Cakkhupāla who accidentally steps on some insects.

11. While receiving *mettā* from the Buddha, the sick Maṭṭhakuṇḍali dies on his miserly father's veranda and is then reborn in the Tāvatiṃsa heaven.

12. The Buddha reconciles a battle between two women that spanned several lifetimes.

13. Repenting his evil actions, the ill Devadatta wanted to seek forgiveness from the Buddha. Just before reaching the front gate of the Jetavana, he fell into a pit of quicksand and drowned.

14. The Buddha and Anāthapiṇḍika take care of a sick *bhikkhu*.

15. While resting with his army in a dry riverbed after slaughtering the Sakyans, Prince Viṭaṭūbha, son of King Pasenadi, is swept away in a flash flood.

16. King Pasenadi was infatuated with the beautiful wife of a poor man. Wanting the woman for himself, the king made the poor man his servant and gave him an impossible assignment, telling him that he would be executed if he didn't complete it. Due to his good karma of the past, some *devas* helped the man accomplish the task. That night, the king felt extremely guilty and was unable to sleep. The next morning, the king went to the Buddha to repent for his selfishness. The Buddha calmed his mind down with an inspiring Dhamma talk, and the king then set the couple free.

17. Koka the hunter is attacked by his dogs who mistake their master for the *bhikkhu* that they were supposed to attack.

18. After raping the Bhikkhunī Uppalavaṇṇā, Nanda is consumed by a fire.[183]

19. After Paṭācārā goes crazy from a series of tragic events where all her family members were killed one by one, the Buddha consoles her with the soothing Dhamma and she becomes an *arahant*.

20. Realizing that death is inevitable, even for her baby, Kisāgotamī attains *nibbāna*.

21. King Pasenadi was disappointed that his queen gave birth to a daughter instead of a son. The Buddha explained to him that girls are just as capable of being successful as boys are, and that he should not superficially discriminate between the sexes.

22. Aṅgulimāla runs after the Buddha.

23. Ciñcamādṇavikā's lies are exposed when her fake pregnant stomach falls to the ground.

24. The Buddha performs the Twin Miracle.

25. The First Council at Rājagaha.

26. The Third Council at Patna.

27. The *arahant* Mahinda, Emperor Asoka's son, converts the Sri Lankan King Devanampiyatissa while he is on a hunting expedition.

28. The *arahant* Nagasena answers the questions of King Milinda, one of the heirs of Alexander the Great.

29. Anagarika Dharmapala at the Mahābodhi Temple in Bodhgayā.

30a. On October 14, 1955, Doctor Bhimrao Ambedkar and half a million untouchables renounced the Hindu caste system and embraced the Buddha's teaching by taking refuge in the Triple Gem and vowing to practise the Five Precepts.

30b. Bhante Saṅgharatana, founder of the Nava Jetavana Mahāvihāra, and Doctor Shankar Dayal Sharma, the vice-president of India, consecrating the temple on December 31, 1988.

Dhamma Suvatthi, Jetavana Vipassana Meditation Centre

This tranquil 9-acre meditation centre is situated across the street from the Jetavana Archaeological Park. As the exact boundaries of the original *vihāra* are unknown, it is quite possible that Dhamma Suvatthi ('Well-Being of Dhamma') is located on part of the original grounds. As the place where the Buddha spent more time than anywhere else, Shravasti offers a uniquely vibrant historical Dhamma atmosphere, and this centre is perhaps the most suitable place to benefit from that energy through practice.

Ten-day courses are held twice a month, with a capacity for about 50 students. As with many centres, old students in the tradition are also welcome to come for shorter self-courses at this simple, yet well-built meditation centre. Meditators are encouraged to come and experience one of the most spiritually and historically important seats of Dhamma.

Contact:
Dhamma Suvatthi, Jetavana Vipassana Meditation Centre
Katara Bypass
Shravasti–271845
Uttar Pradesh
Tel: [+91] (0)5252-265439 or (0)522-2700053 (office in Lucknow)
E-mail: info@suvatthi.dhamma.org
Website: http://www.suvatthi.dhamma.or

Sleeping & Eating

Sāvatthī's monasteries offer the friendliest budget options for pilgrims. Some favourites are the **Korean, Burmese,** and **Sri Lankan.** At the time of writing, the donation system at the monasteries was widespread—travellers simply donate an amount they feel acceptable in exchange for their stay. The new **Sri Lanka Ramayath Guest House** is also a good option for budget travellers while the more expensive **Pawan Palace** and **Lotus Nikko** hotels will satisfy those looking for some semblance of luxury.

If you decide to spend the night in Balrampur for some reason, some budget- to mid-range options include hotels **Maya, Pathik,** and **Tourist Bungalow.**

Coming & Going

Shravasti is located in north-eastern Uttar Pradesh, and can be reached from Balrampur (19 km, by bus or shared/private rickshaw) or from Bahraich (47 km, by bus). There are regular **buses** from Gorakhpur (200 km, 7 hours) and Lucknow (131 km, 5 hours) to both these places.

Travel by **train** is also possible for much of the journey. If coming from Kushinagar (via Gorakhpur) or Kapilavatthu (via Naugarh), hop on to the Kapilavastu Express 5322/5321 (Gonda-Gorakhpur) that stops in Balrampur.

Trains from all over India stop in Lucknow, such as Shatabdi Express 2003/2004 (New Delhi-Lucknow), Rajdhani Express 2309/2310 (Patna-New Delhi), Vaishali Express 2553/2554 (New Delhi-Barauni via Muzaffarpur and Gorakhpur), and the Lucknow Mail 4229/4230 (New Delhi-Lucknow).

The nearest **airport** is in Lucknow (131 km), and is served by daily flights to/from Delhi, Mumbai, Kolkata and Patna. (See below for more information on Lucknow.)

Excursions

Rapti River (Achiravati River)
Shravasti is situated within an inward curve of the Achiravati River. Only 1.5 km from town (a short walk from the Aṅgulimāla and Anāthapiṇḍika stūpas), the river is a nice place to sit and contemplate Paṭācārā's heartfelt story.

> Paṭācārā was the only daughter of overly protective parents who never allowed her to leave the house. One day, she fell in love with a servant and they eloped to a far-off village. When she was pregnant with their second child, however, she wanted to give birth in her parents' house in Sāvatthī, as was the custom at that time.
>
> On the way, they were caught in a thunder storm, so her husband went into the forest to gather branches to make a shelter. Paṭācārā

waited all night for him, but he never returned. In the early hours of the morning she went into labour and gave birth to her second son in the rain. After regaining some strength, she lifted her newborn in one arm and took her other son by the hand, and went into the forest in search of her husband.

In the forest, Paṭācā found him dead from a poisonous snake bite. She wept bitterly and felt like dying, but she knew she had to continue for her children's sake. When she reached the Achiravati River, she noticed that it had swollen during the storm, and that it would be too deep for her older son to cross alone. She left him on the bank, telling him to come when she signalled. While she was wading across the river, carrying her newborn high over her head, an eagle swept down and stole the baby from her. Paṭācārā frantically waved her arms at the bird, trying to save her baby. The older boy, thinking that his mother was calling him, jumped into the river and was swept away by the swift current. Utterly miserable, Paṭācārā continued on for several days, only to find that her entire family had died that same night when their house burnt down.

These tragic events drove Paṭācārā crazy. She tore off her clothes and roamed about the streets of Sāvatthī totally naked. But by good-fortune, she came across the Buddha while on his alms rounds. With great compassion, he calmed her down, and taught her the Dhamma when her mind was ready. She soon became an *arahant*, and spent the rest of her life helping *bhikkhunīs* develop in the Dhamma.[184]

Sitadwar (*Mahākassapa Stūpa*)

Fourteen kilometres from Sāvatthī, towards Lucknow, is a grass-covered stūpa with a small Hindu shrine on top and a colourful Hindu temple at the base. Local monks from Sāvatthī say that this stūpa was built over the hut where Mahākassapa lived at the time of the Buddha's death. Beyond the mound is a circular garden whose grass and flowerbeds cover some unknown ancient ruins. Just to the left of the garden, there are three small stūpas known by the locals as the *samādhi stūpas*. Locals say these are stūpas built over the remains of unknown forest ascetics. This quiet place is great for meditation, and there is no entry fee to the park.

Lucknow

Scattered around this British-influenced city are the massive mausoleums of the Nawabs. These tombs were built by decadent Muslim rulers, who controlled the region from 1724-1856. These monuments are interesting to visit and offer good places to observe Lucknow's local culture. Another notable place in Lucknow are the ruins of the Residency, a Raj-era compound and the sight of the bloody 1857 Indian Uprising.

You can also check out the **State Museum** near the Lucknow Zoo in the Banarsi Bagh section of town. The museum has a decent collection of Buddhist sculptures and is open everyday, except Mondays, from 10:30 a.m. to 4:30 p.m.

If you need to spend a night or two in Lucknow, the best options are in the Hazrat-ganj area, about 3 km north-east of the train stations. Budget travellers can try their luck at the **Homestay Lucknow**. The **Charans Club and Resort** and **Mohan Hotel** are popular mid-range choices. For European-style comfort, you can try the **La Place Sarovar Portico, The Picadilly**, or **Vivanta**.. Hazratganj has a wide range of places to eat. For pure vegetarian, treat your tummy at the **Brindavin South Indian Vegetarian Restaurant**. If you are in Lucknow in May or June, take advantage of the region's great mangoes.

Lucknow has two bus stations. **Buses** departing from Charbagh Bus Stand, near the train stations, offer service to the region's major cities. Buses to Delhi, however, depart from Kaiserbagh Bus Stand, located just west of Hazratganj on J. Narain Road.

Lucknow also has two **train** stations. Charbagh Train Station serves trains travelling east-west between Delhi and Kolkata. These trains may also stop at Lucknow Junction Train Station, which additionally serves trains travelling to destinations in the south. The two stations are quite close to one another; be sure to verify which station your intended train departs from to prevent confusion.

Lucknow's **Amausi Airport** is 15 km south of the city. Indian Airlines and Air Sahara both offer daily flights to Delhi and Mumbai.

If while en route you find yourself spending more time than you planned in Lucknow, you can meditate at **Dhamma Lakkhaṇa** ('Characteristic of Dhamma').

Contact:
Dhamma Lakkhaṇa, Lucknow Vipassana Centre
Asti Road, Bakshi Ka Talab
Lucknow–227202
Uttar Pradesh
Tel: [+91] (0)522-2508525/ 278 2795
E-mail: info@lakkhana.dhamma.org

Sankasya (*Saṅkassa*)

Glory of the Buddha

After performing the Twin Miracle (*yamaka pātihāriya*) in Sāvatthī, the Buddha is said to have ascended to the Tāvatiṃsa heaven, where he spent the rains-retreat (*vassā-vāsa*) preaching the Abhidhamma to celestial beings, including his mother, who was reborn there as a *deva*. All who heard these precious analytical teachings became *sotāpannas*.

During that time, at Saṅkassa, Sāriputta taught the Abhidhamma to a group of 500 bhikkhus. By the end of the rainy season, every one of these monks became an arahant.[185] At the end of the *vassā-vāsa*, the Buddha returned to earth at Saṅkassa, descending on a golden ladder decorated with precious stones, created by the gods Brahma and Indra, who descended on their own grand staircases.

When the Buddha arrived, six coloured rays shone forth from his body. He was accompanied by a large following of *devas* on one side and a large following of *brahmas* on the other. The entire town was lit up by this assembly of splendorous beings, and Saṅkassa's citizens were in awe of the Buddha's grand and glorious return.

One local *bhikkhu* approached the Buddha and said, "Venerable Sir, we have never seen such magnificence. Indeed, you are loved, respected and revered alike by *devas*, brahmas and men!" The Buddha smiled and replied,

The wise, absorbed in meditation
Take delight in the inner calm of renunciation.
The mindful and awake,
All beings hold dear.[186]

Today, the Buddha's descent from Tāvatiṃsa heaven is commemorated through festivals in Buddhist countries such as Sri Lanka, Thailand and Myanmar, where the imagery of the three illuminated staircases plays an important role, as it sometimes does in Buddhist art.

Site-Sitting

Saṅkassa Stūpa & Pillar

This stūpa, erected by Asoka, is now a grassy hill with a small Hindu shrine and bodhi tree at its helm. It's quite pleasant to climb to the top and meditate under the shade of the tree, contemplating the Buddha's deep psychological analysis of the mind.

Just before the stūpa is an Asokan pillar with an elephant crown, decorated with beautiful carvings of lotus flowers and bodhi leaves. The pillar is believed to mark the exact spot of the Buddha's arrival from the Tāvatiṃsa heaven.

Sleeping & Eating

The **Sri Lankan** and **Burmese** monasteries offer places to stay in Saṅkassa. Both are clean, quiet, and at the time this book was researched, run on a donation system. The shrine room in the Sri Lankan monastery has exquisite murals painted by one of the resident *bhikkhus*.

Coming & Going

This small, isolated and rarely-visited village (which is also known as Basantpur) is located in central Uttar Pradesh, and can be reached by **bus** or **taxi** from Fatehgarh (37 km) or Pakhna (12 km). Fatehgarh can be reached by **train** or **bus** from Lucknow (150 km), Delhi (375 km), or Agra (175 km). The nearest railway station to Sankasya is at Pakhna, a stop for some local passenger trains coming from Fatehgarh and Farrukhabad.

Mathura (*Madhurā*)

Madhūra is located on the outer edge of the Middle Land, and was not a place of which the Buddha was fond. For followers of the Buddha, the most well-known event to have occurred here was when Mahākaccāna, the foremost disciple in explicating brief sayings of the Buddha, gave a discourse to King Avantiputta on the erroneous beliefs of caste superiority. The brilliant *bhikkhu* explained that whether a person was of high caste or low caste, his karmic destiny depended not on status, but on his deeds.[187]

Despite being a place of minor importance in the life of the Buddha and his senior disciples, the ancient capital of Mathura developed into a vital Dhamma centre during the initial seven centuries of the first millennium. Mathura was once home to 20 monasteries that supported a community of 3 000 monks. After thriving for centuries, however, the Dhamma establishments in Mathura fell into decline with the gradual revival of Puranic ritualism and the later Turkish invasions.

Mathura, locally referred to as Brij Bhoomi, is also believed to be the birthplace of the Hindu deity Krishna. Thousands of Hindu pilgrims travel around the city, its outskirts, and to the nearby temple town of Vrindaban, retracing the footsteps of the beloved Krishna's adventures. Thousands of song-filled temples decorate the banks of the wide Yamuna River in both Mathura and Vrindaban, representing India's devotion to the playful aspect of the Divine.

To get a glimpse of Mathura's past glory, you can visit the **Archaeological Museum**, one of the best museums in India. Much of the beautiful ancient Buddhist stonework that we see today comes from Mathura. There are many exquisite sculptures of the Buddha in various postures, and also a damaged portrait of King Kanishka, an enthusiastic patron of Buddhist art and culture. This is one of the few portraits of a king to survive from ancient India. The museum is open every day except Mondays, from 10:30 a.m. to 4:30 p.m. (July to March) or 7:30 a.m. to 12:30 p.m. (April to June).

Sleeping & Eating

Most travellers like to stay at the 'cheap-and-best' **International Guest House & Vegetarian Restaurant** next to the *Shri Krishna Janmbhoomi*, the spot said to be where Krishna was born. The hotels **Briraj** and **Madhuvan** are more pricey and comfortable, but less culturally interesting. If you need a room in Vrindaban and don't mind being awakened by worship bells at 3:00 a.m., the **ISKCON Guest House** is very clean and has a great pure-veg restaurant.

Coming & Going

Mathura is located on the western edge of Uttar Pradesh, north-west of Agra. The town is well-connected by **train** and **bus** to Delhi (145 km, 3.5 hours) and Agra (58 km, 2 hours). To get to Vrindaban, there are semi-regular buses that leave from the bus stand, and **tempos** that leave from the train station.

Kushinagar (*Kusinārā*)

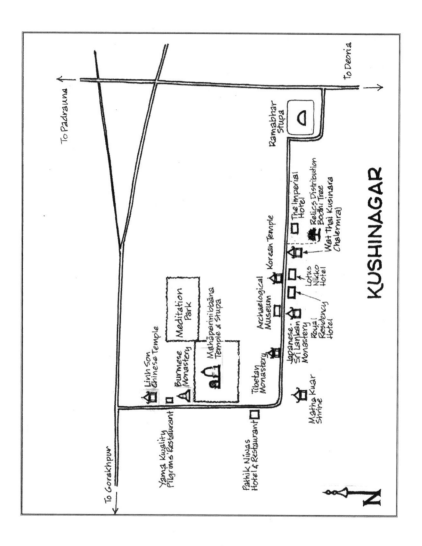

The Buddha's Last Days

After spending his last rainy season in Vesālī, the Buddha announced his imminent passing, and set off for Kusinārā with Ānanda. They stopped in the towns and villages of Bhaṇḍagāma, Hatthigāma, Ambagāma, Jambugāma, and Bhoganagara.[188] In each of these places, the Buddha gave the same comprehensive instructions to the congregated meditators explaining the necessity of deeply understanding morality, concentration and wisdom.

This is sīla, this is samādhi, this is paññā. Samādhi imbued with sīla brings great benefits. Paññā imbued with samādhi brings great benefits. The mind imbued with paññā becomes totally free from the defilements of sense pleasures, becoming, false views, and ignorance.

Thirty kilometres before reaching Kusinārā, the Buddha and Ānanda rested in a small town called Pāvā, where they stayed in a luscious mango grove owned by Cunda the Silversmith, a lay disciple. Cunda was a great admirer of the Buddha and offered him a local delicacy prepared from a mushroom called "Tender Pig" (*sūkara maddava*).[189] Shortly after the meal, the Buddha fell violently ill with dysentery, but bore the pains with perfect awareness and equanimity. The next day, having purged the illness, the Buddha felt fit enough to continue the journey.

After walking several kilometres under the scorching sun, the Buddha began feeling terribly weak and thirsty, and took refuge under the shade of a tree. "Ānanda, please fetch me some water," the Buddha asked, pointing to a nearby stream.

"But Lord, a caravan of 500 carts just passed through here. The water is thick and cloudy," Ānanda protested, not wanting the Buddha to drink such dirty water. "We are almost at the Kakutthā River whose water is clean. It's better to wait for some time than risk drinking dirty water."

"Please Ānanda, do not argue with me. I need water now," the Buddha insisted.

Ānanda relented and took the Buddha's bowl to the stream. As he approached the water, he was astonished to find it clear and unsullied. Ānanda was amazed that he had been the Buddha's attendant for 25 years, and still sometimes failed to recognize the magnitude of his master's powers.

Continuing on their journey, the Buddha and Ānanda met a Malla merchant named Pukkusa. The Buddha spoke to him about the Dhamma, and Pukkusa was filled with happiness. Feeling so grateful for receiving a personal teaching, Pukkusa offered the Buddha a set of robes woven from golden thread. When the Buddha put on the lustrous cloth, Pukkusa and Ānanda were taken aback by how the Buddha's old and tired body glowed with a brilliant radiance, making the robe itself appear dull in comparison.

Before reaching Kusinārā, they came to the Kakutthā River, where the Buddha took his last bath and drink of water. After meditating by the riverbank, the Buddha told Ānanda,

Ānanda, the meal we ate at Cunda's was the Tathāgata's last meal. People may accuse Cunda of poisoning the Tathāgata, so make sure to console him, letting him know that the meal was greatly treasured. Rather than feeling depressed, Cunda should feel glad to have had the opportunity to offer him this auspicious last meal. Explain to him that there are two kinds of alms food whose fruits are far greater than any others. Which two? One is the alms food eaten just before attaining Supreme Enlightenment; the other is the alms food eaten before passing into parinibbāna. The fruits of both these meals are conducive to long life, beauty, happiness, fame, wealth, and heavenly rebirth.

After resting for a short while, the Buddha crossed the Hiraññavati River[190] and went to the Malla's *sālā* grove. The Buddha was fatigued, and Ānanda prepared a place for him to meditate in the resting lion's pose between two great *sālā* trees. The trees, delighted to have the Buddha meditate beneath them, burst into untimely bloom and the flower blossoms gently fell on the Buddha's body. Heavenly *mandārava* flowers and sandalwood powder then fell from the sky, to the tune of divine music that drifted through the air.

"Ānanda, do you see all these wonderful offerings of veneration?" the Buddha asked his attendant. "None of these compare to living a life of Dhamma—the highest offering a being can make."

"Lord, meditators used to visit the Tathāgata to pay their respects. Now with the Tathāgata's passing, meditators will no longer have a chance to do this," Ānanda said.

"Ānanda, there are four places the sight of which will arouse inspiration in meditators. Which four? Where the Tathāgata was born, where the Tathāgata realized *nibbāna*, where the Tathāgata set in motion the Wheel of Dhamma, and where the Tathāgata passed into *parinibbāna*. Any meditator with a devoted heart who dies while on pilgrimage to these places will be reborn in a celestial realm."

Ānanda could not take his eyes off the Buddha's poor physical condition, and he regretted that in spite of all his years of close contact with the Buddha, he had still not reached the stage of total liberation, but merely of a *sotāpanna*. Overcome with emotion, Ānanda ran off to a nearby hut and wept in sorrow and shame. Hearing this, the Buddha sympathetically called him over:

"Enough Ānanda, do not weep. Have I not already told you that all things pleasant are impermanent and subject to separation? So how could it be, Ānanda, that whatever is born, become, and compounded is not subject to decay? How should they not pass away? Ānanda, for a long time you have attended the Tathāgata with bodily, verbal, and mental acts of loving kindness. You have done so gladly, sincerely and without reserve. You have acquired much merit, Ānanda. Keep on striving and you will soon be free from the taints."

The Buddha then turned to a group of nearby *bhikkhus* and praised Ānanda for his wisdom and popularity, pointing out that people were always glad to see him and listen to him when he spoke. These are all positive qualities to be emulated.

Ānanda was still not ready to accept the Buddha's looming demise. Hoping to convince the Buddha to live a little bit longer, Ānanda said, "Please, Lord, it is not fit for you to pass away in this miserable and insignificant town. We should go to a city like Sāvatthī or Rājagaha where there are many devoted followers who would make you a grand ceremony."

The Buddha refused Ānanda's request, explaining that in a past life he was a Wheel-Turning Monarch by the name of Mahāsudassana. At that time, this small town was not insignificant, but a prosperous royal capital named Kusāvatī. If it was fit for the king to die in this place back then, the Buddha asserted, it was certainly fit for him to die here now.[191]

Knowing that he would not live much longer, the Buddha asked Ānanda to send word to the Mallas of his forthcoming death. When the Malla people heard the news they rushed to the *sālā* grove and waited in a long queue to pay their last respects to the Buddha.

A wandering ascetic named Subhadda also heard the news that the Buddha was about to die. He hurried over to the grove hoping that the Buddha would be able to dispel a doubt of his that he'd been carrying for a long time. Seeing the long line of people, Subhadda went over to Ānanda, "Friend," he pleaded, "please allow me to ask the Buddha a question." Not wanting the Buddha to be bothered by philosophical debates in his last moments of life, Ānanda refused the ascetic's request, saying, "Please, Sir, the Buddha is exhausted. He should not be disturbed."

The Buddha overheard their conversation and told Ānanda to permit Subhadda to come forth with his question. He knew that this old man was ripe for awakening and that he too did not have much time left. Subhadda asked the Buddha about other teachers and whether or not they had direct knowledge of ultimate reality. "Forget about them, Subhadda! Concentrate on yourself. Practise the Noble Eightfold Path and you will realize the Truth!"

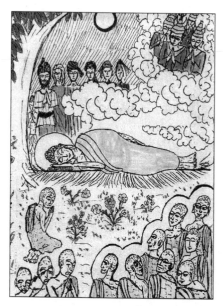

Hearing these words of encouragement and feeling the Buddha's immense compassion, Subhadda asked for immediate ordination. The Buddha consented and Subhadda became the last person to ordain during the Buddha's presence. Subhadda thanked the Buddha profusely and went off to meditate under a nearby tree. Within a few minutes he became an *arahant* and had the honour of being the last person to attain fruition during the Buddha's life.

As his end drew near, the Buddha gave his final directions to the assembled *bhikkhus*, *"Bhikkhus*, do not think, 'the Teacher's instruction has come to an end. Now we have no Teacher!' You should always continue practising the Dhamma. The Dhamma will be your guide when the Tathāgata is gone."

After a few moments of silence, the Buddha looked around at the assembly and then uttered his last words,

Now, meditators, this I declare to you: decay is inherent in all compounded things. Strive with diligence! (Vaya dhammā saṅkhārā, appamādena sampādetha!)

The Buddha then closed his eyes and instantly entered the first *jhāna*. He ascended to the eighth *jhāna* and then slowly descended to the fourth, and from there guided his consciousness to final *nibbāna*. A loud thunder struck and a great earthquake shook and the mighty *deva* king Sakka intoned:

All compounded things are impermanent (Aniccā vata saṅkhārā),
Their nature is to arise and pass away (uppādavaya-dhammino).
When they arise and are eradicated (Uppajjitvā-nirujjhanti),
Their cessation brings happiness (tesaṃ vūpasamo sukho).

Many monks and householders were overcome with grief, and threw up their arms and flung themselves to the ground, crying out, "So soon the Blessed One has passed away! So soon the eye has vanished from the world. Who can we seek refuge in now!" While these people wailed and trounced about, others who were fully aware of *anicca*, solemnly remained silent.

Bhikkhu Anuruddha, the Buddha's cousin, gently reproached the weeping meditators, "Friends, enough lamenting! Has the Lord not already told you that all things that are pleasant are impermanent and subject to separation? So? Why this pitiful display? Whatever is born; dies. Whatever arises; passes away. Whatever is compounded; dissolves. Please regain your composure!"

The *bhikkhus* followed their elder's council and spent the rest of the night around the Buddha's body contemplating the nature of impermanence and listening to Anuruddha and Ānanda recount inspiring episodes from the Buddha's life. Dignity was restored.

The next day, the Malla princes took care of the Buddha's body as if it were the 'king of kings'. They bathed the corpse in the Hiraññavati River, wrapped it in five hundred layers of expensive cloth, and then placed it on the funeral pyre of scented woods. For seven days, people paid homage to the body, offering flowers, incense, music and dance. The Mallas then paraded the body through town and brought it to the Makuṭa Baṇḍhana, their main shrine. When they tried to ignite the pyre, however, it would not catch fire. Legend tells that a host of *devas* had delayed the cremation until Mahākassapa arrived and paid his last respects.

At that time, Mahākassapa and a retinue of 500 *bhikkhus* were somewhere between Pāvā and Kusinārā. They came across an Ājīvika ascetic who had been in Kusinārā when the Buddha had passed on. When the ascetic told them the news, the ignorant *bhikkhus* began lamenting while the awakened ones remained in solemn silence. An old and ignorant monk named Subhadda (not to be confused with the 120-year-old ascetic) exclaimed, "Enough, friends, do not be sad, do not lament. We are better off without him. We have been frustrated by his saying: 'This is allowed; this is not allowed.' But now, we shall do as we like and we shall not do as we do not like."[192]

This set Mahākassapa thinking. He gave the *bhikkhus* an inspiring Dhamma talk on impermanence and encouraged them to go to Kusinārā before the body was cremated. When the group reached the site and circumambulated the Buddha's corpse three times, the pyre spontaneously burst into flames. Everyone fell to their knees, joined their palms, and bowed their heads as the body burned.

When the fire died out, it was evident that the skin, flesh, sinews and oil of the joints did not produce any cinder or ash; only the bones remained. The Malla princes gathered the bones in a golden urn, and worshipped them with dances, songs, flowers and incense.

Shortly after, representatives from other states came along, including King Ajātasattu of Maghada, the Licchavīs of Vesālī, the Sakyans of Kapilavatthu, the Balians of Allakappaka, the Koliyans of Rāmāgāma, the Brahmins of Vetha and the Mallas of Pāvā. They all wanted a share of the relics for their kingdoms. The Kusinārā Mallas refused to give the bones up, arguing that since the Buddha had died in their precinct the relics belonged to them.

On the brink of a violent confrontation, the wise brahmin Doṇa came to the rescue with a suggestion, "Sirs, please listen to my proposal. Tolerance is the Buddha's teaching. It would be wrong for us to clash over a share of the Exalted One's bones. Let us all unite in harmony and in agreement to make up eight parts. Let monuments be set up far and wide so that all may see and develop devotion."

Coming to their senses, they agreed to divide the relics into eight equal shares, and let Doṇa keep the urn. Shortly after the relics were distributed, the Moryans of Pipphalivana arrived, also wanting a share. But since the relics had already been divided, Doṇa gave them the wood ashes from the pyre. Each of the ten groups went to their respective states and erected stūpas enshrining the relics.[193]

Site-Sitting

In the middle of the 5th century CE, a devout Buddhist named Haribala came to Kusinārā and found it totally in ruins. Wanting to revive the glory that the town deserved, Haribala enlarged the original stūpa (erected first by the Malla princes and then later renovated by King Asoka) and also built the famous monolithic sandstone reclining Buddha statue that can be seen today. However, the sacred ground was deserted again after the 12th century Islamic crusades, and left to the whim of the forces of nature.

In the mid-19th century, the British archaeologist Alexander Cunningham and his assistant Archibald Carlleyle rediscovered the lost site. Then in the early 1900s, the Burmese monk Bhante Chandramani fell in love with the holy town and made it his life mission to ensure that it did not fall in to ruin again.

> *When the Buddha finally passed away, it was not just the end of one life. Millions of lives, countless lives, had come to an end. And it was such a good end, after he had helped so many. At that moment there was very strong Dhamma dhātu, Nibbāna dhātu, and the effects have remained for centuries.*
>
> *– S.N. Goenka*

Bhikkhu Chandramani built a small temple (today's Burmese Temple) near the stūpa, which began to attract a steady stream of pilgrims to Kushinagar. Since the early days of Chandramani's renovation efforts, a small town has evolved around the stūpa and a cultural and religious renewal has occurred. This is evident in the growing number of temples and monasteries that make up much of the small town, as well as the new hotels and other amenities catering to pilgrims and tourists alike. Like Sārnāth, Kushinagar is slowly being revived, and is certainly worth a few days' visit.

Meditating in this place where the Buddha breathed his last (after countless aeons of practice!), it's easy to remember the Buddha's 45 years of selfless service to humanity. Whether meditating in the temple next to the beautifully draped statue, or outside by one of the stūpas, the Buddha's profound final words—*vaya dhammā saṅkhārā, appamādena sampādetha*—continue to waft through the air, reminding us to let go of our attachments and put an end to our deep-seated misery.

Nirvana Temple (*Mahāparinibbāna Temple*)

In 1956, the Mahāparinibbāna Temple was rebuilt to celebrate the 2500-year anniversary of the *Buddhasāsana*. The temple houses a magnificent 1500-year-old statue of the Buddha resting in the lion's pose. The statue's base has three small figures representing the people's attitudes at the time of the Buddha's death. The first is of a lamenting Malla woman, the second of an awakened *bhikkhu* meditating on *anicca*, and the third of an unenlightened *bhikkhu* with his head resting in his hands, obviously sulking with grief.

The neat temple grounds feature manicured lawns, flower gardens and large trees (including a few *sāla* just in front of the temple), and is a little oasis in the midst of a noisy Indian town. Chattering flocks of parakeets, flitting about from tree to tree, contribute to the peacefulness and beauty of the park. There is no entrance fee to this living temple and its operating hours are from 6:00am to 6:00pm.

Nirvāna Stūpa (*Mahāparinibbāna Stūpa*)

Directly behind the temple is a towering stūpa that was built over the spot where the Buddha, under the twin *sāla* trees, left the world of mind and matter. When Cunningham and Carlleyle opened the many-layered stūpa in 1876, they found terracotta Buddha figures, an inscription of the *Nidana Sutta* on a copper plate, and pieces of charcoal from the funeral pyre. Meditating near this great, yet simple stūpa helps connect us to the all-embracing nature of the Dhamma.

A little ways from the Mahāparinibbāna Stūpa is a demolished stūpa that local monks say is the spot where the *arahant* Anuruddha passed away. Anuruddha was the Buddha's cousin, famous for mastering the practices of divine eye and for reminding the lamenting *bhikkhus* to contemplate *anicca* over the Buddha's corpse.

Matha-Kuar Shrine

South of the main temple at the crossroad towards the Cremation Stūpa is a shrine that was built in 1927 by Burmese pilgrims. The shrine houses a 10th century golden Buddha statue from Gayā. Local monks claim that this shrine marks the spot where the old King Mahāsudassana (the Buddha in a former life, see above), with his faculties purified and complexion bright, renounced all of his worldly possessions on his deathbed. His wife tried to please him by reminding him of all his treasures, but he retorted that he found them unpleasing, undelightful and unattractive.

> *All things that are pleasing and attractive are liable to change and disappear. To die filled with longing for these things is painful and blameworthy. Desire for these treasures must be abandoned.*

With that said, the king passed away from this world and was reborn in the Brahma realm.[194]

Ramabhar Stūpa (*Makuṭa Baṇḍhana Stūpa*)

This magnificent 15 m high brick stūpa, located in a peaceful and well-maintained park, marks the spot where the Malla princes cremated the Buddha. The trees here provide a nice shaded area for meditation on hot days. Locals call it Ramabhar Stūpa because it is near Ramabhar Pond, about 2 km from the Mahāparinibbāna Temple and Stūpa.

Relics Distribution Bodhi Tree

This huge bodhi tree is said to mark the spot of the Malla's royal council hall, where Doṇa prevented a conflict amongst the eight tribes by proposing to evenly distributing the Buddha's relics.

To get to the tree, turn right on to the narrow dirt footpath immediately after the lovely Thai temple. Follow the path for about 200 metres; on your left, you'll see the massive tree presiding over the paddy fields.

Archaeological Museum

Housing local antiquities, this tiny government Buddha Museum is open Tuesdays to Saturdays from 10:30 a.m. to 4:30 p.m. The museum is located opposite the Japan-Sri Lanka Buddhist Centre, and will hopefully have more to offer in the future.

Wat Thai Kusinārā Chalermraj

This magnificent monastic complex has a shrine containing a relic of the Buddha and has several meditation huts in a bamboo forest for anyone interested in self-retreats. The monastery also runs a clinic that offers free treatments for children and the elderly and charges Rs 5 for adults. Volunteer doctors are welcome in exchange for room and board.

We had just finished sitting at the Mahāparinibbāna Stūpa and were about to go for lunch before continuing our meditation in commemoration of the Buddha's passing, when a group of Thai monks and nuns arrived to celebrate the fullmoon day of Vesākha (April-May). With great big smiles, they handed us flowers and incense, inviting us to join them in their circumambulation of the stūpa while chanting the qualities of the Triple Gem in Pāli. Their fresh-shaven heads, their eyes downcast and the rhythmic cadence of their voices in unison truly gave an auspicious feeling to the sacred day.

After the ceremony, a local layperson offered the monks and nuns not the typical offerings of robes, bowls, medicines, and shaving kits, but cases of Pepsi and 7-Up. We couldn't help but smile when they also offered us some refreshments, not only because it was 40 °C, but, here we were, sitting at the site where the Buddha breathed his last, on this anniversary celebration of his birth, enlightenment and death, with traditional monks in their saffron robes, drinking Pepsi!

That evening we continued our celebration of wisdom by listening to the friendly Saṅgha members chant the paṭimokkha (precepts for

*monks and nuns), followed by an all-night meditation on the imper-
manence of mosquito bites!*

– MD & KG

*Once again, our experience was out of accord with our expecta-
tions; another lesson in letting go. A peculiar thing happened to us
in Kushinagar as I, yet again, became suddenly and seriously ill. It
was a brisk early morning ride in the open-air jeep, but after arriving
and having hot tea in the sunshine I could not get warm, shot through
with deepening fever chills that led to uncontrollable shaking. Fortunately we crossed paths with a group of kind Canadian pilgrims we'd
first met at Sārnāth, who directed me to the Thai Monastery's clinic.
From there I was sent to a pharmacy for treatment.*

*I was made to lie on my side and was given painful shots of both
malaria medicine and antibiotics in hopes of addressing my mysterious affliction. Feverish and disoriented, I lay there on a bunk in the
pharmacy's courtyard for most of our only day in Kushinagar, my
body's position incidentally similar to that the Buddha is said to have
taken for his death in that very place. No profound spiritual visions
followed in my hours of fever, but I did apparently say some pretty
funny things to Shauna.*

*A little too close to death for comfort, those hours provided a chal-
lenging education in the reality of impermanence. After recovering
a little, I was able to make the trip by rickshaw to a few of Kushinagar's sacred sites, where we meditated together briefly in the day's
fading light.*

– Austin Pick

Sleeping & Eating

There are several options for accommodation in Kushinagar. At the time of writing, the **Burmese** and **Tibetan Monastaries** were the only places that still run on
a donation basis. The rooms, however, are very basic and bathrooms are common.
The **Chinese/Linh Son** and **Japanese-Sri Lankan** temples are also really good
budget options. The **Pathik Niwas Government Hotel and Restaurant** is nice
and has good food, though it's a little pricey. Pilgrims wanting 5-star accommodation can choose between the **Lotus Nikko Hotel** and **The Royal Residency**.

The **Yama Kwality Pilgrim's Restaurant** (also called the Yama Café) is run by
a very warm and helpful meditator-couple who have a lot of knowledge about the
pilgrimage sites. The restaurant, which serves good food, is located between the
Chinese and Burmese Temples. The **Chinese Temple** also offers great Asian-style
vegetarian food during the tourist months (October to March). You will find other
food options in the classier hotels or at one of the many street *dhabas*.

Kushinagar is 55 km east of Gorakhpur, a transit hub for the region. Regular **buses** leave from the bus stand near Gorakhpur's train station. Alternately, you can take a shared or private **jeep** (recommended), which departs from the train station or the nearby intersection. Buses and jeeps will drop you at Kushinagar's triple archway entrance. When heading back to Gorakhpur, you can wait by this gateway and hire a jeep or signal a bus to stop. Alternatively, you can go directly to the bus station in Kasia (3 km), where the buses start.

Gorakhpur is well connected to the region's major cities by **train**. Routes include:

- Vaishali Express 2554/2553 (Delhi-Barauni via Vaishali)
- Kashi Express 1027/1028 (Dadar/Mumbai-Gorakhpur)
- Shaheed Express 4674/4673 (Delhi-Darbangha)
- Kushinagar Express 1015/1016 (Mumbai-Gorakhpur)
- Ahmedabad Gorakhpur Express 5045/5046 (Ahmedabad-Gorakhpur)
- Purvanchal Express 5048/5049 (Gorakhpur-Howrah/Kolkata via Patna)
- Avadh Assam Express 5610/5609 (Delhi-Guwahati)

Alternatively, you can come via Deoria (35 km) which is also connected by train to Vārāṇasī.

For those heading to Nepal, beware of the touts trying to sell you over-priced tickets to Kathmandu or Pokhara. It's safer and easier to buy your tickets directly at the stations or on the buses as you go. See Kathmandu's border crossing section for more information.

If you find that your time is short or you are just too tired to continue onwards with the Indian railway and bus system, private taxis can be hired from Gorakhpur (or from one of the travel agents in Kushinagar) to take you to Kapilavatthu (148 km) en route to Shravasti (274 km), or to any of the pilgrimage places in Bihar. This option will be more expensive, but may save much-needed time and energy. Consider sharing the journey with fellow pilgrims.

If you need to spend a night in Gorakhpur to catch an early bus or train, there are some passable budget hotels across from the train station, such as the **Standard Hotel** and **Hotel Siddhartha**. Cheaper mid-range options in the city's centre (about 1.5 km from the train station) include **Hotel Marina, President Hotel and Restaurant,** and the **Arogya Mandir**. You can find plenty of restaurants around the train station, or try your luck at the vegetarian restaurant inside the station. Gorakhpur is a noisy transit centre infamous for its mosquitos; bring a net for your hotel room!

Excursions

Pawanagar/Fazilnagar (*Pāvā*)

Beyond this small town (30 km from Kushinagar) is a grassy mound covering a stūpa supposed to mark the spot where the Buddha took his last meal at Cunda the Silversmith's house. Other than the small **Jain Dharamsala** 1 km from the stūpa, there's no obvious accommodation in this town, so you may want to consider making the journey as a day trip from Kushinagar. There are no direct buses either, so it's best to rent a taxi or jeep if you don't have a private vehicle.

Don

The brahmin Doṇa built a stūpa over the vessel in which the Buddha's ashes had been collected and from which he had divided them to the disputing clans (see above). Doṇa's stūpa today is a large grassy mound with a Hindu temple on it just outside the village of Don. Nearby is a graceful 9th century Tara statue, which is worshipped by locals as a Hindu goddess.

Don village is off the road that goes between Patna and Kushinagar, and can only be reached by private vehicle. From Patna, go through Siwan and Chhapra. From Kusinara, take the road via Gopalganj.

Arogya Mandir Nature Cure Hospital

Arogya Mandir Nature Cure Hospital is one of the few tranquil and clean areas around noisy Gorakhpur. Arogya Mandir can be a good place to stop and re-energize for a few days, especially if you have fallen ill during your pilgrimage. The four-acre property located about 5 km from the railway station was founded by the late Vipassana teacher, health and spiritual writer, and Gandhian freedom fighter, Dr. Vithaldas Modi. Arogya Mandir offers a wide range of therapies such as fasting, enemas, oil massage, steam baths, mud-pack therapy, yoga, brisk walks and badminton. For more information and reservations, visit www.arogyamandir.com

Beyond the
Middle Land

The North:
Delhi

India's bustling capital is usually a source of severe culture shock for travellers arriving in the subcontinent for the first (or tenth!) time. The city's manifold extremes expose your senses to a myriad of contrasting realities: modern high rises hovering over makeshift slums and hutments, spired sandstone temples and domed marble mosques; streets crowded with continually honking cars fender-to-tail against cows meandering amidst the frenetic traffic of rickshaws, motorbikes, pedestrians and vendors. You'll find McDonald's restaurants just steps away from street stalls selling *samosa*, *pakoras*, fresh fruits and mysterious unknown edibles; the delicious aromas of curried vegetables and sandalwood perfumes blending with the awful stench of urine, cigarette smoke and diesel fumes. Sellers and eager touts add a chorus of calls to the sensory confusion, singing "Cheap tickets," and "Come see my shop," while gleeful children play street cricket and well-dressed businessmen talk on their mobile phones, all sharing sidewalk space with aged holy men wearing *dhotis*, chanting mantras and asking for alms along streets where ATM machines spit out rupees a mere stone's throw away from shrines for religious deities offering salvation to both the financially and spiritually poor. The chaotic current of Delhi's mesmerizing and consuming streets—which almost seems sacred, protective and even strangely orderly— prepares you to more fully surrender yourself to your journey in the Buddha's land.

This exceptional city is divided into two sections: Delhi (or Old Delhi) and New Delhi, though the greater capital area now includes a growing suburban sprawl and several satellite cities. Old Delhi, or Shahjahanbad, was the intermittent capital of the Mughal Empire between the 12th and 17th centuries, and today remains the primary Muslim sector, with its innumerable mosques and tombs, *halal* restaurants and butcher shops, markets and forts. **Majnu Ka Tila**, the relaxed Tibetan refugee and foreign tourist centre, is also to be found in Old Delhi. New Delhi was originally designed as the British capital after the imperial government shifted its headquarters from Kolkata, and the city continues to be India's capital. Today, this part of Delhi is a fairly open green space, with wide avenues, tourist ghettos, exclusive gated communities, government buildings and foreign embassies.

Shopping, Activities, Services & Sites

Delhi is a great place to satisfy most of your travel needs or buy souvenirs to bring back home. **Pahar Ganj**, Delhi's ubiquitous travellers' ghetto, is crammed with shops selling all sorts of stuff, though shoppers will have to look hard to find quality products here. Nestled between the Red Fort, Jami Masjid, and Fatehpuri Masjid in Old Delhi is **Chandni Chowk**, a congested yet colourful bazaar where you can get good deals on household items, art, jewellery, carpets and perfumes.

Connaught Place in central Delhi is made up of uniformly concentric ring roads lined with boutique shops, street stalls, restaurants, and hotels. The 3-storied **Khadi Bhavan** in Connaught Place is one of India's best retailers for *khadi*, or homespun cloth. Around the corner in the Regal Building, **The Shop** has excellent, high quality clothing, linen, furniture, ceramics, incense and essential oils; and **People Tree**, an artisan's collective boutique, carries a unique assortment of printed t-shirts, clothing, decorative items and books. **Fab India** and **Soma** are also popular Connaught Place choices for ethical clothing, handicrafts and furniture."

Book lovers will become infatuated with Connaught Place's numerous bookshops and pavement stalls, whose books are much cheaper than in the West. The **New Book Depot** (18 B-Block), **Bookworm** (29B Radial Rd #4), and **People Tree** (in the Regal Building) all have good selections of books on Indian religion and culture. Delhi's pavement booksellers specialize in bootleg copies of popular books, much cheaper but often of inferior quality—look for misspellings on the covers. Sellers, when asked, will often be honest about which copies are counterfeit. Ansari Road in Daryaganj (3 km from Connaught) is lined with bookstores, including the Indian branch of **Oxford University Press** (2-11 Ansari Road). **Motilal Banarsidas**—the leading Indian publisher on anything India—is located at 41 UA Bungalow Road in Jawahar Nagar, not far from Delhi University.

On Janpath, just off Connaught Place, you'll find the **Central Cottage Industries Emporium**, which has, primarily, high-quality goods from around the country; convenient for shoppers but more expensive than elsewhere in India, as with most shops in the city. Around the corner on Baba Kharak Singh Marg are state emporiums selling handicrafts from their particular states. If you're really keen on shopping, trek out to the N-Block and M-Block of the Greater Kailash suburb where you'll find excellent high-end stores such as **Fab India** selling clothes, furniture, kitchenware, bedding, art, handicrafts, jewellery, carpets and more. Fab India also has a smaller boutique clothing stores in Connaught Place (28 B-Block) and **Khan Market**, a high-end shopping enclave in central Delhi.

The **All India Institute of Medical Services** on Ansari Nagar has good facilities, but the more expensive **East-West Medical Centre** on Golf Links Rd. is one of the best places to seek allopathic medical treatment in the country. Check out the US embassy website for comments on medical treatment in New Delhi and the rest of India: http://newdelhi.usembassy.gov/medical_information2.html

If interested in exploring the rich history and sites of Delhi, you can visit the city's several museums, book a guided tour with a travel agency, or venture out alone with the help of a city guidebook, available at any bookstore, the **Government of India Tourist Office** (88 Janpath Rd.), or one of the several Delhi Tourism Corporation offices around the city.

National Museum

The most important place for meditators in the immediate Delhi region is the National Museum, home to about a dozen pieces of bone from the Buddha's body, found at the Kapilavatthu site in Piprahwa. The museum's Buddhist gallery, usually not busy on weekdays, is actually a very quiet place to meditate and absorb the energy of the sacred relics that lay before you there. No one will disturb you, and the few visitors and guards will likely find you mildly entertaining, if not inspiring.

The Buddhist gallery also has an outstanding collection of stone, bronze, terracotta and wooden sculptures that have been brought from several archaeological sites throughout India, as well as ancient Tibetan ritual objects and *thangka* (cloth scroll paintings).

Besides Buddhist art, this immense museum has a fantastic collection of 1 000-year-old miniature Indian paintings; 2 300-year-old Indian jewellery; 1 300-year-old manuscripts made from palm leaves, tree barks, metal and cloth; 2 700-year-old coins; 800-year-old wood carvings; 300-year-old musical instruments and galleries displaying paintings, textiles, weapons and tribal artefacts. Needless to say, it can take several days to fully enjoy everything at the National Museum.

The National Museum is on Janpath Road off Connaught Place, and is open from 10 a.m. to 5 p.m., Tuesday to Sunday. The museum is located next door to the Archaeological Survey of India, which is the place to send complaints about what many feel are discriminatory entry-fee policies at the country's national monuments.

Raj Ghat

On the bank of the sacred Yamuna River is Raj Ghat, where Mahatma Gandhi was cremated after his assassination in 1948. Near the ghat is the Gandhi Darshan, a nice pictography of Gandhi's life, and the Gandhi Smarak Sangrahalaya, which exhibits some of the Mahatma's personal possessions.

Tibet House

This centre, featuring a sizable museum and library, has a unique display of Tibetan Buddhist ceremonial objects that were carried out of Tibet during the Dalai Lama's 1959 flight into exile from the Chinese occupation. The centre is also host to interesting lectures about Tibetan religion, culture and politics. Tibet House is on Lodi Road south of India Gate in Central Delhi, and is open Monday to Saturday from 9:30 a.m. to 5:30 p.m. (closed for lunch between 1 and 2 p.m.).

Sleeping & Eating

Most travellers prefer to stay and eat in **Pahar Ganj**, **Connaught Place**, or **Majnu Ka Tila**. Although not as expensive as Mumbai, guest houses in Delhi aren't cheap. The least expensive and least sanitary options are in **Old Delhi**, but they're far away from all the tourist services, so the next best choice for budget travellers is Pahar Ganj, near the New Delhi Railway Station, with its endless, over-priced restaurants and hotels such as **Vivek**, **Bright**, **Sweet Dream**, **New Shiva** and **Payal**.

Mid-range options include the **Sri Lankan Buddhist Pilgrims' Rest House** (opposite the train station, to the left of the entrance to Pahar Ganj), **Major's Den** (an explicitly substance-free option), **Hotel Sampurn Inn**, **Metropolis Tourist**

Home, and **Hotel Rak International** in Pahar Ganj, and **YMCA Tourist Hotel, YWCA International Guest House** and **Janpath Guest House** near Connaught Place.

Most of the guest houses in Majnu Ka Tila, far north of the city centre, are in the mid-range category and are all of more-or-less equal quality. The relaxed atmosphere here compared to other areas makes its relative isolation worth the inconvenience of distance, especially if you're taking an overnight bus to Dharamsala, many of which arrive and depart from this neighbourhood. The **World Buddhist Centre** in East Kailash (10 km from New Delhi Railway Station and 16 km from the airport) offers a relatively quiet and clean space for weary travellers.

Luxury hotels include **Lasagrita Tourist Home** and **Kailash Inn** in Old Delhi; **Prince Poonia, Relax** and **Vinn** in Pahar Ganj; **Aman Delux** and **Alka Hotel & Vegetarian Restaurant** in Connaught Place, and, away from all the action, **Master Guest House** on Shankar Road west of Connaught Place. Fortress-like 5-star hotels—with their microcosm of restaurants, cafés, hairdressers, shops, lounges, and banquet halls—abound in the New Delhi area: The **Connaught** and **Imperial** near Connaught Place; and **Claridges, Oberoi, Mauryan Sheraton,** and **Metropolitan Nikko,** all located on the fringes of downtown New Delhi.

For those arriving or departing by air at a ridiculous hour, it's possible to stay in Mahipalpur, a village turned boom-town south-west of central Delhi near the Indira Gandhi Airport. All accommodation here is decidedly in the mid- to high-range, but discounts are negotiable when business is slow. **Airport Inn** (A-7, Street No.1) is an affordable option, but directions are difficult in the narrow lanes of the neighbourhood, so look for signs off Mahipalpur Extension, National Highway (NH) 8. To spend your last nights in luxury, the **Radisson Hotel** and **Uppal's Orchid Hotel** are nearby, further south on NH8. Ask your hotel for restaurant suggestions: South Delhi's shopping enclaves offer nice dining and diversions: **Basant Lok, Sunder Nagar** and **South Extension Markets I & II** are all accessible from Mahipalpur by rickshaw or taxi.

Good restaurants abound in Delhi, and the best way to discover them is to ask locals or seek out places that specialize in what you're craving. Recommended places around Connaught Place include the North Indian restaurant **Rajdhani** (all-you-can-eat thāli is at great value), opposite the Khadi Bhavan. For good South Indian fare try **Sagar Ratna** (15 K-Block), **Banana Leaf** (12 N-Block), and **Saravana Bhavan** (two locations: one around the corner from the Khadi Bhavan, and one on Janpath near the Cottage Industries Emporium). For old-world colonial atmosphere drop in at the **United Coffee House,** but be aware that the food doesn't always match the sumptuous décor. Many of Delhi's restaurants aspire for an international standard of excellence, and have prices to match. Budget travellers may need to explore a bit to find affordable places.

Coming & Going

For moving about Delhi, **taxis** and their less expensive counterparts—**rick-shaws**—make life easier, although drivers usually refuse to use the meters or show you the fare conversion cards. Tourists are big business, and you should expect the initial asking rate to be anywhere from double to five times the price accepted by locals. Be aware of the distance you'll be travelling, and ask hotel or restaurant staff what you should expect to pay at a fair price—then don't be afraid to haggle with drivers and wave them off if they refuse to deal straight with you. This is true everywhere in India, but especially in the cities.

Depending on where you're going, the **metro** can be the cheapest and quickest way to get around the city. Delhi's expanding metro system connects several major areas, and will soon provide service to the airport. There are two stations in Pahar Ganj (one at the Railway Station, and one at the end of the main bazaar opposite the Rama Krishna Mission), as well as a station in Connaught Place called Rajiv Chowk. Tickets are cheap, and one- to three-day tourist cards are available for unlimited short distance travel. See www.delhimetrorail.com for routes, schedules and developments.

Intra-city buses in the Delhis are more complicated than in Mumbai. Some are private, some are public, and they both travel similar but slightly different routes. Although generally inexpensive, prices vary between the companies. If you want to travel by bus, ask locals which ones to take and where to get on board. During crowded rush hours, beware of pickpockets and gropers. Be cautious from whom you accept information, as scam-artists may try to mislead you.

As India's capital, Delhi is well-connected by **air** to every major city on the sub-continent. Air travellers should keep in mind that the domestic and international terminals of the **Indira Gandhi Airport** are 5 km apart. If you need to connect, or you end up at the wrong one, there is a regular shuttle service between the two.

Domestic tickets can either be purchased from an agent, or by going directly to the airline's office in the city. The offices of Indian Airlines and Jet Airways are in Connaught Place at F-Block and N-Block respectively, and Sahara Airlines is on Kasturba Gandhi Marg, just off of Connaught Place. International airline offices are generally around Connaught Place or one of its connecting roads, and it's best to find addresses and current office hours on-line. When shopping for plane tickets, it is also recommended to shop for tickets on-line and then compare prices with any travel agent you visit before purchasing—price differences can be significant.

The Indira Gandhi Airport is about 12 km from the Connaught Place and Pahar Ganj areas, and traffic can slow the journey to more than a half-hour. Due to notoriously slow security check procedures, travellers should allow at least three hours before scheduled flight departure for check-in at the airport. See the Mahipalpur section in Sleeping & Eating for accommodation options near the airport.

All city and state **buses** (regular and deluxe) leave from the Interstate Bus Terminal (ISBT) near Kashmiri Gate in Old Delhi. Tickets for these buses can be bought at one of the counters at the bus stand. Private deluxe buses also leave from ISBT, Pahar Ganj, and Connaught Place. Tickets for private buses are sold by travel agents.

Getting **train** tickets in Delhi is perhaps easier than in any other place in India, thanks to the special air-conditioned Foreign Tourist Ticket Reservation Office located on the second floor of the New Delhi Railway Station (open Monday to Saturday from 7:30 a.m. to 5:00 p.m., and Sundays from 8:00 a.m. to 2:00 p.m.). Avoid travel agents and touts near the railway station, who will tell you that the office is closed. Besides the main office at the station, there are also Foreign Tourist Railway Reservation Offices at the airport and at N-Block in Connaught Place. Paying for tickets in rupees requires an encashment certificate or ATM receipt, but US dollars, British pounds and Euros are always accepted. You will also need to show your passport. Remember that you can also book train tickets on-line; see 'Travelling in India' for more information.

Here are a few trains that might get you where you want to go:

- New Delhi Dehra Dun Shatabdi Express 2017/2018 (New Delhi-Haridwar-Dehra Dun)
- Delhi Dehra Dun Kotdwara Mussoorie Express 4041/4042 (New Delhi-Haridwar-Dehra Dun)
- Bandra–Dehra Dun Express 9019/9020 (Bandra/Mumbai-Mathura-New Delhi-Haridwar-Dehra Dun)
- Howrah Dehra Dun Upasana Express 3103/3104 (Howrah/Kolkata-Patna-Vārāṇasī-Haridwar-Dehra Dun)
- Howrah Dehra Dun Express 3009/3010 (Howrah/Kolkata-Gayā-Vārāṇasī-Lucknow-Haridwar-Dehra Dun)
- Delhi Jaipur Express 2413/2414 (Delhi-Jaipur)
- Delhi Ahmedabad Ashram Express 2916/2917 (Delhi-Jaipur-Ahmedabad)
- Delhi Ahmedabad Mail 9106/9107 (Delhi-Jaipur-Ahmedabad)
- Bhuj Bareilly Al Hazrat Express 4311/4312 (Delhi-Jaipur-Ahmedabad-Bhuj)
- Rajdhani Express 2951/2952 (Mumbai-New Delhi)
- Punjab Mail 2137/2138 (Mumbai CST-Igatpuri-Nasik-Jalgaon-Bhopal-Vidisha-New Delhi)
- Dadar Amritsar Express 1057/1058 (Dadar/Mumbai-Igatpuri-Nasik-Jalgaon-Bhopal-Vidisha-New Delhi-Amritsar)
- Nizamuddin Goa Express 2779/2780 (Hazrat Nizamuddin/New Delhi-Bhopal-Pune-Goa)
- Andhra Express 2723/2724 (Hyderabad-New Delhi)
- Poorva Express 2303/2304 (Howrah/Kolkata-Mughalsarai-New Delhi)
- Poorva Express 2381/2382 (Howrah/Kolkata-Gayā-Vārāṇasī-New Delhi)
- Rajdhani Express 2301/2302 (Howrah/Kolkata-Gayā-Delhi)
- Rajdhani Express 2305/2306 (Howrah/Kolkata-Patna-New Delhi)
- Rajdhani Express 2313/2314 (Sealdah/Kolkata-Gayā-Mughalsarai-New Delhi)

- Howrah Kalka Mail 2311/2312 (Howrah/Kolkata-Gayā-Delhi)
- Sriganganagar Udyan Abhatoofan Express 3007/3008 (Howrah/Kolkata-Patna-Mughalsarai-New Delhi)
- Puri New Delhi Purushottam Express 2801/2802 (Puri-Bhubaneshwar-Cuttack-Mughalsarai-Allahabad-Kanpur-New Delhi)
- Bhubaneshwar New Delhi Rajdani Express 2421/2422/2443/2444 (Bhubaneshwar-Cuttack-Kanpur-New Delhi)

Awkward arrival times may add to the initial difficulties of travelling through Delhi. After landing sometime between midnight and dawn (as most international flights do) and spending at least an hour hazily filing through long passport checks, customs queues and money-exchange counters, you'll have ample opportunity to strengthen your equanimity. Besides getting that late night red-eye syndrome and having to wake someone up at 2 a.m. to let you into a guest house, it's likely that you'll also have to deal with dubious taxi-drivers and travel agents. Even if you've already reserved your hotel room before arriving, there's a fair chance that the taxi driver will attempt to convince you that your hotel is full, closed, burnt down, inaccessible due to riots, or has lost your reservation—be firm and refuse to leave the car until the driver takes you to your intended destination.

To avoid these annoyances, go to the Delhi Traffic Police Prepaid Taxi Booth just outside and to the right of the International Terminal entrance; expect an extra service charge between 11 p.m. and 5 a.m. You can also consider taking one of the less expensive yet rickety Ex-Servicemen's Air Link Transport Service (EATS) buses that leave semi-regularly from the airport and stop at the ISBT Bus Terminal in Old Delhi (20 minutes), F-Block in Connaught Place (30 minutes), and New Delhi Railway Station (35 minutes). These buses are not much slower than taxis when travelling in the wee hours of the night.

One of the best ways to combat jet lag is to adapt, as quickly as possible, to the local time schedule when you arrive. Whether you try this method or head for sleep as soon as you hit your hotel, plan for a day or two of rest and slow introduction before striking out to experience India's capital in all its confounding fullness.

Excursions

Dhamma Paṭṭhāna, Kammaspur Vipassana Centre

Dhamma Paṭṭhāna ('Establishment of Dhamma') is located in the vicinity of the ancient town Kammāsadhamma where the Buddha gave the teachings of the celebrated *Mahāsatipaṭṭhāna Sutta*, from which Vipassana meditation in the tradition of S.N. Goenka is most closely derived:

> *This is the one and only way, bhikkhus, for the purification of beings, for the overcoming of sorrow and grief, for walking on the path of Truth, for the realization of Nibbāna: that is to say, the fourfold establishing of awareness.*

> *Which Four? Here, bhikkhus, a bhikkhu dwells ardent with awareness and the constant thorough understanding of impermanence, observing body in body...observing sensations in sensations...observ-*

ing mind in mind...observing mental contents in mental contents, having removed craving and aversion towards the world of mind and matter.

This lovely 7-acre centre is surrounded by agricultural lands and small village hamlets. Unique among centres, Dhamma Paṭṭhāna is reserved solely for old students of S.N. Goenka. Most of the courses held at the centre are the special 8-day *Satipaṭṭhāna Sutta* courses; however, long courses are also held several times each year. The centre has two meditation halls, a beautiful pagoda with 63 meditation cells, 59 individual cottages with attached bathrooms, and a gender-segregated dining hall.

Dhamma Paṭṭhāna is 45 km from the ISBT Bus Terminal in Old Delhi. Sometimes old students driving from Delhi have an extra seat available in their vehicle. For more information, registration, and transportation contact the centre or the city office.

Contact:
Dhamma Paṭṭhāna, Kammaspur Vipassana Centre
City Office:
Vipassana Sadhana Sansthan
Hemkunt Towers, 10ᵗʰ & 16ᵗʰ Floor
98 Nehru Place
New Delhi–110019
Tel: [+91] (0)11-26452772
Fax: [+91] (0)11-26470658
Note: It is also possible to buy books published by VRI at this office.

Centre:
Delhi-Ambala National Highway 1
Dist. Sonapat Haryana
Tel: [+91] (0)130-2482976/-2482976
E-mail: info@patthana.dhamma.org
Website: www.patthana.dhamma.org

McLeod Ganj
(Upper Dharamsala)

This relaxed, picturesque mountain town is a favourite destination for all sorts of travellers with varying degrees of interest in Buddhism, New-Age spiritual practices, healing therapies, Himālayan treks, and full moon trance parties. Being in this eclectic town is like taking a step outside of India. The narrow, hilly roads are dotted with international guest houses and restaurants, cinema halls, arts and handicrafts shops, travel agencies, money-changers, book stores, cyber cafés, and everything Tibetan, from artistic institutions to children's schools and Government-in-Exile offices to Vajrayana Buddhist monasteries. Kashmiri traders, local Gaddi tribespeople and sheep-herders add interesting colour to this fascinating centre of living globalization.

If you plan on visiting in the winter (November-March), don't forget to bring your woollens and thermals; Dharamsala is cold and snowy. However, if you can't spare room in your pack, there's no shortage of stylish, inexpensive warm clothing for sale around town. A good raincoat is necessary if you plan to visit Dharamsala— the rains here don't wait for monsoon!

Site-Sitting

Dhamma Sikhara, Himāchal Vipassana Kendra

Known as the foreigners' centre, Dhamma Sikhara ('Peak of Dhamma') is a centre where many meditators from around the world take their first course. Dhamma Sikhara is located in a 3-acre deodar cedar, pine, oak and rhododendron forest at an altitude of 2000 meters. The contemplative Himālayan atmosphere provides inspiration for meditators striving to dive into the pool of the mind, feel its subtle currents, and turn the tides of suffering toward freedom and ease.

At Dhamma Sikhara it's not uncommon for a single course to be given in up to nine languages, and the centre has adapted its facilities to support this incredible diversity. Dhamma Sikhara can accommodate about 80 students in three Dhamma halls: one main hall where instructions are normally given in Hindi and English, and where the English discourse is held; one hall equipped with about 30 sets of headphones for instructions and discourses in various languages; and one hall for the Hindi discourse, which is also used for group sittings by the community of local and foreign meditators staying in the region.

If you prefer silence during a course, then perhaps this centre isn't for you. Despite being high in the mountains, various noises can be heard from the surrounding villages, including school children, devotional mantras, Bollywood music, Tibetan horns and folk opera, Hebrew Sabbath prayers, mooing cows and baaing sheep. If you want to take up the challenge of centering the mind in the midst of these external energies, and if you want to engage with an international community of

Vipassana meditators, then Dhamma Sikhara is a great place to come for sitting and serving, even if it's just for a couple of hours per day. In addition to deepening your equanimity and compassion, this centre is an excellent place to foster friendships with other aspirants along the path.

Ten-day courses are held twice a month, from the 1st to the 12th and from the 15th to the 26th. Due to the cold winter climate, there are no courses between December and February. This particular centre has an explicit policy of not accepting students who have taken intoxicants 10 days before the course. The centre is located adjacent to the quaint village of Dharamkot, about 1.5 km above McLeod Ganj. From McLeod Ganj, the steep walk is about 20 minutes uphill. Taxis and rickshaws are also available.

Contact:
Dhamma Sikhara, Himāchal Vipassana Kendra
McLeod Ganj, Dharamsala
District Kangra
Himāchal Pradesh–176219
Tel: [+91] 92184-14051/ 92184-14050
E-mail: info@sikhara.dhamma.org
Website: www.sikhara.dhamma.org

I woke up and meditated for an hour before I packed my things and went upstairs for a quick breakfast. There I met Andrew, an Australian, who was also going to the centre to sit his first 10-day Vipassana course. We decided to meet later for lunch and then split the taxi fare up to the centre. Meanwhile I met a South African woman at the internet café who was also on her way to the meditation course.

At noon I met Andrew at the hotel, and we made our way up the steep road towards the taxi stand. On the way we met a Dutch guy, also on his way to the course, and invited him to join us. We had a leisurely lunch and spoke of meditation and reincarnation. A group of people in the restaurant overheard us, and said that they were also going to do the meditation course. It seemed everyone in town was going to the Vipassana centre.

Just after I arrived at Dhamma Sikhara, I was asked to help with registration and to hand out bedding and laundry bags to the students. "It's just like the army," one Israeli girl said.

Afterwards I settled into my room, which I shared with another Dhamma worker named Sharmila. In the beginning we worked non-stop, getting medicine and toiletries for the students and answering questions about the centre. We were three female servers, and we each took turns meditating in the hall and giving the others a break. We also took turns cleaning the toilets. There is nothing like cleaning rubbish bins to dissolve the ego. There I am with a Master's degree, emptying bins with sanitary napkins and soiled toilet paper. As

Sharmila says, "It helps to defleet the ego." I have shiploads of ego, and it would no doubt require a fleet of ships to carry it all away!

During the course I also realized that the human body is nothing but blood, faeces, urine, and mucus, just like the Buddha says in the Satipaṭṭhāna Sutta. I developed great wisdom by understanding that it's pointless attaching so much value and attraction to something that will inevitably decay.

Dhamma Sikhara is situated on a hill in a beautiful cedar forest frequently populated by monkeys. Everyone who works at the centre firmly believes that the monkeys are afraid of men but not women; that they recognize gender and react accordingly. The monkeys often need to be chased away because they are quite aggressive, and have even attacked students once or twice. But it is believed that women should never chase the monkeys away—that only the men should do it.

"What fiddle-faddle," I thought. "Monkeys afraid of men and not women, honestly!" The next time the monkeys were blocking the pathway to the female toilets, I decided to test out this theory. So I took a long stick, as the men do when they chase the monkeys away, and walked right into the middle of the troop. The monkeys all looked at me with bored expressions. They certainly didn't seem to be scared of me. When I walked past a young monkey, he scratched my jeans.

I cultivated mettā, or loving-kindness for him, and very soon he became bored and walked off. I felt a little silly in the middle of the troop, and didn't feel at all like I was chasing them away. Then I saw the large alpha-male yawning lazily, revealing his large sharp yellow-stained teeth, and decided that the experiment had gone far enough. I walked briskly, yet calmly, back to my room.

The monkeys weren't afraid of me; that was for sure. But I wasn't convinced that it was based on my gender. Perhaps a more logical explanation was that I was calm and peaceful, and didn't bang on the ground with the stick like you're supposed to do. I simply didn't buy into the conditioned thinking about gender. I could think of many women who could chase these monkeys away in a heartbeat.

The next day I heard that one of the male kitchen workers

had been chased by some monkeys. Strange, I thought, that the myth about gender still persists. I guess people believe what they want to believe.

On the last day of the course, noble silence ended and everyone came out of the course smiling. The students looked so happy and peaceful. Everyone thanked us profusely for all our help and kindness. We even got 'thank you' cards.

When the course finished, all of the students helped to clean, but the Israelis, especially, did the best clean-up I've ever seen. "I'll do toilets," one skinny girl said. "In the army I was in charge of cleaning toilets." Later, when I went to the toilet, everything was sparkling. I was amazed.

The students continued to thank us as they left. Their gratitude was overwhelming, and I realized, yet again, what a privilege it is to serve others.

– Chantel Oosthuysen

Hiking & Trekking

There are several amazing hikes in the Dharamsala region. **Triund** and **Llaqa** are two spots that offer awe-inspiring views of the Dhauladhar range's 5 200 metre high peaks. From Dharamkot, north of McLeod Ganj near Dhamma Sikhara, take the middle path through the village and then follow the footpath through mixed cedar, oak, pine and rhododendron forests, which diminish as you near the rocky mountain crags that lead eventually to Triund's breathtaking 3 000 metre ridge (7 km, 3.5 hours). To get to Llaqa (also referred to as Snow Line), continue on from Triund for another 5 km, 1.5 hours. Keep in mind that there will probably be too much snow to make it up to Triund between November and March.

Triund makes for a great day trip, and, for the adventurous, so does Llaqa. There are a few tea stalls en route, but it's still a good idea to bring your own food and water in the event they're not open. If you want to spend the night at Triund, you can sleep in one of the nearby caves, stone shepherd huts, or the government forest rest house. The rest house can be booked through the Himāchal Pradesh Tourism and Development Corporation (HPTDC) office in Kotwali Bazaar. Around Llaqa, there are also a couple of caves and stone huts.

For a shorter hike from Dharamkot, take the easy trail through the forest to **Naddi Village** (45 minutes) where views of the Dhauladhar range are impressive.

From Dharamkot it's about 2 hours to the **waterfalls** beyond and to the left of the Galu Devi/Shiva Temple. Follow the route described for reaching Triund, then turn off and follow the arrows painted on the rocks after you've reached the temple.

The **Bhagsu waterfalls**, beyond the Bhagsu temple, also make for a nice hike, except on weekends and holidays when the spot is frequently inundated with hordes of rowdy and sometimes inebriated tourists. You can get to Bhagsu via upper

Dharamkot, lower Dharamkot, or McLeod Ganj. Ask locals for directions. If you hike beyond the Bhagsu waterfalls, be careful on the dangerous rocky trails and take care not to disturb any Tibetan meditators who may be holding private retreats in the surrounding caves or stone huts.

The best time for serious longer treks is generally from June to September, although the trails in some regions open in May and close in October. Consult the **Mountaineering Institute**, located on the footpath between Dharamkot and McLeod Ganj. They have lots of information about trekking in the region and can suggest reliable guides. Lonely Planet's *Trekking in the Indian Himalaya* is a wealth of information for trekkers, and Charlie Loram's *Trekking in Ladakh* provides detailed hand-drawn maps from village to village, including campsite locations, water points and invaluable tips on how to organize a trek.

Day after day, the hours and scenery roll by, yet the breath is ever-present, a constant focal point that keeps me centred. Sometimes it is the only sound to pierce the glacial desert of heart and mind. Walking for one month between Manali and Leh was the most difficult, yet perhaps most rewarding thing I have ever done in my life. I shared this journey with two other women whom I barely knew, yet often wondered: how many times have we walked this Path together before?

Chortens (stūpas), mani-walls, prayer wheels and flags are all intrinsic parts of the Himālayan landscape. These holy icons punctuated the journey, providing token moments to stop, rest, and contemplate the processes involved along the Buddha's path. Originally built to house the remains of saints, Himālayan chortens are also intended to ward off evil spirits. Mani-walls are made up of intricately carved stones, many representing the Buddha or the famous Tibetan mantra "Om Mani Padme Hum." The same mantra, forever on the lips of local Buddhists, is often inscribed on the prayer wheels, which vary in size from small pocket versions to huge cylindrical drums. The creative act of setting a prayer wheel in motion is reminiscent of the rotation of the universe and the Wheel of Dhamma. The five-coloured Tibetan prayer flags, whipping in the air atop every mountain pass, were a welcome sight after a difficult ascent!

During our trek some monasteries gave us a room in exchange for a small donation; others invited us to set up camp nearby. Usually the monks would offer us a cup of butter tea and a piece of tsampa, Tibetan barley bread, to munch on. One afternoon we were invited to stay in a white-washed gompa perched on the edge of a cliff. Our tiny room, nestled around a central cave where a medicinal spring flows, was healing after the long day's walk. That evening we were fortunate to observe the monks create a sand mandala—a gorgeous representation of the cosmos made from colourful sand particles. Once it was completed and blessed with prayers, it was sent to be immersed in the river during a ritual ceremony, thus destroying in an instant days of intricate labour. Anicca!

On our last evening before reaching our destination, Balwant, our faithful friend and horseman, warned us that we must set out at 2:30 a.m. to cross the pass before the snow became too soft for the horses. A smile tickled my chapped lips as we all joined in a song of warmth before dozing off. What seemed to be only minutes later, we began the steep climb. As we ascended, the oxygen decreased, and all sounds, other than the whispered thunder of pure breath, melted away. "I" can smell the trickle of sweat down my back; yet "I" am not this itching three-day old blister. The knot in my throat grows tighter. Who is this struggling "I" whose eye sees not the undivided silent presence? Prayer flags in sight, yet they too will pass away.

The moon has risen, peaked and waned. When I reached Leh, the final destination on this trek, I was aware that many unexplored avenues leading to the heart of the Temple still lay ahead.

– Elissa Crete

Volunteering, Workshops, Therapies & Sites

There's an incredible wealth of activities available in this mountain haven. There are dozens of programmes going on around McLeod Ganj all the time. If you want to do some volunteer work, there are plenty of opportunities to lend a hand by teaching English or computer skills at one of the **Tibetan Children's Village (TCV)** schools, the **Yongling School**, or at one of the monasteries. Local organizations also sometimes need help taking care of newly-arrived refugees. Signs are usually posted around town, or you can inquire at one of the institutions mentioned above.

There are always various performances, courses and workshops going on around town or in the nearby villages of Dharamkot and Bhagsu: language, cooking, yoga, Ayurveda, massage, music, art and philosophy, to name just a few. Posters are usually plastered around town advertising the latest events. Some well-known landmarks for courses are at the **Himalayan Iyengar Yoga Institute, Library of Tibetan Works & Archives (LTWA)** and **Tibetan Institute of Performing Arts (TIPA)**.

When sick, many travellers prefer to restore their health through Tibetan medicine. The **Men Tsee Khang** is the most reputed organization and has branches all over India. There are also several other alterative healing modalities available in the area (Tibetan, Indian, and Western/New-Age); however, make sure the person's credentials are legitimate. Ask locals or other travellers about their experiences.

In addition, there are two main conventional hospitals in Dharamsala. One is a **Himāchal State Hospital**; the other is **Delek Hospital**, a private institution with a staff of Tibetan, Indian and, sometimes, Western doctors. While both are chaotic, the private hospital tends to be more efficient, and you can get blood, urine and stool tests done rather quickly if you arrive ahead of the crowds first thing in the morning.

Dharamsala has a range of Tibetan and Indian arts and handicrafts. If you're looking to do some shopping, browse among the endless tiny shops selling trinkets, clothing, jewellery and stones. Prices vary, so do some comparison and some bargaining. Higher quality items are usually to be found in the well-established galleries throughout town. You may wish to help refugees by buying from supporting shops and organizations, usually well-advertised. There are also a few non-profit co-operatives where you can watch some of the production in action, such as the **Gaddi Women's Co-op** in Bhagsu for local-style clothes, art and homemade foods like nut butters, tofu and soy milk; the **Tibetan Children's Village (TCV) Handicraft Centre** in McLeod Ganj for carpets, paintings, cushions, and statues; and the **Khadi Bhavan** and **Himāchal Emporium** in Lower Dharamsala's Kotwali Bazaar for clothes and material.

Dharamsala's spiritual energy primarily revolves around Vajrayana, or Tibetan Buddhism, and there are a number of important sites associated with the religious and cultural traditions of the Tibetan people.

Namgyal Monastic Complex
Locally referred to as the *Main Temple*, the Dalai Lama's vibrant monastic complex is just south, down the hill from McLeod Ganj. Adjacent to his residence, where he gives monthly public audiences, is the distinctive **Tsuglag Khang Temple**, which houses three magnificent statues of the Buddha and the Bodhisattvas Avalokiteśvara and Padmasambhava. Next door is the **Kalachakra Temple**, with its exquisite murals of the Tibetan "Wheel of Time" *mandala*.

Monks from all schools of Tibetan Buddhism come to Namgyal to study at the Institute of Buddhist Dialectics. Students here learn how to objectively analyse and debate all forms of belief and knowledge, including the Buddha's. For Tibetans, especially those from the Gelug School to which the Dalai Lama belongs, logic is an essential part of understanding the reality of mind and matter. When the monks here aren't engaged in their meditative prayers and peace rituals, you will find them in the lovely courtyard practising debating or playing badminton.

The Dalai Lama usually gives annual public teachings twice a year. One session is held during the monsoon in July/August while the other, more popular session begins after *Losar*, the Tibetan New Year in February/March. The teachings are free, but you'll need to register and get a pass from the **Branch Security Office** on Bhagsu Road to attend; bring your passport and two passport-size photos. The teachings are given in Tibetan, and simultaneous translation is broadcast locally in several languages, so you'll also need an FM Radio and headset. You can buy radios anywhere in McLeod Ganj, or rent them at the **Lha Charitable Trust Office** on Temple Road across from the State Bank of India. Seating is limited for lay people at the Namgyal Complex, and many stake their claim on a patch of ground with a cushion or scrap of cardboard weeks in advance of the teachings.

At the entrance to the complex is the **Tibet Museum**. The museum's heart-wrenching exhibit of the tragedy that the Tibetan people have endured is an inspiration for everyone striving to cultivate compassion and forgiveness towards those who have caused us pain. The nearby **Namgyal Bookshop** sells a variety of books about Tibetan Buddhism and culture (particularly those by the Dalai Lama) as well as postcards and other gift items.

The mile-long Lingkhor pilgrim's path encircling the Monastic Complex is a tranquil place to contemplate the Buddha's teachings. To find the path, continue on the road to the left of Namgyal's entrance. After a minute or so you will see the dirt path on your right. As with all Buddhist monuments, remember to walk in a clockwise direction.

Kangra Art Museum
This interesting museum, just up from the bus stand in lower Dharamsala, houses beautiful local art of the past 400 years. The museum is open Tuesdays to Saturdays from 10:00 a.m. to 5:00 p.m.

Sleeping & Eating

If you're only staying a few nights, it's best to stay in McLeod Ganj. Budget travellers have dozens of guest houses and restaurants to choose from, most of which are of a similar quality. Many of the monasteries and nunneries also offer simple accommodation. At the north-eastern edge of town you'll find a series of quiet Tibetan-run guest houses flanking a steep staircase off Tipa Road. These quite decent budget options, including **Paljor Gakyil** and **Loling** guest houses, feature lovely rooftop views of the Dharamsala region, and can be a convenient location for meditators because the staircase connects to Dharamkot Road, which leads directly uphill to the Vipassana Centre.

Some good mid-range and luxury options in McLeod Ganj include **Hunted Hill House** and **Ladies Venture**, both downhill from the central chorten, past the Post Office near **Lung Ta**, an excellent Japanese restaurant. Also recommended are **Hotel Tibet**, near Nick's Italian Restaurant, and hotels **Bhagsu**, **Surya Natraj**, and **Him Queen**, all on Hotel Bhagsu Road off Temple Road, up the street from the HPTDC Tourist Centre.

In addition to those already mentioned, McLeod Ganj is home to many popular cafés and restaurants. **Lhamo's Croissant Café** on Bhagsu Road is an excellent place to escape the noise and push of Dharamsala's often crowded streets, and is decorated with photographs and pieces from the Norbulingka Institute. Try the family-run **Jimmy's Italian Kitchen**, with two branches near the central chorten, for what is perhaps Dharamsala's best Italian. **The Pizzeria** in Dharamkot, however, is famous for wood-fire baked pizza.

Many places, such as the **Green**, **Om** and **Shangrila** guest houses/restaurants, sell boiled and filtered water at prices lower than bottled water. Avoid using disposable plastic whenever possible, as it's a problematic source of pollution.

If you plan on staying for a longer period of time, you should consider renting an apartment in McLeod Ganj, either near the Namgyal Complex or below the Post

Office. Around Dharamkot and Bhagsu villages there are several guest houses, rooms with kitchens, and houses for rent. It's advisable to spend a night or two in a guest house while you explore available options. **Rishi Bhavan** and **Chopra House**, both downhill from the Vipassana centre, are good, quiet places to start.

Keep in mind that there is usually a shortage of rooms in McLeod Ganj during the Tibetan New Year (*Losar*) when Tibetans and foreigners alike flock to receive blessings and hear the Dalai Lama give his annual public teachings.

Coming & Going

To get to Dharamsala, you have several options. The most comfortable route is to take a **train** to Pathankot (90 km, 4 hours to Dharamsala) or Chakki Bank (95 km, 4 hours to Dharamsala), which are usually on the lines heading to Jammu Tawi. Regular **buses** run from these towns to Dharamsala. From Dharamsala, regular buses and **shared jeep-taxis** make the run uphill to McLeod Ganj (10 km by road, 4 km by foot path). Private **taxis** are also available in Pathankot, Chakki Bank, Dharamsala and McLeod Ganj.

As another option, it's possible to take the **Kangra Valley Narrow-Gauge Train** from Pathankot, which departs seven times daily from Track 4. After an up-to-five-hour journey to Kangra Mandir Station, it's another hour by auto-rickshaw and bus to Dharamsala and McLeod Ganj. This is a scenic but substantially longer haul than a direct bus from Pathankot, and thus only recommended for the adventurous.

If you're willing to sacrifice comfort for expediency, daily regular, deluxe and sleeper **buses** run from Delhi (570 km, 13 hours). Buses depart in the evening from Pahar Ganj (near New Delhi Railway Station), Majnu Ka Tila (North Delhi), or the ISBT Bus Terminal, and arrive in McLeod Ganj the following morning. You can buy your tickets from one of the many travel agents around Delhi, or directly from the bus station. If you're susceptible to nausea, be warned that much of the road to and from Dharamsala is winding and rugged; consider travelling by sleeper bus or train, as lying down helps to minimize nausea.

Daily buses departing from the road near McLeod Ganj's taxi stand make the same journey in reverse, and most terminate in Delhi's Majnu Ka Tila neighborhood. Buy your tickets in advance from any of Dharamsala's tourist agents.

Regular and deluxe buses also go to and from Amritsar (200 km, 7 hours), Manali (250 km 11 hours), Rishikesh (550 km, 15 hours), Dehra Dun (500 km, 14 hours), and Shimla (317 km, 10 hours), among other places.

Flights from Delhi, Shimla and Kullu to Gaggal, which is about 25 km from McLeod Ganj, are also available a few times per week.

Excursions

Norbulingka Institute

This little paradise was established to teach and preserve traditional Tibetan art such as thangka painting, embroidery, woodcarving and sculpting. The Institute is decorated with colourful buildings, an exquisite temple, charming shrines, peaceful gardens and Himālayan views. If you enjoy Tibetan artwork, a visit to Norbulingka is a must.

Norbulingka is about 15 km from McLeod Ganj and can be reached by taxi or bus. If you take a bus, get off at Sidhpur and follow the signs to the Institute (it's about a 15-minute walk). The Norling Guest House and Café offer lovely mid-range rooms and great food for those wanting to stay for a night or few. There are crafts and souvenirs produced at the Institute for sale, and while often expensive, the works are high-quality and purchases benefit refugee artisans.

Bhim Ka Tila, Chaitru Stūpa

The stone and brick remains of this ancient stūpa probably date back to the time of Asoka or just afterwards. This stūpa, now totally covered with grass, trees, a flower garden, and a tiny Hanuman statue, is the only significant monument from ancient times that indicates Dhamma activity in the Kangra Valley, though historical records suggest that the region was once home to several important monastic centres. You can easily imagine today's peaceful park, with its spectacular views of the Dhauladhar range, once serving as a monastic complex full of nature-inspired *bhikkhus* striving for enlightenment.

Chaitru is 18 km from McLeod Ganj. To get there, take the road towards Gaggal. The stūpa, which looks like a hill, is 3 km before Gaggal on your right-hand side.

Dehra Dun

The capital of Uttarakhand state in the foothills of the Himālaya, Dehra Dun is most famous for being home to several scholarly and research centres such as the Forest Research Institute, the Indian Military Academy, the Wildlife Institute of India and the Survey of India (where you can get excellent maps of the country). If you're not here for academics, the only real reason to come to Dehra Dun is to catch a fast train to Delhi or attend a meditation course at Dhamma Salila.

Site-Sitting

Dhamma Salila

This peaceful centre, nestled away in the Doon Valley, is a wonderful place to get in touch with oneself and work to remove the obstacles of grasping and false views. Situated on the bank of the Noon River, Dhamma Salila ('Water of Dhamma') is a tranquil haven where the only disturbances are the flowing waters of the river and the cries of soaring eagles. Dhamma Salila has simple facilities that can accommodate about 75 students in double rooms. The centre's pagoda, charged with Himālayan vibrations, is one of the finest in India.

Arrange transportation to Dhamma Salila through the centre's city office. Otherwise, take a bus from Mussoorie Bus Stand to Jantanwala Village (1 hour). From the Santala Devi Temple, it's a short 10-minute walk to the centre. If you come during the monsoon season, when the forest is at its greenest, prepare to get wet, as getting to the centre requires crossing the river on foot. Dhamma workers are usually on hand to help you wade through the waters, which are sometimes waist-deep. During the winter, the river is partially dried up and you can easily cross without getting drenched. *Anicca*!

Contact:

Dhamma Salila, Dehra Dun Vipassana Centre
Village Jantanwala, near Santala Devi Mandir
Uttaranchal
Tel: [+91](0135) 210-4555/ 271-5189
E-mail: info@salila.dhamma.org
Website: www.salila.dhamma.org

City Office:
16 Tagore Villa, Chakrata Road,
Dehra Dun
Uttarakhand
Tel: [+91](0135) 265-3366
E-mail: info@salila.dhamma.org
Website: www.salila.dhamma.org

Sleeping & Eating

There's not much reason to stay in Dehra Dun, but if you do, the best budget spot is the **White House,** just north of the Clock Tower. Decent mid-range options include the **Shahenshah** and the **Ajanta Continental** hotels. For good South Indian vegetarian food, stop in at **Kumar's** near the Clock Tower on Rajpur Road. Other decent restaurants can also be found along the same stretch.

Coming & Going

There are daily **flights** to Delhi from Dehra Dun's airport, 20 km east of the city. However, the best way to travel to and from Delhi is to catch one of the **express trains,** such as the New Delhi Dehra Dun Shatabdi Express 2017/2018 or the Delhi Dehra Dun Kotdwara Mussoorie Express 4041/4042 (which both stop in Haridwar). Some other express trains include:

* Bandra-Dehra Dun Express 9019/9020 (Bandra/Mumbai-Mathura-New Delhi-Haridwar-Dehra Dun)
* Howrah Dehra Dun Upasana Express 3103/3104 (Howrah/Kolkata-Patna-Vārāṇasī-Haridwar-Dehra Dun)
* Howrah Dehra Dun Express 3009/3010 (Howrah/Kolkata-Gayā-Vārāṇasī-Lucknow-Haridwar-Dehra Dun)

If you can't get a train reservation, long-distance **buses** depart from the Old Delhi Bus Stand in central Dehra Dun and, more commonly, from the Interstate Bus Terminal (ISBT) in Clement Town (5 km south of Dehra Dun). Regular buses head to Delhi (6 hours), Rishikesh (1.5 hours), Haridwar (2 hours), and Lucknow (14 hours). If you're heading to the mountains, go to the Mussoorie Bus Stand next to the train station.

Excursions & Activities

Mussoorie

This hill station above Dehra Dun is very popular with tourists from Delhi. The only real reason foreigners visit Mussoorie is to take an intensive Hindi course at the Mussoorie Language School. Although courses are offered year round, it's advisable to avoid the hot season (May-July), when the town is crowded with tourists. Winters in Mussoorie are typically quite cold. Coming at other times of the year, you'll be better able to appreciate the nice walks and fine views that this hill station has to offer.

To get to Mussoorie, take a bus, taxi, or shared taxi from Dehra Dun (1 hour), Rishikesh (2.5 hours), or Haridwar (3 hours). There are also daily buses to/from Delhi (8 hours).

Rishikesh

This holy Hindu town and New-Age hotspot at the foot of the mighty Himālaya is a great place to learn yoga and Ayurveda, and is also a good starting point for trekking or rafting. The Ganges River flows right through the middle of town, and there are innumerable ashrams, temples, yoga schools, astrologers, ayurvedic centres, guest houses, and vegetarian restaurants on each bank.

Activities abound in the areas of High Bank (on the hill overlooking town), the communities around the Laxshman Jhula and Ram Jhula bridges, and Swarg Ashram (on the eastern bank at Ram Jhula). Some recommended places to learn yoga

without sectarian frills are at the **Yoga Study Centre** near Koyalghati, **Omkarananda Ashram** at Ram Jhula, and **Parmarth Niketan** and **Ved Niketan** in the Swarg Ashram area. As with all of the suggestions in this book, the best way to find the place that suits your needs is by exploring for yourself and talking to other travellers. Also, because Rishikesh is quite spread out, it's most convenient to stay somewhere in the vicinity of where you'll take classes. Go to areas of interest and then look around to see what's available.

The Swastigram Ayurvedic Kendra located between Dehra Dun and Rishikesh was co-founded by Dr. Myriam de Valicour, an Ayurvedic doctor and Vipassana meditator from France. The principle aim of the centre is to integrate natural health, environmental sustainability, and inner awareness. For more information about treatments, accommodations and prices, visit www.swastigram.com.

There are regular buses to Rishikesh from Delhi, Dehra Dun, Haridwar and Dharamsala. You can also catch a train to Haridwar and then take a bus or taxi to Rishikesh. Refer to Dehra Dun's Coming & Going to see some trains that stop in Haridwar.

Jaipur

Known as the Pink City, a nickname inspired by the vaguely pink-hued architecture of the old city, Jaipur is the capital of the great desert state of Rajasthan, where the colour pink is traditionally associated with hospitality. Most travellers find this to be true of Jaipur, which is known for its warm and colourful culture, bustling markets, peaceful buildings, local craftsmanship, high quality jewellery and precious and semi-precious stones. Although its noisy buzz can be a little overwhelming at times, Jaipur is an excellent place for shopping and site-seeing. The city is also home to one of the most well-established Vipassana Meditation centres in the world, the beautiful Dhamma Thalī.

Jaipur's Old City, to the north-east, is partially enclosed by a defensive wall with major gates offering access from different parts of the modern city, such as Chandpol Gate in the west, Singh, Ajmer, New, Sanganeri and Ghat Gates in the south, and Suraj Gate in the east. The old city is characterized by long avenues lined with bazaars, where shops are generally grouped into artisan's quarters according to their wares. Many of Jaipur's most distinctive sites, including the City Palace, Hawa Mahal ("Palace of the Winds") and Jantar Mantar are all clustered in the center of the old city. Modern Jaipur is spread out beyond the walls to the south and west of the old city. Station Road and Mirza Ismail (MI) Road, both extending from Jaipur Railway Station in the south-west to the old city in the north-east, form a sort of triangular area where most travellers' amenities and activities can be found.

Site-Sitting

Dhamma Thalī, Rajasthan Vipassana Centre

Since 1977 meditators from around the globe have been coming to meditate in this tranquil place, which is the second largest Vipassana centre in India after Dhamma Giri. The beautiful 4-acre property is situated in a bowl-shaped valley surrounded on all sides by forested hills that protect the centre from Jaipur's noise and city vibrations. The only sounds one is likely to hear are the constant bird songs and monkey screeches, the odd roar of a tiger, and the morning devotional chants from a nearby ashram.

Dhamma Thalī[195] ('Place of Dhamma') can accommodate up to 300 meditators in single and double cottages, all connected by intricate stone pathways that wind through lovely flower gardens. The four Dhamma halls and well-designed layout of the centre make it possible to run several courses at once. With more than 200 individual cells in five concentric rings, the centre's three-storied octagonal pagoda stands as if it were a mountain, echoing the power of the Dhamma. This central structure exhibits a graceful blend of Rajasthani and Myanmar architecture, expressing both appreciation for local artisanship and gratitude to the country that preserved the practice of Dhamma for millennia.

In the centre's early days, only a few courses conducted by S.N. Goenka or one of his Assistant Teachers were held each year; otherwise the facilities were used for self-courses and management meetings. Today, however, Dhamma Thalī is a full-time centre. Each year the centre holds an average of seven long courses, three *Satipaṭṭhāna Sutta* courses, two Special 10-day courses, seventeen regular 10-day courses, two children's and teenagers' courses, and several 3-day courses. There are also facilities for meditator-scholars to pursue *pariyatti* work with a branch of the Vipassana Research Institute.

Meditators are encouraged to stay here for longer periods and take advantage of this well-established centre and the wisdom and experience offered by the local community of meditators. It's easy to take day trips or excursions between courses, visiting Jaipur or any of the numerous surrounding sites, including the incredible ancient forts at Nahargarh (perfect for sunset) and Amber (pronounced 'amer'), as well as the Galta Monkey Temple.

Dhamma Thalī is located east of Jaipur in the village of Galta, only 12 km from Jaipur Railway Station, and is easily accessible by rickshaw or taxi.

Contact:
Dhamma Thalī, Rajasthan Vipassana Centre
P.O. Box 208
Sisodiarani Baug–Galtaji Road
Jaipur–302001
Rajasthan
Tel: [+91] (0)141-2680220
Fax: [+91] (0)141-2576283
E-mail: info@thali.dhamma.org
Website: www.thali.dhamma.org

I had heard that the centre in Jaipur was one of the most established in India and felt encouraged to go, given that it's only four hours south-west of Delhi. A German friend who doesn't speak much English mentioned there were "animals" around the centre. I was not exactly sure what she meant but I was anticipating a recluse-type meditation experience in the deep jungle. Rajasthan, however, offers desert landscapes instead.

It was getting late by the time I'd finished checking my e-mail at a cyber-café in downtown Jaipur and then settled on a reasonable price with a cycle rickshaw driver. After about half an hour through town, we passed underneath an ornate pinkish archway and began to climb uphill. We passed a very large temple complex that brought to mind the maharajas and desert pilgrimages I had seen in pictures.

My reverie was cut short when the driver stopped and made me understand in Hindi and sign language that he was not going any farther. I had no idea how much further the centre was, so I asked him to please continue. I reminded him of the price we had settled on, but he was resolute in his repeated imitations of what seemed to be a tiger. I began mimicking his performance and was met with lots of vigorous head-wobbling and repeated tiger pantomimes. Evidently, he was afraid of being mauled, and I began to wish I'd taken a morning bus to Jaipur.

I watched him descend toward the city and then began to walk uphill. Every shadow was a leopard and every breeze carried my scent to an army of attack-cats. I comforted myself with the thought that if Vipassana meditators had been eaten on their way to the centre, I would have probably heard about it. The road grew narrower and finally the sign "Vipassana" appeared on my right. Everyone at the centre was asleep. Day 0 was turning into Day 1. The centre was an oasis of tranquility in the vast Indian night. I took out my sleeping bag and slept beneath a small grove of trees.

The next morning, I presented myself at the office and joined the course. On Day 11, I spoke with a server from France and he encouraged me to stay on. We wound up being roommates for most of the next two months. Christophe had spent the last five years in Asia, the majority of that time sitting and serving at various Vipassana centres. During many hushed pre-sleep conversations, he helped me understand many things about India and Dhamma in general. But more than any specific advice he offered, his joy itself was the most inspiring aspect of our relationship. For the first time I began to appreciate the meaning of taking refuge in the Saṅgha. Those more developed in Dhamma than I are helpful to me simply by their presence!

After serving two courses, I sat my second Satipaṭṭhāna course. The cool stone pagoda, where so many other earnest meditators had worked, offered both dhammic and physical shelter from the coming summer heat. After the course, there was an e-mail waiting from my fiancée asking if I would meet her in Bombay so we could start our yatra together with Goenka-ji. In the process of telling Christophe about this possibility, I realized my time at Jaipur had nearly come to an end.

When I think back on my Jaipur experience, I realize how much I learned about both Rajasthani culture and about myself. Although long-term service anywhere in the world is rewarding, one of the particular benefits of serving long-term in India as a Westerner is the opportunity to be an immediate resource for Western meditators who may be sitting their first course in a foreign land. Leaving Jaipur was difficult for me, as I had grown to love the centre and staff. I look forward to returning someday to deepen my Dhamma practice.

– Jonathan Mirin

I recently finished a 30-day meditation course in Jaipur. It was an inspiring experience in a beautiful place. What I remember best about the course, aside from the meditation, is the peacocks, which live in large number in the dry forestland around the meditation centre.

They are big, goofy, beautiful birds, which I only saw a few times, not due to their shyness but due to the meditation discipline of keeping one's eyes downcast.

Far from shy, they frequented the area next to the meditation hall and the residences, making their loud and outlandish noises. One disadvantage I have as a meditator is that I'm easily distracted by sounds, so having a whole new set of birdsongs took some time to put aside. Being a musician with some understanding of music theory, I tend to analyze birdsong musically. Peacocks, when they get in a tizzy about something, often make a kvetching sound like very large kitty cats meowing to come inside. When more contented (at least, this is how I'm interpreting it), they make a sound like a low pitched blast on a truck horn or a trombone or saxophone, followed immediately by a second tone more than an octave higher. I had no idea what this was when I first heard it.

The meditation centre hosts a bunch of other wild or semi-wild beings, including many other birds and numerous insects. Black ants lived in my toilet bowl and we meditators calmly shared the outside drinking water taps with bees who were busily sucking up water as well. Occasionally the bees gave me the willies. I also saw salamanders and a 6-inch lizard in my room a few times. Then there were the monkeys, which I didn't even realize were there until halfway through the course, when I glanced up and saw some in the trees. Later I walked past a family of monkeys on the stone path and they barely moved aside. All this animal activity was a wonderful backdrop to the incredibly inspiring experience I had at this beautiful centre.

– Peter Buchanan

Shopping & Activities

Jaipur abounds with showrooms and emporiums that specialize in selling Rajasthani crafts to tourists at a high markup, though they can be otherwise convenient places to shop. These include the stores along Amber Road, as well as **Rajasthali**, the state-government emporium near Ajmer Gate on MI Road. Depending on what you're looking for, you may find better value and quality in the old city's lengthy bazaars, which are famous for fabrics and textiles, but your best bet may be any of the numerous shopping centres and boutiques along MI Road.

Anokhi, on Prithviraj Road in central Jaipur, is renowned for high-quality block-print clothing, fabric and bedding, all produced by local artisans. Anokhi doesn't have much for gents, unfortunately, but the building is also home to an upscale café, an English bookstore, a housewares boutique and two excellent restaurants (see next section).

Although many emporiums offer Rajasthan's famous blue pottery, one of the best places to purchase is at **Kripal Kumbh**, the home studio of award-winning artist Mr. Kripal Singh.

Prices are surprisingly reasonable and his assistants do an excellent job packaging parcels for travel. Accept no imitations: Kripal Kumbh is a modest house near Jaipur Inn.

Jaipur is also famous for gemstones, which are easily found along Johari and Siredeori Bazaars in the old city. There are plenty of scam artists, so if you don't know your gems it's a good idea to find a trustworthy local to bring you to honest dealers.

Tailored clothing can by made within about a week's time by the brothers at **Jodhpur Tailors**, near Karni Niwas Guest House. It's possible to place an order and have a fine suit made while sitting or serving at Dhamma Thalī. You'll simply need to return for a final fitting before your suit is finished. Fine women's clothing in the Indian style, particularly *salwar kameez* sets, can be found at **Pratap Sons** in the Saraogi Mansion shopping centre on MI Road.

Jaipur is home to what is perhaps the most famous Bollywood theatre in India, the impressive **Raj Mandir Cinema** on Bhagwandas Road off MI Road. This lavish, gaudy theatre is an excellent place to take in the latest hit Bollywood films, which screen several times daily.

Sleeping & Eating

Popular budget options with meditators are **Jaipur Inn** west of the old city's Chandpol Gate, **Diggi Palace** near the Ajmer Gate, and **Hotel Pearl Palace** off Ajmer Road near the 4-Star Country Inn.

One of the best mid-range options is the beautifully decorated **Arya Niwas** on Sansar Chandra Road, around the corner from the Main Bus Station (on-line reservations recommended). The lovely, clean rooms in the new addition of **Karni Ni-**

was guest house are great mid-range value, and feature genuinely hot, pressurized showers! Karni Niwas is behind the landmark 4-star **Hotel Neelam**. The nearby **Atithi Guest House**, off of Motilal Atal Road, and **Madhuban**, near Bani Park, have also been recommended.

Jaipur has several outstanding luxury options, including **Samode Haveli**, a converted estate on the north edge of the old city near Zorawar Gate, and nearby **Raj Palace**, once an actual palace. **Jai Mahal Palace Hotel**, south of the Railway Station, is another former estate set on 18 acres of land featuring extensive gardens. The previously mentioned **Country Inn**, not far from the Railway Station on MI Road, is an ultramodern microcosm including a health spa, excellent restaurant and, at street level, a **Subway Sandwich Shop**.

In addition, most of the other guest houses and hotels listed here have good restaurants on the premises or within walking distance nearby. There are cheap vegetarian restaurants and sweet shops all over the place; however, a few outstanding recommendations include **Natraj Vegetarian** and **Golden Chinese Dragon** on M.I. Road near Ajmeri Gate, and **LMB** on Johari Bazaar, all particularly tasty and a little pricey. The top floor of the Anokhi building on Prithviraj Road boasts two world-class restaurants, **Little Italy** and a companion restaurant serving Indian food, where the service and décor are enough to make you forget you're in India for an evening.

As with all cities in India, Japiur's taxi and rickshaw drivers will want to take you to a hotel of their choosing, where they earn a commission that you'll pay for. This is such a problem that an increasing number of guest houses will provide transport or give you specific instructions on how much to pay drivers if you call or book ahead. Otherwise, you can avoid hassle by taking advantage of the pre-paid auto-rickshaw stands at the train and bus stations. During the summer months from May to September, when Rajasthan is at the height of desert heat, most hotels offer 25–50% discounts.

Coming & Going

Jaipur is well-connected to the rest of India by air, rail, and road. The Rajasthan State Transport Corporation (Main) Bus Station sends off regular and deluxe **buses** to every corner of the state, including Agra (4.5 hours) and Delhi (5 hours, good road!).

If you travel to/from Jaipur by **train**, here are a few convenient ones to choose from:

- Mumbai Jaipur Express 2955/2956 (Mumbai-Jaipur)
- Jaipur Bandra Aravali Express 9007/9008 (Jaipur-Ajmer-Ahmedabad-Bandra/Mumbai)
- Sealdah Jaipur Express 2985/2986 (Sealdah/Kolkata-Gayā-Mughalsarai-Agra-Jaipur)
- Jodhpur Express 2307/2308 (Howrah/Kolkata-Gayā-Mughalsarai-Agra-

Jaipur-Jodhpur)
- Delhi Jaipur Express 2413/2414 (Delhi-Jaipur)
- Delhi Ahmedabad Ashram Express 2916/2917 (Delhi-Jaipur-Ahmedabad)
  Delhi Ahmedabad Mail 9106/9107 (Delhi-Jaipur-Ahmedabad)
- Bhuj Bareilly Al Hazrat Express 4311/4312 (Delhi-Jaipur-Ahmedabad-Bhuj)

Excursions

Bairath (formerly Viratnagar)

On the periphery of this small town are two important sites associated with Emperor Asoka, who used to come here to get away from the political grind in Patna. The first is the foundation of a stūpa and ruins of a small monastery, believed to mark the spot where Asoka was meditating when he attained stream-entry during his 13th year after coronation. The ruins are located near a huge rock on top of Beejak Kee Pahari, a hill that overlooks the town. To get to the hill, go to the police station/ Panchayat Bhawan on the main road and then follow the dirt road for about half a kilometre. At the end of the road, follow the pathway for 20 minutes to the top.

The second important site in Bairath is on Pandu Hill, site of Pandave Cave Temple, several empty caves and an illegible rock edict. The four readable edicts found here were taken to the Indian museum in Kolkata. In the first one, Asoka wrote that after two years of practice he finally entered the Buddha's noble Saṅgha (i.e. reached the first stage of enlightenment). The second one reads that the gods had mingled with humans. Some scholars interpret this as a reference to people who were practising divine spiritual disciplines, perhaps Vipassana. The third edict reads that people from the highest to the lowest castes had become godly through these practices. The fourth inscription reads that Asoka was convinced that enthusiasm for Dhamma would increase one-and-a-half times.

To get to this site, cross the market from the bus stand and walk 1 km slightly uphill. The cave temple is below the peak and the rock edict is on a small path off to the left, about 100 m before the temple.

Bairath is 90 km (about 2 hours) from Jaipur and can be reached by taxi or bus going towards Alwar. Regular and express buses leave regularly from the Sindhi Camp Bus Stand in Jaipur. The only places to stay overnight are at the government Dak Bungalow or at the Jain Temple not far from the Pandave Caves.

Pushkar

Situated on the edge of the desert, this mellow lakeside holy town is a popular place for Hindu pilgrims coming to worship at the only temple in India dedicated to Brahma. Other than the time around the November full moon, when Pushkar hosts its famous Camel Fair, the town is fairly quiet and a good refuge from life on the road before or after a stint of sitting and/or serving at Dhamma Thalī in Jaipur.

All around Pushkar Lake are holy ghats, shrines, guest houses, vegetarian restaurants and Rajasthani handicraft shops. When taking a walk by the lake, keep in mind that it is a pilgrimage site. Photos, shoes and revealing clothing aren't appropriate and may offend. Unless you want to pay for a costly puja, it's best to avoid priests who approach you with a flower and a smile. Pushkar is also well known for its skilled tailors, relaxing yoga classes, talented Indian classical music teachers and performers, and treatments in Ayurveda and massage. Some are better than others; learn from other travellers' experiences. Although many travellers head for more distant parts of Rajasthan to experience the wonders of India's deserts, Pushkar is also a fine place to go camel trekking for short- or long-distance excursions.

Budget accommodation, good restaurants and travellers' amenities abound in Pushkar. Due to the number of people who pass through the popular town, rooms often seem to be in short supply. **Payal Guest House** and **Inn Seventh Heaven** are recommended, and the nearby **Honey & Spice Café** is not to be missed. The **Om Shiva Buffet** restaurants (there are two, same menu but different owners) are great value.

Pushkar's nearest train station is at Ajmer, half an hour away by bus. Although travelling by train can be more comfortable, it's often faster to travel direct to Pushkar by bus. Buses on their way to Ajmer often stop in Pushkar, so you can take a Jaipur-Ajmer bus (2.5 hours) or Delhi-Ajmer bus (7 hours). If you do arrive in Ajmer by train, be aware that you'll then need to take a rickshaw to Ajmer's bus station, where you can easily get a local bus to Pushkar. Some convenient trains to Ajmer are:

- Jaipur Bandra Aravali Express 9007/9008 (Jaipur-Ajmer-Ahmedabad-Bandra/ Mumbai)
- New Delhi Ajmer Shatabdi Express 2014/2015 (New Delhi-Ajmer)

Kathmandu

For centuries, Kathmandu has had the allure of an almost mythical, exotic and far-flung place accessible only to the adventurous, and in some sense this certainly remains true. Nepal is among the poorest nations in South Asia, a conflicted country struggling to develop and modernize, and this is perhaps nowhere more dynamically evident than in the capital city itself. Kathmandu is in fact one of the only real cities in Nepal, and tourism, one of the country's largest industries, is enthusiastically supported by a wide array of amenities, accommodation, restaurants and shopping opportunities. To some travellers Kathmandu feels like "relaxed India," while others find that the noise, congestion, trash, pollution and hassle of the city rivals any in South Asia. Of course this is largely a matter of perception, timing and luck. Kathmandu is nevertheless a city of tremendous history and cultural diversity that has much to offer.

Most places of interest to travellers are in the old city, so it's convenient to think of **Durbar Square** as the center of Kathmandu, though in reality the modern city extends far to the east and north. Surrounding Durbar Square, the old city is a jumble of over-crowded medieval lanes punctuated by many *chowk* (pronounced 'choke'), intersections or crossroads that often serve as open-air markets and meeting places. Adjacent to Durbar Square is **Freak Street**, Kathmandu's original traveller's haunt established by the hippies of the 1970s, while further to the north stretches **Thamel**, the consummate backpackers' ghetto. Kanti Path, a major road bisecting Kathmandu from north to south, forms the division between the old city to the west and the new city to the east. Two large landmarks punctuate Eastern Kathmandu, the central **Tudikhel** parade ground and the **Royal Palace** to the north. Be aware that the outlying towns of Patan and Bhaktapur also have Durbar ('Palace') Squares, so always specify which Durbar Square you intend to go to when travelling by rickshaw or taxi.

Kathmandu lies in the center of a wide, roughly circular valley ringed by forested mountains. The traditional home of the Newar people, the Kathmandu Valley has always been a crossroads of intermingling cultures, traversed by travellers and traders for millennia. Amidst these diverse influences, Newari culture has developed its own characteristic style: a unique synthesis of Hindu and Buddhist beliefs and aesthetics reflected in everything from festivals to fine architecture. The Kathmandu Valley is home to more than 130 important monuments, seven groups of which were accorded UNESCO World Heritage status in 1979. With a venerable tradition of spiritual inquiry, the valley is also known for its places of worship and practice.

Site-Sitting

Dharmaśringa, Nepal Vipassāna Centre

Dharmaśringa ('Summit of Dhamma') is located in the foothills of the Himālaya, perched among hills overlooking the Kathmandu Valley about 12 kilometres north of the city. The centre's land covers nearly four acres and is bordered by a beautiful wildlife reserve. An abundant water supply nourishes the lush terraced gardens that characterize Dharmaśringa's grounds, where flowers bloom throughout the year. Far from the noise of the city and situated at an altitude of about 1 500 metres, the centre is a cool and quiet place ideal for meditation.

Established in 1987, Dharmaśringa is now one of the most well-developed centres in South Asia, and can comfortably accommodate about 250 people. Multi-storied residences offer both dormitories and single rooms, and Nepali-style vegetarian meals are served in two separate dining halls for men and women. All courses at Dharmaśringa are conducted in both English and Hindi, as the majority of Nepali students understand at least one of these languages well. However, auxiliary Dhamma halls are often used for giving instructions and discourses in a variety of additional languages and dialects.

Dharmaśringa also has a separate complex for old-student courses, complete with accommodation, dining halls, meditation facilities and a large 84-cell pagoda. These facilities, including the pagoda, are only used for long courses and *Satipaṭṭhāna Sutta* courses.

In response to a long-standing problem of students chatting with one another during courses, Dharmaśringa has developed a rather strict approach to maintaining rules and regulations, which provides old students, in particular, with a dynamic opportunity to strengthen one's effort and equanimity.

10-day courses are held from the 1st–12th and 14th–25th of every month, though this may vary during the festival season in October and November. One-day courses are held on the 26th of every month, and *Satipaṭṭhāna* courses are also held several times a year.

All course registration is handled by the Vipassana City Office in Kathmandu. Even if you've submitted an application on-line or by mail, it's strongly recommended that you check in with the city office when you arrive in Kathmandu to ensure that you've actually been registered. On the morning of the day the course begins, all students are required to present themselves with passports and relevant paperwork to the city office at 12 p.m. You'll need a passport-sized photo and a copy of your passport (which can be made in a nearby office but will slow your registration, so better to obtain one earlier). Once everyone is registered, free transportation to the centre is provided, though there's often a long wait for the buses.

The city office is located south of the Electric Commission on Kanti Path Road, in the basement of the Jyoti Bhawan building, which is also occupied by a motorcycle dealership. There is no street-side sign for the Vipassana Office, and you'll need to enter the building's gate to reach it, so look carefully because it can be hard to find. The office is open Sunday to Friday from 10 a.m. to 5 p.m., and group meditations for old-students are held every evening (except Saturday) from 5-6 p.m. in a quiet nearby building; check in with the office first if you can.

Contact:
Dharmaśringa
Muhan Pokhari, Budhanilkantha
Kathmandu, Nepal
Tel: [+977](1) 371-655/ 371-077

Kathmandu Vipassana City Office:
Jyoti Bhawan Kantipath
P.O. Box: 12896, Kathmandu, Nepal
Tel: [+977] (0)1-4250581/-4223968
Fax: [+977] (0)1-4224720
Website: www.shringa.dhamma.org

I had just completed 10 days of service at Dharmaśringa, and planned on hiking nearby Sipucho Peak with a Nepali friend I had made during the course. I often like to go hiking after a meditation course, to immerse myself in the natural world and move my body after so many days of introversion and stillness. The gate to Shivapuri National Park lies just a few feet up the road from the meditation centre, and after paying a small entry fee, my friend and I were soon sauntering up the old jeep road through the beautiful, vibrant woods. With a dense tropical forest that includes a host of resident monkeys and large stands of Himālayan oak and alder trees, Shivapuri National Park covers one of the mountains overlooking the Kathmandu Valley. Until recently it was owned solely by the Nepali king, but is now a park managed by the government.

On the way up to the peak we happened upon Nagi Gompa, a nunnery in the Tibetan Buddhist tradition that lies on a flat hilltop on the mountainside. The Gompa's immense rectangular buildings, painted yellow and crimson, are surrounded by open fields and smaller outbuildings. Literally hundreds of garlands of prayer flags were fluttering in the wind, strung among the branches of a resident tree that also serves as a gathering spot for the nuns. From this vantage point one has views over the entire city of Kathmandu, which is breathtaking despite the smog and smoke below.

We walked through the nunnery, stopping at the ornately decorated ritual hall to observe about a dozen nuns chanting; a Westerner sat on a cushion to one side, meditating. We left the hall, and walked across one of the fields to where the trail continued up the mountain. On the way, we ran into another foreigner who was hanging his laundry to dry, a gentle-mannered American who had been living in Indian and Nepali monasteries and nunneries for close to ten years. A serious student of Transcendental Meditation, he let me know about his arrangements for staying at the nunnery: he paid about $3 a day and was given a room in the foreigners' dormitory plus three meals a *day. My friend and I continued up the mountain, passing a group of villagers who were gathering fallen branches for firewood.*

Upon reaching a water temple built into a ravine, featuring a cloth-draped statue of meditating Shiva, we couldn't find the trail to continue up to the peak, so my friend and I started down again, a little disappointed. But I had a plan for myself in mind, and back at the nunnery, I asked the first nun we saw about staying, and was directed to the kitchen. There I met the nun, Sonum, who was in charge of all the foreign guests, a gentle and kind woman of about forty years who understood some English. After I discussed with her the possibility of my return to Nagi Gompa, my friend and I made our way back to the park entrance and hopped on a bus for Kathmandu. I only stayed in the Valley two nights, however, before I was back at the nunnery.

When I returned, after walking the few miles from the park entrance carrying my belongings, Sonum welcomed me heartily and showed me my room. The other foreigner I'd spoken to had told me about a cave on the side of the mountain that was sometimes used by meditators, and when I asked Sonum about it, she led me up the trail towards the peak. After about five minutes of steep climbing, we veered off to the right on a smaller, almost hidden trail, which brought us through the woods and over a small stream, ending eventually at the bottom of a steep staircase carved into a boulder, which led up to the cave. And this was no ordinary cave!

Complete with a bathroom (which unfortunately was out of order), a door, a patio with a view of the valley, and two windows, the cave was more of a studio apartment in the middle of the woods: the perfect spot for solitary meditation. She told me that a few years prior, two young Western men had stayed here for about 2 months, only coming down to the nunnery twice each day for lunch and dinner. It looked to me as if the cave had not been used much since then: the floor was covered with a half-inch of dirt. But together we cleaned it up, and Sonum said I could use the cave as much as I wanted for meditation; I could even stay here if I wanted. Though that was tempting, and I could think of no better place for a self-course, I decided to stay in my room in the main nunnery, closer to the kitchen and working toilets, and closer to the people who lived there.

A Nepali layman was the head chef for the nunnery, and a young orphan girl helped him. Sonum and the few other nuns with whom I had contact, including the abbess, were very warm and accommodating, with that softness and joyful presence so many of the Tibetan people possess. It was very pleasant down there during the mornings and evenings, spending time with the other residents. But because of its beauty and proximity to Kathmandu, during the middle of the day the place took on the character of a noisy tourist attraction.

These were the times I spent meditating in the cave, which turned out to be a very strong place to sit. I spent down time reading inspiring books and walking on the forest trails, even reaching the peak once. The days had a wonderful flow: I would wake up, meditate in my room, then have breakfast and coffee with some of the folks there, after which I would walk up to the cave to meditate and read, leaving only to take a walk or to return to the nunnery for lunch and dinner, and perhaps to spend some time in the ritual hall, listening to the chanting and music of the nuns.

Nagi Gompa, I was told, incorporates more traditional Tibetan music—with horns and drums—than many other nunneries and monasteries throughout the region. It was a very relaxing week, punctuated though it was by bursts of practice in the cave. It was a nice break from the more intensive schedule at a Vipassana centre, where one is always expected to be either meditating or working.

Indeed, to my surprise, the nunnery proved to be a place of supreme relaxation. Towards the end of my visit, my American friend revealed to me that he had a small DVD player and TV unit, and together we watched the latest Brad Pitt movie! The next night was Tom Cruise's masterful Risky Business followed by a DVD of a Grateful Dead concert, all of which were pirated copies that my friend had bought in town.

After months of travelling and meditating in monasteries and meditation centres in India, Burma, and Nepal, what a joy it was to feel like I was back at home, relaxing in the living room with a friend. But the next morning I did something which I could only dream about back home: waking up in the dark, I left my room to watch the blanket of lights in the Valley flicker off, one by one, as the hazy glow of the sun rolled over the hilltops. With the soft breath of satisfaction entering and leaving my body, and my mind sensing, at least a little, how privileged I really was, I leaned into the hill and walked back to the cave for a final, blessed, sit.

– Eric Eichler

Shopping, Activities, Services & Sites

There's no shortage of shopping opportunities in Kathmandu. Shops of interest to travellers are primarily crammed into the streets of **Thamel**, and offer a range of clothing, Nepali and Tibetan arts and crafts, trekking gear, books and media, decorative housewares and assorted religious iconography. Much of what's available has a certain hippie flavour, but there is also an active trade in high-quality home furnishings, including wall hangings, sculptures and antiques. **Freak Street** has a smaller selection of similar shops, often with somewhat lower prices.

Bargaining is the name of the game in Kathmandu, as in the whole of Nepal. Always shop around to compare prices, and when buying works of art, make an effort to inspect quality closely and speak with several dealers about the artists and origins before making a purchase.

Bodhnath is an excellent place to find high-quality Tibetan jewelry, icons, arts and crafts, and while the shops here are generally a bit more expensive than Thamel, a number are run by Tibetan refugees. See *Bodhnath* later in this section for more info.

A fantastic place to shop for Tibetan *thangka* paintings is the **Lama Thangka Painting School** showroom, where you can watch artists at work, tour the amazing gallery and browse through myriad paintings in the sitting room. The showroom is on the south side of **Durbar Square** in **Bhaktapur** (see *Excursions* for details). Similar, though generally less impressive establishments can be found throughout the Kathmandu Valley.

Kathmandu city has perhaps the best range of bookshops on the subcontinent, many of which carry a wide range of titles on Buddhism, Hinduism, regional culture and history. Among these are **Mandala Bookpoint** (on Kanti Path south of the Vipassana City Office) and **Pilgrim's Book House** (in Thamel). **United Books** (in Thamel, with a smaller branch in the Saturday Café at Bodhnath) has an excellent selection of literary fiction and non-fiction, both new and used. Most bookshops sell postcards and stamps, and will post them for you, too.

Kathmandu's most famous local shopping street is **Asan Tole**, which stretches diagonally through the old city from Durbar Square to Kanti Path, passing as it does through Indra Chowk and several other crowded market intersections. Travellers are likely to take most interest in the textiles, clothing and carpets available here. This area is quintessential Kathmandu.

Nepal's capital city is famous for festivals of all kinds; check out **ECS Magazine** in bookshops or on-line for a schedule of coming events: www.ecs.com.np/index.htm

There are several reputable medical treatment centres in Kathmandu. **CIWEC Clinic**, north-east of Thamel across from the British Embassy, is trusted by expatriots and has dental services as well; the **Nepal International Clinic** is perhaps equally good and said to be a little less expensive. There are also other places that may be able to provide for special needs, but the state hospital is to be avoided.

A wide range of naturopathic and alternative healing therapies is available in Kathmandu, some of which are more reputable than others. Ask other travellers for good places. Bodhnath is known for good massage and traditional Tibetan medicine. The office of **Dr. Tsering**, a skilled Tibetan allopathic doctor who speaks English, can be found on Phul Bari Road across from Lotus Guest House in Bodhnath. See *Sleeping & Eating* for more.

While exploring the busy lanes of the old city and buzzing activity of Durbar Square, travellers are sometimes preyed upon by pickpockets, scam artists, forceful would-be tour guides, beggars and coercive holy men. Take caution to avoid interacting with these people whenever possible, and don't hesitate to be forceful and take strong action if being harassed. Giving money only brings more beggars;

we recommend presenting yourself with folded hands and giving *mettā* instead! This remains true at Kathmandu's spiritual sites as well.

Swayambhunath (Monkey Temple)
One of the most important sacred sites in the Kathmandu Valley for both Buddhists and Hindus, Swayambhunath is a place of multiple meanings ensconced in mythology and legend. Situated atop a hill overlooking Kathmandu city from the west, the site of the present stūpa has long been a revered place of spiritual power.

According to Mahāyana legend, the Buddha travelled to Kathmandu sometime after his enlightenment to give thanks to previous buddhas atop Swayambhunath hill, where he also gave teachings on right conduct. It is said that Emperor Asoka also visited the hill in the third century BCE and erected a temple or monument that was later destroyed. The earliest archaeological evidence is an inscription indicating that King Manadeva ordered work done at the site in 640 CE. The present structure, a white-domed *chaitya* or stūpa topped by a golden square and pinnacle bearing Nepal's ubiquitous "Buddha eyes," probably dates from the 13th century.

Sometimes called the Monkey Temple because of the furry inhabitants that hang about, Swayambhunath features diverse religious iconography, from Tibetan prayer wheels and the Great *Dorje* (Sanskrit: *vajra*, a symbol of enlightened mind) to Hindu statuaries and temples devoted to a number of gods and goddesses. There are five monasteries belonging to different Buddhist schools on or around the hill complex, and the Tibetan Kargyud Gompa holds short chanting services everyday around 4 p.m., which are open to the public.

The views from hill are very fine, and although the complex is often crowded with tourist activity, it's possible to meditate on the patio space around the stūpa. If you plan to do so, bring something to sit on as the ground is usually filthy. Never trust your belongings to the monkeys. And remember to walk in a clockwise direction around the stūpa.

There are two ways to reach Swayambhunath. The traditional pilgrim's route is to walk up the steep eastern stairway to the top of the hill. It's also possible to take a taxi or rickshaw to/from the entrance on the western side of the hill, near the National Museum. Many travellers prefer to walk up the stairs and then take transport from the west entrance back to town, or vice versa. Be aware that the park at the base of the eastern stairway is frequented by peddlers and drunks; it's not advisable to pass through after dark. There is a small admission fee for the complex.

Bodhnath
Also referred to as Boudha or Boudhanath, this impressive stūpa is one of the largest of its kind in the world. Situated along an ancient trade route from India to Tibet, Bodhnath has long been an important centre of Buddhist culture and religion. Following the Chinese invasion of Tibet in 1949, large numbers of refugees resettled around Bodhnath, and the area is now one of the largest and most openly accepted communities of Tibetans-in-exile. Clean and prosperous, the township around the Great Stūpa is alive with Tibetan culture and active Buddhist study. The

area is home to hundreds of monks and nuns in residence at dozens of monasteries, many named after those destroyed by the Chinese in Tibet.

Accounts vary as to the origins and construction of the stūpa, but it is generally believed to have been established as a sacred site in the 6th century CE. The present structure is probably the result of restoration or reconstruction work undertaken in the early 16th century. The Great Stūpa is known to house a number of important relics, though there is some speculation as to what is actually entombed. The stūpa is said to enshrine one of the historical Buddha's bones, and Tibetans believe that it contains bone relics of the Buddha Kaśyap.

Regardless of what's inside, the active devotion of Tibetan and Newar Buddhists gives Bodhnath an unmistakable spiritual atmosphere, and it's a pleasure to visit in the early evening when hundreds gather to perform *kora*, a walking meditation where practitioners circle the stūpa in a clockwise direction, often while spinning prayer wheels, chanting, or simply chatting with friends and family. Daily *kora* at Bodhnath is both a religious and social occasion. Because the *mandala* of the inner courtyard and stūpa surface are open to the public during the day, the Great Stūpa is a conducive place to sit and meditate, observing the flux and flow of people and pigeons in this peaceful settlement.

Bodhnath is also an excellent alternative to staying in hectic Kathmandu—see below for details. Located a few kilometres north-east of Kathmandu city, Bodhnath is easily reached by taxi, and buses run regularly from the city bus station. It's also possible to walk between Bodhnath and **Pashupatinath**, Nepal's most important Hindu temple complex. This interesting 30-minute route is well indicated on many tourist maps available throughout Kathmandu.

Sleeping & Eating

Kathmandu is absolutely teeming with accommodation options. Most travellers head for Thamel, the hyperactive tourists' district where you can find pretty much anything, though many meditators prefer the more relaxed energy of Freak Street, which doesn't lack for amenities either. Though somewhat removed from Kathmandu proper, Bodhnath is an even more ideal location for those seeking a quieter, contemplative atmosphere. Be aware that various parts of the city will be without power for a few hours each week on a rolling schedule, because there's not enough electricity production to meet the city's needs. Ask your guest house about their situation.

It's important to note at the outset that many streets in Kathmandu have multiple names, some of which may not be recognized by taxi drivers or other locals. Therefore it's always best to give a well-known landmark as your intended destination. Maps are available at any bookstore and will help to prevent unnecessary complications. When negotiating on room rates at guest houses and hotels, always take a look at available rooms before agreeing on a price. It's often effective to tell guest houses your room budget and how many nights you intend to stay, and then allow them to make you an offer.

Thamel is demarcated to the south by a road that runs east from Chhetrapati Chowk. Thamel's two main streets, JP School Road (JP Marg) and Thamel Marg, extend parallel to one another northward from the Chhetrapati Road. Numerous side streets connect the two and branch off in other directions. A decent on-line map (though lacking most street names!) can be found here: www.lirung.com/map/map_thamel/thamel_map_e.html

Budget accommodation abounds in Thamel. **Kathmandu Guest House**, off JP Marg, is the district's most commonly given landmark, and offers a wide range of rooms from budget to mid-range, plus a variety of services. Many travellers insist that better value can be found elsewhere, and other recommended budget options in central Thamel include **Hotel Horizon, Hotel Red Planet, Acme Guest House** (all fairly close to Kathmandu GH), and **Thorong Peak Guest House** (on Thamel Marg). A range of budget places can also be found in Paknajol, a less hectic district north of Thamel. For a clean and quiet place still close to Thamel's action, **Hotel Hama** (on a sidestreet near Chhetrapati Chowk) is great value, and features a pleasant courtyard garden.

The best mid-range options in Thamel are **Nirvana Garden Hotel** and **Tibet Guest House**, both near Hotel Hama. Other nearby mid-range places are to be found a little ways east in the neighbourhood of Jyatha, situated off Tridevi Marg between Thamel and Kanti Path Road. These include **Hotel Blue Horizon** (side street off Tridevi Marg) and **Mustang Holiday Inn**, down a side street off Jyatha Road where there are several other similar places.

Three somewhat unique mid-range options are available in western Kathmandu, near Swayambhunath. **Benchen Phuntshok Dargyeling Monastery** (www.benchen.org), across from the Military Hospital near the National Museum, runs a spotless guest house with views overlooking the valley and a vegetarian restaurant situated in a peaceful garden. **Tergar Monastery** has comfortable accommodations and space available for individual meditation retreats. Something of an institution, **Hotel Vajra** (www.hotelvajra.com) offers lovely rooms and features a Buddhist library and frequent cultural performances. Hotel Vajra is near Bijeshwori Temple on Swayambhunath Road.

The city has a number of luxury hotels, most of which are located some distance from Thamel. These include the 4-star **Malla Hotel** north-east of Thamel; **Shanker Hotel**, a former palace north of the Royal Palace; the famous **Yak & Yeti Hotel** south of the Royal Palace; and **Dwarika's Hotel**, decorated with ancient Nepali woodcarvings and located east of the city near Pashnupatinath.

Kathmandu has an incredible variety of eateries, the bulk of which are in Thamel, where you can find very decent and often interesting interpretations of most world cuisines. The neighbourhood's numerous rooftop restaurants are particularly popular. It's easy to find places to suit your tastes and your budget no matter where you are in the city. A few notable recommendations include the European-style **Galleria Café** above United Books in Central Thamel, an excellent place to escape the noise below with a cup of joe; **Lotus**, a marvellously inexpensive little Japanese place next to Blue Diamond Guest House in Thamel (on the second floor); and

Dudh Sagar, a tasty South Indian restaurant (try the *mixed chaat!*) a few minutes walk south of the Vipassana City Office on Kanti Path.

Freak Street (actually Jhochhen Tole) is an excellent alternative to Thamel. Extending south from Kathmandu's Durbar Square, this older travellers' district puts you close to the sites and rhythms in the heart of the old city. Relaxed and a little run-down but still lovable, Freak Street offers pretty much everything Thamel does without the sensory overload. All accommodation is in the budget range, and good places include **Monumental Paradise, Century Lodge** and **Annapurna Lodge**. Freak Street's restaurants don't offer the same variety as those in Thamel, but are great for cheap eats. **Kumari Restaurant** and **Ginger Café** are quite nice, as are the cakes and treats at **Snowman**.

Visitors to Durbar Square are required to pay a small entry fee, so for those staying on Freak Street it's best to obtain a **Visitor's Pass**, which allows unlimited access and is valid for the duration of your visa. Passes are easily obtained at the Site Office at Basantapur Square, a large open antiques market area at the southern end of Durbar Square where Freak Street intersects Ganga Path. There is a small fee for the Visitor's Pass, and you'll need your passport and two passport-sized photos. The Visitor's Pass is also recommended for anyone sightseeing over several days in Kathmandu, as you're likely to pass through Durbar Square more than once. When you first arrive at Durbar Square on your way to Freak Street, just tell the entrance attendants that you're going to stay there; they'll usually let you go through without paying the entry fee. If you do pay the fee, save your ticket and it will be credited toward your Visitor Pass when you register at the site office.

As one of the world's most important centres for the study of Tibetan Buddhism, Bodhnath is also a great place for meditators to stay, especially after a course at Dharmaśringa. Bodhnath tends to be a little more expensive than Thamel or Freak Street, but most feel the calm and quiet is well worth the extra cost. Several monasteries run guest houses to help support themselves, the best of which is **Lotus Guest House**, next to Tabsang Gompa on a backstreet just east of the stūpa. **Dragon Guest House, PRK Guest House**, and **Shechen Guest House** have also been recommended. **Hotel Norbu Sangpo** has a good reputation as a mid-range place. There are several good restaurants in the stūpa courtyard area with lots of vegetarian options, among them **Saturday Café** and **Sakura** (authentic Japanese). The amazing vegetarian food at **Stūpa View Restaurant** is complemented by lovely rooftop views of the Great Stūpa.

When staying for a few days or longer anywhere in Nepal (and other places on the subcontinent as well) it's often possible to buy large 20 litre jugs of filtered drinking water (the kind used in water coolers). You can have a jug sent to your room and use it to fill your reusable water bottles, rather than buy numerous expensive and wasteful disposable plastic bottles. Ask your guest house/hotel to arrange a water jug for you, and request that they deliver it to you unopened, to ensure safety. Then simply return the jug when empty!

Coming & Going

Getting around Kathmandu is fairly easy. Cycle rickshaws offer a convenient means of moving through the crowded lanes of the old city, which are also enjoyable to explore on foot, though not necessarily for long distances. Taxis, auto-rickshaws and buses are available for longer journeys within the Kathmandu area, but be aware that transport can be hard to come by after 8 p.m., when prices increase and the city begins to shut down for the night. As with all cities on the subcontinent, be prepared to negotiate prices with taxi and rickshaw drivers, and bring a face-covering when travelling by open-air vehicle, as the pollution from Nepal's low-grade fuel can be horrendous.

Kathmandu's **Tribhuwan International Airport**, 5 km east of the city centre, is connected to several major cities throughout South Asia. The immigration process at this no-frills airport is very straightforward: to obtain a visa, you'll need to fill out a form and present it along with your passport and one passport-sized photo (which you can have taken in a convenient booth) and the visa fee of $US 30 (payable in any major currency). You'll need passport photos for many things throughout your journey, so consider getting a double order at the airport. Be sure to exchange some money for Nepali rupees at the exchange counter in the immigration hall, as you won't have another opportunity until you get into the city. You'll need a receipt to change any remaining rupees when leaving the country, so ask for one and save it. The immigration process is often very slow, and you can speed things along by bringing passport photos with you, or even by securing your visa before you arrive. Otherwise, expect a queue.

There is a pre-paid fixed-rate taxi service from the airport to the city center; make arrangements in the downstairs lobby after passing through the baggage claims area. Otherwise the numerous waiting taxi drivers clambering for your attention outside the airport will almost certainly take you to a hotel of *their* choosing, rather than your intended destination.

The best way to purchase plane tickets is on-line or through a reputable travel agent. Many airlines have offices in central Kathmandu, but locations and numbers are always changing, so allow a travel agent to make arrangements for you if you can't find what you want on-line.

For travelling throughout the Kathmandu Valley, **local buses** are the cheapest method, though many destinations are close to Kathmandu city and can be affordably and much more comfortably reached by taxi. Most valley buses depart from Ratna Park Bus Station on the eastern side of Ratna Park in the city. Notable exceptions are buses to Bhaktapur, which depart from a bus stand on nearby Bagh Bazaar, just north of Ratna Park. See *Excursions* for more info.

It's also possible to travel long-distance throughout Nepal by local bus, though this is often an arduous, lengthy, uncomfortable and even dangerous undertaking that we recommend against. Local long-distance buses depart from the Kathmandu Bus Terminal (Gongu Bus Park) some distance north of the city on Ring Road.

The preferred method of long-distance travel is on the **intercity tourist buses** operated by a number of companies, including **Greenline** and **Golden Travels**. These companies cater to travellers, and offer serviceable ("deluxe air-con") buses, regular schedules and meal stops. Depending on your destination, lunch is usually included in the ticket price. Tickets should be booked at least 24 hours in advance and are most easily purchased through a reputable travel agent or your guest house/hotel. If you make a booking with one of the companies directly, they may require that you come to pick up tickets the day before your travel date; do so, otherwise your reservation may not be kept. Regular tourist bus service is usually available for Pokhara, Chitwan National Park and Lumbinī, but this may vary due to road conditions and political unrest—always check with the company or a travel agent to verify that buses are operating. Tourist buses either depart from their respective company offices or from the intersection of Kanti Path and Tridevi Marg. Confirm time and place with your travel agent.

Border Crossing

Many travellers choose to travel overland between Nepal and India, and the most convenient place to cross over is at **Sonauli**, a dusty run-down border town. It's also possible to cross at the restless frontier outpost of Birganj further to the east (north of Bodhgayā, Patna, and Vaishali), but the roads from Birganj to Kathmandu are bumpier than the roads between Sonauli and Kathmandu.

At Sonauli the immigrations and customs offices are open 24 hours on both the Indian and Nepali sides, but the border is closed to vehicle traffic between 10 p.m. and 4 a.m. If you arrive during this time it's usually not a problem to wake the office officials and then cross the border on foot. There are banks and currency exchange places on both sides. Both sides also offer a few passable accommodation options, but the Nepali side has the better choices, including **Hotel Plaza** and **Nepal Guest House**; if you need to stay on the Indian side your choice is the **Rahi Tourist Bungalow**. In either case, don't expect much. On the Nepali side the nearby town of **Bhairawa**, 4 km from Sonauli, is much more accommodating; try **Hotel Everest** or the mid-range **Hotel Yeti**, where most tourist groups stay and discounts are often available. The 5-star **Hotel Nirvana** also offers discounts that apparently make it worth the money after hard travel. Head to **Kasturi Restaurant** for decent Indian vegetarian eats. Bhairawa also has a regional **airport** servicing Kathmandu and Pokhara.

State and private buses depart from both Sonauli and Bhairawa in the morning and evening for Pokhara and Kathmandu (both 8–10 hours). Taxis are a good alternative, being faster and more comfortable, especially if you can find other travellers to share the cost. **Lumbinī**, only 22 km from Bhairawa, can easily be reached by regularly departing local mini-buses, which are cheap but very slow. It's also possible to hire a taxi to Lumbinī, but they may expect you to pay for a return trip even if you're only going one way. Return trip fares include two hours waiting time. See the *Coming & Going* section for Lumbinī for more info.

Many travel agents in India and Nepal sell 'direct' or 'through' tickets for the journey to/from Kathmandu to Vārāṇasī, but all travellers, regardless of tickets, will have to change buses at the border. These tickets are notorious for being problematic, as scores of travellers report being forced to buy an overpriced new ticket after crossing the border—this is especially common when crossing into India. It's therefore advisable to book a bus to Bhairawa or Sonauli, cross the border, and then book another bus continuing into India (or vice versa). Because tourist buses don't offer service to the border on either side, you might consider travelling in relative comfort to Lumbinī and making that your first/last stop before journeying further.

Travelling into India, it's a 3-hour trip from Sonauli to Gorakhpur, a travel hub where you can then take the train to Vārāṇasī (5.5 hours), Lucknow (6 hours), Delhi (sleeper, 16 hours) and Kolkata (sleeper, 23 hours). Gorakhpur is also the transfer point for Kushinagar. See the *Coming & Going* sections of these respective locations for more info.

When travelling into Nepal, you'll need to catch a bus from Gorakhpur by 3 p.m. in order to catch a same-day night bus to Pokhara or Kathmandu from the Nepali side of the border. Two-month Nepali visas can be obtained at the border for US$30 (dollars only, no rupees), with a passport-size photo. Three-day pilgrim visas for visiting Lumbinī are free. Nepali visas are available upon arrival, but you must obtain an Indian visa before arriving at the border. Travel agencies in Pokhara and Kathmandu can arrange visas for you if you don't have one already. These visas are expensive and aren't always legitimate, so it may be best to go to the embassy in Kathmandu yourself.

Excursions

While the Kathmandu Valley is usually quite stable, Nepal has been fraught with political conflict for years, and journeying elsewhere in the country can be difficult and dangerous. The southern Terai region bordering India is particularly volatile, and transport strikes and road closures are not uncommon. Nepal is generally fairly safe for foreigners, but everything depends on the current situation. Stay updated by regularly checking with international media sources, embassy websites and tourist information outlets.

Patan

South of Kathmandu city across the Bagmati River, Patan (also known as Lalitpur, 'City of Beauty') was once the capital of an ancient independent kingdom and is in fact the oldest city in the valley. Though often considered an extended part of Kathmandu, Patan retains a distinct character and proud heritage as an artisan's city, rich in culture and history. Patan has a long Buddhist legacy, and was important in the transmission of the tradition from India to Tibet. The ancient capital's plan is said to have originally been designed as a Dharma-chakra, or Wheel of Dhamma, the perimeter of which is marked by four mounds (*thurs*) attributed to Emperor Asoka, who is said to have visited the valley in 250 BCE. The northern Asokan Stūpa is the best preserved, while the southern is the largest. Patan's Durbar Square forms the center of this configuration, a beautiful if somewhat touristy square packed with well-preserved palaces, temples and monuments that together form one of the valley's most important World Heritage Sites. There is an entry fee for the Square. Patan is easily accessible by taxi and makes an excellent day trip from Kathmandu. It's also possible to stay there if you're so inclined, though options are somewhat limited.

Bhaktapur

Like Patan, Bhaktapur ('City of Devotees') was once an ancient capital of the valley. Only 12 km east of Kathmandu city, this important Newar centre is known today as a sort of living museum, because much of the town's ancient character is preserved by a carefully limited development plan and the support of a German restoration project. There is a substantial entry fee for foreigners (US$10), but the majority of visitor's don't mind paying what amounts, at least in part, to a project contribution. Walking through the streets of Bhaktapur is like journeying back in time, and the town is said to resemble Kathmandu as it looked thirty years ago, before the modern influx of cars and concrete. Bhaktapur's Durbar Square rivals the others in the valley, and houses and temples throughout town have some of the best-preserved decorative woodcarving and brickwork in Nepal.

While the Royal Palace is now a National Gallery and the town also boasts a few unique shops and showrooms, there isn't a lot "to do" in Bhaktapur per se; rather, with limited motor traffic and lots of atmosphere, it's a lovely place to spend the day exploring on foot. There are a number of cafés and restaurants around Durbar Square, and also several around the equally impressive Taumadhi Square, including **Marco Polo Restaurant**. Bhaktapur is also host to several festivals and music events throughout the year, most of which take place at night. Check with ECS Magazine or any tourist office in Kathmandu. If there's an upcoming event, consider staying in Bhaktapur for a night or few to enjoy the town more fully. There is a limited range of available lodging. The entry fee gives you a valid pass (stay or return visits) for one week. Bhaktapur is famous for a yogurt curd desert called *ju-ju dhau* ('king of curd') – if you visit, don't miss out.

Bhaktapur is easily accessible and usually takes about 45 minutes by bus (see *Coming & Going*). The last bus back to Kathmandu departs at dusk, and may take up to double the usual time due to traffic. Consider departing earlier or taking a taxi.

Pokhara

Situated on Nepal's second largest lake, and framed in clear weather by a gorgeous expanse of white mountains, Pokhara is the major tourist destination outside the Kathmandu Valley. Well positioned to serve as a hotspot for trekking and adventure sports, Pokhara is a fairly relaxing travellers' haven with no shortage of amenities or activities. In fact the Lakeside district, the town's center of activity, feels a lot like one of Thamel's quieter avenues plopped down in the middle of the countryside.

Lakeside is the best area to stay, and most budget places are to be found here, including **Noble Inn** (set back on a side street), and **Hotel Temple Villa**, **Hotel Octagon** and **Nature's Grace Lodge** (all near one another on another side street).

Yeti Guest House has a great location, but watch for rising prices: like an increasing number of places, they've taken their *Lonely Planet* endorsements to heart. It's also possible to stay at the southern end of the lake in Damside, a quieter but somewhat run-down and inconvenient area. The north end of Lakeside is a good alternative for those seeking an accessible escape from the main activity. Mid-range places tend to be pretty good value in Pokhara, and many of them are right on the lakeshore. Try **Hotel Fewa** (with separate stone cottages), **Hotel Stūpa**, **Hotel Meera** or **Hotel Hungry Eye**.

There are two modern hospitals in Pokhara, both said to be over-crowded; there's also a private clinic not far from Lakeside called **Celestial Healthcare**, which has good services and caters specifically to insured travellers.

Pokhara has three bus stations: the Main Bus Station, east of Lakeside and north of the Airport; the Baglung Bus Station, north of town on the highway, which provides service for some trekking start points; and the Mustang Bus Stand in Damside, which provides service for most tourist buses to/from Kathmandu and elsewhere, as well as a number of buses connecting to the Annapurna region. This is the most important bus station for travellers, but always check with your travel agent and make sure you have a clear understanding of the place from which your bus departs. Pokhara is a pretty bicycle-friendly town, and rentals are widely available.

Pokhara offers a range of courses, activities and adventures, including yoga, rafting and paragliding, but is most famous as a base for trekking in the nearby Annapurna range. You can bargain for great deals on facsimiles of name-brand trekking gear at dozens of Lakeside shops, and easily find all the books, maps and information you'll need to embark on a journey in the Himālaya. You can also often buy books and gear from returning trekkers, which is helpful for them as well, so speak to people at your guest house or even on the street.

There is an **Annapurna Conservation Area Project (ACAP) Office** in Damside where you'll need to get a permit for the Annapurna region; bring the correct fee (2000 rupees), your passport and two passport-sized photos. For a small additional fee, several Lakeside travel agents are happy to secure your permit for you. There are lots of companies at which you can arrange organized treks as well as hire guides and porters, and many guest houses provide similar services. Some of the major trekking companies are based in Kathmandu, so if you're interested in hiring someone, you many want to inquire when you're still in the capital. The majority of people hiking the Annapurna Circuit hire at least one porter per two or three people, but for experienced trekkers this is by no means necessary. However, it's rumoured that the government may begin to require that all trekking groups be accompanied by a licensed guide or porter.

Regardless, you'll definitely need a good guidebook. Two recommended titles are *Lonely Planet Trekking in the Nepal Himalaya* and the more detailed *Trekking in the Annapurna Region* by Bryn Thomas. Search Pokhara's bookshops for other titles and second-hand copies.

About two-thirds of all trekkers in Nepal visit the Annapurna region. The area is easily accessible, guest houses in the hills are plentiful, and treks here offer incredibly diverse scenery, with both high mountains and lowland villages. Also, because the entire area is inhabited, trekking in the region offers unique cultural exposure and experience.

There are three major trekking routes in the region: the **Annapurna Circuit** (average 17 days: begins in Besisahar, ends in Naya Pul) which circles the entire Annapurna massif and crosses one of the highest mountain passes in the world; the **Annapurna Sanctuary** (average 9 days, begins in Phedi) a return route which goes to Annapurna base camp; and the **Jomson Trek** (8-12 days, begins in Naya Pul) which covers the western half of the Annapurna Circuit and takes you to Jomsom and the holy sites of Muktinath. The Jomsom Trek requires you to either return along the same route or fly back to Pokhara from Jomsom, which is what most people do. This trek, however, is increasingly disturbed by a road-building project and no longer comes highly recommended. As an alternative to Jomsom, we recommend the **Manang Trek** (12-14 days, begins in Besisahar), which takes you up the eastern side of the Circuit instead. You'll have a chance to experience the beautiful Manang Valley and can then fly back to Pokhara from nearby Hongde. Neither the Jomsom nor Manang trek requires you to traverse the Thorong La, the high mountain pass that lies in between those two destinations. Make flight bookings with a travel agent *before* setting off from Pokhara if you intend to fly back.

Not everyone who comes to Pokhara sets off on intensive multi-week treks, and the town is also a good starting place for other short treks of one to four days, such as routes to Ghorepani or Ghandruk. Some enjoy excursions to nearby villages for great sunrises, sunsets and mountain views. The short hike to the **World Peace Pagoda**, overlooking Pokhara from across the lake, is an excellent day trip, and can be combined with a boat trip across the lake. Pokhara has a lot to offer and is deservedly popular.

Relaxed in the lowland along a lake, and framed by our first tentative glimpses of the high mountains, Pokhara made an excellent place for us to wait out the rains and make preparations for the trek we'd eventually decided to attempt: the Annapurna Circuit, a well-established 200-odd-mile loop that follows ancient trade routes towards Tibet, circling the Annapurna massif and crossing at its apex one of the highest mountain passes in the world.

Though we'd climbed Mt. Fuji together, this venture was to be Shauna's first experience of multi-day trekking, and one of my most difficult, requiring real endurance to complete the circuit, which takes a minimum of about 17 days. We elected to carry our own packs, which was necessary for all the trekking I've done previously, whereas about 80% of the people we met had hired guides/porters to take their loads. And because the trek is so well established, passing through villages where food and lodging is readily available, it's not necessary to carry sleeping bags, tents, food or cooking gear. That put our packs at about 30-35 lbs., very real but also quite reasonable, in my estimation. Shauna, however, would perhaps disagree...

A few days after arriving in Pokhara, the monsoon finished its un-expected encore, bowing out to the breaking sun, and the weather finally held. Saddled and psyched, we set off on a morning bus ride, which took us several hours further into the foothills, and by day's end we were hiking along a crude road with school children on their way home from one village to another. For the next three days we journeyed through the sub-tropical midlands, terraced rice paddies and languid banana trees improbably presided over by the great white bulks of distant peaks, drawing ever closer as we followed the Marsyangdi River deeper into the labyrinthine folds of the range.

Despite its precipitous scale, the Annapurna Conservation Area isn't exactly wilderness, at least what we were able to see of it; the river courses and trail networks are all actively inhabited, the hills ter-raced for rice and, where it's too steep and cold in the higher reach-es, for maize. We pass through dozens of various-sized villages, and see more secreted away, almost invisible among the high recesses of rock and frond. And the circuit trail we follow isn't merely a hiking trail, but a high mountain highway, where all goods must be carried in and out by men, or more commonly pack-mules, which pass us in long trains, littering the track with dung that dries and grinds to scat-tering dust in the hot slog of our first several days of hard hiking.

Our own difficulties are put into a certain perspective by the weath-ered porters who pass us, often only in flip-flops, with absurd loads supported by a rope across the forehead: we see a man carrying several sheets of 8'x4' corrugated tin; several men with cages full of chickens; a teenager porting for a hiking group, with three folding metal tables; a group of local boys walking, each casually carrying a freshly-severed cow's leg; and one old man, tidily dressed, carrying his invalid wife in a plastic deck chair on his back.

Culture informs much of our experience during the trek, and we re-ceive a rather strange reception in the sooty Hindu villages in the midlands, where people often regard us unsmilingly, with a look of faint curiosity shading into something like envy, even disdain. But the people seem to grow warmer as the mountains grow colder and we ascend in altitude, crossing into the Tibetan-influenced lands of the alpine and high desert regions, where Buddhist chortens and prayer walls dot the landscape, offering us safe passage.

There is something of the Wild West here too, especially in Chame, where we arrive in time to witness an annual horse competition: Ti-betan cowboys flying down the main street on half-wild ponies. And in the high twisted-juniper deserts above 10,000 feet, in landscapes that remind me of the American South West, we pass through medieval villages of stone and mud, strikingly similar to Pueblo complexes.

It is harvest time here, and villagers thrash their wheat, buckwheat and barley by hand, leaving grains and great stacks of firewood to dry on flat rooftops.

We rest a few days in the Manang Valley, giving ourselves time to acclimatize to the increasing altitude, and hike up to a small hermitage high in the cliff side, home to Lama Teshi, a 91-year-old monk known as the 100-Rupee-Lama because—for 100 rupees—he will offer blessings to trekkers for safe travels and long life. Shauna is radiant with the simple joy of this man as we share tea and watch him rather fastidiously count his money, childlike and unflinchingly kind...

We need such blessings, because snow begins to fall as we approach the Thorong La, the high pass that we must cross to complete the circuit. Even in normal conditions the pass is a fairly serious mountaineering proposition, requiring at least six hours to reach the village on the far side. When we wake before dawn the next morning to steady wet snow we're torn with a difficult decision: if we go, we risk worsening conditions and dangerous temperatures, not to mention the possibility of altitude sickness. But if we wait another day, we risk worsening conditions and the possibility of the pass closing, or of being snowed in here at the very basic accommodation of Thorong Phedi, one of two base camps for the pass. We are ill-equipped for such conditions, and the snow is too wet, visibility too poor. Though most at Thorong Phedi decide to go over in the snow, we wait.

Our decision turned out to be an excellent one; the snow broke at about 2 p.m., and the next morning we awoke to a glittering net of stars and crystal clarity. We set off at about 5 a.m., climbing into the sunrise, the narrow track quickly packed to ice by those preceding us, dark shadows against the glowing crest of fresh snow. We suffer little from the altitude, but with full packs the going is slow, our pace deliberately measured as we cross through the frosted other-worldly expanses of the abode of snow, the sky deepening to an impossible richness of darkest blue, peaks piling to the heavens and with our own heads afloat, I find myself suddenly emotional, overcome with a sense of something equally deep within, a sense of relief at having chosen well, but something more too, something more than altitude or exertion, but connected to this breath, gratitude for breath, for breathing, for being alive... After a challenging initial ascent, the pass is a long rolling white oblivion where distance is impossible to judge, where everything seems to stretch and reach and lengthen, an oasis for ice giants. We are strung along to the extent of our endurance by a series of false summits, high knolls that only show us we've got farther to go until, at last, we find that the height is beneath our feet, standing on top of the world. At its height the Thorong La is 17,769 ft. (5416 m), higher than Everest Base Camp, higher than any peak in the continental United States.

There is, unbelievably, a small, crouching teahouse there at the top, serving (at about a US$1.50 a cup) the most expensive tea in Nepal, a little thimble of fire for frozen hands in that cold void, strong stuff for spirits already flying. We hang for a moment in the thin air, and then begin the long, icy, treacherous descent, step by careful, sliding step...

For the next week we descend again from high desert through the alpine regions south of Marpha and eventually back into sub-tropical rice-lands, following the great Kali Gandaki River on its journey to India. But there is a road being built along this entire stretch, already continuous from Muktinath to Lete and frequented by motorcycles and jeeps. In a few years this place, these agrarian villages and expansive landscapes will be openly accessible and inevitably changed. The trek itself may cease to exist.

Still, when we watch the sunrise from Poon Hill on our last morning, shy sunrise plotting points for the day's rotation and kissing the broad faces of Annapurna and Dhaulagiri with first light, those great and ancient mountains seem utterly beyond the bustle of morning hikers and distant highways, enduring and ever-white.

– Austin Pick

The West:
Mumbai

Mumbai (formerly Bombay) is the largest, wealthiest, most propulsive city in India, a booming metropolis filled with everything from Bollywood glamour to crowded, appalling slums and, sandwiched between these extremes, the dreams and aspirations of millions. Most meditators usually avoid Mumbai's intense clamor and limit themselves to the tourist areas where it's relatively easy to do some shopping, eat comforting international food, and check e-mail before travelling to other destinations. While there's nothing wrong with that approach, especially when your time is limited, exploring Mumbai's endless bazaars—nestled amongst 19th century Victorian buildings, modern sky-rises, decrepit shantytowns, and ancient temples—can make for an unforgettable adventure. If you're interested in discovering what this "Gateway to India" has to offer, refer to one of the many guidebooks widely available around the city, take an organized city-tour, or as one friend loves to do, hop on to a random city train or bus and see where it leads you...

Tales from Mumbai

The Buddha spent his life in Northern India, and there is no historical record of him ever travelling to India's south-western coast. Nevertheless, we include these legends as inspiration:

> A sea-merchant's ship sank and the entire crew drowned, except for one sailor who caught hold of a plank of wood that carried him safely to shore. When he reached the shore he realized he was naked, so he covered himself by tying the plank to his body. He found a bowl on the beach and started begging for his food. Passers-by gave him enough to eat and called him *Bāhiyadārucīriya* (*Bāhiya* for short—the man who wears wood for clothing). After a short while, locals took him to be a religious saint and spoke in praise of his austere living.

> One day, a *Mahābrahmā*, who had been Bāhiya's friend in a previous life, came to visit him. Bāhiya's jaw dropped as he gazed at the splendid light emenating from the god's body.

> "Bāhiya, my old friend, pretending to be a saint is a foolish thing to do," the *Mahābrahmā* admonished, "Stop it right now! Go to Sāvatthī and meet the Buddha for proper spiritual guidance."

> "Thank you, Lord. I will go right away," Bāhiya said, with a strong sense of urgency in his voice. He then immediately started running to Sāvatthī. Within one night, perhaps supported by *Mahābrahmā*, Bāhiya ran more than 1 300 km from Mumbai to Sāvatthī! He looked

around the large city when he arrived, unsure where he might find the Buddha. But moments later, the Buddha appeared from around the corner, and Bāhiya instantly knew it was him. He ran up to the Buddha and fell to his knees.

"Please, Venerable Sir, please teach me the proper way to Truth," Bāhiya begged, panting and dripping with sweat.

"Bāhiya, this is not the proper time to teach the Dhamma. Please wait until the alms gathering is finished and the meal has been eaten."

"Venerable Sir, I cannot wait a moment longer. Perhaps I will die before then or perhaps you will die before then. Please teach me right now!" Bāhiya persisted.

"Ok, Bāhiya, pay close attention," the Buddha began, sensing that this man was going to die very soon.

When you see a form, be aware that it is merely a sight; when you hear a sound, be aware that it is merely a sound; when you smell an odour, be aware that it is merely an odour; when you taste a flavour be aware that it is merely a flavour; when you touch something, be aware that it is merely a touch; and when you think of anything, be aware that it is merely a thought.

A wide smile came upon Bāhiya's face as this simple yet profound analytical teaching penetrated his mind. He asked permission to join the Saṅgha, and the Buddha agreed, instructing him to get a set of robes, a bowl and the other requisites of a *bhikkhu*. While walking mindfully on his way to retrieve them, a mad cow jumped in his path and gored him to death. When the Buddha and some other *bhikkhus* found his body, they cremated it and enshrined his remains in a stūpa. That evening some *bhikkhus* asked the Buddha how someone could attain liberation so quickly. He responded,

Hearing a single couplet pregnant with meaning
That leads to peace,
Is better than a thousand couplets
Composed of meaningless words.[196]

At the end of the rains retreat, Bhikkhu Puṇṇa bid farewell to the Buddha, telling him that he planned on going to teach the Dhamma in his native land of Sunāparanta (not far from present day Mumbai), a very rough and brutal area.

"Puṇṇa, the people there are fierce and uncivilized. What will you do if they verbally abuse you?" The Buddha asked this, wanting to see if this *bhikkhu* was really ready to take on such a mission.

"Then Lord, I will think that at least they did not hit me."

"And if they do hit you?"

"Then I will think that at least they did not stab me with a knife or kill me."

"And if they do stab you with a knife or kill you?"

"Then I will bear my fate with equanimity and forgiveness."

The Buddha praised Puṇṇa's wise attitude and gave him blessings for his journey. After Bhikkhu Puṇṇa arrived in Sunāparanta, his noble composure attracted hundreds of disciples, who practised the Dhamma properly and realized enlightenment.[197]

Site-Sitting

Global Vipassana Pagoda

For meditators, the primary place of interest in Mumbai is the newly constructed Global Vipassana Pagoda (commonly referred to as the Global Pagoda), a replica of the Shwedagon Pagoda in Yangon, Myanmar. Organized through the efforts of Vipassana teacher S.N. Goenka, the Global Vipassana Pagoda is a graceful expression of gratitude towards the Buddha, his teachings, and to all the countless meditators who have maintained these teachings with sincerity. The pagoda is especially commemorative of Sayagyi U Ba Khin, who was responsible for returning the Dhamma to India from Myanmar, and pays homage to the country of Myanmar itself, which preserved the tradition for more than two millennia.

The 100 m tall central pagoda is now the largest free-standing dome structure in the world, and can accommodate more than 8 000 meditators! This is an excellent place to meditate not only for the sheer number of people who come here to purify their minds, but also because the Buddha's relics are enshrined at the center of the pagoda's ceiling, and are believed to emanate powerful vibrations that assist meditators in that task, truly making the site an island of calm amidst Mumbai's vast sea of people.

One of the aims of the Global Vipassana Pagoda is to inform people of the life and teachings of the Buddha. A museum, information centre, art gallery, library, and meditation centre (see below) will be available for visitors to learn more about who the Buddha was, what his teachings were, and how they are applied to the benefit of humankind.

To get to the Global Vipassana Pagoda, take the train to Borivali Station. Exit at the west gate of the station, and then take an auto-rickshaw or bus 294 to Gorai Bus Depot. Then hop on to a Ferry from Gorai Jetty (next to the bus stand) to Esselworld (an amusement park). As you approach the Esselworld entrance on the right, bear left and go through the gate, then follow the signs to the pagoda.

One day courses for old students are held at the Global Vipassana Pagoda every Sunday from 11 a.m. to 5 p.m. Students are advised to call the site office in advance to obtain a gate pass. One-day course applications can also be downloaded from http://www.dhamma.org/en/schedules/schpattana.shtml

Contact:
Global Vipassana Foundation (administrative offices)
Green House, 2nd Floor
Green Street, Fort
Mumbai–400023
(Opposite the Old Customs House)
Tel: [+91] (0)22-22665926/-22664039
Fax: [+91] (0)22-22664607
E-mail: admin@globalpagoda.org
Website: www.globalpagoda.org
(For the actual physical location of the Global Vipassana Pagoda,
see Contact information for Dhamma Pattana, below.)

Dhamma Pattana
Dhamma Pattana ('Port of Dhamma') is an integrated part of the Global Vipassana Pagoda complex, and features residential and meditation facilities that allow old students to practise seriously and benefit from the powerful atmosphere of the Global Vipassana Pagoda itself.

The second small pagoda at the Global Vipassana Pagoda complex is reserved exclusively for the use of Dhamma Pattana students, and contains a hundred meditation cells so that each course participant can meditate in an individual cell.

Dhamma Pattana offers 10-day, 3-day, 1-day and *Satipaṭṭhāna* courses for old students in the tradition. There are plans to conduct long courses at this centre in the future.

Contact:
Dhamma Pattana Vipassana Centre
Near Esselworld
Gorai Creek, Borivali (West)
Mumbai–91
Tel: [+91] (22) 33747518 / 28452238/ 28452261/ 28452111
Fax: [+91] (0)22-28452261
E-mail: info@pattana.dhamma.org
Website: www.pattana.dhamma.org

Shopping, Activities, Services & Sites

For those wanting to pick up souvenirs for friends and family back home, check out the **Khadi Bhavan** or **Fab India** on MG Road at Fort. Both are great for ethically manufactured clothing, cosmetics and handicrafts. If you're staying in Colaba and you don't have much time to shop, you'll find almost everything you might want at **Chuni Lal** or **Sakari Bhandar** general stores. In and around the World Trade Centre near Cuffe Parade, you'll find **State Government Emporiums** from all over India selling their regional goods. Prices are usually a little higher, but it's easier to get your Kashmiri carpet from the emporium than it would be lugging it back from war-torn Kashmir.

If you're looking for a shopping adventure, dive into the narrow, chaotic and colourful lanes of **Kalbadevi, Javeri**, and **Bhuleshwar** bazaars where you'll find jewellery, handicrafts, music, antiques, furniture and clothing. To get there, hop on to bus #1, 3, or 21 from Colaba or Flora Fountain in Fort.

Lovers of books on Indian religion and culture can spend hours at the pavement stalls on Churchgate; however, there are much better selections and less pressure from vendors at some of the bookshops. Try the **Motilal Banarsidas** book depot by the popular Mahalaxmi Hindu temple near Malabar Hill, the **People's Book Stall** on Veer Nariman, or **Bharatya Vidya Bhavan Bookstore** at Wilson College. For a wide selection of Dhamma books, videos, and CDs visit **Dhamma Granth** on-line at www.dhammagranth.com or contact bhupendra@dhammagranth.com. They will deliver your books to you anywhere in Mumbai for free with purchases over Rs 600.

Prince of Wales Museum

Although Mumbai has several cultural centres (Gandhi Mani Bhavan, National Gallery of Modern Art, Jehangir Art Gallery, Hanging Gardens, Victoria Gardens & Museum), the majestic Prince of Wales Museum deserves mention for its fine collection of Buddhist sculptures. The museum also contains the best paintings, images, and bas-reliefs from the famous Elephanta Caves, rendering the stomach-churning boat-ride, overly crowded site, and hefty entrance fee to Elephanta even less appealing.

The museum is located at Kala Ghoda (the end of MG Road), a small area of museums and galleries between Colaba and Fort. The museum is open from 10:00 a.m. to 6:00 p.m. everyday except Mondays. The entry fee for foreigners is US$5.

Sleeping & Eating

Mumbai is divided into two general districts: North and South Mumbai. North Mumbai is known for being home to the nouveau riche, with neighborhoods such as Juhu, Bandra, Chembur, Jogeshwari, and Santa Cruz having been transformed into areas of exclusive suburbs, corporate high-rises, shopping malls and world-class luxury hotels.

South Mumbai is made up of the well-known areas of Colaba Causeway, Fort, Marine Drive, Churchgate, Chowpatty Beach, Nariman Point, Malabar Hill and Kemp's Corner. Due to its rich history, tourist amenities, diplomatic representation, and proximity to the main railway stations, most visitors tend to stay in South Mumbai.

As with all cities, accommodation in Mumbai isn't cheap. Shoestring budget travellers are forced to stay in one of the cockroach-infested hotels around the lively CST (formerly Victoria Terminus—VT), one of Mumbai's major train stations. The only budget option at Colaba is a dorm bed at the **Salvation Army**. If you find the above unappealing, your best bet is to accept the fact that you will have to dish out at least Rs 500 for a double room and saunter around the causeway until you find an available room in one of the dozens of hotels. Favourites amongst meditators are the **Hotel Lawrence** in Fort (the area between Colaba and CST), **Fernandez Guest House** and **Hotel Prosser's** in Colaba, and **Bentely Hotel** on Marine Drive. These places are tricky to find and they usually fill up quickly, so it's recommended to make reservations in advance. If you don't have luck at one of these spots, try the decent 3-storied **Hotel Sea Lord** in Colaba.

Popular choices in the luxury group are the **Chateau Windsor** on Churchgate, the **YWCA International Centre** at Colaba, and **Marina, Lesser's,** and **Sea Green** guest houses on Marine Drive. If you want to experience Mumbai's best, spend your dollars at one of the top-end hotels such as the **Taj Mahal International**, the **Ritz**, or the **Oberoi**. Near the airport are hotels such as **Suresh** and **Lila**, where non-guests can enjoy excellent buffet meals and use the hotels' shuttle service to get to the airport.

At present there is little choice available for accommodation around the Global Vipassana Pagoda. Clean budget and mid-range rooms are available at the **Maxwell Hotel**, about 5 km from the Global Vipassana Pagoda. Buses pass near it and most rickshaw drivers should know where it is.

The dearth of accommodation that Mumbai suffers doesn't spill over into restaurants, as Mumbai has the widest variety of delicacies in India. Wherever you go, it's nearly impossible not to find a restaurant or food stall. You can feast on great vegetarian Indian dishes for as little as Rs 20 and as much as Rs 2 000. If it's been a while since you've had "authentic" food from home and you don't mind spending the extra rupees, check out the **Pizzeria** or **Not Just Jazz by the Bay** (lunch buffet) on the corner of Veer Nariman and Marine Drive, or the **Mandarin, Hong Kong,** or **Rooftop Rendez-Vous** in Colaba.

No matter where you choose to stay, it will be expensive compared to the rest of the country. The competition for rooms during the main tourist season (October-March) can be intense, so it is advisable to book a room in advance. If you choose to take a taxi when you leave the airport, it's best to get a pre-paid ticket from the taxi-booth. Avoid taxi drivers who don't accept pre-paid tickets; they often work for particular hotels and will almost certainly try to take advantage of you.

Coming & Going

While exploring the city's nooks and crannies, you have several options of getting around: by foot, taxi, bus or train. **Taxis** are convenient, but the drivers almost always refuse to use the meters or show you the fare conversion cards. They would much rather charge you a rate that is anywhere from double to five times the normal price. Your haggling skills will be put to the test in Mumbai. And a taxi isn't always the quickest way to get around, as Mumbai is notorious for traffic jams at nearly any time of day.

Mumbai's **intra-city public transport** system is one of India's finest. The double-decker buses are practical because they're frequent, cheap, travel all over the city, and are less polluting than private vehicles. Most locals are really up-to-date with the routes, so ask fellow passengers for info. Rush-hour tends to be very crowded so beware of pickpockets and gropers. If you find the buses crowded, the electric trains are even more so, and often involve an aggressive, yet amiable scramble to get on and off the train. When you're on the train, don't be shy to ask someone to tell you when your stop is coming up and which side the platform will be (the sides change from station to station) because the trains don't stop for very long and it's easy to miss your station. Locals know the best place to stand when preparing to disembark: follow their lead.

Because Mumbai is the financial capital of India and the main entry point into the country, the city is well connected to all major destinations. There are two country-wide **train** systems that run through Mumbai: Central and Western. Trains running east and south are on the Central line; trains heading north are on Western.

It's best to purchase tickets yourself at CST or Churchgate. Both stations have tourist queues, which are open from 9:00 a.m. to 5:00 p.m. with a 30-minute lunch break at 1:00 p.m. In addition to regular tickets, these queues offer tourist-quota tickets on most trains, which cost more but are sometimes the best (if not only) option for securing the seat you want. To get these handy tickets, you'll need to show your passport and your encashment (or ATM) receipt from wherever you converted your money into rupees. You can also pay directly in any major foreign currency. You might find the following trains helpful:

- Mahanagari Express 1093/1094 (Mumbai CST-Igatpuri-Nasik-Bhopal-Allahabad-Vārāṇasī)
- Mumbai Howrah Mail 2321/2322 (Mumbai CST-Igatpuri-Nasik-Jalgaon-Mughalsarai-Gayā-Howrah/Kolkata)
- Lokmanya Tilak (LT) Vārāṇasī Express 2165/2166 (LT/Mumbai-Igatpuri-Nasik-Vārāṇasī)
- LT Gorakhpur Express 1027/1028 (LT/Mumbai-Igatpuri-Nasik-Vārāṇasī-Gorakhpur)
- Kushinagar Express 1015/1016 (LT/Mumbai-Igatpuri-Nasik-Bhopal-Lucknow-Gonda-Gorakhpur)
- LT Rajendranagar Express 2141/2142 (LT/Mumbai-Nasik-Jalgaon-Mughalsarai-Patna)
- LT Rajendranagar Express 3201/3202 (LT/Mumbai-Igatpuri-Nasik-Jalgaon-Allahabad-Mughalsarai-Patna)
- Gitanjali Express 2859/2860 (Mumbai CST-Igatpuri-Nasik-Nagpur-Bhubaneshwar-Howrah/Kolkata)
- Mumbai Howrah Mail 2809/2810 (Mumbai CST-Igatpuri-Nasik-Jalgaon-Wardha-Nagpur-Howrah/Kolkata)
- Vidarbha Express 2105/2106 (Mumbai CST-Igatpuri-Nasik-Jalgaon-Wardha-Sevagram-Nagpur)
- Sevagram Express 1439/1440 (Mumbai CST-Igatpuri-Nasik-Jalgaon-Wardha-Sevagram-Nagpur)
- Tapovan Express 7617/7618 (Mumbai CST-Igatpuri-Nasik-Aurangabad)
- Devgiri Express 1003/1004 (Mumbai CST-Igatpuri-Nasik-Aurangabad)

- Mumbai-Pune Intercity Express 2127/2128 (Mumbai CST-Lonavala-Pune)
- Deccan Express 1007/1008 (Mumbai CST-Lonavala-Pune)
- Sinhagad Express 1009/1010 (Mumbai CST-Lonavala-Pune)
- Udyan Express 6529/6530 (Mumbai CST-Lonavala-Pune-Bangalore)
- Mumbai Hyderabad Express 7031/7032 (Mumbai CST-Lonavala-Pune-Hyderabad)
- Mumbai Hyderabad Hussainsagar Express 7001/7002 (Mumbai CST-Pune-Hyderabad)
- Kutch Express 9031/9032 (Mumbai Central-Ahmedabad-Bhuj)
- Rajdhani Express 2951/2952 (Mumbai-New Delhi)
- Bandra-Dehra Dun Express 9019/9020 (Bandra/Mumbai-Mathura-New Delhi-Haridwar-Dehra Dun)
- Punjab Mail 2137/2138 (Mumbai CST-Igatpuri-Nasik-Jalgaon-Bhopal-Vidisha-New Delhi)
- Dadar Amritsar Express 1057/1058 (Dadar/Mumbai-Igatpuri-Nasik-Jalgaon-Bhopal-Vidisha-New Delhi-Amritsar)
- Mumbai Jaipur Express 2955/2956 (Mumbai-Jaipur)

If you choose to travel by **bus** from Mumbai, then you have a wealth of options. Trains are much more comfortable and convenient for long distance journeys, but buses are cheaper and often easier to get tickets for, especially when booking on short notice.

You can travel by a **state bus** departing from the hectic State Bus Terminal, located opposite Mumbai Central Railway Station. These buses travel all over Maharashtra. It's also possible to find regular and deluxe **interstate buses** that go to the states of Gujarat, Goa, Karnataka and Madhya Pradesh. Some private companies offer **deluxe bus** services as well. It's best to buy your tickets directly from the company and not from an agent outside the railway station; agents usually charge a heavy commission, often 2 or 3 times the real price.

There is an extensive network of international and domestic **flights** to and from Mumbai. If you haven't purchased your ticket from home or on-line, you can find dozens of international and domestic airline offices at Nariman Point between Maharshi Karve Marg and Marine Drive. If you choose to fly domestically with Indian Airlines, there is also an office in the Taj Mahal Hotel in Colaba. Both airports are far from the tourist areas in southern Mumbai and take from 1 to 3 hours to reach, depending on traffic. If you're on a really tight budget and choose not to go by taxi, take a local train from Churchgate to Vile Parle and then a bus to the domestic airport. From there you can catch an airport bus to the international airport.

Igatpuri

The majority of Western travellers who visit this little town come to invest time at the Vipassana International Academy, the headquarters for Vipassana meditation in the tradition of S.N. Goenka. Between courses, you can meander through the town's narrow lanes lined with colourful fruit and vegetable stands and small shops, each one consisting of an open room either separated from the dirty road by a gutter or raised a couple of feet above it. Although most of these shops are sparse and tend to sell similar things—soap, grains, sugar, biscuits, cheap notebooks and pens, umbrellas, plastic sandals—there are also specialty shops to meet your internet, tailoring, hairstyling, photography and postal needs. **Baba-ji's**, a shop between the train station and the town's single ATM, is known to carry a good assortment of snacks and comfort foods.

Site-Sitting

Vipassana International Academy (VIA):
Dhamma Giri, Dhamma Tapovana & Vipassana Research Institute
In a wide valley surrounded by the ancient Sahyadri Mountains, the Dhamma Giri pagoda's golden spire soars above a re-forested hill. VIA is located on a vibrant 80-acre property dotted with flower gardens, fruit trees and a unique blend of Indian and Burmese architecture. It's an excellent setting for those working to eradicate the self-centredness, false sense of control, and restlessness of mind that prevents us from living in the present moment.

On the 16th of December 1974, a few hundred yards from the sleepy railway station in Igatpuri, a small group of seven men, all Vipassana meditators, slowly made their way up a deserted hill. Mr. S.N. Goenka, whom the others addressed as *Guru-ji* ('revered teacher'), had his foot in a cast, and hobbled along painfully with a crutch. When the group reached the top of the hill, they found a desolate land with crumbling ruins and a few scattered trees. Nearby, they could see bodies burning in a cemetery. "Guru-ji, this place could hardly be ideal for a meditation centre," one amongst the group said nervously.

Mr. Goenka smiled. "On the contrary, this is the ideal place. You can see the ultimate fate of this physical body for which we have so much attachment." The

Dhamma teacher paused as he experienced the vibrations on the lonely hill. "We were not looking for this place," he said quietly. "This place was looking for us."[198]

The site was soon named Dhamma Giri ('Hill of Dhamma'), and the first 10-day course was held in October 1976. Since then Dhamma Giri has grown to become the largest Vipassana meditation centre in the world, offering courses continuously for students from around the world.

Dhamma Giri has comfortable, gender-segregated accommodation for more than 600 meditators, including a separate accommodation block for *bhikkhus* attending courses. The meditation complex stands on the highest part of the site, appropriately named the Plateau of Peace (*Shanti Pathar*). At the center of the complex is Dhamma Giri's distinctive crowned pagoda, which is a replica of the famous Shwedagon Pagoda in Yangon, Myanmar. Based on the unique design of a "meditator's pagoda" created by Sayagyi U Ba Khin, Dhamma Giri's pagoda is a hollow structure containing 400 meditation cells for individual meditation, arranged in concentric rings. On either side of the pagoda are two meditation halls—one for women and one for men—each with a capacity of about 400. The four other halls at Dhamma Giri are used for longer courses, children's courses, foreign language instructions and discourses, conferences, and group sittings for Dhamma workers.

Down the hill from Dhamma Giri is **Dhamma Tapovana** ('Meditation Grove of Dhamma'), a smaller, similarly-structured centre reserved exclusively for old-student courses designed to deepen the veteran meditator's practice of awareness and equanimity. The first ever 60-day course was held to inaugurate the centre in the early months of 2002. In order to create the most supportive atmosphere possible, access to Dhamma Tapovana is restricted during courses. The course schedule is available on-line and at the VIA Office.

Adjacent to Dhamma Giri is the Vipassana Research Institute (VRI), which conducts and publishes research into the theory, practice and social applications of Vipassana meditation. Every year, VRI also holds an intensive 9-mouth Pāli course for serious old students. Participants divide their time between meditation, service and study. For more information about this program, send an e-mail to the director of VRI at info@giri.dhamma.org or check the website: www.vri.dhamma.org

Dhamma Giri is perhaps unparalleled among Vipassana centres in its ability to confound our sense of self-importance. The intense atmosphere helps many meditators discover not only the deepest aspects of our profound attachments, but also how to find release in the peace of the present moment. Meditators should also be warned that Dhamma Giri is a dynamic and often noisy place with constant construction and renovation, train whistles and talkative staff. Part of the centre's power rests in its ability to destroy our expectations and refusal to comply with our notions of what a perfect Dhamma centre should be. When meditators spend time at VIA, they often learn that the centre only becomes 'perfect' when the individual learns to let go of projections and expectations.

To get to the centre from Igatpuri's railway station, you can either take a rickshaw or taxi. Drivers often charge foreigners more than the local rate, but during the winter months, when the foreign meditators arrive in large numbers, drivers as well as local merchants in town earn a considerable amount of their annual income. You many want to consider this before haggling over what amounts to a small difference in your local currency. Alternately, the centre is only about 1 km from the station and is not difficult to reach by foot.

For sitting or serving at Dhamma Giri and Dhamma Tapovana, fill out an application form available on the website and send it—as early as possible—to the management by e-mail, fax or post. VIA receives a large amount of correspondence, so call or e-mail to follow up on your application and ensure acceptance.

Vipassana International Academy
Dhamma Giri Vipassana Centre
Igatpuri
Nasik–422403
Maharashtra
Tel: [+91] (0)2553-244076/-244086/-243712/-243238
E-mail: info@giri.dhamma.org
Website: www.giri.dhamma.org

I went to Dhamma Giri and was rather unexpectedly asked to give service for the Teacher's Self Course. I welcomed this invitation because it's what I'd hope for when I applied eight months prior, but at that time I was told there were already plenty of servers and there would be no space for me to attend. I was disappointed by this, so I talked to several of my friends and teachers at the Vipassana centre in Massachusetts, and they urged me to go to Dhamma Giri anyway; it's a very special place, they said, and I should see it even if I can't take part in the course. One teacher recommended that I make it especially clear that I'd like to serve, by e-mailing again from the US, calling when I got to India, calling again after my 30-day course in Jaipur, and then showing up and offering to serve.

However, when I finally arrived at Dhamma Giri and talked to the course manager about serving or sitting, he said (nicely), "Absolutely not. You see, the course is very full. You should have applied months ago." I reminded him that I had tried and been turned down, but that a teacher had recommended the strategy outlined above. He responded, "I don't know why people keep giving that advice. It's really not the way things work here." Maybe not, but the next day when the manager saw me he said, "Did they tell you? We lost all our Spanish interpreters—they're either sitting the course or have left. So we want you to serve." I ended up translating one sentence into Spanish for the entire course, and watering plants the rest of the time, which was fine because I was happy to be doing anything at all to help in that marvelous place.

– Peter Buchanan

Sleeping & Eating

Since Igatpuri offers very little in accommodation, it may be best to arrive at Dhamma Giri the day the Vipassana course begins. Only old students who plan on volunteering should arrive early, with permission from the management. If circumstances require you to spend the night in town, you can find a cheap and cheerless hotel room opposite the railway station. Alternately, you can spend approximately US$100 for a room at either **Manas Resort** or its cousin, **Manas Lifestyle Resort**, both located a few kilometres from the railway station. The latter spa's **Baithak Restaurant** has a vegetarian buffet. Igatpuri's main drag has several *dhabas* to eat at and a colourful market from which to purchase fruits and vegetables.

Coming & Going

A great way to get to Igatpuri is by **train**; the town is well connected by rail from all parts of the country. See Mumbai's *Coming & Going* section for a list of trains that pass through Igatpuri. If you plan on heading to Igatpuri on the day that a course is starting, the early morning commuter train *Tapovan Express* via Mumbai is a good option. Consider purchasing your ticket ahead of time on-line (www.irctc.co.in), especially if you're travelling during the Indian holiday season. Getting a train ticket is usually easy, but Igatpuri is a somewhat popular vacation place for affluent Indians during the winter months. Expect the journey from Mumbai to take about 3 hours by train.

Some meditators prefer hiring a taxi from Mumbai or even taking a taxi directly to Dhamma Giri from the airport. This method may be more convenient but is fairly expensive and much less comfortable than the train due to the poor quality of the roads. If you take a taxi from the airport, be sure to hire one from the prepaid booth. By taxi you can expect a journey of about 3 hours during the day, or 7 hours during the night. Travelling by highway at night is widely considered to be quite dangerous.

Excursions

Day Hikes
A great way to spend a day between courses at Dhamma Giri is to venture out on a nice hike up the mountain that forms the centre's stunning backdrop, which is part of the ancient Sayadri Range. To get to the top, take the footpath that begins behind the Sayagyi U Ba Khin Village and follow it beyond the small Hindu shrine. When you get up to the first broad plateau, keep to your right until you get to a second plateau, where you find yourself between the two mountaintops in a position that overlooks the villages in the adjacent valley. Unless you are a *very* skilled rock-climber, avoid the steep and dangerous path on your left that leads directly up to the top. Take the path on your right that proceeds along the side of the mountain and overlooks the valley villages. The path makes a gradual descent towards the villages below, but then cuts to the left and up towards the top of the mountain. The spectacular views of the entire valley and the inspiring academy make the effort well worth it. To get to the top from Dhamma Giri takes about 1 hour.

Another great hike leads to an ancient Buddhist cave that is now used as a cow-shed. Follow the above instructions up to the second plateau. Rather than going alongside the mountain, take one of the paths leading down towards the villages. Once you get to the large pond, keep going through the rice paddies until you come face to face with a mountain. The cave is at the foot of it. If you have any doubts, just ask any villager you pass for the *gufā* (cave). To get to the cave from Dhamma Giri takes about two hours.

Beware of going on a hike during or just after the rainy season (June-September), when the vegetation is still lush. Not only do the tall grasses make it quite easy to lose your way, but dense vegetation is an ideal habitat for deadly snakes. These hikes are best taken during the winter or hot season, when seasonal foliage is minimal.

Pandu Lena
Perched high up on a characteristic Deccan hillside is a group of 24 Buddhist caves dating from around the 1st century BCE. Although the artwork is less impressive than at Ajaṇṭā and Ellora, the area is quiet and peaceful because few tourists visit Pandu Lena (except on weekends). The caves are a pleasant 10-minute hike up the hill. Bring a lunch and spend a few hours meditating in the caves and appreciating the spiritually inspired sculptures and architecture.

To get to Pandu Lena from Igatpuri or Nasik, you can take a bus, shared-taxi, or private taxi, with which you'll probably have to arrange a return trip. To return to Igatpuri or Nasik by bus, wave one down as it passes the Pandu Lena entrance.

A couple of years ago, I went to the Vipassana International Academy (VIA) in Igatpuri for nine months to study Pāli, the language spoken by Gotama the Buddha. The Pāli Programme was an experiential learning opportunity for me. I joined other students from all over the world to combine Pāli studies with meditation and volunteer service on the 10-day silent meditation courses at Dhamma Giri.

The Pāli Programme follows the same approach the Buddha took towards teaching the Dhamma: practice, study and service. We studied the Buddha's different discourses such as the Mahāsatipaṭṭhāna Sutta, the Mangala Sutta, the Karaniyamettā Sutta, and the Ratana Sutta. Living and studying beside my fellow meditators, I lived as much like a nun as one can without taking robes. During our daily routine of service, as challenges of life or meditation arose, the Buddha's words helped clarify the purpose of meditation—the practice of equanimity with awareness in all situations.

During my study period at VIA, we took a field trip; but this was no ordinary field trip. Our Pāli teacher took us to the Nasik Caves, an hour's drive from the Academy. The caves were once part of a monastery for bhikkhus living the holy life in search of ultimate truth. Just as the bhikkhus had done so many years ago, we meditated and chanted the Ratana Sutta, a discourse that praises the jewel-like qualities of the Buddha, the Dhamma, and the Saṅgha. Sitting in the cave with my teacher and classmates was like stepping back in time, experiencing the devotion and persistence of the ancient monks' efforts as they worked towards gaining enlightenment. The power of this experience brought home the significance of my nine months of study and practice. With awareness and equanimity, we paid respect to the ancient Dhamma communities who diligently passed on the practice of Vipassana from generation to generation.

– Kim Heacock

Nasik
Nasik is considered one of India's holiest cities, and is one of four sites for the famous Kumbha Mela, a dramatic Hindu festival held every 12 years. The old part of Nasik city is filled with colourful and narrow winding streets, charming temples, shrines and the bathing ghats that stretch along the holy Godavari River. Downstream is the sacred Tapovan where Hindu ascetics congregate around a few meditation caves including the Sita Gupta Cave, the site where, according to the *Ramayana*, Sita was stolen away by the evil Ravana and where Lakshman cut off Ravana's sister's nose (*nasik*), thus giving the city its name.

To get to Nasik from Igatpuri, you can take a bus, shared-taxi or private taxi. A few trains are also available throughout the day, but the Nasik train station is about 8 km outside of town. If coming from elsewhere, see Mumbai's *Coming & Going* section for trains that pass through Nasik.

Dhamma Nāsikā, Nasik Vipassana Centre
The 11-acre piece of land for this charming centre was generously donated by the Nasik Municipal Corporation. Situated halfway between the booming city of Nasik and the pilgrimage town of Trimbak, the ancient mountains surrounding Dhamma Nāsikā ('Nose of Dhamma') create a peaceful haven for meditation. Dhamma Nāsikā is an intimate Deccan alternative to the animated buzz of Dhamma Giri.

The current centre has capacity for 80 students, featuring a lovely meditation hall, a wonderful pagoda, double and single rooms with attached bathrooms, and a simple dining hall. Dhamma Nāsikā continues to expand, and is being constructed in phases. The centre's master plan is to provide for 500 meditators, with separate meditation halls for men and women.

Due to space constraints most courses are currently only offered to a single gender, either males or females. This includes *Satipaṭṭhāna* courses. Check the centre's course schedule for more info, and to register for courses.

To get to the centre from the Nasik Central Bus Stand (CBS), take a city bus to Shivaji Nagar Satpur then an auto-rickshaw or taxi to the centre.

Contact:
Dhamma Nāsikā, Nasik Vipassana Kendra
Opposite Water Filtration Plant, Shivaji Nagar, Satpur
Nasik–422007
Maharashtra
Tel: [+91] (0)253-5616242
E-mail: info@nasika.dhamma.org
Website: www.nasika.dhamma.org

Trimbak
This pilgrimage town is located at the place where the mighty Godavari River, which reaches all the way to the Bay of Bengal, trickles from its source at a modest spring. Trimbak's major sites are off limits to non-Hindus, including the magnificent Trimbakeshwar Temple and the Gangasagar Bathing Tank (whose waters are supposed to wash away bad karma). However, the trip out to Trimbak is still worthwhile for the area's natural beauty, pleasant walks and devotional culture.

Regular buses travel between Trimbak and Nasik (about one hour). It is also possible to hire a taxi for the day from Igatpuri.

Ajaṇṭā, Ellora & Aurangabad

From the reign of Emperor Asoka in the 3rd century BCE up to the 18th century, rock cut caves in the Deccan plateau were the prime real estate sought after by the ascetic community. The 1 200-plus man-made caves exemplify not only some of humanity's greatest works of spiritual art, but also serve as a fine example of religious co-existence, as Buddhist, Hindu, and Jain ascetics learned to live side-by-side in harmony.

Ajaṇṭā Caves

In 1819 British officer James Alexander rediscovered the Ajaṇṭā caves while on a tiger hunt in the jungles of the western Deccan region. Spotting their prey at the Waghora River, Alexander and his hunting party followed the tiger upstream to a large horseshoe-shaped canyon, where they found a series of caves chiselled out of the mountain: portals richly decorated with magnificent arches, ornate pillars, and detailed sculptures.

The Ajaṇṭā complex was first commissioned by Emperor Asoka as a gift to the Saṅgha, and monks lived and meditated here for the next 800 years. After that period the caves were abandoned, probably due to their remoteness, as Buddhism declined in India. Of the 30 excavated caves, five were used as meditation/prayer halls and feature a votive stūpa in the middle; the others were quarters used for sleeping and meditating. Like at the region's other cave complexes, some of the sculptures have been taken away to museums or stolen away to the homes of private collectors. However, numerous works can still be seen at Ajaṇṭā. Early cave sculptures depict symbols of the Buddha (bodhi tree, throne, footprints, stūpa and Dhamma Wheel) and episodes from his life; while later sculptures, fashioned by *Mahāyāna* artists, depict exquisite images of the Buddha and *bodhisattas*, royalty and celestial beings, geometric designs and floral patterns.

Although lack of light, antiquity, humidity damage and cement restoration make it difficult to see the detail and colour of Ajaṇṭā's wall paintings, it's not difficult to appreciate these brilliant works, which were made with a variety of mineral dyes painted on canvases crafted from clay, cow dung, straw and a lime plaster finish. These superb murals not only detail the lives of the Buddha and *bodhisattas*, but also portray glimpses into the lives of celestial beings, royalty, monastics and the laity. The intricate details of bodily and facial expressions, clothing, jewelry, musical instruments, weapons and tools all provide a glimpse of what life may have been like in India some 2 000 years ago.

When you enter any one of the impressive caves—with their artistically bordered doorways, decorated columns and tranquil Buddhas—you may be inspired to meditate and chant the Triple Refuge, Five Precepts, and qualities of the Triple Gem, as the sounds dramatically amplify due to the cave's structure.

To see panoramic views of the caves, follow the path below the caves through the small park for about 10 minutes. To get even better views, continue uphill for about 20 minutes until you reach the lookout point.

Ellora Caves

Between the 6th and 12th centuries, local rulers and wealthy merchants who stopped at Ellora while passing by on their trade routes, excavated Buddhist, Hindu and Jain temples and monasteries. There are 34 caves at Ellora: 12 Buddhist, 17 Hindu and 5 Jain. The caves all face west, so it is best to go in the afternoon. The Buddhist caves are to your far right as you face the curve of the Hill, then come the Hindu ones, and finally, the Jain cave temples to the far left.

Although not very far from Ajaṇṭā, Ellora's Buddhist architecture and sculptures have a different flavour as they draw inspiration mostly from the Vajrayāna Buddhism and later Hindu schools. While the intricate sculptures at Ellora are as remarkable as those at Ajaṇṭā, Ellora's uniqueness lies in its majestic architecture. For example, the smooth and level floors and ceilings and the solid supporting columns of the three-storied Buddhist temple and the 30 m tall Kailash Hindu temple, which is the largest monolithic structure in the world, were carved not by machines but by thousands of skilled human hands.

If you are interested in getting detailed explanations of Ajaṇṭā and Ellora's various caves, temples, monasteries, sculptures and paintings, it's worth hiring a guide or purchasing one of the pictorial guidebooks available at the main gates.

Both Ajaṇṭā and Ellora are open every day from 9 a.m. to 5 p.m., but Ajaṇṭā is closed on Mondays, and Ellora is closed on Tuesdays. The entry-fee for foreigners is US$5 at both sites. Remember to bring a torch to the caves: they're dark inside! Although the caves aren't usually overwhelmingly busy, weekends and holidays can be crowded with tourists and persistent hawkers.

Aurangabad Caves

Lacking the grandeur of the UNESCO World Heritage Sites of Ajaṇṭā and Ellora, the 6th and 7th century Aurangabad caves are usually ignored by most tourists, which for the meditator may be all the more reason to go. While Ajaṇṭā and Ellora may be quiet and great for meditating on some days, other days they may be overrun by tourists or school children. Just a couple of kilometres away from Bibi-Ka-Maqbari—a mausoleum known as the 'Poor man's Taj Mahal'—the quiet Buddhist caves at Aurangabad can make for a great day of peaceful meditation.

If you end up staying in Aurangabad and want to join a group sitting, contact:

Ajaṇṭā International Vipassana Samiti
Near MGM Medical College
N-6, CIDCO
Aurangabad–431003
Tel: [+91] (0240) 234 1836/ 237 7291
E-mail: info@ajanta.dhamma.org
Website: www.ajanta.dhamma.org

Sleeping & Eating

It's probably best to stay in Aurangabad when visiting Ellora, which does not have much to offer in terms of accommodation other than the expensive **Hotel Kailash**, whose rooms overlook the caves. Budget options in Aurangabad include the excellent **Shree Maya** (not far from the train station in the Bharuka Complex), the well-kept **Youth Hostel (YHA),** and the decent **Hotel Ajinkya** (near the bus stand on Nehru Place). Higher-range luxury hotels include the **MTDC Holiday Resort** near the railway station and **President Park** not far from the airport. The 5-star **Taj Residency** is also available to pamper you after a hard day of travelling and exploring. All these places feature restaurants, and employees are usually happy to recommend their favourite local eateries.

Although the few accommodation options around Ajaṇṭā are expensive, some people find that staying near the caves beats travelling several hours to the nearby towns. At Ajaṇṭā your choices include the **Traveller's Lodge,** which is right next to the caves, or **The Holiday Resort** in Fardapur, where there are regular buses and taxis making the 5 km journey to and from Ajaṇṭā. If staying in Ajaṇṭā or Fardpur does not appeal to you, take a taxi or one of the hourly buses from Fardpur to **Jalgoan** (2 hours), a fairly relaxed and prosperous town where you can hop on a train or bus to Mumbai, Igatpuri, Delhi, Kolkata or Hyderabad. Jalgaon has limited but quite good budget accommodation, including the **Hotel Plaza** and **Anjali Guest House**—both are good, clean options with vegetarian food available on the premises or nearby.

Coming & Going

Most meditators seem to visit this region with little time on their hands—usually before or after a stay at Dhamma Giri. If this is your situation, then we find that the quickest and most efficient way of visiting these places (other than hiring a private taxi for the whole journey) is to travel by **bus** or **train** from Mumbai (10 hours) or Igatpuri (8 hours) to Aurangabad, where you can stay the night and visit Ellora, 1 hour away.

For faster service at a higher price, you can also **fly** to Aurangabad's Chikalthana Airport, which is directly linked to Mumbai, Delhi and Jaipur. To get to Ellora (30 km) from Aurangabad (and back), hop on to one of the **state buses** that leave every half hour, squish into **shared jeep-taxis** which leave from the bus stand, or hire a **private taxi** or **auto-rickshaw.**

Early the next morning head out on the 3-hour, 165 km trip to Ajaṇṭā (if not spending a day at the Aurangabad caves), pass a few hours at the caves, and then head to Jalgoan (2 hours) in the afternoon to catch a night train or bus to Mumbai (8 hours) or Igatpuri (6 hours).

Alternately, you can follow the same itinerary in the opposite direction. Spend the night in Jalgoan, and then start out for Ajaṇṭā early the next morning by bus.

Bring your baggage with you and store it in the cloakroom near the main ticket office while touring Ajaṇṭā for the day. When finished, catch an evening bus to Aurangabad. The next day you can explore Ellora, then return to Aurangabad for an evening meal before catching an overnight train to Mumbai or elsewhere.

Important: Be aware that Ajaṇṭā is closed on Mondays, and Ellora is closed on Tuesdays. Plan your visits accordingly. Whichever of the above routes you follow, if you are going by train, it's imperative to make ticket reservations ahead of time.

You can also come and go to Aurangabad and Jalgaon by train or bus from Pune, Delhi, Hyderabad, Bhopal and Kolkata. Here are a few trains that pass through Jalgaon and Aurangabad:

- Mumbai Howrah Mail 2321/2322 (Mumbai CST-Igatpuri-Nasik-Jalgaon-Mughalsarai-Gayā-Howrah/Kolkata)
- LT Rajendranagar Express 2141/2142 (LT/Mumbai-Nasik-Jalgaon-Mughalsarai-Patna)
- LT Rajendranagar Express 3201/3202 (LT/Mumbai-Igatpuri-Nasik-Jalgaon-Allahabad-Mughalsarai-Patna)
- Mumbai Howrah Mail 2809/2810 (Mumbai CST-Igatpuri-Nasik-Jalgaon-Wardha-Nagpur-Howrah/Kolkata)
- Vidarbha Express 2105/2106 (Mumbai CST-Igatpuri-Nasik-Jalgaon-Wardha-Sevagram-Nagpur)
- Sevagram Express 1439/1440 (Mumbai CST-Igatpuri-Nasik-Jalgaon-Wardha-Sevagram-Nagpur)
- Punjab Mail 2137/2138 (Mumbai CST-Igatpuri-Nasik-Jalgaon-Bhopal-Vidisha-New Delhi)
- Dadar Amritsar Express 1057/1058 (Dadar/Mumbai-Igatpuri-Nasik-Jalgaon-Bhopal-Vidisha-New Delhi-Amritsar)
- Tapovan Express 7617/7618 (Mumbai CST-Igatpuri-Nasik-Aurangabad)
- Devgiri Express 1003/1004 (Mumbai CST-Igatpuri-Nasik-Aurangabad)

Pune

With over forty colleges, Pune (pronounced Poona) is alive with youthful energy, nightlife, entertainment and culture. Pune also has several places of interest for the visitor: Raja Kelkar Museum, Shanwarwada Palace, Gandhi National Memorial Empress Botanical Gardens, and the 8th century Panchaleshwar Temple. Pune is also famous for the Osho Commune International (OCI), a spiritual shopping mall for Westerners and affluent Indians. If you are interested in learning a non-sectarian form of Hatha yoga, the Ramamani Iyengar Memorial Yoga Institute (RIMYI) offers month-long courses for all levels and has special programmes for those with medical problems. For more information, visit www.bksiyengar.com. Pune is an active spiritual hub, and there are two Vipassana meditation centres in the vicinity.

Site-Sitting

Dhamma Puṇṇa, Pune City Meditation Centre

This urban Vipassana centre, located in the heart of Pune, sits on about 3 acres of land and has capacity for 90 meditators. Meditating at this city centre is a good place to confront our expectations and desires for what the world should be like, and to come up with realistic resolutions for destroying these habitual drives.

Courses at Dhamma Puṇṇa ('Merit of Dhamma') are usually conducted in English and Hindi, but a few courses each year are conducted only in Marathi and Hindi; check the schedule for details. Besides the regular 10-day courses, several children's courses and a special 10-day course for educators are conducted annually. The educators' course is followed by a 5-day conference around the theme of Vipassana and Education. This special 15-day event is usually held every May.

Dhamma Puṇṇa hosts a group sitting from 6 p.m. to 7 p.m. daily, and additional group sittings are also held at various sites around Pune throughout the week: check the old student pages on the centre's website for more info, and call ahead before attending. One-day courses are conducted on the fourth Sunday and fourth Thursday of every month from 8 a.m. to 5 p.m. Registration is necessary for these one-day courses.

Dhamma Puṇṇa is about 7 km from Pune Railway Station. The centre can be reached by taxi, rickshaw, or public bus. If you choose to go by bus, take the Pune Muncipal Transport (PMT) bus to Swargate Bus Station and then walk or take a rickshaw to the centre, which is opposite Nehru Stadium about 1 km away.

Contact:
Pune City Vipassana Samiti
Dadawadi, opposite Nehru Stadium, near Anand Mangal Karyalaya
Pune–411002
Maharashtra
Open daily between 10 a.m. and 6 p.m.

Tel: [+91] (0)20-24468903
Fax: [+91] (0)20-24464243
E-mail: info@punna.dhamma.org
Website: www.punna.dhamma.org

Dhammānanda, Pune Riverside Meditation Centre

In 1997 this beautiful 23-acre centre was established on the banks of the sacred Indrayani River near the villages of Markal and Aḷandi, where there is a long history of spiritual practice. The tranquil environment of Dhammānanda ('Joy of Dhamma') and its surroundings support meditators during the deep process of introspection. While the meditation hall at Dhammānanda can seat about 125 meditators, there is presently only accommodation for 60 meditators in double rooms and dormitories. In addition to regular 10-day courses, Dhammānanda also offers Teenager and *Satipaṭṭhāna* Courses several times a year.

To get to Dhammānanda, take a taxi or Pune Muncipal Transport (PMT) bus #257 from Pune Municipal Bus Stand or Pune Railway Station Bus Stand directly to Markal (1 hour), and then walk or take a rickshaw/taxi to the centre, which is about 1 km away. Alternately, you can take a bus to Aḷandi (45 minutes) and then take a rickshaw or shared jeep-taxi to Markal (20 minutes). If you go via Aḷandi and have spare time, it's worth visiting the colourful temples dedicated to the local saint Jyaneshwar.

Contact:
Pune City Vipassana Samiti
(address and telephone as above)
E-mail: info@ananda.dhamma.org
Website: www.ananda.dhamma.org

Registration for both Pune centres is usually handled by the City Centre's office, which is open everyday between 10:00 a.m. and 6:00 p.m.

Sleeping & Eating

If you plan on spending a night or few in Pune, there are several restaurants and budget, mid-range and luxury hotels to choose from around **Koregaon Park**, near the Osho Commune International, or around **Wilson Gardens**, not far from the railway station. If you're craving food from home, you may find some comfort at the **German Bakery** and **Zen Restaurant** at Koregaon Park.

Coming & Going

Pune is well connected to most major cities in India by **air** and by **train**. Pune's airport is located 8 km north-east of the city, and is accessible by rickshaw and taxi.

You can also find regular and deluxe **buses** that head to all corners of Maharashtra. If you're going south of Pune (including Goa) by bus, depart from the Railway Bus Stand (PMT Depot); if you're travelling north, depart from the Shivaji Nagar Bus Stand, located west of the city center. A third bus stand, Swargate, offers service to cities in the southern state of Karnataka.

If you choose to travel on a deluxe bus (recommended), make sure you buy your tickets from a bus operator or reputable travel agency, rather than from a 'travel agent' hanging around the Railway Station. These guys are usually scam artists who charge heavy commissions and sometimes sell fake tickets.

For travel to Mumbai, the **train** is the safest and most convenient option. Here are a few useful trains that pass through Pune:

* Mumbai-Pune Intercity Express 2127/2128 (Mumbai CST-Lonavala-Pune)
* Deccan Express 1007/1008 (Mumbai CST-Lonavala-Pune)
* Sinhagad Express 1009/1010 (Mumbai CST-Lonavala-Pune)
* Udyan Express 6529/6530 (Mumbai CST-Lonavala-Pune-Bangalore)
* Mumbai-Hyderabad Express (Mumbai CST-Lonavala-Pune-Hyderabad)
* Mumbai Hyderabad Hussainsagar Express 7001/7002 (Mumbai CST-Pune-Hyderabad)
* Jhelum Express 1077/1078 (New Delhi-Mathura-Bhopal-Pune)
* Nizamuddin Goa Express 2779/2780 (Hazrat Nizamuddin/New Delhi-Bhopal-Pune-Goa)
* Chatrapati Sahu Maharaj Gondia Maharashtra Express 1039/1040 (Nagpur-Wardah-Pune)

Karla & Bhaja Caves

Karla Caves

Karla is a fine example of early Buddhist rock-cut caves dating from around the 1st century BCE. Climbing up 450 steps (lined with souvenir shops) you'll reach the main cave, which has a beautiful votive stūpa, cells that were used for sleeping and meditation, and fine carvings of devotees, elephants and lions. Unfortunately, an imposing modern Hindu temple has been built at the cave's entrance, and several of the other caves have been converted into modern Hindu shrines and picnic spots. The Karla complex is often inundated with pop-music blasting from transistor radios and politicized religious discourses blaring from megaphones; most meditators feel it doesn't offer a conducive place to meditate, and isn't worth the Rs 250 entrance fee.

Bhaja Caves

The experience at Bhaja caves is totally different from the Karla complex. The Bhaja caves are older, feature more votive stūpas and sculptures, offer spectacular views of the Sahyadri Mountains, and provide a quiet place to meditate. Other than the gatekeepers and a few village children, tourists tend to ignore the 18 caves at Bhaja, making it an ideal place to spend a few hours exploring inside and out.

Sleeping & Eating

Although it's manageable to visit Karla and/or Bhaja as a day-trip from Mumbai or Pune, it's also possible to spend the night in Lonavala, the town closest to the caves. Budget options include the hotels **Swiss Cottage** and **Janata**. A decent midrange choice is the **Hotel Chandralok**, which serves excellent vegetarian *thālis*. The **Fariyas Holiday Resort** is a good spot for those seeking a luxury hotel.

Lonavala is also known for the Kaivalyadhama Yoga Institute, where you can learn yoga and receive naturopathic treatments. The well-run institute attracts a number of foreigners, and requires that you stay at least one week in order to get any benefit from their facilities. For more information, visit www.kdham.com

Coming & Going

There are several **buses** and **trains** that stop in Lonavala while travelling between Mumbai (3 hours) and Pune (2 hours). Refer to Pune's *Coming & Going* section for trains that stop in Lonavala.

If you choose to visit the Karla and/or Bhaja caves as a day-trip and you're travelling to Lonavala by train or bus, it's advisable to hire a **rickshaw** or **taxi** for the trip and have them wait for you at the caves to take you back to the station. Otherwise, you risk missing your return transportation.

Nagpur

Nagpur is famous for several reasons. It is renowned for growing the country's most delicious oranges, has some of the country's greenest and cleanest neighbourhoods, is located at the exact center point of India, and has never suffered from a natural calamity. Perhaps more important than any of these interesting details is that Nagpur was the place where Dr. Bhimrao Ramji Ambedkar—the brilliant jurist who chaired the drafting of the Indian constitution—and half a million of his followers, all untouchables, converted to Buddhism by taking refuge in the Triple Gem and vowing to practise the five precepts. Today the majority of Nagpur's 2 million citizens are neo-Buddhists, many of whom have not only entered the Buddha's way by word alone, but by walking on the path through practice. Various meditation courses are offered at several places around Nagpur.

Site-Sitting

Dhamma Nāga, Nagpur Vipassana Centre

Dhamma Nāga ('Protector of Dhamma'), located on the outskirts of the city in Mahurjhari Village, is a good place to meditate and interact with Indian Buddhists who are dedicated to transforming the perils of Indian society through the practice of both *pariyatti* and *paṭipatti*.

The meditation hall at Dhamma Nāga can comfortably seat 200, but at present the centre only offers comfortable accommodation for 50 male and 50 female students. Construction on the centre's pagoda began in 2005. A tract of land adjacent to the centre is being developed as the Vipasshi Gram (Vipasshi Village), a residential community for meditators similar to Dhamma Giri's U Ba Khin Village.

Dhamma Nāga is around 15 kilometres away from Nagpur Railway Station. Students are advised to go to the centrally located City Office in Nagpur by noon on the day the course begins; bus service is provided to take students to the centre and bring them back at the end of the course.

Contact:
Dhamma Nāga, Nagpur Vipassana Centre
Mahurjhari Village
Near Nagpur–Kalmeshwar Road
Nagpur
Maharashtra

City Office:
Kalyanmitra Charitable Trust,
Abyankar Smarak Trust Building
Abyankar Road, Dhantoli
Nagpur–440012
Tel: [+91] (0)712-2548686
Fax: [+91] (0)712-2539716
E-mail: info@naga.dhamma.org
Website: www.naga.dhamma.org

Dikshabhumi Stūpa

Dr. Ambedkar was educated at Columbia University and the London School of Economics, where he earned degrees in economics, politics, law and philosophy. As an earnest social reformer, Dr. Ambedkar understood the fragility of appointed political power and the deeper strength of religious power. Needing a spiritual practice to enable his people to uplift themselves in a dignified manner, Ambedkar chose the Dhamma's empirical and rational approach to morality rather than the blind belief typical of many other traditions. He also saw tremendous potential in the Dhamma's teachings of equality, solidarity, and the possibility of individual and social transformation. On October 14th 1956, Ambedkar and his followers vowed to practise the Dhamma as a way of combating the Hindu caste system and establishing a respectful identity. The Dikshambhumi Stūpa, located in the middle of town, marks the spot of this historic event. Every year in September or October, Nagpur is host to the Hindu **Dussehra Festival**, when thousands gather to celebrate the life of Dr. Ambedkar. For more info see: www.ambedkar.org

Sevagram

If you are interested in the exemplary life of Mahatma Gandhi, a visit to the 40-acre Sevagram Ashram is a must. This 'Village of Service' is where Gandhi lived for 15 years, and today functions as an agricultural and housing cooperative, a research centre, and a museum that contains the Mahatma's spectacles, spinning-wheel, books, presentations on rural economics, and a special photo-gallery of his life.

You're allowed to stay at Sevagram as long as you join the daily prayer services and spin *khadi* cotton for 30 minutes a day. Accommodation and vegetarian meals are simple and inexpensive. It is best to make sure there is available space by calling [+91] (0)7152-84753/-84754. Otherwise you can stay at nearby Paunar, the ashram founded by Vinobe Bhave, a follower of Gandhi who walked all over India encouraging rich landlords to share their land with the poor. Bhave's persistency resulted in the redistribution of approximately 4 million acres of land. Vinobe Bhave was also a personal friend of S.N Goenka, and was the first to encourage Mr. Goenka to teach Vipassana to children and prisoners.

To get to Sevagram, take a bus or train from Nagpur (75 km) and then walk or take a rickshaw to the ashram. Most trains on the central line going to, or coming from Nagpur stop in Sevagram or nearby Wardha. For more info see: www.mkgandhi.org

Sleeping & Eating

Most of the travellers' amenities are to be found along Central Avenue, located a short 10 minute walk east of Nagpur's train station. Decent budget hotels include **Blue Moon** and **Skylark**, and reasonable eats can be had at two nearby South Indian restaurants, **Krishnum** and **Shivraj**. If you're looking for more upscale accommodation, **Hotel Hardeo**, 1 km east of the train station, has a good reputation.

Coming & Going

Located in the center of town, Nagpur Junction **train** station connects the city to most major destinations, making train travel to and from Nagpur the most convenient option for travellers. The overnight *Mumbai Howrah Mail* service connects Mumbai and Kolkata via Nagpur, and five daily express trains connect Nagpur and Mumbai via Jalgaon. Other frequent trains offer service to the north and south.

Nagpur Airport, 8 km south-west of the city center, offers several daily **flights** to and from India's major cities, including Delhi, Mumbai and Hyderabad. Less frequent flights are available to other cities as well.

Regional **buses**, as well as longer distance services, depart from Nagpur's central MSRTC Bus Stand, 2 km south of the train station. Daily semi-deluxe and deluxe buses travel to Jalgaon and Hyderabad.

Sanchi (*Sāñcī*)

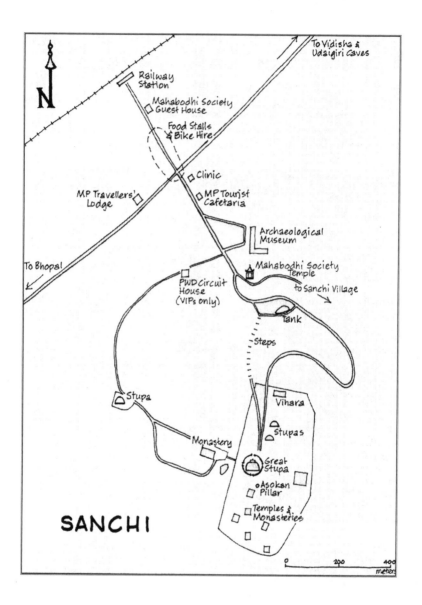

The hilltop site of Sanchi is situated 46 km north-east of Bhopal in central Madhya Pradesh. Despite being a noisy little drive-through town, Sanchi is well worth visiting for its remarkable Archaeological Park, which features some of the finest examples of Dhamma architecture, including a humble Mahābodhi Society temple that is home to the relics of the Buddha's two leading disciples: Sāriputta and Moggallāna. Sanchi is also a good base for excursions to other Asokan stūpas in the region, many of which can be reached by bicycle.

Site-Sitting

Archaeological Park
Situated on a hill at the edge of town is one of the best archaeological parks preserving Dhamma architecture in all of India. The monuments here suffered severe damage from negligence, amateur archaeologists and greedy treasure hunters in the 19th century, when the site was rediscovered after having been forgotten for centuries. Fortunately, restoration and reconstruction efforts began in the early 20th century under John Marshall of the Archaeological Survey of India (ASI). Current maintenance is supported by the United Nations World Heritage Site committee, which has done a wonderful job beautifying the park, making this site a terrific place to visit.

Sanchi—also to refered to as *Chetiyagiri* (Hill of Stūpas) by the Sri Lankan *Mahavaṃsa* chronicle—was an ancient monastic complex that flourished between the 6th and 11th centuries. Remains of more than fifty stūpas, pillars, monasteries and temples abound here.

The **Great Stūpa**, initially constructed by Emperor Asoka near the birthplace of his wife, was later enlarged by the Satavahana rulers around 70 BCE. This stūpa is believed to have enshrined the Buddha's remains, but Alexander Cunningham did not find anything when he opened it in 1851.

The 16 metre high, 37 metre diametre brick and stone monument is crowned with a triple-umbrella and encircled by a stone railing with four gateways (*toraṇa*). The intricate carvings of the gateways depict scenes from the Buddha's life and from his previous lives as a *bodhisatta* related in the *Jātaka* tales, as well as epi-

sodes from the lives of previous Buddhas, Emperor Asoka's life, and subsequent events in Dhamma history. You will notice that these *toraṇa* don't portray any direct images of the Buddha, only symbols that imply his presence: lotus flowers, bodhi trees, dhamma wheels, footprints, thrones, umbrellas and stūpas. The pathway winding up and around the stūpa enables the pilgrim to mindfully circumambulate three times.

Although we don't have space here to narrate every scene from the *Jātaka* tales that can be seen among the *toraṇa* carvings, it's worth recounting one tale in particular: the story of Prince Vessantara (the Bodhisatta's second-to-last birth in human form).

> Prince Vessantara was an extremely generous, sympathetic and compassionate man. When he heard that one of the neighbouring kingdoms was suffering from a terrible drought, Vessantara gave them his father's auspicious white elephant, which was known to have the power to create rain. His father was furious, and banished selfless Vessantara and his family to the forest.
>
> Sakka, the *deva*-king, wanted to test Vessantara's sincerity and offered to bring his family, without Vessantara, to live in a celestial pleasure realm, which was certainly better than the forest. Without hesitating, the prince told Sakka to take his family and leave him to live alone. His family's comfort and security, he said, was more important. Sakka was delighted with the prince's behaviour, and reunited him with his family, father, elephant and kingdom.

Stūpa 3 is also an important spot for meditation as this is the place where Asoka enshrined Sāriputta and Mogagallāna's bone relics with precious stones and charred pieces of sandalwood from the funeral pyre in two grey sandstone boxes. The relics remained here for approximately 1 900 years, until Cunningham discovered and had them sent to a London museum, where they were kept for many years. From 1947-1952 the sacred relics travelled to Sri Lanka, Burma, Nepal and Ladakh. A portion of the relics were then sent for permanent holding at Kaba Aye Zedi in Yangon, while the other returned to Sanchi and are now stored in the Mahābodhi Chetiyagiri Temple.. In 1953 the sacred relics returned to Sanchi and are now stored in the Mahābodhi Temple next door to this stūpa. Stūpa 3 is located next to the Great Stūpa and is almost identical to it, except being smaller, only having one *toraṇa*, and having a 2-tiered umbrèlla.

Another great spot for meditation is at the isolated **Stūpa 2**, located halfway down the hill to the west, beyond Monastery 51 and the **Great Bowl**, where householders used to leave food for the *bhikkhus*. Stūpa 2—with its beautiful carvings of flowers, animals, mythical figures and devotees—enshrined the relics of ten regional *arahants* from three different periods, the first from Asoka's days. Fewer people visit this site, making it easier for meditators to experience the peaceful energy of the place.

There is an admission fee for the Archaeological Park. Anyone interested in explanations of the park's ruins and of the various scenes on the *toraṇa* should purchase one of the handy booklets sold at the gate or at the neighbouring temple. You may also consider hiring a tour guide. The park is open between sunrise and sunset, and is especially lovely at these times, when the sun's rays brilliantly radiate their fiery colours upon the monuments' bricks.

Mahābodhi Chetiyagiri Temple

The Mahābodhi Temple, adjacent to the Archaeological Park, houses the relics of Sāriputta and Moggallāna, the Buddha's two chief disciples, who were known as the *bhikkhus* leading in wisdom and supernatural powers, respectively. Unfortunately, the relics are locked up in the basement and only revealed to the public once a year, on the last Sunday of November, when they are paraded around the stūpas and then returned for safekeeping until the following year. Fantastic oil-on-canvas paintings of the Buddha's life and of subsequent historical Dhamma events decorate the simple temple's walls.

Even though the relics aren't accessible, the temple still makes for a strong spot to meditate, and is a good alternative if you don't wish to pay the Archaeological Park's admission fee on a return visit. The posted hours for the temple are from 8:00 a.m. to 5:00 p.m.

Archaeological Museum

Most of the items in this museum are from excavations around Sanchi, including stone statues, terracotta pots and iron tools, as well as John Marshall's photographs, notes and drawings of the relic caskets featuring the Brahmi-inscribed names of Sāriputta and Moggallāna. The most noteworthy objects are the polished lion capital from one of the Asokan pillars, a sandstone Buddha statue that was found near Stūpa 5, and expressive carved statues of the Bodhisattvas Padmapani, Vajrapani and Avalokiteśvara. While at the museum, please remember to follow its strict rules: "no cooking or picnicking...and visitors may not sleep, run, sing or commit nuisance." The museum is open Saturdays to Thursdays, 10:00 a.m. to 5:00 p.m.

Sleeping & Eating

The cleanest option for pilgrims travelling on a budget is the **Railway Retiring Room**; however, it is not nearly as charming as the friendly **Sri Lanka Mahabodhi Society Guest House** (referred to as the **Dharamshala** by locals). The **Jaiswal Lodge**, across the road from the Mahabodhi, serves decent food. If you want a room priced in the mid-range, check out the **Traveller's Lodge & Restaurant** on the Bhopal-Vidisha Highway or the **Tourist Cafeteria** next door to the museum. Many meditators find that the constant train whistling at night is reminiscent of Igatpuri.

Coming & Going

Although there is a railway station in Sanchi, almost all the trains stopping here are slow local passenger trains and only worth the trip about as far as Bhopal. Your best bet is to take a **train** to Vidisha (10 km) or Bhopal (45 km) and then a **bus**, **taxi** or **rickshaw** to Sanchi. If you need to buy train tickets, the **Traveller's Lodge** on the Bhopal-Vidisha highway has a computerized railway reservation office. Here are some common trains that pass through these towns:

- Punjab Mail 2137/2138 (Mumbai CST-Igatpuri-Nasik-Jalgaon-Bhopal-Vidisha-New Delhi)
- Dadar Amritsar Express 1057/1058 (Dadar/Mumbai-Igatpuri-Nasik-Jalgaon-Bhopal-Vidisha-New Delhi-Amritsar)
- Mahanagari Express 1093/1094 (Mumbai CST-Igatpuri-Nasik-Bhopal-Allahabad-Vārāṇasī)
- Kushinagar Express 1015/1016 (LT/Mumbai-Igatpuri-Nasik-Bhopal-Lucknow-Gonda-Gorakhpur)
- Jhelum Express 1077/1078 (New Delhi-Mathura-Bhopal-Pune)

Excursions

Satdhara, Sonari & Andheri Stūpas

Since most people come to Sanchi for a quick in-and-out trip, these nearby semi-preserved stūpas do not receive many visitors. Nevertheless, if you have the time, these places are worth the visit. Cunningham discovered two relic caskets containing Sāriputta and Moggallāna's bone relics at Satdhara, and local monks claim that two of the Sonari stūpas and three of the Andheri stūpas contain *arahant* relics. The *nibbāna-dhātu* and marvellous landscape make a trip to these sites worth the effort to reach them. These sites are also interesting because they give an idea of what Sanchi may have looked like prior to the process of renovation.

If you plan on just visiting Satdhara (10 km), you may enjoy renting a bicycle for the day. If the bicycle people can't tell you how to get there, ask one of the monks at the Mahabodhi Society Guest House. If you want to visit Sonari (16 km) and Andheri (20 km) as well, then think about hiring a taxi.

Udaigiri Caves

The twenty amazing Hindu and Jain rock-cut cave sanctuaries carved out of the sandstone hill here are another testimonial to India's creative spiritual energy. The caves, carved between the 4th and 10th centuries, contain magnificent images of Vishnu, a lingam with Shiva's head emerging out of it, Kartik (Ganesha's brother) and Mahavira. Udaigiri (13.5 km), which means 'rising sun on the hill,' is situated in a pleasant rural area, making for an enjoyable bike or horse-cart ride from Sanchi.

Kutch

Kutch, the westernmost part of Gujarat state, is one of the most difficult places for people to survive agriculturally in India, due to monsoon floods that cover the land with silt from the sea and fresh water rivers. However, due to this rugged terrain, isolation, and limited tourism, Kutch has preserved its indigenous culture better than most places in India, and many seekers of the divine find the austere landscape to be a powerful source of inspiration.

Site-Sitting

Dhamma Sindhu, Kutch Vipassana Centre

Situated near the sleepy village of Bada, just 1 km inland from the pristine shore-line of the Arabian Sea, this amazing 35-acre Dhamma centre is one of the finest places in the world for meditators to channel the mind's outgoing energies inward. The gentle sea breeze, beautiful gardens, array of birdlife, and loving local community of meditators all help to create a powerful atmosphere for personal introspection.

Dhamma Sindhu ('Ocean of Dhamma') attracts serious meditators from all over the world, many of whom come to attend the long courses that are held here several times a year. During these special times, serious meditators are given the rare opportunity to pay attention to the waves of sensations that constantly wash up onto the shores of our consciousness: arising, crashing and returning to the ocean calm, only to arise again…

The centre's excellent pagoda has 160 cells, most of which are underground, which helps to regulate the temperature. Dhamma Sindhu's three meditation halls have a combined capacity for up to 475 meditators, but accommodation—in the form of single or double rooms with attached bathrooms, and dormitory-styled rooms—is currently limited to 180 residents. All rooms have solar-powered water heaters. Beautiful tree-lined avenues connect the various buildings and provide shade and inspiration during students' contemplative walks.

Foreign meditators usually enjoy volunteering at Dhamma Sindhu because of the large number of international students, the variety of tasks, and the

Eight Ways the Dhamma Resembles an Ocean:

1. Both become gradually deeper
2. Both preserve their identity under many changes
3. Both cast out dead bodies
4. Just as rivers lose their identities when they enter the ocean, so do monks when they enter the Dhamma
5. Both are never full nor empty
6. Both have one flavour: the ocean has the taste of salt; the Dhamma has the taste of liberation
7. Both are full of treasures
8. Both are a dwelling place for mighty beings

– from *Mahāparinibbāna Sutta*

friendly atmosphere. There is also a great Dhamma library in English, Pāli, Hindi and Gujarati. Between courses, a great way to spend the day is by walking to the pristine, uninhabited beach. The walk is about 45 minutes, and if you go in the early morning, you may catch a glimpse of flamingos, pelicans or even dolphins.

The best time to visit Kutch is between November and March, when the days are warm and the nights cool, and malaria is suppressed (malaria-carrying mosquitoes prowl in the evenings from August to October and April to June).

To get to the centre, take a bus, train or plane to Bhuj, then a bus to Mandvi (60 km, 1 hour). From Mandvi, you can take a bus or rickshaw (private or shared) to Bada (22 km, 45 minutes). If you hire a private rickshaw, the driver will take you all the way to the centre. If you take a shared rickshaw, you can pay the driver a little extra to take you the final 1 km to the centre, or you can walk. Taxis are also available from Bhuj.

Contact:
Dhamma Sindhu, Kutch Vipassana Centre
Village: Bada, Taluka: Mandvi
Kutch–370475
Gujarat
City Tel: [+91] (0)283-4223076
Tel: [+91] (0)283-4273303
Fax: [+91] (0)283-4224267/-4288911
E-mail: info@sindhu.dhamma.org
Website: www.sindhu.dhamma.org

On January 26th, 2001, Gujarat's Kutch district was struck by a magnitude 7.7 earthquake that devastated many homes, villages and lives. Leah Thompson was serving a course at Dhamma Sindhu, near the epicentre of Bhuj, when the earthquake struck. This is an excerpt from her diary entry written the following day.

> *I need to record, to the best of my ability, what I experienced yesterday. Exhaustion/dread is what I woke up with Day 1, as a server on a 10-day course at Dhamma Sindhu in Gujarat. Thoughts kept rolling in my mind about leaving the centre, going home to Canada, skipping out on the upcoming 20-day I had planned...but I carried on, simply knowing that this would all change and no matter where I went, I could not escape existence.*

> *So I sat as usual for the group sitting at 8 a.m., asked one woman to raise her head from the famous sleeping-crouched position, and then, suddenly, there was a slight shaking of the floor, and then the whole building. I remember knowing that it was an earthquake. Then everything got surreal, as if I were watching a movie. A few people started getting up and rushing out, but it was when the centre manager yelled something that everyone got up and ran for the door. I thought he was irritated that people were panicking but it turns out he yelled "get out" in Gujarati.*

I got up and put myself in the doorway of the female teacher's entrance, but as I watched the people outside, the open sky seemed much safer than the dancing walls on either side of me. I don't remember getting up, or what it felt like to walk, maybe I simply don't want to recall. I went towards the women on the ground outside the hall, seeing one woman hugging her friend, and I instantly bent down to hug them. Then I saw the cook behind me and went over to hug her; she responded with a squeeze of the arms and I remembered that this is their way of hugging. I saw eyes, crying eyes, and I saw fear, and I wanted my family. I felt surrounded by strangers sharing fate, and the sensations in my body were like no horror movie has ever given me: mere liquid for abdomen, intense lower back pain for 10 seconds, bones like they'd been in a car accident, and throat and chest exploding. I really felt anicca, and realized the power of nature. I saw that I have no control; that what I think is solid can turn to liquid, can dance beneath my feet, and that ultimately I cannot choose sensations or death...I realized how intellectual my mind is, how little control I have over it, how fearful I am, full of aversion to pain, sickness and death, and how meaninglessly I spend my mental energy. Confronting anicca, anattā, dukkha—confronting change, substancelessness, and suffering—this is what India is all about for me. I see local meditators reacting with a bizarre calm—though fear is there, there is no DRAMA, all is just as it is... I am so grateful, for here, for NOW—surrendering to Dhamma, to nature, to life. I have no choice but to surrender, and in consciously doing so, I am aiming for peace.

– Leah Thompson, *January 27th 2001*

I recently took part in a 30-day silent retreat at Dhamma Sindhu, located near the soothing Arabian Sea. The people in this region are incredibly warm and courageous. In spite of the incessant calamities they're forced to endure—severe droughts, torrential rainfalls, devastating earthquakes—they still possess character strength that most of us have never needed to muster. One unique feature of these people that struck me was the way in which they say "Namaste"—the standard Indian greeting that is an acknowledgement of the Divine quality within. For the people I encountered, it's not merely a way of saying "hello," but is an actual recognition of this soulful quality. Whether the person was a camel driver, school kid, goat herder, farmer or village woman carrying a clay pot of water on her head, s/he would look deeply into my eyes with folded hands while uttering this age-old greeting. It's no wonder the golden sandy shores of this region have been home to Indian saints for the last 2500 years, and is also believed to be from where Emperor Asoka sent his children Mahinda and Saṅghamitta to transmit the Dhamma to the island country of Sri Lanka.

After returning from this month-long period of reflection at Dhamma Sindhu, friends now often ask me how I found this intensive experience. Although I find it impossible to accurately tell what happened, what I can say is that it was truly adventurous and clarifying. Adventurous in the sense that the mind travelled to all the realms of existence possible for this psycho-physical continuum labelled as 'Kory.' The journey consisted of various trips to the worlds of anger and love, hatred and compassion, lust and sympathy, greed and generosity, bliss and agony, appreciation and arrogance, joy and pain. This experience was also very much clarifying for me because at a deeper, experiential, non-intellectual level, I realized how ignorant I really am concerning the vast intricate complexities of this mental and material world. How could a fortunate person such as myself —born into a loving and comfortable family, surrounded by warm and stimulating people, and given the precious life opportunities of education and global travel— ever have the nerve to complain about anything? This experience has deepened my appreciation and gratitude towards each and every one of you. Thanks.

– KG

Activities, Sites & Excursions

Mandvi
If you feel like being a little more extroverted before or after a course, Mandvi is a nice little beachside town in which to wander. The boat-builders are fascinating to watch and there are several handicraft shops selling Kutchi village embroideries, tie-dyes, block prints, and wool and cotton weaves. If you need to catch up on your correspondence, there are a few internet cafés and a post office.

Navjivan Nature Cure Centre
This 5-acre oasis, located halfway between Bhuj and Mandvi, is a wonderful place for detoxing after weary travel and for recuperating after a course at Dhamma Sindhu. The tasteful architecture, flower and medicinal gardens of Navjivan are complemented by the surrounding organic fruit plantations and vegetable gardens which feed the centre. In additional to this, lush meadows, picturesque ponds and cattle-grazing grounds make it a special environment for health and healing. Navjivan is run by naturopathic doctors who provide daily consultations and prescriptions for various forms of therapy: herbal treatments, mud baths, massage, physiotherapy, pancha karma, magnet therapy, enemas, fasting, specialized diets, yoga, meditation and more.

Navjivan offers different types of courses throughout the year, and the minimum length of stay is 3 nights. For more information and reservations, call [+91] (0)283-4281430/-4281431/-4294357, fax [+91] (0)283-4281471 or visit www.navjivannaturecure.com

Ananddham Nature Cure Centre

Ananddham Nature Cure Centre in Kharoi village (about one hour from Bhuj) is a great place to heal or re-energize after hard travelling around India. Ananddham, run by the former doctors of Navjivan Nature Cure Centre, provides fantastic and affordable treatments by experienced Ayurvedic and Naturopathic health-care professionals. The centre is located on a tranquil 18-acre property where guests can take part in a variety of healing activities such as Ayurveda, naturopathy, yoga, meditation, massage, steam bath, hydrotherapy, mud therapy, magnet therapy, enema treatment, acupuncture, acupressure, reflexology, physiotherapy and fasting. Much of the food is locally and organically grown. Room and board starts at Rs 500 per day. Visit www.ananddham.com for more information.

Bhujodi

Kutch is reknowned for its weaving and detailed embroidery, and is a great place to buy a variety of textile goods: shawls, bags, bed linens, pillow covers and personal accessories being popular choices. A side trip to Bhujodi is worthwhile if you wish to visit some shops to buy woven wool and cotton textiles. Stroll around the small town (just past the shops that are at the entrance to the village) and you will inevitably be invited to visit with a family and see their works in progress. To get to Bhujodi, take a rickshaw from Bhuj (12 km), or catch a local bus toward Ahmedabad and ask the driver to drop you at the turn-off for Bhujodi. It is about 2 km to the village; you can walk or hire a rickshaw.

In the lobby of the Prince Hotel is **Qasab**, a small shop that sells textile goods with high quality embroidery made by a co-operative of women in the area, the Kutch Mahila Vikas Sangathan (KMVS). Established in 1989, KMVS aims to empower women through an increase in their sustainable income. Today the co-operative includes more than 1 200 artisans, their motto being 'The work you buy is an expression of our pride.'

Sleeping & Eating

If you want to spend the night in Mandvi, the **Rukmavati Guest House** near the bridge is popular amongst meditators, and the **Osho Restaurant** has spicy vegetarian *thālis* that are very good. In Bhuj there is the **Hotel Annapurna** for budget accommodation— the restaurant serves great *thālis* which you can customize: you choose which dishes to include, and pay per dish. **Prince Hotel** has both mid-range and more luxurious options, and has two good restaurants to visit: **Bhakti Garden** and **Toral**. **Hotel Nilam** is also popular for South Indian, vegetarian and noodle dishes.

Coming & Going

Bhuj is the main entry into the Kutch area. The two main overnight Mumbai-Bhuj trains are the Kutch Express (9031/9032) and the Sayahi Nagari Express (9115/9116). If coming from Delhi, you will need to take the Al Hazrat Express

(4311/4312) to Gandhidham (125 km), and then take a bus or taxi to Mandvi. Please check out the Indian Railways website www.wr.indianrail.gov.in for special trains during major holidays.

Private or shared **taxis** from the Bhuj railway station can take you to Mandvi (58 km), the Vipassana centre in Bada (80 km), or one of the nature cure centres (60 km for Ananddham and 35 km for Navjivan). **Rickshaws** are available for Bhuj, but will take too long to go anwhere else. If you'd rather travel to the Vipassana centre by state or private **bus**, take one to Mandvi, and then a bus, rickshaw or taxi to Bada. (The direct Bhuj-Bada bus stops many times and takes 5 hours to travel 80 km!) It's a 5-minute walk to the centre from Bada's bus stop.

To get to the region by **air**, there are daily flights available from Mumbai.

If you are going to the Vipassana centre, check its website first before coming, as there is usually a list of local old students who help meditators reach the centre from Bhuj and Mandvi on the days that courses begin.

The South:
Hyderabad

Hyderabad, the capital of the south-eastern state of Andhra Pradesh, has long been an important city, renowned for its rich Muslim heritage and now competing with Bangalore to be one of India's premier technology centres. This unique blend of tradition and modernity is beautifully represented in the city's crowded markets, interlaced with splendid 16th and 17th century Islamic architecture. Hyderabad shares the more relaxed rhythms of South India with cities like Mysore and Pondicherry.

Hyderabad is divided into four distinct areas. Old Town straddles the Musi River and is home to the city's famous Mecca Masjid, a four-hundred-year-old mosque that has capacity for about 10000 worshippers at a time. North of the Old Town is Central Hyderabad, a transport hub including a travellers' haunt called the **Abids District**, where most budget accommodation can be found. Further north beyond Hussain Sagar Lake is **Secunderabad**, another transport hub with several train stations. Finally, the neighbourhoods of Jubilee Hills and Banjara Hills, to the west of the Hussain Sagar, make up the city's modern, affluent district, nicknamed **Cyberabad**.

Site-Sitting

Dhamma Khetta, Vipassana International Meditation Centre (VIMC)

In 1973, the late Andhari businessman Shri Ratilal Mehta found the liberating path of Vipassana and enthusiastically dedicated the rest of his life to selfless service. Overjoyed by the immediate results he felt and wanting to share his good fortune with others, the wealthy merchant donated his family land and financed the construction of the world's first permanent Vipassana centre. In 1976, S.N. Goenka inaugurated the centre by planting a sapling of the original Bodhi Tree from Bodhgayā and named the centre Dhamma Khetta ('Field of Dhamma'). This marked the beginning of Vipassana history in the modern era.

Dhamma Khetta is located in a small village named Sahabnagar (13 km outside of Hyderabad on Nagarjuna Sagar Rd.). The lovely 5.6-acre property can accommodate about 200 students per course and the huge Dhamma hall has been well designed to provide proper ventilation, muted light, and insulation from both noise and heat (which you'll be grateful for if you meditate here in the hot season). Adjacent to the hall is a graceful Burmese-style pagoda with 72 cells in three concentric rings, making the centre an ideal place to sit courses of 10 days or longer.

Ten-day courses are held from the 1st to 12th and 15th to 26th of every month, except when there are *Satipaṭṭhāna* or long courses. Check the website for details. Come pay tribute to this historical centre and observe sensations under the centre's Bodhi

Tree, whose growth from a tiny sapling into a massive tree is symbolic of how the Dhamma has flourished in this great field of merit.

To get to the centre from Hyderabad, you can take a bus, taxi or auto-rickshaw. If coming by bus, take any bus that heads towards Ibrahimpatnam and disembark at Gurramguda bus stop. From there you can go to the centre by rickshaw or by foot. Walk 300 metres ahead (you will see a Vipassana sign board), turn left and continue for another kilometre.

If you are arriving by train and don't plan on staying in the city, you can catch a taxi or rickshaw from Secunderabad railway station. If you choose to travel by bus, take 277 or 290, which leave every half-hour. Another option for rail travellers is to disembark at Nampally or Kacheguda railway stations, and from there catch a taxi or auto-rickshaw, or take a bus to Nalgonda X Rd., then change to a bus bound for Ibrahimpatnam.

Alternately, the VIMC offers a wonderful, hassle-free bus service on the first and last day of every course. Buses leave from the city office at 9:00 a.m., 11:00 a.m., 1:00 p.m. and 3:00 p.m. Also, every Sunday there is a bus service to take students to the centre for 1-day courses. The VIMC bus leaves for the centre from Emerald House S.D. Road in Secunderabad at 8:00 a.m., and from Gandhi Gyan Mandir in Koti at 8:15 a.m.

Contact:
Dhamma Khetta, Vipassana International Meditation Centre (City Office)
Gandhi Darshan Building, Inside Exhibition Grounds
Hyderabad-500001
Tel: [+91] (0)40-24732569/-24240290/-24241746
Fax: [+91] (0)40-24613941
E-mail: info@khetta.dhamma.org
Website: www.khetta.dhamma.org

"Buddhaṃ saraṇaṃ gacchāmi, Dhammaṃ saraṇaṃ gacchāmi, Saṅghaṃ saraṇaṃ gacchāmi." We chanted, and thus began my first 20-day course. I had only done 10-day courses before and was feeling apprehensive and unsure of my ability. Would I be able to sit for 20 days? Or would I have to leave? I made a strong determination to stay for the duration of the course, no matter what it took. I had endured too much to give up now.

Thankfully, the weather was mild, 27°C, which is a lot better than the predicted 33. I spent most of the time in my meditation cell, a dark room where I couldn't see my hand in front of my eyes. The darkness ensures that there are minimal distractions. The cell even came with its own mosquito net, a real help since the centre is in a mosquito infested area.

What to say about the meditation? It can't really be described, only experienced. The aim is to remove mental defilements and reach the pure state that the Buddha attained some 2500 years ago. So I medi-

tated, and removed some of the flotsam and jetsam accumulated in my unconscious mind. At first it was hard. There were so many distractions. Every couple of hours the Imam from the nearby mosque would chant prayers over a microphone. The Hindus were celebrating the Ganesh festival, which lasted for 18 days of the 20-day course. Every evening I could hear loud music, drumming and chanting as devotees honoured one of their favourite gods, the chubby elephant-headed remover of obstacles. The further into the festival, the louder the music became, with some added fireworks to test my samādhi. India is constantly busying itself with religious and spiritual activities. Here we all were engaged in some practice, whether it was Islamism, Hinduism, or Vipassana meditation.

"Eyes downcast, eyes downcast," Goenka-ji, the Vipassana teacher, said on the evening discourse cassette tape. And with each passing day, I moved into deeper levels of the unconsciousness to remove impurities. I struggled to quiet the mind. And every day I had the same thoughts, over and over again. Perhaps it was because of my daily morning banana that I had now developed a monkey mind, I thought. Towards the end of the course I got so bored with my own thoughts that I decided to try and stop thinking altogether, just to have a change. And then it became clear that thoughts are just like every other thing in this universe—impermanent. And there really is no point assigning any importance to them. They arise and pass away. This is the law of nature. Everything arises and passes away. And with this realization I let go, just a little, of things I had become so attached to. What's the point in fretting about things that will inevitably pass away? In my room, under the safety of my mosquito net, I continued the practice. And there really was no difference in sitting for meditation, or lying down, or showering, or walking. The food lost its flavour, and I was eating only for nourishment and not for taste. Everything was simple and clear.

On Day 20, mettā day, I felt so much lighter. There was no one for me to talk to. I was the only Westerner there and the other three female students did not speak English very well. So I wandered around by myself, looking at the beautiful trees and birds and butterflies at the centre. In the evening there was another of the regular power cuts but since my eyes were no longer downcast, I was able to observe fireflies flying so slowly that they almost looked stationary. The female manager employed me in the kitchen in the late afternoon, to make sure I was properly extroverted and ready to face the world again. With the female kitchen workers, I sat on the kitchen floor and helped them de-seed silk cotton. We opened brown pods as big as hands, and removed the silky substance from inside. It was uncanny to see how much cotton came out of such a small little pod. Then the women stuffed the cotton into pillows that would be used at the centre.

The next morning I had my last wash at the centre. There were no showers, so we used the bucket system, which worked much better than the actual showers I've had in India. For breakfast we had a small bowl of khīr (rice pudding) and then it was time to take the bus back to Hyderabad. "May all beings be happy," I chanted silently on the bus, looking at the manic traffic. May all beings be peaceful, be liberated.

– Chantel Oosthuysen

Shopping, Activities & Sites

If you enjoy Indian bazaars don't miss the famous **Thursday Market**, where traders come from all over the region to sell their wares, most notably silk, pearls, precious metals and Hyderabad's famous glass bangles. The market is held in the Old Town adjacent to the Mecca Masjid.

Lumbinī Park

Meditators may enjoy a visit to Lumbinī Park, situated on a small island in the Hussain Sagar and home to one of the world's largest stone Buddha statues. The 17.5 metre tall statue sits in the middle of the lake and is only accessible by boat. There is a boat service every day (except Mondays) that takes people on the 15-minute ride to the island.

The quaint park is 4 km from the Hyderabad Railway Station in the Nampally district of Central Hyderabad, and is a great place to catch often-spectacular sunrises and sunsets.

Museums

Facing the city stadium, the **Archaeological Museum** has a small collection of Buddhist artefacts found in the area, along with life-size replicas of paintings from the Ajaṇṭā Caves. The museum, however, is most celebrated for its 4000-year-old Egyptian mummy. The museum is open everyday (except Fridays) from 10:30 a.m. to 5:00 p.m.

The massive **Salar Jang Museum** contains over 35 000 antiques collected by Salar Jang III, a former Muslim ruler. On display are Indian and European paintings, outstanding Arabic calligraphy, religious objects from the major traditions, precious jewellery, intricate woodcarvings, weapons, rare manuscripts and a variety of clocks. This collection is not to be missed by museum enthusiasts. The museum is open everyday (except Fridays) from 10:00 a.m. to 5:00 p.m.

Sleeping & Eating

Most travellers prefer to stay in the areas of the Old Town and Central Hyderabad, surrounded by all the historical monuments. The bulk of the hotels and restaurants are on Nampally, Station, and Bank roads in the Abids District, between the Hyderabad (Nampally) Railway Station and the General Post Office (GPO). Although most of the cheap hotels are similar in quality, **Hotel Suhail**, in the alleyway behind the GPO and next to the Ramakrishna Cinema, has been recommended as decent. Otherwise, just go with your intuition. The hotels **Saptagiri, Aahwaanam, Jaya International, Taj Mahal,** and **Siddhartha** are good options in the mid-range. The opulent **Ritz Hotel**—with its gardens, tennis court, restaurants and fine views of the city—is a luxurious choice. The hotel, a former palace, is not far from the stunning white marble Birla Temple (between Hyderabad and Secunderabad).

Coming & Going

There are three main **train** stations: Hyderabad (also known as Nampally), Secunderabad and Kacheguda. Keep in mind that most of the long distance trains depart and arrive in Secunderabad (only a 20 minute auto-rickshaw ride away from Hyderabad), so it's best to check a timetable or go to the tourist counter at one of the stations to determine what's available and from where the trains depart. If going to the Abids District, it's best to get off at Kacheguda Station.

Some major trains that pass through the area are:

- G/S Bangalore Express 5091/5092 (Secunderabad-Gorakhpur)
- Hyderabad Chennai Express 7053/7054 (Hyderabad-Chennai)
- Andhra Express 2723/2724 (Hyderabad-New Delhi)
- Hyderabad Howrah East Coast Express 7045/7046 (Hyderabad-Bhubaneshwar-Howrah/Kolkata)
- Secunderabad Kakinada Gautami Express 7047/7048 (Secunderabad-Bhubaneshwar-Howrah/Kolkata)
- Secunderabad Howrah Falaknuma Express 2703/2704 (Secunderabad-Bhubaneshwar-Howrah/Kolkata)
- Secunderabad Rajendranagar Express 7091/7092 (Secunderabad-Vārāṇasī-Patna)
- Secunderabad Rajkot Express 7017/7018 (Secunderabad-Ahmedabad-Rajkot)
- Secunderabad Bikaner Express 7037/7038 (Secunderabad-Ahmedabad-Bikaner)
- Hyderabad Mumbai Hussainsagar Express 7001/7002 (Hyderabad-Pune-Mumbai CST)
- Hyderabad Mumbai Express 7031/7032 (Hyderabad-Pune-Lonavala-Mumbai CST)
- Manmad Kacheguda Express 7662/7663 (Kacheguda-Aurangabad-Manmad)

There are **bus** stands all over Hyderabad, but the three main ones are: Imlibun, Jubilee (Secunderabad), and Koti. You can catch both inter- and intra-state buses from Imlibun or Jubilee, and local buses from Koti.

Hyderabad is also well connected by **air** with flights to Mumbai, Delhi, Bangalore, Chennai and Kolkata. The Hyderabad airport is at Begampet, 8 km from the Abids.

Nāgārjunakonda

The ancient ruins of this important Buddhist center are located 150 km south-east of Hyderabad in the state of Andhra Pradesh. From the end of the 2nd century BCE to the beginning of the 4th century CE, Nāgārjunakonda was the heart of Buddhism in South India. During that time the city was called Vijaypur; the city is now named after the 2nd century Buddhist saint Nāgārjuna, who established the Middle-Path School (*Madhyamika*) and authored the famous *Mulamadhyamikakarika* ('Fundamental Verses of the Middle Way'), in which Nāgārjuna strives to dismantle all speculative opinions by showing how they are all inherently self-contradictory.

During Nāgārjuna's time, most monks were entangled in philosophical and metaphysical views and spent their days not in meditation, but in ceaseless debates over principles that rarely corresponded with reality. Seeing the folly in their behaviour, Nāgārjuna rejected these constant verbal battles and encouraged the monks to return to the middle path leading towards liberation from misery. Only by experience, he taught, can a *bhikkhu* understand the Four Noble Truths and the teaching of Dependent Origination. The Buddha's teaching, he reminded them, was not speculative, but empirical.

Little is known about Nāgārjuna, and much of the biographical information about him is shrouded in myth and legend. He is often credited with founding the *Mahāyāna* tradition, but his writings show almost no interest in the *bodhisattva* ideals so central to *Mahāyāna* Buddhism. In his essay "Intuitions of the Sublime," Stephan Batchelor helps identify why Nāgārjuna is such a unique and important figure in the history of Buddhism: "Nāgārjuna recovered the core liberating insights of the Buddha's teaching and articulated them in an original and compelling language. He opened up the possibility of tradition being animated as much by contemporary voices as by reference to ancient discourses and encyclopedias."[199] Nāgārjuna was a central figure in the revitalization of Buddhism in India during his time.

Site-Sitting

Dhamma Nāgājjuna, Vipassana International Meditation Centre

Eighteen centuries ago in Sriparvata Hills, beside the Krishna River, Nāgārjuna (Pāli: *Nāgājjuna*) established a university and meditation centre. Many monks, nuns and lay people from all over the Indian subcontinent came to learn the Dhamma from him and later helped to spread the Buddha's practical teachings all over South East Asia.

The Andhra Pradesh Tourism Development Corporation is honouring the Buddha and Nāgārjuna by developing a 285-acre park named Sriparvatha Ārāma. Thirty-five acres of the park have been allotted for a Vipassana centre, Dhamma Nāgājjuna. The centre's master plan will incorporate three sub-centres: one for

10-day courses, one for long courses, and one for Vipassana seminars and research facilities.

The 10-day course centre is completed, but accommodation is limited. Due to current space constraints many courses are currently only offered to a single gender at a time. Check the centre's course schedule for more info.

Contact:
Dhamma Nāgājjuna, Vipassana International Meditation Centre
Hill Colony,
Nagarjunasagar
Andhra Pradesh–502802
Tel: [+91] (0)944-0139329
E-mail: info@nagajjuna.dhamma.org
Website: www.nagajjuna.dhamma.org

Nāgārjunakonda Museum

Excavations in the 1950s and '60s have revealed an entire world of Buddhist life, including the remains of stūpas, monasteries, temples, statues and sculptures of scenes described in the *Jātaka* tales. Prehistoric remnants also suggest that humans have been active in this region over a period of 200 000 years. After the government decided to flood the area by building the Nāgārjuna Sagar, one of the largest dams in the world, the Archaeological Survey of India carried all of its findings to the Nāgārjunakonda Museum, built on an island in the middle of the world's third largest artificial lake. The museum is accessible by ferry service everyday at 9:30 a.m. and 1:30 p.m. Each ferry stays at the island for only 30 minutes before making the return trip, so it's best to take the morning ferry out and return on the afternoon boat. The museum is closed on Fridays.

Sleeping & Eating

For accommodation in this tiny town there are a few options to choose from, including **Project House**, **Nagarjuna Resort**, **Konda Guest House** and the **Youth Hostel**. The **Vijay Vihar Complex**, uphill from the Project House and priced in the mid-range, has excellent views and a good restaurant that is worth visiting even if you're not staying there. Accommodation can be tight in town, so consider booking ahead.

Coming & Going

Nāgārjunakonda is situated 150 km south-east of Hyderabad by the Krishna River in the Sriparvatha Hills. If you want to make a day trip to Nāgārjunakonda, the most convenient way is to hire a **taxi** or take one of the government deluxe tour **buses** from Hyderabad. If you want to spend the night, you can take an ordinary state bus or hop on a deluxe bus for a one-way ride. The nearest **railway** station is at Macherla, 22 km away, accessible by bus.

Kerala

Kerala is India's south-western most state, and a world unto its own. Distinguished by a long coast and meandering backwaters that define much of the geography, Kerala is a place of unique natural beauty. The fertile tropical climate is complemented by a relaxed culture coloured with rich colonial history and renowned for some of the most progressive social politics in the country.

Beginning in 1957, Kerala brought to power the first freely-elected communist government in the world, initiating a system that continues to effectively govern the state according to democratic-socialist principles. Nuanced communist parties abound, and people are apt to complain about local politics, but Kerala has some of the best education, health and social services in the country, and the highest literacy rate anywhere in the developing world. For many travellers, the friendly, laid-back atmosphere of Kerala offers a welcome respite from the sensory-overload so common elsewhere in India.

Unlike most other regions, Kerala isn't dominated by its larger cities; the state is a destination in its own right. Trivandrum (Malayalam: Thiruvananthapuram), the capital city, serves as the gateway to Kerala's southern reaches, but Cochin (Malayalam: Kochi), the largest and central-most city, is the main transport hub for travellers. Cochin consists of two main areas, hectic mainland Ernakulam and the charming island town of Fort Cochin, where we recommend you spend at least a night or two. Other great locales include Alleppey (Malayalam: Alappuzha), which offers access to Kerala's magical backwaters; Varkala, a lovely beachside vacation town, and Munnar, a rural hill station.

Site-Sitting

Dhamma Ketana, Kerala Vipassana Centre
Dhamma Ketana is situated on a tranquil 5.2-acre former homestead in Cheriyanad, a rural village near Chengannur town, south-east of Cochin. The centre is located among coconut groves in a very peaceful and rural environment with relatively little disturbance, and in spite of its apparent remoteness, the site is well connected by road and rail.

Dhamma Ketana ('Sign of Dhamma') was established in 2006, and the current facilities are rustic and rather spartan. Much of the centre operates out of an old converted Keralan country house on the property, but construction on new accommodation has expanded the course capacity to 50 students. Although Dhamma Ketana has few amenities to offer, the spirited community of local meditators is striving to develop a truly international centre. All courses are conducted in English and Malayalam. Foreign students are truly welcome, and foreign servers are always needed.

Dhamma Ketana suffers from the tropical heat of South India, and sitting courses in this climate can be arduous. Foreign students are advised to attend only during the cool season (October to March) when temperatures are usually quite reasonable. Expect warm afternoons, and dress accordingly. Mosquito nets are provided for all beds at the centre.

The centre is easily accessible. Travel by train or bus to Chengannur or Mavelikara, both about 8 km away from Dhamma Ketana. From either town, hire an autorickshaw and ask the driver to take you to Ottappees at Cheriyanad. Expect a 15-30 minute ride, depending on road conditions. You may pass the centre while driving; if so, ask the driver to stop. Otherwise it's a short walk to the centre from the village junction of Ottapees. A good map is available at the centre website.

Contact:
Dhamma Ketana, Vipassana Meditation Centre
Mampra P.O. Kodukulanji (via) Chengannur
Alleppey District
Kerala–689508
E-mail: info@ketana.dhamma.org
Website: www.dhammaketana.tripod.com

Sleeping & Eating

We recommend passing through **Cochin** en route to Dhamma Ketana. The city's islands are famous for their eclectic blend of Indian, European and Chinese cultural landscapes. Cochin's charm is found in its ancient temples, palaces, churches, mosques, synagogues, Kathakali performances and laid-back atmosphere. Budget and mid-range accommodation on the island of Fort Cochin include the tourist homes **Tharavadu, Elite** and **Grace**. If you're looking to bask in luxury, check out **Malabar House**. If you stay on the mainland in Ernakulam, economical rooms can be found at **Basoto Lodge** and hotels **Sea King** and **Hakoba**. Hotels **Paulson Park, Sangeetha, Aiswarya** and the **YMCA**, are good mid-range choices, while the **Taj Residency** is the primary high-end spot. Go to **Arul Jyoti** or **Jaya Café** in the mid-range **Woodland's Hotel** for vegetarian fare.

Coming & Going

Both of Kerala's two main cities, Trivandrum and Cochin (Ernakulam), are well connected to other cities in India by **air, rail** and **bus**. To get to Dhamma Ketana, take a train or bus to Chengannur or Mavelikara, both about 8 km from the centre. From either town, hire an auto rickshaw and ask the driver to take you to Ottappees at Cheriyanad: expect a 15-30 minute ride, depending on road conditions. You may pass the centre while driving; if so, ask the driver to stop. Otherwise, it's a short walk to the centre from the village junction of Ottappees. A good map is available at the centre website.

The East:
Kolkata

When most people think of Kolkata (formerly Calcutta), they often conjure up images of unending filth, heart-wrenching poverty, crumbling colonial architecture, habitual floods or famines and chronic political unrest. As India's second largest city and the site of intense inundation due to forces of nature, Kolkata is a dynamic and struggling metropolis. By taking time to soak in the city and encounter its population of 14 million, however, visitors are also likely to discover the richness of one of India's most vibrant cities, long known for its arts, culture and easy-going attitude.

Monsoon Warning: If you're visiting during the rainy season (between June and September), keep in mind that Kolkata gets the most rain in all of India, if not the world. During severe storms, manhole covers are removed to accommodate the waters, and several people die each year by falling into the sewers. When it rains, do as the locals do and wait for the streets to drain. If you absolutely need to get someplace, stay close to the walls of buildings. Aside from being dangerous, walking in floodwaters can also be harmful to your health. As elsewhere in India, Kolkata's garbage collection and sanitation is poor, and floodwaters are thick with refuse. Umbrellas are of little use here; long raincoats offer more reliable protection. Even better: visit during other months of the year!

Site-Sitting

Dhamma Gaṇgā, Vipassana Centre
Situated on the banks of the sacred Ganges River in a suburb of Kolkata, Dhamma Gaṇgā's tranquil atmosphere is supportive for meditators striving to observe the ever-changing flow of mind and body. When arriving at the centre after travelling through the noisy city for an hour, most people are astonished at the quiet surroundings of the centre.

Formerly the residence and office of a wealthy merchant, the property was purchased by local meditators in 1988, becoming the first Vipassana centre in eastern India. The large, almost medieval looking 3-storeyed building was constructed in the early 1900s and can accommodate up to 50 students.

Dhamma Gaṇgā is a peaceful place to contemplate the Ganges of Dhamma within. 10-day courses are held twice monthly; *Satipaṭṭhāna* and 3-day courses for old students are offered several times a year.

Contact:
Dhamma Gaṅgā, Kolkata Vipassana Centre
Bara Mandir Ghat; Harishchandra Dutta Road
Panihati (Sodepur)
Dt. 24 Parganas
West Bengal–743176
Tel: [+91] (0)33-5532855

City Office:
9 Bonfield Lane
Kolkata
West Bengal–700001
Tel: [+91] (0)33-2421767/-2428043
E-mail: info@ganga.dhamma.org
Website: www.ganga.dhamma.org

Activities, Sites & Volunteer Opportunities

Indian Museum
This impressive 19th century museum is not to be missed by the Dhamma pilgrim.
Welcoming you to the museum is an original Asokan lion capital, giving a taste
of the Dhamma art that the museum houses. The archaeology gallery has a vast
collection of Buddha statues, as well as Asoka's massive Barhut Gateway, which
depicts the Buddha's life. There is also the rock edict found in the northern Rajasthani town of Bairath (formerly Viratnagar), in which Asoka declares that after two
years of practice he entered the Buddha's noble community (i.e. reached at least
the first stage of awakening).

The most important exhibit for meditators are the Buddha's relics in the Terracotta
Gallery (if you find it's closed, don't be shy; ask the staff to open it for you). If
you can, bring a magnifying glass so you can closely inspect the relics before
meditating.

The museum is on the corner of Sudder St. and Chowringhee Rd. and is open
10:00 a.m. to 5:00 p.m. everyday, except Mondays. Weekends are usually more
crowded, so if you feel like having a more tranquil meditation in the presence of
the relics, try to go on a weekday.

Asiatic Society
The Asiatic Society on Park St., built in 1814, was the first museum in Asia, and
exhibits an Asokan stone edict from Orissa, an array of Tibetan Buddhist cloth
paintings (*thangka*), a vast library and interesting botanical specimens. The museum is open Monday to Friday, 8:00 a.m. to 7:00 p.m.

Mother Theresa's Missionaries of Charity
Mother Theresa was the quintessence of selflessness, dedicating her entire life to
serving humankind by nursing the wounds of Kolkata's downtrodden. The 'Saint
of the Gutters' established several projects, including Nirmal Hriday (for the dying), Shanti Nagar (for lepers), Prem Dan (for the mentally ill), and Nirmala Shi-

shu Bhavan (for children). If you are interested in supporting these projects by scrubbing floors, dressing wounds, cooking food, taking care of children or the ill, and acknowledging the starkest misery imaginable, go to Mother Theresa's House/Missionaries of Charity at 54A Jagadish Chandra (JC) Bose Rd. The phone numbers are [+91] (0)33-2452277/-2447115/-2491400. Volunteers are asked to donate at least one week of their time.

Last month I had one of the most moving weeks of my life. I volunteered with the Missionaries of Charity, the order of sisters set up by Mother Theresa in the 1950s. My first three days were spent at an orphanage with handicapped children who were abandoned by their families. These kids, starving for love and attention, were a huge handful. I fed them, washed their sheets, massaged their warped bodies, sang them songs, and tickled them until they gave me the widest smiles. These little beings taught me how precious life can be.

The next three days were spent at a home for the dying. Impoverished people are collected from the slums and brought to the home in order to live their remaining days with slightly more comfort and dignity. When I wasn't washing their plastic bed sheets, I was feeding them, administering medicine, or massaging their atrophied limbs. Being in a room full of so many destitute people on the verge of death was unlike anything I had ever encountered before, both mentally and physically. Some moments I felt waves of love and compassion flow through my consciousness, while other moments I felt as if I were going to completely break down from heartbreak and exhaustion. During these emotional storms, my practice of observing the breath anchored me amidst the perils of depression.

My last day of duty, which was more of a visit than anything, was at the Titagarh Leprosy Centre in a small village about one hour outside the city, where more than 400 patients and their families live. The centre has a school, health clinic, an artificial limb centre, and a handloom unit, whose 50 looms produce the sarees and bedsheets for all the sisters in India, as well as the bandages and gauze for all the missions in Kolkata. The centre also trains people in carpentry, agriculture and animal husbandry. Watching the patients overcome their physical limitations was truly one of the most beautiful things I have ever seen.

Although my week of work here seemed insignificant to the lifelong commitment of the Mother's nuns, deep down I know that it was not. The experience here has given me an entirely new perspective on the fragility of life and the radical importance of fully living every moment with appreciation, gratitude and a sense of what it means to serve selflessly.

– American 'Dhamma Bum'

Rabindra Bharati Museum

> *For Rabindranath Tagore, inner peace began with the cultivation and elaboration of a sense of the intimate, loving relatedness to a personalized divine presence. He gave this felt relationship centrality in every event in every moment. He permitted his daily experience to resonate between immediate facts and cosmic concern…God didn't exist as a separate old man in the sky, but there was a heartbeat evolving within every moment.*

> – Paul Fleischman, *Cultivating Inner Peace*

Dr. Fleischman's words about the legendary Nobel Prize Laureate remind us to keep life in proper perspective, filled with love and action. The Rabindra Bharati Museum, also known as Tagore House, was the birth and death place of Rabindranath Tagore. Besides his accomplishments in poetry and prose, Tagore also painted and composed music. Anyone visiting Kolkata who is interested in the life and works of Tagore should not bypass this fascinating storehouse of original works.

The Borderland

I saw, in the twilight of flagging consciousness,
My body floating down an ink-black stream
With its mass of feelings, with its varied emotion,
With its many-coloured life-long store of memories,
With its flutesong. And as it drifted on and on
Its outlines dimmed; and among familiar tree-shaded
Villages on the banks, the sounds of evening
Worship grew faint, doors were closed, lamps
Were covered, boats were moored to the ghats. Crossings
From either side of the stream stopped; night thickened;
From the forest-branches fading birdsong offered
Self-sacrifice to a huge silence.
Dark formlessness settled over all diversity
Of land and water. As shadow, as particles, my body
Fused with endless night. I came to rest
At the altar of the stars. Alone, amazed, I stared
Upwards with hands clasped and said: 'Sun, you have removed
Your rays: show now your loveliest, kindliest form
That I may see the Person who dwells in me as in you.'

– Rabindranath Tagore

The museum is open everyday from 10:00 a.m. to 5:00 p.m., except Saturdays when it closes at 2:00 p.m. It is located at 6/4 Dwarakanath Tagore Lane, not far from the famous **Marble Palace**, one of the most eccentric museums of art in the world, with its Victorian bric-a-bracs next to masterpieces by Rubins, Reynolds, Murillo and Titian.

Belur Math

On the west bank of the Hooghly River, north of the city, is the headquarters of the Ramakrishna Mission founded by the renowned Hindu mystic Swami Vivekananda in 1897. Swami Vivekananda is best remembered for his impassioned speech calling for inter-religious tolerance and harmony at the Parliament of World Religions in Chicago in 1893. Belur Math is a tranquil corner of the city and a wonderful place to contemplate universal compassion. In line with the Mission's message of the unity of all religions, Belur Math's main building resembles a temple, mosque, and church, depending on the angle it's seen from. The premises are open everyday from 6:30 a.m. to 11:00 a.m. and 3:30 p.m. to 7:00 p.m.

> *Greed brings woe,*
> *while charity is all happiness.*
>
> – Ramakrishna

The powerful **Dakshineshwar Kali Temple** across the river is the spot where Sri Ramakrishna, Vivekananda's guru, lived, meditated, and awakened to a deep understanding of our common humanity.

Sleeping & Eating

Despite all the budget tourists who pass through Kolkata, there always seems to be a lack of available rooms; it's best to book ahead, or arrive in the morning so you have time to look around. The Chowringhee area (Sudder Street and its neighboring lanes) is a travellers' haunt, full of guest houses, restaurants, money changers, travel agents and internet cafés.

Those travelling on a budget can try their luck at the **Salvation Army Guest House, Hotel Maria, Modern Lodge, Times Guest House, Tourist Inn, Neelam Guest House** and **East End Hotel**.

The **Mahābodhi Society** on Bankim Chaterjee St. (opposite the 'swimming pool,' near College Street), is a bit far from the tourist conveniences and has potentially beautiful rooms that lack proper care. The strengths of this place are that you can meditate in the shrine room, which has Buddha relics; there is also a free homeopathic clinic downstairs in case you get sick.

If you decide to volunteer with the Missionaries of Charity, **Monica House** or **Connie Chatterjee House** (women only) next to the Mother House on JC Bose Rd. are both great, family-style choices.

Chowringhee also has a few mid-range choices, such as the **Gujral Lodge, Lindsay Guest House** and **Hotel Lindsay**. North of Chowringhee, in the BBD Bagh area, you can stay at the **Central Guest House** or **Broadway Hotel**. For those who want to live in the style and comfort of the Raj, the **Tollygunge Golf Club** (on the outskirts of town) may be for you. If you want to be closer to the action, Chowringhee offers the museum-like **Fairlawn Hotel** or **Lytton Hotel**. Kolkata is one of the few cities where you can find five-star hotels such as **The Oberoi Grand Hotel** and **The Taj Bengal**.

The Chowringhee district is filled with restaurants and it's best to follow your intuition. Outside of Chowringhee, there are some interesting eateries to explore including **Suruchi** on Elliot St. near Lower Circular Rd. (the same road as the tram tracks). This restaurant is run by the All Bengal Women's Union, a cooperative that prepares dynamite Indian food and sells locally produced arts and crafts. Keep in mind that the restaurant is open for lunch until 5:00 pm. **The Hare Krishna Bakery** on the corner of Russell and Middleton is totally vegetarian and has all sorts of baked goods, macaroni and pizzas. It's best to go early for a wider selection. **The Health Food Center** at 8/1 Dr. U.N. Brahmachari St. (Louden St.) has a variety of dried fruits, nuts, bread, good cheese, cookies and cereal. Their mission statement is "Eat food: Don't allow food to eat you."

Coming & Going

When hanging around any of the bus or train stations in Kolkata, make sure to be extra careful with your belongings as these stations are notorious for pickpockets and thieves.

Kolkata has two major **train** stations: Howrah and Sealdah. Unless you're travelling north to Darjeeling or Siliguri, you will most likely be using Howrah station, which is on the west bank of the Hooghly River. Kolkata has two tourist reservation offices: 6 Fairlie Place (near BBD Bagh) and 14 Strand Rd.

Both offices are open Monday to Saturday from 9:00 a.m. to 1:00 p.m. and 1:30 p.m. to 4:00 p.m., and on Sundays from 9:00 a.m. to 2:00 p.m. If you find these places overly crowded, ask where you can find another computerized reservation office that is not limited to foreigners, as these are often (but not always) less busy. The best alternative to these offices, as always, is to make on-line reservations at your own convenience.

Some convenient trains that arrive in and depart from Kolkata are:

- Poorva Express 2303/2304 (Howrah/Kolkata-Mughalsarai-New Delhi)
- Poorva Express 2381/2382 (Howrah/Kolkata-Gayā-Vārāṇasī-New Delhi)
- Rajdhani Express 2301/2302 (Howrah/Kolkata-Gayā-Delhi)
- Rajdhani Express 2305/2306 (Howrah/Kolkata-Patna-New Delhi)
- Rajdhani Express 2313/2314 (Sealdah/Kolkata-Gayā-Mughalsarai-New Delhi)
- Howrah Kalka Mail 2311/2312 (Howrah/Kolkata-Gayā-Delhi)
- Howrah Gayā Express 3023/3024 (Howrah/Kolkata-Gayā)
- Sriganganagar Udyan Abhatoofan Express 3007/3008 (Howrah/Kolkata-Patna-Mughalsarai-New Delhi)
- Muzzafarpur Express 5227/5228 (Howrah/Kolkata-Muzzafarpur)
- Howrah Gorakhpur Express 5047/5048/5049/5050 (Howrah/Kolkata-Hajipur-Gorakhpur)

- Howrah Dehra Dun Upasana Express 3103/3104 (Howrah/Kolkata-Patna-Vārāṇasī-Haridwar-Dehra Dun)
- Sealdah Jammu Tawi Express 3151/3152 (Sealdah/Kolkata-Vārāṇasī-Pathankot-Jammu Tawi)
- Jodhpur Express 2307/2308 (Howrah/Kolkata-Gayā-Mughalsarai-Agra-Jaipur-Jodhpur)
- Sealdah Jaipur Express 2985/2986 (Sealdah/Kolkata-Gayā-Mughalsarai-Agra-Jaipur)
- Howrah Ahmedabad Express 8033/8034 (Howrah/Kolkata-Jalgaon-Ahmedabad)
- Howrah Mumbai Mail 2809/2810 (Howrah/Kolkata-Nagpur-Wardha-Jalgaon-Nasik-Igatpuri-Mumbai CST)
- Howrah Mumbai Mail 2321/2322 (Howrah/Kolkata-Gayā-Mughalsarai-Igatpuri-Mumbai CST)
- Gitanjali Express 2859/2860 (Howrah/Kolkata-Igatpuri-Nasik-Nagpur-Bhubaneshwar-Mumbai CST)
- Lokmanya Tilak Express 1051/1052 & 2101/2102 (Howrah/Kolkata-Nasik-Igatpuri-LT/Mumbai)
- Howrah Bhubaneshwar Dhauli Express 2821/2822 (Howrah/Kolkata-Bhubaneshwar)
- Howrah Bhubaneshwar Jan Shatabdi Express 2073/2074 (Howrah/Kolkata-Bhubaneshwar)
- Howrah Hyderabad East Coast Express 7044/7045 (Howrah/Kolkata-Bhubaneshwar-Hyderabad)
- Howrah Secunderabad Express 2703/2704 (Howrah/Kolkata-Bhubaneshwar-Secunderabad)

For those who want to attempt the rougher journey to or from Kolkata by **bus**, it's most convenient to use the bus stand north of the Maiden, near Chowringhee. Unless necessary, it is advisable to travel by train.

Kolkata has **flight** connections to almost every major city in India, and is a great place to find cheap flights to other Asian countries. Kolkata's airport is about an hour away from the city. You can catch a direct bus from the Indian Airlines office that leaves about every two hours (check timings at the office). Alternately, you can hire a taxi from the pre-paid kiosk on Sudder St.

Dhauli (*Kalinga*)

Dhauli is located near the capital city of Bhubaneswar in the eastern state of Orissa. Around 260 BCE, Dhauli became the site where Emperor Asoka took part in the bloodiest conquest of his reign. Rather than feeling courageous and powerful, the horrific massacre disgusted 'Asoka the Terrible,' forcing him to question whether his policies of 'might makes right' were the best ways to expand his empire.

Site-Sitting

Dhauli Hill

Shortly after the Kalinga war, Asoka learned the Dhamma and returned to Dhauli, where at the base of Dhauli Hill, he inscribed edicts into a rock detailing his shift in attitude, his evolved views on proper governance, and principles of *sīla*. The rock edicts are found on the main road at the base of Dhauli Hill.

The graceful Shanti Stūpa crowns the hill, testifying to the Dhamma's magnificence and the peacefulness that the Buddha's teachings offer humanity. Meditating at this tranquil spot helps us remember the Buddha's path of non-violence and compassion, which prescribes not battles with other beings, but with our own mental defilements of greed, hatred and delusion.

Bhubaneswar is the closest place to find a roof over your head and a bite to eat. The Orissan capital is crowded with extravagant Hindu temples (many of which non-Hindus are prohibited from entering), a state museum and tribal research centre, and a fascinating botanical garden. The ornate Hindu and Jain caves on Udaiagiri and Khandagiri hills are worth a visit if time permits. The hills face each other and are located a couple of kilometres west of the city.

Sleeping & Eating

Most of the accommodation is in the vicinity of Bhubaneswar's train station. Budget travellers can try their luck at the hotels **Janpath**, **Gajapati**, or the **Venus Nivas**. Mid-range options include the **Tourist Rest House, Kenilworth Hotel & Rooftop Restaurant** and **Hotel Prachi Bhubaneshwar**, while luxury alternatives include the **Hotel Kalinga Asok** and the temple-like **Oberoi Hotel**, located on the outskirts of town. You can find an excellent vegetarian meal at the pricey **Hare Krishna Restaurant**, or a cheaper, yet tasty *veg-thāli* at the **Modern South Indian Hotel** behind the Rajmahal Hotel. Refer to the previous section for food and accommodation in Bhubaneshwar.

Coming & Going

Dhauli is located 8 km south of Bhubaneshwar on the road towards Puri and Konark. You can easily reach there by **bus, rickshaw** or **taxi**. Bhubaneshwar is connected by **air** and **rail** to most major Indian cities. Some convenient trains are:

- Gitanjali Express 2859/2860 (Mumbai CST-Igatpuri-Nasik-Nagpur-Bhubaneshwar-Howrah/Kolkata)
- Hyderabad Howrah East Coast Express 7045/7046 (Hyderabad-Bhubaneshwar-Howrah/Kolkata)
- Secunderabad Kakinada Gautami Express 7047/7048 (Secunderabad-Bhubaneshwar-Howrah/Kolkata)
- Secunderabad Howrah Falaknuma Express 2703/2704 (Secunderabad-Bhubaneshwar-Howrah/Kolkata)
- Lokmanya Tilak Express 1051/1052 & 2101/2102 (Howrah/Kolkata-Nasik-Igatpuri-LT/Mumbai)
- Howrah Bhubaneshwar Dhauli Express 2821/2822 (Howrah/Kolkata-Bhubaneshwar)
- Howrah Bhubaneshwar Jan Shatabdi Express 2073/2074 (Howrah/Kolkata-Bhubaneshwar)
- Howrah Secunderabad Express 2703/2704 (Howrah/Kolkata-Bhubaneshwar-Secunderabad)
- Puri New Delhi Purushottam Express 2801/2802 (Puri-Bhubaneshwar-Mughalsarai-Allahabad-Kanpur-New Delhi)
- Bhubaneshwar New Delhi Rajdani Express 2421/2422/2443/2444 (Bhubaneshwar-Kanpur-New Delhi)

Lalitgiri, Ratnagiri & Udaigiri

All located near Bhubaneswar in the state of Orissa, these three ancient hilltop monastic complexes are off the beaten pilgrimage path, and thus receive few visitors. At all of these sites, you will find the standard temple, monastery, and stūpa ruins that flourished between the 6th and 12th centuries. Although the ruins at Ratnagiri have the most extensive set of monuments, it was at Lalitgiri where relics of the Buddha were discovered.

Sleeping & Eating

Besides a few chai stands, there is nowhere to eat and there is no accommodation around these sites. Your best bet is to either make a longer day trip from Bhubaneshwar or shorter one from Cuttack. If you stay in Cuttack, **Hotel Adarsh** in the Banwarilal Moda Market is a decent budget option for a bed and a bite to eat; while **Panthanivas Tourist Bungalow** in Buxi Bazaar and **Hotel Ashoka** in College Square are decent mid-range choices.

Coming & Going

If you want to visit all three sites in one day from Cuttack (75 km), you need to hire a **taxi** to bring you around to the sites. You can also take a state **bus** from Cuttack to Lalitgiri (60 km) and then hire an **auto rickshaw** to take you to Udaigiri (8 km) and Ratnagiri (5 km past Udaigiri). From Bhubaneshwar, taxis are available, but very costly. You can take a bus to Cuttack (1 hour), and then move from there.

Timeline of the Buddha's Life

Western scholarly sources state that the Buddha's birth was 563 BCE. Most Buddhists, on the other hand, believe his birth to be in 623 BCE. While impossible to know the precise dates, we use the Buddhist system for the following timeline:

- **623 BCE**: Siddhattha Gotama, the Buddha-to-be, is born in Lumbinī into the royal Sakya family.

- **607 BCE**: The 16-year old Siddhattha weds the beautiful Koliyan princess Yasodharā.

- **594 BCE**: The 29-year old Siddhattha leaves the royal boundaries for the first time and sees the 'Four Sights': an old person, a sick person, a corpse and a saint. He is shocked by the first three sites as he did not know what age, disease and death were, but is inspired by the saint's serenity and resolves to find a way out of suffering. Shortly after his son Rahulā is born, Siddhattha secretly leaves the royal household at night in search of liberation.

- **588 BCE**: After six years of practising absorption concentration meditations and extreme asceticism, Siddhattha attains Enlightenment in Bodhgayā and then travels to Sārnāth to teach his discovery to his former ascetic companions.

- **587 BCE**: Siddhattha, now the Buddha, returns home to Kapilavatthu to teach the Dhamma to his family and clan members.

- **586 BCE**: King Bimbisāra offers the Buddha and newly formed Saṅgha his royal park, the Bamboo Grove (*Veḷuvana*). The Buddha accepted the donation and from that point onwards *bhikkhus* were allowed to dwell in permanent monasteries.

- **567 BCE**: The Buddha announces that Sāvatthī will be his primary dwelling spot for the rest of his rainy-seasons so that meditators would know where he was and could receive instructions directly from him. From that time onwards, the Buddha spent every rains-retreat (20th to 44th) in Sāvatthī except his last one, when he stayed in Vesālī.

- **543 BCE**: After the spending his last rainy season in Vesālī, the Buddha walks to—and passes away at—Kusinārā. Three months following his death, the First Buddhist Council is convened and the Pāli canon is formed.

Glossary

This glossary lists words you may come across while on pilgrimage. It covers a broad smorgasbord of categories. More detailed lists specific to food and language can be found in the 'Travelling in India' section of this book.

The following abbreviations have been used to indicate the source-language of the word (where it is not English), or in the case of 'N', to indicate a proper noun (name).

H	Hindi	S	Sanskrit
N	Proper Name	T	Tibetan
P	Pāli	U	Urdu

A

abhidhamma (P); **abhidharma** (H): higher dhamma; analytical details of the entire field of mind and matter

ācariya (P); **ācārya** (H): teacher

acchā (H): 'ok'; 'I understand'

adhiṭṭhāna (P): strong determination

adinnādāna (P): taking what has not been given

adivasi (H): tribal person

agarbhati (H/S): incense

aggasāvaka (P): disciples

aggi (P); **ag, agni** (H): fire

ājīva (P): livelihood

amla (H/S): Indian gooseberry

anāgāmī (P): one who will be reborn at most one more time in a high celestial plane (See Note 1 for more details)

ānanda (H/S): bliss

Ānanda (N-P): The Buddha's cousin and personal attendant for the last 25 years of his life; heard and memorized all of the Buddha's teachings; recited the teachings at the First Council in Rajgir

ānāpānasati (P): awareness of respiration

Anāthapiṇḍika (N-P): title meaning one who gives food to those who are hungry

anattā (P); **anātma** (H/S): no-self, without substance, without essence, without ownership

aṇḍa (P): dome

angrezi (H): foreigner

ani (T): Tibetan nun

anicca (P); **anitya** (H/S): impermanence

arahant (P); **arahat** (H/S): liberated being; one who has eliminated all mental impurities (See Note 1 for more details)

ārāma (P): park, forest

ariya (P): noble one (See Note 1 for more details)

ariya aṭṭhaṅgika magga (P): Noble Eightfold Path leading to liberation from suffering

ariya-sacca (P): noble truth

Āsāḷha (N-H/S): June-July

ashram, aśram (H/S): spiritual community centre; retreat centre

Asoka (N-P); **Ashoka, Aśoka** (N-H): Indian emperor of 3rd century who spread the Dhamma throughout Asia

attā (P): self

auto rickshaw (H): three-wheeled motorized vehicle; usually referred to as 'auto'

avatar (H/S): incarnation of a deity

avijjā (P): ignorance; illusion

ayurveda (H/S): Indian herbal medical system

azan (U): Muslim call to prayer

B

bābā (H/S): Indian saint; father; term of respect

babu (H): low level clerical worker; derogatory term

bachāo (H): help!

bachchā (H): child

bachché (H): children
bagh (H): garden
bahadur (H): brave
bahut acchā (H): very good
baksheesh (H): bribe, tip
bandar (H): monkey
bandh (H): closed; general strike
banyan (H): Indian fig tree
bala (P): force, strength
basti (H): Jain temple
Bauddh (N-H): Buddhist
barā (H): big
bāzār (H): market
ben (H): sister
bhagavā (P): the Enlightened One
Bhagavān (H/S): God
bhāī (H): brother
bhakta (H/S): one who practises bhakti
bhakti (H/S): devotion
bhāṅg (H): marijuana
bhaṅga (P): total dissolution; apparent so-
lidity of body is felt as subtle vibrations
Bhante (P): Venerable One
Bhārat (N-H): India
bhāva (P): process of becoming
Bhavan (H): building
bhāvanā (P/H/S) –mental development,
meditation
bhavatu sabba maṅgalaṃ (P): may all
be happy
bhikkhu (P); bhikshu (H/S): monk
bhikkhunī (P); bhikshunī (H/S): nun
bhojnalay (H): simple restaurant;
cafeteria
bideshi (H): foreigner
bīdi (H): small, hand-rolled tobacco leaf
containing tobacco
bindī (H): forehead mark
bodhi (P): supreme wisdom
bodhi-dhātu (P): vibration of bodhi
bodhisatta (P); bodhisattva (H/S):
someone striving to become a Buddha
who is on the verge of enlightenment but
renounces it to help others attain it
bojjhaṅga (P): factor of enlightenment
Brahma (P/H/S): creator god in Hindu
tradition
brahmācaraya (P); brahmācari (H/S):
living life of purity; chaste

brāhmin (P/H): a member of the Hindu
priestly caste (highest)
Buddha (N-P): fully enlightened being
Buddha-Dhamma (P); Bauddha-
Dharma (H): Buddha's teaching
Buddha-dhātu (P): vibration of the
Buddha
Buddha-sāsana (P): era when Buddha's
teachings are present
Buddhānussati (P): remembering the
qualities of the Buddha
burka (U): one-pieced garment worn by
Muslim women that covers them from
head to toe.
bustī (H): slum

C

cakka (P): wheel
candra (H/S): moon
cantonment: administrative and/or military area left over from the British era.
caste: a person's hereditary socio-economic position
cetiya (P); caitya (H) : Buddhist temple or
place of meditation
chalo (H): 'let's go'
chang (T): Tibetan barley beer
chappals (H): sandals
charas (H): hashish
charpoy (H): rope bed
chauki (H/S): high seat
chela (H/S): disciple
chomo (T): Tibetan nun
chorten (T): pagoda
chowk (H): intersection; marketplace
chowkidar (H): guard
chuba (T): dress worn by Tibetan women
citta (P); citra (S): mind
crore (H): 10 million

D

dacoit (H): robber
Dalit (H): preferred term for members of
the 'untouchable' lowest caste
dāna (H/P): donation
dargah (U): burial of Muslim saint
darshan, darśan (H/S): seeing, observing; viewing a deity or guru
deva (H/P/S): celestial being
deva-loka (P): celestial plane

dhaba (H): street vendor (food)

dhamma (P): Nature; Buddha's teaching; characteristic; element

dhammacakka (P): wheel of dhamma

dhammacārī (P): one who practises the dhamma

dhammadāna (P): donation of dhamma

dhamma-dhātu (P): vibration of dhamma

dhammadūta (P): messenger of dhamma

dhammaniyamani (P): rule of law

dhammānussati (P): remembering qualities of dhamma

dhammavihārī (P): one who dwells in dhamma

dhanyavād (H): thank you

dharamśala, dharamshala (H): pilgrim's rest house

dharma (H/S): law of nature, religion

dharmika (H/S): religious person

dharna (H): nonviolent protest

dhātu (P): vibration

dhobi-wallah/-walli (H): laundry-man/-woman

dhotī (H): a traditional sarong-like cloth that wraps around the legs; worn by Hindu men

dhyāna (H/S); **jhāna** (P): state of mental absorption

dibbacakkhu (P): divine sight

diṭṭhi (P): view, belief, dogma, theory

dohā (H): two-line poem, couplet

domanassupāyāsā (P): mental anguish

dosa (P): aversion

dukkha (H/P/S): misery; dissatisfaction

dupatta (H): women's scarf

E

ekāyano maggo (P): one and only path

eve-teasing: sexual harassment

F

fakir (U): Muslim religious mendicant

fil-lem (H): movie

G

gadi (H): vehicle (i.e. motor-gadi; rail-gadi)

gandā (H): dirty

gandha (P): fragrant

gandhabba (P): celestial musician

ganj (H): market

gaon, grām (H): village

garam (H): hot

geyser (H): hot water heater

ghat (H/S): steps and/or a landing on a riverbank; range of hills

ghazal (U): sad love song

ghee (H/S): clarified butter

giri (P): hill

giri (H): love song

gompa (T): Tibetan Buddhist monastery

grihastha (H/S): householder

gufā (H): cave

guṇḍā (H): hooligan

gurdwara (H): Sikh temple

guru (H/S): respected teacher

H

Harijan (H): name given by Gandhi to 'untouchables'

harmika (H): dome

hasti (H): elephant

hathi (H): elephant

hizra (H): witch-like eunuch

I

icchā (P): desire

imam (U): Muslim religious leader

indriya (P/S): sense doors; strengths

Indra (N-H/P): ruler of the celestial world

Ishwar, Iśwar (H): epithet for God; lord

J

jaldī (H): hurry; early

janata (H): people

jara (P): old age

jātaka (P): birth-stories of the Buddha

jāti (P): birth

jhāna (P); **dhyāna** (H/S): state of mental absorption

jhugee (H): slum; *bustī*

jhula (H): bridge

-ji (H): honorific suffix (i.e., Goenka-ji, Mata-ji, Gandhi-ji)

K

kāmacchanda (P): craving for sensual pleasures

kameez (H): woman's shirt

kāmesumicchācāra (P): sexual misconduct

kamma (P): volitional action

kammanta (P): action

karma (H/S): volitional action

karuṇā (P): compassion

kaprā (H): clothes

kata (T): Tibetan prayer scarf usually given to a respected lama

kataññū (P): grateful

katori (H): small bowl

kāya (H/P/S): body; body sense door

khadi (H): homespun cloth

khandha (P): aggregate, heap, accumulation

kharāb (H): bad

khīr (P): rice pudding

kilesa (P): impurities

kīrtan (H/S): devotional singing

kitāb (H): book

kshatriya (H/S): member of warrior and/or administrative caste

kund (H): lake

kurta (H): shirt

kusala (P); **kushala** (H/S): wholesome

kuṭi (P): hut

kuttā (H): dog

L

lakh (H): one hundred thousand

lakkhaṇa (P): characteristic

lama (T): Tibetan teacher or monk

larkā (H): boy

larkī (H): girl

lhamo (T): Tibetan opera

lobha (H/P/S): craving

lok (H): people

loka (H/P): realm

Losar (N-T): Tibetan new year celebrated in late February/early March

lungi (H): sarong-like cloth worn around the waist

M

magga (P); **marg** (H/S): path, road

mahā (H/P/S): great, big

mahāl (H/U): palace

mahāparinibbāna (P) **mahāparinirvāṇa** (H/S): nibbāna when a Buddha passes away

mahāpurisa (P): great being

mahāraj (H/S): king

mahārani (H/S): queen

mahātma (H/S): 'great soul'

Mahāvīr (N-H): last great Jain teacher (Tirthankar)

Mahāyāna (N-S): 'Great Vehicle'; refers to a type of Buddhism developed several centuries in India after the Buddha's death and currently practised in North and East Asia

maidan (H): open grassy area in a city

maitrā (H/S): loving-kindness

majjhima desa (P): the middle land

mandal (H): shrine

mandāla (S/T): Hindu and Buddhist circular symbol depicting the universe

mandir (H): temple

mantra (H/S): mystical formula of incantation

māra (H/P/S): personification of evil

maraṇaṃ (P): death

masjid (U): mosque

mātā (P); **mata** (H): mother

math (HS): monastery

maulavi (U): Muslim priest

medhi (P): base

mela (H/S): festival

memsahib (H): married western lady

mendi (H/U): henna

mettā (P); **maitrā** (H/S): loving-kindness

mettā-bhāvanā (P): cultivation of loving-kindness

miga (P): deer

moha (H/P): ignorance, delusion, confusion

moksha (H/S): liberation

mūdra (H/P/S): ritualistic or meditative positioning of the hands

mullah (U): Muslim teacher or religious leader

musā-vāda (P): wrong speech

N

nadi (H/S): river

nāga (H/P): snake, serpent; celestial snake with human face

nāma-rūpa (P): mind and matter

namaste (H); **namaskar** (S): respectful Hindu greeting with hands together

namaz (U): Muslim prayers

namo tassa bhagavato arahato sammāsambuddhassa (P): I pay homage to the Enlightened One (traditional prayer to the Buddha uttered before chanting or meditating)

ñāṇa (P): knowledge

neem (H/S): a tree whose bitter leaf has several medicinal properties

nasik (H): nose

nekkhamma (P): renunciation

nibbāna (P): extinction; liberation from cyclical existence; unconditioned

nibbāna-dhātu (P): vibration of nibbāna

nijhatiya (P): the practice of meditation

nirāmisa (P); **nirāmish** (H): vegetarian; purity

nirvāna (S): extinction; liberation from cyclical existence; unconditioned

niwas (H): residence

O

om (H/S): sacred Hindu and Buddhist sound symbolizing ultimate reality

P

paan, pān (H): a mixture of lime paste, spices and betel nut wrapped in a betel leaf; generally chewed after a meal

paccekabuddha (P): awakened individuals who do not teach others of their discovery either because they lack the necessary perfections (*parami*) to do so or because there are no students at that particular time who are able to understand their ennobling message (See Note 6 for more details)

pagoda (H/P): Buddhist spherical monument topped by a sphere; contain sacred relics; contain meditation cells in the tradition of Sayagyi U Ba Khin.

pāṇātipāta (P): killing living beings

pañcasīla (P): five precepts (abstain from killing, stealing, sexual misconduct, false speech, and intoxicants)

pañcavaggiya (P): five ascetics

panchayat (H): village council

pandit (H): wise person; expert

pāmojja (P): tranquillity

paññā (P); **pragya, prajnā** (H/S): wisdom

pāpa (H/P): sin

pāramī (P); **pāramitā** (H/S): perfection

paridev (P): lamentation

parinibbāna (P): final extinction; passing away of the physical body of an enlightened being

paritta (P): protection

pariyatti (P): sufficient intellectual knowledge of Dhamma

paṭiccasamuppāda (P): chain of conditioned arising which explains how suffering is caused by ignorance

paṭimokkha (P): precepts for monks and nuns

paṭipatti (P): experiential knowledge of dhamma

peta (P); **preta** (H/S): ghost

phala (P): fruit

phassa (P): contact

phul (H): fruit

pīti (P): pleasant sensation, bliss, rapture

pradesh (H): state

praṇām (H): respectful greeting

prāṇāyāma (H/S): breathing exercise

prasād (H/S): food offered to a deity and then consumed by the worshippers

pubbenivāsānussatiñāṇa (P): knowledge of all post lives

pūjā (H/P/S): worship; respect

Pūjya (H/S): title of address: Respected, Revered, Venerable

pukkah (H): proper; ripe

puṇṇa (P): merit

purānā (H/S): old, ancient

purdah (U): custom of keeping Muslim women in seclusion

R

raga (H/S): classical rhythm and melody pattern that forms the foundation for spontaneous musical compositions

rāga (H/P/S): craving

raj (H): rule; sovereignty

raja (H/S): king

rani (H/S): queen

rasa (P): taste, flavour

rickshaw (H): three-wheeled passenger bicycle

rūpa (H/P/S): form; matter

S

sacca (P): truth

saddhā (P): faith, devotion

sādhak (H/S): student

sādhanā (H/S): meditation

sādhu (H/P/S): well said

sādhu (H): Hindu religious mendicant

sagar (H): lake; reservoir

sakadāgāmi (P): once-returner, i.e., will only be reborn one more time before final liberation (See Note 1 for more details)

saḷāyatana (P): six senses

salwar (H/U): women's trousers

samādhi (P): concentration

samādhi (H/S): unification with the divine; burial of a saint

sāmaṇera (P): novice monk

sambhar (H): spicy South Indian lentil soup

sammā (P): right; proper

sammāsambuddha (P): one who has attained full enlightenment without any guidance, and then teaches the way to others.

sampajañña (P): continuous awareness of impermanence

saṃsāra (P/S): cyclical existence

saṃyojana (P): fetter

saṅgam (H/S): confluence of two rivers

saṅgha (P): community of enlightened beings; community of monks

saṅkappa (P): thoughts

saṅkhāra (P); **saṃskāra** (S): formative reaction; the part of the mind which reacts and creates suffering

saññā (P): perception; the part of the mind which recognizes and evaluates

sannyāsins (H/S):

sāńs (H): breath

śant, shānt (H): calm, peace

satguru (H/S): root guru ; eternal guru

satsang (H/S): religious discourse

sati (P): awareness

satipaṭṭhāna (P): establishing the awareness of anicca, dukkha, and anattā

satya (H/S): truth

satyagrāha (H/S): nonviolent civil disobedience; lit: 'insistence on truth'

scheduled caste: official term for untouchable castes

sevā (H/S): service

sevāk (H/S): male server; volunteer

sevīka (H/S): female server; volunteer

sīla (P): morality; ethical integrity

sīlavatī (P): nuns on ten precepts

sitar (H): stringed instrument

Śiva, Shiva (N-H/S): Hindu god of destruction

śivāmbu, shivāmbu (H): auto-urine therapy

skhandha (S): aggregate, heap, accumulation

śloka, shloka (S): verse

soka (P): sorrow

sotāpanna (P): one who has entered the stream of Dhamma (i.e. the first of four stages of enlightenment and will be reborn a maximum of seven times)

śraddhā, shraddhā (H/S): faith, devotion

śrī, shrī, shree (H) (S): honorific prefix; Mr., Mrs.

stūpa (S/H); **thūpa** (P): Buddhist shrine erected over the relics of a saint; caitya; pagoda

śūdra, shūdra (H/S): member of labour caste

sufi (N-U): Muslim mystic

sukho (P): happiness

śukriya, shukriya (U): thank you (Muslim areas)

suññāgāra (P): empty room; cell

śūnyagār, shūnyagār (H): empty room; cell

surya, ravi (H/S): sun

sutra (H/S): discourse

sutta (P): discourse

swami (H/S): lit: 'lord of the self'; Hindu monk

T

tabla (H): pair of percussions

tal (H): lake

taluk (H): district

taṇhā (P): thirst; desire

tantra (H/S): mystical Hindu and Buddhist practice

tāpa (P/S): burning; purification practice

tathāgata (P): lit: 'thus gone'; an epithet of the Buddha (See Note 62 for more details)

thāli (H): metal plate; all-you-can-eat meal

Theravāda (N-P): doctrine of the elders; refers to Buddhists of South Asia

tempo (H): large auto-rickshaw

thangka (T): Tibetan cloth painting

tika (H/S): mark that devout Hindus put on their foreheads

tipiṭaka (P): lit. 'three baskets'; collection of the Buddha's teachings

tonga (H): two-wheeled horse-carriage

toraṇa (P/H): archway over an entrance to a sacred space

tripiṭaka (S): lit. 'three baskets'; collection of the Buddha's teachings

U

ublā huā (H): boiled

uṇhisa (P): lump on top of head (indication of a Buddha)

uṇṇa (P): mark between eyes (indication of a Buddha)

upādānā (P): grasping; attachment

upāsakā (P): lay disciple (male)

upāsikā (P): lay disciple (female)

upekkhā (P); **upekshā** (H/S): equanimity

uposatha (P): bi-weekly observance of eight precepts for Buddhist laity and recitation of the monastic code by the Saṅgha

V

vācā (P): speech

vala (P): sand

varna (H/S): a person's hereditary socio-economic position

varśā-vāsa, varshā-vāsa (H/S): rains retreat

vassā-vāsa (P): rains retreat

vaya-dhammā saṅkhārā, appamādena sampādetha (P): All compounded existence is impermanent, strive with diligence (last words of the Buddha)

vāyāma (P): effort

vedanā (H/P/S): sensation, feeling; the part of the mind which feels

vaggiya (P): ascetics

vajrāsana (P): diamond throne

Vajrayāna (N-S): Diamond Vehicle, refers to Esoteric Tibetan Buddhism

vana (P): grove

Vesākha (N-P); **Vaishākh** (N-H): month beginning with the full moon at the end of April or beginning of May (day of Buddha's birth, enlightenment, and death)

videshī (H): foreigner

vidyā (H/S); **vijjā** (P): knowledge; awakened intelligence

vihāra (P); **vihār** (H): monastery

vinaya (P): monastic discipline

viññāṇa (P): consciousness, cognition; the part of the mind which cognizes

vipassanā (P); **vipashyanā** (H): insight

viriya (P): effort

vishrām kareṇ (H): take rest

W

wallah (H): male suffix indicating '-man' (i.e., dobhi-wallah, chai-wallah, Mumbai-wallah)

walli (H): female suffix indicating '-woman' (i.e., dobhi-walli, chai-walli, Mumbai-walli)

Y

yakkha (P): demon; nature spirit

yaśti, yashti (H/S): shaft

yathā-bhūta (P): 'as it is,' reality

yatra (H/P/S): pilgrimage

yatri (H/P/S): pilgrim, tourist

yoga (H/S): unification with ultimate reality

yogī (H/S): one who practises yoga

Z

zamindar (H/U): landowner

Notes

1 Traditionally, noble people (*ariyas*) are those who have had some taste of the fruits of liberation. They include stream entrants (*sotāpannas*) who will be reborn a maximum of seven times and will not be reborn in a lower state of existence, once-returners (*sakadāgāmins*) who will be reborn only once before final liberation, non-returners (*anāgāmins*) who will reappear spontaneously in a special celestial world to continue their meditation work before attaining *nibbāna*, and *arahants*—fully liberated beings who have left behind cyclical existence. The stream-entrant has completely abandoned the first three of the ten fetters (*saṃyojanas*): personality views, doubt of the path and attachments to rites and rituals. The once-returner also removes the first three fetters plus greatly reduces the next two: craving and aversion. The non-returner totally eradicates the fourth and fifth fetters. The *arahant* discontinues having any desire for rebirth in the human or heavenly realms (the sixth and seventh fetters), and totally removes any traces of the last three fetters: conceit, restlessness, and ignorance.

2 M, 142

3 M, 143. Commentators explain that it is important for the donor to remember not to take the individual monk or nun's personal qualities into account, but to see that person as a representative of the entire Saṅgha. Even more important is that the donor should remember to give with a wholesome and pure mind free from attachments.

4 Sn, 4:5

5 Dhammika 1999:22

6 *Sammāsambuddhas* are those who become enlightened for the benefit of all beings and dedicate their entire lives to serving humanity. *Paccekabuddhas*, on the other hand, become enlightened but do not teach others of their discovery either because they lack the necessary perfections (*paramis*) to teach or because there are no students at that particular time who are able to understand their ennobling message.

7 DhA, 14:9

8 Dh, 195-6

9 Luxford 2001

10 Dhammika 1999:23

11 Even though it was (and still is) considered sacrilegious to open a stūpa, Asoka did it anyway with the intention of multiplying the Buddha's influence. It is believed that he opened only seven of the original eight because the guardian *nāga* spirit at the Ramagram Stūpa refused to let him do so.

12 The number 84 000 was a standard Asian way of saying many.

13   See the "Questions of King Milinda" (*Milindapañha*), a work of great clarity and insight, which came to be recognized as a part of the Pāli Canon.

14   S.N. Goenka explains that the Buddha taught the Dhamma. He neither preached the religion of 'Buddhism,' nor did he call himself or his followers 'Buddhists.' Nowhere in the 146 volumes of the Pāli canon and commentary literature are these terms found. Goenka stresses the importance in distinguishing between the Dhamma and Buddhism because the former refers to something universal and accessible to people from every religion, culture, and class, whereas the latter is limited to a particular group of people.

15   Queen Māyā had been endowed with certain characteristics that made her fit to bear such a special child. She was in good health and followed the five precepts scrupulously. She was free from lustful thoughts and in return, none were ever directed towards her.

16   There is a debate as to the exact date of the Buddha's birth. Most Buddhist traditions believe that Siddhattha Gotama was born 623 BCE and died 543 BCE. Modern Western scholarship, however, dates these events sixty years later: his birth in 563 BCE and death in 483 BCE.

17   Early Pāli commentators write that there are eight causes for a Great Earthquake: natural forces, psychic powers, when a *bodhisatta* descends into his mother's womb, when he is born, enlightened, gives his first sermon, announces his forthcoming death, and when he dies. Years later while narrating these super-natural occurrences to some of his students, the Buddha told them that it is even more impressive that "a Perfect One's feelings of pleasure, pain, or neutrality are known to him as they arise...are present... and subside. His perceptions and thoughts are also known to him as they arise, remain, and subside."

18   Sn, 3:11

19   Dh, 197-199; DhpA, 15:1

20   D, 14

21   Pali commentators explain that all mothers of a *bodhisatta's* last birth die within a week because the womb that carried him should not receive any other being after him. These mothers are said to be reborn in the divine realm of the contented (*Tāvatimsa*).

22   Sn, 3:11; A, 3:38

23   DhpA, 13:2. A few years later, King Suddhodana reached arahantship while dying in the arms of his son.

24   VinMvKh, 1

25   D, 32

26   DhA, 4:3

27   A, 8:25

28   VinMvKh, 1

29   M, 101

30 Dhammika 1999:41

31 At the time of the Buddha, the Bodhgayā area was called Uruvelā due to the large amount of sand (*vala*) there. The name was soon replaced with other names evoking the great event, such as Mahābodhi (Great Awakening), Bodhimanda (Area of Awakening), and Vajrāsana (Diamond Throne). When King Asoka visited around 260 BCE, he referred to it as Sambodhi. The name Bodhgayā seems to have come about some time in the 18th century, probably to distinguish it from neighbouring Gayā. (Dhammika 1999:44)

32 The course of the river has shifted over the years and now flows about half a kilometre away from the Bodhi Tree.

33 The bowl is said to have eventually sunk in exactly the same spot where the bowls of the three previous buddhas also sank.

34 M, 36; J, 1:69; Dh, 153-4

35 Dharmapala's touching biography by Saṅgharakshita describes the hardships he faced in restoring Bodhgayā and Sārnāth, and discusses the monk's founding of the Mahābodhi Society, whose aim is to revive the Dhamma through social awareness and education in India and around the world.

36 According to the 7th century Chinese pilgrim Xuan Zang, the shrine was just north of the Ratanacankama Cetiya, which today must be the foundation of the large structure just beyond the gate on the northern side of the Mahābodhi Temple's railing. Interestingly, the statue on this structure faces the direction of the original Bodhi Tree. (Dhammika 1999: 67)

37 The famous first sermon in Sārnāth was the first time someone awakened as a result of listening to the Buddha's teaching. During the teaching at the Ajapāla Tree, the brahmin did not have direct realization of *nibbāna*, but did leave the discussion with a positive impression on his mind.

38 VinMvKh, 1; Ud 1.4

39 Some say Ukkala was an ancient city near present day Yangon; others say it was a city in the state of Orissa, along the east coast of India.

40 VinMvKh, 1

41 M, 26; VinMvKh, 4; S, 6:1

42 Doyle, T. Bodhgayā: Journeys to the Diamond Throne and the Feet of Gayāsur (1998)

43 Sn, 3:2; M, 12; M, 36

44 S, 35:28; VinMvKh, 1

45 Ud, 7

46 M, 7

47 VinCv Kh, 7; DhA, 12:7

48 Sn, 2:5

49   The name comes from a time when the Bodhisatta lived as a golden deer
     in this park. One day he risked his own life to save the life of a pregnant
     deer from a hunter. The king, moved by this selfless and compassionate act,
     decreed that the park would be a protected area from hunting, thus enabling
     the deer to graze without fear of being killed. Eras later, the royal protection
     was still intact. (*Nigrodhamiga Jātaka*, 12)

50   After this meeting, Upaka fell in love with a hunter's daughter. He left the
     ascetic life and married her. His new wife, however, treated him terribly.
     After years of torment, Upaka left his wife, and by chance met the Buddha
     again. This time he joined the Saṅgha, diligently practised the Dhamma, and
     reached the stage of *anagāmi*.

51   The five aggregates are: material form, consciousness, perception, sensation
     and formative reaction.

52   Craving for being can either refer to the desire for eternalism or perma-
     nence, or can mean the wish for a rebirth in a heavenly realm. Craving for
     non-being can either refer to the desire for annihilation or denial of life, or
     it can mean the wish to be reborn in one of the formless planes of existence.

53   M, 26; S, 54:11

54   S, 22:59

55   Fleischman 1999:85

56   M, 27

57   VinMvKh, 1

58   When the great stūpa was demolished by Jagat Singh, a local king in the late
     eighteenth century, to provide building material for a market, a stone box
     was found containing the Buddha's bone relics, along with some gold and
     jewels. The ignorant king kept the gold and jewels, but cast the relics into
     the Ganges River. The stone box that held the relics and casket is now in
     Kolkata's Indian Museum.

59   Dhammika 1999:77

60   During the Buddhas time, this area was still part of the Deer Park.

61   The relics were found in Taxilā (Pali: *Takkasilā*), an ancient centre of educa-
     tion destroyed in the twelfth century. Taxilā is located in Northern Pakistan.

62   Cited from Dhammika 1999:82

63   Sn, 3.1

64   Bhesakala Grove has not yet located.

65   VinMvKh, 1; DhA, 1:8

66   VinMvKh, 1; Dh, 183

67   VinCvKh, 6; S, 10:8

68   Dh, 147; DhA, 11:2

69   DhA, 21:5; Dh, 296-301

70 M, 97

71 Causing a Buddha to bleed is one of the six heinous crimes that result in innumerable aeons in hell. The other five are: matricide, patricide, killing an Arahant, causing a schism in the Saṅgha and raping a *bhikkhunī*. (A, 5:129)

72 VinCvKh, 7; S, 17:36; S, 9:13; DhA, 12:7; DhA, 1:12; A, 7:17

73 The names of these five mountains are Vebhara (Hindi: Vaibhara), Vepulla (Vipula), Paṇḍava (Ratna), Gijjhakūṭa (Sona), and Isigili (Udaya).

74 VinMvKh, 1

75 "I pay homage to the Blessed One, the Liberated One, the Fully-Enlightened One."

76 Dh, 399; DhA, 26:16; S, 7:2

77 S, 21:10

78 Dh, 347; DhA, 24:5

79 M, 144; MA, 144

80 S, 1:10; M, 133

81 S, 61:14

82 Most Theravāda Buddhists accept this version of history, but due to the lack of historical evidence regarding the councils, most modern scholars believe that the majority of the Abhidhamma was added at a later stage, and that there were significant modifications and additions to the entire canon before it was written down. (For one such example, see Etienne Lamotte's *History of Indian Buddhism*.)

83 VinMvKh, 8

84 M, 74

85 A, 6:55; Vin Mv Kh, 5

86 M, 29

87 D, 32. According to tradition, the *sutta* was initially recited by the Four Great Celestial Kings (*cātumahārājikadevā*), and then repeated by the Buddha to his disciples. These *devas* are revered for the protection they provide to sincere meditators.

88 DhA, 25:11

89 D, 16; A,7:20

90 VinMvKh, 2

91 VinCvKh, 7; Nhat Hanh 2002

92 Today, the ruins of this ancient city are found in Pakistan.

93 M, 55. Similarly, the Buddha did not enforce any rules about vegetarianism on his lay students. They were expected to practice the precept of not killing, but were allowed to eat or purchase flesh if it was not killed for their sake.

94 Besides being tormented with remorse for falling under the influence of Devadatta, which caused him to murder his father, Ajātasattu was haunted by thoughts that his own son, Prince Udayibhadda, might one day kill him, which in fact did eventually happen. He was also ridden with fear of vengeful enemies he made during his many conquests of neighbouring states. Incidentally, these conquests formed the nucleus of the first major Indian empire.

95 D, 2. See Bhikkhu Bodhi's excellent translation and commentary of the Discourse on the Fruits of Recluseship.

96 Dhammika 1999:99

97 S, 40; DhA, 10:7

98 This fort around the city was built by Ajātasattu in fear that the neighbouring King Pajjota, an old ally of King Bimbisāra, might want to avenge his friend's murder.

99 S, 47:13

100 D, 21

101 Tathāgata is an epithet of the Buddha, meaning "thus gone." The Buddha usually referred to himself as the Tathāgata, rather than using the discriminatory 'I' or 'mine.'

102 VinMvKh, 1

103 Dhammika 1999:107

104 The exact location of the Ambalaṭṭhikā has not been determined yet.

105 D, 1. See Bhikkhu Bodhi's outstanding translation and commentary of the *Brahmajāla Sutta*.

106 M, 61

107 The 13th century Tibetan monk Dharmasvamin's biography provides a moving eye-witness account of the tragic loss of Buddhist culture in India. Dharmasvamin was one of the last pilgrims to visit the sacred sites before their disappearance. His book is filled with stories of travelling with caravans, avoiding dangerous Islamic crusaders, and dodging greedy bandits. Narrowly escaping from the destruction at Nālandā, Dharmasvamin carried his old teacher on his back and hid in a small nearby temple where they continued studying, meditating and praying.

108 D, 11

109 Mahāvira is an epithet for Nigaṇṭha Nātaputta. Mahāvira spent 14 of his rainy seasons in Nālandā.

110 M, 56

111 D, 16; Ud, 8:6; VinMvKh, 6

112 This Gotama's Gate is yet to be found.

113 Today's Gotama's Ghat.

114 This park, said to be south-east of the city, is still not located today.

115 Most *bhikkhus* whose views differed from that of the elder Moggaliputta Tissa went on to develop their own separate institutions whose lineages exist to this day in various evolved forms.

116 Bhikkhu Mahinda Thera and Bhikkhunī Saṅghamitta Theri (Asoka's son and daughter) went to Sri Lanka; Bhikkhus Soṇa and Uttara Theras went to Myanmar; Bhikkhu Majjhantika Thera went to Kashmir and Afghanistan/ Pakistan; Bhikkhu Mahādeva Thera went to Mysore, Karnataka; Bhikkhu Rakkhita Thera went to the southern tip of India; Bhikkhu Yonaka Dhammarakkhita Thera went to Kutch, Gujarat; Bhikkhu Mahādhamma Rakkhita Thera went to Trimbakeshwar, Maharashtra; Bhikkhu Majjhima Thera went to the Himālaya, and Bhikkhu Mahārakkhita Thera went to Greece. (VRI, 1988: 23)

117 M, 34

118 Nyanaponika Thera & Helmut Hecker 2003:182

119 M, 51

120 D, 4

121 Sn, 2:1

122 See S.N. Goenka's *How to Defend the Republic*

123 In many ancient Indian cultures, attractive and talented courtesans were not usually in positions of subordination, but often rose to high positions of influence and wealth.

124 VinMvKh, 6; D, 16. This celebrated setting might be identified by the today's village of Amvara; however, there is no concrete evidence as of yet to back this claim.

125 Thig, 252-270

126 D, 16

127 D, 16

128 Dhammika 1999:129

129 VinCvKh, 10; A, 7:51

130 A, 3:83

131 M, 35. Although understanding the Buddha's line of reasoning at an intellectual level, Saccaka remained an unawakened worldling as he had not deeply penetrated the teaching at an experiential level.

132 M, 36. The commentaries explain that even though Saccaka neither reached any stage of liberation nor took refuge in the Triple Gem, his encounters with the Buddha left a strong mental impression on him which came to fruit in a later life when he was reborn in Sri Lanka and became a well known *arahant*, Bhikkhu Kāḷa Buddharakkhita.

133 M, 105

134 D, 16; Ud, 6:1; A, 8:70; A, 4:1

135 A, 3:65

136 In the second century CE, the imperial-minded King Kanishka looted Vesālī and brought the begging bowl to his capital in Peshawar (Northern Pakistan). During the Islamic invasions, the bowl was shifted to Kandhara in Afghanistan.

137 D, 16

138 Dhammika 1999:145-7

139 Only the ruins of the Ghositārāma have been found.

140 S, 66: 31

141 DhA, 7:7; Dh, 96

142 DhA, 23:1

143 Dh, 21; DhA, 2:1

144 Dhammika 1999:134-6

145 Scholars identify Balakalonakara with Balakmau, a village 18 km from Kaushambi and 5 km from Bharwai railway station.

146 M, 48; M, 128; Dh, 3-6; Dh, 328-30; DhA, 1:56; DhA, 23:7; VinMvKh, 10; Ud, 41

147 Dhammika 1999:136

148 The Kumbha Mela also happens in three other cities: Haridwar, Nasik and Ujjain. About every three years, one of these cities hosts the event. The story behind the gathering begins with some demons trying to steal a pitcher (*kumbha*) filled with the nectar of immortality (*amrit*) from the gods. During a twelve-day struggle, four drops of nectar fell from the sky on to these four Indian cities.

149 M, 86; DhA, 13:6

150 Dh, 282; DhA, 20:7

151 Dh, 100; DhA, 8:1

152 Dh, 69; DhA, 5:10

153 Dh, 2; DhA, 1:2

154 DhA, 9:1

155 DhA, 9:9

156 Dhammika 1999:160

157 VinCvKh, 6; S, 10:8

158 Dh, 264-5

159 Dh, 306; DhA, 22:6

160 Sn, 2:4

161 M, 87

162 Dh, 325; DhA,15:6; Dh, 204; DhA, 23:4; S, 3:23

163 DhA, 8:13

164 Dh, 13; DhA, 1:9; Sn, 21:8; Ud, 3.2

165 M, 62

166 M,147. The Blind Man's Grove has not been identified.

167 Ud, 6:4

168 M, 63. See M, 72 for a similar scenario with the philosopher Vacchagotta.

169 DhA, 13: 9

170 A, 9:20; Sn, 22:102

171 Dh, 364; DhA, 25:4

172 Dh, 3; DhA, 1:4

173 Sn,1:8; DhA, 3:6

174 Dh, 1; DhA, 1:1

175 Dh, 37; DhA, 3:4

176 Ud, 5:4; Dh, 131-2; DhA, 10:3 has as a similar story except the boys are beating a snake instead of a fish.

177 Dhp, 57; DhA, 3:214

178 DhA, 4:8

179 DhA, 16:3

180 Ud, 8:8

181 The five hindrances are: sense desire, ill-will, agitation, laziness and doubt. The three fetters are wrong view of self, doubt in the path, and attachment to rites and rituals. Giving up these three fetters is a prerequisite for attaining the first stage of liberation: sotāpannahood.

182 M, 107

183 The Dhammapada commentary, however, narrates that he was swallowed up by the earth.

184 DhA, 8:12

185 The Abhidhamma that we have today is believed to come from the exposition given by Sāriputta. However, the final shape of the Abhidhamma that we have today took several hundred years to develop.

186 Dh, 181; DhA, 14:2

187 M, 84

188 Bhaṇḍagāma has not yet been identified; however the other villages have been identified with Hathikhala, near Hathua; Amaya, 10 km south-west of Tamkuhi; Jamunahi, 14 km NW of Hathikhala; and Bodraon, 10 km west of Fazilnagar (Dhammika 1999, 165).

189 There has been debate whether this dish was a mushroom, a bulbous root, or the flesh of a pig. We could probably rule out pig's meat, as Cunda was an informed disciple and probably knew that monks could not accept meat if they had heard, seen, or suspected that it was prepared for them. It's also interesting to note that legend says that all Buddhas eat this same dish as their last meal.

190 Hiraññavati River is now a stream called Hirakinari, near the cremation stūpa.

191 The Buddha seemed to have a liking for this spot as it said that he had died here in seven of his previous lives. Commentaries also point out that the Buddha foresaw his upcoming meeting with the old ascetic Subhadda who was to become the last *arahant* during the Buddha's life and he knew that the *brahmin* Doṇa would reconcile the hostile parties wanting a share in his relics (see below).

192 Hearing this foolishness, the elder Mahākassapa foresaw the necessity of organizing the Buddha's teaching and community in order to prevent erosion of the Buddha's work. S.N. Goenka says that we should develop gratitude towards Subhadda; otherwise we might not have received the teachings today.

193 The entire story of the Buddha's last days is found in D, 16. Three hundred years after this event, King Asoka opened nine out of ten of the original stūpas (except Ramagama), took out a portion of the relics, and then redistributed them throughout his empire in 84 000 stūpas.

194 D, 17

195 Dhamma Thalī (meaning 'Place of Dhamma), is not to be confused with thāli, which means plate!

196 Dh, 101; DhA, 8:2

197 M, 145; S, 35:88

198 Vipassana Research Institute. The Rise and Spread of Dhamma in India. On-line: www.vri.dhamma.org/archives/dsindia.html

199 Batchelor 2000:20

References & Recommended Reading

The following books were indispensable to us in writing *Along the Path*.

Ajahn Chah. 1992. *Food for the Heart*. Wat Pah Nanachat.

Ajahn Sucitto & Nick Scott. 2004. *Rude Awakenings: Two Englishmen on Foot in Buddhism's Holy Land*. Boston: Wisdom.

Ajahn Sumedho. 1991. *The Way It Is*. London: Amaravati Publications.

Allen, Charles. 2012. Ashoka: The Search for India's Lost Emperor. London: Little.

Allen, Charles. 2004. *Search for the Buddha: The Men Who Discovered India's Lost Religion*. London: Carroll & Graf.

Arnold, Edwin. 1952. *The Light of Asia*. London: Routeledge and Kegan Paul.

Basant, Bidan. 2009. Lumbini Beckons. Self-Published.

Batchelor, Stephen. 2000. *Verses from the Center: A Buddhist Vision of the Sublime*. New York: Riverhead Books.

Bhikkhu Ariyesako. 1999. *The Bhikkhus' Rules: A Guide for Laypeople*. Sanghaloka Forest Hermitage.

Bhikkhu Bodhi. 2000. *The Connected Discourses of the Buddha: A Translation of the Saṃyutta Nikāya*. Boston: Wisdom.

Bhikkhu Bodhi. 2000. *The Noble Eightfold Path: Way to the End of Suffering*. Onalaska: BPS Pariyatti Editions.

Bhikkhu Nyānamoli. 2004. *The Life of the Buddha*. Seattle: BPS Pariyatti Editions.

Bhikkhu Nyānamoli & Bhikkhu Bodhi. 1995. *Middle Length Discourses of the Buddha: An English translation of the Majjhima Nikāya*. Boston: Wisdom Publications.

Burlingame, E.W. 1995. *Buddhist Legends: 3 Volume Set* (English Translation of Dhammapada Commentary). London: Pali Text Society.

Cummings, Joe. 2001. *Buddhist Stūpas In Asia*. Melbourne: Lonely Planet Publications.

Cushman, Ann & Jerry Jones. 1998. *From Here to Nirvana: The Yoga Journal Guide to Spiritual India*. New York: Riverhead Books.

Delacy, Richard. 1998. *Hindi and Urdu Phrasebook*. Melbourne: Lonely Planet Publications.

Dendon, Yeshe. 1978. *Health through Balance*. New York: Snowlion Publications.

Dhammika, Shravasti. 1999. *Middle Land, Middle Way: A Pilgrim's Guide to the Buddha's India*. Kandy: Buddhist Publication Society.

Dhammika, Shravasti. 1996. *Navel of the Earth*. Singapore: Buddha Dhamma Mandala Society.

Dhammika, Shravasti. 1985. *The Edicts of King Ashoka*. Kandy: Buddhist Publication Society.

Doyle, Tara. 1998. *Bodhgayā: Journeys to the Diamond Throne and the Feet of Gayāsur* (Unpublished Doctoral Thesis). Boston: Harvard University.

Francis, H.T. 1994. *Jataka Tales*. New Delhi: Jaico Publishing House.

Fleischman, Paul. 1999. *Karma and Chaos: Essays on Vipassana Meditation*. Seattle: Vipassana Research Publications.

Fleischman, Paul. 1997. *Cultivating Inner Peace*. Seattle: Pariyatti Press.

Geary, David., Sayers, Matthew. & Abhishek Sigh Amar (Eds.). 2012. *Cross-disciplinary Perspectives on a Contested Buddhist Site: Bodh Gaya Jataka*. London and New York: Routledge.

Goenka, S.N. 2006. *The Gem Set in Gold*. Onalaska: Vipassana Research Publications.

Goenka, S.N. 2003. *How to Defend the Republic*. Igatpuri: Vipassana Research Institute.

Goenka, S.N. 1998. *Satipaṭṭhāna Sutta Discourses*. Seattle: Vipassana Research Publications.

Goenka, S.N. 1987. *The Discourse Summaries*. Igatpuri: Vipassana Research Institute.

Hart, William. 1988. *The Art of Living: Vipassana Meditation As Taught by S.N. Goenka*. Igatpuri: Vipassana Research Institute.

Hetherington, Ian. 2003. *Realising Change: Vipassana Meditation in Action*. Igatpuri: Vipassana Research Institute.

Horner, I.B. 1993. *Book of Discipline—6 Volume Set* (English Translation of Vinaya Pitika). London Pali Text Society.

Hutanuwatre Pracha & Jane Rasbash. 1998. *Globalization from a Buddhist Perspective*. Kandy: Buddhist Publication Society.

Ireland, John. 1998. *Udana and Itivuttaka*. Kandy: Buddhist Publication Society.

Lamotte, Etienne. 1988. *History of Indian Buddhism*. Paris: Publication de L'Institut Orientaliste de Louvain.

Lay, U Ko. 2002. *Manual of Vipassana Meditation*. Igatpuri: Vipassana Research Institute.

Lerner, Eric. 1988. *Journey into Insight Meditation*. New York: Schocken Books.

Lessell, Colin. 1993. The World Traveler's Manual of Homeopathy, New York: C.W. Daniel Company Limited.

Levitch, Timothy Speed. 2002. Speed on New York on Speed, New York: Context Books.

Luxford, John. *Words of Dhamma* (CD ROM).

McCrorie, Ian. 2003. *The Moon Appears When the Water is Still: Reflections of the Dhamma*. Seattle: Pariyatti Press.

Mendis, N.K.G. 1997. *Questions of King Milinda*. Kandy: Buddhist Publication Society.

Mishima, Yukio. 2001. *Confessions of a Mask*. New York: Peter Owen.

Narada Thera. 1991. *The Buddha and His Teachings*. Kandy: Buddhist Publication Society.

Nhat Hanh, Thich. 2002. *Old Path White Clouds: Walking in the Footsteps of the Buddha*. New Delhi: Full Circle.

Norman, K.R. 2001. *Patimokka*. London: Pali Text Society.

Norman, K.R. 1997. *Theragāthā*. London: Pali Text Society.

Norman, K.R. & C.A.F. Rhys Davids. 1997. *Therīgāthā*. London: Pali Text Society.

Nyanaponika Thera. 1997. *Numerical Discourses of the Buddha: An English Translation of the Anguttara Nikāya*. Boston: Altamira Press.

Nyanaponika Thera & Helmut Hecker. 2003. *Great Disciples of the Buddha: Their Lives, Their Works, Their Legacy*. Boston: Wisdom Publications.

Rhys Davids, T.W. 1985. *Buddhist India*. New Delhi: Motilal Banarsidas.

Roerich, Gregory. 1959. *Biography of Dharmasvamin*. New Delhi: Jayaswal Research Institute.

Saddhatissa, Hammalawa. 1994. *Sutta Nipāta*. London: Curzon Press.

Saddhatissa, Hammalawa. 1990. *Buddhist Ethics: Clear and Practical Advice on How to Live the Moral Life*. Boston: Wisdom Publications.

Sangharakshita. 1995. *Flame in Darkness: The Life and Sayings of Anagarika Dharmapala*. Pune: Triratna Grantha Mala.

Schumann, H.W. 2004. *The Historical Buddha: The Times, Life and Teachings of the Founder of Buddhism*. New Delhi: Motilal Banarsidas.

Seneviratna, Anuradha (ed.). 1987. *King Asoka and Buddhism: Historical and Literary Studies*. Kandy: Buddhist Publication Society.

Svoboda, Robert. 1999. *Prakriti: Your Ayurvedic Constitution*. New Delhi: Sadhana Publications.

Trevithick, Alan. 2006. The Revival of Buddhist Pilgrimage at Bodh Gaya (1811-1949): Anagarika Dharmapala and the Mahabodhi Temple. New Delhi: Motilal Banarsidass.

Walshe, Maurice. 1992. *Long Discourses of the Buddha: A Translation of the Digha Nikāya*. Boston: Wisdom Publications.

Warder, A.K. 2004. *Indian Buddhism*. New Delhi: Motilal Banarsidas.

Weare, Garry. 2002. *Trekking in the Indian Himalaya*. Melbourne: Lonely Planet Publications.

Vipassana Research Institute. 1985. *Mahāsatipaṭṭhāna Sutta: The Great Discourse on the Establishing of Awareness*. Igatpuri: Vipassana Research Institute.

Vipassana Research Institute. 1990. *The Importance of Vedanā and Sampajañña*. Igatpuri: Vipassana Research Institute.

Vipassana Research Institute. 1991. *Sayagyi U Ba Khin Journal: A Collection Commerorating the Teaching of Sayagi U Ba Khin*. Igatpuri: Vipassana Research Institute.

Vipassana Research Institute. 1999. *The Manuals of Dhamma*. Igatpuri: Vipassana Research Institute.

Vipassana Research Institute. 2002. *For the Benefit of Many: Talks and Answers to Questions from Vipassana Students, 1983–2000*. Igatpuri: Vipassana Research Institute.

Voltaire, Francis. 1950. *Candide*. London: Penguin Classics.

Index